SPECTRAS ARISE
TRILOGY
OMNIBUS EDITION

SPECTRAS ARISE

TRILOGY

OMNIBUS EDITION

Print Edition ISBN: 978-0-9853192-8-1

CONTENTS

CONVICTION

A SPECTRAS ARISE
NOVELLA

1. ALL BETS ARE OFF

We humans may be technologically savvy and capable of living in steel cans that fly through space at speeds no one believed were possible seven hundred years ago, but something in us will never forget that we came from dirt. And we don't feel like ourselves unless we're crawling in it.

That's what I'm telling myself as I prepare for my match inside the earthen-floored fighting cage, up next. Prep started at midday and revolved around the attempt to drown the monsters in my brain with another cup of forbidden—or should I say *fermented?*—fruit. It was a natural progression to once again find myself here, competing in the Terra Feara Cage Fights. My soon-to-be opponent is already covered in grime, her preceding matches having ended with her taking only a couple of spills and quick victories. They'd dragged her first two victims out by the heels. Now I sit in my corner, swilling the last of my ill-gotten liquor and waiting for the bettors and debtors to place their final marks and the referee to give her and me the go signal.

Booze is prohibited by the Political and Capital Administration of the Advanced Worlds, the Admin, and I'll end up with something heavier than a wrist slap by my Corps platoon leader for being shitfaced today if he finds out, but fuck it. I'm on leave, I'm on Obal 8, technically my home world, and I need something with a hell of a lot more punch than Betty the Fighting Bear over there can give me to forget about our last mission, the one that had made Central decide my unit could do with some R&R. As if R&R could erase the memory of those slaughtered non-citizens on Ohm Lumi, or replace it.

It hadn't been that hard to find the contraband I'm swallowing. Obal 8 might be an Admin-governed planet, but I am an enterprising soldier. Ha! Just call me Aly "Enterprising" Erikson. The thought strikes my funny bone harder than it should, and when I tilt my head back to laugh, the late-evening radiance of the system's three suns combines and swirls nauseatingly, making me grip ahold of my stool hard in order to keep from tipping off it. Closing my eyes, I stay where I am for the moment, leaning back against the sun-warmed composite wall of the cage. So I'm a lightweight with the booze, so what? I earned this.

Earned it? Or bought it with someone else's blood? My eyes part in a careful squint, still looking into the sky, and the miners' faces, the non-cits on Ohm Lumi, emerge from the prickly gleam like angry spirits. They'd had children with them; we'd had a squad of fifteen weapon-toting soldiers with only the vaguest idea of what they'd done to deserve the barrage of destiny we were about to unleash on them. A Corps gun depot looted, a few soldiers injured, the non-cits disabling weapon DNA triggers so they could launch some kind of go-nowhere armed insurrection. My unit's job was to neutralize them, any way our leadership saw fit.

Follow orders. Just follow orders.

"Ready your weapon, Erikson."

"No, sir, I'm not shooting at kids."

"Those aren't kids, those are hostiles with guns aimed in our direction. You will return fire."

"No."

"Erikson!"

"Erikson!"

The squat, bald man refereeing the fight shouts my name again, and this time I realize I'm in the cage, not back there, not back in that dark mine with walls painted with blood.

"You ready to fight?" the ref says.

All fifty or so years of his hardened attitude toward the kind of person who uses her own body as an offering to the demons of pain and suffering give his voice a "fuck if I care" edge. I know how he feels. Instead of answering, I stand, reel for a second, catch myself with a hand to the cage wall, then move to the center. Big Betty—what had the fight list said her name is? Doesn't matter, she's Betty to me—meets me there. Despite the liquor-saturation level of my brain, I'm reminded that citizens and non-citizens both have other juices and drugs besides alcohol to give them whatever chemical boost they want. The one Betty's hopped up on lends the expression fixed on her dirt-streaked face a rigid, fierce aggression that could scare a viper. It's instantly clear to me that no matter what I do to her, she's not going to feel it; the juice in her veins will block any damage or pain I could inflict. So I better knock her down first—and make sure she can't get up.

The Bear has ten or fifteen kilos on me, and just under that number in centimeters of height. I've seen her a couple of times at the fights before, though never as my opponent. But she's a citizen, soft, not a Capital Military Corps graduate with ten years of physical combat training and twenty-four years of anger to channel into the bout. A bad temper can discharge a hell of a thumping. And now I have this new thing, this guilt thing. It's got nowhere to go but crazy. My liquor-addled brain sends up a flare of compassion for her. Poor girl.

She stares at me, smirking like she knows something I don't, which elicits a second flare, one that warns weakly of danger. I quickly remember to put in my mouth guard. I grew up a citizen and have the good teeth, which I'd like to preserve, to show for it. No reason to wreck this face more than necessary. Betty watches me insert the guard, then smiles broadly, revealing a face full of metal that looks as solid as a gun butt. These matches aren't fought with gloves. I'll have to remember not to hit her in the jaw, which will make it harder to knock her out. Bummer.

As the ref tells us the rules—which we both know and which he knows we both know, but the crowd demands its show—Betty and I stare each other down. I have to force my eyes not to cross while I try to focus, but the adrenaline drip of the looming fight starts sobering me up, little by little. I'm good in the ring, and this is where I always come when leave brings us back to the Obals; lots of the gamblers who know me are going to make some currency tonight. In a society with proscriptions against harming self or others (unless you're a soldier)—no drinking, no smoking, no guns allowed—you have to find your fun wherever else you can. Bien Gang is a citizen city, but being located near a Corps base makes it a soldier's playground, and soldiers have turned it into the twenty-sixth century's gladiatorial arena. Reminding me again that we are all animals, all from the same dirt.

The watching crowd, maybe fifty or sixty citizens and soldiers, wait in silence while the ref belts out the regs—no biting, no eye gouging, no kicking in the groin—and he pauses dramatically with a fist in the air before giving the signal to sound the bell. As soon as his arm drops, the crowd surges, first their bodies crowding against the transparent cage walls, then their voices, shouts, jeers, curses, cascading over Betty and me like a vicious waterfall. The newbies out there think Betty will win. Part of me can't wait to rub their faces in their coming disappointment.

She's quick, though, and lands the first punch. I feel it coming intuitively and sidestep and duck, but not fast enough. Her ragged knuckles graze my cheek and ear. Nothing I can't handle. More fight-ready adrenaline surges, and I rush into her. She tries to swing again, but I dodge and throw my arms around her neck like I'm hugging an old friend, swing around and get a hip into her midsection, then throw her body over me and land with my full weight atop her. She grunts like a kicked dog, and I hold my advantage, getting an arm back around her neck and putting her in a side headlock, trying to squeeze her throat closed. The crowd is roaring, a hydra of excitement and rage. I barely hear it, my own heartbeat too loud in my ears.

This is almost too easy flits through my head. Then it isn't. Somehow, she squirms low and flips onto her stomach, breaking my hold. I drop a couple of hammer blows on the back of her head, trying to make myself heavier on her back, but she bucks and I'm off. And then she's wrapping her legs around my chest, trying to get a solid grip on my dirty, sweaty arm to get me in an arm bar. I get my elbow against her inner thigh before she can, sliding it down to wedge it against her kneecap. I press with all my might, folding myself around her leg using my abdominals to try for enough force to dislocate her knee. She has to roll away, releasing her tenuous grip on my arm, and we both lunge to our feet.

Circling, breathing heavy, not feeling the bruises already forming. This is what I call fun, or a distraction from reality, which is the same thing these days. Movement in the mass outside the cage walls catches my eye, a familiar face. I glance, but it isn't a familiar face, or it shouldn't be familiar. It's a miner, one of the dead ones, the black dust from Ohm Lumi clumped obscenely in his bloody hair.

She strikes me in the gut with a kick that would drop a horse. Every light in the world coalesces and flashes dazzlingly inside my head as I go down, then my vision pinholes. She's already beside me, kicking me in the back, the kidneys, the hamstrings. I feel the thuds, but I don't, still trying to shake the vision of the dead noncit. Survival instinct takes over, and I spin around with my feet to her, still lying on my back. Now she has to go through my legs to get to me. She gets too close, and I land a kick on her meaty thigh, just inside of the same knee I'd already strained. She wobbles, enough time for me to scramble backward and to my feet. I don't let my eyes leave her again. Can't afford another guilt-sopped hallucination.

My back screams at me, the muscles feeling like jelly that's about to liquefy and drop me to the ground in a puddle. She's breathing hard, I'm breathing harder, my solar plexus still trying to unclench after the kick she'd given it. But I'm not losing this fight. Too many of my friends have bets on me, for me. I'll never be rich, but I want to at least be comfortable when I get out of the Corps.

Closing the gap between us fast, I feint low, then launch a haymaker. She's not expecting it, and I connect with her ear. She stumbles, and I lose my balance—*fucking booze*—and stumble with her. Luck is with me as we go down in a heap, me on top again. This time I wrap and hold her with every muscle in my body, squeezing thighs, arms, and feet together to immobilize her. I have her in a complete lock from behind, her body practically in my lap. She's grappling me, trying to get an arm free to pull my leg away, but I'm not giving up. She jerks forward, and I almost come loose, but a second later I'm sliding one arm farther under her armpit and across her body, gripping my wrist with my other hand, and locking everything tight once more across her neck and against her chest. I feel her arm flailing wildly, flapping uselessly toward my face. If I can just hold on, she'll be oxygen deprived and unconscious in a few more seconds. My own breathing strains, all my muscles beginning to cramp from the exertion of keeping her trapped. Heaving myself flat on my back with her over me, in a final effort I get my thighs higher around her midsection and squeeze, squeeze, squeeze! Her flailing arm drops toward the dirt in what might be a tap out or might just be her going limp. Either way, the ref calls it and the bell sounds again.

Letting my body finally go slack is blissful relief. I push her off me and use the cage wall to help me stand. The ref grabs one of my arms and raises it, and sweat runs from my hairline into my eyes, stinging and making me squint. Another victory. I wonder fleetingly what it would feel like to be happy to have won.

The cage door is opened, and a couple of my opponent's friends come to help her. She's already awake, and I'm at least glad about the fact that I hadn't really hurt her badly. Some of the locals chant my name, and I risk a look into the crowd to see smiles of victory—I knew money stood to be made, and a good crowd of spectators knew it too.

Then I catch something that pleases me considerably less. A squad of uniformed Corpsmembers pushing their way through the mass, directly toward me. Greg Tollhut, a friend, leads them.

"Erikson! Why haven't you been answering your coms?" he asks when the squad reaches me.

"Why the hell are you in uniform?" I return, scooping up my shirt from the bench beside the cage and putting it on.

"Leave's been canceled. You're in deep shit for not reporting in."

Fuck.

2. INSUBORDINATION

If you're going to be insubordinate, at least have the guts to do it with conviction. Maybe not the smartest philosophy a soldier can adopt, but it's made me the woman I am today. A Tech One Sergeant just starting my second week as a lavatory scrubber of the lowest class. God, soldiers can be a disgusting lot.

I don't regret telling my platoon leader, Tech Two Sergeant Smith, that it was my right to abuse my body and make extra coin any way I wanted, be it with contraband substances or illegal cage-fight betting, and he could strap his head to a missile and launch it into his own ass if he expected me to tell him who had placed my bets for me. This was only the tail end of the verbal assault I'd launched, which included comments about how he was no more than a bottom-feeding, soulless robot who couldn't find a box of grid squares without Daddy Corps to hold his hand, and there may have been some questions about the mental competency of his parents for having bred someone of such staggering intellectual challenges.

I'd still been less than fully sober.

He'd been less than understanding.

No one can blame me for my hostility. For the last three months we've been skipping from settlement to abandoned mine to trading post in the Delta Quadrant, forcibly "neutralizing" every non-citizen camp that's even been rumored to be involved in illegal activities. Normally the Corps overlooks these types of low-priority illicit happenings, leaving it up to private Admin security crews to clean up their own messes. But Corps Central Command on the Obals has been twitchy lately, playing hardball with everyone and everything. The units assigned to my long-range enforcement ship, the PCA *Thor's Hammer*, all think it has something to do with the minor uprisings rumored to be happening on some of the other Corps fleet ships. We've all heard about it. Though few details filter down to grunt level, enough bits and pieces have for us to make educated guesses. Whatever's really going on, it has the Admin worried. And when the Admin is worried, the Corps goes to work.

Mowing down tired, beat-up backwater planet dwellers, that's what the Corp is calling work now? So what if I'm exaggerating a little—I consider myself entitled when the odds are so heavily stacked in the Corps's favor. Yeah, most of these non-cit fighters are armed, but they may as well be using blowguns and slingshots. We are the Capital Military Corps, the most advanced military in the history of humanity. The battles aren't even close. Hence, my problem with Smith and every other Corpsmember who's content to just do as told. *Yes, sir. Salute. Shoot.* Stick a fucking fork in me; I am done. I'd rather scrub these dingy pisspots till I drop dead of dysentery than look into the eyes of another walking corpse. I can't be the bullet anymore. Not at the cost of myself. For whatever *that's* worth.

Dropping the bristle brush so recently issued in replacement of my AK-80 Corps carbine, I get to my feet and stretch my back, the cracking of my vertebrae playing a punk beat from ass to neck. One thing about being boots-on-the-ground that beats this task is at least being able to move around and keep my recently pummeled muscles from turning into overtightened guitar strings. You get used to all the fresh air—though *fresh* is hardly the word—and legroom when you're running through the dirt. Six years playing soldier have made parts of me feel sixty.

"All units report to stations. All units report to stations."

The alert comes over the general coms, wiping my mind clear of any and every errant thought. More curious than concerned, I walk to the sink and begin washing the cleaning fluid and grime off my hands and forearms. Moments later, Smith rushes in, his face whiter than the bleached latrines.

"What's the matter, Smitty? Sand in your mangina?" I comment. "You look like you're forming a pearl."

"Shut up, Erikson, and get back in uniform. We have a situation."

"So it would seem." My words may border on disobedient, but I can feel the tension. Something not good is going on.

No longer dawdling, I collect my uniform jacket and fasten it on as I head past him toward the troop transport bay. Outside the lavatory, the sound of double-timing boots reverberates through the corridors. The whole gunship is on alert? This shouldn't be happening . . . unless—

"What the hell's going on, Smitty? Are we under attack?"

"Come with me," he orders, and this time I shut up and do as I'm told.

Instead of heading to the shuttle bays, where I'm stationed as first navigator during a general alert in case the *Hammer*'s smaller gun shuttles need to launch, he leads me toward the heavy-gun deck.

"We got a problem with one of the gunners, Enlistee First Class Tollhut. You know him, right? You two are close?"

"Yeah." Greg? We go back to the Academy, and he'd probably saved me from worse punishment by coming to find me at the fights last week instead of waiting around and letting someone else do it.

"He's barricaded himself inside one of the bugsuit bays. You have to talk him out."

I snort, thinking he's joking.

"That's an order from Major Evans."

But Smitty doesn't have this good of a sense of humor. "What do you mean 'barricaded himself in'?"

"Look, Erikson, this is need-to-know, but I've been authorized to tell you. We have the PCA *Frontline* locked in our sights—"

"You mean locked in our sights because we're rendezvousing with them," I interrupt. Our leave had been canceled due to urgent orders for the *Hammer* and our sister gunship the *Szablya* to intercept and escort the PCA *Frontline*. We weren't told why, only to get there posthaste.

"Shut up and listen. Central tasked the *Hammer* with putting the cruiser out of commission. Full stop. They've had some kind of onboard rebellion, and Corps Command reports they're threatening other Corps ships. Right now, they are our enemy. Tollhut's unit is on the assignment, but he went batshit when he got the fire command. Now he's threatening *us*, the *Hammer*. You have to talk him out of the bugsuit bay until we can restrain him."

The autoclave that's become my brain spins too fast. I can't believe any of what I'm hearing. An entire Corps fleet cruiser has, what, mutinied? That's over fifteen thousand soldiers who are, apparently, no longer soldiers. And we've been tasked to fire on them? To destroy them? The level of lunacy at work in those two situations is beyond me. But what he's saying about Tollhut is worse.

I don't know what to say, so I start with a pointless question. "Why me?"

"I volunteered you."

That warms me up. "How could Tollhut be a threat to the whole ship?"

Smitty doesn't bother explaining, just lets the comment "You can't let him get into one of those suits. He could seriously fuck us. Good luck" do it for him as we arrive in the main armory.

We stop at the perimeter of a ring of troops on alert outside one of the ship's six Goldblum Squad Leveller—aka *bugsuit*—bays. The suits are mechanical urban-assault body weapons that can turn a regular soldier into a walking swathe of destruction. Their enhanced sensory analysis processors and attunement to the wearer's nervous system radically change the way a soldier reacts to battlefield situations, making one unit of bugsuited ground troops all a strategic op needs to wipe out, or neutralize, hundreds of targets. If Tollhut starts walking through the *Hammer* with one on, he could indeed, as Smitty put it, seriously fuck us.

Major Evans, as usual, is leading from the rear and approaches us. "Tech One Erikson, you've been briefed." He's not asking.

"Yes, sir."

"Get that man out of there."

"Roger, sir."

Smith taps me on the arm as I face the bugsuit bay hatch. "Where's your sidearm?"

"In my locker. It didn't seem necessary for toilet detail." But it seems pretty goddamn necessary now.

"Just get it done." He waves at the soldier nearest the hatch controls, which have been gutted. Either Tollhut had destroyed them so no one could enter, or the guard had so he couldn't exit easily. The Tech has a bypass board attached and gets busy opening the hatch.

My breath sounds too loud in my ears. The hatch retracts.

Inside, cargo bins and storage bunks have been shoved in a hurried frenzy toward the entryway, a wall of metal and plastic. I can't see anything beyond, but the sound of movement confirms Greg is up to something.

Stepping forward, I gingerly push against a looser-looking obstacle. "Tollhut? You in here, buddy? It's Erikson."

The sounds pause, then resume. "Don't come in here, Aly. You and David need to get somewhere else, somewhere safe."

"Safe from what, Greg? What's going on? What's with the drama?" I make room to get a look toward the rear of the bay, past the rows of suspended bugsuits. He's doing exactly what I'd hoped he wasn't—getting outfitted.

"They didn't tell you, did they?" he says, the sound of the bug-suit's many connectors clicking home punctuating his words. "We've been ordered to fire on the *Frontline*. They want us to shoot down *our own brothers*. You're always talking about it; can't you see? This is where the line is drawn. *This* is what separates humans from the monsters in Corps uniforms."

"C'mon, you know I'm just blowing smoke when I bitch about the Corps." This statement flares out and dies like a dud round—because he knows I'm *not* just blowing smoke, I'm dead fucking serious when I say the Corps is corrupt. Lately it's been worse; lately I haven't been able to keep my mouth shut about it—like with what happened on Ohm Lumi—and I'm one insubordinate-bordering-on-insurrectionary comment from getting thrown into lockup. But that's not the problem right now. Right now, I have to keep Tollhut from getting loose and turning his fellow soldiers into a chow-hall hamburger surprise. "We all blow smoke occasionally. If you have an issue with the chain of command, you gotta go through it. But not like this," I add hastily. Going *through* it is exactly what he's about to do. "You listening, buddy? You have to come out of there. As one of your battle buddies, I—"

I hear him say "Switch to full-auto" and know the time for discussion is over. Wasn't doing any good anyway. I can't convince myself; there's no way I was convincing him. "Move out, everyone!" I yell, but I don't know if they hear me.

The blast of a cement-mixer grenade overrides everything, turning the world into noise. I feel the impact of something hitting me from behind. Strangely, it doesn't hurt, but when my chin hits the deck, all the lights in the hold fade to gray.

3. CUTTING LOOSE

"Come on, come on, Aly! Get up, get moving!" The alarms ripping through the ship's speakers almost drown my brother's voice, but his tugging on my arm doesn't leave any of the situation's urgency to guesswork. "The *Hammer*'s going down. Get up!"

"I'm up," I manage to say, no doubt my weak voice lost beneath the blaring alarms. My vision is fuzzy, worse even than my head, but I can make out the shock on David's, my brother's, face clearly. Is the air filled with smoke? Between his hand pulling me up by my arm and my body's own primal drive to survive, I make it to my feet, sway for what feels like minutes while my brain, equilibrium, and legs negotiate a treaty, then finally find my focus. "What the hell happened?"

"No time, come on." Not letting go of my arm, he pulls me through the armory—or what's left of it. Crates, shattered suits, and blast marks are scattered everywhere. An explosion. And—

"Tollhut!" I yell.

"He's dead." David jerks me to the side of the bay, just avoiding a stampeding group of soldiers heading aft toward the evacuation pods. "Took at least thirty of us with him. No one could stop him before he got to the main engine cooling deck. Crazy bastard."

"I'm good, David. You can let go of my arm." It's too much to think about. How does a guy like Tollhut, someone who'd been next to me in the trenches, watching my back while I watched his, cool and calm on every mission, just lose it like that?

He throws me a quick glance, then drops my arm. "You sure you're all right?"

Swiping my hand across my face, I feel a painful knot on my chin, but not too bad. "Yeah, just a bruise. How did you find me?"

"Everyone on the ship has been ordered to evacuate. I ran into Tech Sergeant Smith at the evac pods, and he told me where you were." With a quick jerk of his head, he moves out.

"Wait, let's get to the squad gunship hangars."

"No, Tollhut caused too much damage. All the airlocks are disabled. The ships can't cut loose."

If they can't cut loose . . .

"What? You mean it's the pods or nothing?"

Instead of answering, he spins the manual release for the armory's small-arms locker room. "Grab as much as you can, Aly. I think we're going to need it."

My body feels cold and my skin breaks out in gooseflesh; it's from more than the mild concussion. Evac pods. No more than coffin sized. In a few minutes, I'm going to wish I'd stayed unconscious.

"Aly, move!" His tone is drill-sergeant-on-adrenaline sharp. Life-or-death sharp.

My feet get moving toward my own arms locker, but I'm less than a meter inside the room before a bellowing explosion shakes the fleet gunship from inside out, and I'm flung into an array of lockers. Shaken but not hurt, I get up faster than last time and hurry to slam my palm against the reader to my own locker after a glance at David tells me he's okay. Pulling out my torso body armor, I quickly buckle it on, then grab my AK-80 and the two magazines of ammo I always keep handy—but, dammit, more would be so much better!—and pack the mags away. The question of why we're grabbing weapons and ammunition when we should be abandoning ship doesn't even cross my mind. Guns are as important as oxygen. If you don't have the basics covered, nothing else matters. That's another soldier's philosophy.

David shoves his cargo pants pockets full, grabs his field radio and shoves that in a backpack, and says, "Let's get to the pods."

He and I are in separate units that are attached for mutual support during ground operations. Hence our barracks and evac pods are on the same crew deck; lucky for me, or he'd never have seen Smith and found out where I was. We haul ass toward our pods aligned along the ship's aft flank. The rollicking shriek of the alarms and the blow my chin took set off a high-pitched whine inside my ear, tinnitus, and the two tones merge into a vibrating hum that threatens to make me lose my mind, *just like Tollhut.* We see only a few crewmembers on the ten-minute sprint; most have already evacuated, becoming so much floating dust in space in the tiny e-pods. I must have been out for several minutes—enough time for Tollhut to get past the squad at the bugsuit bay, rampage his way to the engine cooling deck and destroy it, and then get himself killed. How many soldiers had he taken with him? Thirty, David had said.

A new wave of shock smashes into me. Tollhut could have killed me too, but he hadn't. But what he'd done to the *Hammer*

would have meant a slow death instead if David hadn't come looking for me. Profound gratitude for my brother, who wouldn't leave
me unless I was a cold cadaver, quakes through me. My brother,
my lifeline.

Then another thought strikes.

What about the PCA *Frontline*? Had they known we were targeting them? Will they retaliate if they did?

Suddenly the evac pods are sounding even less inviting than
they had. Nonweaponized and lacking any defense, they're nothing
more than a box to wait in until someone comes along and reels us
in. Or blows us up.

Coming to a sudden stop, I say, "David. David!"

He puts on the brakes and spins, mistaking the alarm in my
voice for something more imminent.

"We can't launch. We were about to fire on the *Frontline*.
We'll be target practice for them!"

He looks momentarily stunned, but pragmatism is his guiding
star. "No choice. The *Hammer* is done for."

Maybe we are too. Regardless, I speed up again, and the two of
us reach the last hatch to the launch-tube corridor. David quickly
enters the open code, but nothing happens.

"You try."

Same result.

"Dammit." He slings his carbine around his back and bangs
open the cabinet in which is housed the locking manual release
arm. It gives with a heave, and the airlock seal releases with a loud
thock! Without hesitating, he grabs the hatch's door wheel to spin
open the locking bars.

"Hold on."

"No time," he grunts.

"No!" I grab him by the shoulders and forcefully jerk him
back. "You feel that? No pressurization. There's a breach on the
other side of the door."

He curses, then steps in front of the ship's visual console next
to the hatch, a terminal linked to the ship's main systems for calling
up quick reference information. Every hatch includes one. This one
is still functioning, and he quickly pulls up the alert grid, which
shows what I already know.

"The explosion ripped the hull wide open on this side. We have maybe five minutes before we're breathing space." He looks pale. "We'll never make it to the starboard pods."

What little saliva remains in my mouth flash dries, coating my tongue and throat with a sick flavor of fear and adrenaline. "The bow. The flight deck evacuation raft. We can make it."

His eyes widen, and he's about to say something, something about how there's no way in frozen hell it will still be there or, if it is, the flight deck brass will let us aboard, but I'm already moving at triple time up the corridor. The echo of his boots lets me know he's on my heels.

The flight deck life raft is the largest on the ship and located directly above the flight deck itself. More than just a simple evac pod, it's the commander and her crew's last-minute getaway craft, the notion of a captain going down with her ship as antiquated as old Earth. Though I've never been inside one, I know it's roomy enough for six crew and stocked with survival gear and necessities for up to three weeks. Built for flight, not merely for escaping, it's docked on the outer hull, and the airlock leading inside is small, made only for people, therefore not a threat to the overall ship's integrity if breached. Most importantly, it can be opened even when the ship's internal security shuts down the main dock airlocks. The engineers reasoned that if the flight crew is trying to evacuate, the main ship must be doomed.

The hatch to the final corridor leading to the evac craft is still open when David and I get there less than three minutes later. We careen through—and stop short at the sight of blood on the walls and the floor, and the smell of a recently discharged firearm inside.

"Is that . . . ?" But I know immediately the body at my feet is Command General Fischer. And beyond him lie Major Evans and three others, contorted and very dead. The entire flight deck crew.

David drops to the floor, pulling me down with him, as a round flies past us. "Don't shoot! It's Tech Sergeant Erikson and Aly Erikson!"

"Eagle Eye?" I know that voice. Enlistee First Class Bernthal. "That you and your sister?"

"Yes!"

"Bernthal," I yell, cautiously getting to my feet, "the *Hammer* is history. Let us on the evac raft."

He says nothing for a second, then: "Aly, you can come, but not Eagle Eye."

It's as clear to me as my own name what happened here. Bernthal probably had this plan in mind long before he ever expected to need it. If the ship was ever compromised, he'd hijack the flight deck craft, ambush the command crew, and have it to himself. It's a legitimately good idea—for a morally bankrupt parasite.

"You have room for us both," I yell.

"I got room for you, sweetheart, but not you, Eagle Eye. You didn't back me up after those Admin bureau*rat*s got wasted on Chum Miro. It's your fault I got reprimanded and lost two stripes. You go right ahead and be the good little soldier you are and die with your comrades."

David stands up beside me, and Bernthal sights down his carbine, ready to fire.

"C'mon, Bernthal! Don't do this," I plead, knowing it won't do any good. "We're almost out of time."

"No, you're out of ti—"

His head jerks back, and a shower of red smears against the airlock door behind him before I hear the shot that hit him. David and I both swing around with weapons at the ready, prepared to go down fighting.

Tech Two Rebecca Soltznin from the 701st Ground Division stands behind us, the barrel of her Bowker O9 pistol still aimed forward. I know her from the chow hall but have never had duty with her.

Less than a handful of heartbeats pass between the three of us, all standing statuelike, our weapons and our nerves about to cook off. David's the first to react. "Come on, Tech. We have to go."

Relief floods over her face, and the three of us pass through the airlock, leaving a trail of bloody footprints along the floor.

The craft is easily piloted, made for survivors who may not necessarily be in top flight condition. David takes one of the two seats at the helm, and I strap in beside him. Once the outer airlock and the ship's hatch are sealed, blocking out the death knell of the *Hammer*'s alarms, the silence is almost ethereal, like a grave.

"Screens open. Thrusters online. Pressure and life support optimal." David goes through a basic checklist, his hands moving across the console. "Aly, get on radar. What's around us?" What he doesn't have to ask, but what we're both most concerned about now is, where's the *Frontline*? "We're clear in five . . . four . . . three . . . two . . . clear."

The craft releases from the *Hammer*'s hull smoothly, like the pull of a trigger, and the thrusters push us upward. As we begin to rise away, leaving the gunship beneath us, dots of hundreds of white evac pods float away in the horizon outside the viewscreens, made infinitesimally small juxtaposed with the endless blackness of space. As we rise higher, more of the gunship comes into view, vapor from the numerous hull breaches on the ship's underside and flanks spilling into the vacuum and disappearing in the same second.

"Aly, have anything?"

I'd been too absorbed in what's happening around us to get on the radar or nav-system yet. "Gimme a sec."

"Hurry." He continues to put distance between us and the *Hammer* while speaking to our passenger. "Soltznin, right?"

"That's right, Tech Sergeant."

"Just call me David. Thanks for saving our asses. Why didn't you get out with the rest of your company?"

"My company was trying to stop that psycho in the bugsuit. We were all still on the cooling level when it started to melt down. No one but me made it out of there, as far as I know. The damage escalated so fast I couldn't get directly to my evac pod, and I had to navigate up from belowdecks through the maintenance sections. I finally ended up back on main near the flight deck, and I overheard you and . . . that other soldier."

"Lucky for us."

"We're less than a day from Spectra 5," I interrupt, finally locating a potential destination. "I've heard of its moon Dramma Sdutti. Supposed to be a low-traffic zone for Corps or Admin. Miners and non-cit settlements, mostly. Livable but low-tech with nothing much the Admin wants anymore. Might be just the right place to recalibrate, make a plan. Coordinates are set."

David automatically engages the craft's main drive, and within a second we feel the powerful engine readying us for hyper.

"Wait. Shouldn't we make for the *Frontline*?" Soltznin asks.

A sudden alarm blares through our main coms console, still linked to the *Hammer*'s systems. "Oh, Christ, it's going," David whispers, then slams his palm against the control stick, launching us into full acceleration instantly.

A blinding, no, *blazing,* flash of greenish-white light fills the viewscreens, fills my vision, fills the world. It disappears instantly as we hit hyper. Immobilized in my seat by the immediate change in pressure, all I can do is grit my teeth and hold on until the life-support systems compensate and I can breathe again. Moments later, the ship settles into cruising speed and the internals balance out. Released from the shock of such an instant jump, I quickly focus on the system readouts on my side of the flight console, praying everything is still functioning optimally. No reds, no alarms, and no burned-out sensors.

Finally, I turn to David, seeing the same dazed but coherent expression I'm sure I have. "All okay?"

He nods, and the tension locked across my chest releases. Looking back at Soltznin, I ask, "You all right?"

She blinks heavily, then says, "What was that?"

"The *Hammer*'s reactors blowing," David answers.

"You mean . . ." She pauses, wrapping her head around the destruction. "All those people in the pods. There's no way they had the distance to . . . I'm going to be sick." She leans forward abruptly, putting her head between her knees, and one hand covers her mouth. As I watch, her back arches violently as she fights against the heaving, but she holds it in, controlling the urge to vomit. After a second, she leans back and closes her eyes, her face a green-gray pallor.

I give her a few more seconds. "Got it together?"

Her eyes open slowly, but a little pink blooms in her cheeks. "I'm fine."

We float silently for a while, taking in the fact that we may be the only survivors. Around five thousand troops dead. It's almost unfathomable. Faces of friends begin to flicker through my mind, Webb, Holmes, Meeker . . . Tollhut. David and I had been on the *Hammer* for nearly six years and probably would have served our full time in service aboard it. Everything I'd known, *everyone* I'd known, everything I'd owned, now gone, completely obliterated in the fallout. Like it never existed.

Eventually, Soltznin says, "We have to get to the *Frontline*. Tell them what happened and send in a rescue party. Not everyone can be dead."

Neither David nor I answer right away. He stops monitoring the ship's systems and looks over at me, his pale green eyes serious. I stare back, not able to articulate exactly what I'm thinking in any useful way, except to shake my head. Tollhut's eyes, the expression I'd seen on his face through the makeshift barrier, come to mind. That haunted, wild darkness in them. He'd known that once we started firing on our own, there would be no going back, no right side to be on. I repress a shiver as the memory of his face starts to merge with memories of the faces of the dead from Ohm Lumi. Maybe we'd already been on the wrong side. Maybe he'd known it.

"Aly," David says quietly, "what did you mean when you said the *Hammer* was going to fire on the *Frontline*?"

"It's why Tollhut lost it," I tell him. "The *Frontline* is compromised. The insurgency, onboard revolts or whatever they are, we've all been hearing about—I guess the ship was overtaken. Smith told me that was the *Hammer*'s real mission, not to join them but to overtake and subdue them." I quickly sketch out everything Smith had said and how it had led to Tollhut coming unhinged.

"What?" Soltznin says when I'm done. "No way. There's no way the Corps would authorize the destruction of a fleet cruiser." She frowns and her eyes crawl over my face, looking, I suppose, for confirmation or negation, something to tell her either I'm joking or I'm nuts.

"Look, Sergeant. I know it's hard to believe, but it's true. Tollhut is, *was*, a heavy gunner on main ordinance. His company was directed to prepare for the assault. He went bonkers because he wasn't going to open fire on another ship full of troops."

"So he destroyed the Hammer instead? Do I look like an idiot?"

"I've known him for a long time," I argue, getting defensive. "*Knew.* He probably didn't want to destroy the ship. He most likely just meant to stop it."

"Well, he pretty much fucking did."

"Look." David jumps in calmly. "It's not easy for any of us to believe. But the point is, if we wait around for the *Frontline*, we're putting ourselves in their hands. I think we might need to—"

Soltznin says, "Exactly. We're soldiers. We belong with other soldiers."

"You mean like Bernthal?" I say. "The private you just shot on the *Hammer*? He was a soldier. Or what about Tollhut? You'd have put a bullet in him too, if you'd had the chance. Help me out here. What exactly is your definition of *soldier*?"

"Whoa, whoa, whoa, Aly. Cool it," David says.

Soltznin's gaze could melt steel, but I meet it without flinching.

"We go to the *Frontline* and we're signing up for a war," I continue, my voice dropping to a softer volume. "I for one am done fighting other people's wars, Soltznin. I don't want anyone else's blood on my hands. If you feel differently, you're free to do whatever you want—after we get to Dramma Sdutti."

She doesn't say anything more, and her eyes drop to the deck for a few seconds, as she thinks her options through. Sighing, she says, "The *Frontline* will find the survivors on its own, if there are any. And if this, I don't know, soldier's *rebellion* is real, we won't have to sign up for it. It'll find us. Let's just get to Dramma Sdutti."

4. ADRIFT

In the fourteen hours it takes to reach the moon, a craggy-faced planetoid with hot, dry plains between deep canyons and ancient rock formations, and not much else, we go over every inch of the evac craft to assess what resources are available to us. Though I have doubts that Soltznin believes what I'd explained about the *Frontline*, no one mentions the fate of the *Hammer* again. It's too raw, too close to home. We are adrift, leaderless and directionless. Thinking too much about the *Hammer* might lead to something worse: hopelessness.

First and foremost we need food and water, but extra weapons and ammo will give me, at least, more peace of mind. Lastly, non-trackable currency and something to wear besides the pattern-adjusting Corps combat uniforms could go a long way to helping us shed our military identities and blend in with the locals, but that's asking too much from a Corps craft. Going underground requires being incognito, and until we decide our next step, that's the only way we're going to stay ahead of danger.

After a tease of a catnap I feel as refreshed as a used snot rag, but manage to rally somewhat after a half pot of instant coffee, hold the water. It's an old trick that's been around as long as coffee and soldiering have. Chew the caffeine-infused crystals and grit your teeth against the flavor. The hit to your adrenals is nearly instant, and it may make you feel like crawling out of your skin, but any residual fatigue or lack of awareness gets wiped out. The Spectras aren't known for their welcoming populations and generally aren't as well policed as the Admin-regulated Obal planets. If you're walking around on a Spectra or one of their moons, you're in charge of your own ass, and you'd better be ready to watch it.

The craft's scanners show no Admin or Corps traffic in the vicinity as we sweep past the moon's largest outpost, a non-citizen trader's settlement called Iron Downs and our best chance for securing the things we need to blend and regroup. The three of us gather around the navigation holoprojection to decide where to land.

"I know it's a hike, but we don't want to get a craft like this too close to the city," David says. "Let's land in the shade of these rocks four klicks northeast. They'll create enough interference to help us hide the ship from most long-distance radar, and with the cloak engaged, we'll be basically invisible to anyone not knocking at the hatch."

In agreement, I turn to the controls and put us on course. Addressing Soltznin, I start, "Tech Two—"

"Look," she interrupts, "it's probably best if we drop the military speak. Just call me Soltznin."

I nod and give her a quick grin. "Right, Soltznin. You and I will go into the Downs, and David, you stay with the ship." He opens his mouth to protest, then shuts it. Right now the ship is our lifeline and only asset. Neither of us wants to leave it in the hands of a stranger, even if that stranger had saved our lives. "The first thing we need to do is get some currency."

"You planning to rob someone?" David asks, half joking.

"No, trade. This ship makes us a target, but I bet there are at least a dozen scalpers on this rock who would be willing to take it off our hands for a reasonable price."

David and Soltznin both turn their eyes to me sharply. "Aly," he says, "this is our transportation. Without it we're stuck here."

"Yeah, true. But do you have somewhere better to be?"

The question dangles in the air, not going away on its own. I see the full impact of what it means settling into the lines of their faces. Because I'm right; if we're not rendezvousing with the nearest fleet cruiser, we are no longer soldiers. We are deserters.

Deserters.

The Political and Capital Administration of the Advanced Worlds is based on a bedrock principle, that all people are one of three things: citizen, soldier, or nothing, more commonly known as a non-citizen. But now we're entering new territory, a territory that subverts those three basics, a territory of criminals, lowlifes, malefactors—and deserters. Occupants of this territory have two guarantees: no sympathy from the rest of society, and death.

"Aly . . ." Unsure what to add, David trails off.

But my focus is on Soltznin, who seems to be doing her best to absorb the impact of this revelation without giving her own thoughts about it away.

After a second, I continue, "So we're all agreed." I don't make it a question and turn back to the console to begin the landing sequence. "Be ready. We'll be down in a minute. David, will you take over? I want to get geared up."

I feel his eyes linger on me for another moment, trying to understand what's going on in my head, but then he gives up and takes the controls.

While checking the action on my AK-80 carbine and putting as much ammo as I can fit into my equipment vest, I outline the plan I've been pondering since we left. "Our VDUs are synced. Soltznin, if anyone questions us, we're still playing soldier, at least until we can ditch these uniforms. Our story is that we're here on routine patrol. We'll check in with David every hour. If we miss a check-in . . ."

His eyebrows raise in a query, but there really isn't an *if*. If we don't check in, he either waits or starts searching. What happens then is well beyond the boundaries of any plan we could conceive of at this point.

"Aly," he comments, "maybe it's best if we all go. Getting split up could just make things harder."

"I hear what you're saying, but this ship is the only collateral we have. If someone isn't here to guard it, we're fucked."

"We could be fucked either way."

He lowers us into the patch of shadow beneath several spires of rust-red rock that rise a hundred meters or so from the ground. By the time the landing gear clunks down, Soltznin has her own equipment tight and right.

"Just guard it the best you can," I say. "See you soon, brother."

ON OUR WALK TO IRON DOWNS, I'm encouraged by the sight of a landing field with at least fifteen spacecraft docked on different tarmacs or simply on the earth, from transports to intra-planet hops. This is one of the most frequented non-citizen trading ports in the quadrant, and I'm sure we'll be able to take our pick of hooligans willing to deal in contraband goods like the *Hammer*'s shuttle. The Obal planets' laws are only applicable when someone, usually someone in a sharp suit and with a lot of armed backup, is here to enforce them. The non-cits of the Algol system make their own laws and are very, very inventive when it comes to enforcement.

"Soltznin, how much time have you spent planet-side since you've been in the Corps?"

"Maybe half my term."

"Good, so you're familiar with this type of trader's post."

"You don't have to worry about me, Erikson. I think our biggest concern will be making sure we don't get grabbed by any slavers. Dramma Sdutti doesn't have a reputation for tolerating the type, but that doesn't mean they aren't around. They'd be disguised as merchants or smugglers of trade goods, not necessarily out to buy hot Corps ships, so we shouldn't have too much trouble avoiding them."

She delivers the comments in a dry tone that I have a hard time reading. Maybe she doesn't appreciate the implication that I'm questioning her judgment, but I relax a little anyway, knowing she's not going to need her hand held. My six years of active combat duty have put me in the mix with locals, both citizen and non-citizen, enough times to have learned quickly how to judge friend or foe. But, more importantly, I've learned a little about the criminal enterprise side of things, so I'm confident—*enough*—that I can interpret the language, both verbal and non, used by the black marketers we need to find. Still, a faraway voice in my head is telling me I should have gone into spook ops and learned the arts of integration and lying instead of navigation and infantry when I'd had the chance. Unfortunately, subtlety has never been my strong trait.

The outpost is a small city, which by my estimate and based on the limited information found in the evac craft's reference database has a fluctuating population averaging around five thousand inhabitants. Most of the buildings are constructed from the local stone, few rising more than two stories, and generally topped by domed roofs. An abundant aquifer of mineral-heavy water lies beneath it, providing the basis for the location, but the area doesn't have any other appealing features that I can see. People come and go to pick up or drop off whatever's profitable, but few put down roots. This transient lifestyle, more than anything else, will help us blend in as just another couple of here-today–gone-tomorrowers.

That is, once we get out of these uniforms.

Between what David, Soltznin, and I had in our pockets, we may have just enough currency to make that possible. As she and I step into the city proper, I experience the first real moment of relief since the *Hammer*'s explosion. Vendors, many hawking simple, cheap textiles and clothes, dot the main thoroughfare linking the northern and southern ends. Every available hint of shade provided by the squat buildings is occupied, and Soltznin and I identify a good option in short order.

As we approach the racks of pants, shirts, and jackets, a woman who I take to be the vendor rises from a chair perched against the building's rough, sandy flank.

"I got papers for everything I'm selling," she informs us, her glare of loathing as clear as the raised purple scar running from the side of her throat down the top of one breast and disappearing into the low-cut collar of her shirt.

For a moment, I consider using the angle of Corpsmembers tasked with confiscating nonregistered trade goods to get clothes from her for nothing. I'd willingly bet the price of a cosmetic surgeon who could remove her disfiguring scar that any papers she may have legitimizing her wares are as false as my story would be. But then I think better of it. Why lie? My loyalty to the Corps died on Ohm Lumi. Yet being a soldier still serves my purpose as cover, for now, and this is a smallish outpost. Word will get out soon that two Corpsmembers—two Corpsmembers with *no apparent back-up*—are wandering around hassling people if we don't employ risk avoidance every chance we get. Better to refrain from antagonizing the locals.

"We're not here to check your papers," I answer. "We want to trade."

Her eyes, already deeply sunken inside a nest of loose wrinkles, seem to narrow. "I don't deal in Admin bills."

"How about these?" I pull off and open the carrying pack I'd brought, which is filled with the extra uniforms we'd found on the evac craft, then tilt it so she can get a good look inside. "Maybe you know a market that you could get a good price?"

Her eyes bounce from the uniforms to my face and back twice, gauging my intent. Then she reaches inside and feels the material, as if for authenticity. "What you want for them?"

Easier than I expected, and trading the uniforms could let us hold on to our currency for better uses. Dropping the bag, I leaf through the garments on her racks and quickly select items that will fit David and me. Soltznin does the same, never taking her right hand from the stock of her Bowker.

"These should do. And how about a couple extras in exchange for the uniforms we have on?"

The vendor quickly zips the pack and nudges it behind a heavily laden rack with her foot. "They're yours. You want to trade up the *uniforms*"—she almost sneers the word—"you're wearing, you can take them off over there." Her chin lifts toward an alleyway just across the street.

Too easy. Suspicion suddenly lays a rough hand on my heart and squeezes. "You know, I think we'll just keep them, but I'll have that bag back."

Shrugging, she pulls a keycard from the pocket of her pants and waves it across the lock in the door of the building behind her. When she turns around to start collecting the extra uniforms to put inside, I let the AK strap drop from my shoulder and cradle the carbine in a fashion that assures anyone watching that taking aim and pulling the trigger will come as easily as drawing a breath. If they give me a reason.

"Second thought," I say casually, "my friend and I could change in there." I glance to the doorway, taking in as much of the gray interior beyond as I can.

"No, that's—"

"I think, yes," I cut in. Her quick protest tells me it'll be safer inside there than in the alley. I'm not doing much to avoid antagonizing the locals, however.

This time she does sneer. "Fuckin' Corps deserters. You scum may leave the Admin, but you're still double-dealing cockroaches."

"Hey, lady, we're just modest girls who want to use your indoors to change clothes. No need to hurt our feelings." I keep my tone dismissive, hiding the surprise and curiosity her statement evoked. Corps deserters? There have been others?

The vendor pulls the clothes free and flings them messily inside, her move a tacit consent. "I'll stay out here and keep watch," I tell Soltznin in a low voice. "You go first."

She enters carefully with the clothes she'd picked draped over her shoulder, then returns in less than two minutes. "It's clear. Just a squat, but she has a lot of uniforms in there."

Nodding, I repeat the action and step back into the street feeling, for the first time in ten years, like anything but a soldier. Part of me wants to question the woman about where she'd gotten all those uniforms and what she knows about the apparently high volume of deserters coming through the outpost, but I can see she has had more than her fill of us. It's time to move on.

At this time of year on this moon, there should only be a few hours of semidarkness to stand in for nightfall, but in the hour since we'd left David at the craft, the planet has shifted enough to make the light from our three suns resemble dusk, which I fully welcome. It takes the edge off the heat and cuts the glare from the overbright sky. It'll be easier to see if someone is coming at us with less-than-friendly intentions if we're not fighting the glare.

Checking in with David as we put distance between us and the vendor, I let him know we're good so far. A couple hundred meters down, the street opens up into a wide circle. In the center is what appears to be a public water pump and well. Two boys, teenagers who look somewhere between thirteen and sixteen, stand at it, filling a tank cinched to the back of a four-wheeled sand quad.

Soltznin and I approach, and the teenagers barely glance at us, engaged in watching a porn on holovid being projected from a device sitting on the quad's front fender.

"Hey," I greet them, and they glance at us disinterestedly. "Can you point us toward the nearest trade station that deals with . . . transport craft?"

This gets their attention, and the oldest asks, "Why? You want something? I can hook you up with sandbikes, hover runners, whatever lights your fire."

He's in the strange no-man's-land between adulthood and still filling out, with awkward, gangly arms, legs that seem too long, and a skinny, sunken torso, but with broad shoulders and good height that hint at the powerfully built man he'll soon be. His voice is already rough and deep, as if he either smokes or doesn't have a good enough air filter to keep his lungs free of whatever this moon's atmosphere likes to rain on its inhabitants.

Soltznin and I had donned nasal filters from the craft, just in case. Most of the Spectras and their moons had seen abundant Admin-controlled mining operations, and the Admin set up at least rudimentary terraforming and atmosphere conversion stations while the mines produced resources and turned profits. But planets with mines that aren't operating at full capacity anymore don't see many maintenance crews to keep the things running. A few of their stations have even been pulled apart by enterprising but shortsighted (and now likely dead or diseased) scavengers. As deserters, this is the kind of environment we're likely to spend the rest of our lives in, short or long. Better get used to it.

"Sandbikes may come in handy later, but right now we're looking to trade something bigger. Know a place?"

The tinny sound of the porn holo still projecting from the quad punctuates my question with amusing grunts and moans. The boys seem oblivious of the interference, but the oldest stares at me as if he might be imagining me as the star of his own private skin flick.

"We might know a place," he answers slowly. "Want a ride?"

The unintended double entendre makes me chuckle, and the kid's eyebrows crease in anger. So he's a tough, maybe even a scout for slavers. This is a dead end.

"Come on." I nod at Soltznin.

We begin walking toward a left-hand branch of the roundabout that looks more trafficked and busier, when the crunch of footsteps on the gravel behind me sends my senses on alert.

"Look, lady." A hand drops on my shoulder. "We—"

Before he can tell me what "we" want, I drive the stock of my carbine into his gut, then spin around and drop him in the dirt with a leg sweep. The eye of my barrel comes to rest between his.

"Don't hurt me!"

Surprised, I realize it's the younger boy. Jerking my eyes toward the older one, who remains beside the quad, I realize he's too shocked to move. This one is clearly still a kid, nothing hard or adult in his smooth, hairless baby face. In fact he looks exactly like a scared child with a psycho bitch pointing a gun at his head should.

Taken aback a little by my own instant ferocity, I move a step away and swing the carbine up to my shoulder. "You shouldn't sneak up on people."

Soltznin has drawn her Bowker and holds it with the barrel toward the ground, her finger locked on the trigger. The look in her eyes isn't one of surprise or concern for our well-being. It's pure disgust, but directed at whom?

The older boy's paralysis breaks, and he rushes up to the younger one's side. "Pete, you okay? Jesus, lady, he's just a kid," he admonishes me, his voice stripped of the tough-guy attitude.

Getting back on his feet, the younger boy dusts himself off. Slightly chagrined but looking determined, he continues, "I just wanted to say we know someone who can maybe help you with your transport."

"And who's that?" My voice is a flat threat, letting them know that any patience for tricks I had got dropped in the dirt along with the kid.

"Our dad. He's not a regular trader, mind you."

The word *slaver* flits through my mind again.

Soltznin says, "Ignore them, Erikson. Nothing but scavengers. We need to find someone authentic."

"No, no, c'mon! Too many ships been coming through lately, if you visit the regular traders, they'll give you next to nothing. My dad can give you top dollar."

"No thanks," Soltznin says and starts walking again.

I stare at the boy's face, full of disappointment and possibly desperation, for another second. Why is he so keen on having our business? Do we look vulnerable, easily taken advantage of? Or is he desperate for another reason? And could that work to *our* advantage?

"Hold up, Soltznin. Take us to your dad, kid. But if you and your brother"—I lay a frank glare, full of the promise of reprisal, on the older boy—"do anything I don't like, I guarantee I'll get even in ways that make watching porn the closest you'll ever get to hooking up with a girl. You read me?"

The youngest one swallows with obvious fear, but the older one rearranges his features to look hard-bitten again. Without a word, he steps over to the quad and shuts off the holovid. Pete joins him and gets up on the passenger seat, turning his eyes to us and waiting.

Soltznin steps over and grips my arm. "We don't need to take chances like this. There must be dozens of other options."

I match her low tone. "Yeah, but we don't need to advertise ourselves. The more people who see us walking around, the more of a target we become. We can keep a lower profile this way, and maybe the kid's being honest; maybe they can offer a better deal. Nothing to lose, if not. We'll just cut them loose and look for a better buyer on our own."

Her frustration isn't hidden, but she says nothing more.

"How far?" I ask, approaching the quad.

"Just at the end of that lane," the oldest answers and points to the side street opposite the one Soltznin and I had intended. "You can both sit on the top of our water tank. I'll go easy."

If you're setting us up, kid, I won't.

5. DEATH'S DOOR

I'd informed David of the plan on our way down the street, and now we sit inside a modest four-room dwelling, made from the same hard rock as most of the other buildings, across from a middle-aged man with yellow-white hair and eyes with sclera to match. The air has a sour smell, not of unwashed bodies, but as if someone is, or recently was, dying. A brief look at the kids' father, Mick Temple, is all it took to know who. He could be as young as his late thirties, but whatever's wrong with him has withered him to old age.

After introductions, the conversation hasn't gone the way I'd wanted, which fails to surprise me. "Look, Temple, your boys told us you could give us what we want for our ship. Now you're telling us you know someone else who can, but not you. You're wasting our time." The '80 hasn't left my knees since sitting down, and I run my finger over the trigger guard as I talk, just to emphasize my irritation.

"What my boys told you is true. I can get you what you want for your ship. I know a smuggler, but he won't deal with people he doesn't know." His skeletal fingers steeple in front of his chest in a "let's be reasonable, shall we?" attitude, and he continues, "Especially not Corps. You need me to introduce you."

My lips twitch. He can tell we're military? I guess I have to get used to the fact. Maybe we can change clothes and modify our lexicon, but there's apparently nothing we can do to shed the stain years of enlistment have left on our hides. The Corps-issued guns don't help either.

"You mean you'll introduce us for a percentage," Soltznin says from her position near the doorway.

Temple nods, not needing to say anything else.

Curiosity gets the better of me. If he wants to play the Corps card, then I'll make him sweat for it. "How is it you aren't worried that we're just setting you up and plan to arrest you for dealing in contraband?"

"Lots of deserters coming through here lately. This rebellion we're hearing about—it's making the Admin nervous. My guess is the Corps doesn't have time to play cat-and-mouse games with lowly non-cits like us right now. Too busy trying to put a plug in the dam that's keeping the whole Corps from coming apart."

"What do you mean? What have you been hearing?"

He eyes me closely, his sickness not dampening his intelligence. "The newscasts aren't saying much, but then, the Admin runs those. Loose lips sink ships, but they also sink governments. Same way a viral epidemic will."

I'm completely lost at this point and glance at Soltznin to see if she knows what he's talking about. Her eyes have grown hard, her viperous stare an unveiled threat. He seems unconcerned, but it makes me nervous. Why her hostility?

She says, "Forget about him. We can find a real buyer on our own. Let's go."

"Not likely, but I won't try and stop you," he says, his attention on her for the first time.

"Don't underestimate us, old man."

It should be obvious to him she's not talking about underestimating our ability to fend for ourselves. The threat in her eyes has moved into her hands, and her fingers are laced tightly around the Bowker, ready to draw at any provocation, real or perceived.

"Dad?" Pete, who's been sitting off to one side listening, says, doing a good job of reading the tense situation as if he's been dealing with this kind of thing his whole life.

"Keep in mind," Temple goes on, "if the Corps gets this under control, it's going to get bad for deserters like yourselves. The best thing you can do is stack up as many odds in your favor as you can, now." He stops talking for a second, his eyes losing focus as he considers something privately. "Between you and me, I don't think they're going to fix it. The Corps, I mean. This is just the trickle coming through a crack, but cracks have a way of busting wide open before the right people take them seriously. I think we're going to see a lot more like you before this gets locked down. If it does."

He takes a deep inhalation that seems to get caught up in some kind of blockage in his lungs and chokes it out in a rattling cough that lasts for a while. Long enough for me to wonder if he's going to choke to death. His older son steps up and begins patting him gently on the back, helplessly trying to ease the fit. A few more seconds go by before the hacking diminishes, leaving him wheezing and red faced. Eventually, he takes a sip from a cup the boy holds out, then resumes, his voice even deeper and rougher than before. "Enough of your type end up out here in the Spectras, we might catch the Admin's attention. But for now, we gotta take advantage of the situation."

Soltznin has a hand on the door, ready to go, but I stand fast. I want to know what he meant by epidemics sinking governments. "Why are you sick?"

He snorts a brief laugh. "You breathe our air long enough, you'll know why."

"You said something about an epidemic, is that what's wrong with you?"

"No. The newscasts are calling it the Crower's Croup. It's killing people faster than any Corps unit could dream of doing."

The name rings a bell. "We've heard it was a small outbreak, localized to just a few of the Obal moons." I can see Soltznin from the corner of my eye, trying to get my attention with her insistent stare. I ignore her.

"You've heard . . . you don't hear much, huh?" Another mocking laugh. "Why do you think that is, soldier?"

I say nothing.

"Because *they* cooked it up. The Croup isn't anything but a lab virus the Admin's been testing on people like us, the Spectres. But something happened, and it's outta the labs and into the system, being passed around by soldiers and citizens. Hasn't got out here to Dramma Sdutti yet, but with the way you Corps are starting to peel off, eventually it will. I wouldn't be surprised if it's the reason the military is starting to rebel."

It's my turn to laugh, but there isn't much humor in it. "You're sick as well as paranoid. I don't know where you get your 'news,' but—"

"We're going now, Tech *One*." Soltznin puts an emphasis on my rank, as if military chain of command matters anymore. But she's right. Temple's road leads to nowhere.

I stand up, attentive to the way Temple's eyes follow me, but neither he nor the kids move. Following Soltznin out the door without a look back, I work on shaking the unease his doom-and-gloom words bred in me.

Before we've gone more than a few steps, we hear a plaintive "Please." Turning, I face the youngest. "Please," he repeats, "we need—"

"Look, kid—Pete, right?"

He nods.

"Pete, we can't help you." I look into his face for another second, his helplessness holding my gaze like a magnet. I start to follow Soltznin, then have an idea. Digging in my pocket, I pull out two of the nasal filter sets that make air like what's on this rock breathable and hold my hand out. "You can have these."

The kid knows what they are, but he doesn't reach for them, waiting for the conditions.

Which are: "In exchange for that quad we rode here."

"Done." The older brother has stepped out to find out what's going on and overhears me. He swipes for the filters, but I pull them back too quickly.

"What kind of power does it use?"

"Batteries."

"Is there a spare?"

He hesitates, not liking how quickly the potential deal is stacking in my favor. I offer, "These will last six to eight months. That's with continuous use. They won't do anything for him"—I glance pointedly toward the dwelling's interior—"but they will do you two a world of good."

"He's dying," Pete says. As I look into his face, the sadness I expect to see there isn't. Instead, his expression is pinched and hard, a good facsimile of anger to cover up the fear that skulks just beneath.

"I'm sorry." It's a useless nicety, but it's all I have.

The older one still stares at me, his own anger not hiding anything but more of the same.

"What's your name, kid?" Stoic, sullen silence. "What's your brother's name, Pete?"

"Drew."

Drew shoots his younger brother a sneer that promises retribution, but I cut in before he can let his boiling angst out on the wrong victim. "Drew, you know your dad's days are numbered. Where's your mother?"

"She took off. Left us behind."

His words trigger in me an unexpected bubble of compassion, and I'm suddenly seeing these kids as more than just a means to an end. Because I know what it's like to be left behind. The only gift my and David's mother ever gave me before she split was an older brother who actually gave a damn about me.

I continue, still talking directly to Drew, "What I'm offering you isn't just a way to keep yourself from getting sick like your father. It's a chance for your future. And not just yours, but Pete's too. Because who do you think is going to watch out for him when your dad's gone?"

For the first time, the rough exterior he's consistently shown—except when he'd given his old man a drink of water to staunch his coughing fit—cracks. His eyes widen, showing a tiny bit more sparkle than was there a moment ago. The struggle going on inside him isn't as hidden as I know he hopes it is, but I don't show that I can see it. He's learning to be a grown-up in a hard way, but he's already learned that out here he doesn't have an alternative.

His eyes drop to Pete. "Fine, deal," he finally says, his voice much softer than his words.

"Good, now—"

I'm cut off by David's voice coming through my VDU. "Aly, Soltznin, get your asses out here. I got trouble."

6. BUZZARDS

I thrust the filters at Drew and push by him back inside, rush past their father, who stares in surprise, and bang through the door at the dwelling's rear where we'd originally come in. Soltznin marks my every step. The quad is still where we'd left it beside another two. Drew must have removed the water tank while we'd been speaking with his father. A bonus.

"Where's the backup battery?" I yell.

The kid has followed us and points without hesitation to a compartment that had previously been under the tank. Soltznin opens it, looks inside, and gives me a quick nod.

"You drive!" I tell her, taking the passenger seat. Speaking into my VDU, I call, "David, we're ten minutes away. What's your situation?"

Soltznin triggers the engine and gets us moving, leaving the kids and their dying father behind like so much dust in a windstorm.

"Scavs are closing. I can see at least four ATVs. Maybe ten people total. I locked up the craft, but it'll only be a few more seconds till they get here."

"Where are you?"

"Took cover on one of the rock pinnacles inside an impression about ten meters up. The only way they'll get to me is with artillery."

"David, what if they have some?"

"Hurry."

Soltznin gets us onto a track outside of town instead of going through it. Fewer obstacles, but a bumpier ride. The set of craggy pinnacles is visible, though barely more than a shadow at this distance. The suns are low enough that the entire horizon is melting into a uniform deep red and gray. I leave my VDU on, its camera feed showing just the edge of David's face as he squints at the approaching chaos, and the shadowed wall of the rock indentation he's perched in. "Push it," I somehow manage through a jaw that feels too tight to move.

As we draw closer, clouds of red dust from the ATVs hover in the still air, reducing our visibility. But also providing us cover. The interlopers are assembled in a ring facing the buttoned-up craft. We have the advantage of being nearly noiseless on the battery-powered quad, and they aren't expecting company from the rear.

"David, are you sure they're a threat? Could just be—" The sound of a shot ricocheting off the front faring of our quad cuts me off. "They're firing! Cover us!"

I yank my eyes from the VDU and bring my carbine up, immediately sighting in on the two men from the leftmost and closest ATV and squeezing off a shot. Through the noise of their still-running engines, I can't hear if my shot hit its target, but the way the man on the right crumples awkwardly against his vehicle tells me my aim was good. The other immediately drops behind the ATV, using its sparse size for cover. The action draws the attention of the rest, but too late for three of them, who are picked off by David from his fortuitous vantage point. He isn't called Eagle Eye for nothing.

That leaves six, at least by David's count. The dust and shadows of the rock make it hard to know for sure. The quad doesn't move fast enough for anyone with even a moderately decent firing group to miss, but the only cover out here is behind the rock spires, and Soltznin keeps pushing toward them as David and I continue to fire at the parked scavs. They've all hit the deck behind their own vehicles. Their vantage reduces their chances of hitting us, but I still feel much, much too exposed.

Within a minute, Soltznin passes the evac craft and our assailants and pulls the quad up short just before barreling into a bench-sized boulder at the edge of the field of rocks. We both dive for cover among them.

"David, we have good cover, but it'll be hard to hit anything from here. What can you see?"

"Four more of them. Three pinned down behind the two ATVs on the right and one on the ground behind the first one you took out."

I turn to look at Soltznin. "What do you think we should do?"

"I don't know, but they could have friends on the way, so we better do it *now*."

She's right. Swallowing against the hard knot in my throat, I decide. "I'm moving closer, see if I can get a better shot."

"We got your back," David responds, and Soltznin gives me a thumbs-up.

Staying low, I push through the strewn boulders as quickly as I can. The ground slopes up, leaving the angle of sight better for the scavs. Every time I rush from the cover of one sandstone slab to another, a shot follows me, always whining too close off a rock for me to draw a comfortable breath. My lungs feel as if they're being squeezed by a fist, and sweat begins to slip down my neck into my shirt. I have to force myself to stop and put my back against a boulder for a few seconds to calm everything down, my heartbeat, my breathing, my jittering nerves.

"Aly, you good?" David asks.

"Just having a personal moment."

Suddenly Soltznin's voice rings out. "You scavs have one chance to get out of here before we cut you down."

Her words, infused with the authority of a seasoned squad leader, batter the rocks with their force, and I take the unexpected moment of distraction to leap forward several meters to the cover of a slab directly behind the evac craft's port wing foil. The sound of my boots against the gritty rock redraws the scavs' focus, but not fast enough for them to put a stop to my progress. I drop to the ground and find a funnel of open space between the rocks, just large enough for me to get a good visual on someone's carelessly exposed foot. His scream when I shoot off everything from the arch to the toes could break glass.

In typical scav style, they barrage the rock I hide behind with a useless volley, using up too much of their ammo and achieving nothing except to assure the three of us that they have no plans to decamp. Like rabid dogs, their jaws are clamped tightly, tenaciously, and maybe fatally to this quarry.

David's spire looms to my left as I face the craft. Looking up, I can just see the barrel of his carbine aimed down at the vultures from the darkness of his rock depression. Now what? Only a minute or so has passed since I started forward, but with the exception of one less foot, our accosters don't have any more of a disadvantage, and I still don't have a clear shot. With about ten meters between them and the craft, they can't move forward and use its frame as cover without risking full exposure, and I'm sure our display of firing skills hasn't made them eager to risk it. We're at a stalemate.

On my VDU, keeping my voice low: "I'm going to have to kamikaze it."

"Hold on, Aly, let me think," David responds.

No. Thinking is only going to make me reconsider. "You two start suppressive fire in three . . . two . . . *now*!"

Relying on their discipline more than my faith, I run down the slight slope, bent forward and firing at every potential target, my senses lit up like the core of a supernova. It's only adrenaline, but this isn't the first nor will it be the last time adrenaline saves my life. The sound of David and Soltznin's cover fire is almost as faint as drops of water in a deep cave as my brain cycles into a sense that supersedes sound or sight and becomes something stronger, far more powerful. A sixth sense known as survival.

An explosion of blood, which to my overattentive focus appears a thousand times redder than normal, erupts across one of the ATVs as its driver rises too high and one of David or Soltznin's bullets ghosts him. I've covered the gap between me and the nearest ATV at the speed of arterial spray and shoot the man behind it before he realizes I'm there. My aim isn't perfect this time and only hits him in the shoulder. Before I can finish the job, one of the other scavs sees me and fires in my direction. His shot *does* finish the job, unintentionally hitting the scav I'd shot in the shoulder, and my target goes down for good with half the brain matter he used to have.

I take cover behind the slimed ATV, now only meters from the other two sets of scavs. They know I'm here, but they can't get a good shot without exposing themselves to my cohorts. Of course, neither can I.

"Aly?" David asks.

"I'm clear."

"Can you draw them out?" Soltznin chimes in.

"Any ideas how I might do that?"

Silence.

The clock, if there were a clock, would be ticking. The buzzards, if there were buzzards on this rock, would be flying overhead. My patience, if I had any patience, would be at its limit.

But battles are often won in the silences between shots, and I'm just not ready to become the next bleeder on this dusty piece of earth.

Soltznin: "I'm moving in. Erikson—both of you—keep your eyes open."

My turn to create a distraction. "Boys, you know you're not going to win this one!" I yell.

"You shouldn'ta landed where you don't have any friends," one of them responds. "We're going to tear you up and feed you to the rats! That ship is as good as ours."

"Speaking of friends, you're down to two, buddy." A wild shot whines through the air above me to illustrate how little my new conversationalist thinks of this observation. "Good idea. Use up all your ammo. You're going to win this fight for us."

This is received with an angry silence.

I hear Soltznin advancing through the rocks, drawing closer. With me so near, none of the scavs dares move into position to fire at her, making her approach much easier. David's vantage from above and she and I working on the ground could be all we need to beat them with our better aim and experienced military tactics. If we're lucky.

"I'm just behind you, Aly. Coming to your position in—"

I hear it at the same instant she does. Another vehicle approaching. With the shadows cast by the three lowered suns, I don't see anything but a dark speck about a hundred meters out, approaching from the same direction Soltznin and I had come from. It's moving slowly, but the engine is louder than the battery-powered quad's. Friend or foe? Or just an innocent passerby? There's no way to tell at this range.

"David, can you see what that is?"

After a second he gets back to me. "It's an ATV or a quad, boxy, like a land trans, but too small to be a regular trans. It's moving way too slow, though, like he's getting a read on you."

"Take a shot," Soltznin says decisively, and I don't argue. Yeah, it might be a hapless local with no ill intent, but given the people we've met today, none of us are willing to bet on it. "Just take him out, Tech Sergeant," she repeats.

David's end is quiet, but I can imagine him at this moment. Calming his breathing, in and out through the nose; hardening his solar plexus and the muscles in his shoulders as his body completely stills; blinking his eyes slowly, deliberately, before bringing his carbine stock to rest naturally against his cheek. His right pointer finger hooked through the trigger guard; his right thumb cocked along the upper breech. The center of his pupil in-line directly in the center of the scope. An in-breath, an out-breath, and . . .

An explosion ten times louder than rifle fire cracks through the artificial stillness, and a fireball drenched in black smoke careens upward from the destroyed ATV five meters away. Then once more, and the second ATV joins the first in instant, total cremation. I flatten my body against the packed earth, as if trying to press through it, the only thing I can do to escape what my mind simply cannot understand. Something much bigger than a bullet just blew up those vehicles, and the scavs just became the outcome of a very bad day at the range. All I can think is that I'm next, and these last few hours of being a deserter were the only taste of freedom I'll ever have.

But I'm *not* dead.

"Aly, get out of there!" David yells, his voice so loud I hear it from his perch as well as clanging from my VDU.

Scooting backward to try and put the gory ATV between myself and the approaching quad—where else could the artillery, if that's what it was, have come from?—I simultaneously and clumsily try to emplace my carbine atop one knee to be ready to take a shot. The new vehicle no longer moves toward us but has stopped about twenty meters distant. As I stare, the roof swings upward and open, like a trapdoor, and someone's head and shoulders appear.

"Don't shoot!" the gunman yells. "It's Drew!"

7. BROTHERLY LOVE

The moment passes like a languid breeze on a humid day while I try to make sense of what I just heard. Drew? The sixteen-year-old with the cruiser-sized chip on his shoulder? Wrapping my mind around the concept that this kid really just incinerated the scav team with some kind of explosive projectile weapons takes the last bit of energy I can spare.

Blinking several times, more to clear my disbelief than my sight, I take a closer look. His pinched, freckled face and gangly, overly long arms are unmistakable, even at this range.

I get to my feet and relax my grip on the AK. The fact that my body remains in one still-healthy piece is enough for me to forgive him for following us out here and scaring the living shit out of me. That, and the fact that he'd saved our asses.

Into my VDU, I say, "David, Soltznin, hold your fire." Then out loud: "What the hell are you doing here, kid?"

David asks, "Aly, do you know who that is?"

Forgoing the VDU altogether, I turn and wave at him until his face appears outside the dimness of his enclave. "He's one of the kids we met in town. Sold us the quad. I think it's safe to come down."

Gauging the danger to be on hold, Drew climbs clear of his weaponized vehicle and approaches. Wisely, his hands stay at shoulder height.

When he's close enough, I ask again, "What are you doing here?"

Soltznin has stepped clear of the boulder field and stands beside me, adding, "More importantly, where did you get that ordnance?"

Drew stops a few steps away, but he doesn't say anything. His eyes are wide, taking in the destruction he'd caused and never even looking toward Soltznin and me.

"Kid." I keep my voice calm. "You can put your hands down now."

Realizing they're still upraised, he drops his arms quickly with an embarrassed glance at us. As I watch, his face slowly loses its shocked expression and begins to reassemble into the mask of worldly hardness he's spent his formative years trying to create. Once more, his behavior reminds me of me, of being forced into growing up and toughening up before feeling ready. Because there isn't a choice.

"I'm not going to ask again," Soltznin says, her tone steely. She holds her Bowker in her palm, lowered but still threatening, and I'm surprised by the irritation I feel at her.

"Did your dad send you after us?" I ask.

"Uh, yeah. He, uh, he knew there was trouble, and he wanted to know what might happen."

He wanted to see if there was a chance he could benefit from our "trouble" more like, but I don't take it personally. "That took some balls, what you did."

He shakes his head, unsure if my tone is admiring or mocking.

"You got that artillery from the smuggler Temple was telling us about, didn't you?"

He nods. "We bought it for protection."

"Well, it works," I say. "Nice job, kid."

David, down from his eagle's nest, joins us. "This the kid who said he could get us a buyer on the e-craft?" I nod, and after taking a look at me, he continues, "Are you sure you're not hit, Aly? There's . . ." He gestures at my face and neck.

With the hand not holding my carbine, I wipe my cheek. My fingers come away covered in sand-infused, coagulating blood. "Ah, shit."

Drew loses it, doubling over and stumbling away a few steps as whatever his last meal was rumbles out of him with the velocity of a rail gun. The sound of his retching is the only noise on the still plain.

"None of it's mine," I comment, waiting for the kid to get it together. "You know, if this smuggler can get his hands on something like that quad and that kind of firepower, he may be the real deal. Exactly the kind of person we could use to flip the ship."

"None of these fucking scavs can be trusted," Soltznin says.

"Your point?"

"My point is this whole idea needs to be rethought. We don't belong out here." She starts to say more, then pauses, getting control of what sounds like a change of heart.

Carefully, deliberately, I say, "We can't turn back now. We're deserters, Tech Sergeant. Or should I just say 'non-citizens'? There isn't any going back." My eyes flick to David, looking for backup. But that's not what I see.

He says, "Look, little sis, we need to consider what Soltznin is saying. If the Corps finds us out here, deserters . . . this may not be the right move—"

I cut him off. "Let's discuss this later. It's late and we could lose more light. We need to set up a watch and defense. Who knows what other kind of company we'll get, and we're not in a position to go anywhere right now."

David nods in agreement, reluctantly, and Soltznin says nothing.

"I'll help." Drew, recovered, stands nearby listening closely.

"Help what?" I ask.

"I can help you keep watch."

Soltznin snorts dismissively. Drew's eyes narrow at her.

"Thanks, kid," David says, "but you shouldn't be out here in the first place. This"—he waves a hand toward the smoking ATVs—"isn't something you want any more to do with."

"Look, helmet head, I know everyone around here, and everyone knows me. If they see me here, they'll think twice about bothering you."

"They see *this* and *this*"—Soltznin holds up first her Bowker, then a modified CCIX rifle she's pulled from the hand of one of the dead men—"and they'll think twice. We don't need help from a scav. Especially a little one like you."

"Soltznin—" I start angrily.

"Forget it. He isn't sticking around. Can't you see he's trying to play us?"

"Yeah? That's why he just mulched four guys into tomato soup vapor? 'Cause he's trying to trick us?"

"Jesus, wake up, Tech." Her voice is filled with the same disgust her expression has held since we landed. "You're nearly as delusional as the vermin that crawls on these rocks."

I start toward her, planning to feed her my fists, but David gets between us first. "Stop."

Having to go through him to get to her makes me pause, but neither she nor I drop our eyes.

"He just dug our asses out of a seriously deep hole. I think the least we can do is give him the benefit of the doubt," David says, his head swiveling between us as he tries to read our intentions. "Kid—"

"Drew," I interject.

"Drew—why do you want to help us?"

The kid says nothing for a moment, and I drop the glare-down with Soltznin to glance at him. He looks nervous and uncertain, but eventually answers. "Because of what she said." He juts his chin toward me. "Pretty soon it's just going to be me and my brother. I got no choice but to figure out how to make . . . how to . . . how to take care of him."

David stares at the kid for a few seconds, then looks at me. His blue-green eyes shine with compassion. If I thought I knew what the kid was going through, David could be his Gemini twin. My brother had taken care of me in the same way. He'd been all I had as a little girl, and he knew it. What kind of burden could that have been? All I have to do is look into this kid's eyes to find out.

David says, "Sure, yeah, okay. Why don't you work perimeter with us till tomorrow? We could use a hand."

Soltznin grinds a boot into the dusty earth and executes a brutal about-face. She reaches the sealed e-craft hatch and enters the opening code before anyone says another word. Whatever. She doesn't have to like it, as long as she remains outnumbered.

But David's comment, *This may not be the right move*, makes me wonder if she is.

8. WANK PATROL

As a gray-purple dusk rolls over the landscape, David and Soltznin sort through the weapons at our disposal and lay out a base of operations inside the e-craft while I take Drew on a walk to set up an outdoor perimeter.

I explain as we go: "Our ship is only lightly armored, mostly to protect against minor debris while in flight, but it will repel any small-arms fire, even a direct hit by the type of projectile you used. Deploying these telemetry robot sensors will let us know if anyone is sneaking up by broadcasting movement or changes in environmental ambience to the receivers inside."

I drop a pile of self-propelled autonomous sensors in the dust, each about the size of my fist. Another prize we'd found aboard the evacuation craft. The Corps is nothing if not prepared. Using a central remote operator for all five units, I turn them on and let the operator box run through its autochecks to ensure they're all at optimal functioning and get a baseline read of the area. I won't deploy their movement alert system until we're tucked in for the evening.

To his credit the kid pays close attention, and I continue, "But what to do in case anyone unwelcome shows up is our biggest problem. They might not be able to get us inside the ship, but that doesn't do us any good if we can't get out. One advantage is David's sniper post." I turn and point out the emplacement. "We'll just rotate shifts up there. Three hours each." Trying not to be obvious, I glance back at the kid. "Except you."

"I'm a good shot," he says defensively.

"You may be. But I have a rule. I don't trust my life to strangers." Holding his coffee-colored brown eyes with mine, I wait to make sure he understands.

After a second, he nods and looks away. "So you want me to stay inside the ship?"

"How many rounds does your quad have left?"

He thinks for a second. "Four."

"Outstanding. You volunteered to help us, so you can help us by doing what you already know how to. Wank patrol." He gives me a look of complete confusion. "Perimeter watch," I explain. "You can spend the night in the quad, and be ready to use it if we tell you to. Whoever's in the perch will cover you—if needed." I don't add how much I hope it isn't.

"Uh, why do you call it 'wank patrol'?"

"Because if you're lucky, it'll be boring enough that jerking off is the only way to fill the time." I doubt, however, he'll still be awake after an hour or two of the mind-numbing monotony that defines battlefield circulation control.

Still, he seems to accept the role with a hint of enthusiasm. After a second, he surprises me by asking, "The guy, David, he's your brother?"

"Yeah."

"And you were in the Corps together, huh. What was that like? Why did you desert?"

It's a guess, but I think the kid is fishing for an out, encouragement to pursue a path that might reasonably offer him and his younger brother a chance at a life once their father dies. I'm torn about what to tell him. On one hand it's true, the Corps, for all its soul-crushing requirement of blind obedience, will keep him and his brother from starving to death or worse on some backwater rock. On the other hand, as non-citizens their chances for even passing the physical requirements to get in are as slim as their chances for making it out here on their own, and their futures would be no less violent, and likely just as limited. My own loathing for everything the Corps has become probably clouds my reasoning, sure, but I'm not going to lie to the kid.

"We deserted because being in the Corps is slavery. You might think it's rough out here in the Spectras"—I'm not about to sugarcoat anything—"but just try to imagine what it's like when your commander tells you that wiping out a mining colony full of noncits for insurrection is your *duty*. I wanted to be a soldier of justice, but that's not what the Corps does anymore."

His expression doesn't change, but the confusion lurking behind his eyes is clear. He probably isn't used to being preached to, but I continue. "You don't want to find out what that does to you, kid. And my advice is, don't try."

"So you deserted because you don't like taking orders. Sounds chickenshit to me."

He's doing his best to sound tough, but it makes me chuckle. "Sure, chickenshit, whatever you think. You've been around long enough to have it all figured out, right? C'mon, let me go over your quad. I want to see what exactly it's capable of."

He follows me to the vehicle without another word. It's as stripped down and basic as a retrofitted all-terrain vehicle could be, but its simplicity makes it effective. Steel plates have been welded to its frame to give it weight, and the undercarriage hosts tracks instead of tires, adding to its heaviness and balance, but also making it slower than it would be otherwise. It's not made to engage an enemy, only to stop them. The mortar tubes ride along the tracks' skirts, and a steel shell topping it serves as a solid barrier to any small-arms fire. Essentially, this little beauty is a boy-sized tank, but with real, lethal weaponry.

"You load it from inside?" I ask.

He nods, his expression thoughtful and faraway.

"Kid. You think you can handle a night in here?"

This brings his attention back to the present. "Why couldn't I?"

Because being inside that tiny cabin would feel a little like being inside a corpse locker. I don't voice this thought. It's my own, private little phobia. "Because you're only sixteen years old," I comment instead, getting tired of his overblown "I'm a badass motherfucker" act. "This isn't a game, Drew."

"I know that."

"No, I'm not talking about standing sentry out here in the middle of nowhere while a bunch of deserters relax inside a stolen e-craft, as if it's a fucking holiday. I'm talking about your *life*. You aren't going anywhere but underground in lots of little pieces if you think you really have it all figured out. I'm not trying to bash you, kid. I'm trying to do you a favor. But playtime is over. Stop pretending you're a grown-up and start learning how to be one."

His glare could incinerate stone. He'll have to work on his poker face.

"Aly, how's it going out there?" David's voice coming through my VDU takes a front seat to the tension.

I hold Drew's eyes as I answer, waiting to see a spark of either understanding or further rebelliousness. I need to know what exactly I'm dealing with. "We're just sorting out the kid's quad. Sentries are online and ready to be released."

"Good. See you in a few."

The kid seethes for another few seconds as I pretend to double-check the quad's interior. Not that I'm actually going in there myself. Uh-uh.

His voice has lost most of its edge—a good sign—when he says, "I have a plan."

I bite. "Yeah?"

"I'm going to work for a smuggler."

Hiding my doubt, I comment, "And your brother?"

"He'll come too. He can be useful, he's smart, and he can already shoot pretty well. Not as well as me, but he's good enough."

"Sounds like a plan. Now you just have to live through the night." Crawling off the quad and activating the sentries, I ask offhandedly, "Is it the same runner your pops knows?"

He nods. "Besides, when I tell him what I, uh, did today, it'll give him more confidence in me."

Is that pride in his voice? I decide it's my civic duty to set him straight. "Kid, this smuggler is nothing but a bullet bouncer, a gunrunner. The only thing they ever care about is how big their take is. It's not about confidence, it's about how many other scavs they have to go through to get what they want."

Drew says nothing.

"You want to be a smuggler? Then I'll make you a deal. I'll give you one percent of my split for the e-craft if you give me your word you and your dad aren't planning some kind of cheat or backstab on this sale. If you make sure to keep things on the level with this smuggler, I'll make sure you get your own share of the take. And if you don't . . ." My eyebrows arch in promise, making the "if you don't" part as clear as if I'd spoken the stakes aloud. "Deal?"

"Fuck yeah!" he says instantly. This time, I'm glad for his piss-poor poker face. This kid doesn't have the spirit of a criminal, even if he has the goal to be one. Not yet anyway. But in a few years, after life out here on the border of civility, who knows?

I reach out and he shakes my hand.

"Does this runner we're going to meet have a name?"

"János Rajcik."

9. CHAOS THEORY

"Drew's tucked in. I put him and his midget mortar chucker on sentry duty outside for the night. That's a solid piece of equipment."

Soltznin sits at the pilot bench monitoring our visual feeds, and David is stretched out on one of the bunks. For the first time since landing on this rock, the tension in my muscles releases briefly, like a flag going limp after hours of being buffeted by a hurricane. Then I catch a glimpse of my reflection in the nav seat console. The grit and gore I accumulated in our surprise firefight have dried to a hard shell. Instead of doing what I want to—grab something to eat, then get horizontal for a few hours—I head immediately for the ship's onboard wash station.

"So much for new civvies," I mutter, disgusted at the state of my recently acquired clothing.

After I peel off the stained duds and wedge myself into the tiny shower stall, the overpressurized recycled water blasts into me with exuberance, but the sting against my crusty skin feels a thousand times better than the tacky blood spatter I'd been wearing. Once I'm done scraping it all off, I feel almost renewed, almost ready for the next surprise.

And I don't have long to wait.

David slouches casually on the bunk when I come out, his long legs splayed out in front of him, looking laid back and relaxed. Except for his face.

"What?" I ask, running my hands through my damp hair to pull out the tangles.

His glance toward Soltznin sets me back on edge, a feeling that's becoming default. She stands rigidly with her back to the controls, nearly at parade rest, waiting for him to broach whatever topic it is he wants to broach. I think I already know what it is.

"Soltznin and I have been talking. We think we"—he rubs his hand across the forty-eight hours of stubble sprouting from his jaw—"need to discuss other options."

"We need to get back to work," Soltznin puts in more firmly.

Forcing myself to take a long, deep breath before responding takes an order of magnitude more self-control than I'm used to. Despite this, my throat still constricts around my words. "What do you mean by 'back to work'?"

"We're Corps," Soltznin says. "That's where we belong."

"Tech Sergeant, you need to burp your brain and let some of the crazy out."

"Aly . . ." David starts, but he doesn't seem to know where to go with it.

As I stare at Soltznin, my mind grinding into high gear trying to find the perfect words to describe exactly how wrong she is and exactly where she can cram her loyalty to the Corps, I'm hit with a sudden reality. A certainty. And I don't need to fight about it, with either of them. It's a truth, irrevocable, final. "I'm not Corps. And I won't ever be Corps again."

"Look," David tries again, "have you thought about what comes next? What are we supposed to do out here in the Spectras with almost no currency? And fugitives from our units at that? I'll tell you what—we wait to get arrested. And then being a soldier is going to become a whole lot less of a thrill than *not* being one."

Deliberately, I cross the flight deck and sit at the navigator's bench next to Soltznin to let her know she's not taking this ship anywhere I don't want it to go. But I keep my eyes on David. His coppery hair, a few shades lighter than mine, is growing long, almost too long to be in regulation. It would help him pass as a civilian if he planned to try it. *If.* I stuff down the panicky dread that thought brings. I haven't been without my brother . . . ever. Losing him would be like losing a limb. That thought takes my mind back to the memory of the people on Ohm Lumi, their struggle to survive against the odds, against the Admin, against the Corps. They hadn't been bad people, just desperate. And they hadn't been the only ones in the last couple of years that had found their fates dictated by a system that puts the lives of non-citizens on the same level of importance as garbage, and just as disposable. That's what I'll be, what I am, if I don't listen to Soltznin and David's reasoning.

But I can't go back to the Corps.

"You think I don't get it, David, but I do get it. I get that it's going to be hard to stay ahead of the sweep crews that'll be sent out to round up deserters like me after this rebellion or whatever it is gets mopped up. I get that it will be dangerous to try to live, even just try to hide, among non-cits and smugglers out here on the fringes. I get that I'm probably going to have to fight for everything I need. But do *you* get that every time you've pulled a trigger for the Corps, you've been nothing but a puppet?"

"Jesus, you're always so goddamn dramatic."

"Yeah? Well, it's pretty fucking dramatic when every single one of your friends just got shredded into so much space trash because the Corps thought it would be fun to play target practice with its own ships. What about Bostich, Vos, Wiggins? They're dead, David! Because of the fucking Corps. And you want to go back?"

"Leave my squad out of this!"

"I guess I should, right? Because they *are* out of it; they're out of everything now. Just like we'll be if we turn ourselves in." My voice has risen to the point of nearly yelling, and I know I'm making things worse. But chaos theory owns me right now, and it's so much easier to be angry at him than to be scared I might lose him.

He jumps off the bunk and paces the short distance across the hold, turns, and paces back, his breath heaving as if he's just run a race. Back in control, he faces me and says quietly, "Being a soldier is all I know. What else could I be?"

"How about alive?"

He looks at Soltznin for backup. The skin of her face is hard, shiny, and set, the picture of a woman whose mind is made up. He faces the stacked bunks once more and puts his forearms on the top, leaning into them with his back to me. The only answer I'm going to get.

Ignoring the implications of my words, I continue, "Tomorrow, we can meet with this smuggler the kid knows, we can sell the ship, and then split the payoff. From there, we can all go whichever direction"—my voice goes husky for a second, and I have to swallow to get it back—"we feel like we need to. For me, that's anywhere but back to the Corps. I won't fight for a side I don't believe in anymore. From here on out, I fight for myself. Period."

My glance jumps back and forth between them as I speak, and now it settles on Soltznin, mostly because I'm afraid of what I might see in David's face if he turns around. The surface of a lake couldn't be more blank, and I have no idea what she's thinking.

"If that's the call you want to make, Erikson," she says. "We sell the ship, then we go our separate ways. Agreed."

Speaking into the wall, David says, "Agreed."

Swallowing once more, I stay quiet, not trusting my voice to be steady. After a moment, Soltznin adjusts the internal climate switches to keep us from cooking—even in the evening, this planet is warm—and lowers the lights.

"We need to set up our rotation. Tomorrow could have a few surprises," David says, his voice deeper than usual.

I clear my throat. "Speaking of surprises, there's something you should know. The kid told me who his gunrunner contact is. You'll know the name: Rajcik."

A fugitive for at least fifteen years, anyone in the Corps who's ever been tasked with transport traffic security has heard his name at least once. The criminal went from thievery to smuggling to black-market arms dealing in a steady progression of worsening crimes, but no one has been able to catch him yet. He's big time, dangerous, and by all accounts, fucking evil. Still, for what we need, there could hardly be anyone more suited.

Soltznin looks like she's swallowed something rotten, and David says, "Looks like we came to the right place, then."

"Yeah." And because there's nothing else to discuss, I finish with: "I'll take first watch."

10. STAINS THAT STAY

Drew survives his night in the armored ATV, only looking moderately worse for wear after so many hours in its cramped confines. We radioed his father, Temple, last night, and he arranged our meet up with Rajcik for early morning in a heavily trafficked local tavern. With no real darkness on this planet because of the Algol system's three stars, morning and evening, even for a canteen, make zero difference to those with business to transact.

Soltznin and Drew guard the ship while David and I meet Temple and Rajcik. Soltznin seems to have reached a point of equilibrium and just wants to get this over with as soon as possible so she can do whatever she can to regroup with the Corps. Sweep and patrol ships can always be counted on to show up eventually, and I have no doubt one or two functioning non-Admin satellites orbit Dramma Sdutti, which she'll be able to buy access to in order to contact a local patrol and get picked up. By now, the Corps has to be investigating the *Hammer*'s destruction, and Soltznin and David shouldn't have any trouble convincing them that they're stranded survivors. Despite the stress of all the coming unknowns, I still maintain hope that there may have been others.

Rajcik and Temple and David and I sit at a round table in the basement of the building that houses the tavern and a few other smaller apartments. Light fixtures, covered by years of plaque from smoke and other unidentified air particulates, dangle from the exposed steel beams crossing the ceiling but do a poor job of illuminating anything. Their yellow-blue tinge makes everyone milling inside look like a jaundiced, freshly dead body. The exception is Drew's father. Already sallow, he just looks like an animated corpse, minus the freshness.

Rajcik is dark skinned and muscular to the point of being intimidating. He sits across from David and me with rigid but relaxed alertness, the whites of his eyes, bright and clear, seeming to defy the dingy light. One hand has held on to a glass the entire time we've been here, about twenty minutes now, but he's never taken a drink. I've had ample time to observe the layers of white scar tissue that cover his knuckles, and it's not a stretch to imagine those hands beating men to death. A lot of men.

The surprise-that-shouldn't-be is how quickly he'd agreed to buy our e-craft, and for our asking price, which tells me that he's already had someone out to our landing area to assess it. That, or he thinks we'll be easy marks and is doing what it takes to appease us before ghosting us. But maybe this isn't the case. Even with his notoriety, he wouldn't have lasted this long as a thief among thieves if he played everyone he dealt with. The criminal underclass has its own justice system, and even the most ruthless "businessman" isn't above the criminal code.

And our business is nearly concluded.

"Temple," the smuggler says, "go up and tell MacCready to pull the land trans to the front. We'll meet you upstairs."

Temple rises, leaning heavily on the table for support, then trudges to and up the stairs.

David is about to rise to follow when I interrupt. "One more thing," I say to Rajcik, "I want to include as part of the purchase a selection of . . . let's call it 'personal aids.'"

The smuggler's eyes, as dark as mineshafts, regard me with blatant cunning. After a moment, he says, "No."

His abrupt dismissal takes me aback. Before I can clamp down on my reactions, my eyes widen the tiniest bit, not so much in surprise as in irritation. But I know better than to show any more emotion. "Okay, then no deal."

David's head snaps around to look at me, surprised at my declaration. Then he looks back at Rajcik. "Deal's on. You can buy guns from someone else, Aly."

Rajcik says nothing, but his tongue snakes out and licks his lower lip, as if savoring something. Taking this as agreement, David finishes standing and drops a hand heavily on my shoulder, a warning not to further complicate things. "You'll want to follow us to the ship," he tells the smuggler.

"Sit down." Still holding the glass, still not drinking from it, he continues, as if we'd both complied without question. "No, you don't need guns. What you two need is a job."

"Excuse me?" I ask.

He leans back in his seat and stretches his legs out farther beneath the table, looking utterly at ease. But I don't miss the tension in his forearms and shoulders, the way his left hand has dropped to his lap where it's near a weapon strapped either to his calf or possibly under the tabletop. "You're already carrying enough for self-defense. So what could you use more weapons for? Rob a few people, maybe even steal a ship—if you can fly one—but then what?

Take it to the next rock and repeat the process until the Admin or Corps run you down, or some other deserter with less to lose gets the drop on you?"

"You don't know wh—" David begins angrily.

"I know exactly what I'm talking about, *deserter*. Everyone in this room knows it." His eyes rove from one side of the canteen to the other, blazing with intelligence and ferocity. "You don't leave the Corps without bringing some of it with you. In your case, I'd say it's more than you want. It's like a deep stain, more than skin deep. It's in your muscles, the way you walk, the way you had every head counted and threat assessed before you were a meter inside the room. You even smell like Corps. Dirty."

"Look, asshole—"

"David, wait." I put a hand on his wrist. "We're not Corps."

Rajcik's lips stretch across his teeth, revealing their luminous whiteness, in something approximating a smile but more closely resembling the skin covering a dried-up mummy's skull. "I didn't say you were Corps. I said you're deserters."

"And you want to turn us in? Looking for a reward?"

Strangely, his eyes fall to my hand, still on David's wrist. "Drew told me you two served together. Brother and sister."

Momentarily confused by the subject change, I answer automatically. "Yeah."

"You look like a good team, like you know how to fight together."

"Answer her question," David says. "Are you planning to turn us in?"

"Do you really think I'd tell you if I were? Come on, you both look smarter than that." His left hand rises from beneath the table and presses flat next to the glass in his right. Like a peace offering, he finally lets go of the glass and puts that hand down, too. But there is no peace in his cold eyes.

It's like a deep stain, more than skin deep. Hadn't I thought almost the same thing yesterday? I scrutinize him, looking for some indication of his intent, and my eyes wander over his face and neck. His large Adam's apple is tattooed over by a standard 7.62 bullet case about the size of my fist, the meaningful end pointing up toward his chin. The ink is black and thick and makes the skin it covers stand out more than normal, like more scar tissue. It's a prison tattoo, but it carries none of the false bravado that a lot of the revolving-door cons in the system flash like paper-tiger flags. Rajcik is authentic; I can see it in his cruel face and hear it in his severe voice. My brother and I may wear Corps inside and out, but something tells me the stains on Rajcik's soul are far darker.

Which, in a strange way, makes my own dark guilt seem lighter. That comforts me.

"What kind of job?" I finally ask.

"Bigger jobs than this," he answers. "The truth is, I rarely bother selling one-offs like yours. But this infighting happening in the Capital Military Corps is leaving security gaps, creating unique opportunities for Corps impersonators, and making it easier for me to stick a shiv between their ribs—in a manner of speaking. Your e-craft went up in value almost overnight. Make you happy?"

The question isn't supposed to be answered, and he continues, "And one more thing. You two caught my eye, and I'm looking for new help. It's dangerous, but I think you can handle that. The pay is twenty-five–seventy-five split on everything we unload. I take the twenty-five, and my crew splits the rest."

"Sounds like a good reason for your crew to make sure as few as possible ever come back from a sale. Is that why you're short-handed?" David doesn't bother trying to keep the contempt out of his voice.

Rajcik's expression doesn't change. "Smart. I knew it."

I already know what David's thinking, and despite my surfacing interest in Rajcik's proposal—I'll leave trying to decide if it's genuine or not for later—I stick with my brother. "Not interested, Rajcik. Now, do you want to see my list, or should we go to your competition?"

Rajcik looks over my shoulder, and I read an acknowledgment in his expression. Jerking around in my seat, I notice a woman I hadn't seen yet standing next to the stairwell, as if guarding it. I would have remembered her—the scars covering her face and part of her scalp, even the backs of her hands, are hideous, disfiguring. Her posture is vigilant, and she holds a bulky Corps-issue CCIX carbine at her side, ready to be brought into action.

I turn back, seeing that David has noticed her too, and start to rise, cursing the realization that we've just walked into a trap. Then Rajcik says, "Wait here. I need to speak with my colleague."

He gets up and walks past the two of us without concern, knowing we aren't likely to do anything rash, not with no exit points to escape through should bullets start flying. From my seat, I watch him and the scarred woman speak together, their voices low, for a few seconds. Eventually, he nods, then comes back and stands beside the table, telling us without words that our transaction is almost concluded.

Nothing in his face has changed, but like an animal, I feel the shift. He stares at us with the same unbreakable gaze, but not like a wolf deciding whether the rabbit has enough meat on its bones to be worth the chase. What's his game? What had he and the woman been discussing?

"I'll get you what you need," he says. "But I don't have it nearby. Meet me in a week. Same place. We'll make the trade for the ship and the guns at the same time." Not bothering to wait for our answer, he heads toward the stairs. The smoke in the air seems to seek him out, a gray-blue plume drawing around him in a wizardlike cloak.

On my feet immediately, I ask, "Don't you want the list?"

He stops and turns. "I'll have what you want." Appraising us for another second, he finishes with: "If you change your minds about the job before the end of the week and want to meet sooner, contact me through Temple. And if you don't show . . . not many of your kind last long out here on your own."

The two of us stare at his retreating back as if it might be on fire. Breaking the silence, David says, "It might have been a mistake contacting him. Aly, you don't want to get involved with him. *I* don't want you to get involved with him."

"You've always had my back, big brother."

We exchange a heavy glance. There's really no argument. His point is 100 percent true, but he knows my trajectory is fixed and can't be changed. I don't blame him for wanting to stay in the Corps; I can't, he's sacrificed more than anyone should have to, for me. But that odd comfort I'd felt at recognizing Rajcik's cruelty, maybe much worse than mine could ever be, it resonates. If I'm not choosing the side of the Corps, which side am I choosing? What the smuggler is offering is a place to dig in, put the question of sides aside and maybe just live for myself alone. At least for a while. Could living in the shade of someone else's crimes veil me from memories of my own? Part of me wants to find out. Most of me wants it to be true.Part of me wants to find out. Most of me wants it to be true.

11. THE PROBLEM WITH TRUST

David breaks into my dark thoughts. "A week. What the hell are we going to do for a week?"

I shake my head, answering, "And what will Soltznin's reaction be when we tell her the situation? I won't hold my breath for a 'well done' or a 'that's fine.'"

With no reason to hurry, we stick around the tavern long enough to finish the drinks we'd ordered. Daytime on this moon vacillates between hotter than smoking lava and too hot to live, and neither of us jumps for joy at the thought of having to negotiate the sufferfest temps for that long. Even though the e-craft's climate control will keep us comfortable, being stuck on the e-craft will get old fast.

"We need to move the ship," he eventually says. "Stay ahead of the scavs who may try to gank it out from under us. That is, if Rajcik and his crew aren't already in the process of doing so."

His words jolt me, and I set my glass down with a clunk. "You're right. Let's go. Make sure Soltznin and the kid aren't in any trouble."

With a final gulp, David rises and follows me up the stairs.

Into a nest of Corps soldiers.

Seven carbine barrels point in our direction. The squad of armored troops wielding them form a half-moon near the front wall of the canteen, and I'm surprised by how intimidating they appear now that I'm not one of them. As I absorb this, the quiet inside the bar hits me; not a single civilian is left to enjoy the establishment's fine refreshments. The Corps had cleared the place out quickly, efficiently, and silently, waiting for us.

David and I become statues, except for our hands, which we move away from our weapons ever so cautiously. We both know that drawing them would be instant death.

"That bastard," David curses. "He turned us in."

Soltznin appears and pushes forward from behind the formation. "If you mean that scav smuggler scumbag, he got away, Tech Sergeant. He'll be caught eventually, but it's you two that are the biggest problem. Now solved."

"Soltznin! What the hell?" David says.

"You have to be crazy to think I was going to let you *mutiny* against the Corps, Erikson. You're no better than that gunrunner.

Neither of you." Her eyes come to rest where I stand in silence, my fury paralyzing my ability for rational thought, much less speech.

"Get your hands in the air. Tech One"—she turns to the nearest soldier and flicks her Bowker in our direction—"relieve them of those arms." As he approaches us, she continues, "Stealing and intent to sell Corps property is just the beginning of your crimes. I'm sure Central Command's justice counselors will have a few to add to that."

The soldier pulls the carbine from my shoulder and roughly pats me down, then yanks my arms behind me and quickzips my hands. Soltznin had been biding her time, waiting until David and I were out of range so she could reconnect with the Corps. She'd never intended to go along with our plan, that much is clear to me now. What I can't tell is which is more enraging: her turning us in or her double-crossing David, who she knows planned to return to the Corps after helping sort me out.

David says, "Crimes? You mean like shooting another soldier aboard the *Hammer* so you could take the evacuation craft for yourself?"

Before he says another word, Soltznin, her face contorted with rage, whips the Bowker against his temple, sending him to his knees. Reflexively, I lunge, but the Corpsmember still has my arms and holds me back.

She leans over David, who raises his bleary eyes to her. "Open your mouth again, Tech Sergeant, and I'll be your executioner as well as your savior. Understood?" He says nothing but holds her eyes with his until she turns around. "Let's get them to the scout."

The Tech holding my arms prods me toward the door, dislodging a crazy-sounding rage-laugh from me. The situation holds a certain sick humor. Less than forty-eight hours have passed, and I've gone from soldier to deserter to prisoner. It would have rounded out well if I'd taken Rajcik's offer and become a smuggler, too. Guess I'll never find out how well that description would have fit.

THEY'D BROUGHT US BY LAND trans directly from the colony to the red-and-green anodized Corps security scout, which sits grounded beside our smaller e-craft. Soltznin's adopted unit had to have been told where to find the ship; the e-craft's cloaking feature would have kept it well hidden from anyone who wasn't specifically looking for it.

Soltznin. She must have transmitted an SOS either sometime last night when she was the only one awake on watch or as soon as David and I had left to meet Rajcik. No wonder she'd become so noncombative about the plan to sell the e-craft and go our separate ways. She'd wanted to make the road to betraying us as smooth as possible. *Trusting people*—might as well just arm a grenade and shove it down my throat. It's faster and achieves essentially the same outcome.

The scout's not meant to carry prisoners, so David and I have been locked into a storage room serving as a makeshift holding cell for going on two hours. The patrol unit is waiting until the troop transport ship this scout and crew are attached to returns to local orbit before we launch to join them. From there, it will be a transfer to the fleet cruiser PCA *Galatea*, which *does* have formal prisoner accommodations, and finally to one of the two Admin-governed central planets that have the military infrastructure to deal with our situation, Obal 8 or Obal 3, to stand trial. With the havoc of the Corps rebels' insurrection, whatever passes for justice in the Ministry of Security these days is unlikely to show much leniency for David and me. The example of Ohm Lumi and half a dozen other recent missions proves it.

Soltznin's pistol-whip hadn't made David bleed, but a purple-and-yellow sunset bruise adorns the side of his head and cheek-bone. Of the few, maybe just one, positives in the situation is that they'd freed our wrists before locking us in. I'd pounded on the door for five minutes demanding medical care for him, at least some cold pads, before David asked me to stop, the noise making his buzzing bee of a headache turn into the whole hive. It wasn't doing any good anyway, other than letting me vent some of my fury and frustration. But now that I'm sitting here counting down minutes to our judgment, I'm realizing there is a lot more fury where that came from, and it wants nothing more than to vent in the form of a barrage of automatic fire straight into Soltznin's smug fucking face.

With the room cleared of everything but us, David and I both sit on the floor and lean against the wall, quietly thinking over the shitstorm we're flapping in. For fifteen minutes, I've been warring with myself over whether or not to point out to him just how twisted and misguided his allegiance to the Corps is, given how willing its other members are to make whipping boys of their own compatriots.

Soltznin is bad enough, but she's just one example of an epidemic of self-serving opportunists who happen to wear Corps uniforms—just like Bernthal had been, just like the *Hammer*'s commanding general had been, just like nine out of ten of them are. If being Corps means anything, it means having a thoughtless ability to take life with no remorse, especially if it benefits you. Tollhut had been right. The Corps turns people into monsters.

My remorse, it seems, has finally caught up with me. The only reason I'm here now instead of in uniform, attached to the Galatea's crew and hunting down other deserters, is because my remorse at being the tool of a force with no conscience has finally turned my stomach, maybe my soul—if such a thing existed—inside out. It isn't as if I want to die for it, though. I'm not some kind of space opera hero, or a martyr, willing to sacrifice myself for the good of the oppressed masses. Jesus Christ. No, that is not me. But if desertion comes at the price of death, I'd at least like to know my last act in life was for some purpose greater than anything I've done up to now, which isn't too high a bar to set, really.

12. A DEAL'S A DEAL

"What was that?"

My head jerks up at the sound of David's voice. I'd started to doze with my forehead pressed into my knees.

Then I hear it, too.

Gunfire.

We both jump to our feet, bracing for . . . who knows? Running bootsteps pass our doorway, their owners not pausing to give us a heads-up on what's going on. But the sound coming from outside, though faint, is definitely gunshots, multiple, and not just small arms. In fact, it sounds like the patrol unit is getting a dose of the local hospitality just like we had the day before.

David and I are both on our feet instantly. The firefight's cadence picks up, then we hear running again, coming from the other end of the corridor outside our storage closet. A retreat?

Four rapid shots burst past the doorway, sounding to my ears like funeral bells. Then silence.

I look at David. He stares back. We both shrug and do something incredibly stupid. Together, we pound on the door, yelling to be let out. Confined by the small room, our voices sound hollow and powerless. But it's a bad idea to be found by accident if scavs have overrun the Corps squad and are in the process of stealing the ship. They can have it, but we need them to know we're not part of the patrol unit. Maybe they'll even let us go.

"Shh!" David says suddenly, and I catch what he'd heard. Shouting comes from somewhere in the ship, but I only hear garbled, distant syllables, not enough to make out what's being said. "They know we're here."

With no other options, we both stand back from the door and tense into fighting stances.

"Aly and David Erikson?" someone says from just outside.

"Yeah," says David.

"Stand back."

Our visitor—rescuer or rival?—disengages the lock, and the door slides open. A tall, fit blond man stands in the corridor, his Kaldor 75 pistol aimed casually in our direction. "Rajcik thought you'd still be here." His icicle-blue eyes skate over me in one long sweep, and the side of his mouth twitches in a grin that says he likes what he sees. "Now I get why he wanted new meat on the team. Good news, you've unofficially been pardoned. This ship's not Corps anymore."

He motions us out, and we follow him cautiously toward the scout's embarkation ramp as I piece together what had just happened. It's clear enough that Rajcik and his smuggling crew, of which our doorman is a member, attacked the patrol unit and won. He knew we were aboard, which means—

We step out into blazing afternoon sun, the heat and piercing light hitting me like a bullwhip. In a second my eyes adjust, and I absorb the sight of five hideously mangled uniformed bodies lying in unusual, almost theatrical, sprawls around the ship's ramp. David and I step past them into the shade cast by the scout's starboard elevon foil, instinctively moving out of the glare. The quiet and dead soldiers are all the info we need to see that the danger, for now, has passed.

Rajcik has his back to us, shielding his eyes as he scans the sky to the east. I follow his gaze and see another ship, a small shuttle like the type used for a planet-side hop, coming in to land. Unlike normal civilian crafts, this one sports a protruding turret over the engine intakes, with a barrel measuring at least thirty mike-mikes. I glance again at the corpses, now understanding why they so closely resemble shredded meat. Clearly Rajcik is a take-no-prisoners kind of smuggler. The thought should disgust me, but I seem to be fresh out of sympathy for my ex-fellow Corpsmembers.

The shuttle settles with a quiet hum about ten meters away, and Rajcik turns and appraises us. "So which one of you has a four-leaf clover in your pocket?"

"You knew they were coming for us, back at the bar. You left us as bait, didn't you?" David accuses him, having drawn the same conclusion I have. "You didn't even warn us!"

"Why would I?" Rajcik asks, his voice menacing. "You don't work for me. I'm not your friend. And I'm sure as hell not interested in saving your asses at my own expense."

"Then why this?" I ask, gesturing at the litter of corpses.

Instead of a response, he reaches out and pats the scout's stern, as if it's a cute, cuddly puppy. "I answered that question back at the canteen. This is worth quite a bit in common currency. But that still leaves your e-craft."

As the sentence finishes, his attention jerks away and focuses sharply on something behind me. Before I can spin around, Mick

Temple erupts into a shambling run toward us from the cover of several small land transports parked a dozen meters distant. "Drew!"

David suddenly grabs my shoulder, and I turn.

"Everyone get the fuck on the ground, or this scav dies." Soltznin, holding Drew in a chokehold with the Bowker pressed to his cheek. The panic in her expression is only moderately tempered by the fury in it.

"Soltznin!" I yell. "What are you doing? He's just a kid, for Christ's sake!"

She stands at the threshold of the scout's embarkation ramp, half-in and half-out, not even acknowledging me. Drew looks frightened, pasty white. More like a child than a teenager. They must have been detaining him in a different holding area on board. Wherever it was, Rajcik's crew overlooked it, and Soltznin—lucky again—had been there too. Did she go straight for the kid to use as a shield when the shooting started? The thought turns my stomach. One of his eyes is blackened and swollen, and his lip is split. Whatever she'd done to get the drop on him, it's clear he'd gone down fighting. Good kid.

"You"—she juts her chin at Rajcik, who stands still and alert, one hand grasping the stock of a Sinbad auto-pistol, the other still resting on the scout's metal skin—"tell everyone on that shuttle to get out here. Now!"

Rajcik doesn't move.

"And drop that pistol!"

He still doesn't move.

From my periphery, I make out the blond guy and the scarred woman from the bar standing at the ready nearby. How many more of Rajcik's crew are around, tucked under cover?

I try again, keeping my voice as reasonable as I can. "Soltznin, look. Just let the kid go. You can get back on the scout and take off to whatever fleet cruiser you want. There are way too many of these smugglers for you to fight, you must realize that." Subtext: *You're going to die the second you let down your guard.*

"Dad," Drew cries.

"Let him go, you bitch!" Temple yells, fear giving his voice enough strength to overpower the sickness weakening him.

She glares at the group for a second, then focuses back on David and me. "Fucking traitors, both of you. Cowards."

She adjusts the arm clamped tightly around Drew's throat and starts to say something else. Before she can, the kid reaches up and grabs it, simultaneously letting his body go as limp as one of the corpses at his feet. Soltznin is pulled off balance and staggers as he yanks her arm away, straightens his legs, and lurches forward.

She shoots him directly between the shoulder blades. His body leaps into the air, his arms spread wide, as if he's trying to fly like a bird. Then he collapses into the red sand, twisting as he comes down so that he lands on his side, his head turned to the sky. I can't pull my eyes from his face, even as the sound of Rajcik's Sinbad echoes Soltznin's pistol shot.

"NO! Not my son!" Temple screams, rushing forward to stumble and fall next to the body of his dead kid.

David's hand is still on my shoulder, and he squeezes it hard, ready to pull me into flight if we need to. But we don't. Soltznin lies in a pile, blood pumping from a gash in her throat, her eyes desperate, pleading.

The world goes sharp-edged and gray. All noise wicked away to a subtle background hum. Again with the killing, the kids dying for no reason besides being born non-citizens, the Corps taking life like it's nothing more than an exchange of currency. I want to laugh at how it's going to end for Soltznin.

Instead of going to Drew—I can't bring myself to look at him and have his face join those of so many others like him in the caskets of my memories—I approach Soltznin, absently kicking her Bowker off to the side. Her hand presses to the wound, the sleeve of her uniform becoming instantly drenched with dark red. I feel nothing for her, neither hatred nor concern nor resentment. A matching stain spreads over her jacket on the same side, where a second shot from Rajcik landed a few centimeters beneath her collarbone. I merely stare. Numbness protects me right now, Drew's pointless death too disturbing to allow through my armor. If that makes me a coward, so be it.

Temple's sobs sound like gravel and glass crunching beneath tires. Someone comes up beside me. Rajcik. Soltznin's eyes leave mine and look at him. He squats and wraps his fingers around the hand covering her wound, pulling her arm away and holding it. His expression as he watches her bleed to death is the coldest void in the galaxy. She doesn't struggle. In a second, she's gone.

Numb.

The smuggler rises. "MacCready, bring the case."

"Fucking mess," David says. "What a fucking waste."

I seek out his green-blue eyes with mine, wondering what happens next. I had it all figured out, but after this nothing feels like it makes sense, not right now anyway. Maybe not ever.

The blond smuggler steps up to us and drops a metal case, about the size of an ammo box, at our feet. He turns to Rajcik. "We need to split. She may have had time to warn the ship that's been moving in from nightside since yesterday. It's probably her ride."

Rajcik nods, then says to David and me, "What's in that box is for the e-craft. A deal is a deal." He turns back to the man he'd called MacCready. "You and Ortiz take that one. I'll fly this. We'll settle them in the bunker for now. Meet us there."

MacCready answers, "Got it," then gestures to the scarred woman, who follows him to the e-craft.

Rajcik faces us again. "You have five minutes to get anything you want off that ship." He pauses and stares acutely into my eyes, as if watching the chaos happening in my mind, and liking what he sees. "Or—you can stay on board and fly with MacCready to our depot. My offer hasn't expired." He then gives me that mummy-skull smile again and walks past us up the ramp and into the scout.

I look at Temple, still kneeling over Drew's body, his tear-wet face a dead gray color, his eyes haunted and bleary. Like he's already a ghost.

A deal's a deal.

Squatting, I open the case MacCready had dropped. Inside are several thousand marks of common currency. I scoop out half and walk over to Temple.

"If you're going to bury him, you better do it before that Corps ship sends down a patrol. You don't want to be anywhere near here when they find these bodies."

Temple doesn't acknowledge me.

I kneel and shove the currency into his hand. "Take this and whatever Rajcik paid you, and take your other kid, take Pete, off this rock. Buy him false citizen papers and find him a way to the Obals. Whatever it takes. You have to make sure this doesn't happen to him. You got it?"

His fist tightens around the cash, and slowly his eyes meet mine. He doesn't speak, but I think he does get it.

I turn back to David. "I'm going with them."

David puts a hand up and rubs his forehead hard, as if he's try-ing to wipe out all memory and impressions of everything that has just happened, maybe more. I hear him sigh heavily. He bends over, closes the lid on the currency container, and picks it up. Then he walks up to Temple.

"Here." The metal case hits the ground with a dry clunk and falls to its side. "I'm so sorry. Let's go, Aly."

13. FLAWS AND CONVICTIONS

Rajcik's depot is a remote abandoned mine descending so deeply into the planet's crust that not even the Corps's most powerful geophysical spectrometer is going to penetrate. The cold, dark hole is a partial luxury right now, a respite from the hell above, but not the hell inside.

We're aboard his flagship, the *Temptation*. Originally assault ships manufactured for Corps use, the line was decommissioned a few years earlier and all the surplus sold as salvage. Rajcik's made some modifications and reconfigured the hull's interior to haul more cargo, also building a quick-launch ejection bay for the shuttle carrying the Nagasaki, the retractable long-range orbital that had turned the security patrol into flesh confetti. Though the Corps had yanked out all the weapon capabilities before selling the ships, Rajcik's overhaul allows it to fight again.

David and I haven't spoken much in the last few hours. The fact that he's come with me tells me all I need to know about what he's thinking. We're sitting in a sectioned-off nook in the cargo hold, killing time with canteens of water that are untouched as Rajcik and his crew decide what they're going to do with us.

He sighs, the breath ending in a noise like he's choking. For a second, I think he could weep.

"We are so fucking flawed," he says. "How could it all go so wrong?"

Seeing my older brother starting to crack doesn't help me hold together my own fragile shell. Encouragement isn't my specialty, but I try. "Everyone is flawed, David. We aren't any worse."

The words drop from my mouth like the sigh of a war-weary veteran. But then, that's all we are. Shells of people who missed out on the good things life was supposed to offer—through no fault of our own—and were left to scrape through the waste that remained. That's what led us here, and that's what I have to hold on to or go crazy. Maybe, like David is doing right now, we can't help but pick at the scars left by the mistakes we've made, even if our mistakes were the only choices we had.

The furrows in his forehead deepen, and he turns to look at me. The soldier in him is trying to bear the weight of this truth, though the slump in his shoulders seems like it will never straighten.

"Maybe it's our flaws that prepare us to do what's right," he comments, the shadow of a half smile crossing his mouth.

I'm too tired to return it. The hope in his words is real, but I'm not capable yet of feeling much hope. The memory of Drew's dead face and his father's keening agony haunts me, no matter how much I try to forget it. The Corps and the things the Corps has done through my good soldierly hands haunt me. If I ever want to escape seeing Drew's glazed eyes, I have to become the ghost that haunts them in return. Maybe Rajcik is the way to do that.

Sensing my resolve, David gives me a nod. Standing, he starts toward the hatch. "Let's meet the rest of our new crew."

"They can't be any worse than Soltznin, right?"

He shrugs. "Like you said, we all have flaws."

"And demons," I whisper, not knowing if he hears me.

The scarred woman Rajcik had called Ortiz is working in the hold, organizing crates and inventory. She wears a sleeveless shirt that reveals well-muscled, though almost equally scarred arms. My eyes follow her automatically, and I realize the mark I've been observing high on her right deltoid is actually a Corps tattoo. She, too, had been one of us. One of *them*. Her being here, among this crew of cutthroats, gives another stir to the nauseating mix of emotions going on inside me. She'd been a cog in the death machine; now she's not. It's a choice, the same one David and I had made. Now, like her, we have to find a way to live with it.

Rajcik steps into the hold, walks over, and pushes a crate at me with his foot. "Open it."

The crate is packed with a stolen shipment of handguns, all tagged for Corps.

"Do you know how to disable the DNA readers on these weapons?" The look on my face must be all the answer he needs. "Teez," he says, "come show them."

Ortiz walks over, but before she says anything, Rajcik pushes the crate's lid shut, then sits down atop it. He holds a finger up, telling her to wait one. "Couple of things you need to know. The Admin Ministry of Security has put out a bulletin, warning that all deserters will be charged with treason and executed. That's what you have to look forward to if you're caught. If you're going to be part of my crew, getting caught isn't an option. I have trade secrets to protect. Do you understand?"

Do we understand? I stare into his face, where the meaning of his statement glows in his eyes. *Don't get caught or you die, one way or another.* I snort humorlessly.

Surprisingly, Rajcik smiles, as if we're sharing an inside joke. "Don't worry, though. We're smarter than the Admin or the Corps. And now we have you two, which only increases the advantage. After what went down today, I can see you're loyal, and loyalty is a commodity I can use."

David and I say nothing.

"Second thing, and this is good news. We're hearing that a group of wire-rat subversives has managed to fuck up the central Corps personnel database. They've lost the data on at least half their forces, including lifemarker IDs and DNA."

David jolts. "You're saying the Corps can't track us?"

"Exactly. If your records are part of the data that was destroyed, and the Admin's backups have been hit too, you no longer exist."

"If they catch us, they won't be able to tell we're deserters," I comment. The full weight of this realization slams into me. *I don't exist.* Is this the freedom I wanted?

Does it matter?

"We take off in an hour for a job. You get to start earning your keep." He stands and nods to Ortiz. Before he exits through the hatch, he pauses and turns back. "You need to know that whatever the Corps might do to you if they catch you will never be as bad as what I will if you cross me." He remains still, studying us, ensuring we understand completely.

Involuntarily, my eyes drop to his scarred knuckles, and I clench my teeth against what I might say. An ally isn't necessarily a friend, or even truly an ally. Soltznin proved this. Whatever comes in David's and my future, I won't make the mistake of trusting someone again, but I know I can believe Rajcik on this. He's a man of pure conviction. And that's all the truth I need.

CONTRACT
OF DEFIANCE

SPECTRAS ARISE TRILOGY

BOOK 1

> It is better to go to defeat with free will than to live in a
> meaningless security as a cog in a machine.
> ~ Isaac Asimov, *Foundation's Edge*

ONE

Maybe running for my life during a firefight with a squad of Corps soldiers isn't the best time to be having second thoughts about my occupation, but I have to ask myself, why the hell did I become an arms smuggler? I could have been an engineer!

David vaults over a discarded tool caddy like a champion hurdler and I follow on his heels, clipping one foot on a drill and pinwheeling my arms to keep my balance without missing a step. This is a race where the loser dies.

The rest of our crew already has the holodisc, so now it's just a question of distracting the Corps until they can get safely back to the *Temptation* and off of Obal 3. We can handle that. Our body armor doesn't provide as much protection as newer-issue Corps gear, but at least it's lighter, and we're starting to lose the two squads on our heels. We had enough time to deploy decoys around the station before being detected, and their shots aren't coming anywhere near us.

Still in the lead, David slams through a swinging door to his right. As I veer through, a round flies past my ear, whistling like a miniature surface-to-air missile and knocking the door from its hinges. That was close! *Most* of their shots aren't coming near us anyway.

The launch docks are just ahead and we propel toward them. David slams the heavy blast door behind me as I tumble in, barely making it through before the squad fans out behind us and fills the gap with bullets. Shielded by the blast door, he jams a wad of E-10 wax into the lock system, hoping to fry it and buy us some time, and we keep moving. Two rights, two lefts, then down a flight of stairs to sub-dock three and we'll be at our escape shuttle. Almost there.

Almost.

A door to our left blows open and automatic fire stutters down the passage. Regular rounds. They must have realized seeker rounds were useless. I'm suddenly spun sideways as a round grazes my ribs, but the low impact does no damage to the armor. We make it into the concealment of the stairwell door that leads to our shuttle's dock. Locked! Smoke hangs in the air, burning my lungs with each ragged breath as I lean out of sight. David frantically scans the corridor but can't see through the haze.

"Bypass it. I'll keep them busy."

He fires down the corridor as I pry the face off the locking system and rip wires free until I can short it out. It hisses as the bolt slides free.

"Shit!" David yells.

Warm, sticky blood speckles my face. I jerk my head back and see it pouring from his left shoulder. He's pressing one hand over the wound, and I can't tell how serious the damage is. If the bullet struck bone, he has major problems.

Pulling him toward me, I try to get us both through the door, but he resists.

"It's open, come on!" I yell.

He lets go of his shoulder and pushes me backward with his good hand—hard. His eyes are squinted and his face pale, but the message in his expression is clear. *Get out of here!*

"What are you doing?!"

"Keep going. Don't stop. Get to the shuttle and get out of here," he says.

"No, David, I'm not leaving you!"

"Get back to the crew and finish the job. And little sis, whatever you do, don't let Rajcik out of your sight."

Before I can stop him, he throws his carbine into the corridor and yells, "Don't shoot! I'm unarmed!" He gives me a final push through the door and slams it shut, the sound like a coffin lid.

For a split second, I'm stunned, unable to believe he'd do this. Surrendering to a squad of Corps soldiers is a death sentence for deserters like us. A muffled voice outside commands, "Hands behind your head! Move forward slowly!"

They know there are two of us, and they'll be coming through the door in seconds. The only chance David has is if I can get help. The shuttle should be docked outside, and if I'm going to go, it has to be now. I take the stairs two at time, jumping over the rail when I'm still about two meters from the deck. Landing hard thanks to the body armor, I crumple to one knee, but ignore the sting and keep running.

My mind is filled with one stuttering mantra: get to the shuttle and rendezvous with the crew. I'm working on reflex now but I'm torn. Part of me wants to double back and ambush the squad holding David, but one against ten is asking to be shredded, and the rest of me says today is not a good day to die. It's the crew or nothing.

Bursting into the docking bay, I sprint all the way through. Where's the shuttle? The only thing in the cavernous bay is a modified and very used ISPS—Intersystem Propulsion Shuttle—sitting in the middle with its loading ramp open. Am I in the wrong bay? I keep running, not wanting to make myself a target to anyone that might be in the ship. If I get to the control room on the other side of the bay, I can stop and check my VDU.

I get to the blast door and start working on a lock bypass, but it begins sliding open before I finish. Fueled by pure reflex, I hit the man coming through in the throat with the stock of my AK-80 pulse carbine. Caught by surprise, he collapses backward, gagging and going limp when his head hits the floor. As I hop over him to get inside, the left side of my neck suddenly burns with liquid fire, as if I'm being branded, and the bullet pings against the wall in front of me. The shot probably would have gone through my skull if I hadn't been jumping when it hit me. Spinning ninety degrees, I land on my side and start firing back at the soldiers streaming across the bay. They quickly duck and cover behind scattered equipment. Climbing over the man I knocked out, I note with some regret that he's no soldier, but at the moment I have other concerns. Once inside the cover of the control room, I try to drag him in so I can close the damn door, but his body is too heavy.

The squad closes on me fast and a soldier springs through the doorway before I can get the man moved. I fire one-handed, aiming for his vulnerable neck, and he goes down like a felled tree, blood spraying the walls and me. He must have thought I'd exited through the rear door or he wouldn't have charged through like that. His mistake.

Everything falls quiet outside. I lean against the wall next to the doorway, listening and waiting. I can almost hear them breathing, and now I have two bodies to get out of the way if I'm going to be able to close the control room door. What are my options? I could dive for the second exit, but I'll be exposed. If I wait for them to move in, they'll have plenty of time to call backup and surround me. My options, clearly, are shit.

There's no more time to think it through. Scooting backward, I risk a glance through the reinforced porthole into the bay. There's movement out there, a couple people coming down the ISPS's ramp. They keep low, moving carefully, trying to avoid being seen. What are they doing? Doesn't matter—they may be just the diversion I need to get the soldiers off my back while I haul ass to the escape shuttle. If they'd just make some noise.

There are two of them. The bigger one is built like a champion fighter, and tall enough to have to hunch when standing beneath the ship. The other is about David's height, with dark brown hair and a several days of beard growth. They move with too much practiced stealth toward the front end of the bay to be civilians. Former Corps maybe? As they disappear from my line of sight, I want to scream in frustration.

"Put down that weapon!" It's one of the soldiers, but he's not talking to me.

Another voice rings out. "We don't want any trouble. Our mechanic is in the control room. We just want to get him out. No trouble."

"This is a Corps-controlled hangar. Put your weapon down and show yourself."

This is the moment and I lunge for the rear door. But the day just gets worse and worse as a soldier tackles me from behind. My ribs take both our weight as we hit the floor and I grit my teeth against a scream of pain. The soldier gets his feet planted and yanks me up by both arms, forcing me to drop my carbine. Fighting back, I kick against the wall and throw him off balance. He staggers backward, loosening his hold enough for me to jerk one hand free. I spin sideways, snatching at his sidearm as I do. It comes clear of the holster, and I shoot him right below his armpit where the body armor is thinner to allow for articulation. A look of anguished surprise freezes across his features. My other arm, still entwined with his, twists painfully as he falls, pulling me back to the floor. I yank it free and jump up, immediately taking a shot mid-torso by another soldier. The range is so close that it feels as if my entire chest collapses as it blows me back into the second doorway. Gasping, trying to force my lungs to suck in air, I watch helplessly as he aims, preparing to blow my head off.

A rifle report echoes across the dock, and the soldier is thrown into the wall behind me. The shot was well aimed, tearing through his neck, and he crumples lifeless to the floor.

Tendrils of acrid smoke from the volume of shots fired waver through the room as I lie bleeding, my lungs struggling to expand. Lurching to the wall, I lean into it, listening. Footsteps approach quickly and cautiously. There's no time to think, only to react. I check the soldier's pistol and then my own. Empty, dammit! I holster mine and scan the room, but the bluish smoke conceals any other weapons. Pulling an NKT bolo from my equipment vest, I lower into a crouch beside the doorway. Black dots shoot across my vision, making it hard to concentrate, and my legs shake, wanting to spill out from under me. Yeah, engineering would have been a better choice.

The black barrel of a rifle materializes, framed in the doorway. Trying to get the drop on the gunman, I lunge, staying low, and thrust the blade up, aiming for his vitals. But I'm too shaky. The blade barely nicks his thigh. As I pull back, prepping for another attempt, a galaxy of stars explodes through my head.

TWO

No blackness is as dark or deep as unconsciousness, and rising out of the murk takes as much effort as waking the dead. Slowly, as if time has been stretched, I float back toward awareness, the still layers of my torpor gradually being disturbed by the suck and whoosh of an air exchanger.

After a while, nausea creeps in and rudely yanks my addled consciousness out of its insensate serenity. Not the kind of immediate nausea you feel right before throwing up, but the penetrating queasiness of vertigo. A familiar feeling. Having suffered other concussions, it's easy to pin the cause on the bludgeoning my skull took right before I checked out.

It takes considerable effort to focus. Where am I and how the hell did I get here? Why am I not dead? Images flash behind my eyes. Soldiers, David, the dock control room . . . it comes back to me in pieces, starting from the blackout and rewinding to when my team had been discovered in the data warehouse on Obal 3. We were there to collect a holodisc with intel for our next job, the big one that will finally give David and I enough capital to get as far away from the Admin as a ship can go. When the security squad closed in, we ran, trying to draw them off so our crew could get away. The lingering cacophony of the firefight echoes in my head, making the transition into this subdued atmosphere incongruous, like the feeling of shrapnel wrapped in velvet.

A dull ache slowly shrink-wraps my body from my cheekbones to the arches of my feet, becoming unbearable within a few minutes. Jesus, I feel sick, and stiff. I try to reach up and rub my eyes, but my arms are immobile, clamped to whatever I'm lying on. The realization that I am completely and irrevocably screwed crashes over me like a jet of freezing water and I finally jolt fully awake.

Lights pierce my optic nerves and spear directly into my bruised and fragile brain. A flicker at the edge of my consciousness threatens to tug me back down, my mind unwilling to accept the harsh brightness or my uncertain fate. Craning my neck in each direction causes the skin to tug painfully where the bullet grazed me. I'm strapped to a gurney, in a room about five-by-three meters. Cupboards and medical equipment line the walls and the air has that sterile bite that dries the mucus in your sinuses, like a sensory deprivation cell. Which means I'm not in a hospital but on a ship. The med supplies lack any insignia or labels, so not military. Could be transport or cargo. Maybe I haven't been pinched by the Corps, but I'm not sure. They sometimes hire civilian contractors, but not usually for prisoner transport. Then whose ship is it? Could be the ISPS that was docked in the bay of the control room I'd ended up in. But why?

No one has come in to check on me, but a large two-way mirror dominates the wall to my left and there's a security and observation camera hanging from the ceiling.

"Anyone there?" I try to shout, but my throat is dry, lined with felt. How long have I been here? Lifting my head makes my stomach jolt and brain feel like a rotting cantaloupe. There's an IV stuck in the bend of my left elbow. Someone has taken my clothes and dressed me in a sleeveless, shin-length gray robe, which allows me a good look at the multicolored explosion of bruises running along my arms. My aching ribs force me to lie back down, and a groan wants to crawl out of me, but I won't give whoever's watching the satisfaction. Trying to wiggle my wrists from side to side to test the tightness of the restraints is useless. They're made of a thick banding material, and there's no way I can tear through them. At least they aren't chafing the skin off my arms.

The doors slide open with a grating metal sound and I jerk my head to look, the wound in my neck stinging and making me hiss in pain. *Here we go, Aly. Wake up and get on top of this.*

A striking woman, easily a head taller than me, with a spiderweb patchwork of tiny lines around her eyes, strides toward me, her gaze dark and level. She's dressed in a sleeveless top and baggy cargo pants made of a vinyl-cotton hybrid similar to the fabric of military uniforms, and wears a snug ambidextrous-draw shoulder holster complete with two pistols. She looks as if she knows how to draw them fast enough to matter. Behind her is a man that I think I recognize as the scruffy, ex-military type from the hangar. He also carries a pistol, this one on a belt. Same cargo pants and a black utility jacket over a washed-out gray T-shirt. Simple, nondescript clothing. And, most importantly, not Corps. They watch me coolly. I stare back at them with the same consideration.

The woman starts us off: "I'm Captain Eleanor Vitruzzi, and you're a passenger on my ship." I don't miss the inflection she puts on the word *passenger*. She means *prisoner*.

"This is Strahan, the one who nearly deflated your skull. Consider yourself lucky, after what you did to our mechanic." Her posture is relaxed and in control, but her eyes betray tension. Anger, maybe curiosity.

"You're probably disoriented right now because of the tissue regeneration stimulants and painkillers you're on. They should wear off in a few hours." She analyzes a monitor near my right shoulder and checks my IV drip as she speaks. "Your ribs look like you got hit by a cannonball, but nothing is broken. And the wound on your neck is superficial. In fact, you're incredibly lucky." She pauses, letting me absorb the information, and then continues, "Now why don't you tell us the rest of the story?"

This is not the way I want this to go. I want out of these restraints and I want my guns. Neither of which is likely, so I start by trying to negotiate with something small.

"Look." I clear my throat. "I don't know you and I don't know why I'm here. But I assure you, I have no problem with you, and as far as I know, you don't have one with me. So let's be civil. Take off these restraints and tell me what I'm doing here." My voice gains momentum after the first few words. I've always been a quick healer.

Vitruzzi looks at me with skepticism for a moment, and Strahan's scowl deepens. Surprisingly, she starts unbuckling the restraints.

"Captain!" Strahan challenges, but Vitruzzi frees both of my wrists.

She stares directly into my eyes and says, "She's right, Karl. No reason to think she's a threat to us. She's unarmed, and we are civilized people." Softening her tone slightly, she finishes, "This can't be comfortable and you need to get some blood moving if you're going to recover."

Strahan takes a step back and rests his hand on the grip of his pistol, ready for anything. I have to be careful what I do here, and what I say. I don't want to set these people off, but I have a few questions of my own.

I sit up as slowly and carefully as I can, more because of the sickening complaint from my ribs than any fear of alarming them. "So who are you? Admin? Where are we and what do you want with me?"

Vitruzzi takes another few seconds to look me over before she answers. "We're in flight, three days from Obal 3."

She continues to talk, but my mind is spinning. We've been flying for three days! I barely hear the rest of what she says before I'm on my feet, yelling, "I've got to get back there!"

"Hold it! Sit down." The tone of command.

I comply as my head seems to fill with concrete, threatening to pull me face first into the hard floor, and shifting gray veils materialize in front of my eyes. With an effort, I continue, "Look, my name is Aly Erikson and you've got to take me back to Obal 3. My brother and my crew are there, and I need to find out what happened to them."

Neither of them comments, just look at me. Anger suddenly tears through the tight fabric occluding my brain, making my next words rough and raw. "Why the fuck did you kidnap me? I haven't done anything to you!"

Strahan's eyes narrow further, but Vitruzzi seems unperturbed. It's almost as if she's holding back a chuckle. What's the joke? If my head wasn't so fogged up I'd be more on top of things. What am I missing?

"To tell you the truth, we brought you on board for your own safety."

Urgency cleaves through my body like a plasma torch. I need to find Rajcik and the rest of the team. At this point, I don't even know if they made it off Obal 3. If they did, they may know where David is. These thoughts pulse in time with the pain in my head, blocking everything else out. The last glimpse I had of David's face, pale and severe as he surrendered so I could get away, floods my mind. Hold on, brother. I'm going to find you.

She continues, this time with a hard edge to her voice, "If you think nearly killing an unarmed man is nothing, you have a disturbing lack of empathy for others."

The memory of a face comes to mind. "The blond guy . . ."

"That's right. His name is Bodie Murdock. He's a damn fine technician and a member of my crew. Lucky for you, he's going to make it."

"I can explain that. I didn't mean to hit him that hard. I was trying to get away from the Corps, and when he came out of the control room—it was just reflex."

"You almost killed him." Strahan's voice is granite.

I didn't want to hurt the guy, but it was instinct, and something tells me Strahan would have done the same thing under the circumstances. Maybe already had. I'm thinking of the soldier who'd been about to shoot me in the control room, and the rifle shot that had come out of nowhere, ripping his throat out. It had to have been someone from the ISPS who'd saved my life. Maybe intentionally, maybe not.

Vitruzzi continues, "So let's talk about what's fair. We saved your ass on Obal 3. You can just think of it as a neighborly gesture among people with common interests. And now we're going to give you a chance to make it up to us."

This just got more complicated. I force myself to stay still, though every muscle in my body is ready to fight. I could jump them, steal their ship and fly it back to Obal 3—in my dreams. In my shape, I'd be dead before I got to the door. One thing, at least, is clear. They're not Admin, and if they haven't turned me in yet, they probably aren't planning to.

But what had they been doing on Obal 3 in the first place? It's a small planet, mainly an outpost used by the Admin for launching security operations in that quadrant. The only reason for citizens to be there is if they're under contract with the Admin. And the kind of citizens contracted by the Admin are the law-abiding kind, which leaves out kidnappers and people who shoot Capital Military Corps soldiers.

Vitruzzi watches me closely as I piece all this together. She seems to have relaxed a little, but Strahan looks as if he might be considering what I'd taste like spitted and roasted. His build is medium, neither bulky nor lithe. He could be a wrestler or a runner, but the rigid set of his shoulders and chronic, brooding scowl that carves deep lines across his forehead indicates his default setting is pissed off and dangerous. There's no mistaking it—I can see by the way he holds himself that he's ex-Corps. His at-the-ready stance and casual awareness of everything in the room makes it as obvious as if he were still wearing a uniform. It's hard to know what kind of switch might be flipped if he decides he doesn't like what I say.

She continues, "So here's the deal. We heard a security transmission that your crew was smuggling something from the data warehouse. It sounds like they got off world, but you were left behind. Why? Were you running a diversion?"

"I don't know what you're talking about." Why make it easy for them?

Her eyes don't leave my face, and her expression remains very calm. "It doesn't matter. The thing that does matter is that we have you, and your crew has the structural and security holodisc for the Fortress."

My eyes begin to widen, but I clamp down on my surprise. How the hell does she know that?

"Now, here's where you get to answer some questions. What's your team planning on doing with them?"

This is not what I want to be happening right now. As I lean forward to hide the emotions rampaging across my face, my ribs moan in protest. I'm not telling them a damn thing.

"I'm losing patience," Strahan warns.

What do they want? A cut? There's no way in hell Rajcik will give them a percentage, not even in trade for me. At this point, the crew may even think David and I have both been arrested and have already started making their way to the Fortress to complete the job. If that's the case, my leverage here amounts to nothing. If this situation could be worse, I don't know how.

Completely without warning, Strahan's grip locks around the neck of my smock, pulling me to my feet. My head spins, but I still have the reflexes to strike out and try to dislodge his grip. The exertion and pain are too much. My knees give out, spilling me on the floor, half out of the smock. Waves of nausea leave me huddled, shivering on the cold tile. Warm, fresh blood from my neck drips down my shoulder.

"Karl, let her go!" Vitruzzi's voice is sharp, but not angry, not out of control. She is definitely in charge here. He lets go, and I see his booted feet backing up through my half-opened eyes. My head is reeling, yet my senses are hyper-acute and strangely disconnected, as if I'm watching everything around me through a high-rez telescope. Grains of dust and debris the size of sand seem to be miniature planets set in the dimples of his boot leather, their details as clear as my own name. I can even smell the smoky residue of the firefight. Is it coming from my hair? I have to get off this floor. Summoning more will than strength, I pull myself up, holding on to the gurney to stay upright.

"If you ever touch me again, you're a dead man. Get me?" Of course my threat is hollow; we can all see what kind of shape I'm in. But my silence isn't doing me any good, so I'll dangle them a little rope.

"Look, you're right. I'm a smuggler working with János Rajcik. We deal mostly in arms, and you probably know as well as I that we could lift enough from the Fortress to live a long, comfortable life." I look for any sense of recognition in their faces. Anyone in the system working in law enforcement or crime will know Rajcik's reputation, but their faces remain stony. Either they're very good at hiding their thoughts, or they're completely clueless. If they haven't heard of Rajcik, they're small time.

Vitruzzi asks, "Why didn't you fly out with the rest of your team?"

She must be trying to suss out my value to my comrades. It's no use evading her questions. I have nowhere to go, and considering the fact that we're most likely a couple astronomical units from the nearest planet's orbit, neither do they. All we have right now is time and distance, one too short, the other too long and getting longer. Somehow, I have to convince them to let me go. I'll tell them as much of my story as possible. If I'm lucky, they'll have a little sympathy. Really lucky.

"My brother and I were drawing off fire, making for a short-range shuttle stashed in . . ." And I remember. The shuttle wasn't where we'd thought it would be. Their eyes stay on me, and I shake off my confusion and continue, "We got pinned down by Corps and David was arrested. I escaped and ended up in your dock's control room. And then you," I look pointedly at Strahan, "killed the remainder of the squad." I pause, giving him a chance to elaborate on that point, but he doesn't.

"So here I am. I'm cut off from my team and you're harboring a fugitive, which probably isn't the smartest move you've ever made. If you're looking for a percentage of our take, I can't promise you anything. We only stole the holodisc, nothing that can be split."

It's a risk to tell them this much, but what difference does it make? Vitruzzi made it clear: I'm their prisoner. I have nothing to bargain with, so they can do whatever they want to me. If they were going to kill me, they wouldn't have gone through the trouble to fix me up. I have a feeling that these people aren't cutthroat smugglers willing to spill blood out of convenience. I hope like hell I'm right.

A look passes between them, but I can't tell what they're thinking. Finally, Vitruzzi turns back to me. "All right Erikson, we're going to be in the sky for a few days. Maybe you'll think of something else you want to tell us before we get where we're going."

"Which is?"

"Spectra 6."

I mentally flip through navigation charts in my mind to figure out how far that is from Obal 3. It has to be a week at least. Alarms shriek in my head, but I manage to keep my tone at least semi-reasonable. "Wait. You don't understand. My brother's been arrested and I have to try and rescue him. There's still a chance! Look, take me back, let me rendezvous with my crew, and I might be able to get you in on the deal. We can work something out so it won't be a waste of your time. But your chances for making any bank on this get worse with every kilometer that passes between me and my team."

The corners of her mouth drop into a frown. "It would be suicide to take you back to Obal 3. By now they'll have the planet locked up like a holding cell and every Corps search-and-destroy team in the quadrant will be looking for your crew." She crosses her arms resolutely. "Face it, you're better off here than anywhere else right now. Why do you assume we want a cut, anyway?"

She's testing me, and I almost laugh at the absurdity of the question. But I don't have the energy to haggle anymore. "Why else would I be here?"

She stares at me blankly, long enough for me to figure out that my question has pissed her off.

She walks to the cabinets and comes back carrying tissue glue and cleaning solution. "We're not pirates, Erikson. My crew and I have a contract with the Admin, and some of us are citizens. But we're not going to turn you in. Which you've already figured out." She hands me the solution and some gauze and motions for me to clean off my neck. The bleeding has stopped on its own, which is a good sign. "All we want is the holodisc."

Strahan finally relaxes. The verdict is in: I'm not nearly as threatening in my weakened, bruised, and spinning state as I want to be. Reaching into the breast pocket of his jacket, he pulls out a small box of cigarettes and shakes one loose.

They seem sincere, but what could they possibly want the holodisc for? Vitruzzi has one thing right: the disc contains all the plans for the Fortress—a space station designed by the Admin as both a containment and development site for its covert research, mostly in biological warfare, the kind that regular people would shudder to think about. Nuclear and chemical munitions development is its secondary purpose. Its location, and until now, its infrastructure, are only known to the scientists and soldiers who operate there, and the few leaders in the Admin's hierarchy who keep the station funded. Most citizens don't even know it exists. It's the Admin's bogeyman, the nightmare leviathan of an advanced military industry.

And Vitruzzi, this down-and-out captain of an obsolete and ramshackle transport ship, wants me to believe that I was kidnapped for a copy of the holodisc? That I'll happily hand it over as a thanks for saving my skin? This has to be the joke she was trying not to laugh about earlier.

I hold her eye, waiting for the punch line, but her expression is somber. Letting my glance jump to Strahan's face, the amusement I expect to see isn't there either. Nothing. They're serious.

"So that's it, huh? A copy of the holodisc? And if I arrange it, you'll let me go?" She doesn't nod. She doesn't need to. I can't think of a reason for anyone besides my crew to want that disc. It's worth next to nothing on the black market because no one besides us is crazy enough to get anywhere near the Fortress, much less smuggle weapons from it. I won't bother asking Vitruzzi what she wants with the disc. If I were her, I wouldn't tell me anyway.

Trying to sound convincing, I continue, "Yeah. I think we can work that out." Which is about as likely as me growing wings and learning to breathe nitrogen. Even if I could contact Rajcik and the team, there's no way in frozen hell that he'll ever, *ever*, let anyone else have a copy of the disc. The deal he made with T'Kai to get his hands on it was practically signed in blood. But what else can I say?

Which brings up a more important question: How do they know about the disc and our intent to steal it in the first place? Rajcik has been on the Admin's top-ten most wanted list for years, and if Kurosawa T'Kai, the Admin's director of the Ministry of Science and Engineering, is ever tied to those plans being leaked to him, T'Kai will be tried and fried before the sun sets. Everyone involved knows the risks, and no one else should know about the disc. *No one.* So, either T'Kai had changed plans and betrayed us, or . . . what?

I bring my attention back to the present problem. "When can I contact my people?"

"We'll be on Spectra 6 in about four days . . . ."

Impatiently, I cut in, "We need to get back to the Obals *now*. There's no time to lose."

"Not going to happen. Spectra 6 is the only place with the kind of equipment we need to send encrypted communications across citizen-controlled satellites. Once we get there and you get in touch with your people, we'll decide how to proceed. When will they make their move on the Fortress?"

If I tell her it will be soon, it might speed up her willingness to get back to the Obals. But she'll see right through me if I lie. "My best guess is that we'll . . . they'll be ready in a couple of weeks. That'll be too soon for the Admin to make major changes to the Fortress's security protocols, even if they find out we have the details. Which, according to the contact who provided them, they won't." I watch them carefully as I say this, trying to catch any hint that might reveal how much they know. But they're too good at this game; their faces are as smooth and expressionless as a missile housing.

"So we have some time. Where were you supposed to rendez-vous with your team?"

She gets right to the point, but I'm tired of answering questions. "Look Vitruzzi, I've been incredibly cooperative, considering the circumstances, and I'm done until you give me something in return." I'm pissing in the wind, but I'm exhausted, angry, and have a sinking feeling the whole shitstorm is just a prelude to a catastrophe. "What about giving me back my clothes and weapons? At least my gear."

Strahan lets out a sarcastic grunt and drops his cigarette butt into a sealed trash canister. Vitruzzi decides to be more accommodating. "Sure. Karl, let Desto and the rest of the crew know we've got a guest on board." Strahan exits and she turns her hard gaze back on me. "I'm going to let you out of here, Erikson, because I know that you know there's nowhere to run, and we're your only chance of finding your brother and your crew. We've got an arrangement here, and as long as you keep as level about it as you are right now, we'll all come out of this with what we want. But the minute you fuck up, no one on this ship will hesitate to send your ass into cold space."

THREE

An hour later, my weapons are still MIA, but I manage to twist myself into my returned clothing. It hurts in spectacular ways and makes sweat pop out on my forehead, harshly reminding me of the beating the Corps squad dealt me. As Vitruzzi fills the gash on my neck with tissue glue, she hands me a mirror and I see my contused face for the first time. Pulling my shoulder-length auburn hair back with one hand reveals ghoulish streaks of green, red, and black bruises shrouding the side Strahan had thumped with the butt of his rifle from hairline almost to the tip of my slightly pointed chin. The eye on that side opens a little more than halfway; Vitruzzi did a good job of keeping the swelling down, and I count myself lucky not to have a fractured skull. I've seen uglier, but not much.

She works efficiently, not wasting movement. She's done this before. When I ask her if she's a doctor, her reply is a curt nod. Captain of a transport ship and doctor— everything about Vitruzzi dispenses authority. I've already sized her up in my mind, a habit from years of never trusting anyone who's breathing. She's muscular, a little taller than me, and dexterous. Her efficient movements betray no weakness or hesitancy. Something about her eyes tells me she's seen a great deal of the darkness of the human psyche but is still resolutely humane. She lives a hard life, relying on order and control to make sense of it.

When I was still Corps, I met a handful of non-comms, and even fewer officers, with the same presence of leadership. Her type is a rarity though, especially out here on the fringes. It makes me wonder what brought her here, and why she's resorting to petty extortion when she could be working in a cush hospital on one of the Obals or running a department in one of the Ministries. As I size her up, I realize two things. She's dead set on getting that disc, and it'll be a brutal fight if I don't hold up my end of the deal.

When she's done, we walk out of the infirmary together and run into Strahan standing outside. Wordlessly, his familiar scowl still firmly set, he follows us to the galley.

I glance through the window of the first door we pass, posted INF 1. Sleeping on the gurney inside is a shaggy-headed blond man with a full beard, wearing a smock similar to the one I'd worn earlier. I recognize him as the man I'd knocked out to get inside the dock control room. His neck and chest are encased in a stiff metal brace with an attached mouthpiece covering the lower half of his face. The device looks as if it would be worn by an underwater diver.

In the Corps, I'd been a Tech 1 Sergeant and a navigator on mass deployment troop carriers. The ISPS is much smaller than the ships I'd been assigned to and I examine it curiously as we make our way forward. The Admin originally commissioned these to be Corps micro-ops combat ships, usually as backup fighters. They travel light and fast, but with enough room and storage for a squad of about ten to live on for a couple of months without resupplying. This one's been refurbished for use as a transport vessel, probably for low-volume supplies. It's a fairly old model, and has seen rough use. Scars appear here and there where the metal has been welded and patched, indicating damage, most likely from small arms.

As we ascend a metal staircase beyond the infirmary rooms, I hear three or four new voices. I can't make out what they're saying until Vitruzzi presses the opening sequence on the control pad to the galley door. It slides open and three heads swivel toward us.

"Everyone, our guest, Aly Erikson. Desto," she nods toward the other man I'd seen with Strahan on the dock. "Show her where things are." Turning to me, she says, "Erikson, I have a feeling you're smart enough not to make trouble, but that's not a lesson I'm going to learn the hard way. Strahan will be your shadow while you're on board. Where you go outside your own bunk, he goes." Without sparing a second for my protests, she leaves the galley.

They all stare at me and I stare back. Music wafts into the room from an invisible source, its tinny sound and basic beat creating an urgent backdrop to the room's uncomfortable tension. The words are hard to hear, something . . . reckless . . . feckless . . . *Rudie can't fail.* I recognize the song, a flawlessly preserved relic from Earth. The band had been called the Clash.

A smallish woman with hair so short it stands on end is the first to speak. She glides up to me, her eyes slipping over my features—hairline, eyes, nose, cheeks, mouth, neck—probing every centimeter of my skin as if reading a data log. With a friendly grin, hand outstretched, she says, "I'm Venus. I fly this rig. I fly it, and Bodie fixes it. He should be okay, just so you know. No permanent damage the captain says. And just so you know, any enemy of the Admin is a friend of mine." Energy seems to pour out of her palm into mine as if I'm holding a live wire.

"Dr. Kellen Vilbrandt." This comes from a wiry man sitting at the table, sizing me up with a veiled expression. He's young looking, with a long, pale face and black hair. Something about his feigned casualness puts me on edge. That name: Vilbrandt. It causes a faint spark of recognition. Should I know this guy? My brain is still too addled, I can't remember. If I do know him, I hope it comes to me before I need it to.

Desto steps in front of me so closely that his massive build blocks everything else from my sight. With a boxing glove-sized hand, he takes mine and shakes it. "*Mr.* Bomani Desto." He spins "mister" with a touch of sarcasm, making fun of Vilbrandt. "If there's anything you need while on board, you just let me know. Making you comfortable is my *specialty*." Judging by the tightness of his grip, sheer power is another. I can't miss the lewd suggestion in his introduction. A man with his strength doesn't have to be polite.

My mouth decides to fire before engaging my brain. "You must be the brains of the crew."

Instead of being insulted by my sarcasm, a low-pitched chuckle radiates from his throat, and he says, "You're all right."

Without letting go of my hand, he pulls me relentlessly toward the wall of cupboards making up the galley storage.

"In here is everything we have to eat. Most of it is pure slop, but nutritious slop. Not much needs cooking, which means not much to clean. We like to keep things simple on the *Sphynx*." He turns to face me, and suddenly his expression is savagely serious. "We like simple *very* much. Meaning, we aren't going to have any more problems with you, right?" The threat tears through his campy exterior, and I know he won't hesitate to break me in half if I give him a reason.

Staring hard into his unflinching eyes, I acknowledge his question with a slight nod, extract my hand from his grip and step up to the nearest cupboard to examine what's inside. It's not in my interest to give anyone here the impression that I'm harmless or easily intimidated. Regardless of the deal Vitruzzi and I struck, I have more important things to think about then making nice with a bunch of strangers.

I feel more than hear him walk away. Damn he's quiet. Now I see how he and Strahan had gotten the drop on the Corps squad. Grabbing a nutrient bar that might be palatable, I walk back over to the galley table and have a seat, hoping the solid food will settle my shaky limbs. The pressure of chewing creates a reverberating beat in my head, but I'm ravenous and eat it fast.

They don't talk much while I eat, and their quiet observation of me should make me uncomfortable, but I'm too distracted by Venus. She's fidgety, frenetically animated, and stays in constant motion: picking things up and putting them down, wiping off counters, sometimes bobbing her head up and down with the music and staring off into space. Her incessant activity draws my glances again and again.

"Don't let Venus bother you. She can't help it." Desto leans toward me, grinning at my discomfort.

The ceaseless activity makes me feel as if I might jump out of my skin. Trying to stay calm, I start a conversation. "So Venus, you're the pilot? You seem a little young to be flying a . . . transport ship. Where did you learn?"

Thankfully, she stops drawing random figures in the air with one finger and looks at me. "I started out flying a mining shuttle between my moon and Spectra 5. I have natural abilities that make me very good at flying ships."

I take the bait. "What are those?"

"Well, you know Spectra 5 was where the Admin used to have a curienite mine. I was born with a mutation in my brain from the stuff. My folks mined it their whole lives, so it was built up in their systems. Like poison, you know. Except, it didn't work like poison. It changed my brain. I just have naturally faster reactions, um, to, well, everything."

Vilbrandt interrupts, "Basically, her synaptic connections exceed most people's by a power of ten. It's as if she's always in fight-or-flight mode. Her sympathetic nervous system is constantly stimulated because her mind works too quickly to filter or counteract sensory input. It's somewhat complicated to explain." He looks around at us with an expression that suggests he's speaking to a roomful of idiots, and continues, "She also has an adrenal-inhibiting response to offset the cortisol that would naturally build up in someone with her physiology, which keeps her from just burning out. It's amazing, actually."

We all look at him the way children examine a fascinating bug. "What kind of doctor are you?" I ask.

"I was a biological engineer."

Venus says with a cheerful grin, "I'm harder to catch. Which makes me an excellent pilot."

"Makes it harder for you to chill out and let us relax, is what," Desto says, grinning at her as if she were a favorite sister.

"That's very interesting," I comment. "Having mutations, I mean, adaptations like yours seem like the kind of thing the Admin would exploit. I'm surprised you're not locked up in some lab."

"Oh, they took all kinds of samples of my DNA and even some brain tissue when I was still a kid. But I guess they figured, you know, why let all this talent go to waste?"

I wonder how many human guinea pigs the Admin has tortured trying to copy her phenomenal biology.

"I have a perfect flying record. Been doing it since I was fourteen. Never crashed anything that still had energy to fly." She grins proudly and pours water from a glass into a pitcher, then back in the glass.

The atmosphere in the room seems to be thawing some and I dredge up a small grin in return. Finished with my nutrition bar, I'm ready for another and help myself. Strahan hasn't sat down, instead opting to lean stiffly against the door we'd entered through, the same expression stamped on his face. He still looks as if he wants to toss me straight out the nearest hatch into thin—nothing.

After sitting down to enjoy, if that's the right word, my second bar and a glass of water, I watch the rest of the crew carefully, cataloguing my impressions of them. Desto and Venus ease into familiar conversation as if they'd been flying together for a while, but Strahan keeps his sullen distance. Kellen also says very little, and I notice the others don't try and engage him. I get the impression that he's not totally at home here, maybe a new crewmember. Our eyes meet several times. He's watching me as much as I'm watching them.

In a few minutes, Desto draws Strahan into the conversation. "You know, Karl, you didn't have to smash her head in. You're supposed to hit the pretty ones lower so you don't mess up their looks." He winks at me.

Strahan remains silent.

Desto doesn't let it go. "Erikson, you know, we're about three more days from Agate Beach. You got your own bunk, but if you get lonely, I'll make sure you know how to find me. No need for anyone around here to get cold at night. Just take a look at Karl over there—that's what happens to a body that doesn't get enough love."

This elicits a sneering smirk from Strahan that serves as a silent warning no one can mistake. *Shut up, Desto.*

I'm not so easy to embarrass. "You know, Desto, if I get that lonely I think I'd be better off finding something battery powered to keep me company. You don't look like you've had much companionship lately. Must be rough being cooped up on this ship with no one else from your species."

He laughs so hard the dishes in the cupboards rattle and Venus joins him. Kellen's lips only curl into a ghost of a grin, as if his mind is on other matters. Still laughing, Desto gets up, slaps me good naturedly on the back, nearly causing me to choke on my food, and heads toward the opposite galley door. "Venus, you and I better get back up to the flight deck."

"Erikson, it's a pleasure to meet you. I hope you find your stay with us . . . accommodating." Kellen's eyes latch into mine, forcing me to pay attention. His comment is strange; what does he mean? I don't respond, and with a nod, he leaves too. That leaves Strahan and me.

"Come on. V—the captain—says you're healthy enough to leave the infirmary. I'll take you to your bunk."

He leads the way out of the galley door and for the first time I notice that he carries his right leg stiffly, limping slightly. So, I'd hit him after all. No wonder he's so unpleasant. He waits for me to get through and then points me toward a corridor lined by the crew quarter doors. We're nearly at the end before he tells me to stop. Punching a code into the keypad opens the metal doors to what will be my bunk. One half-meter step up separates the corridor floor from the cabin.

Lights come on. "This is it: bed, sink with a couple liters of water, can. If you need anything else, ask me, and I'll ask the captain."

I nod, irritated at being treated as a prisoner. But if I weren't here, I'd probably be dead. For the moment, like it or not, I'm completely at their mercy, and our agreement makes us business partners. It doesn't do me any good to continue provoking anyone. Trying to dispel some of the animosity, I say, "Thanks. I realize things could have gone much worse for me."

Oblivious to my sincerity, he leans into the room and points out another keypad inside. "Just punch in lima-nine to turn the lights on and off. I'm locking the door. You can't open it, so don't try."

Fine, we're not playing nice. "And I'm sorry about your leg." I don't try to soften the sarcasm in my voice.

For the first time, a hint of a grin turns up the corners of his mouth. "Well, I guess I'm lucky. Ten centimeters up and to the left, and Desto would have a lot more to laugh about." He thrusts his chin forward, signaling me to go inside.

The gas-filled ceiling glows a murky white as his footsteps recede down the corridor, illuminating my newest cell-slash-room. There's a narrow bunk to my left, embedded in a niche between sets of drawers below and shelves above. All empty. Another smaller door to the rear leads into the head with a nonbreakable metal mirror, a sink with a bottle of water hooked up to the tap, and a toilet. The identical setup to every Corps crew quarters I've ever lived in. After removing my boots, I stretch out on the bunk.

Despite days of unconsciousness, I'm now more tired than groggy. The drugs Vitruzzi had been giving me are finally wearing off, and I have some time to sort out everything that's happened since jumping out of my last nightmare into this one. How am I going to find David and convince Rajcik to deal with Vitruzzi? Does she think she'll be able to trade me for the disc? I'm enough of a realist to know that that may not be enough of a bargain for Rajcik. His loyalty isn't to people, it's to profits. Even though we've smuggled and sold enough illicit munitions together over the last six years to outfit a private army, I wouldn't bet my life on his loyalty. And what had David said right before being arrested? Don't let Rajcik out of my sight. What did he mean?

When I followed David, two years my senior, into the Admin Corps Military Academy, I thought the life of a soldier would be a thousand times better than my other option: civil service. Our mother abandoned the family when I was three, leaving me a burden on our dad—*David's* dad. The old man never believed I was his. The only impact our mother had on my life was teaching me what it felt like to not matter. I thought the Corps would make me part of something real and noble, that I'd be protecting the perfect and faultless order of The Political and Capital Administration of the Advanced Worlds. Like all fourteen-year-olds, I was naïve.

By twenty, I'd seen more combat than I could take. The Algol triple-star system was supposed to be peaceful and prosperous, with humanity happily ensconced in the orderly and beneficent arms of the Administration. If that were the case, why had I been ordered to arrest or neutralize more Admin-condemned non-citizens than I wanted to count? The people we targeted didn't seem like much of a threat to orderly society to me; most of them didn't even have weapons beyond whatever crude, handmade junk they could piece together for their own protection.

I began to ask questions of my CO, and when he wouldn't answer, I asked people further up the chain. The more questions I asked, the harder it became to get answers. David warned me to keep quiet or I'd be arrested, or worse, for disobedience. But he knew I couldn't. He saw the same shit go down as I did and had no more ability to stomach it than I did. It was only a matter of time before the hammer fell and I was extinguished from the Corps like a smothered candle.

Then the Rebellion hit. David and I helped take over our combat craft, crashed it on a moon off of Obal 8 called Dramma Sdutti, and, like hundreds of other soldiers who weren't caught and exterminated, disappeared from the Admin and the Corps.

When we met Rajcik, he instantly knew us for what we were. Deserters were all over the system for a while, before the Admin rounded most of them back up. He recognized the advantages of having people from our backgrounds on his crew, mine as interstellar ship navigator and David as an infantry platoon leader. We were smart, knew weapons, and had a detailed library of knowledge about Corps tactics and operations.

We joined him, not out of greed, but out of a shared disgust and enmity for the Admin and its clean, orderly, monstrous totalitarianism. Rajcik operates from a core that's fueled by pure hate, planning every heist and operation with the intent to damage the Admin as much as possible. After what I'd been commanded to do as a soldier, I can relate to that.

These thoughts occupy my brain while I lie stretched on my bunk, aching along every streak of the rainbow of bruises covering my body. The darkness and the quiet bring a sense of lucidity again. Despite starting to feel more like myself, uncertainty and fear for David still gnaw at my guts like a rodent. I get up again and try the door. Strahan hadn't let me see the code he had input in the keypad to open it, but I try a couple random sequences for the hell of it. No luck, but there's nowhere for me to go anyway. All I can do is lie here and think about how I'm going to find my brother. If he's alive.

FOUR

I'm suddenly awake. I don't know how long I've been asleep, hadn't even noticed myself doze off, and I'm disoriented. By reflex I roll off my bunk, reaching for the pistol that should be taped to the bottom, but my fist hits a drawer instead. My door is sliding open, though it's too dark to see anything but a man's shadow. Before he gets more than halfway into the room, I shoot off the floor, ignoring the protest from my ribs, grasp his wrist, and using the momentum of my lunge, twist his arm behind his back, slamming him against the wall.

"What the fuck are you doing in here?" I keep my voice low so that no one can hear me except the intruder.

"Relax! It's K-Kellen! Vilbrandt! Jesus, you're breaking my arm!"

"What are you doing here?" I hiss again, pushing his limp hand farther up his back so that it's nestled between his shoulder blades.

"I just want to talk to you! That's all, just talk, please!"

His voice is a strangled screech and his body is taut with pain. If I push a fraction more, his shoulder will pop out of its socket like wet driftwood snapped in half. Instead, I loosen the pressure just slightly. He draws a relieved breath.

"What about?"

He cranes his head around so he can look at me with one wide brown eye. "Do you know who I am?"

"Why would I?" But I remember the feeling I'd had a when I'd met him. Why is he familiar?

"You don't recognize me? I'm Dr. Vilbrandt. I used to work for Director T'Kai."

And it hits me. "You're the head of human subjects R&D in the medical branch of Science and Engineering. Or you were. The newscasts said you were sent to prison for selling information to smugglers."

"Yes, that's right. But I wasn't selling information, that was a lie T'Kai created when I discovered *he* was leaking information. To you. Can you . . . would you let go of me?"

"You're lying!" I give his arm another shove to encourage him to tell the truth.

"Oww, Christ!" He sucks in a tortured breath. "Where do you think Vitruzzi found out about the disc?"

Surprised, I pause. Could Vilbrandt actually have found out what T'Kai was up to? Or is he a plant, sent by T'Kai to round up my crew because he'd gotten cold feet? If that's the case, everyone on this ship is in on it.

Sweat begins to drip down his neck and, at this point, I don't think he'll be able to use the arm for a couple of days. His voice is desperate. "Please, please, Erikson. It's true. I don't have any proof, but just hear me out."

The door is open and I could run for it. But where would I go? He hardly seems fast or strong enough to be a threat, so I'll give him a chance. "If you do *anything* I don't like, I'll kill you. I think you know I can do it." Turning on the lights, I release him and take a step back.

He turns around slowly, smart enough to keep his hands where I can see them, and reaches up with his undamaged arm to rub his injured shoulder. His lips are pressed into pain-tightened slits, his eyes equally narrow. There's a smear of blood behind him on the wall where his lips impacted when I jumped him.

"I worked for T'Kai—"

"You said that."

"Yes. I did. A month ago, he asked me to meet him at the Ministry of Engineering to retrieve a sequence of data. All of our testing data on human subjects are stored there."

Human subjects data. He's talking about experimentation. Research on the effects of new weapons—chemical, biological, nano, all of it. There's no proof that this kind of thing occurs, the Admin is careful. But anyone who's been in prison or the underground long enough has heard the stories.

"As head of R&D, I am, *was*, supposed to be informed of all data being accessed, even by T'Kai. I wasn't made aware of any retrieval authorizations given to him, specifically for the Fortress, but he needed my access signature to query the system. When I insisted on seeing his authorization, he threatened me. I remitted to his authority, and didn't say another word about it. But I went back later and used his access code to see the logs of what he pulled. That's when I discovered he created the disc that went to your crew."

He looks young, too young to be as high in the Admin echelons as he is. Which means he's very smart, and talented in ma-
nipulation. Listening to the way he talks, his precise phrasing, his
clipped syllables, and the sneering disdain in his voice for T'Kai
illuminates an ego that is anything but small. His type is dangerous,
mostly to themselves because they have a hard time believing anyone could outsmart them. He, and what he stands for, makes the
spit in my mouth taste sour and my fingers twitch to slap him.

"You just happened to have T'Kai's access code?"

"It came in handy, didn't it?" There's a new menace to his
voice that sends cold pinpricks of suspicion up and down my spine.
He must notice my reaction and moderates his tone. "I mean, I
thought it would, so I acquired it. Perhaps it wasn't ethical, but
someone in your line of work should understand."

His somber eyes are wide with deep, dark circles beneath them
as if he hasn't been getting a lot of sleep. He has an angle, but he's
taking his time in revealing it. Impatience makes the blood throb
dully behind my eyes. Saying nothing, I wait for him to continue.

"When he realized what I knew, he had me arrested. I was
locked in a holding cell on Obal 10 while he made up all those lies,
slandering me, ruining my career. I was given no trial, no lawyer,
no defense. He saw to that. Then he had me shipped to the Fortress,
trying to wipe out my existence. But I escaped."

I chuckle, the sound more a threat than amusement. I'm beginning to regret not breaking his arm and giving him the chance to
shovel me such crap. The Fortress isn't a facility people escape
from. Especially soft, spineless scientist-types like him.

"You escaped the Fortress. Are you some kind of magician?"

"I worked there for years. Given the liability the Admin would
face if someone with my in-depth knowledge of the station's research activities were holding a grudge, I concluded some time ago
that I should create my own insurance should the Fortress ever become something other than my laboratory."

He's not going to tell me exactly how he escaped, if he really
did, but I have no trouble seeing the picture he's painting. Even the
Admin's own don't trust each other. Despite the impossibility of
his story, there's a ball of disquiet growing in my stomach. If T'Kai
knew we were compromised, why didn't he change the rendezvous? Maybe he *did* get cold feet on the deal. For all I know, he
could have tipped off the security on Obal 3 himself. If we'd been

caught, he already had a convenient scapegoat locked away to pin the leak on, and any trail leading back to him would have been wiped clean. Which could mean Vilbrandt's story about being framed is true.

"Once I was free, I headed out here to the Spectras where no one would know me. I needed time to figure out a way to clear myself and send T'Kai where he belongs. Then I met Vitruzzi and Strahan. I overheard them talking to people about the Fortress, trying to find out where it was."

"Why?"

"Didn't Vitruzzi tell you this? Apparently friends of theirs were arrested for stealing energy and imprisoned there. Vitruzzi wants a copy of the disc because they're going to attempt a rescue." He chuckles as if the idea amuses him.

It's as if a light is switched on, illuminating all the answers I'd been missing. I was right about Vitruzzi. She has a good gig out here as a legally contracted transport ship. She's not the criminal type, and she's sure as hell too smart to try and break into the most highly secured installation in the system for some petty thievery. But when you throw people she knows into the mix, people who are friends and allies, it makes sense.

Vilbrandt's story is too simple, too full of coincidence. I know he's lying, or at least not telling me everything, and it sets my nerves on edge. "So you just walk over to Vitruzzi and tell her you know where it is? And about the disc? Do I look stupid to you?"

He takes a seat on the bunk, still cradling his shoulder. "But that *is* what happened. I knew that helping them get the disc would help me clear myself, you see? With a copy, I can turn myself in and prove that T'Kai is responsible for it being leaked in the first place. It's the only evidence that could possibly carry any weight."

"And she brought you aboard?"

"Exactly. Once Vitruzzi understood the advantages of having both the disc and someone who knows the Fortress from the inside, she would have done almost anything to have me join her crew. She's very desperate to save her friends. I'm sure you're aware of the theories about what happens to human subjects in the Fortress."

"They aren't theories." It's a statement, not a question. "And you were in charge of that."

His expression doesn't change; there's no remorse in his eyes. "I didn't choose to be, I simply went where I was assigned, where our government thinks I'm best suited. My own Hobson's choice, if you like."

The urge to slap him returns, stronger, but I rein it in.

"I explained the smuggling operation your team planned as I knew it. Vitruzzi is a legal transporter of Admin armaments and arranged a pick-up on Obal 3 the same day. She'd intended to set up a meeting with your crew to negotiate for a copy of the disc, but things turned out differently."

I listen carefully and have to admit that, laid out like this, the pieces of his story are cohesive, maybe even plausible. Except the part about him escaping the Fortress. "I already told Vitruzzi I'd get a copy for her. So what do you want?"

"It's simple. I know what your team is planning to steal, and I want to be involved."

"I thought you wanted to get your career back."

I don't miss how quickly he buries the exasperation my remark provokes. "I may or may not be able to prove T'Kai's involvement, and I could still end up on an examining table with my insides liquefied by some very unpleasant disease for trying. Money is starting to sound much better to me than revenge. And if you cut me in, introduce me to your boss, perhaps we can cut T'Kai out. And I'll still have my revenge."

This man, a scientist who had probably ordered more than a few instances of the same kind of research he just described, thinks he can convince me to do something every nerve in my body tells me not to. A visceral knot of resistance tightens in my guts and I don't bother to hide the threat in my voice. "What is it exactly that you think you know?"

His expression doesn't change from that same wide-eyed vulnerability, but there's a shift in his attitude, something subtle. My nerves go on full alert again, as if I'm not talking to a man but a poisonous viper. "The Nova, Erikson. I know about *that*."

The spit in my mouth takes on the consistency and taste of oil run through a diesel engine. How does he know so much? Keeping my voice neutral takes some discipline. "Why should Rajcik cut you in? It would be easier to just kill you."

His voice drops to a sharp, sinister edge, and his expression is vulpine. "I've been there. I'm a living map and I can get you in and out of the Fortress faster than any schematic. You must realize, as senior biogenetics researcher, I had full security and administrative clearance. And the time to create back doors." He gives me a look of impossible hubris. "I can go anywhere I want in the Fortress and no one will ever know."

I gaze at him levelly. "Bullshit."

"What good would I be doing myself by lying? Why else would I be trying to get back? T'Kai's worst mistake was not killing me when he had the chance. And perhaps there are other gems on the Fortress your boss can appreciate. There's no reason not to help each other."

You're a retrograde, sociopathic, Admin rat. That's plenty reason. I'm not convinced, but if what he says is true, his participation could be the difference between my crew's success and failure. Rajcik could see it that way too.

"Think about this, Erikson." His eyes leave my face and begin wandering around the room, as if our conversation is of very little interest to him. The practiced casualness in his voice keeps my attention. "I saw how you handled the security squad in the dock on Obal 3, and you were able to fire one of their weapons. The only way you could do that is you were also Corps, with an active DNA signature tag. A deserter? One of the lucky ones whose records were destroyed during the Rebellion? And your brother also. Am I right?"

I let the silence answer for me, his shrewdness surprising. He may be more dangerous than I realize.

"You know stealing Corps property is a capital offense. And if you are deserters, the Admin is within its rights to sentence you as they see fit. Your brother is a prime candidate to become an R&D test subject. I'd almost bet my life he's already on his way to the Fortress."

He lets that sink in, craftily aware of the kind of effect the idea has on me. I hadn't let myself think that it might be a possibility, but hearing it spoken sends a shockwave through my body that nearly makes me stagger.

His eyes scan my face the way a fly crawls on a wall. "I'm probably the best chance you have to save his life."

"How the fuck did you get in here?"

We both jump at the grating sound of Strahan's voice. He's standing in the doorway, eyes burning furiously, holding a pistol in his right hand.

"Captain Vitruzzi gave me the code." Vilbrandt quickly rises from my bunk and takes a step backward, away from the menacing edge of Strahan's gaze. "I thought I could illuminate the situation for Erikson, help her see how important her cooperation is." The vulnerable, slightly scared expression returns to his face, as if it's a mask he slips on when needed.

Strahan looks as if he might be contemplating shooting him anyway. "Captain wants us all in the galley. *Now.*"

Vilbrandt surreptitiously glances at me, his look beseeching. *Keep this between us.*

I will . . . for now.

FIVE

As we enter the galley, Venus rushes toward me with her impossibly frenzied energy. Instinctively, I reach for my Sinbad, which isn't there, uncertain what the girl's intentions are.

Instead of jumping me, she says, "Hiya. How are you feeling?"

Her friendliness is more unexpected than a fight would be. "Like a planet landed on me."

Vitruzzi motions me to the table. Handing me a bottle containing half a dozen white pills to dull the lingering, but finally fading, soreness, she says, "Erikson, this is Murdock." To her left stands the blond man from the control room.

Uncomfortable with the casual introduction to a man I'd nearly killed, if not by accident at least by necessity, I nod meekly. He's taller and stouter than I'd realized on Obal 3. Stiff bandages still enshroud his neck, but the metal apparatus is gone. One of his lips is swollen, probably from landing on his face when he'd fallen. He lets me stand here for a few seconds without saying anything but then cocks one side of his mouth back in what I take to be a grin. His keen blue eyes light up, the crow's feet beside them deep, reaching back toward his temples.

"'Meet ya." He is clearly straining to force the words from his battered throat.

Self-consciously, I find myself trying to explain, "Uh, look, I'm sorry about . . . that. I was in trouble and it was, um, just the circumstances."

"No hard feelings," he manages to whisper. His voice sounds like sandpaper scraping along wood, barely there. It's obvious that speaking causes him some pain.

"Hey, what's a smashed trachea among friends?" Venus trills, giggling. There's something not right about the kid.

Vitruzzi intervenes, "Everyone listen up. I received a message from Patrick this morning. He set up a trade with smugglers on R'Kadia for a supply of solar seeds, and we're going to make the exchange. We need as many as we can lay our hands on for the trip to the Fortress. We'll be within range of R'Kadia in an hour, and should be down in two. The man in charge is named Fitzsimmon. Not a pretty . . ."

Sirens shriek inside my head, drowning out Vitruzzi. I don't have time—David doesn't have time—for us to be making pit stops all over the system! Stay cool, Aly. Vitruzzi is captain here and if she's like most officers I know, she doesn't like to be questioned. Let her talk and then try and get her to change her mind when the crew isn't around.

"We'll land about fifteen klicks from their complex and take the Rover from there. I'll drive. Desto and Karl, you'll come." She looks at me. "Erikson, I want you to help us."

My eyebrows aren't the only ones that rise in surprise. All heads turn toward me. Did I hear her right?

"We're a gun short with Bodie still recuperating, and we need a replacement."

"V, you can't be serious!" Strahan nearly shouts. "We can't give her a gun! You want to give her a chance to shoot one of us?"

Vilbrandt sits bolt upright in his seat and asks, "Do you really think that is a wise move, Captain? She *is* nothing but a criminal." He knows that if something happens to me, he'll never get a chance to join Rajcik.

I keep my mouth shut, hoping the situation sorts itself out.

Her words are like blunt objects, pummeling them. "When did you get the impression that this is up for discussion?"

The muscles in Strahan's jaw clench hard, about to pop through his cheeks, and Vilbrandt slumps in childish capitulation.

She continues, "The operation runs out of an old mine. The Administration abandoned the site, but the men we're dealing with use the remaining structures to run a smuggling op. They bring in and sell whatever they can, and it turns out they have about as many solar seeds as we can use right now. They're dangerous, but they're the only people within a month's travel with energy for sale, and they're willing to deal. I don't trust them and I want to make sure we have enough firepower with us to convince them we're not an easy mark. That means you, Erikson."

"Do I have a choice?" I'm sure it's a purely rhetorical question.

"No. Desto, get the Rover ready. Make sure the grenade launcher is full. Strahan, show Erikson where the rest of her gear is."

"Captain, can I have a word with you?" Strahan isn't ready to let this issue go. I'm not sure I am either, but if it means not being locked up, it might be worth it.

Her reply is curt and absolute. "No. Anyone else have a problem with this? No? Good." She looks the crew over, ready to squash any disagreements with pure rage. "And Karl, our guest won't be needing a shadow after this."

Vitruzzi exits and everyone else disperses to attend to their duties. Without looking at me, Strahan stomps out toward the crew quarters. I follow him, keeping my footsteps light to avoid attracting his attention. I don't need to bring any more shit down on my own head than I have to. Stopping in front of my door once more, he turns toward a storage locker in the opposite wall. Another keypad is mounted beside it.

"The code is alpha, zed, omega, two, one, zed, same as your bunk," he grunts, and stalks off, jaw still clenched.

It's been a while since I've provoked this kind of raw hostility in anyone. Shrugging, I start sorting out my gear.

BODY ARMOR, EQUIPMENT VEST, AK-80 pulse carbine, Sinbad pistol in my left side holster, Mini-Derg laser concealed within a boot-sheath; the only thing missing is my NKT bolo. I strap everything on in efficient movements honed from the hundreds of times I've done it before, as if slipping into a second skin. The familiarity of my gear makes me feel more in control of an otherwise uncontrollable situation, and I'm pleasantly surprised at finding they'd picked up my carbine from the dock control room floor. The carbine has saved my ass too many times to count and I think of it as a lucky rabbit's foot. The sights are calibrated and the stock is specially molded so the weapon fits like an extension of my body. It would have been easy to spot—the only weapon present that wasn't military issue.

It's been twenty minutes and we should be hitting R'Kadia's orbit soon. They'd given me my gear, but my magazines are all empty. It's time to catch up with Vitruzzi. Heading back up the corridor, I run across Desto and get directions to the flight deck.

I approach the cockpit quietly out of habit and catch Strahan and Vitruzzi in conversation.

"She's a liability, V. You know that. The longer she's aboard, the more likely it is the Admin'll pinch us and everything we've worked for will be over. We don't need her on R'Kadia. It's not worth the risk. We have no idea what she'll do."

"Relax. She needs us right now as much as we need her. And she knows it."

"Yeah? We could lose our citizenship, our contracts, the *Sphynx*. We don't need the disc to get Zeta and Doug and the rest. We've got Vilbrandt and he's just as useful. I don't trust her. And I think you're wrong—we don't need her."

"Karl, you don't trust anyone who hasn't taken a bullet for you, so why should she be any different? Besides, I trust Vilbrandt even less. He worked for the Admin, after all."

"So did we . . . once."

There's a pause, and then Vitruzzi takes a deep, resigned breath. "Point taken. But our chances are doubled with both the disc and Vilbrandt's cooperation. You know I'm right. I'm not giving up on Doug and Zeta and I'll be surprised if you are."

"But we don't have . . ."

It's time to stop eavesdropping. Scuffing my boot on the metal floor just loud enough to be heard, I step through the hatch into the flight deck. They both turn toward me, slightly surprised at my intrusion. Immediately, Strahan brushes past me toward the exit. I give him plenty of room to pass.

The cockpit is smallish, just enough space for the navigator's seat and the pilot's controls. Nobody sits at them now; we're on auto. The ceiling is low, and two jump seats line the walls to either side of the cockpit's rear, stowed in the recesses built to hold them.

"Got a second?" I ask.

"Yes. I wanted to speak with you anyway."

Leaning against the stowed jump seats, I try to seem relaxed. I want things to go smoothly, just this once. "I haven't thanked you for the way you patched me up. I'd be in bad shape right now if you hadn't, so thanks for that."

She nods, impatient for me to get to the point.

"But we have a problem. Is this side trip to R'Kadia absolutely necessary? The longer we stall, the harder it's going to be to regroup with my team and get you what you want. My brother's life is on the line."

"You really think he's still alive?"

"Maybe not, but my first priority is to find out."

She ponders my words for a moment, measuring how determined I am. "Vilbrandt told you about our missing friends? Doug and his crew?"

I nod.

"Did he tell you why the Admin arrested them?"

"Theft. Stealing energy." She's deviating from the point, but I have no leverage to stop her. Gritting my teeth, I wait for her to continue.

"They're not civilians, but they're not criminals either. We all live in an independent settlement on Spectra 6. We don't bother the Admin and they don't give a damn about us. But it isn't easy, and sometimes we have to be creative in finding the basics we need to survive. Three weeks ago Doug and a crew of four, all good people, tried to jack some solar seeds from an Admin warehouse on Obal 8, and got caught."

"I thought you said they aren't criminals."

"Don't argue semantics with me, Erikson. You know as well as I do that the Admin doesn't have the right to hoard the system's seeds. People on the outer planets need them, citizens or not."

I let it rest, not wanting to provoke her.

"We have no alternative. We need the seeds for energy, both at home and for the *Sphynx*. We won't get far without them. Spectra 6 may not be close to Admin oversight, but it's not plush with resources either." She steps over to the navigator console and inputs the course-sequencing diagram. "If you're worried about how long it will take, we're only going about ten hours off our course. Look at this chart." Pointing to a moon orbiting Spectra 5 in the system's Delta quadrant, she continues, "Here's R'Kadia. And we're headed to Spectra 6, right here. It's on the way, just a quick detour. If you help us get these seeds, you'll get your ride back into the Obals and we can finish our other business. If not . . ." She allows the statement to hang.

She's using me, but if I were Vitruzzi, I'd play the same cards. Her friends and my brother, both in Admin custody, both probably being held at the Fortress. What wouldn't I do to try and rescue David? Doesn't matter, the similarities between us end there. Vitruzzi isn't trying to come out rich in this deal, she just wants to do what she can for her friends.

Facing the fact that I'm not going to change her mind, I bring up another issue. "How much do you trust Vilbrandt?"

She regards me cannily before answering, "I don't. I know he's trying to make a deal with you, but it doesn't matter, does it? Listen to me carefully, though. If you and he try to double-cross us or get any of my crew hurt, you'll be dead before you ever see the Fortress, or your brother."

There's no mistaking the promise in her words. This is the second time she's threatened me, and the message is coming through loud and clear. Her loyalty to her crew is fierce. "David is my brother. I'm not going to do anything to jeopardize whatever chance he still has."

"We have an understanding then."

Can an alliance formed out of desperation and distrust end any way but badly? We'll soon find out. "One more thing, I'm low on ammo. Do you have any 5.7 millimeter rounds, about three magazines, and . . ."

"Go to the cargo bay. Desto can sort you out."

SIX

Desto isn't in the main cargo bay, but there's a wide blast door at the rear that's partially open. Curious, I approach quietly and peer inside. Just left of the door sit several rows of missile transport tubes chained securely to the wall. A glance at their stenciled labels confirms: this is serious firepower. AU5 Glower missiles, perfectly suited for striking planetary targets from orbit, and farther down the row, RFX Murphys, which wouldn't be out of place in a full-blown fleet action. Beyond them, an entire wall is dedicated to ammo bins, holding rounds and magazines for about everything I've ever used. Another wall houses neatly stacked crates stenciled with the names of different weaponry components and military-issue equipment. It's an ammo vault. How and why do they—?

"Glad to see you found your way down here." My head jerks back in surprise toward where Desto works, his back to me. Impressive—my entry had been completely silent. I've known people who have developed that sixth sense, that internal radar that never quite shuts off, usually soldiers or survivors with a good deal of combat behind them. What's Desto's story?

"It's not that big a ship. But by the arsenal you have here, I'd think I was aboard a fleet cruiser."

With an amused grunt, he says, "Just tools in our toolbox. So what do you need, sweetheart?" Uh-huh. No answers here, I guess.

"Just some 5.7."

The bemused grin never leaves his face. "For that little AK-80 of yours, right? Yeah, we've got some right over here," he says, moving farther along a stack and taking out a regulation, standard-issue crate of Corps ammo.

I feel a twinge of annoyance at his dismissive reference to the carbine I carry. "It's light, handy, lets me move fast, and it's never jammed on me in a fight. Plus, I can carry more ammo."

He smiles, not missing the opportunity to crack a joke at my expense. "Miss often, do you?" Before I can respond, he continues, "You should try one of *my* toys sometime." He steps past me to some lockers closer to the door opposite the missiles and pulls out a large, dark-colored rifle scabbard.

"Thresher M-2209," he says, slipping the scabbard off and hefting out the heavy weapon with ease.

Holy shit. I haven't seen one of those since early in my Corps training. A squad-level weapon, used to supply more punch when standard rifles and carbines wouldn't do. Not long after I'd joined, it was dropped in favor of lighter, smaller-caliber weapons with smart ammunition. Just remembering its brutal recoil makes my shoulder ache.

"Now," he continues, "unless you hit them in the head or heart, it might take two or three rounds with 5.7 millimeter to put somebody down. With the 7.9 in the '209, here," he sights down the barrel affectionately, "one round is all you need."

"Old fashioned, isn't it? Christ, the grip is made of wood! And the ammo is heavy as hell."

"Yeah, it's nothing like caseless, but this baby can't be spoofed or jammed, either. And body armor doesn't help. At best, your insides are still going to be pounded into salsa. As for the weight . . ."

"Right. Of course." What was I thinking? This guy could probably hold one in each hand without much trouble.

He hands it to me. Well used but definitely not abused. Examining the wooden fore grip closely, I notice something else. What I at first thought was the standard checkering to give the shooter a better hold is actually an intricate carving of planetary scenes, starscapes, ships, and people. A tapestry of his life?

"Is this—?"

Vitruzzi's voice rings over the intercom: "Approaching atmosphere. We should be entering in five minutes. We'll hit dirt in less than an hour. Everyone who's going, meet me at the Rover. Out."

"Better get your ammo loaded up." Desto takes the Thresher and slings it across his back. "Anything else?"

"Yeah," I answer, snapping back to practical reality. "I need something to replace my bolo."

He looks around thoughtfully. "I have a Torcher that would fit in your vest."

"Not the same as a knife, and I'm not crazy about lasers."

"Something we agree on." He snaps a knife off his own harness and tosses it to me. "Here you go. I've got another one."

Business concluded, we walk out into the cargo bay to finish prepping the Rover, the *Sphynx*'s auxiliary land transport. The bay is about twice the size of the weapons vault, room enough for plenty of cargo. There are stairs leading up from either side to the crew quarters and galley level, ending at a landing that runs the circumference of the bay. In the middle of the floor, a hatch to its short-range shuttle is surrounded by yellow paint to mark its border. A few crates and boxes lay around, but the space is mostly empty. The Rover sits to one side, secured to the deck by heavy cables. It's a four-wheeled all terrain vehicle, covered by a bubble made of clear, bullet-resistant plating. The metal upper frame provides adequate strength to withstand a rollover but is sparse enough that the passengers have a 360-degree view outside. Four interior bucket seats are arranged back to back, two facing forward and two backward. Gray material covers them, worn and thin, and in some places torn away, revealing solid metal plates underneath that were probably built to withstand an external blast. Attached in the front and rear are a set of cargo racks that look sturdy, designed to carry a lot of weight.

Strahan enters the bay and, passing me without a glance, opens one side of the Rover's hatch. It swings up on a set of center-mounted hinges on the top bar like a giant clam. After loading two rifles into racks attached to the seat frames, he secures a smallish crate to the cargo rack.

"Can I help with anything?"

"Just stay out of my way."

And just like that, my patience gives. "What's your problem, Strahan? Did I steal your lunch money in another life or something?"

He drops the cam strap securing the cargo and focuses on me for the first time. "I think you're dangerous, Erikson. People like you will do anything for profit. I think Vitruzzi made a mistake bringing you on board, and I'm not going to give you a chance to prove me right."

Icy cold fury rushes through my veins. His comment hits me somewhere deep inside, a visceral strike with the force of a tank. Sucking breath through my clenched teeth, I face him woodenly. "Don't think for a second that you know me, Strahan. You don't know anything about me."

"Just stay where I can see you. I'm not getting stabbed again." His tone, still level, is dismissive.

Vitruzzi and Desto approach and Strahan jumps aboard the Rover. Desto nudges me and says with an impish grin, "Don't worry. That's how he shows he cares."

"Get ready. We should be down in about ten minutes," Vitruzzi says, and turns to me. "Here, put this on." She hands me a small, white breathing apparatus, and points toward my nostrils. "It'll filter out things you don't want in your lungs. You'll feel light-headed at first because the air is mostly oxygen, but you'll get used to it. Just remember to breath through your nose as much as you can."

I press the flexible device into my nostrils, and the walls and floors begin to vibrate furiously as we penetrate R'Kadia's atmosphere. On most military ships, it's best to be strapped into something for this part, but no one seems worried. My stomach does a lazy flip-flop as we begin decelerating, and I brace myself for the sudden shock that usually occurs when breaking through the troposphere. The vibration increases for a few seconds, making the shipping crates rattle, but then, just as suddenly as it had started, the bumpiness ends and we're sailing smoothly through the air, like fish through water. Whatever else they'd done to this craft, modifying their atmospheric thrust compensation could be the most impressive.

Venus's high-pitched, girlish voice floats out from the intercom: "Setting us down in five, Captain. Looks like a nice day outside, no weather issues. Temp is thirty-four degrees C."

As the ship maneuvers through rising air currents from the ground, we all take our seats in the Rover, Vitruzzi at the wheel next to Strahan, Desto and I beside each other in the back. Once we're on the ground, she remote-opens the cargo bay door and then we're out, rolling over rough sandy terrain.

I've never been to this moon. It's bright out, but I don't see any of the Algol stars illuminating the landscape. It must be approaching night here. Brownish-green plants dot the landscape, but not many, and they are all short and dry looking. Not a very habitable planet, but the air is relatively clear. We cruise along quickly, eating up kilometers, as the *Sphynx* shrinks behind us.

Vitruzzi speaks into the com unit, telling Bodie and Venus to be online for a quick retrieval. Her actions are sure and direct, not nervous, but alert, ready for anything. I turn around in my seat to look ahead. We've gone about halfway and are quickly approaching the entrance to a canyon with steep sloping walls.

Desto suddenly tenses up next to me and I turn around quickly to see what has set him on edge. There's a flash of light, as if from a solar panel, behind us on a hilltop to the east.

"Vitruzzi," Desto warns.

"I know, they're signaling each other. There's another one up there." She points ahead toward the western cliff.

"They must not be using radio. They're signaling each other so we can't pick up what they're saying," Strahan says.

"Only people who have something to hide are worried about other people hearing them." Desto sounds angry.

Vitruzzi slows the Rover, trying to buy us some time to prepare for whatever might be coming at us.

I scan the horizon before us, spotting another signal flash on the western wall above us. Almost directly beneath it, a spur of crumbling rock creates a sharp corner. The canyon walls narrow and begin a short curve west just past the spur. I have an idea.

"Vitruzzi, if we can get the drop on them, they'll have to re-think whatever ambush they might be planning."

"Do you have any suggestions?"

"Those rocks up ahead. The signalers above won't be able to see us when we're right next to it, and the eastern wall will block the group behind us. They won't know it if we stop. Someone can scale the slope and overtake that signal station right above it. If we do it fast, they'll never know we're coming."

Vitruzzi backs off the Rover's accelerator a fraction more, thinking it through. Desto chimes in, "I'd be happy to crash their party."

"All right, let's try it. If they're planning to attack us, they'll do it outside the mine where there's less chance for crossfire and better cover. If we can snag them up, they may lose their nerve, or at least buy us more time. Desto, get ready to jump out when I stop. Stay low, use the cover in those boulders. Radio us when you have things under control. But don't take any chances. If it's too hot, get back to the Rover and we'll make a break for it. Try and beat them back to the ship. Ready?" Retreat is Vitruzzi's last option. They must need these seeds pretty badly.

In a moment, we're passing the spur. I watch the signal station fade out of view behind us as the walls conceal our position. Vitruzzi slows just enough for Desto to open the clamshell and leap out, becoming quickly obscured by dust kicked up from the tires.

We catch brief glances of his ascent as he scrambles up the steep slope: a hand, a foot. He's stealthy, not dislodging a single rock. As he nears the top, he moves farther around the corner, toward the mine entrance, until we lose sight of him altogether. Vitruzzi brings us to a stop a few meters past the spur and we wait in stillness. Only a couple of minutes pass, but the tension makes time warp and extend.

There's no sign of Desto for several long seconds, and then the radio on the Rover crackles to life. "*Sphynx* crew, do you copy?" An unfamiliar voice.

"This is Captain Vitruzzi. Who do I have?"

"Suarez. Your friend asked me to extend you a welcome to our mine. Fitzsimmon is waiting for you. Just keep heading to the entrance." The radio transmission wasn't perfect, but his voice doesn't convey much warmth or welcome.

"Let me speak to my guy."

A pause. "Hey, Captain. Looks like we've got some new friends." Desto lets out a satisfied-with-himself chuckle. "It's handled. Me and these guys will meet you in the mine. Out."

Vitruzzi starts driving forward again. The maneuver worked, but my stomach still clenches in a tense knot. These people have something planned, and it's pretty clear it's not something we're going to like. Another sixty meters and I can see where the mine begins. The canyon narrows and leads to a derelict but still functional barricade marking the entrance to a dark tunnel. As we roll toward it, I hear a small engine off to our left. It's Desto and the men from the signaling station coming down a graded road in another ATV. As we meet at the entrance, we can see three men in the cab with him. Desto's flash-suppressed pistol is out, trained, more or less, on the driver's skull.

Desto is on the radio again. "Captain, the mine is deep, it's about three klicks in to their HQ. Follow us. Out."

Switching on a set of lights, Vitruzzi pulls in behind Desto's hijacked ATV, staying close to present less of a target. Soon, we pull into a wider, dimly lit area with a steel and concrete cargo elevator marking the end of the tunnel.

"Karl, I want you and Erikson behind me. Keep your eyes open." Vitruzzi and Strahan push each side of the Rover's shell up and we all climb out.

"Captain Vitruzzi. Did you bring what we arranged?" A stooped man with septic green eyes and teeth that match approaches, squinting suspiciously. He's armed with a slung rifle and a pistol holstered in a chest harness. Another man, similarly armed, walks beside him. They're exactly what I'd expected from carrion smugglers of this sort; the type that's always looking for ways to steal what could easily be bought for cheap. They don't distinguish between entities like the Admin who have the resources to cover their losses, and honest people who are forced to make dangerous deals just to get by. For men like Fitzsimmon, the goal is profit, no matter who it hurts.

The men Desto had corralled move up next to Fitzsimmon. With a look of contempt, he motions them aside. Desto stands beside me.

"I have it. Let's see the seeds."

"They're underground. We'll go get them together."

"No. Bring them out here or we're gone."

He grunts derisively, not willing to give any ground. The cave is littered with cargo, most of it in bins or under tarps, and I can't make out what anything is in the gloom. There are too many hiding places. Hot and cold pinpricks jig down my spine, a hypersensitivity that assures me we're moments from open hostility. The depth of the mine and distance between us and the *Sphynx* cuts off communication and any help the rest of the crew can provide. Vitruzzi and Strahan face off with Fitzsimmon, poised to draw their weapons.

Her next words astonish me. "Desto, get back in the Rover and keep watch up here. Karl, Erikson, let's go." She faces Fitzsimmon. "We'll come down and get the goods. The money stays up here. After we have the seeds loaded on our ATV, you'll get your price."

She must have a lot of faith in Desto to leave him up here alone. She must also be crazy to separate us like this. What choice do I have but to go along? Strahan stares unblinking and unafraid at the men before us. Confident, but wary.

Fitzsimmon turns and opens the elevator. A massive blast door rumbles upward, exposing a wire-caged platform. One of the men from Desto's group slides the cage open and he and another man move inside. Desto steps inside the Rover and shuts the hatch. Fitzsimmon waits for us to get on the elevator, closing the door behind us.

The elevator is spacious, with plenty of room for six of us. The descent takes close to a minute and the hard stone walls passing by outside the elevator cage radiate deep, earthen cold that increases the farther we descend. One yellow light hangs from the wire mesh, turning the condensation from our breath into golden vapor. The floor is plate steel, made to haul heavy equipment and earth.

"I have to say, it's your lucky day—you needing solar seeds and we just happen to have some." Fitzsimmon stares straight ahead as he's talking, trying to divert our attention and keep us off guard. "Acquired them from a crew whose ship crashed on the other side of the moon. They were happy to give 'em up since that bird was scrap. Only needed a tiny bit of convincing. Who says crime doesn't pay?" Scavenger. He and his group had probably murdered the wrecked crew and taken everything they could. He turns to us and flashes a seedy grin, clearly thinking of us as his next opportunity.

The elevator hits bottom. Another thick blast door rises and we're looking into a large room, about forty meters deep, with concrete walls and heavy steel and concrete struts bracing against the earth. An alternate shaft enters the chamber ten meters above the floor on the far end. There may once have been a ledge running the perimeter of the upper story, but it has long since fallen apart or been used for scrap. Fitszimmon steps out of the lift, Vitruzzi right behind him. I follow with Strahan at my right elbow, and feel the other two men breathing on the back of my neck.

As we walk forward, Fitzsimmon tells us that the crates up ahead hold our seeds. I know it's a lie. He's trying to get us out into the open where we lose the advantage and can't escape behind the blast door into the elevator. Furtively, I look around, trying to see what other surprises are in store for us. This room is well lit, at least better than the tunnel above. There's movement above us, coming from the second-story entrance. Crates are jammed into the opening, but my battle sense tells me there's someone behind them, covering the room from the better vantage point. Envisioning the ambush they have planned is as easy as if I were watching it on a video screen. My nerves start firing, raw adrenalin squirting into my muscles. After I clear my throat to catch Strahan's attention, he gives me a sidelong glance and I hold out a finger in front of my stomach, shifting my eyes up to the opening. His chin drops almost imperceptibly, acknowledging the situation, and I breathe more easily. I'm here with professionals. Good, maybe we have a chance.

A crackle explodes from Vitruzzi's radio, like a fission bomb, blasting the silent tension into pieces. "Captain, they fucked us! Get out of there!" Desto's voice is sharp, sudden, absolute. *It* is *on!*

SEVEN

My elbow smashes into the nose of the man behind me too fast for him to react. He flies backward off his feet. Going with the momentum, I fall on top of him and roll to the side. Pistol already out, I shoot him in the head then dive for a concrete support to my left that holds the roof in place. Rapid firing cascades into the cavern from above, and Vitruzzi is crouched behind a stack of crates about seven meters to my right, returning fire. I look behind me and the other man is lying on his face, not moving, blood pooling beneath him. Did Vitruzzi shoot him, or was it crossfire? Strahan grapples in the middle of the floor with Fitzsimmon. He's completely in the open, but Vitruzzi is keeping the man above from getting a clean shot at him, and I join the barrage with my carbine.

The elevator motor rumbles, signaling that we're about to have more company. Shit! This party is getting out of hand. The blast door begins to gape and I press my back against the support beam, firing a barrage under the door. Screams and blood flood out, followed by two heavy thuds. Suddenly two surprised and agonized faces stare at me from under the door and I aim carefully, finishing them off before they can fire a single shot.

Turning back, I see Strahan crouching over Fitzsimmon's lifeless body, firing his pistol toward the upper entry. He's in the open, completely exposed, and the return fire isn't abating. There must be at least two shooters up there. I glance at Vitruzzi; her magazine has to be close to dry. She suddenly drops with her back to the crates and grabs at her ammunition vest. Got to make a move. "Vitruzzi, Strahan, make for the elevator! I've got it!" I yell.

She breaks immediately and I flinch as a bullet ricochets from the corner of the beam I'm hiding behind, less than a fist's width above my head. Shrapnel stings my hands and tiny beads of blood well up, but I keep firing—can't let those bastards get a clear shot.

"Strahan!" Vitruzzi yells in alarm. I look over in time to see him dive behind the crates where she had been hiding, blood mixing with the grit on the dirty floor beneath him. He twists awkwardly onto one knee and continues firing. Vitruzzi is behind me with good cover in the elevator, loading a second magazine. The display counter on the carbine's stock reads three shots from dry. I pop off two and grab a new magazine, reloading it before the final shot so I don't have to chamber a round. No one fires, and no targets are visible. Whoever is up there has the luxury of waiting us out. They have better cover and a better vantage point. If we move, Strahan and I will be easy targets, but we have to get to that elevator.

I'm crouched on the ground, my back to the beam. I can see Vitruzzi's barrel and one eye from her cover in the elevator. I look over at Strahan. His jaw is clenched, eyes narrowed to slits.

"Strahan," I call. "Where are you hit?"

"My goddamn leg!"

"Can you walk?"

He tries to bring his foot underneath him but gives it up with a gasp. His glance is furious. No fear there. Making a decision, I turn back to Vitruzzi and signal for her to open fire at the shooters, pointing at myself, then at Strahan, and lastly back toward the elevator. She nods and brings her gun around.

Rifle blasts echo throughout the chamber. Rocketing from behind the beam and staying low, I lunge for Strahan. Firing his pistol with his left hand, he swings his right arm over my shoulder. I spring upward as hard as I can with almost his full weight on my shoulders. Christ, he's heavy! Doesn't matter, moving forward. I can feel him lurching with his good leg, trying to improve our speed. We're not fast enough—a bullet hits me in the back, smashing into my body armor like a sledgehammer, instantly propelling us forward a few meters. My lungs go limp as the impact pushes all the air out of me. This can't keep happening. But we're in the elevator! I stumble over one of the dead men's legs and Strahan and I hit the floor. The blast doors shut with agonizing slowness as bullets skid off the ground outside. Finally, the doors seal.

Wheezing, I'm finally able to suck in air and re-inflate my lungs. Vitruzzi is on the radio. "Desto! Do you copy? What's your status? Over."

"Captain, they've shut me in the Rover. Broke the latch from the outside. I can't open it, but I'm alone up here."

"We're in the elevator. We should be up in less than two minutes. Do not shoot when the doors open! Out."

"Strahan, how are you doing?" Blood saturates his right pant leg above the ankle and his face is ashen. Two bright red spots flame over his cheeks, making his eyes glint like gemstones. "I'm going to take a look at this, all right?" Gingerly pulling up his pant leg, I see a clean hole going all the way through the bottom of his calf. He watches me, sweat beading up on his brow. "I don't see any bone. Looks like you got lucky." Ripping a sleeve from his shirt to bandage the wound, I tie it extra tight to aid in supporting his weight. We're not out of this yet. "What do you think now, huh? Still think I'm dangerous?" I'm just trying to distract him, not really paying attention to what I'm saying. But his response grabs my attention.

"I think we're even." His burning eyes catch mine and hold them for a split second.

The elevator stops and Vitruzzi hits the button to open the blast doors. We wait. Nothing happens.

"Shit." She hits it harder. Nada. "They must have rigged it. Desto, do you still have control of the Rover?"

"Yeah, I just can't get out." He's angry, an irate animal caught in a cage.

"All right, I want you to launch a rumbler."

"V, no grenade is getting through that blast door."

"I know. Hit the wall to your left. Hit it is many times as you have to. Smash through it."

"Copy."

"Okay, get down. There could be some debris."

Strahan pulls his knees up, wincing, and Vitruzzi and I crouch against the far brace, covering our faces with our arms just as we feel a blast. Dust fills the shaft. Another blast, and another, the sound pummeling my eardrums like a hammer. The elevator light is burst by a flying rock. I pray that the impact doesn't damage the elevator cables. It's a long way to the bottom.

"Captain! There's a hole, climb through!"

I open my eyes but can't see anything except a disquieting red glow coming from below. They must have the doors open down there, but they won't be able to shoot up the shaft this far—unless they have a pulse launcher. Vitruzzi slides the cage door open, grunting as she struggles to get the warped rollers to give. There's just enough space between it and the blast door for her to fit. Squeezing through, she climbs around the cage until she's next to the jagged opening.

"I'm going to try the controls from outside. If they still work, I'll open the blast door for you. If not . . . Karl?"

"I'll manage," he says, and pulls himself up using the elevator wall.

Maneuvering through the crater in the tunnel wall, she disappears. Moments later, the door rumbles open and I take Strahan's arm again. "Let's go."

The tunnel is nearly dark. Vitruzzi runs to the Rover and begins working at the driver's side latch with a knife pulled from her ammo vest. Desto crouches inside, poised and ready to shove it open as soon as the latch breaks free. As Strahan and I limp forward, beams of light bounce along the walls, speeding down the tunnel toward us.

"Wait!" he yells, jerking me to a halt. "Over there."

Two metal containers marked "Solar Focusing Amalgam" sit beside one of the rough stone walls. A tarp lies crumpled on the ground next to them, blown off by the concussion from the grenades. Exactly what we came here for.

"Those bastards," I manage to pant. "Come on, we can't carry them." We make it to the Rover as Desto finally kicks open the hatch.

"Vitruzzi, the seeds are over there! We can still get them."

Her forehead wrinkles for a half second, gauging the situation, wondering how much time we have. Then she says, "Desto, bring the Rover! Come on, Erikson."

Strahan lets go of my shoulders and takes aim down the tunnel. Whoever's coming is moving fast, but I can't hear anything, only see the lights approaching. Vitruzzi and I get to the crates and work together to quickly load them on the Rover's cargo racks.

"Let's move!" She jumps in, scrambling over Desto to the passenger seat, and I'm right behind her. Desto passes Strahan, slowing down enough for us to haul him over the side. Vitruzzi and I pull the hatch closed but it won't latch, so I hold onto it using the closing strap. Desto presses hard on the accelerator, forcing us into a spin, and then the Rover lurches straight ahead. A four-wheeler comes into view from the tunnel entrance, cruising at top speed. The next instant, I'm thrown into Strahan as Desto turns sharply, losing my grip on the hatch. It flies upward, smacks against the other side, and slams back down with a thud. I manage to grasp it again, and wrap it tightly around my fist as I hold my breath, just waiting for a blast to hit us. Then Vitruzzi says, "Take this you fucks." A hollow thump comes from beneath us, and the tunnel is filled with dazzling brightness as the four-wheeler explodes.

"Got him!"

We speed through the smoky blaze, momentarily riding up on debris. In seconds, we break through the tunnel entrance and back into the open air. Twilight has hit and the sky above us is a mix of purple and red clouds, shifting like the superheated plasma of supernova remnants. It's not until Strahan shifts beneath me that I realize I'm still sitting half on top of him. I pull myself back into my seat. Finally, the *Sphynx* comes into sight.

VENUS PILOTS US OFF the moon the instant we roll into the cargo hold and seal the hatch.

"Whew! That was the shit, wasn't it?!" Desto jumps off the Rover, grinning like a deranged butcher. Still sitting, I lean back and take in the ceiling, letting the fact that we survived sink into both my senses and muscles before I trust myself to stand.

"Damn woman, you know how to keep a firefight from getting dull, don't you?" It takes me a minute to realize he's talking to me, and I drop my eyes to see his outstretched hand ready to help me out.

Still winded, I say flatly, "You're nuts."

He laughs, grasping my hand and pulling me out. With a wink, he says to Strahan, "She's as smart as she looks. Come on, let's get you to the infirmary." The two of them start off.

"You should come too, get that hand cleaned up," Vitruzzi says, staring at me keenly. What is she thinking? I'm a complete stranger, a dangerous stranger who had nearly killed one of her crew, and yet she'd taken a major risk on me, gambling I would come through for them when the shit hit the fan. And I had. Where does that leave us now?

Without a hint of mockery, she says, "Thank you, Erikson."

STANDING IN INF 1, I wince with every cement fragment I pluck from my knuckles. Vitruzzi cuts through Strahan's pant leg as he sucks down a cigarette like a jonesing opium addict, teeth embedded in the filter, smoke pouring simultaneously from the end of the butt and out through his flared nostrils.

As Vitruzzi runs a scanner above Strahan's wound, a to-scale three-dimensional image appears in the air. It takes me a minute of staring before I can make sense of what I'm seeing.

"Cybernetic tissue?"

Strahan replies around the cigarette, "Yeah. Lost the real one from the knee down when I was still in the Corps. Proximity grenade. That, and these." He waves the last three fingers of his right hand at me.

Vitruzzi speaks with the distracted tone of a teacher as she works on the wound. "Most of the leg is still natural tissue, only the nerves and bones are synthetic. Titanium fibula, tibia, and tarsals, and semiconducting fibers tracing the neural pathways. His muscles and blood vessels re-grew easily once the structure was replaced. We haven't been able to perfect the neurological system yet, but the synth-nerve fibers are a functional replacement." She returns her attention to Strahan. "The bullet went through, but it made a mess. I can suture things back together and put you in regeneration brace, but you'll be hobbling for a few days."

Finished cleaning the scrapes on my hands, I have nothing left here to do and move toward the exit, expecting them to say or do something to stop me. But only their eyes follow me out.

Now what?

Now, I wait.

Once in my bunk, autopilot takes command, and I follow the same, almost ritualistic, pattern I always do. Throwing a rag I'd found across the cabin's bench, I begin tearing down my weapons and laying them out, uniformly, methodically, piece by piece until the bench is covered with a smorgasbord of black metal. I attack the pieces using a cleaning kit from my belt, scraping each of them clean until they gleam like living embers. Knowing my weapons function smoothly and flawlessly, that they'll be reliable when I need them, gives me the extra edge of confidence that can mean the difference between living and dying. Soon, the smell of gun oil infuses the pandemonium of thoughts whirling through my head, transporting me back to Obal 3. All I can think about is David, guessing how much danger he's in, weighing his chances.

Common sense tells me to accept the probability that he's dead already, but I don't believe it. *I can't.* Capturing smugglers alive is Admin SOP. The Soldier's Rebellion had left a mess behind that they're still trying to clean up, and deserters control many of the system's black market operations and smuggling rings. With the destruction of the Capital Military Corps' central personnel database and part of the backup, the Admin lost the ability to reference or track the identities of soldiers who'd deserted or who had simply been lost, their ships obliterated in the uprising. It was a blow that nearly crippled them . . . for a while. Thousands of deserters like

David and I simply disappeared from existence, anonymous and untraceable. In order to clean up the system and regain control, the Admin's best option is live capture and interrogation. All information is potentially valuable. Because of this, I let myself believe David is still alive. But for how long? Five days have already passed.

Picking up the bolt of my AK-80 pulse carbine and scrubbing the carbon residue vigorously from its short barrel, I try to imagine what would have happened after David surrendered. He threw out his weapons and went quietly. They'd have had no reason to kill him. But citizens and non-cits carrying weapons get them a guarantee of a quick trial and judgment, followed by an inevitable capital sentence.

The mechanical process of cleaning and checking my weapons keeps me occupied while I let my mind wander freely. My own version of meditation. Unique, yeah, but it keeps me from bugging out. Next to the AK sits my Sinbad auto-pistol, already cleaned and reassembled, and the Mini-Derg XM2 laser that lives strapped to my right calf. The only piece that can be disassembled and replaced on this small but expendable weapon is the battery. As I press the cold metal into the holster, my mind jumps to thoughts of the Fortress itself.

Designed and built in secret, the Admin never intended the space station to be exposed; yet they still prepared for the possibility. Instead of locating it on a planet or moon, it was designed to be mobile, keeping it virtually untraceable. I've never seen it, never met anyone who claims to have been on it until Vilbrandt, but I've heard the stories, and I'm a firm believer that every myth contains some truth. My years in the Corps are enough proof that any government with unlimited power is a government with a reason to hurt people. Sometimes they don't even need a reason. My naiveté died the first time they commanded me to take aim and fire at an innocent.

Hot tears of fear and frustration seep into my eyes. Blinking against them, I slam my fist against the bench and force myself to just STOP thinking. I'll go crazy if I let myself imagine what might be happening to David, but Vilbrandt, with his sidling innuendoes about the types of research done on the Fortress, hadn't made it any easier. Soon I'll be back in contact with Rajcik and won't have time to sit around being tortured by my corrosive thoughts. I hope.

If Vitruzzi's guess is right and Rajcik and the crew made it free and clear with those plans, they're already preparing for the assault on the Fortress. David and I should have rendezvoused with them three days after the mission, two days ago, so Rajcik has probably already written us off. But if I can contact him and make some kind of arrangement to get Vitruzzi the disc, there may still be time to find my brother.

Resuming my ritual, I wipe the AK's bolt spring down with the rag and a drop of oil, mentally weighing the likelihood that Rajcik will be willing to deal with Vitruzzi. Maybe he doesn't need David and me for this job, but then, we've operated as a team for six years. He knows he can rely on us when the shooting starts—and there will be a lot of shooting—and he may be counting on the same level of mutual reliance to increase the odds for success. On the other hand, when have I ever seen Rajcik make a deal that could put a payoff in jeopardy? Never. Our lives might not mean a damn thing to him, and Vitruzzi and her crew can write their friends off for good.

These thoughts continue chasing each other in a maddening circle until I hear footsteps echoing up the metal walkway. I prefer the silence, and slivers of disappointment and irritation cut through me. Reluctantly, I raise my head to see Strahan standing in my doorway.

"You need any help with those?"

"What—are we friends now?"

With a dark frown, he spins around to leave, but then hesitates. Turning halfway back, he says, "You know Erikson, maybe I was wrong about you."

"Maybe you were."

"At least I'm willing to admit it." Abruptly, he stomp-limps away.

Clicking the carbine's barrel into place, I try to ignore an unexpected tinge of regret.

EIGHT

My weapons can't get any cleaner and my thoughts can't get any grimmer. I'm completely helpless, at the mercy of Vitruzzi and her crew, and it's infuriating. With nothing to do but wait for time to pass until we reach Spectra 6, I decide to make my way to the galley. The Sinbad is hidden beneath my bunk, the carbine lies on the bench, and the Derg is attached to my calf. Normally the gun is hidden inside the baggy material of my pants, but this time I attach the holster to the outside. I'm not leaving the weapons locked up where they'll be useless if I need them in a hurry.

I run into Vilbrandt at the staircase leading up to galley level. The stairs are so narrow I have no choice but to wait for him at the bottom. That's part of it. The other part is that the thought of brushing against him makes my skin feel slimy.

"Congratulations on your successful mission." A red glow seeps through a vent beside him as he reaches my level, casting a mesh shadow over his face that gives his pale features a sallow, sickly glow.

The memory of his protestations when Vitruzzi had announced my enlistment on the mission makes my teeth clench. "What kind of shit were you trying to pull with Vitruzzi?"

Of course he knows what I mean. He's a quick one. "You're important to me, Erikson." His tone is sibilant and calm. "If anything happens to you, I stay poor *and* a fugitive. I'd rather you not risk your life for these . . . people, if you don't absolutely have to." His eyebrows arch, and he ends his sentence on an upward note. The message is clear: he doesn't think there's *any* reason I should risk my life for Vitruzzi's crew. Prick.

I want to throw him off guard and ruin that smug calm of his. "She knows you're trying to deal."

"She's an intelligent woman. I think she has more of a criminal mind than she lets on. Why wouldn't I try to make a deal with you? I have nothing to lose, and everything to gain."

His callousness makes me feel as if I'm biting tinfoil. How many people are this cold, this disconnected from normal human emotions? I'm beginning to see why T'Kai was so quick to try and have him erased. It's unnerving to be around someone this unapologetically avaricious.

"I told you I couldn't guarantee anything."

His smile is a squashed worm writhing on a hot sidewalk. "Just introduce me to Rajcik. I'm quite certain he will see the benefit of involving me in this enterprise."

"We'll see." His slippery gaze follows me up the stairs as I maneuver past him.

DESTO AND BODIE SIT in the galley drinking bottles of what looks like flat, warm beer. The fermentation process in space is an imprecise science. Constantly changing pressure and inconsistent matter in both the air and water make for interesting, and usually questionable, brews. Alcohol of any kind is as illegal as weapons are on the governed planets, and plants as marginally useful as hops don't often warrant room in artificial growing environments. There's something to be said for the people who continue trying to develop the beverage.

They nod to me as I enter, much of their earlier coolness seeming to have thawed. Helping out on R'Kadia has earned me some good credit. This newfound trust, or at least indifference, could come in handy.

Rummaging through the cabinets in hopes of finding something, *anything* more appetizing than travel-packaged nutrition bars turns out to be a pipe dream. I haven't eaten more than a few bites of food since waking up almost twenty-four hours ago, yet my appetite has been minimal. Must be a side effect of the drugs and whatever Vitruzzi had been pumping into me through the IV. Surviving a firefight usually makes me ravenous, and my insides feel as hollow as a balloon.

As Desto and Bodie, whose voice now resembles large stones rolling along a streambed, talk, I sit with them and jump in with an observation, "The amount of seeds we got could turn a solid profit. There are a least fifty kilos there."

"We don't need them for cash," Desto says. "We just use them to keep the power on and the *Sphynx* flying."

"Right, sure," I nod, pretending to consider the statement, but I have other ideas. "Have you thought about what you're going to offer Rajcik for the holodisc?"

Desto gives me a flat look, his expression completely blank.

"I'm just asking."

"Aren't you enough?"

"Let me get this straight. The options are my crew either hands over a copy of the disc, or you'll kill me?" I pause, hoping to read something in their expressions that says that's not what they intend. Bodie's clear blue eyes squint slightly, as if the idea makes him uneasy—all the proof I need. "You're not going to do that, so it's not really much of an incentive for Rajcik, is it? I'll be straight with you, he would kill me himself if he thought it would help his cause."

"What cause is that?" asks Bodie.

"He hates the Admin and he'll do whatever he can to sabotage it, as long as it's profitable."

Vitruzzi walks in, Strahan limping doggedly behind her. The brace he wears is a sophisticated piece of medical equipment. Not much bigger than a boot, it fully encloses the lower leg and creates a hydro chamber that combines with sensors. These attach to the surrounding tissue and detect the optimal nutrient and chemical necessities of the wounded area. While running continual tissue scans, it releases biochemical components directly into the bloodstream to expedite healing. In the Corps, I'd seen them used to repair soldiers' broken bones in less than four weeks, and flesh wounds even more quickly. It's surprising to see such a useful and expensive piece of equipment outside of an Admin medical station. Then again, it's surprising to meet a doctor out here who knows how to use one.

Vitruzzi must have overhead us. "So your boss has an agenda. In that case, suppose you tell us what he plans to steal from the Fortress?"

"That's not part of our deal."

An angry vein begins pulsing in her forehead, a warning that she's losing patience, but her voice is steady. "Erikson, you did a good job back there and we might not have made it without you." She glances at Strahan, who eases into a chair next to me. "But I'm not going into this deal without knowing *all* the details. I didn't press the issue before because I wanted to be sure you weren't bullshitting us. But I've heard of Rajcik, I know some of the things he's accused of. If we're going to deal with him, I have to know what he's planning. This isn't negotiable."

Damn. The fun just keeps getting better and better. "Weapons. High-tech munitions."

"There are lots of illicit arms all over the place. What does the Admin care if you steal a few more?" Strahan asks.

Bodie follows up with his own question, "And why steal weapons from the Fortress? I can name ten different locations that you could break into with a fraction of the effort that would take."

My eyes shift to Vitruzzi whose eyebrows are now creased together, the vein pulsing like an accusation. If she hasn't already guessed our plan, she's about to.

They would have some good points if we were just after a nominal return. But Rajcik wants to strike deeper. He wants to show the Admin how vulnerable they are, prove that their most well-protected facility is still no match for him. It's a personal vendetta, a primal, gut-stick fight that he's bringing to their doorstep.

Sighing, I take the plunge. "The Fortress is the only place you can find a weapon like this. It's experimental, secret. The only reason we know about it is T'Kai got greedy, and it was the best carrot he could dangle to get Rajcik involved. It's called the Richter Mini-Nova. The technology is new, but it's the same concept as a chain reaction fusion bomb."

Bodie whistles, almost appreciatively. "Someone could do a lot of damage with a bomb like that."

"Or kill a lot of people." Strahan's voice is icy. "Whom exactly would you sell something like that to?"

"Back to the Admin. They won't want it out in the system. Can you imagine the kind of backlash there would be if citizens knew they are designing weapons like this?"

"And what if they don't buy it?"

This is the part this crew won't like. "They will definitely pay after we threaten to detonate it if they don't."

Alarmed, Bodie sits up straight in his chair. "That's crazy! You'll kill thousands of people!"

Keeping my gaze steady, I scan the room, drawing them all in so that they'll listen carefully. "Millions, actually. The experimental aspect of the device uses antimatter. If it's detonated above, say, a city like Tunis, it'll be completely wiped out, and most of the continent with it. They've finally perfected a way to end worlds, to obliterate everything."

The look on Strahan's face, all of their faces, is a livid mix of horror, disgust, and loathing. A natural reaction, really.

"But you have to understand, we would never *actually* detonate it. I may be a smuggler, but I'm not a psychopath. Neither is Rajcik. The Admin will pay, they won't risk that many lives."

"You're out of your mind if you think you can get away with this. No one will recognize your bodies after they catch you," Vitruzzi says.

The same thoughts had occurred to me when Rajcik first brought up the idea. It's a risk, the biggest risk conceivable. "If we can break into the Fortress, we can handle the Admin. It's worth it."

"So you're suicidal and crazy," says Desto.

"Maybe, but if they build something like this, they should be prepared to deal with the possibility of it getting into the wrong hands. Rajcik's just using their own tools against them. Why should something with that much destructive potential even exist? Maybe the Admin isn't quite as benevolent as it makes itself out to be." My impromptu speech surprises me. *Don't forget,* I tell myself, *you're just in this for the money. When you start taking sides, you start losing the initiative.*

Strahan leans back in his chair, his lips twisted into a sarcastic grin. "That's just beautiful, Erikson. You work for a man who wiped out a squad of thirty soldiers to escape from Keum Libre, a prison he no doubt deserved to be in, and help him steal a bomb that could potentially wipe out the population of a planet. And you make out that it's the Admin's fault? That's rich."

Bodie stares at the table, his face sagging in dismay. Desto and Vitruzzi mirror each other's disbelief. Ignoring Strahan, I keep my mouth shut. I knew they wouldn't want to hear this.

Finally Vitruzzi asks, "And if they call your bluff? What will you do with a weapon like that? Put it in storage? Wait for a good buyer? You can't think something like that would be safe anywhere. Except where it is right now."

Her tone isn't patronizing, but my temper is starting to burn anyway. "You think leaving it at the Fortress is safe? Have you thought about why the Admin is building it in the first place? How they plan to use it?"

"None of this shit matters right now. V, Erikson and her insane plans are not our problem. We need to figure out what it will take to get that disc from Rajcik so we can help Mason and the rest." Everyone listens to Desto, the deep bass of his voice flooding the room. My earlier comment about bargaining chips must have hit a chord with him, and I'm starting to think he's had his own taste of the criminal world.

After a moment to consider, Vitruzzi straightens up, her eyes never leaving my face. "All right, Erikson. Your plans for the Fortress are your business. I just hope you know what you're doing." She punctuates this comment with a glare that says this isn't over. "So tell me, what do you think we should offer Rajcik for that disc?"

"Nothing. He won't give them up." Their faces register, not surprise exactly, more like exasperation. "I know that's not what you want to hear, and you don't have a damn thing to lose if you toss me out the cargo hatch right now. But if there is a chance, I'm it. I've known Rajcik for a long time. He trusts me, as far as anyone can trust anyone." This is a major exaggeration of Rajcik's confidence in me, but they don't need to know that. "He might listen to what I have to say and be persuaded. As long as there's something to persuade with."

"As in?" Strahan asks, but Vitruzzi answers for me.

"He needs energy just like anyone else, right?"

I nod in agreement. "Those seeds would probably draw his attention long enough to at least think about the trade you're proposing."

Venus's voice sounds off over the intercom. "Captain, thirty minutes to touchdown. Brady's on the link for you."

Vitruzzi walks to the intercom and presses the speaker. "I'll be there in a second." Turning back to face the table she states, "We're home. Erikson, we've got a com boost that will link you to wherever you need. That will be the first order of business when we land." With those words, she leaves.

NINE

Venus engages the *Sphynx*'s backup thrusters, gliding us to our landing zone with the precision and lightness of a machine-operated feather. The landing gear slides into deployment with a mechanical hum, and in a few seconds we're settled firmly on the earth. The kid is amazing.

My hands want to twitch while we wait for the loading doors to open, and I clench them into tight fists. They don't need to see how on edge I am about facing a group of strangers on this unfamiliar planet.

Alone.

I've been working as part of a team my entire life, first in the Corps, then with Rajcik's crew. Knowing you're the only one who can save your brother's life, the only family you have, is more than pressure, it's gut-wrenching dread. He needs me. For the first time since I followed my big brother into the Corps, I'm alone in the universe, with no one to rely on but myself.

As the ramp lowers, I take a long look around. We're inside an enormous mine, another dried-up Admin operation, yet the place is alive with activity. Giant fixtures rigged to the ceiling wash everything in a brutal white incandescence. People and ships pack the space, everyone and everything involved in different activities. I realize immediately that this colony of non-citizens is big, and organized.

Nothing throughout the cavern appears disorderly or random. A crew to the right of the *Sphynx* is working together to operate a giant crane. Attached to its loading chains is another ship, this one a small shuttle that is probably used for intra-atmosphere transport. Another group at the end of the cave carries supplies in and out of an enclosed area. Judging by the carts loaded with bags of chemical fertilizers some of them push, they're working in a greenhouse or growing room. The space is filled with everything from earthmoving equipment, to generators, to stacks of building material—all the tools a colony needs to build and maintain an independent infrastructure. There are more supplies and equipment than you see in typical settlements on most of the uncivilized planets by a power of ten.

How much does the Admin know about them? From what I can see, their operation is advanced and self-sufficient, at least enough so to draw unwanted Admin attention. Not everything in this cavern could have been legally obtained, and a well-organized enclave of non-cits, no matter how anonymous or noncombative, is usually considered a threat. At least a hundred people are at work in this mine alone. Who knows how big this place is or what else they've got going on?

The ramp hits the dirt and the *Sphynx*'s crew quickly disembarks. A middle-aged man waits at the base, and I stand at the top of the ramp watching as he exchanges greetings with everyone. Vitruzzi waits next to me. Glancing in my direction and cutting her eyes toward the door, she invites me off.

We step onto the gritty floor and she and the man embrace, arms wrapping tightly around each. They hold onto each other for several tender seconds, their affection overshadowing everything around them. Up to now, her attitude had been cold, efficient, and impersonal, deep-freezing any thoughts I might have had about her inner motivations, the things that drive her to take the kind of chances she has in the last few days. This glimpse into her real life, the life not involved in kidnapping and smuggling, finally drives home how important her friends are to her, and how much she's willing to risk to help them.

After a few seconds, she extracts herself from the man's hug. "Patrick, this is Aly Erikson."

His face is deeply lined by hardship and years of work. A stark white scar runs from his right temple down his cheek, neatly parting the salt-and-pepper stubble covering his jaw, and branches into two lines next to his mouth, one stopping at his top lip and the other ending at the angle of his chin. It's a stern face but not cruel. He jabs his hand toward me.

"Patrick Brady."

His attitude is as gruff as his handshake. I return the gesture but say nothing. The strength in his grip reminds me of how on my own I am. I feel as if I'm standing on a chair with a noose around my neck.

His eyes linger on me for a moment, sizing me up before dropping my hand. I look at Vitruzzi. Time to send the message.

"Patrick, I'll meet you later," she says. "We'll be in the com room for a while."

"Yeah. Bring her by when you're finished. We have things to discuss." Dismissing me, he runs his hand down Vitruzzi's wavy black hair to her shoulder, leaning forward to kiss her. The rest of the crew is already gone, attending to other things. Brady steps back and Vitruzzi turns to me.

"This way."

We walk through the chamber to a lift on the northern wall of the cavern. The ride up lasts a few seconds and we enter a room housing an impressive collection of satellite and radio communication equipment. I settle into a chair in front of a large video display, while her hands move over the controls, activating the necessary channels.

"All communications are scrambled, dissected, and bounced over multiple com nodes throughout the system. We'll have to direct the message to a contact on Obal 8 who will put it back together and transmit to wherever you tell him. The shorter the message, the better, but say what you have to." Her dark eyes bore into mine to emphasize her next statement. "A lot of people are depending on this."

David is one of them. Looking into the video feed, I take a few seconds to think about what to say, then switch it on. "*Temptation* this is Erikson. Situation stable. Need mission status and new rendezvous location. Out." I bite back the urge to press for information about David. It's not likely Rajcik knows anything, but it's hard not to ask. Turning around, I say, "Short and sweet. Just tell your contact on Obal 8 to transmit to uplink 548 in Delta Alpha. If he encodes it, send the key to uplink twelve, same quadrant. Rajcik will get the message."

She types the directions into the satcom computer and inputs the transmission code. "For what it's worth."

Deep lines materialize around her mouth and eyes, only pronounced when she thinks no one notices, when she forgets people are looking to her to be in charge. The lines are like a map of her burdens, but they also reveal the inner strength with which she manages them. Right now, we have a lot in common. Too much. We're both afraid people we care for are going to die at the hands of an enemy who, reason tells us, should be anything but. She leans back in her chair, her focus on people millions of miles away. I recognize the difficult position she's in, wanting to do what's best for her crew, people who depend on her, and having to rely on me, a smuggler, a criminal, someone who shouldn't be trusted no matter how much she needs to. I wish we were on the same side, as real allies instead of collaborating out of necessity.

"Now what?" The sound of my voice brings her back to the here and now.

"We wait," she says, the lines smoothing back into calm authority. "Hungry?"

"Yeah. And I could use a shower."

TEN MINUTES LATER we're aboard the Rover and leaving the cave through a long, well-lit tunnel. Emerging into the brightness of midmorning, I can see the outlines of three small moons fading to ghostly circles high above, and the hot ball of Algol A. Spectra 6 doesn't appear to be much different than any of the other outer planets I'd been too, at least in terms of climate. Dry and hot, with negligible life-supporting material thanks to its proximity to the star. The Spectras that were once rich in minerals or ore lack much else that makes them appealing or livable to people. Once the Admin took what it could from them, they were abandoned. People still manage to populate some of them, but the living is harsh and tenuous. Those who come out to the Spectras have learned to forget, if they ever knew, about nice things—things like fresh food, civil structure, and law enforcement. Like packs of hyenas, those who live here have to become half-savage and dangerous in order to survive.

For all the harshness of the landscape, the settlement is good sized. A multitude of housing structures, mostly assembled from scraps of metal and discarded junk, rise out of the coarse and sandy ground like ancient relics, cleverly built into the strange and abundant rock formations that cover the surface so that they almost seem organic, growing naturally from the earth. Though most of the materials are probably scavenged, nothing about the settlement seems accidental or derelict. It appears there have been people here for a long time, making use of whatever they found, and making the best of it. With the scarcity of anything besides rock and dust as far as I can see, I can't help but wonder about the people living here and what it is that makes them tick.

A quick ride takes us to one of the dwellings, a sand-colored structure with an arched roof peppered with photovoltaics, and she leads me inside. The building is round and the front entrance opens into a main room with a kitchen and table and chairs. Dusty skylights nestled between the solar panels shed enough light on the interior to see clearly. It's cooler in here, well insulated. The walls are probably filled with dirt and a fan system circulates the air inside. All in all, it's surprisingly comfortable, another indication of a relatively advanced long-term settlement. These people are well beyond simply trying to survive out here. Brady is waiting for us, and I sit at the table across from him.

"You've got friends here, Erikson, so it wouldn't be a bad idea to try and trust us." Brady's statement is abrupt and unexpected. He stares at me as if I'm something he might have scraped off of the bottom of his shoe. Vitruzzi sits next to him, very still, her back rigid.

Looks as if that shower's going to have to wait. Cursing silently, I keep my features still and impassive. Why can't anything be simple?

I shift a little in my chair, trying not to explode with frustration, and wait for someone to start telling me what Brady is talking about. I could demand answers, but it wouldn't do any good. They have the advantage here and the only thing I have is a complete lack of options and patience. Both are excruciating.

Shoving a cup with some orange liquid and a plate of food across the table toward me, Brady continues, "Eleanor has told me about you, Erikson, and I did a little digging, too. You're ex-Corps, like Desto and Karl—special tactical operations. It surprises me that someone in spec-ops would end up in your shoes. Usually, once those dogs get the taste for blood, they never lose it."

Is he trying to make me angry? I sit motionless in my seat, holding his eyes with mine. He's long past pretending to be friendly.

"But then, you haven't have you? Just changed flavors." There's a harsh, bitter edge to his voice, and suddenly I understand. He mentioned I was ex-Corps, like Desto and Strahan, but *not* like him. The scar on his face, his obvious hatred for spec-ops soldiers—he's a non-cit of course. Born and raised on a desolate rock in the outer planets with cancer-causing dust in the air. Treated like a machine or worse by some Admin resource extraction franchise—used, abused, then tossed when it became too expensive to keep him working or the mine dried up.

Then what? Did he fight back? Did he become a problem the Admin needed to deal with? Yeah, it makes sense that he'd hate me, or at least, hate what I was. Corps special operations squadrons are in charge of eradicating insurgent threats throughout the system. The long arm of the law. My unit's mission is, *was*, to police the massive and scattered non-cit populations of sixteen Obal and Spectra planets and well over a hundred moons within the Algol system. And police them hard.

The ship David and I had been stationed on, PCA *Thor's Hammer*, operated as an enforcement craft. Mostly we were put down on what the Admin termed "insurgent enclaves" to deep six all rebellious activity. We were trained to be efficient, and that's exactly what we were. Like all good soldiers, we weren't supposed to think about what we did. We just followed orders, and the orders were always the same: exterminate all threats, no questions.

Long-suppressed memories of those firefights begin to float up from beneath the swamp rocks I'd buried them under in my mind, as if they are the noxious contents of a broken sewer line bubbling to the surface. Soldiers with pulse rifles, grenades, missiles, and armored land cruisers deployed from orbiting long-range warships, fighting against people in rags with a few handguns and maybe some homemade dynamite. My stomach clenches as I recall the methodical ruthlessness with which we utterly squashed all the petty resistance they'd tried to mount. The way we'd killed every man, woman, and child on those planets so no one would live to tell about what had happened to them. Just folks who wanted to live without Admin interference, on their own terms. People like Brady.

His grim face is set as he watches me process these thoughts. Staring at his unflinching eyes, I remain speechless and my anger evaporates, leaving a cold and empty void. Why wouldn't he hate me? I represent all the atrocities that soldiers like me had done to people like him.

The room is hushed and tense. Finally, Vitruzzi breaks the silence, "Erikson, we want to offer Rajcik a trade. He gets twenty kilos of solar seeds for a copy of the disc."

Her all-business tone lets me escape Brady's accusing gaze. "Seems like a good idea," I comment glibly. They don't have anything else that Rajcik would care in the least about.

"And his crew and some of us team up in a rescue mission for your brother and our friends."

I take a drink of liquid Brady gave me and nearly choke on it. Coughing, I ask, "You're kidding me, right?"

No. She's not kidding. Not joking, not pulling my leg, not having a laugh at my expense. She's serious. Another glance at Brady confirms that they are both serious.

Enunciating my words as clearly as I can, I promise them, "That . . . is . . . NOT . . . an option."

"Why not, Erikson? We up our odds with every able-bodied fighter we have. You know it. If Rajcik is as clever as we've heard, he'll know it."

"Did you forget what I was doing when you *kidnapped* me?" I use the word deliberately, trying to incite enough hostility that they'll drop the idea completely. "I was smuggling. Smuggling plans to steal a weapon so dangerous it could destroy an *entire planet*. And you want to team up? Maybe I have some screws loose, but you people are completely nuts."

Pausing, I read their faces, looking for an indication that they realize their idea is ludicrous. "Besides, Rajcik isn't the group-effort type. He probably won't even be willing to trade for the seeds."

Vitruzzi's expression doesn't change from the same calm focus. Maybe I persuaded her that she's pushing her luck with her proposal, or maybe not, but I'm willing to bet she doesn't like what I said. Brady's pinched stare has gone from sour dislike to outright detestation. He leans forward slowly, putting all four legs of his chair back on the ground and gets up stiffly from the table, as if he's about to walk the plank.

Superficially, it seems like a smart move to pool our resources. I've seen how tightly Vitruzzi and her crew work together, and it's apparent that they can handle themselves in a tough situation. And as much as I hate to admit it, confirmation that Desto and Strahan both share my military background makes me trust, if not them, at least their abilities. If all we had to do was break through the Fortress's security, let ourselves in, grab David and their friends, and get the hell out, I might even be willing to go along with her idea. But this isn't just a rescue mission. There's a monumental payoff involved, and if I know János Rajcik, anyone or anything that tries to remap his intended course of action will be eliminated.

Disgusted, Brady turns his back and walks to the kitchen. Vitruzzi waits calmly, trying to will me to reconsider. She doesn't know how stubborn I am. Or how dangerous Rajcik is.

Finally, she says, "Have it your way, Erikson." She stands up, concluding the discussion. "Meet me at the hangar at 1600 and we'll see if Rajcik has responded."

"So what am I supposed to do until then?"

"Whatever you want. I'll take you over to Venus's and you can get that shower. Come on."

As I pass in front of Brady, he reaches out and grabs me by the arm. I tense up and face him, ready for whatever might be coming, but the look on his face isn't what I expect. I see weariness and resignation just under the surface of his weathered skin. His anger is still there, but subdued. We look at each other for a drawn out second and then he lets go. The message is clear: *Don't be a fool.*

VENUS'S DWELLING IS SIMILAR to Brady's, just a bit smaller and wildly untidy. No one is home when Vitruzzi drops me off, but she assures me Venus will be around soon. Inside, electronic consoles, maps, unidentifiable parts, and machine schematics are strewn everywhere. An engine of some sort lays disassembled on part of the floor, pieces of it and other mechanical equipment dumped helter-skelter all around it like an asteroid field. It's difficult to tell what's supposed to be furniture and what's just taking up space.

The room is dim, and after a short search, I'm able to locate the controls for a ceiling panel. Activating it rotates the panels toward the brightest part of the sky and catches the light, reflecting it back inside, but the room doesn't look any better.

It probably wouldn't be difficult to steal a land transport and run. But where would I go, and what good would it do me? As far as I know, the only communication link-up on this planet is here in this little settlement and I don't think I could manage to steal an interstellar craft and fly it by myself. Could I get Vilbrandt to help me? I dismiss that thought immediately. Even if he knows anything about flying, I don't trust him any farther than I can throw him and definitely don't want to be in a situation where I'm forced to rely on him.

Forget it. The best thing for me to do right now is wait, no matter how difficult it is.

A narrow door leads into the bathroom. The shower is a round metal cylinder that requires an upward step of about half a meter to get inside, the lower portion a catchment and filtration system to either recycle the water or direct it to another use. Stripping down and leaving my clothes on the floor, I carefully balance the 'Bad on the top of the stall. Pushing the single round button on the wall dumps enough water on my head to get my hair and body wet. The temperature is lukewarm, probably regulated to stay exactly that. Finding a soapy gel in a tube on the floor, I lather up. It feels good to be in a shower with real water. Ships don't carry much more than the essentials for the crew's basic needs. Showering is done using a dry enzymatic powder that breaks down, rather than rinses off, all the dirt and grime on your skin, and is then scrubbed off with a microfiber towel or blasted off with an air blower. Washing in space is a little like being in a sandstorm.

When I'm finished, I push the button twice more and rinse off. I don't have a towel, so I stand inside for a few more moments to drip dry.

I'd like to take a look at my bruises to see how much discoloration remains, but the mirror is nearly hidden by image captures. People, animals, landscapes, ships—everything imaginable is pinned to the wall, pictures on top of pictures until all I can see of some are the corners, the rest buried underneath layers. I stare at them, thinking that they're a perfect representation of how I perceive Venus. Scattered, filled with bits of information that is so profuse and disconnected that even she can't make it make sense. Or maybe it does make sense to her, but I'm at a loss.

A sliver of mirror remains, enough to see just my eyes. At thirteen, my first boyfriend had told me that they were the shape of elm leaves. He said it trying to sound smart and seductive, awkward coming from an adolescent boy, especially since neither of us had ever seen a real elm tree. Years later, I ran across a model of one in an Earth relics museum and discovered that the boy hadn't been wrong. My eyes do slant to severe points at each corner. But they are blue instead of green.

"Sorry, I don't have any towels. The air is so warm, usually you dry off right away anyway."

I whirl, caught completely by surprise. "You shouldn't sneak up on me like that!"

"Oh, okay." Her focus is on a small video display unit in her hands, totally unaware that she'd startled me, or of the fact that I'm still half-naked. I've been on ships long enough, where the only privacy is in your head, that it doesn't really bother me. It's the way she seems so detached that makes me nervous. Not in a distracted way, but as if she's wired into a different frequency than most people altogether. Without a glance up, she motions toward my pistol, still on top of the shower stall. "Don't forget that." Then wanders back into the main room. I finish dressing and join her.

She's cleared a small table of its clutter. On top lies the same tray of food that Brady had given me. At the time, I hadn't been in the mood to eat, but now I feel hunger gnawing away at my stomach. I sit down on top of a crate and lift a square sandwich to my lips. Real bread! Venus sits opposite me and remains engrossed in watching the handheld VDU. Her feet tap a rhythm on the floor that would make a tap dancer tired in seconds. I have to take deep, calm breaths to cope with the incessant motion.

Suddenly, she looks up and levels her plutonium green eyes on me, disconcertingly like a cat's in a dark room. "Did you know I lost my family because of the Admin? In a mining . . . accident." She sneers the word, making it a curse. "My little sister and my parents. My brother died before that, from the chemicals that got into our food, our water, everything. The same chemicals that made me a freak killed him. Strange, isn't it?" I don't know if she wants me to answer, but I'm glad I ate so fast. I'm losing my appetite.

"I wasn't there when it happened. I might have saved them if I had been. But it was already too late when I found out. I should have died too, but it happened at night and I don't sleep much."

I'm not sure I want to hear this story, but I have to ask, "What kind of accident?"

"I'm from one of the moons off of Spectra 5, Acculmi. The mine was an old one, almost nothing left in the ground. That's why they started shipping us to the mine on Spectra 5. There hadn't been any maintenance or reinforcement on Acculmi's structure in years, except what we did ourselves. Requests for better equipment, parts, anything that could keep things running went without response. It was going dry and they knew it, so they weren't going to be bothered with putting any money into keeping it in good order. We were all non-cits anyway. Cheaper labor." She puts down the VDU and clasps her hands together tightly, almost as if she doesn't trust what they might do.

"So we had to start finding other ways to get what we needed. We didn't report all the ore we extracted, which was practically nothing anyway, and sold what we skimmed to whoever would buy it."

After a pause, she continues, "It just collapsed one night with eighty people inside. We'd had to move inside because our sun shields were badly deteriorated. I was out flying when it happened, testing some of the modifications I'd been making to our shuttle. I heard the dispatch from the mine; they were begging for help. And then . . . I picked up a communication between the Admin flight control and one of their patrol ships close to our orbit. The patrol ship asked if they should send a medical team to the mine."

My stomach cramps painfully as I wait for what she's going to say next. I already know.

"The flight ship controller just asked him why he thought that was necessary." A scary, half-crazed laugh bubbles out of her throat. "I got back to the mine as fast as I could, but there were only a few people who made it out. We couldn't dig deep enough to get to the lower chambers and we didn't have the kind of equipment we needed. I don't remember how many days we worked, trying to find anyone who was still alive. Their cries for help . . . there were less of them every hour. But eventually, we just had to give up. There was nothing we could do.

"Not long after that, a patrol ship finally landed to survey the situation, see if there was anything left to salvage. I stole it."

She looks me fully in the face for the first time since she'd started the story, a wet sheen of tears highlighting her eyes. "I was going to get revenge, you know? I was going to fly straight into the first Admin ship I found and blow them all up. I was crazy. I lost my whole family, my friends. Everything I had. You understand that, right?

"I got as far as Spectra 6 without seeing a single Admin ship. I hadn't eaten for days and had burns from a fire that broke out on the ship. There's an outpost on the other side with a smaller settlement than this one. The fire took out part of the hydraulics and I crashed. Fortunately, Captain V and Karl found me. I was delirious. I don't really remember it. When I got back to normal, they told me how sorry they were that they hadn't been able to find any other survivors. I'd been raving the whole time, so they knew most of my story. But when I told them I'd flown the ship alone, they didn't believe me for a while. They said that ship couldn't be flown without a crew." This time her laugh is genuinely amused. "They'd never met *me* before."

"What kind of ship did you steal?"

"A DC Class gun ship."

"What?" It's my turn for disbelief. DCs are interstellar cruisers with the capacity for thirty crewmembers, four of which are essential to fly it. "How could you keep it flying, much less control it?"

"Took some rigging, and like I said, no time for eating or sleeping. But I got the flight trajectories loaded and made that baby do things it was never designed for. Kept on it for three days but I lost it anyway. Without a full crew I couldn't look to the engine and once that fire started, I was done for."

It's a fascinating story, I'll give her that. Fascinating, but impossible. Or is it? I've already seen how fluidly she handles the *Sphynx*, a ship design known for having quirks in atmosphere that makes being aboard one feel as if you're riding a roller coaster through a blast zone. Something in her makeup has made her the kind of person who can read ships, understand and intuit the vagaries of flying and weather the way a master sculptor understands marble. And the modifications done to the ISPS, who better than the pilot to know what to do?

"The captain took care of me until I got back into my head again. Her and Karlie talked me out of killing myself. Even if I had managed to find an Admin ship and run into, it wouldn't have brought my family back. She asked me to take the *Sphynx* up one day, to see if I really could fly it, and that's why I'm here now, and not atomized space dust."

It's almost hard for me to match the image of a caring and concerned Strahan with the surly grunt I've dealt with, but it's easier with Vitruzzi. It's been a while since I've met people with a genuine sense of human decency. People who actually give a damn about others, not just percentages.

"Do you know why I'm telling you this?"

I honestly don't, and shake my head.

She looks at me as if I might be a little slow. "Because Cap'n V, Karlie, and Pat are not stupid, Aly. If they were, they'd have been dead a long time ago. They don't make decisions at random. They've been at this game a long time. They're smart, and they always do what's right for people who deserve it. Do you get it?"

"It seems to me as if they make a habit out of kidnapping unconscious people and making them part of the crew." I know my words are unnecessarily frosty, but I can't seem to help myself.

"Yeah, I guess you could look at it that way. But you could also look at it like they help those that need it. Even when there's a risk." She gives me a tranquil smile, her heart-shaped face and pale skin making her look like a marble angel. "The captain is a doctor, after all." And then, with a rapid change of mood to which I'm becoming accustomed, she stands up and walks toward the door. "I have to help Bodie with some maintenance on the *Sphynx*. Help yourself to anything you can find, or wander around. Whatever you want. See you later." And she leaves.

TEN

Restlessness and anxiety set my nerves on fire while my brain lists twenty different horrible things that might be happening to David while I sit uselessly on this rock. My watch has set itself to local time. It's only 1130, so I have some time to kill before meeting Vitruzzi. I've been alone for half an hour and no one has shown up to keep tabs on me, but I know they can't trust me that much. I probably have a shadow, most likely someone I haven't met, someone I wouldn't recognize if I saw them around. Probably waiting for me to leave and planning on following me. Or maybe they have video captures hidden in the maelstrom of Venus's dwelling. Could be both. If I cared, it would be enough to make me paranoid.

Fuck it. Sitting here is going to make me crazy. I'll just take a walk.

Being on foot allows me to soak up the warm air, refreshingly welcome after being aboard ship for almost a week. I walk aimlessly around the rambling settlement with no destination in mind. Basically, it's just a small collection of dirt streets that divide the spaces between buildings. It's hard to say how many people live in the area. Could be a couple hundred, could be no more than a sixty or seventy. People occasionally pass me either on foot or driving some version of a beat-up land transport. No one stops to talk, but their suspicious stares make it clear that they're aware of who I am. They all proceed as if they have something important to do. Considering the work I saw taking place inside the mine, they probably do.

Despite my wandering, my mind stays busy thinking over the things I see. Here's a group of people who have done more than fall into the deep end of space and given up. They're really trying to make a life for themselves, make it work despite the Admin restrictions that work against them. Most of the non-cit outposts I've been to in my travels have been destitute sties filled with pirates, degenerates, and criminals—hiding places for the cutthroat and brutal. I had almost forgotten that there are still people in the universe, citizen or not, who want to do more than steal and hide.

By 1200 hours on my watch, Algol A is at its zenith, setting the sky fully ablaze. A crescent of Algol B can be seen on the distant horizon shadowed by the planets between us. The brilliant backdrop only serves to punctuate how alone and unguarded I am.

As if to create a safe barrier between the unknown and myself, my interior navigator leads me back to the mine entrance.

As I walk through the opening toward the main cavern, darkness quickly absorbs the dazzling outside light like an inky sponge. The tunnel is semi-illuminated by deep holes penetrating to the surface along the roof, allowing enough sunlight to provide moderate visibility. The grainy gray glow filters through suspended dust and sweeps over a metal walkway along the left side of the tunnel. As speeding vehicles pass me in both directions, it becomes immediately clear that it's the safest path for foot traffic.

The sound of a vehicle approaches, catching my attention as the hum of its engine slows. It pulls to a stop beside me. In the gloom, I recognize Desto sitting astride a large motorcycle with a gigantic faring and gun barrels pointing out of turrets on either side of the steering apparatus. I've never seen any kind of two-wheeled, terrain-limited vehicle equipped like it before. A bike made for combat?

He gives me his trademark lecherous grin.

"Nice bike."

The grin widens even further at the compliment. "You like it, huh? My own design, with some help from my man, Bodie. He's pretty decent with a wrench. But the guns were definitely my idea. Are you headed to the ship?"

"Just wandering around. Waiting for a chance to pick up communications with Vitruzzi a little later."

He revs the engine loudly, showing off its power. "So you have some time then. Why don't you come with me and I'll show you one of my favorite places on this rock." Noticing my hesitation, he continues, "Don't worry, I promise to get you back in time."

"Are you trying to pick me up?"

"You damn right I am!" He leans closer and winks. "Come on, honey. Don't be shy. We're going somewhere I know you'll love."

"Which is?"

"The shooting range. Let's see how good you are with that little carbine of yours." His very white teeth gleam at me in a challenging smile. "If you want, you can try my gun too. Hop on."

Why not? I'll do about anything to take my mind off the fact that David's been in the hands of the Admin for a week. Almost before I'm seated, Desto guns it and peels out, the sudden velocity whipping my head backward. Without time for a single breath, he slams the footbrakes, making the back wheel skid in an improbably canted arc at the mouth of the mine. Taking a moment to let his eyes adjust and make sure no one is entering, he warns, "Hang on."

We drive fast for about fifteen klicks to a deserted stretch of land. The road we're on narrows as we enter a sprawling cluster of wreckage, chunks of twisted metal, and other scattered debris that covers a range nearly the size of the mine's main chamber. The path continues into the heart of the ruins, forming a twisted circuit.

Desto stops just outside of the perimeter and leans the bike on a reinforced kickstand the size of my arm. I nearly have to pry my clenched fists from his shirt with my teeth as we dismount. The transport is clearly as heavy as it looks, but he handles it as if it weighs no more than a bicycle. Next to us is a loudspeaker kiosk. He picks up the handset and clicks it on.

"Anyone on the range fire twice in the air. Otherwise, watch out." He lowers the handset and waits for a moment, scanning the field. There's no sound to alert us anyone else is here.

"All right, Erikson. Ever ridden one of these?" He gestures toward the bike.

"Sure."

"Good. Right here and here are your triggers, and these toggles adjust the barrels up and down about twenty degrees from center. They don't have a left or right pan mechanism. I couldn't get enough angle out of them before hitting the tank. But that's what steering is for. The bullets are caseless, so don't worry about them ejecting and burning your legs. But the thing that makes it a challenge is the kick. You'll ride forward just fine, but fire those guns and you have to compensate for the recoil." He turns to look me over, gauging my reaction to the task.

The size of the bike is daunting. It will hold itself upright once it gets going; that's not what I'm worried about. It's the fact that if I lean too far on a turn without enough momentum, this behemoth will pin me to the ground as if it were a bulldozer parked on a mouse.

Smirking bravely, I climb on. As I start to pull the bike off its kickstand, a hydraulic activator helps it extend, pushing off the ground and raising the bike to riding position. When I have control of it, I jump on the starter and the kickstand retracts. "Any thoughts on what you want me to hit?" I ask as the engine rumbles to life, growling at the same pitch as Desto's laughter.

"Anything that looks scary, babe."

I visually measure the distance and angle to a blasted old piece of mining equipment, adjust the right gun, and fire. The steering apparatus bucks furiously in my hands, vibrating as if I'd grabbed an electric fence, and jagged metal spikes bloom around the new hole that appears in the mining junk. The bike maintains perfect balance. I glance at Desto with a nervous grin. His return smile is full of both approval and pride. However overblown his libertine act, the guy knows his shit.

I'm about ready to twist the accelerator when he says, "Hold it," and opens a storage box mounted behind the seat. Keeping the bike locked tightly between my thighs, I pull on the pair of heavy plastic goggles he hands me, tighten up the strap, and move out.

Weaving throughout the range, I cover several branches of the circuitous paths, adjusting to the bike's feel. It handles smoothly, only the shocks reacting a little stiffly. But then they're calibrated for a man who easily outweighs me by forty kilos, maybe more. At first, I'm cautious, almost jittery, but nervousness quickly gives way to a sense of natural easiness. The rig almost drives itself. All I have to do is maintain control while firing. Its power is intense, and the accuracy of the guns is a lesson in perfection. I do two or three loops just for fun, carefully aiming at targets that come within range, returning to where Desto waits, with real reluctance. As I pull up and kill its inertia, the bike's heaviness seems at odds with its graceful motion.

Desto's grin is total approval this time. "Outstanding! Where have you been all my life?"

I grin back, weirdly pleased to have made a good impression. "I think I missed a couple, but as fast as it goes, no one would have time to return fire anyway. How do you reload when you're dry?"

"You can't while it's moving. She's more of an escape than an attack vehicle. Spray and pray and get the hell out of there."

We spend the next two hours practicing firing drills. Ingrained military maneuvers, part of my DNA after years of training, come as natural as breathing. Desto shows me some new ones. My shots are either dead on, or close enough to matter, but he never misses. When midafternoon shadows begin to pool between the hulking wrecks, we switch to laser sights and continue practicing. Finally, hunger and fatigue bring an end to the fun.

As we prepare to head back to the hangar, a sudden movement at the north end of the range catches my attention. There's a man there, or what used to be a man. He's deathly pale, dressed in rags, his face covered with red, scaly lesions. He leans against a rusting turbine that once belonged to a midrange transport ship, staring at us with filmy eyes that continually blink and squint. The symptoms are all too easy to recognize.

"Desto, do you know that guy?"

His head swivels on his muscular neck to follow my line of sight. "Solar stoner. Junkies from a little town east of here wander over to the range sometimes. They usually don't have enough of a brain left to figure out how to get back. I've seen a few of them 'accidentally' wander into the line of fire. It's a pain in the ass to clean up."

About what I thought. Sometime in the last couple of decades, a scientist discovered a compound that he hoped would cure the ubiquitous cases of melanoma caused by the system's binary stars. During the testing phase, he discovered that instead of blocking damaging UV light, the compound catalyzes with it and induces feelings of intense euphoria in anyone who ingests it. It has virtually no effect if you stay out of sunlight, but the addictive effects were too much of an instant hook for a lot of people. Word got out, and the process for making the compound with it, and people like the guy at the end of the range started popping up everywhere. If taken over a long enough period of time, the product and overexposure to sunlight turn these pathetic addicts into walking zombies, bodies filled with cancers and diseases, and brains fried like rotten bacon. There's no way to recover from the effects once they've gone that far. Like any junkie, they can be dangerous if they don't get their fix. That is, until they become too weak to do anything but fester and waste away. The name solar stoner is as good as any.

Desto's comment about a nearby town ignites my interest. "There's a town in the area?"

"Yeah, but you don't want to go there. Full of lowlifes and crooks. We keep the Beach free of their kind."

Does he realize the irony in what he said? *I'm* one of their kind.

"We shake down anyone from that gutter-ghetto who comes over here. More than a few have tried to take what we've got. They just don't seem to get it that you have to work for what you get in this life. No free rides. Besides, we're always ready for them, me and her." He pats the Thresher assault rifle that he'd used on the range, now resting in a scabbard along the frame of the bike. "You ready?"

I jerk my chin over to the stoner by the turbine. "What about him?"

"Can't do anything for him. He doesn't have long." He revs the bike and I barely manage to grasp his shirt in time to keep from tumbling off the back.

THE SHORT RIDE BACK to the hangar isn't fast enough to keep my worries from catching up with me. I'm sure it's too soon to have heard back from Rajcik, but every hour that passes could be one hour closer to David's death.

Desto skids to a stop next to the *Sphynx*. As I climb off the beast, Bodie walks over. He grins at Desto, very straight teeth gleaming through the tendrils of his beard and mustache. "Hey man, can you give me a hand with this toolbox?" He indicates a container sitting at the base of a ladder propped against the *Sphynx*.

"Bodie! Bring me that cylinder torque, will you?" The voice belongs to a pair of legs emerging from the rear hydraulic compartment. It's Strahan, leaning so far in that only the tips of his toes are skimming the ground. One of his feet is black-booted but the other is still encased in its brace.

Bodie and Desto both take an end of the toolbox. With his free hand, Bodie tosses me a wrench. "Here, Erikson, hand this to Karl. Thanks."

I approach the legs and hear muted cursing. "I've got your wrench."

"Great, sweetie. Just lay it on the cart there. No wait, hand it to me."

I'm confused for a second and then chuckle when I realize that he thinks I'm someone else. "Here you go."

He emerges from the hatch so quickly it's almost as if the ship spits him out. "Oh, shit. Erikson. I thought you were . . . you sounded like . . . um, I thought you were someone else."

"Yeah, I got that." It's hard not to laugh at his embarrassment as I hand him the cylinder torque. He just stands there for a moment, appearing to be at a loss at what to say. So I make it easy. "Have you seen Vitruzzi?"

A faint red blush still tinges his cheeks. Sensitive after all, it appears. "She's up in the com annex. You know how to get there, right?"

I nod and walk to the lift. When I get to the top, Vitruzzi is sitting in a chair in front of the massive satellite console, listening to something through a set of headphones. I allow myself to hope for a second that it's a message from Rajcik.

"Anything?" I ask.

She swivels around and looks at me with a mixture of disappointment and worry. My own features shift, mirroring hers.

Removing the headphones and laying them down on the desk, she says, "We'll try again at 2000. That's about twelve hours since you sent the first message."

Twelve hours, but the chances are still slim that enough time will have passed for him to respond. It would take approximately three hours for the transmission to get there, another three to get back, with a narrow six-hour window in between where he'd have to be monitoring for new messages from the uplink satellite. It's possible he's not even checking at this point, having given David and I up for dead days ago. Or the Admin could have traced him and severed his access. There are a million things that could keep him from getting that message. Thinking of it makes the balloon of anxiety in my torso swell tight, close to bursting.

"And if there's nothing, what then?"

"Then we'll have to take our chances with Vilbrandt."

I meant what would happen to me if Rajcik doesn't come through with the plans, but I don't pursue the answer. The severity of her expression makes it clear that her biggest, and only, concern is figuring out how to rescue the other crew from the Fortress. I'm here as a token of hope, one that can be chucked if there's no more reason *to* hope.

As if she hears my thoughts, Vitruzzi says, "You know, Erikson, if Rajcik doesn't respond, there isn't a hell of a lot you can offer us."

I keep my features neutral and my eyes very steady. "You can't keep me here forever."

"Nothing is stopping you from running. You've seen that. But I think it's fair to warn you that the Admin has newscast your theft. There's an at-large notice for you and Rajcik both. Everyone with a receiver from here to the moons of Spectra 4 has seen your faces. There's also a reward." She pauses, inspecting my expression.

My features feel as if they've turned to stone, rigid and cold, hiding the fear behind them. T'Kai had agreed that the operation would be anonymous. Any Corps soldier who asked the wrong questions would be charged with dereliction of duty and sentenced indefinitely to Keum Libre. If Vitruzzi is telling the truth, and I have no reason to think she wouldn't be, either T'Kai hadn't kept that part of the bargain or they'd gotten to David and made him talk. It wouldn't surprise me if T'Kai double crossed us; he's a typical self-serving Admin politician, but if it was David . . . I know my brother. If he talked, it took drugs and torture. Imagining how much he'd resist before they could break him turns my guts to antifreeze. And if he told them everything he knew, why would they keep him alive?

"They're calling it theft of Admin property, downplaying it. But they want you and Rajcik bad, that's certain."

"So you could turn me in and collect the reward. If Rajcik doesn't come through, what'll stop you?"

"Besides the fact that my crew and I are the reason they haven't caught you already? Nothing. Except that's not the way I do things. I know something about you, Erikson, that you either don't realize about yourself, or you're trying very hard to hide."

"And what's that?"

"You're not as much of a greedy cutthroat as you pretend you are."

I chuckle rudely.

"You want to know what my proof is? The way you risked your neck to help Karl on R'Kadia. If you didn't care about anyone's ass but your own, you wouldn't have done that. You could have jumped on that elevator without a second thought. But you didn't. It's automatic for you to look out for others . . ."

"When it's in my own interest," I finish for her.

She's quiet for a moment, letting that sink in. "I don't think it's about getting rich for you. We all have our reasons for doing what we do, and I think yours are about getting even, getting revenge. I know what the Corps is like. The stories make it out this far. A soldier has to follow orders, whether she likes it or not. You deserted for the same reason you work with an arms smuggler."

"And what's that?"

"You want to get back at the Admin for trying to make you a killer. That's not you, even if it's easier for you to tell yourself it is."

Vitruzzi's words splash over me with the same harsh effect of alcohol poured over an open wound. She's right, but it's a hard truth. I hide behind my battle-hardened armor so I don't have to think about who I may really be deep inside. I buried the soldier I had been under layers and layers of carefully tended forgetfulness. What kind of person follows the inhuman orders that I had to follow? Telling myself that I had no choice doesn't make any difference. I'm no more willing to know the answer to that than I am to let my brother die without traveling to the edge of the galaxy, to hell if I have to, to save him. So I bury the guilt and I bury the hate I have for the Admin and the Corps. It doesn't matter. It's bigger than the universe. So fuck it, let me forget my feelings, and my reasons, and just get rich. "What's your point, Vitruzzi?"

"What I'm saying is this. Most of the people in Agate Beach feel the same way you do. But instead of giving up, they went the other way. We're *really* living, Erikson. We have friends, family, and a future, and we're doing it our way. We are not controlled and we make our own choices about how we lead our lives. There could be a place for you here, if you want to know what real freedom is."

"But you kept your citizenship. You still work for the Admin. Is that what you mean by freedom?"

My words are unnecessarily callous, and her face hardens. "I'm not a hypocrite. I do what I have to because I'm a doctor. Working for the Admin gives me access to the equipment and supplies I need so that the people here don't die needlessly."

"So you want to pass judgment on me because I don't pretend to be a good citizen? At least I'm honest about being a thief. Where did Brady and your crew get those weapons they carry? Found them in the desert? And what about those solar seeds? Don't try and tell me your *legally* contracted transport operation is squeaky clean. Maybe you think you have me figured out, but your business isn't exactly going to win you a 'citizen of the year' award."

Her reaction is instant and vicious. "Who the hell do you think you are?"

"Hey, am I interrupting?" Neither one of us had heard the lift that brought Bodie up.

Vitruzzi rises, her shoulders stiff and her eyes blazing with anger. "No, we're done. Be back here at 2000." Brushing by me without another look, she steps onto the lift and disappears.

Bodie watches her leave, eyebrows raised in concern and curiosity. When she's gone, he turns to me and asks, "What was that about?"

I already regret what I'd said. What good does it do to make Vitruzzi my enemy? Don't I have enough to worry about? "Nothing important."

"Yeah whatever, Erikson." He stares crossly at me, the way you stare at a child who has tried but not succeeded in lying to you. "It's all right to tell me it's none of my business. Anyway, I'm headed to an observation platform topside to take an air quality reading. Want to join me? It's a helluva climb."

I have four hours to kill, each one promising to be more frustrating than the last. Anything to take my mind off the waiting. "Yeah, sure."

"Here, put this on. It's dark in there." He hands me a light attached to a head harness and we begin to climb up a steel ladder hanging from the wall beside the lift platform. It soon disappears into a narrow tunnel drilled into the rock.

I count two hundred and fifty rungs as we climb before he stops. A giant lock tumbler grates noisily into place, and a waterfall of sunlight blazes past his frame, dazzling my upturned eyes.

"Sorry, I should have warned you. It's pretty bright after being in the tunnel."

I follow him up the last couple of rungs and over the edge of the tunnel mouth, my arms grateful for the reprieve.

We're standing on a small platform, maybe one-and-half by two meters, with a metal railing. From up here, the midafternoon sunlight scorches the planet as far as my eyes can see, turning the goose bumps on my arms from the cool cave into tiny, hot stingers. I feel the way ants must feel when wicked children level a magnifying glass over the top of them, but the sensation passes quickly as I take in the panoramic view.

Bodie unslings his backpack and now holds a small sensor wand in one hand and an analysis pack in the other. He waves it around and checks the readout from the air tester.

"Why check the air quality? Is there an atmosphere converter on this planet?"

"No, I just do it for my amusement. I used to be a geophysicist with the Ministry of Engineering before I came out here. It's habit." Aside from a catch in the back of his throat, as if he's getting over a persistent cough, his voice is almost back to normal.

"Sounds like a good job. Why did you give it up?"

He gives me a reluctant sideways glance before answering. "I lost my citizenship when I quit working for the Admin. We were researching unique life forms on the Obals and trying to convert them into incubators for specimens from the first Earth. You know, cows, horses, that kind of thing. I just couldn't stomach it. I thought we should leave them be and learn to live with the natural environment, at least what's left of it. The Admin disagreed and threatened to strip my funding. Said I was 'jeopardizing essential scientific research' or some shit like that. I decided selling out for a few bucks wasn't worth it. So I quit."

His story explains a lot to me. He's an idealist, what people had once called an "environmentalist." Mental maybe. He doesn't believe the Admin creed that everything exists purely for humanity to exploit.

So being a gunrunning pawn for the Admin is more in line with your worldview. I keep the thought to myself. I nearly killed the guy, and now he's taking me on a tour. He's too friendly to antagonize. Besides, he has his reasons for being out here, as we all do.

He puts the air tester back into his backpack and takes out a bottle of water. Motioning me over to the railing, he says, "Take a look at that view, Aly. Can I call you Aly? Calling you Erikson makes me feel like I should start with 'sir,' or 'sergeant,' or something."

"Whatever makes you happy."

"Beautiful, huh?"

"I guess. Looks dead to me though."

"You'd be surprised. We've been able to mix relatively low levels of growth hormones and fertilizers in the soil to make it viable. Even deserts are full of their own kind of life. You just have to learn what to look for." He takes a swig of the water, caps it, and hands it to me.

I glance at him. Rough exterior, untamed beard, and shaggy hair aside, he certainly seems gentle. Taking a closer look at his eyes reveals a depth and intelligence I hadn't noticed when they were still squinted in pain.

"We've been composting and fortifying soil inside the mine for years. There are some real farmers here who know more about it than I do. They started long before I got here. Most of our food still has to be grown in the typical industrial incubation fashion. You know, growing protein and carbohydrate compounds inside bean pods and banana skins, but we're getting to the point where naturally grown foods are becoming a staple. I had no idea how good a squash could taste until I grew one myself."

I take a long drink of the water and smile slightly at the idea of being excited about the taste of a vegetable. He notices and smiles in return.

Changing the subject, I ask, "So you went AWOL from civil service. Does that make you a fugitive?"

"No, I'm legal enough. Just not a citizen. That's how I can still run transport operations with Vitruzzi."

"Don't you think the Admin would be a little skeptical of your colony's success out here? I mean, there's no way you got all the materials and equipment I've seen since this morning legally. At least, not without boatloads of cash. And there are the guns."

His forehead creases and mouth pulls down in a frown. "We've been careful about keeping the existence of this colony quiet. Outsiders aren't welcome. Everyone living here is reliable and we trust each other. Nothing we do is a threat to the Admin, so why should they bother us?"

"I don't know. Because that's what they do. Bother people who aren't fitting into their grand plan." And what about me? I'm an outsider. And Vilbrandt?

He doesn't say anything, just reaches for the water and takes another drink. Blunt honesty has always been one of my attributes, or possibly flaws. "Bodie, you know that if your crew manages, by some monumental stroke of luck, to get your friends off of the Fortress, the Admin will scour every single planet between the suns until they find you."

His frown deepens. "Maybe. But what should we do? Just let them rot?"

I shrug, unwilling to say it, but that may be exactly what they should do if they want to maintain the relative peace they have out here.

"Right. Well, that's out of the question." There's a bitter edge to his voice. He knows what's at stake.

We stand for another few minutes staring at the landscape in moody silence. I feel as if a load of cement has been added to my already overburdened scaffold of emotions. Am I beginning to care about what happens to these people, this colony? How did I get mixed up in this? I have my own problems, and the future of these non-cits and their hopeless wish to live in a world where the rules make sense should not become one of them.

Finally, he turns his faded blue eyes back on me and says with a stubborn cheeriness, "I have to get back down to the grow room and take care of some things. A few of us are having dinner at my place after that. You're welcome to join us."

His grin says he is not just being polite, the invite is authentic. I mutter an awkward, "Okay," and then, more loudly, "thanks."

I'M HALF AN HOUR early arriving in the darkened communication room, and take a seat to wait for Vitruzzi to show up. Most of the satellite equipment is password protected or encrypted, and I can't make any of it work. My anxiety is mounting, and I'm at the point where I've decided I'm going to take my chances and try to find Rajcik myself if he hasn't come through yet. The people in the town Desto had told me about have to get to this planet somehow. I'll start there.

I spend the time waiting for Vitruzzi thinking over what I'd learned from Bodie's dinner. I don't know if I thought the squash tasted as good as he does, but almost anything is an improvement after eating nutrition bars for the better part of a month. Besides Bodie, Strahan, Desto, and Venus were present.

Their conversations had mostly revolved around the various duties the people of the colony shared to keep the place in working order. Maintenance, digging wells, growing food, the essentials. I kept quiet unless someone asked me something directly but was able to get an idea of the size of the settlement and the dynamic that's making them successful at it.

They call it Agate Beach, apparently an ironic reference to the ore once mined here and the complete lack of any large enough body of water nearby to have a beach. It has been occupied for around fifty years. The first people to make it a permanent home had originally been workers in the mine when the Admin ran it, an they'd stayed when the operation was abandoned. The town Desto mentioned is called Hell's Gate, and lies about fifty kilometers east. All of this served as useful information that my mind had automatically catalogued.

I hadn't seen Vilbrandt anywhere in the settlement since we landed and it had been nagging at me. Seeing no need to keep my distrust of him a secret, I asked about him during the meal.

A secretive glance had passed among them and Strahan's tight-lipped response had been short. "He's around. We're keeping an eye on him." Whatever the reason for their secrecy, his comment was nonetheless revealing. If they're keeping an eye on Vilbrandt, they're undoubtedly keeping an eye on me as well.

After dinner, Bodie offered me a lift to the mine. Needing some quiet, I'd declined and walked back to wait for Vitruzzi.

When she finally arrives, we go through the process of checking incoming communications. Still nothing.

Leaning back in her chair and leveling a look that's neither embittered nor benevolent, but somehow both, she says, "We're going to have to go to plan B. If we're lucky, your team hasn't already started their assault on the Fortress. If they have, we may never be able to beat the Admin security. We'll check the uplink queue one more time tomorrow morning, but we can't afford to wait any longer. I'm sure you feel the same."

Distress and mental fatigue pull the corners of my lips into a frown, and I want to scream in frustration. Where is Rajcik? This is the outcome I'd avoided thinking about, but now I have to decide what to do next.

Again, she seems to be reading my thoughts. "Erikson, you don't have a lot of options, but you're free to do what you want." She stands up and pushes her thick hair back from her forehead, as if what she's about to say is going to be hard for her. "Truth is, we could use someone with your skills and your background to help us. I know that's a lot to hope for, considering your priorities. The only other thing you can do is head to Hell's Gate and barter a ride, if you have anywhere to go."

Disentangling her fingers, she reaches into the cargo pocket on her pants and pulls out a stack of Admin-printed cash. "We brought you here without asking you. Maybe you realize the decision saved your life, maybe not. But this money will get you at least as far as the Obals. Consider us even."

She tosses the money on my lap and walks out to the lift platform. "I'll be here early in the morning. If you're still around, we'll check the queue. Think hard about what you're going to do, Erikson. Your bunk on the *Sphynx* is open if you want to get some sleep."

She reaches out to activate the lift. "Vitruzzi," I say. Her hand stops, hovering above the controls, and she looks at me. "I am grateful. I know I wouldn't have made it."

Without a word, she presses the controls and is gone.

I don't know what I'd expected her to do if the situation came to this, but this isn't it. I sit in the darkening communication room for a couple minutes, listening to the thump of my heart, trying not to hear the whir of thoughts spinning through my head. She's right, there's no more time to wait. I'll leave first thing in the morning. I don't know what kind of town Hell's Gate is, but it's probably best not to walk in there in the middle of the night looking for a lift to the Obals. I pick up the stack of bills she gave me and its heft is a generous reassurance. Especially not with this much cash on me. I may be on the forsaken outskirts of the system, but I'm no longer stuck here.

It's still early and I'm way too wound up to sleep anyway, so I climb back up the tunnel to the overlook Bodie had shown me, some deep part of my brain hoping the tranquil view will quiet my thoughts and make it possible to sleep.

The heavy door thuds open and I reach for the handrail to pull myself the rest of the way onto the overlook. Movement in the corner of my eye alerts me that someone else is already here.

"Oh, sorry." Disappointed, I start to pull the door closed.

Strahan's voice stops me. "It's all right."

"No, that's fine. I'll leave you alone."

"Wait." He takes a step forward and I make out the look on his face. The scowl is permanently affixed but muted in the darkness. "Erikson, actually I wanted a chance to talk to you. Will you stay for a minute?"

I shrug. I've had enough one-on-one time with people trying to talk me into things I don't want to do today. Besides, what's the use? I'm gone in the morning and I'll never even see these people again. But, if that's the case, talking to him now won't kill me, will it? I pull myself over the edge onto the landing.

The sky is blazing with a billion stars, each tiny point a dazzle in my eye. It's beautiful, peaceful in a way that is somehow different from being aboard a ship. Standing here on solid ground, watching them hanging brightly above me, they feel further away and less like a judgment, filling me with the kind of wonder the first *Homo erectus* must have felt a couple million years ago. There's a measure of relief in realizing how utterly small and unimportant our fleeting lives are.

I walk up to the railing and lightly rest my hands along it, not saying anything, just waiting.

He pulls out his cigarettes and casually leans on his elbows a few steps away from me, pulls one from the pack and sticks it between his lips. Lighting it with a match and cupping the flame in his hands so the fragile spark is hidden, he inhales deeply. Noticing me watching, he asks, with the cigarette dangling from his mouth, "Did you want one?"

Shaking my head, I respond, "You'll lose your citizenship if the Admin knows you smoke."

"Yeah, well, they can keep those forty-seven years."

He's referring to life expectancy. For a citizen it's ninety-seven years, for non-cits it's around fifty.

We both turn back and stare out over the expanse of the Spectra 6 landscape. Unbroken blackness crawls away from us, making it seem as if we are in space, not standing on solid earth.

Strahan remains quiet for some time. Finally I say, "So you wanted to talk to me about something?"

Still focused on the distant skies, he replies, "Do you like to fly, Erikson?" The question is rhetorical and he doesn't wait for an answer. "I love it. I dreamed of it when I was still a kid on Obal 10. Wanted to be on those big cruisers and see new worlds more than anything. So I joined the Corps when I was sixteen. No way was I going to be stuck in some landlocked job in the civil service. I worked hard to get assigned to a ship, and when it looked as if I wouldn't get assigned outside the infantry and maybe never go farther than the nearest moon, I worked even harder until I became a pilot. I even thought I was a pretty good one until I met Venus." He pauses, a faraway grin playing at the corners of his mouth, then resumes, serious again, "I've probably seen forty or fifty different moons and planets in this system."

He's getting at something so I just let him talk.

"And you know what I've learned?" He takes another drag on his cigarette. The burning coal reflects in his light-brown eyes, making them resonate with an inner flame. "No matter where you are, it's the people you're with that matter the most."

I bite back a sarcastic response: *Thanks for the lecture*. "Uh-huh."

"Doug Mason is the pilot of the *Sky Serpent*. We used to fly together a lot until Venus came along. He's a good man. Like a brother, really. There's nothing I wouldn't do to get him the fuck away from the Admin."

He turns to look at me full on. "And he'd do the same thing for me. What would you do to get your brother free, Erikson? Is profit that much more important?"

His words are a cleverly laid trap, but he doesn't know the real effect they have on me. I push away from the railing and turn stiffly, facing him. "Is that it?" My voice is sharp and I hope he doesn't hear the way it catches for a second in my throat.

He drops the cigarette on the landing and squashes it with a brutal stomp from his boot. "Yeah, I guess it is. Enjoy the view." Taking one long stride, he disappears down the shaft, leaving me in the wake of his disapproval and disappointment.

The view suddenly isn't quite as serene as before. Who is he to judge me? Part of me wants to follow him down the ladder and unload on him, but there's another part of me that has to admit, regardless of what difference it does or doesn't make, he isn't completely wrong. Rajcik and the rest of my crew are dangerous people. They're not the type to sacrifice profit, and certainly not the type to put themselves in harm's way for others. What good does it do me to find Rajcik? Will he bother to help me try and save David? Why do I even fly with someone I can't rely on in the first place?

The answer is surprisingly simple. There's freedom in knowing exactly how much your life is worth to others. When the answer is nothing, there are no surprises.

The chill night air begins seeping through my clothes, staunching my anger. Time to go back to the *Sphynx* and get some sleep. What are my chances of getting off this rock tomorrow? Best not to think about it yet.

ELEVEN

Standing at the rim of a canyon looking over the little town of Hell's Gate about half a klick away, it's easy to see where it gets its name. It's a densely packed, dirty little pisspot of a town with smoke stacks and mud turning the whole thing into a uniform dingy heap. One flash fire and the whole place would be smoldering toothpicks within minutes. Right now, the town is mostly quiet except for a few stray dogs that move around the outskirts looking for scraps. I idly wonder what happens to people who die here.

Still, for all its ugliness and destitution I can see three inter-planetary vessels sitting outside of town. Hopefully, they're sky worthy. Now I just have to find their owners.

Turning around for one last scan of the labyrinthine canyon system I'd just come through, I feel confident that I haven't been followed and start driving down the hillside's eastern flank. I'd quickly and steadily lost elevation as I drove from Agate Beach into this maze of walls and crags this morning, and the going is now much more gradual after clearing the canyon walls. With a sliver of guilt, I check for confirmation on the navigation console of the ATV I'd stolen. I could probably have found someone to give me a ride here, but I wanted to avoid another encounter bur-dened with accusations and expectations. They'll know where to find the transport, and I'll be long gone.

It's nearing 0900 hours and more people can be seen up and about as I reach the town's edge. The place is gritty and claustro-phobic with buildings haphazardly placed, leaning on each other for support. Trash and refuse are everywhere, tossed carelessly in the streets. The overall area is smaller than Vitruzzi's settlement, but more structures fill the space. The air is redolent of oily smoke and unusual food.

The paths running between the buildings are too small for the ATV, so I ditch it behind a large bin on the edge of town and wave goodbye. Even if I planned to come back for it, I have my doubts that much time will pass before someone steals it or strips it. Un-sure of the best place to start searching for passage, I pass between the two nearest buildings onto the widest of the footpaths running through the cluster's center. Places like this always have a dive where business and drinking can occur, and people with ships seek out those who have something that needs to be shipped. I walk cautiously, but not obviously so. No need to give the impression I'm nervous. Trouble can be dealt with but doesn't need to be invited.

Instincts of self-preservation envelope me in their usual configuration: hyper-awareness, cautious movement, and hair-trigger reflexes. I'm here on business and not to be fucked with.

As I walk, I feel the heat of the morning sun bake into my neck. The bruises from Strahan's rifle butt and the watchcap I wear are the only disguises I have. If bounty hunters are canvassing the area, it won't be hard to recognize me. I just have to keep my head down and look as if I belong. Easy enough for someone with my years of practice.

"Got some spare change? Little money for a hungry man?" says a scruffy beggar, reeking of piss and the disturbing smell of cooked skin, from an alleyway as I walk by. He reaches out to grab my arm, and the red scabs covering his wrists emerge from his own tattered sleeve. His eyes are cloudy and bloodshot, rolling back and forth in his pitted and dirt-streaked face, and he leers at me in a suggestion of a smile. His teeth are all missing.

Moving backward a step before he can get hold of my arm, I answer, "Maybe. Where can I hire a transport ship?"

He coughs in a dry, wheezing crackle. "You're almost there," he answers, and points toward a building a few meters down the street. There's a glowing sign in front, hanging on a slant from its one remaining wire: Van Dieman's Land, and under that, *Roomz & Drinkz*. Perfect.

"Any ideas on who I might need to talk to?"

He shakes his head miserably. I doubt this walking shell has spoken to anyone besides rats, and maybe a dealer, in weeks. I pull out a single bill, hand it over, careful not to let his scaly fingers touch me, and walk on.

The bar has no windows and it will be dark inside. I stand next to the door for a few seconds, glancing inside whenever anyone enters or leaves, getting an impression of the interior and letting my eyes get used to the gloom. It's smoky, the shadows of men and women visible standing around a few tables, but I can't make out many details. Even this early, the place has good business. A man walks in past me without a glance and I slip in behind him, quickly moving beside the wall nearest the door.

Two more men and a woman sit at the bar near the back. The woman and one of the men don't look like much, but the second one wears clean clothes made of good material, and his boots are barely scratched. He hasn't been walking around on this rocky planet much. I'll start with him.

Crossing the room, I come to a standstill beside him—the bar has no seats—and catch the barkeep's eye.

Before I can say anything, I hear: "Erikson. I've been looking for you."

My jaw clenches involuntarily at the sound of that voice. Calmly, but not slowly, I turn around. Before he can speak again, I thrust out my hand and grip the man's crotch in a relentless squeeze. He hisses in surprise and pain, but doesn't try to move.

"MacCready." I have to wait a second for the dryness in my throat to give way before I can go on. "I didn't expect to ever see you again."

Almost two years have passed since I abandoned Marcus MacCready, a one-time member of Rajcik's smuggling crew, on a moon about to be overrun by Corps. I thought he was dead.

"That goes for both of us, Erikson. But don't worry, I've completely forgotten about that, uh, disagreement. Now would you let up a bit? You could be ruining my chances for future generations."

"You and I both know you'll never be anyone's father." I eye his sweat-sheeted face for a second. Even if he does have plans for revenge, this place is far too public for him to settle any scores. Letting go, I ask, "What the fuck do you want?"

He sucks in a full breath, reaches an exploratory hand toward his package, and pushes in next to me. The man who I'd originally intended to talk with side-steps as far toward the other end of the bar as he can, trying to conceal the wary way he glances at us from the corners of his eyes. "Our mutual friend sent me to pick you up."

It's as if his words are cold water suddenly thrown in my face. Keeping my voice low, I say, "You're here with János? Where is he?" The question I don't ask is: What do you mean, our mutual friend?

"Waiting. Let's go." Without sticking around to see if I'll follow, he heads for the door.

My nerves are on full alert. It seems impossible that Rajcik has somehow made it to Spectra 6. But then, in six years working together, I've learned not to be surprised by much of what he does.

The only two ways he could be here so soon are pure luck, which I don't put much faith in, or he somehow followed me here. Either way, this situation has just become more fluid. There may be a chance of getting to David in time after all.

No longer hesitating, I go after him. We step back out into the hot sunlight and MacCready begins walking down the empty street. I want to grab him and force him to answer the thousand questions reeling in my mind, but his pace is too quick, as if time is short.

The sun scorches us and sweat glazes my neck like lukewarm jet fuel. MacCready turns into a narrow alleyway, but I stop. Part of me is eager to follow him and meet back up with Rajcik; the rest of me knows better than to let myself be led into a dead end by this man. Planting myself at the corner of a building, I ask, "Where exactly is he, MacCready? I haven't seen the *Temptation* anywhere."

There's an extensive list of men in the universe that I don't trust, and Marcus MacCready is on the top of it. For good reason. When I'd left him behind, I'd been in a hurry. Unfortunately for him, he'd been standing in the stream of deadly blowback from our escape craft's jet engine. The last thing I'd seen through the craft's image sensors before getting the fuck out of there was his twisting body engulfed in flames consuming his clothes like ravenous devils. A thing like that isn't easily forgiven, and MacCready never impressed me as the understanding type.

My abrupt questioning stops him. As he turns around, pale features fixed in exasperation and impatience, I see his face clearly for the first time. Reddened and pocked skin scours the left side of his head, peeking through in patches beneath his white-blond hair and continuing down his jaw and throat until the scarring is hidden beneath the collar of his distressed jacket. He hadn't been facing me directly inside the dark bar and I had not seen the damage. The burn scars draw the skin of his cheek together the way plastic curls up when it's melting, giving him a permanent sneer.

But it's the look in his anemic blue eyes, corneas the same yellow as a jaundice patient, that triggers the neurons in my brain to fire a high alert. Pure hate, the kind that burns a person up from inside out, threatens to ignite the air between us. He doesn't say anything for several seconds, regarding me, trying to smolder me on the spot. With slow but menacing care, I draw my Sinbad as a warning, but I keep the muzzle pointed toward the dirt. In response, he raises his hand to his jacket, where I assume he carries his own pistol. Rays of sun find their way between the building roofs and pour their spotlights on the scene, illuminating everything with perfect clarity. Before he reaches into his jacket, which would guarantee him a bullet between the eyes, his hand stops and he blinks.

Instead of doing anything stupid, he extends a finger and points up the alleyway. "Our ride is parked just outside town. We're supposed to take it to the ship. Rajcik's gone to a lot of trouble to find you."

He's not telling me something. "Then why did he send you? When did you start working for him again? Show me some proof, MacCready, or our little reunion will end right here."

His sneer deepens, but he reaches into the jacket's cargo pocket, slowly, and retrieves a handheld comsat channeler. Pressing the telecast operator, he says, "Mac for Rajcik."

Holding up the video display so that we can both see it, we wait for a response. In a few seconds, the black screen shifts and I'm looking at the face of János Rajcik in crisp detail. "Go for . . ." My boss's wide, thin lips part to reveal the edges of perfectly even teeth in what represents, for Rajcik, a smile. "Erikson. You *aren't* dead. I only half expected Mac to find you. Get back to the *Temptation* ASAP."

Uncertainty and anxiety bubble up from my guts in an acidic burp. I should be glad to have found my employer and crew again, but the presence of MacCready and unusual twist of events leaves me cold, worried. Still, I lower the Sinbad. "Rajcik, what's going on? How did you find—?"

"We'll have plenty of time for Q&A, Aly. MacCready, how quickly can you get back to the ship?"

"Shouldn't take more than an hour."

"Good. Don't use the comsat again." Without another word, Rajcik severs our connection.

MacCready looks at me and doesn't try to hide his impatience. "You ready to go, Erikson? Or do you want to discuss anything else?"

Stifling the urge to buy myself more time, I holster my pistol. My questions will be answered as soon as I get back to the *Temptation*, and right now reconnecting with Rajcik is the only option that offers me much hope. MacCready takes the cue and begins walking down the alley again. Before following, I take a final glance back toward the town to see what else could be in store. No one on the roofline, no one coming toward us. I look back toward the bar and see—

"Oh, shit." Strahan stands just outside. His back is pressed against the wall of the building and he's trying to wedge himself out of sight inside the doorway. Clever bastard. *Why are you following me?* I can't tell if he knows I've spotted him, but I'm not going to give him any more opportunities. Stepping past MacCready, I start double-timing down the alley. "Let's go."

It branches out into a T-intersection at the end and I turn to get directions. He's standing flat-footed, his jaw set and eyes stabbing me again with hatred. I realize he's about to attack, but too late. His fist smashes into my jaw with tooth-rattling force. I feel an explosion of pain, taste blood, and then my arms are yanked backward, my wrists quickly clamped tightly together with handcuffs. I try to pull free, but whoever has my arms keeps his hold, forcing me to stop before ripping my shoulders from their sockets.

"MacCready, what the fuck?!"

"Shut up!" And he slaps tape over my mouth so I'll do exactly that.

Craning my head backward in an effort to avoid the tape, I get a look at the person holding my arms. Liev Fedchenko, another of the regular crew. His dark, greasy hair covers his bushy eyebrows and he's grinning at me sinisterly, scarecrow teeth protruding from his thick lips. I may be in more trouble than I realized.

"Quit struggling, Erikson, or I'll break your jaw," MacCready warns. "We're taking you to the *Temptation*, but Rajcik didn't specify what condition you'd have to be in. I've had enough fucking trouble from you."

"Forget it, Mac. Let's just get her back. Rajcik wants to talk to her."

He snarls at Fedchenko like a dog but leans away from me. Pulling a rag from his pocket, he unfurls it and pulls it over my head as a hood. I can't see anything, but dust and rankness fill my nose, making me gag. The tape over my mouth forces me to control the reflex in order to keep from choking, and I consciously slow my breathing down, making myself ignore the stench.

"You're either going to walk on your own, or we're going to drag you. What'll it be?"

Because I can't speak, I nod and my shoulders are yanked sideways, spinning me around. Pressure that can't be anything but a gun barrel jabs into my spine, and we walk.

THE DOOR OPENS. Someone approaches, lifts the hood still covering my head partway, and presses something cold against my cheek, making me suck air sharply through my nostrils in a nasal gasp. Then the hood is pulled off.

"Welcome back." Rajcik stands in front of me, holding an ice-pack to my cheek.

I'm groggy and off kilter after the shot to the jaw and lack of clean air. They'd brought me back to the *Temptation*—a decommissioned assault craft, stolen and retrofitted for use as a long-range smuggling ship—and locked me up. I've been waiting for at least an hour, but, somehow, I'm not as relieved to be back as I expected to be. We'd traveled by hovercraft to get here, but even without the benefit of being able to feel solid ground beneath us, the extensive rises and dips we'd glided over tell me we're in canyon country. Rajcik has hidden the *Temptation* amid the walls of the ragged landscape, and I have no idea where I am.

I focus on him, letting my fury at being punched, handcuffed, nearly asphyxiated, and brought at gunpoint back to the ship burn from my eyes in a toxic-waste glare. He stares back with a glint of mania and rage in his own.

If people were dogs, I wouldn't be surprised to see many submissively piss themselves when meeting Rajcik. His hulking frame, grinning-skull face, and the measured threat always looming in his voice never fail to induce a lizard-brain reaction of fear and intimidation, even from the reckless and insane. His muscles fit his frame the way perfectly calibrated elements fit a war machine, both graceful and menacing. On the rare occasions that our jobs had ended up in a hand-to-hand fracas, I'd seen Rajcik move like a vengeful ghost, swift and certain, killing men before they'd even realized they were in a fight.

He examines my expression for a moment, as if trying to decide whether to eat his dinner with a knife and fork or just shove his whole face into the plate, and unceremoniously yanks the tape from my mouth.

I'm furious and confused, but I let the fury talk for me. "What THE FUCK is going on, János?" My jaw feels swollen, a hot lump that pulses with my heartbeat. I can only imagine what my face looks like now, between the damage caused by Strahan's rifle and MacCready's fist. "Let me out of these fucking handcuffs."

He swallows and a large-caliber machine gun round tattooed in black ink bobs up and down with his Adam's apple. With his flight jacket on, only the top of the vast network of tattoos that adorn his skin, winding up and down his arms, neck, and back, is visible. He is covered in savagely inked illustrations, the kind that mean something. It's not about vanity or having a jailhouse record of how many people he's killed or how many women he's fucked. A darker impulse drives his epidermal tableau. A maelstrom of guns, warships, and all the other devices for war and destruction that he buys and sells covers his body in a macabre representation of death in machine form. These are the tools he peddles in defiance of the Admin, always with the intent that they'll be used against it. It's all about money and revenge, which to him equate to the same thing.

Finally unlocking my wrists, he steps back, waiting patiently for me to either calm down or do something stupid like jump him. "I was very surprised to pick up a transmission from you, Aly. I thought you were dead. There were two squads after you on Obal 3." He scans my face, trying to read my thoughts. "Looks like I underestimated you."

He hasn't answered my question. "David and I were trapped. He held them off, while I tried to escape. I think he's been arrested and—"

He cuts me off with unmasked suspicion in his tone. "How did you end up here?"

"That's why I contacted you."

"You contacted me to tell me how you got here?" Sarcasm is frightening coming from him. "I don't think so. You're trying my patience. Now, how did you escape from Obal 3 and whose uplink did you use to transmit?"

This is his favorite dance. Not a waltz, more like the circling of a hungry wolf, the tango of a tiger. He's only interested in discovering why I'm still alive and how he can use this information to his advantage. It hasn't played into his plans that I could possibly have survived the odds we faced on Obal 3, and he probably believes that I've betrayed him in exchange for my life. He'll feint and jab until I admit it, not relenting or allowing anything from me except the answers to his questions, which he thinks he already has. My only chance is to take the lead. I have to be strategic if I'm going to convince him of anything different.

"First, why don't you tell me why you're here? You got my transmission. Why didn't you just respond? You want the story, János, you're going to have to tell me one too."

He tosses the icepack next to me on the table. "MacCready tells me you were being followed. What assurance do I have that you aren't working with someone else?"

So MacCready had seen Strahan too. "Look at my face! You think I'm working for people who did this to me? Besides, is there another gig in the galaxy with a better payday?"

My outburst has the right effect. A vicious smile curls up both edges of his mouth, making him look sharklike, all teeth. I can almost imagine flecks of meat from his last victim stuck between them. The thought makes me shudder. "Hmm." He makes a smacking sound with his lips. "You are consistently reliable when it comes to getting paid, Aly. You would think I'd know by now not to doubt that." Reaching out to lightly brush my throbbing jaw, the gesture more intimate than necessary, he says, "As for this, Mac must have taken the opportunity to recover an old debt."

It takes an effort not to brush away his fingers. "So what's going on? How did you find me and how did you get here so fast? We were supposed to rendezvous on Obal 10. That's at least a week and a half away. Why didn't you stick to the plan?"

"Plans changed."

It's clear that he's not going to give me any straight answers, but I try anyway. "Then why are you on Spectra 6?"

"No, Aly. The question is, why are you on Spectra 6"—his eyes turn feral and dangerous—"with another group of arms smugglers?"

I can almost feel the ground sinking beneath me like quicksand, and I'm suddenly not sure I'll be able to talk my way out of this. There's a shrill edge to my voice as I try. "Cut the shit. I was kidnapped! Get it? T'Kai was sloppy and someone else found out about the holodisc. Or he changed his mind about the gig and outed us. Either way, the people who grabbed me want a copy of their own." Now that I hear the story coming from my own mouth, I realize how unbelievable it is. It doesn't matter that I've spent the last six years working for Rajcik. If I don't convince him of the truth, MacCready's blow is going to seem kind. "You know I wouldn't blue falcon you."

He regards me for a long second with a sly look I can't interpret. "No, you wouldn't. You're not stupid, are you? That's something I've always found curious about you—your loyalty." Then, to my relief, he says, "Tell me what's going on."

It takes me fifteen minutes to explain everything. He listens closely, without interrupting. A grim scowl darkens his features when I tell him about Vilbrandt and Director T'Kai. T'Kai had obviously told him nothing about Vilbrandt or bothered to warn him about Vilbrandt's potential to jeopardize our mission. Rajcik's jaw clenches when I tell him about the Admin's newscast of the robbery, probably promoted by T'Kai in an attempt to cover for himself. He says nothing about Vilbrandt's interest in trading his insider knowledge of the Fortress for a cut, and stays equally mute when I share Vilbrandt's theory that David's captors would have taken him to the Fortress for questioning—and use as a lab rat. His looming silence throughout my explanation has the effect he wants; I grow more nervous and agitated by the second, struggling to keep it under wraps.

He stands in front of me like a wall, his eyes scanning my face as I conclude with Vitruzzi and Brady's proposal. "So these arms transporters are trying to help their friends and they're serious about negotiating with us. They want to exchange a mother load of solar seeds for the disc. It's a solid deal. I've seen the seeds and I know they have them." The expression on his face makes me decide to leave out the part about them wanting to make this a joint operation.

The room is quiet for a few seconds. Then slowly, he recites, "T'Kai, David, who's in the Admin's hands, this scientist Vilbrandt, and a group of non-cit smugglers . . . tell me, Aly, is there anyone in the *fucking universe who doesn't know about my plan*?!"

He leans over me, eyes red-rimmed, furious and wide. His mouth is inches from my face, spittle flecking his lips, his anger like a furnace on the brink of exploding, and for a moment I think he may actually try ripping my throat out with his teeth. I don't budge from the table. Drawing in a long, controlled breath and forcing myself not to move, I refuse to let him see my fear.

His nostrils flare once more, and then he straightens back up. His neck and face are flushed red, glowing the way vulnerable skin sitting too close to an open flame does, making the whites of his eyes stand out vividly. The muscles from his jaw to his neck, each almost as thick as my wrists, are flexed taut. I've seen him look this way before throwing men from the doorways of in-flight transporters. They died. I wonder if it's my turn.

Taking a deep breath, he lets it out slowly and asks casually, as if the conversation had never verged on murder, "Tell me more about Captain Vitruzzi and her crew."

Already his mind is working on an angle he can use to his benefit. The immediate threat appears to have diminished, but I well know that Rajcik can go ballistic without warning if I'm not careful. "Mostly ex-soldiers, legally released. Vitruzzi used to be an Admin doctor. There are about five regulars on her crew and they all seem reliable. From what I've seen, they're not loyal to the Admin."

"They transport arms. How did they get that kind of clearance?"

"I don't know."

His next question is so unexpected, I'm not sure I hear him right. "Do you think we can trust them?"

What's he getting at? Rajcik trusts no one, not even me. "If you mean do I think they're good for the exchange, yeah I do."

"Maybe we can use them."

He's no longer looking at me, his thoughts probing the surface of some new plan. I'm not sure I'll like what he's thinking. "What do you mean?"

"We need a way to get aboard the Fortress. Stealing an Admin ship will be too obvious and they won't let unknown transporters anywhere near their perimeter. This Vitruzzi and her team could be just the diversion we need."

"You mean use them as bait? I don't think that's—" He focuses on me sharply. "I mean . . . what about this? We could make them partners—not for the payoff, just to get in and out of the station." Suddenly no longer in control of my mouth, I barely believe what I'm saying. "They don't even want a cut of the money, just the disc so that they can break in and rescue their friends. If David's there, they're all probably being held together. Their involvement could be a tremendous asset."

He frowns, looking almost as surprised at what I said as I am. "The plan does not change. This is *my* show. Don't forget that."

Leaning close again, he emphasizes, "I'm not jeopardizing this mission for *any* man. Including David."

I hear a stupefied gasp and realize it came from me. "Are you insane? We can't leave him there! They'll kill him!" I'm standing now, face to face with him, both of my hands gripping the collar of his jacket.

Grabbing my arms just above the elbows, he pulls them away with a quick jerk and shoves me back against the table. A shadow of impatient anger passes over his brow like the first ripple of a pending tsunami. "He knew the risks when he signed up for this job. So did you."

Bile begins to churn in my stomach. "You're going to regret this you sonofabitch." My voice is flat, icy, toneless. For the moment, I don't care if he kills me.

He squeezes my wrists crushingly tight, black eyes smoldering into mine. "Does this mean you want off the crew?"

Cold hatred lodges in my throat, making me choke on the threats I want to hurl at him. Instead, I remain tense and silent, rage shaking me.

He stands motionless for a moment, scrutinizing me with insidious attention. Then he drops my hands, and a quick dip of his chin indicates that he's come to some kind of decision. "Maybe you need a little time to think it over. You know I've always liked you, Aly. Because you're smart. Don't do something that's going to change my opinion."

He turns his back to leave before I break out of my paralysis. "There's one thing you didn't tell me, János."

He looks back over his shoulder.

"Why did you bring MacCready back on the team?"

"I can rely on him to do what's necessary."

"I told you what happened last time. He put the operation at *unnecessary* risk. We could have lost the payoff. What makes you think he's reliable now?"

"Don't worry. MacCready knows what his orders are." His face is unreadable, but I can guess what those orders might be.

DAVID. DAVID'S IN TROUBLE and the only chance I had of helping him just threatened to sic his guard dog on me if I make a wrong move. David. How the fuck am I going to get to him?

Maybe Rajcik isn't my only option.

Ten minutes go by and I don't move from my seat on the table. What's the use? I'm as familiar with this ship as I am with my own weapons. I should be, it's been my home for the last six years. There's no way to break through the door to this room, an empty berth for excess gear and smuggled goods. Not even a duct from the ventilation system links into it so there are no shafts I might be able to wriggle through. I'm in a prison that's as secure as any in the system.

My mind is like a flag in a hurricane, whipping and beating itself into a shredded frenzy. Something is very wrong here. It shouldn't surprise me that Rajcik could care less about the jeopardy David is in, but something more has kindled a warning fire at the tips of my nerves. He acts as if he *expected* the two of us to be killed. As if we weren't supposed to escape Obal 3 at all. But what reason would he have for wanting us dead? We've backed this mission completely since the day he told us about it.

And there's MacCready: unpredictable, psychotic, and almost guaranteed to increase the amount of bloodshed in a mission way beyond what's necessary.

When I left him for dead, we'd been following a Corps troop transport for about a week, the kind of job we'd done a hundred times. These ships always docked at some point to rotate personnel on and off remote duty. Our intel told us that this particular crew were tasked with guarding an Admin warehouse full of munitions.

Once the squads had been switched and the troop ship dispatched, MacCready and I ambushed the new sentries. They were slow-witted and clumsy, not prepared for our little surprise, and we'd neutralized them within minutes. Unexpectedly, we also found a handful of citizens serving as supplemental staffing for the facility. Before we realized they had active DNA tags that allowed them to fire weapons, MacCready was winged by a small-caliber handgun. We were able to outmaneuver them, killing one before they surrendered, and he trussed them together while I collected the payload. Less than ten minutes had passed by the time we had everything on board our escape craft, and I'd climbed in to start the engine and check our satellite surveillance feed for company. I can still taste the metallic gush of adrenaline that filled my mouth at the sight of a short-range hovercraft full of soldiers speeding toward the warehouse.

"MacCready, move your ass! Unfriendlies are on the way and they look like they know we're here. Five minutes tops!"

His voice came back via our helmet comlink, furious. "Sonofabitch. These cits got the word out."

Something was keeping him. When I stuck my head outside the EC's cockpit to see what, he was approaching the citizens, pistol drawn. My voice felt as if it were trying to force itself through mountains of sawdust, but I tried to stop him. "MacCready! We don't have time. Come on!"

He'd ignored me and shot the first man point-blank in the face. I heard him mumbling as he turned to the next one, "Goddamn citizen fucks. Don't know when to just shut the fuck up," and raised his weapon to the victim's head.

The sickening shock at such needless carnage only held me immobile for a second, though the terror in their faces will be embedded in my mind forever. There was no time to deal with MacCready if I was going to get out of there before the Corps arrived, so I engaged the forward drive and started the EC toward the open warehouse door. Another shot echoed through the comlink and MacCready began shouting for me to stop. Instead, I overcharged the EC's engine and slammed the thruster-control to full open. A superheated jet of fumes steamed from the exhaust port, instantly turning his running figure into a scorched scarecrow and propelling the EC through the exit like a bullet.

I made it back to the *Temptation*, certain MacCready was dead and happy to have been the cause.

Rajcik accepted the news calmly. He well knew the kind of sadistic man MacCready was, and my decision to leave him behind had kept us from losing both the EC and a pile of arms worth a sizable sum.

Yet, here he is. The thought keeps ringing through my head like a funeral bell. I don't care how he survived, and I'll leave him for dead again or shoot him myself if he gives me a reason. What I do care about is the answer to one simple question: Is he back on the crew because Rajcik intends to replace me?

There's no other explanation. I don't know exactly why Rajcik would decide to cut me loose, but I have to consider that a possibility. He's using me, just like he wants to use Vitruzzi and her crew. Right now, I'm the link between the two, and to get what he wants, he'll have to pretend he's not planning to shake me off. As unreal as it seems, I might have been better off throwing in my lot with the settlers.

But why? Why would Rajcik turn like this? Does it have something to do with David? What he'd said to me when he surrendered—*Don't let Rajcik out of your sight*—what did he know? Is Rajcik planning to double cross us? He hates the Admin, and he loves selling weapons to people that could use them against the Admin, but he needs our help to do it. None of this makes sense.

The room is small and stifling, the lack of airflow making me sweaty and lightheaded. It's almost a relief when the door opens and he comes in. He's back to ask the only question that matters. What will it be, Aly? The answer is easy: live today, fight tomorrow.

"So are you with us?"

I let the silence hang heavily for a minute, satisfying myself with a hint of disdain before answering. "What do you think, János? Of course I'm in. I'm kidding myself if I think David's still alive. Let's make some money."

His lips curl in that frightening half grin. "Excellent. You've just made yourself mission imperative again. Your gear is in the bunkroom. Get it and meet me in operations in twenty minutes."

TWELVE

Most of the crew is assembled around a holographic 3D image of the Fortress hovering over a disc reader when I arrive on the operations deck. Looming silently in the doorway, I survey them before anyone notices me—Rajcik, Fuller Thompson, Liev Fedchenko, Valya Ortiz, and of course, Marcus MacCready. The final member, Ahsan Yadav, brushes in behind me and activates the door. As it slides closed, the noise draws their attention and they turn and look at me with suspicion and disinterest. No questions about what happened to David and me. No happiness to see me. But then, I'm not happy to see them either. This is just the way it is: we work as partners, not as friends. The only person I had cared about in this bunch was David. What's the point of all those years on the take now?

Rajcik speaks, staring fervently at the image of the Fortress. "Our only way in is through disguise and deception. The *Temptation* has to appear to be one of their regular supply ships."

Data readouts are displayed along the screens adjoining the disc reader. T'Kai, for all his treachery, definitely did his job. We have enough information here to practically rebuild the Fortress. Separate menus allow the structural design to be overlaid with the security system grid, which includes pass codes, system schematics, and personnel routines—full disclosure of every operational detail. Combing through the data makes it clear that it would be impossible to infiltrate the space station, much less pirate stolen goods from it, without these plans. Even with the disc, the operation will be anything but easy.

We pay close attention as Rajcik continues sketching out the plan. "We'll cloak our heat signature and use legitimate transport authorization codes, but the dock controller's attention has to be elsewhere. If anything ignites their suspicion or makes them look too closely, they'll lock it down and we'll never get in. Which is why we're lucky to have Erikson back on board." His sly stare rests on me, the pressure of it forcing me to acknowledge the plans he'd already made.

The words stick like napalm in my throat, but I have no other choice than to play along. "During the mission on Obal 3, while David and I were drawing off the soldiers, he was arrested and I ended up getting nabbed by a group of settlers with intel on our operation. It's a long story. The important point is, they also plan to

infiltrate the Fortress and János wants to use them as . . . as bait
to draw off the Admin." I glance at him, making sure I've said
what he wants to hear. He looks satisfied.

Yadav, a swarthy smuggler with a thick mustache and the epi-
canthic eyes of a Mongol, asks grittily, "You been gone over a
week, Erikson. Why should we trust you now? Maybe you're trying to set us up."

Fedchenko and Thompson nod in agreement. Together with
Yadav, the three of them form the dicey edges of a lethal triad. Bottom dwellers in the smuggling cesspool, they'd worked as a team
throughout the system for several years as mercs, murderers, and
guns-for-hire. Alternately picking and robbing their own marks, or
hiring out to the kind of scum that has the money to pay someone
else to do the dirty work, they've been frequent poster boys on the
Admin most-wanted list. Rajcik hired them on for a job on Ohm
Lumi a couple years back, and they've been on the crew since. Neither David nor I ever cared much for their methods or morals, but
the crew's successes have made it easier to ignore them. Rajcik
doesn't answer Yadav's accusation, leaving it up to me to convince
them, testing my commitment.

Now, I have to lie, and lie well. I may or may not have convinced Rajcik that I'm not in Vitruzzi's pocket, or that I'm willing
to use her and her crew as a disposable cover for our robbery and
extortion, but I better convince the rest of them. If I want to work
the situation to my advantage, I can't have five suspicious cutthroats scrutinizing every move I make. I don't want to set up
Vitruzzi's crew to take the fall for us any more than I want to abandon the possibility of saving David. I'm not as detached from my
own moral barometer as Rajcik and most of this group are, no matter what people may think. Unlike Rajcik, I'm not willing to sacrifice others, especially others who've already proven that they're
willing to help me if I ask them to. He couldn't care less about
David. Or me. So fuck him. The trick is making them believe I'm
on their side, but when the chance comes, I'll do whatever it takes
to alter the plan to my own ends.

So I follow my usual tactic. "I don't give a shit if you trust me,
Yadav. If saving your ass on Obal 3, all of your asses, doesn't
prove what I'll do for this payoff, feel free to run the mission without me. And after you fuck it up and end up on some experimental
slab with a probe up your ass, I'll be relaxing on Obal 10 laughing

about it." It helps that I am truly furious. At Rajcik, at myself for being his pawn, at them for being too degenerate to care. At the whole fucked-up situation.

No one speaks for a second that quickly turns into several.

Ortiz breaks the silence. "Don't be fools. Erikson is here because Rajcik trusts her. That's enough."

Ortiz is a veteran on Rajcik's crew. At one time enlisted in the Corps, she'd already been with Rajcik when David and I had come into the mix. I convey my thanks with a quick glance in her direction, but it's hard to look at her too long. Ten years ago, she hadn't made it off her patrol ship when it went down after being struck by orbiting debris, and pocked and mottled burn-flesh covers her face and extremities. Her cowardly shipmates evacuated like gun-toting ants from a burning anthill, failing to follow protocol and assist the injured. After the vessel hurtled into Spectra 4, its auto-controls managing to keep the ship from going into total free fall, a non-cit doctor known to Rajcik had found her alive and helped her recover, in a way. At her insistence, he'd removed her lifemarker, making her untraceable by the Corps. Rajcik had hired her for many of the same reasons he'd hired David and me. Radically scarred inside and out, she's callous and remote, almost automaton, but still lethal and sharp. She speaks very little, but I suspect she backs me most of the time because of our shared link to the Corps, and shared hatred for it.

Rajcik finally speaks up. "This isn't up for discussion." He kills Yadav's accusation by ignoring it, letting me off the hook . . . for now. Fine with me. I've deflected enough bullshit today.

"We've got the equipment to mask our signature. We'll get the calls signs from a supply ship en route, which shouldn't be difficult. I'll have that information within a few days. For now, we sit tight. Aly and I have some arrangements to make. No one leave the ship until you hear from me."

Resentment billows through the room like caustic smoke. Nobody likes being stuck aboard a small interstellar craft for days at a time, especially when it's planet-side. But Rajcik is playing every centimeter of this gig with complete caution. As of now, the only wildcard, the only thing he hasn't precisely calculated, is the involvement of Vitruzzi and her crew. The image of the last time I saw Strahan looms to the surface of my thoughts. Why had he been following me? Can he and the rest of them even imagine what kind of danger they're in?

"Let's talk." He motions for me to follow and together we walk out of operations toward the flight deck. I can almost feel the hateful gazes of MacCready and Yadav, maybe all of them, on my back.

"HERE'S WHAT YOU'LL do." Outside of the flight deck window screens, I see nothing but rust-colored rock walls rising from the canyon floor. It must not have been easy to land the *Temptation* between these tightly abutting cliffs. The cover, however, is excellent. It isn't the kind of place anyone would happen upon unless they were looking for something, and I know I won't get far if I try to escape. Damn you, Rajcik. His mind for strategy is probably the most nimble and ruthless I've ever seen. The Corps would benefit from having him as their Command General, but the rest of the system would be in serious trouble if that ever happened. As dangerous as he is, it's best for everyone that he'll never have that kind of power.

He hands me a disc and continues, "You're going to take this to Vitruzzi and tell her we'll be in touch with further instructions."

"Are these the complete plans?"

He raises a mocking eyebrow at me, daring me to admit that I'd made up any part of the story about Vitruzzi's crew. If I lied to him about their interest in being involved, this would be my last opportunity to come clean. Not that it would matter. If I admitted to even the smallest attempt to mislead him, he'll kill me now. Best to say as little as possible. Finally, he answers, "That disc contains everything she needs to know. Except the location."

"Which you have?" I *knew* there was something he wasn't telling me.

Without answering, he gives me a cold look, and says, "Tell Vitruzzi I want to meet. I'll let her know where and when. Make sure they have the seeds."

"We don't have a lot of time, János."

"I'm aware that there is a sense of urgency on their behalf. However, they've waited this long, and as you said, David is probably dead. Is your impatience coming from the fact that you can't wait to get paid, or is there something else I should know?"

"If you string them along, they may take matters into their own hands."

"Your job is to stay with them and ensure that doesn't happen."

It takes some effort to swallow the golf-ball-sized lump of exasperation lodged in my throat before answering. "Understood."

"Thompson will take you back to Hell's Gate. I'm sure you'll find your way from there." He flicks on the intercom and orders Thompson to meet me at the *Temptation*'s transport shuttle.

He turns to leave, but my next question stops him. "When did you have time to go back to Obal 3 and pick up the shuttle?"

His head swivels toward me slowly, the way a cobra rises from a basket. He's caught and he knows it.

The answer is that he didn't, *couldn't*, have had the time or the opportunity to retrieve the shuttle. If he'd gone back, the Corps would have blasted the *Temptation* out of the sky. Which means he never sent the shuttle to the rendezvous in the first place, explaining why I couldn't find it despite following the directions he'd given me. Had he led the Corps to that hangar, trying to set me up? But why, goddammit? It doesn't make any sense.

He doesn't say anything. He doesn't have to. If I want to leave this room alive, I'm going to have to pretend that I don't know the truth, and he's going to have to pretend to believe me.

"I guess it doesn't really matter, huh?" It's the closest I can come to playing along. "We'll be waiting for your message."

Before I exit through the cabin doors, he grips my shoulder, spinning me to face him. Strong, implacable fingers dig like stakes into my back. Every muscle in my body goes taut, prepared to fight for my life, prepared for anything. "One more thing, Aly. If they try to run, or you do, I'll find you. And end you. Then I'll wipe their little settlement off the face of the planet. If they don't agree to my terms, you make sure they *completely* understand what they have to lose."

This time I don't stop myself from shoving his hand off me. Deftly, he grabs my wrist and jerks my fist toward him, pulling me with it. I try one time to pull my arm out of his grasp, but it's like fighting the vacuum of space. His grip is relentless, demanding I submit.

Bitterly, I respond, "Whatever you say."

He releases my arm and I watch the white marks where his fingers had been slowly begin to fill with red, angry blood. Shoving the disc inside the protection of my armor, I turn my back to him and leave.

THE DOORS SLIDE closed behind me and Thompson, a tall, gangly bullwhip of a man, is waiting in the corridor.

"You ready?" I ask.

He grunts and starts walking in the direction of the shuttle. After a couple of seconds, he says, "I'm glad Rajcik is grounding you. You don't have what it takes to be on this ship. Slags need to stay where they belong—out of our way. Ships are a man's world."

I couldn't like this cockroach any less, and in my current state of mind, there's no controlling my mouth. "Excuse me if I didn't notice where you pissed on the walls to mark your territory. I guess I should be happy that you can even remember to put your dick back in your pants."

He stops walking and turns around, his lips curled into an ugly snarl. Stepping close, trying to menace me, he fumes into my face, "I'll show you where my dick goes, bitch," and grabs at my crotch.

The dumb bastard isn't prepared for my forehead slamming into his nose. He grunts in pain and surprise, the exhalation rising into an out-of-breath screech as my knee connects full force with his groin. He doubles up, holding onto his damaged goods, blood dripping from his nose, making a pattering noise on the steel walkway that's punctuated by desperate attempts to draw air back into his locked lungs. I stand over him in disgust for a moment and warn, "Remember what that feels like next time you think about fucking with me, Thompson."

Still bent over, he turns his red, clenched face toward me and mouths "bitch" between gasps as I walk past him to the shuttle. I don't know what's going to happen next, but I realize I'll never be aboard the *Temptation* again. I'm done with Rajcik, and this crew, forever.

THIRTEEN

On the short trip back to Hell's Gate, Thompson forces me to sit in the shuttle's windowless fuselage to keep me from pinpointing the *Temptation*'s location. He barely plants the landing gear before opening the exterior hatch and telling me to get out.

Fortunately, all the money Vitruzzi gave me is still in the cargo pocket of my pants. It's late in the afternoon and more people shuffle around the area than I'd seen earlier this morning. Odds are good I'll be able to buy a land transport or a few minutes on a satcom link to contact Agate Beach and warn them. Rajcik knows where the settlement is, so there is no need for him to tail me. He's holding all the cards right now. I intend to change that.

Just outside the entrance to Van Dieman's Land, I notice that same solar stoner who had begged money off me earlier lying flat out on the dirt street. No one looks in his direction or even diverts their steps to avoid him. They just raise their feet slightly higher to clear him and keep moving. I can't tell if he's breathing. Either passed out or dead. There's a part of me that recognizes the tragedy, and the irony, in the fact that both states equal the same thing for this guy. Once you've gone too far down the road he's on, there's only one place it will end. For a second I consider helping him, at least get him out of the way of potential traffic. Except it wouldn't really be as if I'm doing him a favor. The sooner it ends for him, the better.

Bullshit. No one deserves to die like that. A man walking past gives me a dirty look as I cut in front of him, veering out into the street and grabbing the stoner's outstretched hand. Still warm. Pulling him into the shade of the nearest building—he's lighter than he looks, unhealthily light—I let go, and he slumps to the side with a deep grunt. A string of yellow drool hangs from his mouth and his eyes flutter. His sunken chest and sharp ribs burn with fever beneath my hand as I shove a few more bills into his shirt. There's nothing else I can do for him.

The bar's dark interior is refreshingly cool despite the smoke-thick air. Like all of the Spectras, being planet-side means either being rendered into an incoherent block of ice by the frost that sinks its deadly claws into your skin, lungs, and brain, or burning up from the relentless heat that fries your motivation along with your sanity. Spectra 6 is more mild than the others I've been to, but it could still be mistaken for hell. Bounty hunters on my trail are still a possibility and I keep a lookout for them or Admin personnel. But my current goal of finding a way to warn Vitruzzi makes me less careful about keeping a low profile. There are more patrons at the bar than before and catching the eye of the barkeep, I nod, beckoning her over. Her footsteps are labored as she approaches, as if she's sick or old, though she looks younger than me. Whatever this town is, it doesn't appear to be a healthy place to live. Her eyes are filmy and disinterested as she waits for my order.

"Is there anywhere around here with a satcom link?"

Her placid stare doesn't change, and she simply stands there as if I haven't said a word. So I drop some cash on the bar.

The bill disappears and she says, "There's an empty table over there. I'll find someone who can sort you out."

Uh-uh. My guess is I'll sit there all day and no one will ever show. In one quick motion, I lean over the bar and grab the arm she used to pick up the money. "I'm not fucking around here. If no one shows up within twenty minutes, that A-bill is going to be the hardest you've ever made."

My patience has already been stretched to its breaking point today and the message gets across. Her eyes widen and she dips her chin in acknowledgment.

Less than five minutes pass before Strahan pushes open the door, scans the interior, and walks up and sits in the chair opposite me. Somehow, I'm not surprised.

He looks me over, eyes resting on my freshly bruised jaw for a few seconds, and then asks, "How happy am I to see you, Erikson?"

"The truth? Not very." He waits for me to continue. "We can't talk here. This place isn't safe and we don't have the time. I need to talk to Vitruzzi right away." I'm a decent liar when I need to be, but I hope he recognizes the sincerity in my face.

He stands up. "Then let's roll."

STRAHAN DRIVES THE four-wheeled Rover through the canyon at a speed I wouldn't have imagined any land craft could manage. His usual taciturn attitude gives me plenty of time to think about how to explain the situation and come up with my next move. The population of Agate Beach is as good as dead if I don't talk them into playing Rajcik's game. The hard-to-swallow fact is, Rajcik only gave up the plans to the Fortress. We still don't know where it is and have nothing left to exchange for the location. The solar seeds are worth a small fortune, but they were also Vitruzzi's only bargaining chip, and Rajcik, technically, has already struck that bargain—the holodisc for the seeds. Vitruzzi didn't realize he would take the opportunity to up the ante at her and Brady's suggestion to team up on infiltrating the Fortress. Now Rajcik will try and force Vitruzzi into carrying out a suicide mission or make her watch Agate Beach be destroyed.

He's already proved that David and I were expendable from the beginning, and now he's willing to sacrifice a town full of people he's never even met to get the Nova. He's obviously well beyond compromise, or even reason, and it's clear to me that even if I stayed on Rajcik's crew and played everything exactly as he wants, I'd still never see a cent of the payoff.

I should be bitter. I should be livid, enraged, filled with hate. But the only feeling I'm still capable of is an overwhelming, crushing urgency to do whatever it takes to get to the Fortress and find my brother. If saving David means throwing in with Vitruzzi and her crew, then that's what I'll do. I know he'd do the same if our circumstances were reversed. If he dies, or if he's already dead, I'm not sure I can face the savage guilt, knowing that I'm the one who left him there.

In the end, that's all this is really about. My brother is the only person in this world that I can point to as evidence that I'm not just another robot, mindless and empty, trained and controlled by the Corps and its Admin puppet master. David is proof that I'm more than that. He's my brother. I'm not alone in the universe, not just another stray that no one cares about. Having a family means coming from somewhere, and knowing where to go when you need help. In a time when space flight is the norm and living planet-side with even half the luxuries of old Earth is something few can appreciate, being part of a family grounds a person. It validates the human in me and keeps me from becoming what the Admin wanted me to be—a nonentity, a tool, a unit. I don't want to be nothing.

Rajcik is prepared to let David die and make me exactly that. With calm, almost detached bitterness, I finally realize the real surprise is that Rajcik hadn't sold us out sooner.

That's all it takes for my loyalty to change sides.

We reach Agate Beach in less than three hours. Brady and Vitruzzi are waiting for us at the dwelling they share. As I take a seat, all eyes are on me, impatient for me to describe what went down with Rajcik. There's very little hope in their expressions, merely cautious examination. They're used to bad news.

Clearing my throat, I begin: "Here's the deal. Rajcik sent me back here to tell you that he would give up the disc in exchange for the seeds we took from R'Kadia." Reaching into my vest, I pull out the holodisc. "Here it is."

Their faces all register the same shocked surprise, but aggressive suspicion is also there. Brady's hazel eyes stab through the air between us, prickling the skin of my face. His dislike for me is palpable.

I toss the disc on the table and continue, "But the problem is that we, that you, don't have the Fortress's location. And he does."

Vitruzzi's voice is grim. "What does he want for it?"

"Simple. He wants to work together." I let them all see the exaggerated benevolence on my face that I'm supposed to be conveying as Rajcik's appointed representative, and all of its exaggerated falseness.

I'm not enjoying telling them this. I'm not trying to build up a dramatic sense of fragile hope in order to shatter it. I want them to understand just how dangerous János Rajcik is. I want them to comprehend that they're in over their heads and maybe they should start picking out their headstones. "Of course you already know what I'm saying is too good to be true. He wants to use you and your ship as a diversion, a set up, so the Admin targets you when we get within range of the Fortress. You get taken prisoner, or just blown to bits, and he slips in and steals the Nova."

No one says anything. I catch Strahan's expression in the corner of my eye. Unlike Brady's face, there's no dislike and distrust. It almost seems to be sympathy.

The outside door opens and Venus, Desto, and Bodie walk in. Nothing is said, but their movements become deliberate and awareness lights up their eyes, perceiving the tension in the air. Desto and Bodie look at me curiously and sit down at the table on either side of me. The corners of Venus's mouth turn downward in unhappy disappointment and she begins fidgeting around in the cupboards behind where Brady stands.

"What did we miss?" Desto asks.

"Erikson here was just telling us how her partners want to use us as decoys so they can get rich," Brady says.

Vitruzzi glances at Brady, the look in her eyes gentle but firm, and says, "Erikson, you've obviously got more to say, so get on with it."

I have to force my voice to stay even, to not give away the stress cracking through my bones like an earthquake. "Rajcik can go to hell. I'm not working for him anymore. The only way I see that we'll be able to get to the Fortress is to play along with him until he gives up the location. Then maybe we can turn his plan around and make him and his crew the diversion *we* need to get in and out undetected."

"We," Vitruzzi says flatly, but her eyebrows arch with curiosity.

"My goal and your goals are the same, at least for now. I don't give a fuck about getting rich anymore." I look directly at Brady when I say this, wanting to drive home how wrong he is, at least about me.

"Why the change of heart?" Strahan asks.

"What I want to know is why any of us are pretending to believe her," Brady cuts in, not so easily convinced. "Isn't it clear she's trying to bait us? She's a criminal, and she's working for a criminal. All of us know exactly what she's capable of." He glares darkly at me and leans forward on the table. "We know about the New Sweden Massacre." Sweeping the rest of the group with his swamp-grass stare, he continues, "Just because she's brought collateral doesn't mean those are really the plans for the Fortress, or that they haven't been rigged in some way. If she doesn't have some proof, I'm pulling the plug."

I've gone pale, my skin tingling coldly from the lack of blood. The New Sweden Massacre had been Rajcik's doing, that's true. But I hadn't been part of it.

The job happened almost a month ago, an easy-money gig appropriating a rebel cache of weapons from a non-cit settlement on Spectra 4. It should have been quick and low-risk—rush in, suppress resistance by threat and superior firepower, and be a memory within the hour. The rebels were a disorganized group, trying to plan some kind of attack on the Corps surveillance ships that sweep through the Spectras regularly. I have no idea what they hoped to get from such an attack, besides dead, and we anticipated that they would have no capacity to fight off a group with our experience. Like I said: easy.

We were on our way in, just passing near an Admin space station, when David had suggested to Rajcik that he and I divert from the operation. He convinced Rajcik that we weren't needed in New Sweden and could take the opportunity to sweep around the station in the *Temptation*'s shuttle to look for potential targets for future ops. He hadn't bothered to ask me what I thought of the plan, just assumed that I'd go along with whatever he proposed. We'd found nothing and rendezvoused with the *Temptation* six hours later. I was angry with David for pulling us off the op on a dangerous wild goose chase, but he'd been tight-lipped and unapologetic. Looking back now, I should have realized something else was going on. Maybe David knew Rajcik was going to go berserk and didn't want us involved.

Two weeks later, I caught a news bulletin detailing what happened at New Sweden. Rajcik and the crew hadn't just overpowered them; they'd killed every person there and blown the settlement off the map. The weapons cache had been paltry, barely worth the energy it took to fly out, and there didn't seem to be a reason for such dire actions. The news had upset and disgusted me, and David had been furious with Rajcik, threatening to kill him if he ever did something like that again. Murdering non-cits for no reason wasn't what we'd signed up for—we'd had enough of that back in the Corps. But it was done. Nothing would change that. By then, we had our sights set on bigger payoffs, and we hit Obal 3 eight days later.

"I didn't have anything to do with that." I'm shaken and I know it shows. For the first time since this whole mess began, I'm defending myself. "Neither did my brother. I don't know exactly what happened in New Sweden, and maybe it wouldn't have if we'd been there. But we weren't."

"Right." Brady thinks I'm lying and doesn't hide the fact. His smug expression shows that he's satisfied that he's won.

All the credibility I thought I had with this group is slipping away. If they already believed me capable of participating in that kind of ruthless slaughter, why bother trying to enlist my help at all? White-hot anger streaks through me. Have they just been toying with me all along, to get to Rajcik?

"Let me ask you something, Erikson. You know what kind of person Rajcik is. What makes you think his only interest in this Nova is profit? Hasn't it occurred to you that he plans on using it? No?

Well it has occurred to me." Brady's eyes are narrow, slitted like a snake's, as he continues, "Which is why I think you're either lying and you're just as much of a low-life-scum-villain as he is, or you're being stupid."

I throw the table aside and lunge at Brady before his last word is out. I don't care that I may be committing suicide; he's gone too fucking far.

My fist flies toward his face and I register that he's pulled a pistol out and is leveling it at my torso. Then my right shoulder shrieks in sudden, sharp pain as someone grabs my arm and forces it behind my back. With a grunt, I'm pulled backward and off balance, not dropping my eyes from Brady's scarred, hate-contorted face. I jerk forward in another attempt, and a knee slams into the back of my legs, buckling them and dropping me face first into the floor. My shoulder protests alarmingly. If I don't stop, it'll be useless for weeks. A knee is planted in the middle of my back and I let myself go limp, knowing I've lost this fight.

"Fuck you, Brady! You don't know what the fuck you're talking about! If you don't believe me, then fucking kill me!"

"Everyone calm down." Vitruzzi's voice is full of collected, icy reason.

Through the water leaking from my eyes, both from pain and rage, I see Desto's coffee-black-no-cream-no-sugar hand pulling my Sinbad free from my side. Just in case.

Vitruzzi says, "Get her up." He stands, pulling me to my feet. The look on his face is more amusement than anger, which frustrates me further. "Patrick, this isn't getting us anywhere. Why don't you give it a rest?"

Brady scowls at her for a moment and slams his pistol back into its holster. Without giving me another look, he stomps out.

Venus has pushed her body tightly against the far wall, her face betraying her distress. The strain is palpable, everyone struggling to keep it under wraps. Strahan rests his hand on the butt of his pistol but doesn't draw it.

My teeth are gritted fiercely against the pain in my contorted shoulder and I have to suck air through my nostrils. After another second, Desto releases some of the pressure, giving me a chance to continue in a more reasonable tone. "I don't care what you do, Vitruzzi. Those are the plans Rajcik gave me. Take them and use Vilbrandt, if you really think he's going to help you, and storm the

Fortress yourself. Good fucking luck. But bet on this. If you don't play along with Rajcik, he's going to do the same thing to your settlement that he did to New Sweden. Do you believe that?"

Well, maybe not so reasonable.

She blinks, tension spreading tightly over her already drawn features, and starts pacing across the room. "We've got our eye on Rajcik. He's not going to get a chance to threaten Agate Beach."

"How can you have your eye on him? I was on the *Temptation*, and I don't even know where it is."

The look she gives me is heavy with resolve. "We traced his location using a tracking chip we implanted on you. We have video emplacements watching his every move."

I almost missed what she said, it was so matter-of-fact. Then realization hits me. "What? What do you mean a tracking chip?"

"We bugged you."

If I'd been mad about being insulted by Brady before, I'm over-the-top, brace-for-the-storm, fucking furious now, but the sharp spike of pain in my shoulder and Desto's unbreakable grip keeps me from letting loose again. I'm forced to stand still, giving my sense of reason time to work out that she's probably bluffing. "Rajcik has the equipment to detect tracking devices," I respond. "If I had one on me, he'd have found it and I'd be dead."

"He couldn't have found it if he tried." She sounds utterly certain.

"What do you mean?"

"You don't know what I did before becoming a transporter, Erikson. Don't make the mistake of thinking you have everything figured out. You're smarter than that, and you have no idea what we're capable of."

There's no bluff in her face. "So you're saying I'm bugged. How?"

"The chip is tiny, bioengineered. It doesn't show up through magnetic resonance, x-ray, or radio frequency scanning, both because it is so small, and because it's masked by your own biochemistry. It hides from scans by cloaking itself in a genetically copied envelope of cells and integrating with the tissue around it. Its mechanical ability allows it to scramble scanners and make them see only normal biological structures. The only way to find it is by introducing viral catalysts in or near the physical instrument. It will copy viral cells, something like a cancer, but only affects the local area, thus creating a telltale lesion. It's only detectable if you know what you're looking for. I designed it peripheral to Admin research protocols, so its existence is unknown. Which makes it useful to us."

I swallow, unable to think of a response.

"I wouldn't have put you in a situation where I believed your life would be jeopardized without telling you, Erikson. I'm a doctor. My goal is to preserve life, not waste it."

"You're the one who told me I could leave if I chose to. Then you have me followed," I shoot an accusatory glance at Strahan, "and you bug me. What about all that bullshit you gave me about trusting you?"

"Did you really think that we would just give up if you decided not to help us?" She stops pacing and stands in front of me, whipping me with her words. "We knew you'd find Rajcik, or he'd find you. And since he has the information we need, we had to take the necessary steps to get to him."

"Do you have control of yourself, Erikson?" Desto asks softly in my ear.

I shrug noncommittally. Maybe I'm being touchy, but hearing my body's been used as a homing beacon makes a little retaliation feel justified. Desto releases my arm anyway and I take a slow step forward, wanting desperately to rub my aching shoulder, but refusing to give them the satisfaction.

"So where is it?"

"Your right shoulder, just under the scar. Scar tissue helps disguise the entry hole."

I pull up my sleeve to look. The scar, a remnant from the flying debris of a badly timed ammo dump eradication, is the only thing visible.

"Don't worry. It won't cause any harm. Almost everyone in the settlement has one."

Bodie and Venus begin picking up the toppled table and chairs. I remain standing, Desto's bulk near me enough of a deterrent to any half-cocked attempt at retribution I may be planning.

Vitruzzi waves her hand at the chair I'd been using before, wanting me to sit. I don't. Her eyebrows crease in anger, and she takes her own seat. After a moment, only Strahan, Desto, and I remain standing.

Bodie speaks for the first time. Leaning forward in his chair, eyes brimming with compassion, he says, "Imagine it from our perspective, Aly. We've all got friends who were on the *Sky Serpent*. We're just trying to help them. You would do the same for your brother, wouldn't you?"

What he says is 100 percent true, and everyone here knows it. I've already betrayed Rajcik, who had, despite our association with the Corps, given my brother and I an opportunity to escape that life and start a new one. You could argue that I owe him something. Or did. His decision to betray us and let David die changed that.

I take one last deep breath to rein in my temper and sit in the chair. "All right. Look. I can't prove anything I'm telling you. But the fact is, Rajcik is willing and able to do whatever it takes to get that bomb. And he won't share the profit or change the mission plan. Not even to try and rescue my brother. So fuck him. There's a chance that David is still alive, and I'm going to find him. That's the truth." And I think Rajcik plans to kill me anyway, but I'll keep that to myself.

Venus walks toward me and, surprisingly, grasps my hands between her own as if trying to reassure me. "We understand, Aly."

Vitruzzi continues to glare at me stoically for a few more seconds. Then she says, "Everyone take twenty minutes then meet back in the command room. Let's take a look at the disc and see what we have."

FOURTEEN

The room empties. Without another word to me, Vitruzzi raises her hand in a halting gesture, motioning for me to stay and wait, and catches up with Brady outside. Their voices carry through the door, modulating between loud and fast and slow and quiet, and bits of the conversation filter in to me.

" . . . trust her."

"When you're responsible for the lives of one hundred and twenty people, Eleanor, you'll think before bringing scum like them . . ."

" . . . no other chance to save Doug and Zeta! We've got Rajcik where we want him . . ."

When they return a few minutes later, Vitruzzi's face is set in hard lines, angry but determined. Brady remains surly and won't look at me. I'd overheard enough for it to be clear that he'd never agreed with Vitruzzi about bringing me to Spectra 6, and would probably prefer to have me dead and buried rather than be given any more opportunity to endanger the settlement. I didn't hear what she said to persuade him, but his opinion of me, no matter how misguided it is, could be an obstacle to a smooth mission outcome. I'll just have to keep as much distance between us as I can and hope that he listens to Vitruzzi. It complicates things, but right now he has to be considered hostile and potentially dangerous.

"Tell us what Rajcik plans to do and what he's capable of," Brady says.

There's no hesitation in my response, betrayal or not. When Rajcik had called me loyal, he'd underestimated how far that loyalty is capable of extending, and there's a subtle eagerness in my voice as I answer, "The *Temptation* isn't your biggest concern. The ship is nothing more than an escape vehicle with a few smuggling holds that allow us to hide stolen goods. Our pilot—I mean Rajcik's pilot—a man named Thompson, is good, but no match for Venus. The *Sphynx* is slower, but it's more maneuverable and takes less time to get up to speed, so she may be able to catch up to Rajcik within atmosphere if she has to. It's the *Temptation*'s shuttle that you need to be concerned about. It carries a retractable, fully auto orbital gun with nuke-tipped ammo."

"You're talking about a Nagasaki?"

"Yes. It stays on the shuttle in order to keep it hidden from Corps ship scanners. But it could tear up Agate Beach in seconds if it gets close enough."

"How close?"

"Within twenty K."

"Anything else?"

"Rajcik won't try to assault the colony by land. I'm not sure how much he knows about the area or about the mine. But if he targets Agate Beach and hits the mine, it could cave in."

The two of them share a long look and both stand. "All right, let's get to the command room."

In my mind, the issue of the tracking device is unresolved, but it's moot at this point. I may hate the fact that I have a microscopic apparatus inside my skin that's concealed by my own tissue, but I have to give Vitruzzi credit. It's difficult to believe that the Admin would let someone with her medical talents slip through their fingers. What's she doing here? Her empathy, compassion, and superlative medical skills don't add up with her choice to live in the gutters of the Algol system and risk her life in a criminal enterprise that's doomed to fail. It all contradicts what she must have come from. The only people who live on the outskirts are people with nothing to lose. The first time I saw her, wearing cross-draw holsters and an interrogator's blank expression, she seemed no different than hundreds of others I've met out here—a small-time crook. By now, I've spent enough time around her and her crew to realize that's not even close to who she really is, or was. I wonder if she has a hard time sleeping at night with the choices she's made.

The three of us take the Rover back to the mine, cold silence our uneasy companion. The tension is thick, but I'm beyond caring. I just want to see some progress. Plans have been set in motion now, and all that's left is to carry them out. To the end.

When we reach the mine's interior chamber, Brady leads the way into what Vitruzzi had called their command room, a chamber carved out of the rock walls beneath the communications annex. It must have been used as the foreman's office when the mining operations were still active. There's a heavy steel door at the entrance that can't be opened without inputting a key code. They keep it secure, and I see why once we get inside.

I don't know what I expected, hadn't even really thought about what kind of technology this rag-tag settlement might have collected, but when I get a look inside, it's almost as if I'm back in the Corps.

The walls are lined with computers and VDUs, scanners, robotic devices, and, most importantly, a holodisc reader. The far corner of the room is stocked with lab machines unlike any I've seen, but they're obviously expensive and highly specialized.

Everyone is standing around the disc reader. I walk up next to Bodie while Vitruzzi loads the disc and quietly ask, "Where does all this equipment come from?"

"This? It's . . . on loan from the local fleet." Meaning it's stolen.

"Yeah, but why is it here? And what are all of those machines for over there?" I gesture toward the bank of computers lining the north wall.

He hesitates before answering long enough to give me the sense he's hiding something. "Uh, those are for geologic analysis. Most of this stuff comes from Ministry of S&E excavation ships. That's how I find replacements when something breaks."

"And is this just a hobby, or is there a reason you're so interested in the rock on this planet?"

He smiles at me indulgently. "Solar seeds are a geologic anomaly. But that doesn't mean they're the only things in the universe that has properties we couldn't even conceive of until we found them. Maybe there's more to find." He pauses. "Besides, you can take the scientist out of the lab, but you can't take the lab out of the scientist."

Whatever that means. Is that really all this stuff is? Or are they up to something else? The more time I spend with them, the more I realize that there is much, much more than meets the eye with these people. If I weren't so concerned about my own problems, maybe I would pay more attention, but right now, I simply don't have the time or energy to investigate.

Lights beam upward from the disc reader, quickly organizing themselves into the shape of the Fortress. With each layer of the full complex illuminated, the hovering display is a chaotic jumble of lines, rooms, walls, ducts, materials, and tunnels. By selecting from different options presented on screen readouts on both sides of the table, variable views can be chosen to see exactly, and only, what interests us at the moment. It's a way to peel back the space station layer by layer and figure out what we're dealing with.

Brady makes the first choice, a schematic showing the location of all security screens, checkpoints, and sensors, and all eyes turn toward the display.

FOUR HOURS PASS LIKE salt grains through a bullet hole, trickling thickly by, every suggestion congealing around one central barrier—we still don't know where the station is. Every possible scenario to infiltrate the space station once we're there has been discussed down to microscopic detail, and the crew's ideas have been well-informed and precise, consistent with the behavior I'm getting more and more used to. Tactical planning isn't a new vocation for them.

Once inside the station, movement should be fairly easy. Armed sentries are posted at the major sensitive areas: the weapons development labs at the station's fore, each entry into the station's command and control center, located in the belly, and the main entrances to the biochem labs at the lower-level stern and scattered around the docking bays. Collectively, the Corps units providing security on the station are a huge force, way too big for us to deal with. But if we can get in without being detected, we'll only have to neutralize the immediate on-site personnel, who will mostly be composed of doctors and scientists. With enough deception, surprise, and luck—mostly luck—we could be in and out before the main security forces know we're there.

Standing a kilometer beneath the surface in a sealed and secured room on Spectra 6, the plan sounds deceptively feasible. Except . . . it all supposes we can first *locate* and then *get inside* the station, which is where we need magic, a miracle, or an army. Rajcik's plan to gain access under the guise of a supply ship could work on two conditions: control of an Admin supply ship, or at least a similarly sized ship with replicable engine signatures, and the personnel call signs and identification numbers of a scheduled delivery run. I can only assume T'Kai packaged these details with the disc for Rajcik, but that doesn't do us any good. If he has them, he didn't include them with the copy he gave me. Besides, from what I've seen around here, there's no ship in the settlement's pool large enough to imitate a supply ship.

Once inside the Fortress we'll have to rely on wits, reflexes, and the ability to adapt. We all know that; it doesn't need to be discussed. It's not knowing the two most important elements of the plan, namely where the station is and how we're going to get in, that overstretches our nerves close to the breaking point, and the strain is beginning to show. Vitruzzi presses her palms to her temples in frustration again, yanking her thick hair, now shiny and lank from repeated handling, out of the way. The lines around Brady's massive facial scar have deepened as his irritation at our lack of resources grows, leaving a dark, severe crevasse running down his face. Desto and Strahan are the only ones who don't seem to be losing focus, their enthusiasm for cracking this problem actually increasing as the options seem to whittle down to almost nothing. Theirs is the kind of determination and intensity that you want for this kind of mission, even if it is a suicide attempt.

Finally, Vitruzzi slaps both her palms flat on the display table, causing the image over it to waver ghostlike for a second, and says, "That's it. We're not getting anywhere tonight. As much as I hate to say it," she gives me an unreadable look, "I think we have to accept that Rajcik may have given us a janky disc. We can't even tell from these where the S*ky Serpent* crew is being held. There's no indication of a prison area or anything like it."

From most people, this kind of speech would sound like an admission of defeat. But from her, it sounds like what it is: frustration, and a subtle but malicious seed of growing desperation. She's not giving up. None of them look like the thought has even crossed their minds. In a strange way, it makes me feel better. We've barely scratched the surface tonight, but being among a group that's willing to face the worst possible odds with total resolve gives me a reason to hope. Maybe I'm lying to myself about David's chances, and about their friends' chances, but if there's any way of pulling this off, we'll find it.

Brady straightens up from where he's been focusing intensely on the sub docks around the station's fore. "We need to take a break. Let's reassemble in three hours. We've got to be missing something. Maybe with a fresh outlook . . ." He trails off.

With a collective nod, everyone agrees. It's late, probably only a couple hours until sun-up. Sleep and some time to clear our heads can't hurt anything. Yet I wait at the far end of the control room as everyone else leaves, their footsteps heavy. I'm just as exhausted and my jaw continues to throb from MacCready's punch, but I can go on feeling like this indefinitely.

Everyone passes through the heavy doors except Vitruzzi. She turns to wait for me, refusing to leave me alone in the command room. "Are you coming?"

"I'd prefer to keep looking. Time is short."

She pauses, considering whether fighting with me is worth the effort, and says, "No one is giving up, Erikson. And for this to work, we all have to be operating at full capacity. You look like shit. Maybe you should try and get some sleep."

Blunt, but true. She's made her point. It has been almost twenty hours since I left Agate Beach early this morning and what I need most right now is the ability to think straight. "Yeah, all right." I follow her out and make my way to my bunk on the *Sphynx*.

IT SEEMS LIKE ONLY seconds have passed since I lay down when my wrist com beeps me back to awareness. Ghostly iridescent lines of the space station's schematics crisscross the darkness, permanently drawn on my mind's eye and I wearily sit up and strap on my boots. As I walk down the metal ramp to join the others in the control room, voices come to me from the front of the ship.

"He ran, just like we expected. Took one of the land crafts. Looks like he's been in the com annex, too. If he convinced Rajcik that he knows what he says he does, he may have already been picked up."

Vitruzzi and Strahan. I stop walking, listening quietly.

"All right, we planned for this. Find Desto and Venus and get the *Sphynx* up in the air. I want you all locked on Rajcik's shuttle within the hour. And check in with Bodie; he's in the control room. Tell him to find out exactly where Vilbrandt is."

That slippery bastard. Strahan said they were keeping an eye on him, but who was watching him when we'd all been at Brady's after I met with Rajcik? Vilbrandt must have gotten impatient and risked contacting Rajcik on his own. Rajcik had been angry when he heard how many people knew about the operation to steal the Nova, but what I'd told him about Vilbrandt may be enough to tempt him to consider whatever scheme Vilbrandt proposes. If Vilbrandt knows what he says he knows . . . Rajcik is no fool. He won't underestimate the value of Vilbrandt's information and may take full advantage of insider knowledge to increase his own odds. Then what'll happen to Vilbrandt? Not what he expects, I'm sure.

Vitruzzi's decision to send the *Sphynx* up, presumably to intercept the *Temptation*'s shuttle, is interesting. What good will it do? The *Sphynx* may once have been weaponized, but now it's just a decommissioned transport ship that the Nagasaki will easily turn into dust.

I emerge from the ramp, ready to jump into the middle of their plan and find out where I fit. Vitruzzi nods at me in a way that indicates she knows I overheard them. "Come with me. It's time to call Rajcik."

"Vitruzzi, there's nothing stopping him at this point from wiping out Agate Beach. What are you going to do?"

Without answering, she walks toward the lift, assuming I'll follow the way any captain assumes unquestioned authority. As if I'm just part of the crew.

On the ride up, Venus, Brady, and Strahan board the *Sphynx* below us and the lift cables begin thrumming in legato vibration as the ship's engines cycle up. Vitruzzi grips the lift's handrail hard enough to make the veins in her hands pop to the surface. It's the grasp of an overboard sailor around a life preserver, which is ironically close to the truth.

Once inside, she quickly dials-in a frequency and sends her voice into the morning: "Agate Beach hailing the *Temptation*, over."

Hardly a minute passes before the VDU lights up and the pinched, sour face of Ahsan Yadav looks out at us. "Yeah."

"This is Captain Eleanor Vitruzzi. Get me Rajcik."

He sneers. "Wait one."

The screen blanks out briefly and then comes back on. Rajcik, sitting at the familiar flight deck console of the *Temptation*, leans back in his seat, relaxed, leveling his discomfiting shark grin at us.

"Captain Eleanor Vitruzzi. Not an unexpected transmission. Did you call to ask for your scientist back?" His eyes shift to me and hold there for an uncomfortable second before he continues, "Maybe to trade one defector for another?"

Realization hits me with the force of a rocketing meteor as it strikes the planet; Vilbrandt had overheard the conversation I'd had with Vitruzzi and Brady and spilled it all to Rajcik. If I ever see that sewer rat again, he'll wish he'd died at birth.

Vitruzzi's voice is all business, almost robotic. "You still have something we need. It's not Vilbrandt."

The tiny wrinkles that deepen around his eyes indicate a hint of annoyance. "Vitruzzi, there's nothing stopping me from wiping you off the map right now. You should remember that. That's right, Aly," he focuses on me for the first time, "Vilbrandt shared your little rebellion. I knew someday you'd turn on me."

Vitruzzi cuts him off. "Rajcik, I just sent you a feed. It's in your best interest to watch it. Right now."

He gazes at her for a moment before reaching forward to his communication console and turning on a second monitor. Simultaneously, Vitruzzi switches on a display embedded below her main screen, letting us see what he's seeing.

A live feed of the *Temptation* appears, docked in a deep ravine and surrounded by steep canyon walls on three sides. A rock cornice hangs over the ship, hiding most of it, but the light glinting off the rear thrusters leaves no doubt what it is.

He looks at his display calmly for a moment, then back at Vitruzzi. "That's very clever, Captain. I don't know how you found my ship, but I feel it necessary to warn you that there's a—"

She cuts him off again, "Short-range shuttle equipped with a Nagasaki en route to Agate Beach. I know. It has been accounted for as well."

Exactly how many cards does she have up her sleeve? Rajcik has revealed something useful: he doesn't know how she found his ship. That means either Vilbrandt hadn't stuck around long enough to learn about the tracking device, or he'd hidden that information from Rajcik. Is he bugged, too? He's smart enough to realize the liability he'd instantly become if Rajcik knew they could track the *Temptation* through him, plenty of incentive to keep it a secret if he is. Even if Vitruzzi had homed in on my tracking device yesterday, how and when they had an opportunity to set up surveillance is a mystery.

She continues, "Now that I have your attention, I want you to listen very carefully. This is what's going to happen. In addition to the disc you've already handed over, you're going to give us the coordinates to the Fortress. Because we're reasonable people, we'll give you ten kilos of solar seeds for them. I'm giving *you* a chance to be reasonable and take us up on our offer."

The black bullet tattooed on Rajcik's Adam's apple ripples as he swallows, and the muscles in his jaw twitch spasmodically. "And why would I do any of this?"

"If you don't, I'll give the command to detonate seismic blasting charges loaded throughout the canyon around you and bury you under so much rock the Algols will burn out before anyone finds you. Then we'll blow your shuttle from the sky." She leans forward a little, her intensity holding his attention like a magnet. "If you don't believe me, Rajcik, I can give you a demonstration."

We're both staring at her, me in surprise, Rajcik in something like demonic hate. Finally he says, "*Captain* Vitruzzi," putting a sneering emphasis on the word 'captain,' "I have exactly zero tolerance for games." The fact that he doesn't say what he wants to say—*prove it*—makes it clear that he's close enough to believing her that he's not taking the chance.

She clicks a switch next to a microphone and, without taking her eyes from the screen, says, "Bodie."

"Yeah." Bodie's voice comes back over the speaker, loud enough for Rajcik to hear at his end.

"Give the crew in the canyon a mild shake along the north wall."

"Roger."

Vitruzzi doesn't say anything, but within a few moments small pebbles begin to jump and cascade down the side of canyon, dust blooming like desert ghosts from the walls in all directions.

Rajcik's image vibrates just slightly as the earth around him shakes. His upper lip curls in a wicked sneer that makes my blood run cold. "All right, Vitruzzi. Now what?"

"Call off your shuttle. Meet me in two hours where your crewmember found Erikson in Hell's Gate. I'll bring your seeds. You bring us the coordinates. If your ship's engines start to cycle, I won't hesitate to bury it. Am I clear?"

Rajcik looks off to his left and gives the order: "Ortiz, tell Fedchenko and Thompson to get back here immediately." Dropping his dark gaze back on Vitruzzi, he threatens, "See you then," and closes the connection.

Vitruzzi sighs deeply and looks at me. The surprise must still be stamped on my face because she says, "You didn't really think all the equipment we have in the control room was just for analyzing dirt, did you?"

"I'm starting to not know what to think."

"We stay prepared, and we stay safe. Let's get moving."

FIFTEEN

Twenty minutes later we're in the *Sphynx*'s shuttle flying low over the canyon system headed back to Hell's Gate. We'll get there early, giving us enough time to scope the surrounding area and see if Rajcik's managed to set up an ambush. Given that up to this point he's had absolutely no idea what Vitruzzi and her crew have been capable of, it's doubtful he could have come up with anything unexpected, but with him, there's never enough margin of safety.

Two rows of crew seats are packed against opposing walls inside the narrow shuttle, filling the fuselage from the cockpit to the engine compartment. Strahan flies with Vitruzzi as copilot, and Desto sits across the aisle from me. I'm focused on the brown dirt speeding by outside the window screens when I catch Vitruzzi glance over her shoulder at Desto. Something in the look puts me on instant alert.

Desto turns to me, his left hand held out. His right rests on the butt of his pistol. "Hand over your weapons, Erikson."

"What?" I look to Vitruzzi sharply, not believing this is happening.

Desto keeps his voice pitched low, trying to keep the situation calm. "Don't make this hard, we just want to make sure everyone stays safe. Give them here, slowly."

Any ideas of resistance melt away at the implacability of his face, as if they are so much useless ice under a burning sun. "Everyone safe? What about me?" I spit the words as I pull out my Sinbad and hand it to him stock first, followed by the Mini-Derg. "I thought we were on the same side."

"We'll watch out for you, Erikson. But we can't take any chances," Vitruzzi responds, deflecting my unbelieving fury with impassivity, and turns back to the front.

I still have my body armor, that's something. But my AK-80 is hung up in the rack at the rear next to the barrel of solar seeds for Rajcik, and it looks as if that's where it will stay. Desto wedges my Sinbad under the belt of his equipment vest near his left hip and deposits the Derg in a pocket.

Sinking back into my seat, I wait for intermission to end and let this bad dream continue.

Soon, Strahan is passing the shuttle over Hell's Gate, taking a couple of low turns while he and Vitruzzi scan the streets, on the lookout for anything suspicious. I've ceased paying attention as I brace for the meeting but catch Strahan point out something to Vitruzzi on the first pass. She nods. My guess is that they've spotted the *Temptation*'s shuttle. Rajcik would have used it to get to the rendezvous.

When they're satisfied that nothing looks out of the ordinary, she turns and faces Desto and I. "This is how it will go down. Bodie is our eyes and ears from the control room back at the Beach, watching Rajcik's ship. Patrick and Venus are on the *Sphynx*, in position to deal with any other contingency." She turns to Strahan. "Once we land, get back in the air and be ready for a quick extraction. The three of us will meet with Rajcik. If you don't hear from me within the hour, tell Patrick. If Rajcik pulls any shit, make sure his ship never leaves that canyon."

As she finishes speaking, Strahan brings the shuttle to a static hover at the town's edge. Desto and Vitruzzi unsnap their harnesses and prepare to dismount.

Pulling my own harness off my shoulders, I ask, "So what exactly do you want me to do?"

She unlocks the shuttle's hatch and pushes it out to serve as our exit ramp. "Whatever comes naturally, Erikson." What the hell does that mean? "Let's move," she finishes.

The bar's atmosphere is like an ancient, primitive cave with danger crouching in every shadow. Rajcik sits with his back to the wall of the dingy room like the deity of cannibals, ready to receive prayers and pleas for mercy. No other customers are present, which I know from my previous visit is unusual. Either the patrons of this particular dive are savvy enough to know when there's too much danger to risk a drink, or Rajcik simply threatened to kill anyone who didn't leave. The only person left is the bar pilot, the same haggard woman who'd been here a couple of days ago, ready to serve.

None of this is interesting or even important to me. At the moment, my full focus is on the smuggler, looking as relaxed as an overfed snake, and the two compatriots he brought with him. It's no surprise to see MacCready's disfigured face to Rajcik's right, and Ortiz sits a short distance off to his left. I can too easily imagine a variety of possible outcomes to this situation, and few of them are good.

An electrical fizz from a broken sign hanging behind the bar suffuses the air, and the clinking of glasses being wiped off by the bar pilot with all the enthusiasm of a condemned criminal adds to the noise. The two sounds combine in a muted nerve-jangling racket, as if part of a symphony played on thousand-year-old instruments that have long since decayed into relics and dust, making my teeth want to grind.

Let's get this over with. As I cross the empty room and sit without pretense, Rajcik's relaxed posture doesn't change. Using more caution, Vitruzzi's dark eyes, their impenetrable blackness exactly the same as Rajcik's, scan the room, pausing briefly when they come to Ortiz and MacCready. She approaches nonchalantly, but her pistols are unhooked, ready for action. Desto remains standing next to the door, guarding against unwelcome intruders and keeping some distance in case of close-quarter firing.

Without waiting for an introduction, she jumps right into it. "Did you bring what we agreed on?"

Rajcik's gaze hasn't shifted from Vitruzzi since we entered the bar, but he says, "I don't like the advantage your bulldog has. Make him take a seat."

For a second, she doesn't move. Then slowly and reluctantly, as if her neck were in need of rust removal, she turns toward Desto and nods to the chair on my left. Naked hostility shadows her features when she looks back to Rajcik.

"That's the one and only demand you get to make. We've done all the negotiating we're going to. Now, do you have the Fortress's coordinates?"

His eyes flicker dangerously, anger glowing in their depths. He isn't used to being spoken to like this and it's pissing him off. Fury vibrates from him, joining the buzz of the broken sign.

After a long silence, he says, "Tell me, Captain. What makes you think you can trust her?" He tilts his chin in my direction without looking at me, and the unexpected question hits me like a sucker punch. He's trying to rattle her, put her on edge, in the process undermining the fragile bond that's begun to form between Vitruzzi's crew and I.

She says nothing, prepared to let him continue and see what he's getting at.

"I ask because I now harbor one of your former crewmembers who has already switched sides twice." He continues, "I ask because it seems you have a problem finding reliable people."

"Make your point," she says.

He leans forward, placing one palm flat on the table and glaring at Vitruzzi. "I'm not convinced your judgment is sound enough for me to trust that you'll hold up your end of our arrangement, if the people in your employ are any indication." His eyes rest on me, dead calm and filled with poison.

Vitruzzi keeps her cool. "So Vilbrandt told you he was a member of my crew?" She lets these words, heavy with the implied accusation that Rajcik is a fool for believing anything Vilbrandt has told him, settle in the vacant space between them, then continues, "This isn't about my crew, or Vilbrandt. Do you want the seeds or not?"

"Where are they? You didn't bring them with you, as we agreed, which leads me to conclude that my assessment of your trustworthiness is accurate. I have no reason to give you the coordinates."

There's an icy shift in the atmosphere, a frigid draft gusting around us that carries the realization that more than one pistol is locked, cocked, and aimed beneath the table. Almost casually concerned with self-preservation, I wonder how many are pointed at me.

Vitruzzi's lips grow tight, the tiny lines around them strained and deep. "Yes. You do. Here's how it's going to go. First, you give us the coordinates. Then we're all going to get up from this table and walk to my shuttle. We'll drop you and the seeds off at your ship and escort you off of Spectra 6. When you're far enough away to make me feel comfortable, we let you out of missile range and you can go wherever you want."

Rajcik sits motionlessly, his eyes lingering in thoughtful consideration on hers for a few moments before looking back at me. "And this is your choice, Aly? You're going to give up the biggest payoff of your life on a rescue mission for your troublemaking brother, who's probably already dead, and people you don't even know?"

My words tumble out before I think about what I'm going to say. "Do you really think that matters to me anymore? That I'd sell out David for a few bucks? Fuck you. If you had any idea what loyalty really is, you wouldn't even ask me that. As far as I'm concerned, you can go to hell, and take the rest of these greedy bootlickers with you." My eyes bounce to MacCready.

MacCready half stands and seethes, "You fucking bitch! I'll . . ."

He's stopped by a casual, "Sit down," from Rajcik, and his lips wrinkle back in a hateful sneer.

Rajcik chuckles. "It's rare that I underestimate someone, Aly. You're no exception."

Before I can ask what he means, he dismisses me and returns his cold stare to Vitruzzi. After a heavy pause, he says, "It occurs to me that you could be an incredible asset in my work, Captain. Have you considered the benefits of becoming a businesswoman of the free market?"

She's hardly moved a centimeter since first sitting down, but the way her face hardens, as if made of drying concrete, and the rapidly beating pulse in her neck show that her patience is starting to dissolve. "I'm not interested."

"Why not?" He leans forward, baring more of his large teeth in that predatory grin. "From what I understand, you have no reason to remain loyal to the Admin. To be their luggage girl. For someone who's lost a husband and a daughter to their deceit—you have more reason than most to want to work for the other side. For my side."

I don't know what Rajcik is talking about, but I can see the way he's getting to her. Her body grows so rigid that her muscles strain against her skin. Desto shifts beside me, his hand coming to rest on the Thresher propped against his thigh, and my palms itch for the feel of my own carbine.

Her voice sounds as if it's being pressed in a vice as she says, "We're not here to discuss that. Now make your choice."

He appears satisfied with the effect his question has on her and leans back in his chair. "Two questions. What makes you think I have the coordinates with me? And if I give them to you, once we're escorted off this rock as you described, what makes you think I won't come back and turn your settlement into so much garbage and dust while you're en route to the Fortress, losing your personal little war against the Admin?"

He's stalling, and I want to jump across the table and carve the smug expression from his face, but Vitruzzi answers him, "Because a man like you wouldn't move an inch without keeping something as valuable as those coordinates with you. Maybe you will try to attack Agate Beach. But not if it means we get to the Fortress before you do. Erikson told us why you want the disc. And whether we're successful or not, once we hit the Fortress, the Admin will be on full alert. If you wait, you'll never get another opportunity like this. A man like you has priorities, doesn't he?" She scans his face, trying to read whether she judged correctly. Aside from a slight flaring of his nostrils, his expression doesn't change. "The truth is, Rajcik, we have no reason to fight with you. Just give us what we want, and we never have to see each other again."

He seems to consider for a moment. "You seem very sure of yourself. And I have your guarantee that you'll give us the seeds?"

My patience snaps. "Goddammit, Rajcik. Just give us the fucking coordinates."

He glances toward me with hate in his eyes. Nothing else on his face betrays the slightest hint of emotion, but that look says my death warrant has been signed and he is only waiting for the ink to dry.

Still looking at me, he reaches carefully into his cargo jacket and withdraws a small data disc. With a carefree flick of the wrist, he tosses it onto the table as if it were nothing more than a piece of trash.

Vitruzzi picks it up and plugs it into the disc slot of a portable VDU. After pulling up the information, she hands it across me to Desto. I catch a glimpse of the screen and see enough to feel confident he's given us what we want.

Desto studies the coordinates for a moment and then nods his head. "Should work."

Vitruzzi retrieves the device and speaks into her comlink. "Karl, be ready for pickup in ten minutes." Stuffing the device into the breast pocket of her jacket, she returns her focus to Rajcik.

"All right. I want you both to stand up and put your weapons on the table. Her too," she adds, glancing at Ortiz.

Rajcik smirks, appearing to be amused by something, and slowly pushes his chair back as he rises. As he raises his hands, the pistol he'd been leveling under the table comes into view. He keeps the barrel pointed toward the floor and flips the grip out to Vitruzzi as the rest of us stand. To an outsider witnessing our synchronized movements, it must look as if a bomb has exploded beneath us in slow motion. Desto reaches out with the hand not gripping his shotgun and takes the pistol. With no weapon of my own, I ball my empty fingers into tight fists, my nerves kindling in anticipation of what could happen in the next few seconds.

No one makes any unexpected movements as Rajcik reaches for the shotgun he left leaning against the table, preparing to give it over as well. Hypervigilance, a side effect of having reencountered someone I left for dead in years past, causes me to glance toward MacCready, and I don't like what I see.

Rage has contorted his features into a terrible grimace and his ice-blue eyes, dangerously lucid, are fixed on me. There's no need to think about what his expression means; instinct screams he's about to pull his weapon and start firing. "Vitruzzi! Watch him!" I yell and immediately turn to Desto, pushing him hard sideways with the full weight of my body and out of MacCready's target area.

Caught off guard by my abrupt shove, Desto loses his balance and we topple to the ground in a frantic jumble. Grabbing the pistol he'd taken from me and rolling onto my side, I fire upward through the table now blocking my view. It splinters down the center and I lunge to my feet, viciously shoving the pistol into Rajcik's chin, relishing the way he flinches from the hot barrel. My body acts on its own—thoughts, sensations, emotions, and conscience all a distant echo, far from the me that's present and handling the situation. Instinct is in control here, keeping me alive. I don't know why I'm pointing the pistol at Rajcik instead of MacCready, but I know it's the right move.

"Fuck! Christ! Fuck!" MacCready wails, leaning against the wall behind him. My shot had hit home. Blood cascades down his mutilated firing arm, which hangs askance, the fabric and flesh mixed in a shredded, smoldering waste. His weapon skitters across the floor away from him as he clutches his damaged arm.

Disjointed awareness strikes me. Everything around me except MacCready has grown completely still. My immediate focus stays on the pistol in my hand, ready to turn Rajcik's head into negative space if he even flinches. Vitruzzi stands a short distance behind me and to my right. I sense that she has one of her pistols aimed at Rajcik's chest and the other at my midsection, but this doesn't concern me. Ortiz also points her weapon at me, and Desto has a bead on MacCready with his rifle. If he fires at this proximity, its spray will cut everyone in front of him, including me, down.

Sharp smoke stings my nose and eyes as I glare at Rajcik. His head is tilted slightly back by the pressure of the gun in my hand,

and his jaw is clenched so tightly that veins stand out at both of his temples. He still holds the shotgun he'd been picking up by the barrel and stares at Vitruzzi, waiting for her to pass judgment.

"Drop them." Her voice demands compliance.

"Do it," Rajcik growls through clenched teeth, thanks to the barrel wedged against his jaw.

Ortiz slowly lowers her own weapon and kicks it forward.

I remain in the same position, the frustration and anger inside me holding me frozen. I want to pull the trigger until my Sinbad is empty. I don't know what stops me.

"Erikson, we got it. Back up," Vitruzzi demands, but I can't. Rajcik has to pay.

"Erikson!" She finally gets through, the sharpness in her tone making my eyes jerk toward her. "Keep your weapon pointed. Step back."

Something—is it compassion?—in her expression carries more force than her words and my legs unlock. As the Sinbad's muzzle leaves Rajcik's throat, he lowers his gleaming black eyes to us, his lips stretched into a snarl. MacCready's face is arranged in an agonized rictus, and he drools with the pain while still holding his butchered shoulder. He's hurt too seriously to be a threat any longer.

"Move," she commands, jerking her head toward the door.

So quickly that none of us have time to stop him, Rajcik turns to MacCready. Like a battering ram, his fist hammers forward and connects with the bump in the center of MacCready's throat with enough force to slam him against the wall. MacCready gasps loudly, as if his voice is made of screeching metal being sheered from the body of a ship, and a fountain of blood erupts from his mouth.

"You won't make another mistake like that, Marcus," Rajcik says, his voice pitched low and quiet as if sympathizing with a dead man's relative. He keeps his back turned to us, unconcerned with the fact that three weapons are aimed at it. MacCready grips his throat with his usable hand, trying hard to suck air through his ruined trachea. Blood bubbles from the corners of his mouth and joins the light, steady stream still pouring from his arm. It's hard to watch him struggling to draw breath, despite my loathing for him.

Rajcik's expression stays blank, as if he's watching nothing more than clouds shift, and without turning he says, "This must make you happy, Aly."

My throat feels tight and gummy, and my response has to be forced out. "Ecstatic."

Vitruzzi jumps in, not bothering to mask the disgust in her voice. "Time to go, Rajcik."

There's a loud croaking sound as MacCready's whole body makes one last attempt for air, then he goes completely still. His eyes continue to stare up at Rajcik, bulging like the eyes of a starved lunatic, and slowly begin to glaze over. His body remains rigidly erect.

I'm still staring at him when Desto puts a hand on my shoulder, gently nudging me forward. "I got the rear. Keep that pointed where it's most useful," he says, nodding toward my pistol.

SIXTEEN

It's been hours, maybe six, maybe more. The days are blending together as we cross the darkness of space. The crew sits in the com room and hovers around the shining image of the Fortress. We've spent another marathon session exhausting every idea, no matter how far-fetched, for cracking the enigma of how to get in. Still nothing to show for it.

Venus stops in and drops off an armload of food. Flight rations never taste good and desperation curbs our appetites further, making it hard to eat. I do it anyway, mechanically forcing down a few nutrition bars followed by some bottles of electrolyte-packed fluids. Physical and mental preparedness are paramount and I'm not allowing anything to inhibit my readiness for this mission. It's the most important thing I'll ever do. The others eat too, talking among themselves and trying to pretend things are under control, but the worry and uncertainty is taking a toll on everyone. If we don't solve the puzzle in the next thirty-six to forty hours, this will turn into a kamikaze mission. Even so, that won't stop us. That's how dedicated they are—*we* are.

"This makes me think of this thing that happened on Ammi Duc when I was still in Terrestrial and Atmospheric R&D." Bodie sits backward on his chair, head resting on his hands. "We had these burrowing creatures beneath the surface that kept getting into the food storage. Every time we'd flush them out and close another line of tunnels, it would only take them a few hours to start an entirely new system. Eventually, the thermals couldn't tell old tunnels from new ones, the critters just kept digging and re-digging so fast. We spent days analyzing their system, trying to find a way to cut them off so they'd leave the food alone. It was mind-boggling. Just like this shit." A frustrated sigh explodes from his lips, blowing the curling hair of his mustache outward.

"So how did you solve it?" Brady asks.

He shrugs. "Only way we could. Exterminated them and collapsed the tunnels on top of them. Not an option I recommend in this case," he adds hurriedly.

"No, I guess not," Desto says, pushing back from the table and starting another round of pacing. "Fuck."

Mental restlessness and fatigue is starting to push me into Crazyville, the same as the rest of them. "I'm going to take a few. Walk around and clear my head."

"Yeah, good idea. I think I'll take a shower. Want to join me, babe?" Desto asks, flashing me a leer that doesn't even scratch the surface of the crudeness of his thoughts.

"Not even if I'd just fallen into a sewer," I respond, but smile wearily, grateful for any attempt to lighten the mood.

"Hey, that's all right. I like it dirty too," he answers with his own grin, and heads toward the community washroom.

Bodie remains behind with Brady and Vitruzzi, none of them quite ready to leave the problem alone yet, and I exit behind Desto.

The silence inside the corridor, punctuated by the distant, rhythmic thrumming of the engines, closes around me like a trap. Walking through it makes me feel alone, isolated in my own anxiety. In reality, no more relaxing than slamming my head against a brick wall a few million times. I have to find something to keep my mind off the situation, give it rest before I throw myself out of the hold out of sheer frustration. I make a left toward the crew quarters, deciding to break down my weapons and clean them. Not that they need it.

When I reach the long corridor leading to the bunks, the sound of a cabin door sliding closed draws my attention. Lights come through Strahan's window, and before thinking about it, I head in that direction. Maybe a little company will be a better remedy for escaping my grim thoughts than an attempt to blank out on routine, which I know will fail.

I hit the buzzer. A second later, he opens the door and stares at me, shirtless and surprised. There's no missing the patchwork of scars, burns and a few roundly uniform bullet wounds, peppering his muscular torso. His brows are ridged in a frown and he doesn't say anything, just stands there.

I have nothing to say either. Lamely, I ask, "How's the leg?"

"Healing."

I should have thought about this before walking down here. Besides the few encounters we've had at the Beach, Strahan and I have barely spoken. We're just soldiers on a mission, thrown into the same mix by random forces. Which doesn't exactly make us friends. What am I doing here?

This was a mistake. "Glad to hear it," I remark, and spin around to walk to my own bunk.

Then I hear him step into the corridor. "Wait a sec, Erikson. I'm sorry. Hold on, will you?"

Maybe he'll drop it if I pretend not to hear him and keep walking. Instead, I turn around. I don't know why, maybe because of the understanding in his voice.

"You came by to talk and I act like an asshole. I apologize, okay? You and I started off on the wrong foot, and things are getting more fucked up lately. I'm just edgy." He gives me a lopsided grin. "I tell you what—I've got a bottle of peacemaker under my bunk. Have a drink with me. We can chat, you know, try to be civil for once. Wait right there." He ducks back into his cabin, re-emerging moments later holding a clear plastic bottle. "What do you say?"

I'm not sure what to make of this. I'm still the outsider here. But four days from now we'll all probably be dead, so what is there to lose?

"Thanks," I say, and step in.

A bunk juts from the left wall, blankets meticulously tucked, a door to the bathroom opens to the rear, and a cargo box that looks as if it may be used for a table sits on the floor against the right wall. It's exactly the same as my cabin. Feeling cramped, I sit down on the box and he follows me in, leaving the door open. Wrestling on a shirt that's the same dull uniform gray that everything washed time and again in a ship's water-recycling system becomes, he says, "Shit. I don't think I have any cups. Hold on a second and I'll go get some."

"It's all right. I don't need one."

With a grin, a look as unfamiliar on his face as it has lately been on mine, he sits down. The top of the bottle comes off with a quick twist. "To comrades," he says, swallowing deeply. His eyes fill with water and he passes it to me.

"Right." I take the bottle, tilt the neck toward him in a salute, and take a swallow of my own. Instantly, my tongue curls up and I have to force my throat to open wide enough for the burning liquid to pass. "Oh my god, what is that?" It streams into my stomach with the same caustic flow as molten lava.

"Like it? I got it as part of a trade for some mining tools we lifted a while ago. We had about sixty bottles, but we're down to just a few. Good stuff." He takes another drink.

You're insane could be written on my face. The stuff tasted as if it were radioactive pond scum filtered through gasoline. He extends the bottle to me, but I shake my head "no." So he puts it on the floor between us. The closeness of the cabin makes it seem like a good idea to have something solid between us.

"How long—?" I start.

"I know—" he starts.

We both stop. This time he waits for me to go first.

"So how long have you and Vitruzzi been flying together?" I'm fidgety and find it hard to sit still, so I grab the bottle for another drink. My throat rebels with slightly less outrage this time.

"Since just after the Soldier's Rebellion. I was in the hospital when it happened, just three months shy of my time being up. I'd been part of a suppression squad, dealing with a manufacturing riot on Obal 4 and lost my real leg. Vitruzzi was my doctor." He takes another long gulp. "She's brilliant. The technology that saved my leg from amputation, bioregeneration, she developed it. I was the first patient to have the procedure done. Took eight months to get everything working right, but Eleanor was persistent. Stubborn, in fact. She wasn't going to fail. Anyway, we had a lot of time to get to know each other."

"So what's she doing flying cargo now?" I still haven't puzzled this out.

"I'd already been planning on buying my own cargo ship when my time was up. Had a few bucks saved, and planned on working as a pilot until I could get the rest together. Flying interstellar cruise ships or corporate jobs. You know, where the real money is."

Strahan's personality isn't exactly a model of the conventionally affable, easy-going cruiser pilot, and I smirk at the idea of him giving deck tours to sliced and molded women in overpriced evening gowns. Catching my expression, he smiles back.

"Yeah, it was just an idea. Anyway, V decided it was time to change careers after the shit hit the fan during the Rebellion. She had the capital and she was able to get the weapons contract because of her standing in the medical branch and high-profile achievements, and we went into business together."

He's avoiding telling me the full story, but I know it's no good to press. There's a reason, probably a damn good one, that Vitruzzi decided to "change careers," as he puts it. "And what about Desto?"

"Bomani? Another deserter. He was into small-time black-marketing on Chum Miro. That's where the *Sphynx* came from. He needed a job and we needed someone who wasn't afraid to break the rules. Desto and Bodie are the best two guys I've ever had at my back."

"Best two guys, huh?"

"Except recently. I mean . . . well, you took care of business out there on R'Kadia. So, now I've got three . . ."

I hadn't intended to fluster him, but his surprising embarrassment is amusing. I take another drink, beginning to enjoy the signature fireball spreading through my guts. If not for the nutrition bars helping absorb the asbestoslike liquid, I would probably have a hard time walking. The room is beginning to feel hot and smaller by the second. We both look at the bottle so we don't have to look at each other. Neither of us are much for small talk, apparently, so I decide to make my exit. Maybe the booze will help me catch a few minutes of sleep. But he asks another question.

"So what will you do once we get your brother off the Fortress?"

It's the first hint of optimism I've heard in regard to David, and it's strangely comforting. "You mean if we don't all get blown into tiny molecules of space-born carbon?" My optimism, on the other hand, is tempered by my realism. "Business as usual, I guess. The black market is fairly competitive, and we've got a lot of experience. We're done with Rajcik, though, if that's what you're getting at."

He gives me a considering look. "Sounds a little pointless to me," he says and hands me the bottle.

He isn't trying to pick a fight or pass judgment; the comment comes across as a detached observation, so I let it slide. Taking the bottle, I bring the subject back to him and Vitruzzi. "If you and Vitruzzi are partners, why is she captain?"

"She's smart, she's capable, and she had the money. I've never been anything but a soldier. It just makes sense. I don't want to be in charge of a ship. This crew is . . . they're more than friends, you know? Eleanor just has what it takes to lead, and it's easier for me to follow. She knows how to keep things from coming unraveled. It's hard to explain."

He doesn't need to. I know exactly what he's saying. It's not hard to take command, but people like Strahan, and like me, reject leadership. Independence is easier; inviting people to rely on you is asking for trouble. It's asking to be let down, or to let them down. And that's hard to live with, that kind of pressure. It just means you have more to lose. People like Strahan and I have seen how ugly the universe can be. We have that joyless ability to look ahead and see all the bad things that can happen, and who wants to be responsible for leading others into them? It's not cowardice—in a twisted way, it's hope. If you're not close to people, you can't hurt them. We're quite a pair.

Swigging another drink from the bottle, I'm astonished to find it more than half empty. We'd killed a lot of it while talking. It's strange how easy it is to be with him, now that we've both relaxed and forgotten to be enemies for a second. Or maybe it's just the rotgut, melting away my instinctive caution and numbing my live-wire nerves. Whatever, it's time to go. "Look, thanks for the drink. I should get going. We don't have much time left before we reach the Fortress."

He gets up too. "We should take another look at the disc in a couple of hours. I know there's something we're not seeing, but it's there. We just have to keep at it."

Is he stalling me?

"Sounds good."

He nods but looks distracted. Nothing left to say, I start to step through the door. Strahan stops me with a hand on my elbow. I turn, and his face is inches from mine. I can feel the heat that radiates from his body. Or is it just me?

No.

Yes.

No.

As delicately as I can, I pull my arm out of his grip.

"Strahan, this can't happen."

"Why?" His eyes are gentle, and the same color as fall leaves right before the icy winter wind takes them. The emotion in them is intense, confining. It's hard for me to speak.

"It's just not possible. I can't let anything complicate this mission."

On a hair-trigger, his face grows hard and his brows knit together. "Dammit, Erikson, are you so focused on killing that you don't know how to live?"

The strike-first-or-strike-back instinct in me makes me want to hit him, but I bottle it. Yanking my elbow from his grip and careening into the corridor, nearly falling down the stairs in his doorway, I lurch toward my bunk. There's a thump against the wall behind me, like a fist striking it in anger, but I don't turn around to look. Maybe it's impossible to get along with someone so like yourself. Maybe it's just impossible for us.

SEVENTEEN

"We should've killed him."

I'm sitting in the navigator's seat in the *Sphynx*'s flight control deck, both hands clasped tightly around the seat mounts, staring across a few hundred meters of space at the *Temptation*'s stern. It isn't that the seat isn't stable; the reason my knuckles are white is because we're about to let Rajcik go.

Venus sits at the helm, swiftly punching through systems checks. Whether she's ignoring me or just can't hear my under-the-breath comment through the din of her own clamorous thoughts isn't important. Vitruzzi made it clear that we're holding up our end of the deal, believing, recklessly in my opinion, that Rajcik might still be useful.

The speed in which new schematics pop on and off the pilot display creates a chaotic strobe effect, fracturing my focus. But Venus seems to be absorbing the split-second information with casual ease, speaking in her customary rapid clip as she does.

"There's a slight tension that we can't work out of the ejector coils, but it's easily offset if we just run the core rotor at .05 amps higher   . . ." Her voice becomes part of the background as she explains each observation, quickly oversaturating my interest.

"Whoa, hold it, Venus. Can you go through that a little more slowly?" A curious image catches my eye. "That can't be what it looked like."

Shrugging, she reverses the system feed, stopping when I point. "There."

A starboard missile launch tube glows from the display in as much stark detail as the real thing.

Scanning the image closely anyway for a few seconds, I just want to make sure I'm not mistaken. "I'd really like to know how you've managed to hide functioning weapons systems from Admin inspections."

"Oh yeah, it's not that hard actually." She smiles. "You see, the missile tubes are here, beneath the cargo bay floor, instead of on the outer flanks of the ship like it was originally designed. Bodie, Desto, and Pat built the new launch tubes after the captain brought the *Sphynx* to Spectra 6. The Admin had just yanked off the launch activators and pulled all the tube plating off. Bodie and the guys rerouted the afterburn jets into the old tubes, covered them with heavier graphite plating, and added a little extra piece. Lead inner walls. Pat took some radioisotope aluminum freezers and lined the tubes with their parts to keep the lead from getting too hot. So, the jets help keep the inside of the ship warm, but the heat can't get to the lead walls, which makes it impossible for scanners to see what's inside. Namely, the missile tubes."

Vitruzzi hadn't been bluffing when she'd told Rajcik we'd be keeping him in missile range. This bird is still hot. I look closely at the schematic and have her zoom out so I can see the outline of the whole cargo bay. As I suspect, the armory doubles as the loading room, and the missile tubes can be fed directly from inside. They're well camouflaged; I hadn't suspected a thing when I'd been there to get ammunition from Desto. The vault being reinforced by blast walls and located midship isn't just a convenient accident. If the ship were attacked or damaged, anyone inside would be safe and able to feed and probably even launch the missiles until they ran out or the threat was eradicated. And from the outside, there's no way to tell what secrets lay hidden in the heart of the *Sphynx*.

"So where are the ejection portals?"

"The hydraulic doors, disguised as off-gassing vents beneath the main engine. If anyone even notices them, they know not to open them without depressurizing first. We've got the real off-gassing chambers linked into the tubes, so if we need to shunt into them, I can either do it from my console, or from the backup console in the armory."

"There's a system controller in the armory?"

"Yep. It's all there, in another room. You get to it using a code in the door keypad."

"Who knows the code and how to operate it?"

She looks up from the display and raises an amused eyebrow. "You have to be in the secret club, Aly." Satisfied with my nonplussed expression, she continues, "Kidding. It's all of us, the regular crew. And Pat."

I almost have to laugh. They've been in total control of this situation from the minute Rajcik landed on Spectra 6. Vitruzzi could say the word anytime and blow him out of the sky inside of seconds. With the *Temptation*'s onboard weapon detection system, Rajcik knows it, which explains why he hasn't tried even once to shake us in the six days that have passed since we left Spectra 6.

Why hadn't they told me any of this? Rationally, it makes no sense for me to resent being kept in the dark, about everything, starting with the tracking device and going all the way to the *Sphynx*'s battle capabilities. Why would they have trusted me with information that could have benefited Rajcik? They couldn't have taken any chances; if I'd been lying about my loyalty to him, I might have given him everything he needed to sweep into Agate Beach and take anything he wanted any time that was convenient for him, even if Vitruzzi's crew didn't go for the joint-effort assault on the Fortress.

Still, a spasm of, I don't know, disappointment, regret . . . some emotion I'd rather not examine twists through me. Almost two weeks we've been together, working side by side, fighting, planning, hell, I've even risked my life for them. What does it take to make them trust me? Accept me as part of the crew?

Venus stares at me quizzically, reading the thoughts play across my face, and I turn away. Forget it. This is how it is. We're partners. Not friends, not comrades. Business associates locked into an arrangement, a contract of defiance against the odds threatening to tear our lives apart. I better get used to it and stop letting things that don't matter distract me.

We've flown more than three-quarters of the distance to where Rajcik's coordinates put the Fortress. Three hours ago, Vitruzzi and Brady informed the crew that the time has come to cut him loose. We're so close now we can almost feel the Fortress's malignancy like a black hole in our flight path. It's a gamble to believe Rajcik will keep his promise and continue his intended mission instead of doubling back to attack the Beach, maybe the biggest gamble any of us have ever been forced to make. Vitruzzi says the settlement has an evacuation procedure in the case of such an event, and the equipment to know if he, or anyone, is coming. While I have my doubts about the settlement's preparedness, each passing day reveals something new and astonishing about these people, pushing those doubts further into the dust.

Vitruzzi hails Rajcik from the com room and I shove my concerns aside, all my focus on what's about to happen. From our seats on the flight control deck, Venus and I watch the linked pilot's VDU.

"This is it, Rajcik. We're done here. Remember, we did everything we said we would. You have your seeds and you have Vilbrandt. I suggest you take both of them and disappear."

Standing up before his video uplink and crossing his arms over his wide chest, his response is woodenly sincere. "Captain Vitruzzi, make no mistake. This won't be the last time we see each other." He lets his gaze linger on her for few seconds and motions to Thompson, standing behind him. "I want you to tell Aly something for me. Tell her I'm sorry to be losing such a competent crewmember, but it was inevitable. I knew that long before she did." He pauses, and a cold feeling begins creeping through my guts. Outside the flight control deck screen, the *Temptation*'s main engines start cycling rapidly in preparation for hyperspeed.

"Tell her she should have trusted her instincts when she realized I hadn't left the escape shuttle on Obal 3." Another pause, and a shadow comes across his features as if he's uncertain whether or not to continue. "She accused me of having no loyalty, and she's right. But loyalty is one of *her* flaws, not mine."

Black eyes shining like crystals, he continues, "Just let her know: I *gave* her and David to the Admin before his misguided ideas of moral superiority convinced him to turn on me. Vitruzzi, are you listening?"

She doesn't respond, and he keeps talking. "Make sure she knows that her brother is at the Fortress. I made that a special part of my arrangement with T'Kai. I'll be there too, waiting for her. And I'll be looking forward to our reunion." His teeth flash in a savage grin. "And one last thing. Give her this; it's *her* payback for the mission. Tell her to enjoy." And he reaches for his console.

"What the hell . . .?" There doesn't seem to be enough air in my lungs to finish the question. Stunned, I rise from the seat and stare into the empty void where the *Temptation* had been before it suddenly disappeared deeper into space, too fast for the eye to see. Rajcik has made his break, out of weapons range already.

The flight control VDU abruptly goes black, then lights up with a new image: a video feed. I instantly realize that I'm staring into a prison cell. Dingy green-painted walls seem to absorb all the high intensity light coming from fixtures on the ceiling, but it's the man sitting next to the wall, his head resting on his knees and his arms around his legs, that catches my attention. It's David.

The cell is completely empty besides him. He's wearing the same clothes as the day I lost him in the Obal 3 sub docks, but now the gray material is spotted here and there with tarnished maroon streaks that can only be dried blood. The fact that I'm looking at my brother in a cell on the Fortress isn't something my mind has to grasp; every cell in my body already knows it. My legs seem to disappear, collapsing from beneath me like so much rushing water. Falling forward, both of my hands come to rest alongside the display, but my eyes don't budge from the console. I feel as if I've been hit in the stomach with a sledgehammer.

There's a tinny clang in the background of the video feed. Alarmed, David quickly raises his head from his knees and my mouth goes dry as I glimpse his hardly recognizable face, thoroughly misshapen and swollen. Bruises cover everything and a deep laceration splits the skin above one eyebrow. His lips are torn in at least two places. But his eyes are the worst. The lids have puffed up to the size of tennis balls, stuck fast to his cheeks by a dried puslike fluid seeping from behind them. There's no doubt that he's reacting to the sound, but he can't possibly see what it is.

As quickly as the image appears, it's gone. I remain leaning over the display, my body devoid of sensation for the moment, just waiting . . . for Rajcik, for the image to continue, for my screams to split the ship open and spill me into space. The room around me begins to recede, shrinking into blackness, and my focus dims down into two tiny points before my eyes. Finally my legs give out completely and I land on my hands and knees, torso clenching in dry heaves.

"Erikson, hey, Erikson. Just take a deep breath."

Strahan's words seep through a disconnected part of my brain. When had he come in? His hands gently grip my shoulders, senselessly trying to help me hold it together. And then everything in me suddenly breaks free from reality, from rational thought, from control.

"NO!" I'm on my feet, flailing madly at his hands. If I get by him, I'll knock Venus from the pilot's seat and take control of the *Sphynx,* chase Rajcik down and kill him, the way I should have back on Spectra 6. The scorching desire propels me into a frenzy, wildly punching Strahan and lunging to get free of his grip, but it's useless. He's too strong, too prepared. My frantic onslaught is no more effective against his restraint than fire against water.

"Take it easy, take it easy, Erikson." He keeps talking, his voice too calm to punch through my anguish. But his grip is relentless and he presses my body firmly against the rear wall, not letting me free. "Calm down. We'll get him. We'll get your brother. Just take it easy."

My body isn't listening to me anymore; it has come undone. This must be what if feels like to plummet so far into hopeless, agonizing despair that you become embedded in the bottom, glued and trapped, drowning in poison. I'm powerless to do anything but collapse against the wall, held up by Strahan. My eyes close, and I hope I never have to open them again.

His warm breath puffs against my cheeks. "Look, Aly, we're going to find your brother, okay? He may still be alive. Are you listening? Don't give up, because we're going to find him. We need your help. *He* needs your help."

I open my eyes and see his face centimeters away, rearranged into an expression I hardly recognize. His sepia eyes are filled with concern, staring into mine. Hot tears burn my cheeks. Patiently, he holds onto me, providing a solid foundation, letting me process the image of my wounded brother, but keeping me from harming anyone, or myself. Finally, my breathing steadies. Time begins ticking again and awareness creeps back. In another few seconds, I take a deep breath, and let it out slowly.

He relaxes some of the pressure on my shoulders and I straighten up. "Are you all right?"

Nodding is an effort, but I don't trust myself to speak yet. The cockpit door opens and Vitruzzi steps hurriedly through, worry stamped on her face. Taking in the situation quickly, she doesn't need to ask how I'd reacted. She looks at me and asks, "That was your brother?"

Swallowing and swiping an arm across my hot face, I answer in a choked voice, "Yeah."

To Strahan: "Do you think that was a live feed or recorded?"

With a final examination to make sure I'm in control, he lets his hands drop from my shoulders. "It had to be recorded. How could he get a live broadcast from the Fortress?"

"Unless her brother's not really at the Fortress. Do you think he could be using him as bait, Erikson? Trying to set a trap for us?"

Vitruzzi's questions pierce the shock-fog enveloping my brain. What would Rajcik have to gain by sending me footage of David, suffering and beaten, other than a sick sense of retribution for our betrayal? No, Rajcik isn't trying to lead us anywhere that we're not already going. He does know me well. He knows we'll be coming to the Fortress and that he's given me all the incentive I need. He knows I won't stop until I find David, or we're both dead.

I shake my head. "No. He's trying to keep us close. He wants revenge." There's no longer any need to emphasize how cruel he can be. They've finally seen it for themselves.

From the corner of my eye I see Bodie and Desto join the group, standing just outside the flight deck hatchway. They must have heard me scream. Venus has turned around to look at me, for once entirely still, a sympathetic frown etched across her pale face. The depth and sincerity of their concern is real, making me uncomfortable. At what point did they start caring about my brother?

Vitruzzi glances around the room, taking in everyone's condition. No one says anything, as if we're all waiting for the next thing to happen. Finally, she says, "Okay, this is it. Karl, you and Bodie take the controls for a couple of hours and give Venus a break. Stay alert. Rajcik is unpredictable. Everyone else, take a break too. We're not going to get many chances from here. We'll all get back together in the com room in four hours. According to the coordinates, we're within three days of the Fortress. That's all the time we have. We need to make some decisions. Any questions?"

No.

"Erikson, can I talk to you in private?"

My legs are stiff as I follow her off the flight deck. Before we're out of range, I hear Desto say in a low voice, "Man, that was some of the most fucked-up shit I've ever seen. For Rajcik's sake, I hope her brother's alive."

Rajcik's a dead man. Whether I find David or not.

WE STEP UP A short stairway into the com room, situated astern and above the flight deck. After closing the door, she turns and says, "Look, Erikson, I know you're only with us because you're hoping your brother still has a chance. But there's something I have to know." Her focus is intense, uncompromising. "We don't know how old that video is. He may already be dead. You realize that."

She pauses, and the words seep like acid into my brain. "Yeah. I know that."

There's deep concern in her eyes, but her voice doesn't waver as she asks her next question. "What if he is? Are you going to stick with us if we get in there and don't find anything, or maybe just his body? I have to know how far we can count on you to go."

It's a fair question, but one I don't have to think about. "I'm in this until the end, Vitruzzi."

She stares at me for another second and nods. There is zero equivocation in my plans, and she knows it. Maybe she can see that if David is dead, the only thing I'm going to care about is revenge. Which means, no matter what, I'm in to the bitter end.

IT TAKES ME A FEW minutes to get myself together after talking with Vitruzzi. Standing in the washroom of my bunk and splashing cold water on my face gives me a chance to think deeply for the first time about how I'm going to cope with it if we don't find David alive. The thought has always crouched in the recesses of my brain where dark and hateful things live, things I rarely allow myself to think about. Now as I stare into the mirror, cold water dripping in rivulets down my nose and cheeks, the same resolve that helped me escape a loveless home, then desert the tyranny of the Corps, and has now freed me from Rajcik's control, is still there. If there's a chance David's alive, I'll search every centimeter of that station until I find him. And if he's dead, nothing in the universe will keep me from finding Rajcik and ending him.

EIGHTEEN

The sound of Brady's voice over the intercom yanks me harshly from a restless sleep.

"Everyone to the com room! An Admin patroller is boarding us. Get your asses up here now!"

Panic and adrenaline send sparks of electric saliva shooting into my mouth. Within seconds, I'm fully dressed, jamming the Mini-Derg into my boot and racing to the com room.

The crew piles inside, everyone strapping on or zipping up the bits of equipment they'd grabbed on the way, and Brady lays out the situation. "They pinged us two minutes ago. Routine sweep ship. They said they're looking for a fugee. I'm sure they mean you."

There's no way to interpret the look he gives me. "How could they know where I am?"

"Not the issue. We have to get you hidden. Go to the ammo vault with Desto." He turns to him. "Hide in the fire control room. We've got legal manifests that put us in the area, so, as long as they don't find you, we shouldn't have any trouble. Stay put until I give the all clear. They'll be here in five."

I'm already on the way to the vault by the time he's done talking, with Desto following closely. Once we get inside the ammo vault, he uses the interior keypad to open a hidden hatch in the floor.

Climbing in behind me, he slides the door closed overhead. "Keep quiet. We'll shake these guys fast. Nothing to worry about."

It takes a few seconds for my eyes to adjust to the dimness, helped by the glow from a console anchored against one of the steel walls. The background hum of the *Sphynx*'s engines begins to grow quieter and a couple minutes pass before they stop altogether. The ship's slowing motion creates the disconcerting feeling of reaching the vertex of an arc, hovering for a moment, and then plunging back downward in an unchecked dive. There's a sharp jerk as the Admin ship's boarding shuttle connects with the external airlock, reinstating the sense of gravity. Standing totally still, I listen with my entire body, trying to hear what may be happening on the cargo deck. Of course, it's futile; the overhead bay floor is engineered with thick steel plating designed to sustain the ship's integrity in the case of a ballistic attack, muting all sound and cutting us off from everything happening above. We're locked in the dark with no way to control the situation.

But not helpless. One benefit of being on ship for nearly ten years in the Corps: I know my way around a flight control deck and weapons systems. A quick investigation of the fire control console and I easily locate and enable the target acquisition sensor. Desto doesn't notice, standing at the top of the stairs with his pistol drawn, waiting for a reason to jump out like a bogeyman jack-in-the-box. The image display lights up sharply with a schematic of the *Sphynx* floating inside a dull green circle, overlaid by a grid pattern. I'm seeing a 360-degree view from the perspective of the ship's current position relative to everything outside. Triangulated guidance points hover in the display's upper corner, waiting to be trained on their objective. The diagram only shows a one-kilometer circumference, which is nothing but emptiness. Placing my fingers on the zoom controls, I'm able to enlarge the visual area. As I do, the image of the ship shrinks on the screen, but now I can make out the Admin sweep ship about three klicks from our stern. Zooming closer, I get a bead on her main generator and bring both missile guidance points to lock on. If anyone at the *Sphynx*'s helm is also attempting to operate the system, apparently this console has override power. Good for me. A single, nonrepulsed missile from the *Sphynx* could blast the Admin ship into dust if I hit it right. And if anyone comes through the hatch besides one of the *Sphynx*'s crew, that's exactly what I'll do. One strike and you're out, two and you're annihilated, you bastards.

Desto turns and sees what I'm up to. "Erikson, what the hell—?"

Both of us suddenly freeze in place as the door to the weapons vault above opens and footsteps belonging to two or three people enter the room. The cargo bay floor may be soundproof, but noise travels more easily from the vault through the hidden hatch. Desto's eyes move in a plane from the hatch, to me, to the console, and he gives me a short nod. He knows what I'm doing.

"Your manifests look legitimate, Captain Vitruzzi. We just have to check every room in case you have a stowaway. Someone you don't know is here, of course." A male voice. Unfamiliar. Probably the Admin ship's commander.

"I understand, Major." Vitruzzi's composure is unearthly; even through the floor she sounds as cool as ever. Knowing she can lie so convincingly marginally increases my sense of security.

"I have to admit," the man continues, "it's rare for a citizen to have such a generous contract. An unarmed ship carrying this caliber and volume of weaponry could create problems if it were to get into the wrong hands."

What is he implying? Is he playing with us? My head is tilted, my ear toward the ceiling trying to hear his voice more clearly, looking for a cue that it's time to render the Admin ship into fragments of unidentifiable space trash. Vitruzzi says nothing, but I can imagine the way her jaw clenches at his barely concealed accusation. More footsteps overhead.

"Sir, everyone on the ship is accounted for. One thing seems out of place. We found an extra bunk that has recently been occupied. It's empty now, but there are no passengers listed on the manifest."

Shit. They found my bunk. There's a grating sound and I picture the insufferable officer rotating on his boot heels to face Vitruzzi. "Captain?"

"We took a non-cit passenger from Letum Uti to Dro'an. Dropped him off yesterday. You can verify that with my nav-planner." That same casualness. There's no hidden challenge in her voice, but if they look and the nav-planner hasn't been fixed to show landings on the two Obal moons—landings we didn't make—we may get a trip to the Fortress after all. Of the one-way variety. My fingers dance jerkily on the targeting console, ready to launch the eagles.

"That's all right, Captain. I know there are numerous difficulties involved in living on the unsettled planets. Anything to make a little extra cash, right?" I can't speak for her, but I'd like to bust the smug bastard in the mouth.

"Thank you, Major."

His portable manifest reader emits a beep as he shuts it off, saying, "Your cooperation has been excellent. I'll make a note of it. We're done here."

Their footsteps retreat and the vault door slides shut again. That was too fucking close, but it doesn't mean they'll be leaving. I'll just keep my eyes on them for a while, see what happens. Fifteen minutes later their shuttle flies into view and docks, their engines spin up, and they're gone. Sitting in the semidarkness waiting for Vitruzzi to give the all clear, I'm thinking now would be a good

time for another slug of that paint thinner Strahan and I had been
drinking a few short hours ago.

"WE'VE SWEPT THE SHIP for surveillance devices. Come on out."

Vitruzzi stands at the top of the hatch and beckons. She
doesn't have to ask twice; two hours of killing time in this dun-
geon, time that should be spent working on the Fortress op, is plenty.

"What did you find?" Desto asks, coming up behind me. Despite the sober inquiry, I can practically feel his eyes crawling over
my ass.

"Usual. Bugs, a couple of imagers. We fried them. Venus says
the ship's out of range, so they're not coming back to ask why."

That's all I need to know.

After grabbing a box of compressed fruit blocks and a jug of
water from the galley, I head directly to the com room, prepared to
spend every remaining minute locked inside with the disc. Three
days left. Three days until I know whether David is alive or dead.
Thirty-six hours until I spill every drop of the toxic sludge that
stands in for Rajcik's blood. Everyone lives for a reason, and I
have two.

Strahan and Bodie walk in. Barely glancing up, I nod and
quickly return my attention to the plans.

"Anything new?" Bodie asks.

"Not a goddamn thing." My voice is strained in frustration.

I feel Strahan's gaze, like a hot ray of light, resting on my face.
When I look up, he's passing me the jug of water. "Let's see what
we can see."

Bodie takes a seat and Strahan leans against the reader, their
scrutiny equaling mine. For a while, no one talks, the time seeming
to pass instantly, and far too slowly. Even after manipulating the
schematic's angle, shifting perspective in new ways, and changing
structural overlays, it still feels as if I'm staring into a blacked-out
window and seeing nothing but my own reflection mocking me.
The plans are impenetrable, like a fucking Gordian knot.

Leaning against the back of a chair, I recite the same litany of
questions we've all gone over a hundred times. How are we going
to get in there? Where are the prisoner cells? How much more time
do they have? What the hell are we missing? Our last chance to
figure out how to achieve the impossible is being shot away like so
many wasted bullets.

According to the plans, a bank of surveillance satellites encircles the station, picking up everything within a ten thousand kilometer perimeter. It's completely impossible to get close to the thing undetected.

That's *if* we're right about where it is.

Brady, proving the word "optimism" isn't in his vocabulary, had earlier voiced the practical reality that the coordinates we have are only good as long as the Fortress doesn't move. At this point, a week after Rajcik gave them to us and two weeks since they were originally stolen, it's entirely possible that the station is no longer where we expect it to be. On Spectra 6, Rajcik had said something to the crew about picking up the call signs for a supply ship en route. Was that all he was picking up? It would have been easy for Rajcik to give us bogus coordinates, and why wouldn't he have? He had told Vitruzzi that he would see us at the Fortress, so it seems that the coordinates are correct, but . . . what if? He could easily have been bluffing.

The unknowns are piling up too high. The only way to maintain my focus, and my sanity, is to assume the station is where we expect it to be and concentrate on the central problem.

With no feasible chance of docking by surprise, the only way to get in is if we're supposed to be there. The security reports T'Kai included with the disc indicate that incoming and outgoing flights have been preplotted for over a month, but the precise schedule is missing. We can reasonably assume that there will be intermittent resupply ships, and we're far enough from any of the Obals or Admin outposts that ship traffic is irregular at best. It wouldn't be impossible to scan all crafts that come within range of the *Sphynx*'s radar and hope we're lucky enough to pick up a supply ship. But the chances that we find one on its way to the Fortress are slim to the point of being almost nonexistent. That's not good enough.

Bodie asks a question about entry and exit points, launching a discussion over the station's traffic patterns, which we guess at based on the number and size of its docks. I pull shipping access points into view, their boundaries highlighted in sharp red within the floating blue lines of the holograph. Looking through the margins of the after-deck diagram into the laboratories, it's hard not to imagine what could be happening to David and their friends in there. And then—

"Look at this," I say, pointing to a docking bay near the base of the station. "You see this bay? It's labeled 'Supply Docking Bay 5.'"

They both look from me to the schematic, then back at me, not sure what I'm getting at. "Look at the dimensions. See how small it is? It can't dock a ship much bigger than the *Sphynx*. And look where it's located, right next to the water storage and reclamation system, on this side, and an incinerator on this side." I point at the image, my finger almost shaking in excitement.

"Then over here, beyond the bay control rooms, are the two main labs. Bio and chemical. The weapons development center is on the other side of the station. If they wanted to bring supplies in from this bay, they'd have to take them through the labs. Think about it. A complex this size is going to need a hell of a lot more room than this little dock for bringing in all the essentials—food, more water, equipment, whatever."

My eyes lock on Strahan's, demanding he understand. "I think this is where they're bringing in prisoners. Human subjects."

Bodie looks at me surprised, but Strahan is nodding his head, excited now too. Standing, he points to a series of small rooms running between the two labs. "Look right here at these rooms, Storage A–J. If you're right, they bring the prisoners in, and take them right to these rooms. These have to be holding cells."

He's right. With the exception of the areas labeled "Living Quarters," no other compartments on the station are configured the same way. Perfect jail-cell size, and located right next to where we know they're testing their inhuman shit on living people.

A fragile tendril of an idea starts growing in my mind. "Yeah, makes sense. The docking bays near the front of the station are much bigger. *That's* where they're bringing in supplies and everything else. But they don't need a big dock for this. And they don't need to advertise it by labeling it what it is, in case some honcho with a weak stomach or sense of puritan morality ever gets a look at these plans."

Bodie still looks slightly perplexed. "So what? They'll be guarding that dock just as closely as everything else."

"Yeah, but if we can land there, we'll be right next to where they're holding David and the others. And the only way they'll be able to come at us is through the labs or from the outside. They'll have to be careful too, or they'll destroy their own water system, which will force them to shut down the whole place. They're not going to want to do that."

"Okay, yeah, I see. That still leaves the problem of docking, Aly. They're not going to let a civilian ship anywhere near it. If we even look as if we might be getting too close, regardless of what our manifests say, they'll send someone to intercept us and probably arrest us."

I have a plan for that too. Walking to the intercom console, I buzz Vitruzzi. "Captain, I think I have an idea. Can we get everyone to the com room?"

NINETEEN

Everyone assembles and I quickly explain our theory. I'm grateful when Strahan jumps in at critical points, giving my ideas some credibility. Brady's face is a mask of cynicism, but he doesn't call bullshit. It's a relief to not have to defend the idea against his automatic suspicion; time is far too short for divisiveness.

After everyone looks over the schematic and sees what we're talking about, I take over. "So Bodie, your question, *the* question, is how are we going to get permission to dock? Easy. We're going to give them a prisoner." They're all looking at me with focused concentration, wondering what I'm talking about. No jury ever handed down a sentence with more conviction than mine as I answer their unspoken question, "Me."

Strahan begins shaking his head. "Uh-uh, Aly. You're not going in there alone, and we're not a registered prison transport anyway."

"You're right. But we know where to get one."

Vitruzzi knows what I'm talking about. "The ship that boarded us today."

"Exactly. I got a good look at them while I was hiding in the fire control room. It's an MCACS—Multi-Containment Armored Carrier Ship. Commonly used by the Admin for prisoner transport. They're probably taking a load to the Fortress right now and got tasked with checking us out because we were in the same region and getting close to the station. Their commander wasn't very interested in doing a thorough inspection of the *Sphynx*; he didn't even want to look at the nav-logs. Why? Because that's not his job. He just wanted to follow orders and wrap up his primary duty—dropping his cargo, the prisoners, at the Fortress."

"What's your point, Erikson? That ship is faster than us, armed, and loaded with security personnel." Brady's playing Captain Obvious, not trying hard enough to understand.

Opting to ignore him, I continue, "Look, they've got twenty personnel max. An MCACS isn't much bigger than we are and all the prisoners are locked up, contained, whatever the hell they do. They're basically an armored transport ship. And they aren't going to be too far away yet. Hell, they may even be following us."

Venus chimes in, "Nuh-uh, I've been keeping my eye on the radars. There's no one out here but us."

I don't want to be a jerk, she's just a kid after all, but the point has to be made. "The minute we underestimate them, we lose our advantage. They can cloak themselves if they want to."

She frowns, slightly stung, but my bluntness stoppers their doubts long enough for me to continue, "It's easy. Just call them back and say you found me on board after all. I'd been hiding or something. They may not believe you, and they don't have to." I stare intently at Vitruzzi, wanting to impress on her the importance of giving the plan all due diligence before rejecting it. The final decision will be hers, and everything rides on what she chooses. "Let them think that being boarded spooked you and made you realize how much shit you were in, so you decided to give me up and pretend like you didn't know anything. It doesn't matter. They'll come back for me because they've been told to. And when they do, we take their ship. The coordinates to the Fortress will be in their nav-system. Brady, if you're right and the Fortress has moved or Rajcik gave us the wrong coordinates, it won't matter. We've *got* to do this."

Their expressions testify to the fact that they think I've gone completely off my nut, but it's the best plan anyone's thought of so far. The *only* plan.

"Venus, do you think you can fly an MCACS?" Vitruzzi asks after a moment of consideration.

Without hesitation, her lips spread into a wide grin. "Shouldn't be a problem. Their engines are modeled after these, but with a higher output. The stabilizers have to compensate for that by creating more drag, but that's offset by a larger bore combuster and higher torque on the turbines."

Does she study ship designs for fun, or is it just wired into her mutant brain? Either way, good news for us. "Then we just have to make the call. People, there's no other choice. We do this or they die."

"She's right." Desto stands, no smile on his face this time. "It may be crazy, and probably impossible, but I've always wanted to hijack an Admin ship. I'm in."

It only takes another second before everyone is nodding. "Okay." I'm also nodding, relief and excitement flooding through me. We may be grasping at the shortest straw ever made, but we finally have a plan. From this point, there will be no more doubt, no more confusion, no more uncertainty or fear. Right or wrong, we are finally, inevitably, in motion.

"The best way to take control is to capture their commander. With a little persuasion, he'll order the crew to stand down. There may be a couple of heroes, but we can deal with them. Once we own the ship, we'll bring Venus on board. Until then, she and someone else can stay here and cover us."

Worry dances circles in Venus's wide eyes, threatening her nerve. I smile confidently, trying to reassure her. As long as we can keep her out of harm's way, no doubt she'll be able to manage the hijacked ship.

Talking fast, I lay out the strategy my mind has already processed. "Whoever stays on the *Sphynx* will provide us with a distraction. Once they're convinced I'm the fugee they've been tasked to find, we'll be forced to make the delivery. Take me to them. They're vulnerable if they split up and their shuttle is launched." I shift my eyes back to Venus. "You keep their ship in firing range. After we're on board—and I don't mean after we dock, but after we're on board and *off* the shuttle—you line up and blow out one of their auxiliary engines. The MCACS can still fly without it, but the strike will confuse them and give us enough of a distraction to take the ship."

"You're saying that four or five of us are going to take out twenty of them?" Desto asks.

"We don't have to kill them. Just take away their initiative and make them *our* prisoners. Once we blow their auxiliary and they realize they're under fire, if they follow SOPs, they'll try to make a run for it. But not if we have their commander hostage." I stop talking for a minute, considering the biggest obstacle to this plan. "But what we really need is a way to jam their coms, make them unable to transmit a SITREP or SOS. The plan hinges on us being able to surprise them, and then use the ship as cover to get inside the Fortress."

"We've got a pulse emitter in the fire control room. If we splice it to our transmitter and draw from the *Sphynx*'s engine, we may be able to scramble their transmissions by overloading all frequencies," Bodie says. "It's old, and it'll take a lot of power from the *Sphynx* to create a big enough electrostatic wave. I'm not a hundred percent it'll even work at all." He looks around the table, one eyebrow raised as if to ask, *I know it's a long shot, but what else do we have?*

Vitruzzi asks, "How much power? Will the *Sphynx* be able to make a break for it if things go wrong?"

"*If* it works, it'll draw . . . maybe eighty percent of the engine's energy. All at once. The only thing on board that will work is the grav-stabilizer and life support. That's for one static pulse, which should disrupt their communications for three, maybe even five, minutes. If they send a transmission, it'll be garbled and anyone hearing it won't know who it came from." He draws a long, slow breath. "I think."

"How long will the *Sphynx* be down?"

"I'd guess about ten minutes."

"Is that enough time?" Strahan asks.

"The MCACS is a small ship, and they don't have much more firepower than the *Sphynx* does. But they're a lot faster than we are, even with a burnt-out auxiliary. Their orders will be to send an SOS and make a break for it. But it will take them a minute to diagnose the damage. If we take their commander hostage before they can respond, we can make him order the ship to stand to. They'll know what we're capable of and do as commanded."

"And if any single thing goes wrong . . ." Brady doesn't finish the sentence.

No one else says anything for a few seconds, thinking over what I've outlined. Strahan's brown eyes are on mine, and this time I meet his gaze. He stares right through my resolute, no-compromises exterior, recognizing the deep fears now pushing me into risks that seem beyond reckless, and he nods. He understands. I, *we,* have no more options.

"Okay. This is how we'll run it." Vitruzzi takes over and we spend the next forty-five minutes ramping up for the mission that decides whether David and the *Sky Serpent* crew live or die.

TWENTY

The *Sphynx* is about two kilometers behind us and the shuttle-docking doors opening on the top of the MCACS are just ahead. Vitruzzi made the call and they'd responded exactly as we'd hoped. It's small and close inside the shuttle. Sweat runs down my back and I see it beading up on Desto and Strahan's temples. Vitruzzi is as impassive as ever, piloting us to the shuttle dock with the same even determination as when she's sewing up one of her crew or lying to an officer of the Administration.

Turning to Strahan, I tell him, "Put me in restraints."

"What?"

"Put some wrist restraints on me. They won't believe us unless I'm cuffed."

"You'll be helpless . . ."

"If you think that, you don't know me very well. Just do it. Fill the lock core with a fingernail's worth of E-10 right before we get off. It'll melt through in about two minutes and my hands will be free. But take this," I hand him my Sinbad pistol, "and keep it in the back of your pants. Stay in front of me. I can fire with restraints on."

We all have guns, all well hidden. We need the Admin crew to let us inside the dock with the doors shut and the airlocks activated if this is going to work. For them to do that, Vitruzzi and the others have to appear to be innocent citizens giving up a known fugitive. Possessing guns is illegal, and if ours are seen, our cover is blown.

"Shit," he mutters under his breath but puts the cuffs on. I try to smile at him while he's balling up the E-10 wax, but it feels forced. He grins back anyway and pushes the Sinbad inside his belt in the small of his back. "Don't pull that trigger until it's clear, got it?"

Vitruzzi eases us down through the open doors and we hit the bay floor with a screech of metal. I hear the hydraulics engage, and the doors above us begin to close. Here we go.

Green lights flash inside the bay indicating the airlock is engaged and pressurized, and Vitruzzi activates the shuttle ramp. It lowers slowly, giving us time to note the positions of the commander and half a dozen other uniformed personnel in the bay. Every one of them has a weapon pointed at us. Vitruzzi takes the lead and begins walking down the ramp, followed by Strahan, me, then Desto. I raise my hands waist high, hovering just behind Strahan's back.

"Be very careful, Captain. I want to see empty hands in the air."

I take my first look at the officer, and to my complete lack of surprise, he is almost exactly as I'd pictured. Regulation cropped hair, barely long enough to be seen beneath his commander's cap, sharp blue eyes attentive beneath the cap's brim, and a rigid stature that makes his starched uniform look nailed on. Distinct lines drape from the edges of his mouth toward his chin, reinforcing the frown that he now levels on us. He's not much older than I am, but life transporting prisoners to the fringes of space has not been gentle on him.

All of us keep our hands in plain view except for me. Once we're all on deck I step only slightly beside Strahan so I can draw the 'Bad without having to shift my body. The others line up horizontally as the crewmen approach to search us. The air tastes electric with tension and I can read in the major's face that he knows something is up.

Just as the first man reaches to pat down Vitruzzi, a voice stoked by urgency booms through the ship's com system, "Major Donnelly, we're getting an unexpected reading on our weapon sensors."

Bodie is locked! *Fire now!* I scream in my head, reaching for the Sinbad. The major's sharp eyes dart toward us, and then the ship bucks crazily, throwing everyone through the air.

The auxiliary engine's explosion reverberates throughout the chamber like water breaking through a dam, forcing my eyes to squeeze tightly shut. A yell followed by a meaty thud comes from nearby and I open them in time to glimpse Desto kneeling over the nearest crewman, trying to disarm him. Vitruzzi lines up a shot at another, and Strahan has Donnelly by the collar, forcing the officer in front of him to use as a shield. Another crewman lines up to fire at me, and I roll aside just in time, then back, aiming for his face with the 'Bad. My shot is off by a few centimeters and only grazes him, but the pain and surprise are enough to make him forget to fire back. His weapon clatters against the floor as he reaches for his wounded neck, allowing me the time I need to take aim at his head. He knows the deal and reaches high.

"Everyone drop them or your commander is dead." Strahan's voice slices through the chamber like a scythe.

As if they were a single unit, the security team freezes. Strahan scans the bay, one arm gripped around the major's neck, the other pointing the pistol he had strapped to his calf at the man's temple.

"Do as he says," Donnelly gasps through his half-closed throat.

"Sir! We've been fired on! Sir, what are your orders?" The same frantic voice as before shouts through the com system.

The men remain still, but it's a fifty-fifty chance they'll disregard their commander's order. It only takes one overhyped gunman jerking his trigger, and like dominoes, the rest will open fire. The docking chamber is small, the walls deflective—it would be suicide to continue shooting standard-issue metal rounds in here, but the human mind doesn't always believe in its own mortality. Rising slowly, I draw the Mini-Derg with my free hand and point it at another crewman, already regretting that I'll be useless to my brother and he'll die alone inside an Admin torture chamber if we lose our momentary advantage. But then Donnelly finds the motivation he needs to force an unquestionable command through his constricted throat. "Drop your weapons, now!"

This time, the remaining crewmen comply, and the room echoes with the sound of rifle butts banging on steel. Desto and I quickly kick them out of reach and wave the men against the far wall with the non-negotiating ends of our weapons. Strahan continues to hold the major in a throat-crushing grip, and the man's face begins turning an alarming purplish color as Vitruzzi approaches them.

Despite being choked, he manages to whisper, "You're making a huge mistake, Captain."

She nods at Strahan, who eases up on the pressure, and Donnelly draws a whooping, pained breath.

Vitruzzi ignores him. "Call your flight deck and get a SITREP. Tell them not to report to any other ship until you get back up there. Am I clear, Major?"

He nods, eyes squinting in fury, keenly aware of the gravity of his situation. Strahan pushes him toward a com console near the airlock.

Pressing the link, he clears his throat and says, "Captain Roby, SITREP."

"Sir, the ISPS fired on us! The auxiliary engine is completely gone. And there's something wrong with the transmitter. We're trying to get a lock on the craft, but it's moving erratically. What are your orders?"

The major shifts his eyes to Vitruzzi, waiting for his orders.

"Tell him to hold fast, you're coming up. Have all crew not dealing with the engine meet you in here."

He gives his subordinates the command. Within seconds, six more men rush into the bay from the forward cabin, completely unaware of the situation, and are quickly subdued. Desto ties their hands and feet to each other, immobilizing them, and covers their mouths with tape. It takes less than two minutes. While he's busy with the crew, Strahan and I provide security, and Vitruzzi interrogates Donnelly for information regarding the location and duty of any remaining crewmembers. Ten minutes later we're standing on the bridge, in control of the ship. I'm having a hard time swallowing the rising sense of dread our unlikely streak of luck brings—there's no way things will go this smoothly again. No way.

TWENTY-ONE

Twenty-four hours have passed. Venus has been at the helm for the last eighteen, but seems as fresh and lively as if she'd slept eight perfect hours a night, each and every night of her life. The good news: no shots were fired when we took the bridge. The bad news: the bridge commander, Captain Roby, immediately changed the ship's course and locked the nav-system when he realized they were compromised. Donnelly and Roby are the only crewmen with the encryption pass codes to get back into the nav-system, and without them we're flying blind. Not part of the plan.

Donnelly consistently denies the ship's destination is the Fortress, but he's lying. He doesn't even try that hard to hide it. So what if we reach the Fortress? He knows it's crazy and our odds of being blown out of the sky, or worse, picked off to be used as more test subjects, are much greater than our odds of achieving whatever idiotic plan we've cooked up, so why bother to try and be convincing?

When the MCACS doesn't make its rendezvous with the station, they'll begin a search and our plan, along with all of us, will be dead in the water. Vitruzzi has been explicitly clear that none of the Admin crew should be needlessly harmed, instantly rejecting my suggestion that we shoot one every ten minutes until Donnelly gives up the codes. I'm not bloodthirsty, but it's as Rajcik once told me: they knew the risks when they signed on.

Brady has been piloting the *Sphynx*, keeping her within firing distance in case we lose control of the situation, while Bodie and Venus keep the MCACS flying. We locked the crew in the galley, rather than with the thirty-eight prisoners aboard, for their own protection, and Desto and I switch guard duty every six hours. I'm standing on my third watch, staring through the galley door at the imprisoned crew, shifting my weight from foot to foot to stay conscious. None of us has slept since intercepting the MCACS and I'm starting to lose the battle against the fatigue threatening to take my eyelids prisoner.

There's a noise in the corridor and I look up to see Desto approaching. "Your relief is here, honey. You ready to catch a nap?"

"No. I couldn't sleep even if I wanted to."

He chuckles. "That's not what it looks like. Go ahead, rack out for a few. I just did and I feel a million times better. Captain started us on a sleep rotation for three hours each, and you're up. Take it while you can get it."

"Is that an order?" I try to keep my tone light, but it doesn't work. My voice sounds gruff and resentful, even to me.

"Does it matter? You need it, trust me."

Even if I don't, my body wants to accept the invitation. My arms drop heavily to my sides and my knees waver, forcing me to lean back against the wall.

"Yeah, that's what I thought. Head up to the top level. It's the bunk nearest the flight deck. Any troubles here?"

"They're as calm as kittens. Keeping the temp at thirty-seven C doesn't inspire rebellion."

A DENSE CURTAIN OF fog moves around me like a shroud. It's cold and damp, a heavy mist, and there's a strange grating sound—metal against metal—coming from somewhere not very distant. I'm on full alert, feeling danger in the mist with me, but none of my senses can locate it. I want to call out to David, to see if he is here too, but I can't risk drawing unwanted attention to myself. Any noise could give away my location, and I won't be able to see it, whatever it is, coming.

I don't know what to do, so I begin stalking quietly toward the sound. If I find it first, I may be able to identify it without being detected.

As I take a few tentative steps, curdles of thick fog blow back from my shape like smoke, quickly replaced by more of the same. Continuing forward, I look down to get a sense of what kind of ground I'm walking on, trying not to make any noise. One more step and the mist shifts for an instant, long enough for me to see that there is nothing. Nothing but black, empty space below me.

The moment this realization hits me, the sense of having solid ground beneath my feet dissolves, and I'm suddenly falling—hurtling—through space, gaining speed though there is no gravity. I feel cold wind and needles of ice burrowing into my skin, as if being stabbed by a million tiny knives. I begin to kick and claw at the emptiness around me, trying to slow myself, to break my fall, anything. I hitch in a deep breath, preparing to scream—

—and wake up gasping. Wild-eyed and panicked, I look around the room and pick out Vitruzzi leaning through the doorway.

"You all right?" she asks.

I can't speak for a second, still partly paralyzed in the free fall of my dream. The haggardness in her face, eyes deep-set in dark pockets, almost mournful, helps bring me back to the present. "Yeah, I'm fine."

Time to get back to work. Leaning down and pulling my boots on, still trying to get a grip, I hear her footsteps as she comes in. She watches me quietly for a moment and says, "We can't wait for Donnelly anymore. We need the pass codes, and we're going to have to make him tell us." She doesn't say it, but I know what she's thinking: *I wish like hell it didn't have to come to this.*

"Are we going to use his crew?"

"No," she answers immediately. "We're not going to make them pay for his mistakes."

"Vitruzzi, you know we can't let any of them go. They know who you are. They know your ship. Even if we pull this off, if anyone lives to report what happened, you and the others in Agate Beach will be targets. The Admin will come eventually."

Anger flashes across her features, but it's not about me. She's angry with them for putting her in this situation, and no one can blame her for it. I still don't know why she gave up her comfortable life on Obal 10 before all this, but the more I see, the more I'm convinced the Admin had something to do with it.

"Let's just get this done." She heads for the flight deck and I follow her.

Strahan stands over Donnelly, who's been taped to the copilot's seat. He doesn't appear to be frightened, but dark smudges beneath his eyes reveal a wary concern and lack of sleep. When we enter, Strahan glances up and the major cranes his head back to look at us.

Vitruzzi positions herself rigidly beside the seat, looming over him. She's relaxed, nothing in her stance overtly threatening, yet no one would mistake her mood for anything but serious. Deadly serious.

"Major Donnelly, give us the pass codes to the nav-system. Now."

"You have control of the ship. What difference does it make?" He's trying to remain curt, but there's an unmistakable strain in his voice.

Strahan pulls a vicious-looking knife from his load-bearing vest and presses the blade against the man's jugular. "Major, you're going to tell us those codes, or you're going to watch yourself bleed to death. I suggest you think very carefully about what you say next. You've got five seconds."

Donnelly's face grows pale, the depressed circles around his eyes becoming more like bruises. Or like the sunken eyes of a corpse. "You'll never get away with this. You'll kill me anyway, even if I give you the pass codes."

Strahan remains stolid, staring the man down with the intensity of a predator locked on its prey. Finally, Vitruzzi says, "Karl, take him to the galley and put a bullet in his head in front of his crew. Then bring the captain to the deck." Her eyes never leave Donnelly's. "Erikson, go with him."

I look from her, to Strahan, to Donnelly. The same resolute calmness is in all of their faces. Venus remains seated in the pilot's station, keeping her head turned stiffly to the front, refusing to acknowledge the scene playing out around her. If only we could all wish it away.

Donnelly stands up after Strahan cuts through the tape holding him to the seat, and without a word turns toward the flight deck door. Vitruzzi, still staring at the seat he'd been sitting in, says quietly, "Last chance, Major."

He steps through the doorway without looking back.

KILLING HIM WORKS. The ship's new OIC, Captain Roby, complies without hesitation, inputting the pass codes himself. Once the nav-system is unlocked, Venus and I locate the Fortress's coordinates. We're all a little surprised when they match those Rajcik originally gave us. He'd kept his word after all, confirmation that he's been baiting us, even as we'd held him captive. It leaves me feeling sick.

We're within eighteen hours of the prisoner ship's scheduled rendezvous. They'd been ahead of schedule before we intercepted them and Roby informs us that Donnelly's plan had been to remain in a holding pattern until their expected window. By reinstating their previous course, we'll be arriving at the Fortress just in time.

I'm sitting in the navigator's station poring through the flight logs when Vitruzzi walks onto the flight deck. Without a word, she takes the pilot's seat. Venus put the ship on auto about two hours ago and left to catch a few minutes of sleep, finally. Or maybe she just needed to put some distance between herself and the horrible shit happening around her.

Glancing up at Vitruzzi, I see the same look in her eyes that I've seen too often in my own. The haunted way the eyes trip around a room, not seeing anything, covered by a dull sheen that says they've seen too much violence and senseless death. A look stained with the knowledge that our own end is coming, and fast. That look is the reason most soldiers don't own a mirror.

"You had to do it, Vitruzzi. It was the only way."

She looks at me gravely. "Have you ever been a parent, Erikson?"

It's a strange question. "You know I haven't." Corps troops are sterilized at in-processing to keep the ranks and population in order and ensure perpetual combat readiness—a Malthusian reaction by the Admin to guard civilization from ever reaching critical mass again.

"I know you've never had children, but that doesn't necessarily mean you've never had to help raise a child. Then, I imagine you've never had that kind of opportunity, the life you've led."

I shake my head. I'm not sure what she's talking about, but her grim tone extinguishes any impulse to interrupt.

"That's just another freedom the Admin takes from people." She stops. Part of me hopes she's done, but after a minute, she continues, "Karl says you're curious about how I became an Admin contractor."

"Yeah. You've got some good people around you, but let's be honest, it isn't much of a life."

She studies me blankly for a second, then begins speaking rapidly, as if the words have been dammed up too long and can no longer be held back. "I was Head Surgeon of the Cyber Prosthetics Unit at Mercy Hope Hospital in Tunis City before I went into business with Karl. My husband was a molecular chemist, working on biological pacification projects. We met at the hospital. A year after we were married, we had a little girl. Evie." She stops again. There's something she wants to say, something painful, and in another second, I'm going to hear it. Only I'm not sure I want to.

"Six years ago, an Admin-engineered virus was brought to the hospital. John couldn't tell me where it came from, but it wasn't hard to figure out it was developed at the Fortress. Everyone had heard the rumors about the place. He was so excited about being part of such a highly sensitive operation. I still don't know why the

Admin exported it. There was no reason to bring it to a civilian population center.

"Somehow, the virus got out, and before they could contain it, twenty-five thousand citizens from Tunis City and the surrounding area died. My husband and daughter included." She continues staring through the flight deck screens, her lips the only part of her body still animated. "I went to work early on a Saturday morning, and that afternoon they locked down the hospital. No one was allowed in or out. By the time the epidemic was contained a week later, my family was dead. I never saw either of them again. All the bodies were incinerated."

I remember the news. It happened right before the Soldier's Rebellion. Rumors claimed the outbreak, dubbed the "Crowers Croup" by the Corps ranks because of how bad it made people cough, so bad it shredded their lungs and throat, was the reason for the rebellion in the first place. Or at least the catalyst. The units sent to quarantine the infected and clean up the mess weren't properly outfitted for the bug, no one was even sure what it was and the Admin spun the news reports to keep people pacified and in the dark. Word was that it was transmitted through body fluids, mucus and saliva, but soldiers were dropping like flies before anyone realized it was airborne. Estimates say fifty thousand citizens died in the Obals—no one bothered to count the non-cits in the Spectras—but over seventy-five thousand soldiers were sent to the cremation chambers.

"I wasn't a very good mother. I worked too much and spent more time with my patients than my own family. My husband was just like me. By the end, we were just familiar strangers to each other. I like to think Evie died knowing that her parents loved her. But most of the time, I doubt she did."

An involuntary shiver traces up my spinal cord. I don't know what to say; not that anything I come up with would matter anyway. I knew people who died from the Croup, but no story I've heard is as horrible as hers.

She stops talking, battling with herself over whether she wants to relive this nightmare by telling it to me, but eventually, she goes on. "The Admin never acknowledged that the virus had come from their experimentation at the Fortress, and everyone who knew the truth was dead, like John.

"I couldn't stay at the hospital after that, working for a government that killed my little girl and then lied to me about it. I dropped off my resignation two days after the quarantine was lifted, and I think the only reason they let me go was because they suspected I knew the truth. They gambled I'd keep my mouth shut if they let me leave without restrictions."

"Why did you?"

A bitter chuckle escapes her. "How could I have proved it? Besides, it isn't hard to guess what would have happened to me if I had tried."

I don't know how she chokes off the rage she must feel over what the Admin did to her and her family without going crazy, but even as she tells me the story, she seems calm. Bitter and hateful, but calm.

She swings the pilot's seat around and looks at me for the first time. "Erikson, I'm telling you this so you'll understand something important: I have no regrets about what happened to Donnelly. That was simple justice. Those scientists on the Fortress, scientists like Vilbrandt, kill people, *people,* in ways that no one deserves, and Donnelly was helping them do it. He got what was coming to him."

There's no trace of guilt in her words. She's not trying to make me see things her way; she wants me to know how far things have gone and the consequences for anything or anyone that gets in our way. If I had not just heard these words, I could have lived fifty lifetimes before seeing this deeply into Vitruzzi. She hadn't brought Vilbrandt on board just because he presented an opportunity. Her motives were never that straightforward. Her plans for him, once he served his purpose, were almost certainly every bit as grisly as what Rajcik will probably end up doing to him. This isn't just a simple mission to save her friends from bad luck. It's personal. It's a vendetta, and it's driving every decision she makes, good or bad. So far, those decisions have been exact, calculated, and flawless, but there's no telling what tiny little nudge might be all that's needed to send her over the edge and out of control. She could be close and no one would know it. If Vitruzzi loses it, it's hard to know how the rest of this crew will react. They're smart, strong, and capable, but like any tower, when the foundation crumbles, it all comes down.

"In a way, I've had more of a relationship with the prosthetic in Karl's leg and the *Sphynx* than I ever had with my own daughter. She was only seven years, two months, and nine days old when she died."

"FORTRESS, THIS IS MCACS F-205, prisoner transport from Keum Libre, requesting clearance to land. Over."

"Roger, Major Donnelly. This is Lieutenant Stevenson. Redirect to the lower docking bays and provide your authentication code."

We've arrived. The monstrosity looms at our bow, gleaming against the blackness like a hellish, mutant asteroid. According to the disc, there are fifteen levels in the bow of the station: two that are strictly traffic corridors spanning the entire length through the center, and ten levels in the stern. The main generators encircle its core, generating the energy needed for both operations and mobility, completely enclosed in an impenetrable structural shell. No way to take those out, even if we had ten ships with ten times more firepower.

We approach facing the two main flight deck levels where the transit ship launch tracks run into the interior, terminating at the station's primary loading bays. The tracks, being the station's most vulnerable design component, are buttressed on each side with jutting missile tubes that ensure nothing gets near without clearance. Prismatic lenses, which capture and relay all visuals from outside, are located directly above the launch tracks' gaping airlocks. Coupled with the segmented design of the station's hull, the overall effect creates the impression that we're flying toward the snatching jaws of a giant carnivorous insect.

Vitruzzi, Venus, Brady, Strahan, and I occupy the prisoner ship's flight deck. We'd left the *Sphynx* crewless and in stasis when we entered into communication range of the Fortress, and everyone now wears the MCACS's security personnel uniforms. I hate it; my own body armor is light and flexible and this stuff is like wearing a lead suit, but we have to look the part. Even so, I removed the lower plates from the torso section to give me marginally better maneuverability and speed. Security guards are hired for size and strength, and their heavy vests are not designed for my short, compact frame. All of us are now ready and waiting for the action to begin, with Bodie and Desto docked in the *Sphynx*'s short-range shuttle inside the MCACS's bay in case there is need, and opportunity, to bug out.

"Fortress, this is Captain Roby, OIC. We've encountered hostile activity and Major Donnelly is in the infirmary. I've taken command. Over," Strahan answers, assuming the role of the ship's second in command.

"Why didn't you send a report?"

"Our coms sustained damage, Lieutenant. We haven't had the chance."

"Describe your situation, F-205. Over."

"We were tasked to pick up a fugitive by the name of Erikson, located aboard a contracted vessel. Their crew resisted us and Major Donnelly was injured during the fugee's extraction. His situation is critical. We need immediate clearance and a medical team ready when we dock. We also have a faulty auxiliary engine that needs maintenance. Over."

"Roger, Captain Roby. What's your authentication code? Over."

He flips off the com. "Shit." The rest of us hold our breath, frantically trying to think of a way to get this asshole to open up the Fortress and let us in. We'd left the real Roby with his crew to keep him from blowing the whistle once we made contact. It's too late to run back to the galley and retrieve him; the hesitation might serve as a warning to the Fortress's boarding command. Before anyone says anything, Strahan switches the com back on. "Lieutenant Stevenson, stand by for authent code. STY-0038-9762-98. Over."

Where did that come from? After a moment the LT's voice comes back. "Captain Roby, that authent code is inactive. It actually belongs to a former Tech 3 Sergeant, Chief Pilot, Strahan, Karl S. Over."

I look over at him, genuinely surprised. It's a dangerous gamble for Strahan to give them his prior active-duty flight officer code. If we manage to get away with this, there's no doubt that he'll be investigated, which will lead back to Vitruzzi and the *Sphynx*, and eventually, Agate Beach. It doesn't matter now. The option of turning back is obsolete.

"So?" He's playing a pissed-off commander flawlessly.

"Sir, we can't let you board without a valid authentication code. What is your authentication code? Over."

"Lieutenant Stevenson, I've got my ship commander leaking brains and blood, a hull full of pain-in-the-ass prisoners and one fugee, and a busted engine. I've got enough problems to deal with today. Don't become one of them. Some goon database tech who can't read his fucking alphabet entering my authent code into the system wrong, is *not* my problem. Do you read me? Now, are you going to clear that fucking dock? Over."

There's a pause after his transmission that feels too long to be anything but a death sentence. Then: "Captain Roby. Please proceed to Alpha Dock, Bay 5. They are clear and waiting for your arrival. Over."

Everyone in the cabin starts breathing again. Strahan looks genuinely pissed off and finishes the transmission. "Good job, Lieutenant. And make sure they have a goddamn mechanic crew on standby when we get there too. Out."

He switches off and the deck falls into total silence. Once we're inside the station, approximately ten minutes from now, all of the planning, running, hiding, and fighting that got us this far will stop, and the real battle will finally begin. I don't know what thoughts are spinning through their minds, but the face of my brother, bleeding, hurt, and afraid, fills mine like a cancer. But instead of enervating me, the image replenishes my determination to get the bastards that did it to him. Whatever the cost.

Finally, Venus breaks the silence. "Captain, what are we going to do with the prisoners?"

Vitruzzi and Brady look at each other and he says, "We let them go."

"We what?"

"If we leave them on the ship, they're sitting ducks. And we don't really want to cart them back to the *Sphynx* if, *when,* we get away. Besides, they'll make a good distraction."

"Do you really think that's a good idea, Brady?" I ask. "We've got enough to worry about without giving them a chance to turn on us too."

"Do you have a better idea?"

I don't. This time I keep my mouth shut.

Vitruzzi takes a deep breath. "I'll go tell them."

The four of us walk through the guard annex to the holding bay. Vitruzzi activates the hatch and the din of voices inside quiets down as we enter.

"Listen up." All heads turn to her. The walkway we stand on is about two meters above two metal-barred cages that separate thirty men and a handful of women. The room is brightly lit, casting garish light over their upturned faces. They look mean, pissed off, and violent, but there's no fear in their faces.

"By now you've probably realized that this ship has been hijacked. We're not here because of you, and now we have to figure out what to do with you. So we're going to let you go." No cheers. No applause. No smiles.

"It's fair to tell you where we're going, if you don't already know. The Fortress." For the first time, murmurs of anger and disquiet wash through the air, quickly whipping into a wrathful gale.

Someone shouts, "You can't cut us loose in there! They'll kill us!" More yelling, interspersed with gems like, "Fly us outta here or you're dead," "I'll fucking hunt you down, bitch," and more similarly empty, useless threats. No doubt about it, these are not the type we'd be interested in recruiting as partners, and I'm not surprised they've been earmarked as future human lab rats. Still, I can't help but feel some sympathy for them. Like Vitruzzi said: no one deserves to die the way they certainly would if we hadn't hijacked the ship and changed their fates. Whether or not their new futures will be an improvement, however, is not so certain.

"Quiet!" Her voice rings throughout the confined space like doom, and they fall silent. "We're not taking you anywhere you weren't going already, so quit complaining. This is the only chance you're going to get. We're not here to save you. But like I said, we're giving you a chance."

Thirty-eight pairs of eyes are now fixed on her, some with murder in them, but some are starting to show interest.

"How many here are deserters?" A little over half of them raise their hands, listening closely now. "There are a lot of guns on this ship. Most of you should still be able to activate them if your records were destroyed in the Rebellion. You're going to have full access. For the rest of you, there are some grenades, maybe some incendiary units. Once we dock, which will be in about three minutes, my crew and I are going to disappear. These doors will open five minutes later and you can all do whatever the hell you want. Claim your freedom. If you're smart, you'll team up and get systematic about dealing with the security shit show that I guarantee will be coming."

She turns and we walk back into the guardroom, an angry furor flooding the bay behind us. Hitting the code, she lets the door close them out. "Karl, get some E-10 in those locks as soon as we land then hustle back to the exit ramp. Let's get these gun cages open."

The entire scenario is a lunatic's nightmare, but the fact is the Admin is going to have a, as Vitruzzi put it, a shit show on their hands very soon. We're dead if they catch us. But if we're lucky, this swarm of gun-toting degenerates with nothing to lose will thin out the Fortress's security force, and we'll just slip silently through their fingers.

TWENTY-TWO

Venus maneuvers into the launch track and hovers at the end until the dock controllers activate the airlock. The vibration of the ship's floor slackens underfoot as she lowers it onto the dock and disengages the engines. The rest of us stand at the exit ramp. Three out of the six of us came from the Corps, but being back in uniform makes cold sweat seep from my pores. Or maybe it's this place.

Staring through the window hatch into the bay, things seem too quiet. "I don't see any mechanics."

The communication console lights up, and a second later the dock controller starts speaking. "Captain Roby, we're experiencing a security situation and need you and your crew to move directly to the debrief room. Just leave your cargo and injured on board. We'll send medics and a maintenance crew soon. Over."

The six of us turn to look at each other. "Rajcik?" Vitruzzi speculates.

I shake my head, not knowing what else it could be. "Unreal."

"Answer him, Karl."

Strahan clicks on the transmitter. "That's affirmative. Out."

Bodie releases the ramp and we walk onto the Fortress, where the coldness of space wraps its burial shroud around us.

The dock is relatively small with only three bays for ships no bigger than the one we're flying. We cross as a group to the debriefing room. No one needs to be told where it is; we've all scrutinized the holodisc long enough to know exactly where to go. As we pass by the prisoner ship's bow, I look up and see Venus staring out at us with worried eyes. She's locked inside the flight deck, ready to get us the hell out of here the instant our mission is complete. I nod and give her a small smile of encouragement. She acknowledges the gesture with a smile in return, and raises her hand to her temple in a mock salute.

There is no one waiting in the bay to meet us. Unusual. Their security protocols are tight enough that we'd anticipated an armed escort but something else must be keeping the soldiers busy. The dock controller didn't sound overly alarmed, but I can almost taste the panic and disorder that's happening somewhere on the station. Whatever the cause for the alert, it's well timed.

As we cross the bay, Brady snaps his fingers. Once he has all of our attention, he points to his throat mic, indicating that it's time to switch them on. By pressing the throat radio sensors against the trachea, we're able to speak much more quietly than normal and still transmit clearly to each other. If there are listening devices around, they won't be able to pick up what we're saying.

Brady's voice carries through my earpiece: "Once we're in the debrief room, we'll split into our teams. Strahan, Bodie, and Erikson, you sweep holding cells alpha through echo, we'll take the rest. If we don't find the crew, we start sweeping the labs."

He's not saying anything we don't already know. This is the plan we decided on days ago, but hearing it spoken now that we're inside the Fortress gives it a heavy finality.

Our group steps into the debrief room, everyone working hard to appear relaxed. As the door sweeps closed behind us, the high reverberating octaves of an alarm erupt throughout the complex. Beside me, Vitruzzi inhales sharply. Adrenaline surges through my body, flooding my motor and sensory neurons in a building storm that will soon settle into a slow drip until this thing is done. The sound of the team breathing around me is loud, rhythmic and heavy, but aside from Vitruzzi's first breath, no one sounds panicked. Looking to my left, Strahan's pupils dilate with the same intent focus as my own. We are ready. I reach forward and input the code that unlocks the debrief room, opening out into the bowels of the Fortress.

Instantly swinging my carbine barrel out and down the left side of the corridor, I glance quickly in both directions. The hallway is clear. Looking back over my shoulder, I give the rest of them a quick nod, and we begin advancing in bounds up the corridor. A set of stairs at the end will take us to level two and the first set of holding cells. Vitruzzi, Brady, and Desto will check these and the rest of us will continue up one more flight to the last five cells. Level three is also where the biological and chemical laboratories are located. Part of me hopes we don't have to search them. Christ knows what we might find inside.

We reach the end of the hallway without seeing anyone and race up the stairwells. Entering the third floor corridor, Bodie trains his rifle down its length. The alarms continue to bounce back and forth against the walls, but there's no sign of other people. According to the disc, SOP in a code five or higher security breach is for non-security personnel to evacuate to a safety chamber on an upper level. If that's where this section's personnel are, the security breach must be severe. Good.

A rumbling boom thuds from behind us, sounding in or near the debrief room. The prisoners must be loose. We don't slow, continuing up the flight to the first level of cells.

The first door is a quick jog down the corridor. Strahan inputs the pass code and it slides open on its track. Simultaneously, we realize we're not looking into a holding cell but into some kind of anteroom, like a guard station. This wasn't in the holograph. What other surprises will we find?

Two chairs are parked in front of a control console. A one-way window looking into an empty cell beyond dominates the far wall. Strahan gets on his mic. "Vitruzzi, Brady, be careful. There's a security antechamber for the holding cells. Over."

Vitruzzi's voice comes back. "Roger. We just discovered that. Let's just hope there aren't any more surprises. Find anyone? Over."

"Negative."

"All right, keep moving."

We exit and race to the next door, ten meters down the corridor. Strahan reaches for the keypad just as the door starts sliding open on its own. With reflexes as taut as overstretched wires, Bodie swings his rifle around and shoots the exiting soldier point-blank in the face, then drops to a knee and fires at another soldier inside as he jumps off his chair. As a bullet tears through his chest wall, a sadly comical expression of surprise affixes itself permanently to the dying man's features. Ensuring no one else is inside, the three of us leap into the room and pull the body of the first soldier through the door with us.

The window to the holding cell is grayed out, not allowing us to see what's behind it. Bodie leans over the control console, searching for the function that will clear it or open the door to let us inside. In a few seconds, he finds it and the glaze begins to dissipate.

A row of stacked bunks line one wall. A lean woman with a galaxy of black curls spread around her lies on the closest, her head turned away from us. A short man who looks as if he could single-handedly trounce a squad of wrestlers stands with his eyes fixed on the one-way window. His jaw is bruised and his lip swollen, and his fists are balled into bludgeons with knuckles that look as if they've been through a shredder. He can't see us, but his rigid stance indicates that he heard Bodie's shots. On another bunk, a small woman with dark brown hair sits upright, also staring at the window.

But no David.

"Karl!" Bodie cries.

Strahan presses the speaker on the guards' console. "Doug, Zeta, Jade—it's Karl and Bodie. We're going to get you out of here."

Instantly, the woman on the bunk jumps to her feet and looks toward the window. Both of her eyes are surrounded by dark bruises shot through with shades of green as if she's been in a hell of a fight. She squints through the remaining swelling and half whispers, "Oh my god, how did you . . .?"

Still on the mic, Bodie says, "Did you think we'd leave you here?"

The smile that spreads across her face is huge. The man, also smiling, responds, "Took you long enough."

Strahan busily cycles through the security codes for the door while I take position by the entrance, ready for anyone who tries to come in.

Bodie stays on the mic. "Are you hurt, any of you? Can everyone walk?"

"We're all okay," Zeta answers. "Just get us out of here."

What's taking Strahan so long? I glance back and see a laser reader buzz to life on the console. "Dammit!" Strahan growls. "Biosensor. We need a hand. Bodie, help me lift this guy. Quick."

They grab the man who was shot in the face by both arms and drag him back to the console. Strahan holds his limp hand inside the wavering red field but nothing happens. He curses and cycles through the operations appearing on the console as precious seconds slip away. I can almost hear a clock ticking.

"What's the problem?"

"I don't—wait! It won't open unless it reads a pulse." He reaches out and grabs the other soldier, laying his fingers against the inside of the man's wrist.

"Anything?" Bodie asks.

Karl's strained grin is almost a sneer as he nods. Yanking the guard's arm violently, he brings his hand up to the sensor. The red light wavers for a moment then turns green. Steel bolts on the security door retract and it slides open.

The three prisoners rush into the guardroom, their expressions a mixture of disbelief and joy.

"Where are C.M. and Kazaki?" Strahan asks.

"Dead," the older woman says.

Bitter sadness tightens their features momentarily, then melts into acceptance. Gratitude that we've found anyone at all will come later, if there is a later.

Facing the woman who'd spoken, I ask, "We're also looking for another prisoner. A man named Erikson. David Erikson. Have you seen him?"

She looks at me curiously. "I haven't seen any others. It's just us."

It feels as if a giant vacuum sucks my heart straight from my chest, collapsing my chest wall in the process and making me breathless.

Then the man says, "No, I saw a guy when they brought us in here. Couple hours ago. They were taking him somewhere on a gurney."

My voice is almost a whisper. "What did he look like?"

"I didn't see much. He had reddish hair like yours, and he looked like he was beat to hell. His eyes were all jacked up."

"Was he alive?"

"I don't know."

I don't know . . . the words chip through my composure as if they were daggers of ice. "Do you know where they took him?"

"No. No idea. I'm sorry."

"V, we've found them. Over." Strahan presses on with the mission.

"Everyone?"

"Just Zeta, Jade, and Doug. The rest didn't make it."

"What about Erikson's brother?"

"We don't know where he is. You haven't seen him?"

"No."

I break into the transmission. "Vitruzzi, I'm going to sweep the labs. I'm not leaving until I know something."

There's a pause. No doubt Vitruzzi is questioning whether she's willing to add more to the risks we're already taking by spending time we don't have searching for David. Then: "We're on our way up to your level. Is everyone mobile?"

"Roger."

"We'll start aft and meet you in the center. Out."

Bodie and Strahan hand extra weapons to Zeta and Mason. Strahan takes point and risks a quick glance outside the guardroom door. He gives us a nod and begins moving down the hall. Bodie immediately follows, then Zeta. Mason goes next. Before I bring up the rear, I turn to see why the short woman hasn't moved out. She is visibly shaking and pale, scared shitless. I don't have time to babysit, so I strip the Mini-Derg from my shin holster and push it into her hands. My face is inches away from hers. "Do you want to get out of here?"

Her eyes, already wide, bulge. *Goddammit, where's your survival instinct?* "Do you want to live?!" I have to be harsh, make her mad, make her realize she doesn't have time to be afraid.

She nods.

"All right." Remembering her name, I add, "That's good, Jade. 'Cause if you're ever going to see the light of day, you better move your ass and keep that gun up. Do you understand?"

She nods again with more energy. Checking again to see if the corridor is still empty, I squeeze the girl's arm—she can't be more than seventeen—and nudge her out the door.

Moving in a ragged formation, we cover the last three holding cells, all empty. The corridor opens up into a semicircle at the end, like a stadium. The schematics show the labs branching off from this central area, but there's little cover inside that nexus. For now, it's clear and we rush to the first lab.

The room is easily as large the *Sphynx*'s cargo bay with a door at the far end leading into a smaller storage room. Nothing moves inside and the lab is dark except for the illumination of several workstation VDUs in rows along the room's center.

I grab Strahan's elbow. "There are four labs on this level just as big. We need to split up if we're going to cover them quickly."

"All right. Bodie, you four check out the next lab." Pressing his throat mic, he says, "V, what's your position?"

It's Brady who answers, "We're taking fire! Stuck in the elevator at the far end of level two. They can't get in, but it's disabled. It's going to take us a few minutes to get to you. Desto is trying to rig it to move."

"Dammit," he mutters.

"Strahan, you and the others watch your asses. It's not the soldiers, it's the prisoners. They're rampaging."

"Fuck." This time he curses loudly. "We need to get down to level two and help them."

I'm *not* giving up the search for David, even if I'm doing it on my own. Strahan shoots me a look, reading my face. With a tiny shake of the head, he turns to the rest. "You four, take the stairs and flank the shooters, but watch your backs. Security could be on us in any minute. Try to get the rest of the crew up here to help cover these labs. Aly, I'll stick with you." He turns back to Bodie. "Let V know you're coming. Let's move."

I'm not expecting the wave of relief that washes over me. Having someone with me is good; having Strahan is ten times better. David's still got a chance, if he's alive.

They take off at a run down the corridor to the stairwell we'd come up. Strahan gives me a nod, and we duck into the lab and scrub the room, finding no one. It's abandoned and it looks as if they left in a hurry. The consoles and lab equipment are still running and several tubes with who knows what kind of biospecimens rest in containers on a few counters. As we approach the door to exit, a noise from outside alerts us that we're no longer alone. Quickly, we crouch behind a nearby cabinet, securing clean fields of fire to the doorway.

"I just need to grab a few things. Won't take a minute."

The sound of that voice throws me, and it takes me a second to realize why. It's Vilbrandt. I'd almost forgotten about him, but the fact he's here now confirms that Rajcik is too. I glance toward Strahan, and the look of contempt on his face makes it clear that he recognizes the voice too. Two sets of footsteps enter the room.

"What's in here that's so important?"

My eyes widen at the sound of the other voice. Ortiz!

"Things! Things that your boss wants! Now please be quiet and let me find what I need."

We stay kneeling silently behind our cover as objects are shoved quickly and haphazardly out of the way while he searches. The Nova is in the station's fore, stored in one of the weapons labs. What could be so important to Rajcik that he would send the scientist to this end? The answer is only too obvious and I stifle a shudder of revulsion. Rajcik wants Vilbrandt to bring back whatever feculent biowarf specimens he's been developing. That kind of shit brings limited interest on the black market. There are still buyers, but maybe Rajcik's not planning to sell it. If I know him, he'll put it to more personal use. Maybe dose the drinking water of an Admin office complex, or just wipe out a military base. With the right resources, Rajcik's brutality has no limits.

I look back toward Strahan, wondering what he's thinking. I have no problem shooting Vilbrandt, in my book he's the lowest form of life, but Ortiz is another matter. She's committed her share of crimes, the same as I have, but she's never displayed the lack of human feeling, or conscience, that some of the others in my old crew have. Inside, she's not a monster, and maybe she would rather help me find David than continue to work with Rajcik. If I can talk to her, maybe I can turn her.

Strahan readies his pistol, preparing to stand and fire. Before he can, Ortiz says, "Drop that shit, Vilbrandt. You're not taking it."

A quick look around the edge of the cabinet shows Ortiz standing in a marksman's pose with her carbine aimed at Vilbrandt's head. He's facing her with several sealed tubes held up and his lips pulled back from his teeth in rabid hate.

"Don't be stupid. Drop it? Do you have any idea what would happen to both of us?" His question is followed by silence, and he continues, "Your boss wants it. You're going to help me get it."

"No, you're wrong about that. I'm—"

Before she can finish the sentence, gunfire erupts in the hallway outside. Instantly, I crouch lower, bracing against the cabinet, and lose visibility of the lab. A pistol fires inside the room, and there's a heaving *gghhhhht!* sound, as if someone got the wind knocked out of them. Before either Strahan or I can move, running footsteps enter and another shot is fired. This time there's the unmistakable sound of someone's head opening up and spilling its contents at peak velocity against the floor and walls. People are yelling, their voices moving down the corridor outside, but the room is quiet. Whoever entered is still here.

"Strahan?"

"Vitruzzi!"

She's standing inside the open door, guns up and ready to fire, looking out into the hallway. At the sound of her name, she jerks her head back toward where Strahan has leapt out of hiding.

"Where's Erikson?" she asks, and I step into the open.

Ortiz lays to my right, blood burbling from her chest. Vilbrandt's body has been blown backward and flops awkwardly over a desk. One fist is clenched around a pistol grip and blood flows in a growing pool beneath him. I didn't need to see what happened, experience explains everything. The scientist had been crafty enough to hide a pistol and shot Ortiz when the gunfire from the corridor distracted her and Vitruzzi fired on him when she came in. The vials he had been holding lay scattered around his body, unbroken.

"We have to move. Venus has been picking up transmissions from security and they're on their way toward us. They could lock down the docks any second and we won't be able to launch."

Strahan bounds around the equipment, ready to get the hell out of here. Despite the urgency, I squat down next to Ortiz. She'd been the closest thing to a friend I had on Rajcik's crew and something about her going out this way triggers compassion for her I didn't know I had.

Her eyes open when I put a hand on her arm and she recognizes me. "Aly." Blood speckles her lips as she whispers, "You've . . . got to stop him. Rajcik. You've got to . . ." She coughs and more blood erupts from her chest.

"I'm sorry, Ortiz."

"Listen." Somehow, she finds the strength to grab my hand. "He's going to drop the Nova on Tu-Tu-Tunis. Kill everyone."

My eyes widen. That sick bastard. "Why?"

"Crazy." A fog begins to dull her eyes and the blood seeping from the side of her mouth has become a dark, thick red. Her chest stops its desperate hitch to draw in air and I think she's gone, then her fingers tighten on mine again for a moment and she whispers, "He has . . . David."

"What? What?" But it's useless, she's dead.

Dropping the Nova on Tunis City? It's . . . exactly the kind of thing he would do. And he has David, just the way he'd promised. Rajcik's duplicity and craftiness and his ability to play multiple hands of poker at once are traits I've always recognized in him, admired even. How could I not have seen that he was playing T'Kai and maybe his own crew in the Nova job? He had certainly played David and I from the start. Do the rest of him know his plan? Do they care?

I look up and see both Vitruzzi and Strahan staring at me, their faces mirroring my own turmoil. Vitruzzi presses her mic. "Patrick, what's the situation?"

"Elevator is operational. Three squads are on the stairs headed for your level. Get down here now!"

As Brady finishes his sentence, a pistol report erupts inside the room. Strahan and Vitruzzi drop instantly, but I'm still crouched by Ortiz's body. Vitruzzi fires through the open doorway and the body of a prisoner falls inward, face down on the floor.

"Get to the elevator."

She covers the entrance, peering down the corridor. In a smooth motion, she brings one of her pistols to shoulder level and fires down the hallway, five, six, seven times. Then she turns back to the room and says something. Oddly, I can see her mouth moving, her eyes wide and emphatic, but I can't hear what she's saying. I feel as if I'm inside a thick plastic bag and nothing from the outside can penetrate. Hearing that David may still be alive has stunned me, making me realize how certain I'd been that he was already dead.

Vitruzzi's eyes shift from me to Strahan and she begins yelling more urgently, pointing at me, but it's as if her voice has been whipped away in a strong wind. Strahan's head snaps back and his eyes widen. I start to rise, but my leg refuses to hold me and I tumble forward, hitting the wall in front of me with my palm. He runs up beside me and kneels, his face inches from mine. "Aly, you're hit!"

Sound returns, bringing a searing shock of pain along with it that suddenly bursts from my left thigh. I look down and see a rip in my pants with blood oozing through, about six inches below my hip. "Fuck." My voice sounds much too calm.

"What's it look like, Karl?" Vitruzzi yells.

He leans forward and pulls the tatters of the rip apart, saying to me, "Shallow. Looks like it went through. Can you walk?"

"Yeah." Through numb lips. With gritted teeth and a timid nausea beginning to take hold of my stomach, I push myself up. No way is this going to stop me.

"Good." He yanks open a pocket in his vest, pulls out a field bandage, and deftly wraps it around my thigh, tying it off with a tight yank. "V, got anything to numb this with?"

She pulls a syringe from a med bag she carries and tosses it to us. Strahan rips through the packaging with his teeth and not bothering with delicacy, presses the needle into my thigh. "Dammit! Careful!" Searing pain rips through my wounded flesh and quickly begins receding to a suggestion.

He gives me a half grin that's calm and cool, not a normal expression for someone outnumbered by both Corps and criminals, all ready and willing to cut him down. "Let's get out of here."

Back in motion, we leapfrog up the corridor to the elevator, passing the bodies of the prisoners Vitruzzi shot. Brady holds the elevator doors open and the rest of the crew is lodged inside. Just as we reach it, we hear the stairwell door at the other end of the hallway slam against the wall.

Vitruzzi steps inside first, crowding against the others when a sudden, explosive *WHOOMPFFF!* echoes throughout the complex. The floor bucks beneath us and the elevator jumps slightly on its rails. Immediately, thick black smoke begins pouring into the corridor from every direction.

"Get in!" Brady yells.

Strahan and Vitruzzi cram into the elevator. I don't.

"What are you doing, come on!" Bodie cries.

"I'm not leaving."

Strahan pushes to the front of the elevator. "You're going to find your brother?"

Nodding, I respond simply, "I can't leave. He's all I've got."

"I'll help," he says, and steps off the elevator, followed by Desto. "We're with you, Aly. We've come this far."

I can't speak, my disbelief more paralyzing than shock. But I know I probably won't get much further alone. My voice shakes as I finally respond, "Rajcik will be in the docks at the front of the station. Nearest the weapons labs." Even while studying how to infiltrate the Fortress, I'd also been calculating what his plans might be. I knew he would never give up, just as I knew instinctively that our paths would cross again.

Vitruzzi scowls, considering the situation. She knows I won't change my course, but she won't abandon Desto or Strahan either. Not when there is any chance, no matter how small. "You've got twenty minutes to get back to the prisoner transport. We'll be waiting." The elevator door closes.

The smoke filled corridor gives us enough cover to duck into the nearest lab before the advancing soldiers see us, and we hunker together for a minute to sketch out a plan.

"The ninth floor is the most direct line to the bow. The connecting corridor, if it's still accessible, is going to have the least amount of cover. If we move toward the docks near the weapons labs and don't run into any security, it should take us five minutes." Strahan looks me directly in the eye, the message *we'll never make it in time* stamped on his face. He's probably right, but that's not going to stop me.

The squad securing our level runs by, not bothering to clear the rooms, apparently just trying to reach the elevator and get away from the smoke-filled hallway, a perfect cloak for an ambush.

"I'll take point. Karl, you get our six," Desto says. He glances outside and breaks for the stairs with us on his heels.

We scramble up the stairwell and reach level nine without encountering anyone. Running fast now, taking chances we wouldn't ordinarily take, we speed directly down the corridor as a unit. There's no time to check if each feeder hallway is clear, and the corridor itself is wide, designed for high traffic. We may as well be running down the middle of a bull's-eye. Desto skates past the opening of an adjoining hallway and a bullet glances from his armor, blowing puffs of fiber into my face. I'm right beside him, running as hard as I can to keep up, and have to duck across the opening, firing blindly as I go by. Strahan doesn't even slow down, skidding across the opening on his knees, firing into the squad racing to catch us. I reach back to grab his hand and pull him back to his feet. We keep running, blowing our lungs out to make it to the next hatch before they can get behind us and fire up the corridor.

We make it.

Strahan stops long enough to disable the entry mechanism with a ball of E-10 wax and catches up as Desto and I reach an intersection. Desto peers around the corner, then jumps backward. With his back pressed against the wall, he signals to us by sliding one hand under the other. *Find some cover!* Then waves a hand in front of his eyes. *Get out of sight!*

There's a doorway right beside me and I slip inside, expecting them both to follow but they don't. The door clicks quietly closed, cutting off sounds from the hallway. Where are they? For a moment the only thing I hear is my breathing, then an unfamiliar voice cries out, "Contact!" and shots begin echoing down the hallway. I hear someone running, more shooting coming from right outside the door, and a stampede of boots rolling down the corridor like thunder. Shadows pass under the gap at the bottom of the doorway. I tense up and press myself harder into the wall, forcing my hand to stay away from the doorknob. It would be suicide to jump into the middle of them.

As soon as the footsteps begin to fade, I try to raise the other two in my throat-mic: "Strahan, Desto, what's your position? Do you copy? Over."

There's no response for a long second, then Desto says, "I sweet talked them into following me, but they couldn't keep up. I'm a floor above you now. I'll meet you at the hangar. Over."

"Copy. Strahan?"

"Right outside." He presses the door open with the barrel of his rifle. "Let's go."

I don't know how he gave them the slip, but the soldiers took Desto's bait and have all double-timed out of the area. Moving quickly, we cover the last hundred meters to the connecting corridor. Luck is with us—it's clear. We take the speedwalking belt running along one side and make it to the far end in just a few breaths. The weapons labs are a floor below us, immediately adjacent to the docking hangars.

An empty guard booth at the end of the corridor provides enough cover for us to stop for a few seconds to catch our breath. The bandage Strahan wrapped around my thigh is holding tight and the wound is barely bleeding. I can't feel a thing. Strahan crouches inside the booth and activates his mic. "Desto, where are you?"

"Coming up on the first hangar, level seven. Looks like there has been some activity. I'm looking at one, maybe two squads of wasted soldiers. Over."

We exchange a knowing look. *Rajcik's work.*

"Hang tight. We're still on nine. We'll meet you at hangar zero-one. Out."

With a nod, we move out, running left toward the end of the corridor where another stairwell will take us down. I bang through the door and train my carbine down the shaft. No one. Strahan's right behind me and we begin descending.

Passing by level eight, my feet barely touch the steps. The sound of the door swinging open above me causes me to jerk to a sudden stop on the next landing and nearly topple over the side. Gripping the rail, I spin around and see a squad pouring through the door between Strahan and I. He manages to come to a stop a few stairs above them and trains his rifle at the three who have crammed onto the landing, but who knows how many are on the other side of the door? I begin reversing direction back up the stairs to get a clean line of fire, but Strahan suddenly turns and starts running back up. The sound of his boots on the metal stairs draws their attention, inciting them to follow. Strahan's voice comes through my earpiece: "Keep going, Aly. I'll shake them and meet you in the hangar. Over."

They don't have a firing solution on him and he has a solid lead. I press my back against the wall to stay out of sight and continue to slip down the stairs. Strahan wouldn't tell me to keep going if he isn't certain he has an out, but that doesn't stop my pulse from going into overdrive. I have the advantage with every soldier in this section probably chasing Strahan and Desto, but now I'm on my own. There are no guarantees in this, no matter how good at the game we are. It's possible that I'll be able to slip into the hangar unnoticed. But then what? Will Rajcik still be there?

Quietly cracking the door onto level seven, I study the corridor and go through. Motorized transports line up along niches in the wall along the wide corridor, ready to transport newly off-loaded supplies to their destinations throughout the station. Dead soldiers crowd the hall a few meters away, their blood streaking the walls. Yet another advantage, but there's no pleasure in seeing the carnage. Judging by the burned and mangled condition of their corpses, whoever did this used an explosive.

"Desto? Strahan? Anyone copy? Over." No answer. Maybe they're already in the hangar.

The wall separating the corridor from the docking hangars is a meter thick and built from high-strength, low-alloy steel with a melting point of over 3,000 degrees, more than capable of protecting the complex from the engine blowback of incoming and outgoing ships. A service tunnel into hangar zero-alpha opens up just beyond the pile of corpses. It has been nine minutes since we left the bio labs, leaving eleven minutes until the crew dusts off and disappears for good. It doesn't matter. I'm not leaving without my brother. He wouldn't leave me.

My VDU displays the saved pass code and I step to the side while the door slides open. Thick blue smoke pours from the gap, enveloping me and creating a fuming cloud in the corridor. Pushing away from the doorway, I fall flat against the floor waiting for a fire to rush out but none does.

What the hell is going on? A fire inside one of the hangars should trigger the Fortress's hull security response, completely disabling all of the doors leading in and out. If the integrity of a hangar is compromised, the entire complex could by destroyed, ripped to pieces by the vacuum of space. Somehow, the internal security defenses have been disabled. The station has taken a lot of damage from the prisoners, but not that much. It has to be Rajcik.

Blaring fire alarms inside the hangar slice through the air, mixing with the ever-present dull *whump* of the general alarm and setting my teeth on edge. Tendrils of the smoke caught in the service tunnel trail out and a quick look through the doorway reveals that it's empty. Still, I can't see much of the hangar beyond. A rotating red strobe light fixed on the entryway roof flashes in circles, giving the tunnel a crazed funhouse kind of effect. I'll be target practice if anyone is guarding the entrance from hangar-side, but I don't have time to look for another way in. Keeping the AK-80 stock pressed firmly to my shoulder and crouching low, I run for everything I'm worth to the other side.

Caustic vestiges of smoke line my lungs, but nothing stops me from reaching the bay. Two parked track tugs sit beyond the entryway, one partially obscuring it, the other about thirty paces forward and to my right. Random crates and barrels are pushed into groups and a catwalk with a control pod for maneuvering a ceiling-mounted crane traces the wall on the bay's left side. Clouds of smoke rise toward the ceiling but no fire. The tracker offers good coverage and I lunge toward it.

The best vantage of the bay floor is the catwalk, but the tracker's left runner conceals me while my eyes adjust to the auxiliary lights flashing in yellow strobes on the ceiling. Climbing up the ladder to the cab lets me peer over the side to see what lies beyond. The *Temptation* sits near the launch track airlock.

How did he get clearance to land? It's hard to believe a ship with the *Temptation*'s notoriety could, but it hardly matters at this point. The ship sits in the middle of the dock, loading door still open and engines cycling in preparation for launch. There is no movement around the ship visible from where I hide and the flight deck screens face the airlock. Whoever's inside the cockpit, probably Thompson, won't be able to spot me. The dock control room is about sixty paces to my right. Either Rajcik or Yadav must be in there prepping the interior airlock to open so the *Temptation* can enter the launch track. Is the Nova already on board?

Carefully climbing back down to ground level, I prepare to move in closer to the ship. The only other crewmember is Fedchenko; Rajcik wouldn't have had time to enlist more cohorts, but he could be anywhere. It's just me against four. Even if I try to raise Strahan and Desto, the mic is useless in this kind of noise.

As if reading my mind, the shrieking alarms cut out abruptly. The good news is short-lived, however, as the dock control room door opens and Rajcik comes through, staring in my direction.

And he's not alone.

He pushes my brother in front of him to use as a bullet-stopper, one of his muscular arms locked around David's neck and the other jamming a Sinbad into his temple. Before thinking of the consequences, I shout, "David!"

Rajcik's arm tightens around David's throat, almost jerking him off his feet and making him unable to respond. Deadly calm, he says, "Aly, you never fail to impress me."

I can't risk the shot. If I expose myself, Rajcik will drop David before I can pull the trigger and I'll either hit my brother or miss altogether. Dammit, Strahan, Desto, get your asses up here now!

Pressing my back into the tug's track, I shout, "You don't have to do this, János! I don't give a fuck about the bomb or the money, just let him go!"

An icy chuckle wafts across the bay to me. The only other sound comes from the *Temptation*'s engines as they slowly gain momentum, building energy for flight. "Negotiations don't work with me, Aly. When will you learn? You and your brother have caused me far too much trouble, and I want retribution."

I risk a glance around the track. He's dragging David toward the ship, his eyes fixed in my direction. David's eyes are blackened and still swollen, but they're open. But he's moving strangely, swiveling his head left and right, squinting as if he's trying to locate the sound of my voice. His eyes never seem to focus.

Rajcik shakes him. "Go on, David. Tell her what I plan to do with the Nova. I want Aly to know before you both die."

My line of sight is cut off as they move behind the track vehicle and continue to close the gap to the ship. If they get on board, there's no way I'll be able to reach them. Sweat drips from my forehead, running down my cheeks and neck into my shirt. Not a muscle in my body relaxes and my carbine stays steady at shoulder level. I have a window of about eight meters from when they become visible on the other side of the tug to when they'll be walking up the ship's loading ramp. Those eight meters are my only chance of stopping Rajcik.

"Tell her!" Rajcik yells.

David's voice, strained by the pressure of Rajcik's tight grip, cuts through the smoke. "He's going to wipe out Tunis City. There was never going to be any extortion. He's just a sick fuck and—" He's cut off.

Christ, he knew? Goddammit, David, you should have told me! If you had, we wouldn't be here right now! This is no time to get angry; I need to get in position for the shot. I hear Ortiz's dying words again, *"He's going to drop the Nova . . . kill everyone."* But how had David known? The reason Rajcik wanted us dead is finally clear. We never would have helped him get the holodisc and steal the Nova if we'd known what he intended to do with it. We would have done anything to stop him, and he knows it. I don't know how David found out or how Rajcik knew he had, but he's seconds away from paying the price for not shooting Rajcik when he had the chance. Unless I can do it first.

I'm going to kill you, Rajcik. If it's the last thing I do.

"There you have it, Aly! Now you can see what a monumental pain in the ass you two have been to me! But I think we're done now. Get out here and say goodbye to your brother." It almost sounds as if Rajcik is laughing, but as they move around the other side of the vehicle, there is no grin on his face. His black eyes are fierce and his lips are pulled back from his gleaming incisors in a snarl. Dragging David along, he shuffles backward toward the open hatch of the *Temptation.* I catch a glimpse of someone's rifle barrel from inside the hatch, providing Rajcik with more cover.

There's a noise above me, a sharp gonging sound like metal on metal. Everyone looks toward it simultaneously. Strahan!

David drives his head back into Rajcik's face and a wet, smacking sound reports across the bay. Then he lunges forward toward me, staying low, and I open fire. A fine, red mist of blood erupts from Rajcik's shoulder as he takes a bullet, but the sonofa-bitch is so fucking fast. He starts running before David gets more than a few steps away and quickly takes cover inside the *Tempta-tion*. Strahan fires a screen of bullets from above me, keeping the shooter inside the ship from getting a clear shot while David runs for his life across the bay.

"RIGHT HERE! I'M HERE!" The sound of my voice helps him make it to the tug in a blind shambling run that proves his vision is jacked up, and I grab him by the shirt, pulling him to safety. Strahan continues to keep Rajcik and the shooter inside the ship busy. Holding David by the arm, I start to run, pulling him toward the tunnel to the other side. Almost the instant we break from cover, automatic rifle reports issue from the dock control room. I leap backward, still holding David and he lands nearly on top of me, just as bullets bounce off the steel floor in front of our feet. We're covered from every angle.

Leaning back against the tracks again, I crane my head up to see Strahan on the catwalk. He has good coverage of the entire dock and is well hidden behind a stack of cargo bins. Whoever's inside the dock control room is completely concealed and has a perfect line of fire between where we're hidden and the tunnel I came in through. Rajcik, firing from the *Temptation*'s loading ramp, also has a direct line of fire at us if we leave the concealment of the tug. Strahan can't hold off both of them and David can't see to either fire or run to the tunnel. Basically, we're fucked.

Tapping my mic, I whisper, "Desto, do you read me? What's your position? Over."

Silence.

The sickening realization that Desto is probably dead washes over me, but I squash it. I have to. Brushing the sweat soaked hair from my face, I call Strahan, "I'm going to try and drive this track-er to the exit. When I stop, see if you can make it to the other side and help us get out of here."

"Roger."

Cutting through the ties on David's wrists, I realize how thin he's become. His clothes hang from his skeletal frame and I'm surprised he even had the strength to run for cover. "Can you see at all?"

"Not a goddamn thing," he says, and then adds, "How the hell did you get here?"

"I'll tell you later. Look, we're hiding behind a track tug. There's a handhold about a meter above you, by your right hand. You're leaning against the step. I'm going to go up first and get it started. When I yell, try to get up. I'll help. You ready?"

"Yeah."

I scramble up the tracker's side and into the open interior. It's too high up for anyone on the ground to get a shot at me, but as soon as they hear the engine crank up, rifle fire begins clacking off the sides. The doors are reinforced and nothing but a direct, level shot is going to get through them. Leaning out from the open left-side door, I call down to David. He reaches up, hand scrambling along the side and I direct it to the handhold. Grimacing, he pulls himself onto the cab's floor, keeping his body low and compact.

Reversing fast, I force the tug into the wall and we come to a shuddering stop. Bullets continue to bounce off its thick tracks, having no effect, but our angle is good; we're between the dock control room and the exit tunnel. The *Temptation* now has the only line of fire and Strahan won't ease up to let them get a shot.

I launch over the side and direct David's feet to the ladder rungs, helping him down. "We've got to run like hell. Just hold onto my shirt."

He nods and we take off at a sprint through the tunnel entrance. The safety door at the other end is still open and I push him against the wall while I check the corridor. Clear.

The sound of rifle fire from the hangar stops. We pause at the end of the tunnel for a few seconds, hoping to hear Strahan. Seconds later, his voice echoes down the corridor from my right. "Hold your fire!"

Appearing through the smoke about twelve meters down the hall, he races to us and engages his mic: "Vitruzzi, Brady, do you copy?"

"Where the hell are you, Karl?"

"Look, we found Erikson's brother, but we're still at the loading docks. We need ten more minutes."

"Dammit, Strahan! You've got eight! Out."

He takes one of David's arms, ready to run.

"Wait," I say. Strahan stops and turns, his expression tense and expectant. "You take David back to the ship. I'll meet you there."

The disbelief on his face might be funny in other circumstances. No, probably not.

David says, "Aly, what are you talking about?"

Strahan looks as if he wants to shoot me himself. "No fucking way. We've got to *go*."

"No! If Rajcik gets out of here with the Nova, a lot of people are going to die!"

"No way, Aly, there's no time!" Strahan argues. "Don't be so fucking stubborn. For once—"

I grab him, both of my hands gripping the straps of his equipment vest, and shout, "He's going to detonate it, Karl! He'll kill millions! I can't let that happen. Take David back to the MCACS, okay? If I'm not there in time, just leave. Don't risk it. I'll find another way out."

David starts to argue, "Aly, no . . ."

"Just go!"

He reaches blindly toward me, his eyes somehow able to find mine and lock onto them. I grab his searching hand. Strahan studies me for a bitter second, grabs David's shoulder, and turns to run. With a final squeeze, David turns away and they double-time down the corridor.

TWENTY-THREE

Gulping a lungful of acrid air, I make my way back down the service tunnel into the hangar. Even Rajcik won't suspect I'm crazy enough to come after him. He's probably dead certain that we're headed toward the escape we should be making—that Strahan and David *are* making. Right now, that's my only advantage. Creeping deftly along the wall, I can't make out any movement in the bay. The smoke that had hung like a thin fog has diminished to a minute tendril, more an oily taste in the back of my throat than something visible. There had been no indication of chemical fire retardant self-ejecting in any of the sectors we've been through, so the fire, wherever it is, must be burning itself out.

Crouched low, nearly squatting, I reach the end of the tunnel and run for the cover of the tracker. The voice telling me I'll never see my brother, or any of them, again makes my hands feel shaky as I train the carbine around the tracker's side, looking for my next move. The auxiliary lights still spin in sinister yellow flashes, but the bay is clear of my old crew. At least from what I can see. Climbing into the tracker's cab, the sound of machinery suddenly catches my attention and I duck low behind the control apparatus. The only thing I can see is the ceiling, and finally the thing I'd missed all along becomes obvious.

The Nova hovers fifteen meters above the bay floor, suspended by a network of steel chains from the ceiling crane. Parked directly beneath it, a four-wheeled electric cart is prepped to carry it on board the *Temptation*. As I watch the weapon's slow descent, my eyes track to the catwalk and the man standing at the controls. It's Fedchenko, and he's completely focused on the bomb. He doesn't know I'm here.

The Nova is surprisingly small, only about two meters in length, cylindrical in shape and narrow enough that two grown men could reach around it by linking their arms. The housing is a dark, burnished steel divided into two segments. I know from the schematics that Rajcik had obtained before the operation that the bigger segment contains the triggering mechanisms. The missile seems so small and nonthreatening that it's hard to imagine it could ever cause the devastation we'd been warned of. Taking careful aim from inside the cab, I wait for the crane to descend farther. When I pick off Fedchenko, I don't want the thing falling.

Tock, tock! I double tap him in the head and as predicted, his body hurls forward, shorting out the crane's circuit board and sending the Nova into a fast descent. It lands squarely on the cart. With Fedchenko, MacCready, and Ortiz down, that leaves Yadav and Thompson, along with Rajcik.

The sound of someone running and then—*holyshit!*—a grenade lands nearly in my lap. I fling myself back through the cab door, landing next to the tug and tucking myself into a tight ball. *KUR-RUMPPFFF!* The blast goes right over the top of me, bursting outward and upward. With my position compromised, I geronimo out from behind the ruined vehicle straight for the cover of the four-wheeled cart sitting between me and the *Temptation.*

Reaching relative safety, I squeeze myself against one of the rear wheels, keeping my carbine at shoulder level. On the other side of the cart, the *Temptation* sits on the bay floor like a menacing predator, loading ramp still open and engines still cycling up. Approximately six meters of open bay lie between it and me. If my guess is correct, my three ex-shipmates are now all aboard, waiting for me to expose myself.

I just start to catch my breath when the cart begins to roll slowly toward the ship. Shit! Must be controlled by remote. All Rajcik has to do is direct it onto the *Temptation,* launch, and he's free.

Not if I stop him.

I fire into the vehicle's tires, first the rear, then the front. Its engine continues to strain against the drag, so I grab a metal rod lying in a tool bin mounted on its side and thrust it into the cart's local control box. Sparks erupt in my face, momentarily blinding me and dotting my skin with burning pinpricks. One side of its wheels makes another half revolution, forcing it into a lopsided turn, and with a whining buzz, it dies. With smug self-satisfaction, I imagine Rajcik inside the ship, wondering how he's going to get the Nova on board. He can't get a shot at me from the ship, and wouldn't want to fire at the Nova anyway. With the bomb as my cover, I'm at the perfect position to ghost anyone who shows so much as an arm outside the loading ramp. David and Karl should be at the MCACS by now. I have maybe five minutes left before they launch and then I'll be stranded on the Fortress with Corps fighters guaranteed to be on their way. My momentary smugness disappears like an empty promise. I need to get the hell of out here.

As I gauge my chances of making it back to the service tunnel, the hydraulic hum of the *Temptation*'s ramp catches my attention. In an eternity that lasts maybe ten seconds, it climbs back up into the ship's belly and seals shut. He's leaving! Relief pours over me like a shower of hot sand, instantly filling me with a crazy excitement, as if maybe this will all be over soon. Rajcik might get away, but at least he's not taking his lethal payload with him.

It's time for me to go. Standing and setting my sights on nothing but the service tunnel entrance, I'm preparing to run like hell when my guts explode in a white-hot nebula of pain. It's as if a phosphorous grenade has just detonated inside my torso. It isn't until I clutch my stomach, my carbine falling from my hands, that I hear the pistol report.

I didn't know it was possible to feel this much pain, and I suddenly understand what it's like to wish to be dead. Then it gets worse. Every thought, every instinct for survival, every driving force that's ever gotten me from one second to the next is suddenly wiped away by pure, visceral agony. All I'm capable of is standing, motionless, my hands gripped to my torso while blood backs up behind them and then starts to stream over the top in a crimson waterfall. A hand clamps onto my shoulder, twirls me around, and Rajcik leers down at me. The look on his face is a demented mixture of serenity and rage.

"Aly, you just never quit, do you?"

I'm stunned, my guts bubbling, unable to speak.

He looks at the disabled cart carrying the dormant Nova, then back at me. "Still," he begins, his tone strangely magnanimous, "a lot of useless people will have you to thank for not being blown into oblivion. Too bad they'll never know, huh?"

Desperately, I look to where my carbine landed, but I'll never reach it before he shoots me again. My hands are plastered to my burning belly, the hot blood continuing to seep between my fingers like grisly lava. With tremendous effort, I reach up and jerk his hand violently from my shoulder, not wanting him to touch me. The movement takes the last of my strength. I would crumple to the floor except for his fist that flies out and squeezes painfully around my throat, cutting off the air I can't draw anyway because of the pain in my guts. Blood drips from his nose from where David had head-butted him, forming a gory mustache, which streaks down his jaw line. Holding me up and staring coldly into my eyes, he casually licks it from his lips as if savoring the taste. Before I can struggle, he jerks me forward and throws me into the floor like an empty sack.

I land on my back and draw air through my clenched teeth. It hurts. He stands above me, glaring. I try to tell him to rot in hell, but a spark of pain shoots from my belly up into my chest and I writhe on the floor, feeling my face contort from the agony. Drawing up into a fetal position, I'm helpless to do anything but watch as he opens a compartment on the Nova's sleek black housing and reaches inside.

Squinting my eyelids against the hot tears welling up, I hear him chuckle. His face grows deadly serious as he leans down over me. "I want you to know something, Aly. You're going to die right here on this floor. When this detonates, your body is going to be the first thing it destroys. You'll disintegrate and be blasted into space like so much human waste."

An uncontrollable shudder, not of fear but of pain, wracks me and makes him pause. He squats down and leans forward, pressing the barrel of his pistol against the floor as a prop. My eyes pick out the fact that he has blood caked under his thumbnail.

"In another nine minutes and thirty seconds, you won't feel a thing," he continues. "But when I find your brother, if he and your new friends manage to get away, he's going to feel *a lot*. His suffering is going to make what you're going through right now seem pleasant. That's my parting promise to you." He gives me a last look of almost fraternal pity, then stands up and walks across the bay to his ship. As he climbs back into the *Temptation*'s cockpit hatch, which he'd used to exit the ship and sneak up on me, the station's inner airlock doors engage and begin to part, allowing the ship to enter the launch tracks. Rajcik is going to escape, and I can do nothing to stop him now.

I need to warn the others. "Vitruzzi, if you're listening, get out of here. The Nova . . ." My throat convulses and I start to cough, another eruption of blood spurting from my ruined stomach. Getting it under control, I finish, "Get out of here. It's counting down."

There's no response, but I'm not going to die here on this floor. I won't give Rajcik the satisfaction. I might, just might, be able to make it to the MCACS. It's an impossible lie, but the thought gives me the motivation I need. I know it doesn't matter, but I don't want to be next to that thing when it blows. Trying to direct my attention away from the molten pain in my guts, I grab the sidewall of the cart's tire, reach for my carbine, and drag my body up into a standing position. Once on my feet and forced to hold my own weight up, pain and nausea twist through me in a secondary explosion. I double over, vomiting bright red blood, and see more blood pattering out of the hole in my torso and onto my boots. I'm not sure if the amount coming from my throat or out of my stomach is more disturbing. The red is so bright, glowing as if it really is composed of phosphorous.

The *Temptation* starts rolling down the launch tunnel. In seconds, the doors close behind it. It's just me and the bomb now, and I can feel my strength evaporating like so much smoke. Have to push hard, get away.

Staggering, I make it across the bay to the service entrance and lean against the smooth metal walls, already needing to rest. The corridor seems to be an endless tunnel blurring in and out of clarity. Slumping against the wall, feeling my insides leaking out, I search for the strength to start walking, or crawling, to the other end. The hatch is down there, and if I can get to the hatch, I can get away from the Nova.

The lights on the ceiling waver and pulse, getting darker with each beat. I've been standing here for less than five seconds, but it might as well be five years. I don't think I can make it.

My arms feel heavy and begin to go numb. Ordering myself to move forward, I push one leg out. As I rest my weight on it, it feels odd, as if my knees aren't bending the right way. I lean onto the leg anyway, grateful that it holds my weight, and will the next one forward. Something clanks beside me, but it sounds tinny and far away. Distractedly, my brain records that I've dropped the carbine. I can't pick it up—too weak. If I bend over I'll fall and that will be it.

Another step, then another. I stumble and brace against the wall with both hands. They leave a wide swath of blood behind. Not good. Warmth is spreading down my hip and thigh. I'm not going to look, just keep walking.

The pulsing lights are getting much darker. A couple more beats and I won't be able to see at all. Is this what dying feels like? Just blacking out and not waking up?

I trip over my own feet once more. But this time, my hands just slide along the metal corridor wall, the blood making them slick. I hit like a dropped corpse, my face banging into the grated floor. Its coldness presses into my cheek. It's not refreshing. It hurts.

Come on, Aly, come on. You got to keep moving.

Reaching out and digging my fingers into the grated floor, I grab and pull with all the strength I have left. I make about five centimeters. Just need a break. A short break.

I rest my cheek on the floor again. Air rushes up through the small squares made by the grate. There's an oily, faintly burned odor to it. My eyes fall closed.

Something wakes me up, or pulls me out of unconsciousness, I can't tell which. Noise. Clattering . . . no, tromping. Boots. They're moving fast. I just hope whoever it is kills me quickly. I don't care, just let me sleep.

"Aly? ALY! Oh shit!"

The runner's speed increases, and then I see Strahan's face above me. "Get . . . out. Nova . . . run," I whisper, feeling blood that had started to dry cracking on my lips.

"Jesus, Aly. I'm going to get you out of here! You're not dead yet!"

Yes, I am, I try to whisper, but then he's picking me up, and the radiation from a thousand suns bursts through me. And it all goes black.

SHRIEKING ALARMS AND LIGHTS. My eyes flutter open, everything around me in chaos. The only pain I feel is my splitting eardrums, as if the nerves in them are being ripped from my cranium. A voice, "ohmygod, it's going to hit us," filled with terror, "HOLD ONTO SOMETHING!" A giant *CRAAAASH!* and the sense of being hurled through space, as if gravity suddenly changed direction, everything around me flying through the air. As the world drains into darkness again, all I feel is relief.

PEOPLE SPEAKING, MURMURS THAT I can't understand. Then, something warm against my cheek, like breath. "Hang on, Aly. You're going to make it. You're strong. Strongest person I've ever met." David? No. Strahan.

LATER.

There's a sound, a low-key beep going off in a constant rhythm. Kinda soothing. I listen for a while before realizing I'm awake. How long have I been unconscious? It's too much effort to open my eyes. Just lay here. *Beep . . . beep . . . beep.* Eventually, the sound becomes annoying.

"Can someone turn that off?"

Air exchangers whispering. Pain everywhere. My nose, my throat, my chin, my guts. My eyes flicker open inside a dim room. In my peripheral vision, I see stands loaded with hanging bags of blood, saline, and other liquids, tubes dangling everywhere, connected to my body in different places. Thankfully, I sense drugs doing their work, dulling out everything, making the pain just an unwelcome visitor, not part of me.

A silhouette looms next to me. "I told you you weren't dead."

"Where's David?" I don't recognize my own voice. I sound like a breathless crow.

"He's okay. He's in the other med-station."

" . . . see him."

"Not yet. You've got to stay still for now. V says you've just started to recover. You need to rest, recuperate."

I have no strength to argue, even if I want to. "Thirsty."

"Aly, you've been shot in the stomach, so I can't give you anything to drink. But here." He rubs blessedly cool ice over my lips. The room seems as if it isn't there, just a gray backdrop. The only thing that comes into focus is Strahan.

" . . . crazy to come back for me."

"Yeah. You're rubbing off on me."

My eyelids start to rebel and slide closed. I sense him still standing next to me and I force them back open. His hands rest on the gurney, his features arranged intently, concerned, maybe even a little afraid.

"Karl."

"Yeah?"

"I . . . owe you."

A tragic grin spreads across his lips and his moist eyes gleam. "Not this time. We're even."

TWENTY-FOUR

Days, maybe a week, go by; I'm too in and out of it to be completely sure. I start waking up more and more, longer each time, my body healing while its monuments to pain shrink in achingly slow decrements. Almost every time I open my eyes, Strahan is there, asking me how I am, if he can get me anything. Vitruzzi monitors every pump, tube, and screen attached to me with clockwork diligence. Everyone visits. By the time we arrive at Agate Beach, most of my many questions are answered.

Why had Strahan come back for me? And how had we made it back to the MCACS before either Vitruzzi launched or the Fortress blew?

On our way back toward Agate Beach, I'm itching for another shot of morphine, sweating like a leaky faucet from the recurrent spasms of pain in my insides, when Desto comes by and fills in that part of the story for me.

About the same time I had persuaded Strahan and David to make a run for it back to the *Sphynx*, Desto finally managed to get back down to the seventh-floor hangar but was cornered by a security squad in one of the weapons labs.

"I had to duck behind the door too fast and it tore my mic right off. Couldn't transmit and tell you what happened. The security squad had me covered. There was no way I was leaving that lab the way I came in, so I headed toward the back door and damned if they didn't throw a grenade. I probably would have bought it, but an explosives testing shield hit me in the back and knocked my ass about five meters through the air. And here's the funny part—those dumbshits threw a grenade into a weapons lab. Something else in there blew up when it went off and burned up half the squad. Incinerated them in a flash so fast they never even had time to scream. That shield was thick and heavy as hell, but it kept me from getting turned into a human torch too. The rest of them must have been worried something else was going to go off because they double-timed out of there like Corps Comp master runners." There's a burn along one of his cheeks, a raw pink furrow that looks painful. Other than that, his glowing smile is as reckless as ever.

"They headed for the next level and I took off the other way, toward the hangar. When Karl and your brother came around the corner, it was nearly the end of it for everyone. I almost shot them, and Karl had me dead to rights. Once we regrouped, Karl heard your transmission about the Nova. He could tell from your voice that you'd bought at least one bullet, but if you could still talk, you were still breathing. So, we gave David a pistol and told him to keep it aimed forward, and we all doubled back to the hangar. We carried you as far as the midstation tunnels before you died. But Captain V and your boyfriend weren't having it."

I blushed when he said that, no doubt in my mind he was talking about Strahan. "What do you mean 'before I died'? And since when is Strahan my boy—?"

He cut me off with a patronizing laugh and left, telling me I needed to get some rest.

The havoc that the prisoners had wreaked upon the Fortress's security grid had not only overridden fire-control protocols and left the entrances to the docking bays operational, but none of the airlocks or launch tubes could be locked down. Despite needing to get the hell out of the area before Corps detachments came to the Fortress's defense, Vitruzzi still had the option of staying put as long as needed. The crew weren't about to leave friends behind if there was even a slim possibility of rescue, and against monumental odds, Strahan and Desto had gotten David and I back to the MCACS, the ship launching at the last possible nanosecond before the Nova blew.

But it was Vitruzzi who explained this part to me. A few hours later, she came into the med-station looking more tired than I've ever seen her, but no less composed. I noticed that the tenseness that had dug itself into deeper and deeper grooves around her mouth and eyes every day since I first met her seemed shallower. She no longer looked like a forty-year-old woman pushing eighty, and I was surprised by how relieved it made me feel.

While she scanned my medical readouts, I repeated the question, "What was Desto talking about? He said I died."

"Yes, you were dead. You had a stomach that was more hole than tissue from the bullet wound, but that was the least of your worries. By the time Karl and Desto found you, you'd lost a critical amount of blood and went into heart failure, flatlined. The MCACS's med-station had the equipment necessary to revive you, but we needed to get you back on the *Sphynx* if there was going to be any chance you'd make it. We launched just as I got your heartbeat back. Then the station blew."

The brief fragment of consciousness I'd experienced was caused by the blast concussion from the Nova exploding. But it had been too close; the blast crippled the MCACS and caused more injuries among the unprepared crew. Most escaped with minor bruises and abrasions, but David had been unable to brace himself because of his sight limitations. He had several broken ribs caused by a heavy gear locker slamming into him, and Venus's right arm was fractured from the blast's force shoving her against the flight control console. Because of having been strapped to a stationary gurney as soon as Strahan carried me on, I was the only one aboard that wasn't hurt. At least, not more hurt. Despite her injury, Venus was able to coax the MCACS back under control and Vitruzzi, escaping with only a few minor contusions, had immediately gone to work helping the injured. With luck and sheer strength of will, the crew patched the ruined ship together enough to fly it within shuttle range of the *Sphynx*. They got me to its onboard infirmary and an emergency surgery kept me alive. Vitruzzi had been accumulating specialized medical equipment for some time through both legal and black-market transactions. Thanks to her criminal initiative, she had what she needed to save me. After the surgery, I'd been interred in a pressure suit and given several blood transfusions, but despite all of it, another four days had passed before I came out of the coma. Vitruzzi hadn't believed I'd make it until I started breathing on my own again, a week ago. Since then, a constant IV diet of tissue regeneration- and hemo-stims has brought me a few steps closer to a full recovery everyday. This is the second time I've woken up from unconsciousness aboard the *Sphynx*. I'd really like it to be the last time.

There are other questions: Like how did we escape being tracked down by Corps ships detached to the Fortress's aid? And what happened to Rajcik? No one has the answer to these. And that worries us all.

WE'VE BEEN BACK AT Agate Beach for two days and I'm at the point where I can stand and even walk a few feet before pain and exhaustion force me prone again. I've asked to be helped into David's room a few times, but so far he hasn't been awake. In his weakened condition—he'd barely been able to stay on his feet while fleeing the alpha-zero hangar—he needs to retain all the energy his body can summon to help him heal and Vitruzzi has kept him sedated. His ribs are knitting gamely, and she's been running tests to determine what the Admin did to his eyes, trying to figure out whether or not he'll ever see again.

The settlement's makeshift hospital occupies three of the smaller rooms inside the mine. Brady had warned the people living here while we were still en route about the possibility of Rajcik attacking them. Since then, everything necessary to keep the settlement safe, fed, and protected has been brought inside the network of underground shafts and caves, leaving the outdoor settlement virtually abandoned. Everyone now lives in a constant state of alert. We can't take any chances that Rajcik won't try and get his revenge. He may not have cleared the station before it flared into a billion blazing fragments. But what if he did? Neither Vitruzzi nor I have forgotten his promise to destroy Agate Beach. Not for a second. The *Sphynx* and her short-range shuttle sweep the skies night and day, and a rotating schedule of locals continuously monitor the radar systems from the subterranean control room.

I hadn't been able to walk off the *Sphynx* on my own two feet and the inability to help out has been frustrating. I'm tired of being an invalid, relying on others. It's time to get back to the Aly who never asks for help and gets it done on her own. Leaning over to pull on my boots is a textbook lesson in misery, but once they're on, I carefully push myself upright and begin a slow, methodical shuffle next door to David's recovery room.

He's stretched out flat on the bed, looking pale, worn, and haggard. If I didn't see the beat of his pulse in his neck, I might think he was dead. Then, to my surprise, his eyes peel open in slow motion as if he's falling asleep in reverse.

"Hey, little sis." Fatigue and injuries make his voice soft.

Lurching to his bedside as fast as I can, I wrap one of his white hands in both of mine. It's not as cold as it looks. "Hey. How did you know it was me?"

"Easy. You're the only one who doesn't walk in and start prodding me or pulling on these tubes sticking out of me."

I grin. "How are you feeling?"

He considers the question for a minute, taking inventory. "I think it will be a couple of days before I'm ready for a rugby match, but nothing really hurts. Captain Vitruzzi is ninety-nine percent sure that the shit that screwed up my eyes—she says they're retinal ganglion-inhibitors—will wear off. That's a relief."

Patches of fading blue bruises still mark his arms and the top part of his chest not covered by his gown. His face is the only thing that looks really bad, even though it's probably the least of his injuries.

"When did you wake up?" I ask.

"Just a couple hours ago. I told Vitruzzi not to bother you if you were sleeping. How are you doing?"

"I'd say fantastic by comparison."

This makes him grin crookedly, only using one side of his mouth so he doesn't reopen the split in his lower lip. Watching him lie there, something inside me, some wall of emotion that I'd defiantly controlled, finally lets go.

"I shouldn't have left you on Obal 3." Guilt withers my words into skeletal leaves that crackle to the floor, and my eyes fill with water.

"Don't be crazy, sis. If you hadn't, we'd both be dead." His eyebrows are furrowed with concern, that older brother expression that always makes me feel as if I'm still seven years old. Squeezing my fingers in his strong hands, he says, "You had to run, and you did. And then you pulled off the most amazing rescue in the history of the universe. *You* did, little sis, you and these people, and you saved my life. Don't beat yourself up, because there was nothing else you could have done."

Wiping away the tears and trying to smile, I say, "Yeah, okay, you're right. You damn near threw me through that door anyway. I'm lucky you didn't break my ribs." He knows I'm just covering it up, but the important thing is that he's safe now and on the mend.

We settle into silence for a while, no sound in the room except filters drawing out the stale air. I know he still needs to rest, but I can't stop myself from asking, "How did you know what Rajcik planned to do with the Nova? And why didn't you tell me?"

He doesn't respond for several seconds. "I couldn't tell you because I didn't want you to get hurt; I figured what you didn't know couldn't be used against you."

"Dammit, David, I'm not a kid . . ."

"Yeah, I know, but it's my job, okay? You'll always be my little sister." His smirk has turned into a grimace, but not from the pain in his body. "Besides, I wasn't sure until after what happened at New Sweden. A couple of nights after Rajcik told us about the Fortress job, I was working in the wiring shaft under the com console. There was a short in my bunk's intercom and I traced it back to the panel down there. As I was finishing up, someone pinged us and then Rajcik came in and answered before I could get out of there. It was T'Kai. I was actually kind of glad to be there, to get to hear for myself what was really going on. We've both always known better than to trust Rajcik."

He shifts, trying to get a little more comfortable, and I think about ending the conversation so he can get the rest he needs. But I don't. "They argued about New Sweden. T'Kai wanted him to pick up a team of non-cits living there and use them on the job. Rajcik refused; he said he wouldn't use anyone on a job that he didn't know. T'Kai threatened him, things got ugly. I could see Rajcik's reflection in the VDU through the floor—I thought the whole deal was about to get blown, the way he reacted. But then he relaxed and gave in. A few days later, right before we were supposed to get there, he asked me about security around Tunis City, wanting to know how to get clearance, how to get close to the Capitol building. I kind of laughed, you know, because it's *impossible* to get in the Capitol's air space. I told Rajcik that a ship, a known ship like the *Temptation*, had no chance. The closest we'd ever get to Obal 10 would be one of its port moons, and then we'd still probably be shot down. It made me really uneasy, Aly. And that's when I started to think he had other plans for the Nova."

"So I got us out of the deal at New Sweden. I thought T'Kai might change his mind and set up an ambush, but I never thought Rajcik would do what he did. Jesus, how could we work for a man like that? When he killed all those people, I realized he was tying up loose ends. He wasn't going to let anything come between the plans he had, not even T'Kai. Whatever excuse he gave T'Kai must have worked, or maybe T'Kai was desperate, I don't know. But I knew it was time for us to cut loose too."

His breathing has sped up and I can see the effort hurts his wounded ribs, so I try to end the conversation. "Forget it. You need to take it easy. We can talk about it later, if you want."

He ignores me. "So after New Sweden, I told him you and I were getting out after the Admin paid up and we got our cut. I thought he'd try to convince us to stay, or threaten to kill us, something. But he acted as if it didn't matter. It was what he said that convinced me he was never planning on selling it. 'You and your sister do what you want, David. After we get that bomb, there won't be anyone left to stop you.' It wasn't hard to guess what he meant.

"The only thing more important to Rajcik than money is destroying the Admin. If he had the Nova, he finally had the opportunity to really hurt them. I couldn't kill him, not with Thompson and Fedchenko in the way, so I waited until we were on Obal 3 and tried to get away."

"You should have told me."

"I know that now. But I was so concerned with protecting you, I didn't know if you'd believe me. And I didn't want anyone else to know I suspected what Rajcik was planning. Maybe they were in on it too, I didn't know. Maybe Ortiz could have been trusted, but there wasn't enough time. The most important thing was getting away from Rajcik as soon as we could. I never thought we'd pull off the assault on the Fortress anyway." He'd sat up on his elbows while relaying the story. Now he eases back down to his pillow with a strained expression. "I'm glad I was wrong about that part, little sis. I mean, he probably had help infiltrating the station from T'Kai, but if you hadn't figured out a way to get in and outmaneuver their security, I wouldn't be here right now." His voice trails off and his eyes close again.

I want to tell him that it's time for him to stop treating me like the little sister who used to come crying to him whenever I skinned an elbow or took another hammering from Dad. But I know it won't do any good. So I don't say anything and watch as he drifts back to sleep.

TWO MORE WEEKS PASS and not a sign of Rajcik. People are beginning to move topside again, but no one takes any needless chances. The colony's radars are watched night and day. I'm stronger now, but Vitruzzi hasn't let me leave the infirmary yet—more because there's nowhere else for me to sleep than because of my injuries. David still has tunnel vision, but his sight is returning.

I'm standing next to the infirmary counter, my weapons broken down and the pieces laid out in neat rows, when the familiar sound of Strahan's boots approach from down the hallway. I catch myself smiling and put the Sinbad's barrel up to my eye before he notices. Staring intently down the barrel, I examine it for any excess carbon.

"Need help with those?"

Lowering the barrel, I see him grinning at me. He holds out his hand, revealing a round, ripe grapefruit. The yellow-pink skin shines with droplets of glistening oil, making it look like the round-est, juiciest, most appealing piece of candy ever made. "I saved you one."

"I haven't seen a grapefruit since I was a kid. Thanks. Some-day you're going to have to show me how you manage to grow these things." Saliva begins trickling into my mouth. I've only been back on solid food for a few days, and the dehydrated nutritional bars I'm so used to eating aren't putting a dent in my appetite. I take the fruit and begin to peel the thick skin off, relishing the sweet smell, and drop the peelings onto my work rag.

"If you stick around, I will."

I don't look at him, but I know he catches the way my hands pause for a moment. "Sure."

"Aly, listen." He reaches out and gently wraps a callused hand around one of my wrists, urging me to stop and look at him. "You are staying, right?"

I gently retrieve my wrist and put the grapefruit down on the rag. "I don't know. I mean, Agate Beach doesn't really need more people, and the kind of trouble David and I could bring—it's not really worth it. Not for you guys, anyway."

His brows wrinkle in a look that says he's not buying my bull-shit. "Who are you trying to convince? You know you're not pro-tecting us by leaving, so don't act like you think you are. We bought our troubles, and we can deal with them. And what would you and David do anyway? Where would you go?" He finishes matter-of-factly, "Your friends are here."

I look intently into his sepia eyes, trying for the first time to imagine what it would be like not to be on the run. To belong somewhere with people who actually care about each other, about me.

"Aly, we want you to stay." He pauses. "*I* want you to stay."

I draw a quick, almost nervous breath and realize: this is what it feels like to be home.

CONTRACT
OF BETRAYAL

SPECTRAS ARISE TRILOGY
BOOK 2

The fall of Empire, gentlemen, is a massive thing, however, and not easily fought. It is dictated by a rising bureaucracy, a receding initiative, a freezing of caste, a damming of curiosity—a hundred other factors. It has been going on, as I have said, for centuries, and it is too majestic and massive a movement to stop.

~ Isaac Asimov, Part I, *The Psychohistorians*, section 6

ONE

I'm rushing over the hot desert skin of the planet, pushing the Rover at top speed just for the fun of it, hitting sandbars and bouncing high off the ground at times. It's good to get out of the mine, and late fall on Spectra 6 has come in with enough of a cool breeze blowing through the brown hills to keep me from sweating rivers every time I step outside. I'm moving too fast to really accomplish what I'm out here for—Bodie asked me to gather some samples of a newly engineered species of brush at the base of these eastern hills—but at the moment, I'm enjoying myself too much to care.

The sand is compacting into hard earth as it rises into the baked hillsides, so I steer the Rover south to flank them and give myself a few more minutes of fast-moving freedom. I come up over a finger of the closest hill, the front tires rising vertically for a moment before falling flat back to the earth—and I see it. A transport ship is sitting on the flat plain two hundred and fifty meters from my position. Immediately, I lay off the accelerator and pray that the sound of the Rover's engine doesn't echo against the hills and give me away. The ship could belong to anybody, including people it would be best to avoid.

A culvert at the base of the nearest hillock provides me plenty of cover to be hidden from the ship's view and I coast into it, kill the engine, and switch on my wrist VDU to contact the control room at Agate Beach, where someone is always listening.

"Beach control, this is Aly. Do you copy?"

"Erikson, it's Mason. What's up?"

"I've got a ship I've never seen before out here by the Torarua Range. Can you get me V?"

"Wait one."

Vitruzzi's image comes into focus on my VDU within seconds. "What's going on?"

"I'm about thirty klicks east of the Beach, at the base of the Torarua Range. We've got some company. Looks like a transport ship. Admin manufactured. Did they contact you?"

"We haven't been hailed and"—she turns to confer with Mason—"there's nothing on radar. Have they seen you?"

"Negative, as far as I can tell."

"What's their status? Does it look like a crash? Can you see any registration marks?"

"No, I just got a quick look before I got out of sight. It doesn't look like a crash. No smoke, no burns, no runners. But they're pretty far from Hell's Gate."

"We've been expecting a delivery from an old friend. It could be him. I'm on the way. Do me a favor and just hang tight. Don't let them see you. But if you can keep them from going anywhere, try. We don't want anyone unexpected flying around the Beach."

"Affirmative."

"We have your grid. Be there in twenty." There's a click as she breaks the link and my VDU screen fades to black.

Cautiously pushing the Rover's clamshell hatch open, I decide to climb to the top of the culvert to keep eyes on the stray. If they decide to launch, I'm not exactly sure how Vitruzzi expects me to keep them from going anywhere, but I'll cross that bridge if I come to it. There's no movement around the ship. From my vantage point, only the stern is visible, and I'm looking straight into the engine outflow chambers. They look clear and operational, and the inner coils have a slight reddish glow. Still hot; they haven't been here long. The fact that our radars at the Beach didn't pick them up indicates that they'd entered the atmosphere from another part of the planet and flown in the direction of the settlement below radar. Whether they intended to use stealth or if it was only coincidence is impossible to know, and it makes me nervous.

Five minutes pass and hot, stagnant air pools in the deep depression, baking my skin as if I were in a convection oven and sending streams of sweat dribbling from my hairline to the tip of my nose. Keeping my movements to a minimum, I switch on my carbine's scope, ratchet up the magnification, and peer through. A light breeze blows a welcome puff of cooler air on my face but also carries the noise of hydraulics. Panning to the left and right helps me pinpoint the cause of the noise, and I finally make out a ramp lowering from the ship's bow, the wind grabbing up a flurry of dust when it hits the ground.

That's all I need to see. Leaping back into the Rover, I yank the hatch shut, slam on the ignition, and jump it out of the culvert at top speed. I don't want whoever is on that ship to get aboard a land trans and head for Agate Beach. It's easier to hold them here than chase them down. Of course, they may be harmless. Maybe lost citizens with broken communication equipment, who knows? Better to find out now, while they're locked down, than after they've reached the settlement.

Pushing the Rover hard, I cover the distance in a few seconds and skid to a stop behind the engines. The smell of super-heated metal and burnt dust fills my nostrils as I run from the Rover to the front of the ship and take a firing position next to the lowered ramp. Raising my carbine barrel, I line up the sight with the center of the opening, ready for anything. Sounds of movement come from inside.

With a raised but steady voice, I order, "Come out slowly. You're covered in every direction."

The movement stops cold and, after a second, a voice carries down the open hatchway. "We're not armed. Coming out. Just keep cool."

That voice . . .

The first thing to emerge from the sloping ramp is a pair of military-issue boots, old and scuffed, made of a dingy pseudo-leather material that's at least five years past a military polish. Their owner jumps to the deck, kicking up wisps of desert dirt. He's about midthirties, close-cropped brown hair, hands exactly where they should be—shoulder height and empty. He's followed by a woman and two more men, all dressed in similar civilian clothing. The last one exits and takes a few short steps forward. Still a couple of meters from the opening, I keep my barrel trained at chest level, but when the man moves forward, I'm dazzled by the sunlight slanting through the ramp struts. My eyes squeeze shut involuntarily at the sudden brightness, and a tiny warning dose of adrenaline shoots into my veins at the realization that I've momentarily given up the advantage.

"I'll be goddamned! Aly Erikson!"

It can't be. The silhouette moves closer, blocking the piercing light, and I'm finally able to focus on him.

"Sergeant Cross?"

"Oh, come on, Aly. You know me better than that! I don't believe what I'm seeing!"

There are hundreds of rocks in this solar system, and the likelihood of running into someone from my past on this one had, until now, seemed like a complete impossibility. It would be like finding a bullet from your own gun tumbling through the floating debris of a long-since-concluded interstellar battle.

Impossible or not, I'm staring at proof that it can happen. Rob Cross. Munitions team platoon leader from the 808th Ground Division. I last saw him a year before the Soldier's Rebellion, when David's and my flight patrol unit stopped dropping troops into hot zones. His detachment was reassigned to another ship. We hadn't kept in touch.

Nearly stuttering with surprise, I ask, "Wh-what are you doing out here?"

"Is that happiness to see me? It's hard to tell." He's standing less than a meter in front of me, smiling in a cavalier way I remember too well. But his eyebrows are raised in a hint of concern—a natural response to the fact that my carbine is still leveled at his heart.

Regardless, it's been eight years since I've seen him, and I'm not that trusting. "I don't believe this is a coincidence."

Before he can respond, the ground around us begins to gyrate as the *Sphynx*'s shuttle descends. No one speaks, the craft's engines too loud to be heard over. I cover my eyes with one hand and let the carbine sag. Vitruzzi's coming in close, not showing the kind of concern she would for someone she doesn't know. Could Cross be the person she's expecting?

When they hit the dirt, the shuttle's door slides open and she steps out, Karl and David following behind. "Cross, it's good to see you. Why didn't you signal us when you got in our orbit? You're three days early."

He turns toward them with a renewed smile, and I finally lower my weapon. "Good to see you again, Eleanor. Her reversals went haywire and caused a wiring issue that sucked all the power from my com system *and* my engine backups. We were hoping to get a little closer to Agate Beach before we had to set her down, but . . ." He shrugs.

"No backup power? I'm *glad* you didn't get any closer." Vitruzzi steps aside, letting me get a better look at David, who stares at Cross with a gape-mouthed mixture of shock and disbelief. I can't help but grin at his incredulity, though my own expression moments ago must not have been so different.

"Rob Cross?" David takes a step forward and peers at Rob, as if questioning his own eyesight.

"I don't believe this. This day just gets better and better!"

The two men embrace in a hearty man-hug like brothers, slapping each other on the back. David asks, "What the hell are you doing out here on the fringes? And with your own transport ship? I didn't think the Corps would ever trust you among civilians." I haven't seen him so pleased in quite a while. The three of us had some good times together, back when we all still belonged to the Corps.

"I take it you know each other," Vitruzzi comments, surprised.

"Know each other? Eagle Eye Erikson's the only man in the system who could keep up with me back in the old days." A huge smile spreads across Cross's face, causing a fan of crow's feet to sweep out in a winning arc. He has the kind of smile that makes a person feel like they've just been reunited with a twin brother or best friend after years of being apart. There's no sign of sarcasm or irony in his face; his expression is complete and genuine openness and enthusiasm. All of a sudden, I feel like I did a few years ago when I woke up to that same smile nearly every off-duty morning. My mind summons the mildly sharp smell of his skin, and I remember too clearly how his body felt next to mine. It throws me off balance for a minute, and I realize I'm blushing.

I pull my eyes away from his face and catch Karl looking at me strangely. Blushing twice as hard, I turn back to the ship, which at this moment is the only safe thing to look at.

"Let's get you guys back to Agate Beach. When was the last time you ate anything fresh? We can talk over some lunch," Vitruzzi says.

"Sounds terrific. And can you spare any viridian heat rods? If we can get those in, we'll be able to get the *Red Horizon* to your mine. I hate leaving her out in the open. You never know what kind of scavengers may find their way out here."

Vitruzzi gets on her com and locates Bodie. A moment later she says, "Bodie and Venus will be here in a few minutes to get you squared away. Were you able to get everything we talked about?"

"Have I ever let you down, Eleanor? Yeah, come on in and check things out. There's at least ninety kilos of scrap steel and enough wire to build yourself a new ship."

"What about the comlink switches? And the seeds?"

"And those."

"Thanks, Rob. It's good to have someone we can rely on."

He smiles again, not quite gloating but close, and focuses his attention back on me. "So what do you say, Aly? You're too quiet. That's nothing like I remember."

I have to clear my throat before I can speak. I woke up this morning thinking I'd be helping Bodie collect specimens from the local plants. Nothing prepared me to be standing face-to-face with an ex-lover, the first man in my life that ever meant more to me than just a pleasant way to kill a couple of hours. "I'm just really surprised. I never expected to see you again." I'm at such a loss for words that I'm nearly mumbling.

"I know! It's amazing, isn't it? You're as beautiful as I remember." One of his crewmen, a tough-looking hatchet of a man, walks between us to get back on the ship, finally breaking through my paralysis.

Time to escape this awkward situation. "Vitruzzi, I'll take the Rover back to the Beach. It looks like you have things handled here."

She shrugs and I turn to climb aboard. Before I can pull the clamshell cover closed, Karl steps over and motions toward the seat. "Mind if I drive?"

I shrug and push over to the passenger side. Before the hatch closes, I hear Rob ask, presumably speaking to David, "So what's that about? She's not angry with me is she?"

"It's a little . . . uh . . . complicated."

TWO

Karl accelerates back to the settlement, and I lean back in the seat, feeling a strange sense of time-vertigo, as if I'm stuck in a black hole's event horizon. My life up to now is in redshift, simultaneously standing still and blurring away at the edges. What the hell had just happened? For a second, it had seemed as if my real life was back in the Corps—fresh out of the Academy and aboard my first duty ship with my older brother and the charming squad leader, Tech 1 Sergeant Cross, who'd caught my full attention the first time I'd seen him.

My swirling thoughts turn sour as they mix with guilt and I glance sideways at Karl. We're a team now, lovers, friends, together as much as we can be—partners. If you had told me six months ago that I'd find someone, besides my brother, that I cared about more than myself, I would have thought you were sadly sentimental and possibly delusional. What Karl and I had been through—the Fortress, the rescue mission to save David, Zeta, Mason, and Jade, and the fact that Karl had risked his life more than once to save mine—had affected me, changed me to my core. His selflessness and perseverance brought me back to life when I should have been dead, and resuscitated the part of me that understood that there was more to being alive than just breathing and making it to the next day. With all that's passed, Karl and the settlers at Agate Beach have become more than friends; they're all my family now.

He drives as if he'd seen me doing more than blushing over Rob, in some kind of fury that I only half register as I silently struggle with the realization that things that had only recently begun to grow stable and steady—both life in the Beach and between Karl and I—may have just become complicated again. When Cross's unit had been reassigned, it was hard on me. The dread I had about the Corps and its master puppeteer the Admin was already rooted deep in my psyche. The loathing I felt for the way they wore out lives—the same way machines wear out gears—for their convenience and greed was taking its toll on me, and my allies were getting fewer and fewer. Even David was telling me I sounded paranoid and needed to keep my mouth shut before the Corps put me on the mentally incapacitated chit and locked me up. Cross's departure left me with no more distractions and no one else to lean on. By that point, I had lost both my lover and my convictions, and my life changed completely.

Karl hits a sandbar going too fast and I jolt back into the present. "Careful, kamikaze, or we're going to have to replace the rear axle again." He remains sullenly silent without even a glance in my direction. "Hey, you okay?"

"Yeah, just didn't see that." He reaches into his vest and pulls out his pack of homemade cigarettes, clamps one between his teeth, and lights it with one hand. He takes a deep pull from the smoke, squinting until the color of his eyes is hidden, and keeps his gaze locked on the baked earth outside the Rover's cockpit.

Yeah, something is bothering him, but I know him well enough by now to know that he won't breathe a word about what it might be until he's either ready to hash it out at full volume or decides to let it go forever. There is no in between with him, and he never hesitates to point out that I'm exactly the same way. He'll tell me what's on his mind when he's ready for me to know.

We're still ten kilometers from the settlement when a shadow quickly overtakes us from behind. I raise my head to see what's going on just as the *Red Horizon* buzzes past in a low bank no more than fifty meters above our heads on its way to Agate Beach. Vitruzzi transmits to Karl's wrist VDU. "We're all getting together at Pat's and my place at 1900 hours for dinner. Can you two make it?"

Karl glances at me before answering, and I don't miss the reluctance stretching the skin around his mouth too tight. "Want to go?"

"Why not?" I try to sound neutral, but the pitch of my voice raises a notch, completely betraying me.

He depresses the transmit button and replies, "See you tonight, V."

THREE

Unable to find Bodie to explain why I hadn't gathered any of his samples earlier, I ditch the mine early and walk to Vitruzzi's. As I enter, I find her and Bodie side by side, hunched over the main room's central table and raptly focused on the fleximesh monitor covering it. They both nod a quick *hello* and return their attention to the meshmo, as Bodie calls it. Like an overprotective librarian, he has assumed control over the variety of scientific and monitoring equipment stored within the mine's control room and this delicate readout device rarely leaves it. Most of the equipment has been painstakingly "acquired" from Admin ships or cities and now makes up the Beach's technical hub. Besides the *Sphynx*, this equipment is the only thing that differentiates the Beach from the kind of anachronistic settlement people must have lived in on old Earth before such "high-tech" advancements as electricity and indoor plumbing.

All right, maybe a slight embellishment, but no one can deny that the Beach is just about as primitive as colonies come in the Spectras—which, surprisingly, suits me fine.

"You see the numbers, V. It can't work," Bodie says as he taps a stream of text and images slowly descending the screen's surface. "It's the same exact problem they documented in the reports we took from the Fortress. If we'd only had fifteen more minutes, I could have taken a complete copy of the data. It was right in my damn hands."

"I know, I know. But fifteen more minutes and we would have been vaporized right along with it. Either way, we don't know what their final developments were. We don't even know if they were successful," Vitruzzi answers.

Brady and Vitruzzi's residence serves as the crew's de facto meeting center during the cooler evenings. Few people bother to knock when they know they're expected, and I'm no exception. Glancing around, it doesn't look like Brady is here, causing me an involuntary twitch of relief. The amount of time we can tolerate each other is inversely proportional with the amount of time we share oxygen molecules, and our fragile truce is strongest when we're miles apart. With him out of the picture for now, I can relax and pay attention to Vitruzzi and Bodie's conversation.

Bodie sighs, and then seeing something on the screen, taps the command to stop its flow. "But look here. This is the thing that really grabs my interest." He points.

The data Bodie has is a by-product of our mission to the Fortress. While the crew waited for Karl and Desto to bring in my brother and I, Bodie had the time to retrieve files from the laboratory computers that had been left unguarded after the prisoners we'd set loose went on attack. I considered it morbid curiosity at first—not realizing those so-called scientists had been working on projects outside of whatever evil shit they could invent to inflict suffering on people—but Bodie had mentioned that most of the information had something to do with soil alteration experiments. "Growing better food, Aly," he'd tried to explain, which naturally reduced my interest from marginal to extinct. I've lived on ship and field rations for more than half my life, having long since given up the ambitious expectation of actually enjoying my meals. So when it comes to food production, it's not an exaggeration to say I know more about the workings of a pulse carbine or interstellar system map and can't be bothered to care much about where my food comes from as long as I have some when I need it.

Still, Vitruzzi's next question yanks my attention to front and center. "Now what the hell would they have been doing on Keum Libre?"

As I step up to the table to get a look at whatever Bodie's pointing at, they move closer together to allow me to see it better.

```
The advanced developmental formula being
tested on Keum Libre has shown favorable re-
sults. Potential increased production is an-
ticipated to be approved and commence within
30-60 days. Director T'Kai has reiterated
that no commercialization foci will be pur-
sued.
```

"Do you think that means what I think it means?" I ask in a voice gritty with anger and disgust. The penal colony is inhabited by only the worst of the worst criminals, the ones the Admin has deemed incapable of rehabilitation and readmission into society. After what we'd heard from the twisted Admin doctor Kellen Vilbrandt and then seen them doing to people on the Fortress, it's no stretch to imagine they'd be doing the same to the inmates of Keum Libre.

"Yeah, it seems like the logical conclusion to assume they're testing stuff on KL's population, but I don't think that's what it is, Aly," Bodie answers. "I think they had a more complete version of this soil application that was working, and they were maybe testing it there. It's a natural environment that no one cares about, so it would make sense to do field tests where results would be more reliable than they would in lab research."

"Sure."

He arches one bushy eyebrow in annoyance at my scorn. "I guess the only way to know would be to make a trip to KL. But that statement about a commercialization focus makes it pretty clear, at least to me, that it wasn't something that would be considered a hazard."

He has a point, and this time I keep my mouth shut.

"What did you say about going to Keum Libre?" Brady steps inside carrying a box full of food, presumably for dinner. He lays it on the counter at the far side of the room, then walks to Vitruzzi and kisses her cheek. With the barest glance at me in greeting, he leans over the table to examine the meshmo.

"I was saying that I think they may have completed the research they needed to do to make this soil enhancement formula work and were probably testing it on KL. If I had even just a sample of the ground from there—"

"Forget it," Brady says. "You know how crazy that sounds? It's a least a week of flying, probably more like two, and there has to be a solid force of Corps or Admin security surrounding the rock. Especially if this formula, or whatever it is, is as valuable as you've been saying. Anyway, we have what we need to keep the settlement running. This 'soil enhancement formula' sounds too good to be true."

Scowling, Bodie folds the meshmo, his frustration evident in his slow and deliberate movements.

"WE'RE FLOATING FIFTY METERS off the bow of this frigate with its engine completely locked thanks to the EM pulse we shot it with. I'm thinking that we fried at least half of the thruster grid and maybe their coms, so it wasn't going anywhere on its own. Erikson's crew searched it top to bottom using both eyes-on and scanners, but there wasn't anything. Their CO—you remember that guy, David? Captain Hobins or Hogans, something like that. What a bastard.

Anyway, he was pissed because he swore the intel on these smugglers was right. My squad's in the airlock ready to escort their crew to lockdown when David's team brought them back on board. They came in and Hobins instantly starts chewing Erikson a new one. Why didn't you find anything? Why was the search ineffective? Did you use the scanners? Et cetera, et cetera. Erikson's just standing there, staring out of the airlock hatch, and then he blurts out, like the captain isn't even there, 'Doesn't this class of frigate have a concave forward hull?' Hobins starts to steam at being interrupted, but one of the other crewman says that's correct and Erikson says, 'Then why is this one's convex?'

"Hobins hadn't ordered a hull scan, and he gets so worked up about Erikson drawing attention to the fact that he makes him suit up and go check it out. Sure enough, the whole shipment of missing mining core-bits is there. One thing you can say about Eagle Eye, he never misses the obvious."

We're all seated around the main room in the center of Vitruzzi and Brady's hexagonal dwelling. Dinner is over and Cross and David are reminiscing about the days when the three of us were stationed on the Corps long-range enforcement ship the PCA *Thor's Hammer*. I glance around the room noting how everyone listens raptly to Cross's story. He's always liked attention.

David picks it up. "The funniest part about it was that the smugglers had left one of their men with the stolen equipment. When I broke into the compartment, he looked pretty surprised to see me. I think he was even more surprised when he realized his whole crew had been arrested and left him out there with no way to get back on the frigate. Since the controls were burnt out, he wouldn't have been able to open the airlock hatch from the outside. And his buddies weren't talking. Honor among thieves, right, Twig?"

He winks at me, no doubt thinking, as I am, about the way we'd been betrayed by our own former smuggling crew. I can only hope the attachments we're developing here won't turn out the way those had. Part of me still struggles against an ingrained reluctance to get too close to the settlers, people I hardly know, but Karl helps me keep from giving in to my old habits. Cutting bait and running every time things get tough is no way to live.

The thought makes me look over at Karl sitting next to Venus. He's been quiet this evening, his forehead crumpled in a brooding scowl. Every so often, he walks outside by himself to smoke, but I'm starting to wonder if he just doesn't want to be around Cross. Ever since the *Red Horizon* landed, Karl's been edgy. Is it because he can tell that Cross and I have a history—though he hasn't asked me about it—or is it something else?

"Man, I though Hobins was going to come apart," Cross says, chuckling over the way our old CO had reacted about being upstaged by his subordinates. "He'd already reported that we hadn't found anything, and then you come back with the entire missing cargo. That guy was your typical company commander—promoted beyond his capacity to be effective, but short of his capacity to realize it."

Everyone laughs, even those who hadn't been in the Corps. A pompous jerkoff too busy stroking his own ego to know when he's wrong is a universal character.

"Aly, do you remember that time he busted us in the armory?" Before I can respond, Cross launches into another tale from our past. "Aly and I were getting in some off-duty 'recreation' in the *Hammer*'s portable arms storage when Hobins comes in and scares the shit out of us. I stood up too fast, trying to get dressed, and ran into one of the arms-locker doors. It latched with Aly's shirt stuck inside and locked, of course. So she grabs her rifle and slings it over her chest just as the captain walks around the corner. We did what we were supposed to—came to attention and saluted. Me with only one leg of my pants on and Aly using her carbine to cover her top, and both of us nearly having a stroke from trying not to laugh. He freaked! Damn, we were so in for it."

I catch myself simultaneously wanting to smile and wanting to run Cross through with my dinner knife. How could he tell a story like that? Here? Desto and Bodie are practically falling off their chairs with laughter. In fact, everyone is getting a good guffaw at my expense. Everyone, that is, except Karl. He rockets from his seat like he'd been stung by it and strides out the door. His sandbike rumbles to life, the noise of its engine fading as he drives away.

The chuckles subside, and Cross asks, innocently, "What did I say?" But he's looking at me knowingly, and I feel hot blood rush to my cheeks for the second time today.

I have to say something in my defense, but David beats me to it, "So Rob, now that you've done the impossible and made Aly speechless, I guess you probably know to sleep with one eye open tonight." He's trying to lighten the mood, but his eyes shift toward me with concern. He knows the deal between Karl and I, everyone here does. If the tables were turned, I'd probably be just as pissed off hearing Karl's old flames talk so openly about their prior excursions. But dammit, this is all out of nowhere and I don't really know what I'm supposed to say. I had not planned on crossing paths with Cross today—or ever—and I'm not sure how to respond to the whole situation.

"Actually, that kind of brings me to a question I wanted to ask." Cross changes the subject, finally, and addresses Brady and Vitruzzi. "With the changes to Admin contracts coming down, we've found ourselves with a few less clients than normal and time on our hands until we can line up another job. I thought we might stick around the Beach for a while. Take a minivacation."

He stops, taking in the silence and quizzical looks that surround him. "I mean, we can make ourselves useful, and we have all the provisions we need. We won't put any strain on your food or other supplies."

"Hell yeah! Give me a chance to win that pile of money back you fleeced from me last time you were here," Desto responds.

Vitruzzi pulls up closer to the table and lays her hands flat against it, as if bracing herself. "What changes to Admin contracts, Rob?"

Sudden understanding settles on Rob's face and his olive skin loses a shade of color. "You haven't heard," he states.

"Heard what?" Brady asks.

Before answering, Rob walks over to the counter and pours himself another glass of water. Turning, he says, almost to himself, "That makes sense. You wouldn't know if you hadn't traveled to the Obals lately." He pauses, taking a long drink. "The Admin started rescinding all of their contracts with non-cit crews or crews with non-cits in them. They're basically closing all Obal space to anyone who isn't an Admin citizen. Some are saying it's a matter of time before they even let anyone leave, citizen or not. There's been so much upheaval, and that facility that was destroyed a few months ago . . . they're on serious crackdown, doing a bigger policing job of the system than I"—he glances at me—"or any of us, have ever seen. They're serious about catching whoever blew up their—whatever it was. The rumor is that an important research facility was destroyed. What kind of research is anyone's guess," he adds as an afterthought, finishing the water and setting the glass down.

My eyes find Vitruzzi's face. If what Cross is saying is true, Agate Beach could be in real trouble. Much of our equipment, a good portion of our food, and all of our medical supplies are brought in from citizen ports. Ports that Vitruzzi and Karl have easy access to given their citizen status and Admin contracts. If they can't leave the Spectras or run cargo for the Admin, this settlement could just dry up and blow away.

"Why don't you want to head back to Obal 10? Isn't that your usual port-of-call?" Brady asks, apparently deciding the subject isn't to be discussed now. Brady and I may have our differences, but the man has shown me in these last couple of months that there is nothing he won't do to keep himself, and the people he feels responsible for, safe. I often wonder what the system would be like if men like him were running it instead of the scum serving as members of the Admin Cabinet of Directorates.

"Yeah, it is. But what's the harm? It would be great to catch up with David and Aly. Eight years is a lot of water under the bridge, and by the look of those raccoon rings Erikson's sporting, I suspect they've got some interesting stories to tell. Am I right, Eagle Eye?" Cross is referring to a residual pinkish discoloration of the skin encircling David's eye sockets. A happy little reminder of the shit the Admin had put in them on the Fortress to test whatever god-awful chemicals they had concocted for whatever unspeakable purpose. David's sight has returned as acutely as ever, but the skin around them seems burned, and it's uncertain if it will ever look normal again.

David says, "I don't see any harm in it, Brady. I'll vouch for Rob."

"I don't have any objections." Vitruzzi adds her piece. "If the material he just brought isn't exactly what we need, maybe he can do another run for us before his next job. Save us some time and trouble, at the least." *Especially if we can't get them ourselves*, she doesn't have to add.

"That would be no problem. Happy to help," Cross responds.

After a few more seconds of quiet deliberation, Brady finally says, "Yeah, okay, fine. Desto or Bodie could probably find room for you and—"

"Don't even worry about it. We're fine sleeping on the *'Rize*. She's really home anyway."

Cross's three companions have said very little all evening, accepting food and drink with reserved politeness and melting into the edges of the group. I notice that even Cross rarely addresses them, and I wonder how long they've flown together.

"The night's young. Why don't you all come over to our place and pony up some of that hard-earned cash in a rematch? I feel like revenge may be mine tonight. Anyone else want to get spanked?" Desto's poker tactics are a local phenomenon. I've learned that the only way to keep from losing money to him is not to play. David and Bodie, however, aren't resigned to their collective losses and get ready to go.

Cross stands up and beams a winning smile at Vitruzzi and Brady. "Thanks again for the hospitality. Agate Beach has become my oasis from the Admin's BS these last couple of years. Tomorrow, whatever you need help with, the crew and I at your disposal."

"Thanks, Rob. I have some ideas," Vitruzzi responds.

Cross looks over at me. "How about you, Aly? Care to join us?"

"No, I've got some things I need to take care of." In reality, if Karl's gone back to the dwelling he shares with Desto and Doug Mason, I'm not sure it would be a good idea for me to show up there with Cross. I'll see Karl tomorrow and maybe find a way to smooth out whatever's going on between us. That, or he and Cross will "smooth" it out tonight. Either way, I'd rather avoid being around if the two of them decide to beat their chests in a testosterone-soaked dick-measuring contest.

"Suit yourself. In any case, it's good to see you again." He walks out with his crew, leaving me to wonder how he could possibly sound so sincere.

When the sound of Bodie and Desto's sandbikes and Cross's team's land transport fades off, I turn my attention back to Vitruzzi and Brady.

"You've known Cross for a while?"

Vitruzzi is collecting plates and piling them in their sanitizing system. "Since I was still on Obal 10. He was already a contractor and helped Karl and I find the *Sphynx*. He's a good man, but it sounds like you know that." Even she can't avoid joking about my obvious embarrassment.

I manage to keep the blush at bay this time. "What about the rest of his crew: Baker, Montoya, Sims? Who are they?"

A crease slides down between her black brows like the drop of rain that precludes a thunderstorm, but it's Brady who responds, "We don't know them."

"V, do you think it's a good idea to have a bunch of strangers hanging around while we're building the transceiver? I mean, yeah, you trust Rob, but these others? They do work for the Admin, you know."

"Jesus, you two are more paranoid than rats in a storm drain during monsoon season. Look, the fact is, the transceiver will be ready for testing soon, and we could really use another ship in the sky to tell us if it's working. I think we should ask Cross. With him and the *Sphynx* and . . ."—her eyes shift away from me and her jaw tightens for a split second—"and a lot of luck, we'll know if our plan is a go, or if it's just wishful thinking."

The plan she's talking about, she and Brady are thinking of it as the best insurance policy money can buy, but I'm not so sure.

She continues, "Rob's loyalty to the Admin only extends up to a point. We can trust *him* if we can trust anyone. I'll talk to him about it tomorrow."

Neither Brady nor I say anything more. At least in this one thing we're united: neither of us likes to show our cards unless we know we have nothing to lose.

Reading the doubt in our eyes, she adds, "If it makes you feel better, I'll ask him to keep it quiet and leave his crew out of it."

"I think that's the best option. Cross is reliable, but that doesn't make him one of us, Eleanor. You know I trust your instincts, but we can't risk too much," Brady says.

I'm not convinced that it's a good idea to let anyone else in on the transceiver. The thing itself might be a harmless communication device, but the way we plan to use it is a one-way trip to the Admin's version of hell if we're caught—but arguing with her isn't going to change her mind. "I'd like to be there when you tell him about the transceiver."

Vitruzzi levels her hard almost black eyes on me in a stare that would make most people uncomfortable, but I'm used to it. "Sure," she says flatly. "See you at work tomorrow."

As I walk out the door, I feel a strange discontinuity turning knots in my stomach. Besides David, I know Cross better than anyone here, and eight years ago I wouldn't have thought twice before trusting him, even with my life. But people change. Things grow unstable, unpredictable. Sometimes, people can be pushed, or they take risks that are too big. And before they even realize what happened, their backs are against the wall and they're doing dangerous, unexpected things just to survive. Sometimes that means sacrifice, sometimes it means betrayal. I can't help but wonder, what has Cross been doing since I saw him last? What kinds of risks has he taken?

It's a subject I know a lot about. In the six years since David and I deserted the Corps, I've made compromises and taken risks that seem insane. That *were* insane. Risks that eventually culminated in being betrayed by Rajcik, nearly losing my brother, and almost dying on the Fortress. The wound has fully healed and I no longer walk listing to one side to compensate for the nerve damage caused by Rajcik's bullet—the only thing he ever gave me—but it could have gone another way. For a while, every decision I made, even the ones that seemed firmly rooted in self-preservation, was the wrong one. My recklessness may or may not have been wise, but David and I are still alive and I've learned a hard lesson. Cross had never been reckless in the same way, at least not when I knew him. But, just as Vitruzzi had said, his loyalty has its limits. Always has.

KARL AND I HAD GONE to Vitruzzi and Brady's for dinner together and his abrupt departure earlier leaves me on foot, but I'm content to walk. Venus had dragged me out of my bunk on the *Sphynx* a month ago, telling me that living underground wasn't healthy, and it's only a short distance to the dwelling we now share. The cool night air of the desert will be a perfect balm to my overheated brain.

At the time, I thought Venus was doing me a favor, but as the weeks have passed, I realize she needs me more than I needed somewhere besides the *Sphynx* to go. Her constant frenzy makes managing routine tasks, such as cooking without burning the place down, a challenge. The only time I've seen her truly calm is when she's at the helm of a ship, and almost as a matter of survival, I've embraced the challenge of ensuring she doesn't kill herself, or me, out of pure absentmindedness. Besides the bathroom and main room, we each have our own room for racking out, but unless we're sleeping, we're never there. The settlement, despite its isolation and limited resources, keeps me busy and there isn't much slack time. It's better that way. The routines I've carved out here bring me a kind of satisfaction smuggling never could.

The western horizon is a deep shade of red where Algol B spins, only fully setting for a few short hours each night. As I approach the dwelling, lights and laughter twine together in an inviting stream that spills from the doorway. Jeremy La Mer—a prisoner from the MCACS we'd hijacked to infiltrate the Fortress—is here. I stand outside for a minute, hesitant to enter for some reason. Hearing Venus and La Mer, their happiness and carefree youth, sends a pang of . . . what? sadness? . . . through me. Karl and I have our fights, *loud* ones, but since the first night we'd spent together—lying out under the shadow of the cliffs to the west of the settlement, the scent of night and desert grasses making me giddy, his hands moving in delicious exploration over my body in a way that left my skin thirsty for more—I haven't considered the possibility that such fulfillment may be temporary. But his coolness since Cross had landed today and the way he'd reacted tonight at hearing Cross's story jams that possibility into my gut in a way that hurts more than any bullet ever could.

There's a crash inside followed by immediate silence. Seconds later, Venus's explosive laughter splinters the air. I take a deep breath and walk in.

"Hey."

"Aly! Jer was just showing me how to convert these broken-down com monitors into signal magnifiers."

The sharp smell of burnt electrical components stings my nose and a full-sized VDU lies shattered at Venus's feet. She sees me looking and says, "I got a little carried away with the testing, but you should see what the sound of radio feedback looks like! It's the craziest wave pattern you can imagine."

"It carried a little more vibration than I expected, but these monitors definitely aren't junk yet," La Mer tells me, a lopsided grin on his face. Wearing that expression, he looks like a kid barely old enough to shave, and I laugh at myself for how much of a battle-hardened harpy I'm starting to sound like—at only thirty.

La Mer is tall, taller than anyone else in the Beach except Desto. His skin is the sable, silky hue of strong black tea, always seeming to glow with a moonlit sheen, even in the day. His eyelashes are long and flirtatious, arrayed around his tranquil green eyes like a corona. It's not in the least difficult to see why Venus fell for him the instant he'd suggested a recode of the *Sphynx*'s engine sequencers to help increase reaction speed. His quiet yet contagious enthusiasm is an excellent counterpoint to her nonstop energy, and his Cimmerian tone is an elegant backdrop to her colorless, nearly transparent paleness. The only surface similarities they share, in fact, are their youth and their brilliant green eyes.

Mason had found La Mer stowing away aboard the *Sphynx* after we'd escaped the Fortress, and his story is an interesting one—which is fortunate for him. It had to be to keep Desto from throwing him out of the airlock. I'm still not certain I believe it, but I have to admit, the sheer unlikelihood of why he'd been taken prisoner is what makes it plausible.

The Corps picked him up on Eruo Pium, one of Spectra 3's habitable moons, and arrested him for treason two weeks before we'd hijacked his prisoner transport. He'd been on the run for six years, and in that time they'd identified him as a member of a network of programming techs and citizen wire-rats who had worked together before the Soldier's Rebellion of 2719, developing, testing, and, eventually, unleashing the software virus that completely wiped out the primary records database for all Corps personnel, then hunted down and erased more than half the data backup logs before the Admin had stopped it. The system-wide manhunt started right after the Soldier's Rebellion and had been going on since. In the Admin's eyes, wire-rats like La Mer are the single biggest threat the government has ever encountered.

They're both smiling at me and I realize I've been standing in the doorway silently for several seconds thinking about all the things that have happened since I'd deserted the Corps. In a way, I have this shy, boyish wire-rat to thank for most of it. If the Corps's records hadn't been destroyed, they'd have probably tracked David and I down a long time ago. La Mer and Venus don't seem to be concerned at my awkward entrance and merely wait for me to come in. I guess they've gotten used to the way I disengage, easily distracted by my own thoughts. It's been this way since Rajcik shot me—surviving a death sentence tends to make a person more thoughtful than they once were. Sometimes I wonder if I'm getting soft.

"Desto radioed us. Said there's a poker game at his and Karl's place. Rob's there. He's an old friend of yours, right, Aly?" Venus asks as she carefully toes the shards of the VDU screen aside.

I walk around the mess toward my bedroom door. "You could say that."

"You're not interested in a hand? I know Desto's insanely competitive, but he really sucks at poker." Venus is the only person in the system who could think Desto isn't a savant at poker. Her ability to read people is almost preternatural. It's a good thing for the rest of us she's too high-strung to play. "You'd probably be able to win a couple hundred dollars, or at least make him take some of your shifts in the grow rooms." My dislike for gardening is well-known throughout the settlement.

"Nah, I'm a little tired. Just going to turn in early tonight."

La Mer's thoughtful eyes are pinned to my face and I catch his gaze. He does me a favor by changing the subject. "Bodie and I should be able to wire in the last pieces of the transceiver in the next couple of days. If Vitruzzi and Brady say it's a go, we could test it by the end of the week. Pretty exciting, huh?"

"That's great news." With my concern over Vitruzzi's plan to ask Cross to help test, I can't quite summon the enthusiasm I know he's feeling.

"Using Admin tooders to transmit to and from the *Sphynx*? It's not just exciting." Venus takes an almost condescending school-marmish tone that is comical coming from someone who's too guileless to be anything but puppy-dog friendly. "It's *brilliant*! They'll never know, and our link ups will be almost instantaneous! No more days of lag between the Beach and the rest of the system. We'll finally be able to communicate and coordinate in real time. Just what they don't want."

Tooders, aka TDRSs, or Tracking and Data Relay satellites. The Admin builds and controls the only reliable satellite network in the system. Therefore, they control the air-to-ground communication throughout. If you control coms, you control everything. Private individuals, mostly citizens, have built and dispersed a handful of open-link satellites in out-of-the-way pockets of space, but they're so distant that messages take from hours to days to get from sender to receiver, and if either party is on the move, it takes even longer.

La Mer's expression is somber. "*If* it works. We can't be sure—I still don't know if my programming will override their lockouts until we test it." He bends down and slowly begins collecting some of the broken hardware on the floor. "It's actually a big risk. If they catch us trying to boost their coms . . . you know, it could be bad."

"Don't worry! You're a genius, Jer. I know it will work," Venus says.

"V is thinking about using Cross to help us run the test," I comment, hoping they'll come up with a reason it would be a bad idea, maybe something that can help me convince Vitruzzi of it.

La Mer turns sharply to face me. "What? Why?" he asks. "I mean, we could use another ship in orbit to test the transmission, but he's not, not really—I mean he's *Admin*."

Finally, another person who gets my concerns. "That's what I told V, but she thinks he's trustworthy." I sigh.

"She wouldn't take any risks she hasn't already calculated. Rob and V go back a few years," Venus muses. "Seems like you and he have too, Aly. You really think he'd turn us in for something like this?"

"I don't know. It's just—shit, never mind. I'm going to turn in. See you in the morning." It's a done deal. Worrying about it isn't going to change Vitruzzi's mind, and La Mer is right. The thing needs to be tested. It doesn't do us any good if we don't know if it works reliably.

"Night, Aly! We'll try and keep the noise down."

To Venus, keeping the noise down means trying not to make anything explode, and I lie awake for another couple of hours while they continue their experimentation. It's not a problem. I have a lot on my mind.

FOUR

In the morning, I run four laps around the settlement, about nine kilometers, grab a quick, tasteless breakfast of watery fortified grains, and head directly to the mine. It's still early—Algol A is draped along the crest of the Torarua Range, not quite high enough yet to beat the planet into smelt-hot submission, and the glittering debris belt around the distant red dwarf that comprises the third star in our system, Algol C, can still be faintly seen in the southern sky—but there is no shortage of early risers in Agate Beach. People here seem to naturally sleep less, having grown accustomed to the five short hours of complete darkness at night during the fall, and less in the summer.

I'm supposed to be working underground with Desto in the weapons vault today, doing overhaul and maintenance. Even in the fall, it gets hot out there, and being underground is usually a respite welcomed by all. A quick ride down the mine tunnel on my sandbike takes me into the main cavern, ready to get busy. The mine's central room is gigantic and the *Red Horizon* sits neatly on its tripod landing gear beside the *Sphynx*. Built for long hauls transporting heavy-volume loads, the *'Rize* is a bigger ship by a factor of about two. Next to it, the *Sphynx* looks barely fit for cross-continent hops.

The *'Rize*'s cargo-hold ramp is down, leaving the ship open to anyone who might want to wander aboard. Curious, I stop my sandbike in front of it and try to get a look inside. No lights on, just a dark hold, even after I pull off my thick, tinted riding goggles. Oh well. I throw the goggles in my back carrier and reach out to kill the bike's engine and park.

"Hey, good morning!" Cross calls, coming down the dark ramp.

My first instinct is to keep going, but there's no reason to be rude. Could I still be harboring some resentment for the way he'd just dropped off the map when his unit was reassigned? After eight years? Being this uncomfortable around him is starting to get on my nerves and I make an effort to answer amiably. "How are you? Sleep well?"

He runs his hand through his tousled black hair, leaving thick sheaves of it standing on end. "Honestly, I always sleep better on the ground than when I'm in the sky."

"You're probably in the wrong profession then."

He looks at me oddly for long enough that I think he must have misunderstood me. Then he says, "Yeah, but the money's good in what I do."

"Which is?"

The crooked grin that spreads across his face embarrasses me slightly. I'm giving him the third degree and I don't know why.

"Same sweet Aly. You've never let anyone off the hook, have you?"

"Sorry," I answer, tossing my leg over the sandbike saddle and dismounting.

Footsteps clang off the ramp and we both turn to see who it is. Baker—I hadn't caught her first name—the ship's navigator, is approaching. She's taller than me, and lean in a featherweight box-er's way. Her long brown hair is tied back and she wears a utilitari-an sleeveless shirt that shows off her wiry arms. The straight-legged pants tucked into her high black boots give away her former Corps status as clearly as if she were wearing rank. Her unflinching blue eyes weigh down on me as she addresses Cross. "We still have some work to do on the reversals." She says it flatly, like a com-mand.

"Yeah. Get started. I'll be right there."

She hesitates for another second, still trying to stare me down and fronting a distinct attitude of dislike. I don't drop my eyes, far too used to this game. Finally, she reverses and heads back into the belly of the ship.

Cross turns back to me with a slight *what can you do?* lift of his eyebrows.

"So, you and Baker?" I ask.

"What? Nah. We just work together."

"We just worked together too, back on the *Hammer*."

"Yeah, but that was completely different."

In what way, I want to ask, but leave it alone. It's none of my business. In any case, if she wants to be jealous of something that doesn't exist, that's her own problem.

"I've got work to do. I'll see you later."

"Okay." I feel his eyes follow me as I push the bike over to a paddock where several others are parked.

Before I make for the vault and a day guaranteed to leave me sooty, oily, dirty, and tired, I do a quick search inside the *Sphynx*, hoping to find Karl. He's not around, so I wander into the control room and find Bodie standing by a table-sized electron microscope that is known, for reasons I've never been able to put my finger on, as Medusa. His eyes are pressed firmly against the viewing lenses, probably indulging in his favorite hobby, i.e., analyzing anything he can fit under a lens or in front of a reader. His recent obsession is trying to splice the staple crops the settlement usually grows in underground greenhouses and grow rooms with the hardier local plants that are adapted to the harsh dry environment of Spectra 6. If we can do a better job of acclimating ourselves and our food sources to the local environment, there's a better chance of the settlement remaining a viable and independent long-term home. He doesn't look up when I come in, totally absorbed in whatever he's staring at, until I get his attention with a gentle tap on his shoulder.

"Oh, hey, Aly. You looking for Desto?"

"No, actually, I was wondering if you've seen Karl? I thought he might be working on the *Sphynx* with Venus today, but neither of them are there."

"He and Doug left on the Rover awhile ago. I think they're taking some of the new parts out to the transceiver."

A brick of disappointment lodges in my stomach. Until I moved in with Venus, Karl was at my infirmary room first thing every day to wish me good morning. Since I've recovered, we've kept up the tradition, always getting together for breakfast or to exchange a few quick words before the day's work takes over. So what's changed with him? Is he really jealous of someone I haven't seen since I was twenty-two years old? He's always been a hothead but this is just irrational. Between him and Baker, it's almost hard to believe there *isn't* something going on between Rob and me. The idea is absurd, and my disappointment starts to morph into a feeling I'm much more used to: anger.

"Want me to send him to the vault when they get back?" Bodie is staring at me the way he'd just been looking through the scope lens, and I wonder what he's seeing in my expression.

"No, I'll catch up with him some other time. Thanks."

"No problem."

I don't have time for this hassle; I have work to do. If Karl wants to sort this out, he knows where to find me.

When I pass by the *'Rize* this time, no one's outside. There's a hydraulic lift built to handle bigger pieces of cargo at the far end of the cavern where it finally dead ends at the heart of the mountain. I take it down past the midlevel subfloor and its network of grow rooms to the lowest subfloor. The lift is a wall-less platform and it settles to the floor at the bottom of the shaft into a dusty, barely lit room no bigger than a closet. The original miners who'd dug up this mountain to extract whatever the Admin was looking for had blasted one last shaft down here before giving up and going home—or dying off, whatever happened to them. Maybe they'd found something, maybe not, but this room is only an antechamber to a tunnel that was once about twenty meters long and five or so wide. Now, all a person standing where I am can see is a rock wall three meters in front of them. It feels uncomfortably like being inside a grave.

There's no sound down here but that doesn't mean I'm alone. The electronic door hiding our ammunition vault—an airlock hatch salvaged from a derelict that a hawker had been piecing out in Hell's Gate—is thick. Any sound on the other side would have to be as loud as a symphony for a person on this side of it to hear. It's controlled remotely by a twelve-digit code, transmitted via the wrist VDUs we all wear. I enter the sequence and watch as the rock in front of me splits along a left seam and begins to slide to the right. Small puffs of pulverized dust shake from the ceiling and rain into the lighted opening.

Rectangular overhead lights hang in meter intervals along the chamber's ceiling. When they're all functioning, they flood the room with blazing white light, sucking a lot of juice from one of the generators in the mine's main chamber. Most of the settlement's power is derived from an array of photovoltaic heliostats that cover an acre of hard desert nearby, and with our three stars, they're never in danger of going dry. Two of the ten light rigs are down right now, but the chamber still incandesces like the center of a fusion bomb, making the cold surfaces of rows of missiles, rifles, thrown projectiles, and assorted electronic surveillance and explosive devices gleam. It's a tomb for contraband military hardware. Vitruzzi thinks of the transceiver as an insurance policy against surprises, but to me, this room holds the real insurance.

"Twig, how are ya?" Desto calls, standing before the open housing of a Glower missile, where he's testing its navigation mechanism.

I move over to the gun racks and start pulling down rags and cleaning compound. "Please don't call me that."

"Why not? It's perfect! You're short, skinny"—a devious smile replaces the frown he'd adopted to feign insult—"and sometimes a little sharp."

"Forget it, okay? That's what my mom use to call me."

"Yeah? Why'd she call you that?"

Irritated, my voice gives off sparks as I answer. "I don't know. She took off when I was a kid." The past is over and I don't like to think about it.

"All right, all right. But if even half those stories Cross was telling us last night are true, you haven't been a kid in a long time."

"Jesus, Desto! Can you just drop it?" I'm a little shocked that Cross would have much to say about our shared past, but then, what else do men have to talk about when they're drinking and playing cards?

"Don't freak, babe, I'm not talking about anything naughty. I'd prefer you showed me that yourself." He winks. "Cross and David were talking about some of the work you all did for the Corps. Back before you grew an unauthorized conscience."

Feeling foolish, I try to ignore him, but Desto's directness and total lack of tact are all part of his appeal. That and the fact that he can quote you exactly what kind of blade, firearm, bomb, or tactical missile you'll need to get the job done to specification for any, and I mean *any*, situation.

"We've all done shit we wished we hadn't, huh?" He doesn't respond, doesn't need to. Desto's had his own taste of the Corps and its explicit antimercy policy. I'd like to get on with work so I can stop wondering about Karl's strange behavior and forget about Cross's unexpected reintroduction into my life. "So, what's on the agenda?"

He hands me a small receiver. "Today, you get to be the target." Meaning, he'll be checking the missile calibrations as I move around to make sure they're tracking.

To keep perspective on the utter dullness of the next couple of hours, I keep telling myself I could be stuck outside in the 35 C heat, working on the transceiver. That isn't enough though, and soon I'm thinking about last's night's conversation again and what Cross said about the Admin rescinding its contracts with noncitizen crews.

We've tested about half of the missiles when I bring it up. "Things are going to get rough out here if Vitruzzi loses her Admin contracts."

Grunting, Desto squats and reseats a Glower in its cargo box, a job that usually requires two men. Straightening up, he answers, "Nah. There's always the black market." Waving me away, he opens the crate for the next one.

"Sure. That's true. But the risks are higher."

Connecting the test rig, he gives me a count of three on his fingers. After confirming that the coordinates locked, he answers, "The stakes aren't high enough stealing from the Admin? Damn. Besides, we already have mostly everything we need. Far as I'm concerned, the less we tango with them, the better."

"And what if they close the Obals to non-cits? Are you ready to be cut off from . . . ?" I let the sentence hang.

"Civilization?" He laughs. "Aly, we may be on the fringes out here, but if that means I don't take orders from anyone, I'm good. Besides, did you book a vacation to Tunis City or something? And, oh yeah, I hear the weather on Keum Libre is fucking great this time of year." Chuckling harder, he wrestles the next box down from its shelf.

Frowning, I wait for him to set the test rig. Desto has a point, but I'm somehow not finding it as easy as him to let go of the idea of never being able to travel to an Admin city. Banished from law and order for good. How do you get used to that?

FIVE

Two hours later, the back of my throat tastes like an oil slick and my hands are a uniform black from carbon dust. Desto suggests we take a break and go topside for some food and sunshine, and I can hardly contain my eagerness. Whatever Venus's reasons for wanting me as a roommate, she was certainly right about people not being built to live underground. Though it makes me wonder why I don't feel this cooped up when in flight for months at a time. It's darker in space than any cave, and there isn't much room on a ship. Still, being in the sky has always felt right to me. There's no explaining it, not even to myself.

When the lift reaches topside, Vitruzzi sees it and walks toward us. "I was just about to come and get you. Cross is free and I'm going to take him out to the transceiver. Do you still want to come, Aly?"

I nod. "And his crew?"

"They're occupied with the *Horizon*. It'll just be him. Desto, join us?"

"My pleasure."

We walk past the *Sphynx* and I notice the Rover parked alongside its loading ramp, but still no Karl. Brady and Cross stand beside it chatting amiably, as if they've been friends for years. Rob's always been the kind of guy that people take an instant liking to, both charming and funny and rarely anything but polite. He's probably been doing pretty well for himself as an Admin contractor. Besides being likable, I remember him as being efficient and reliable, and he'd risen through the ranks back in the Corps at a speed that would ordinarily make people mutter about bribes and blackmail. But it was just Cross's personality and rock-solid capabilities that got him so far. Now as a citizen, his ship, a newer model with solar amalgam-powered engines, reflects at least some measure of the same success, broken reversals aside. Sitting next the *Sphynx*, whose hull is pocked and scraped to raw metal in more than a few places, the *Red Horizon* epitomizes the difference between citizens and non-citizens, those living on the Obals and those living on the Spectras.

Brady gets into the driver's seat and Vitruzzi, Cross, and I load up and roll outside the mine's tunnel, Desto following on his bike. The day is hot already and we extend a shade flap along either side of the Rover's clamshell spine to block the driving sun. Vents along the base of the sideboards let air circulate through the vehicle's cab, but no one would describe it as a cool and comfortable ride. The best way to drive the Rover on this planet to keep from getting broiled is *fast*.

The transceiver sits north of the mine about five klicks, planted atop the first high ridge of the complex canyon system extending between Agate Beach and Hell's Gate. I'd passed through that labyrinth during my first visit to the Beach, trying to get back to Rajcik and my old smuggling crew. Now I know the area as Mecca Flats. Having explored every circuitous crag and peak since settling here, I know how easy it would be to get lost in there, or lose someone else, plus it provides excellent cover from airborne spies.

The top of the ridge sits a couple hundred meters from the valley floor, and there's a vehicle-wide path carved and graded up the gradual slope. The device itself is only about the size of a standard radar dish, oblong and convex, and mounted on top of a metal base that also serves as a battery housing. The batteries can be rotated from a supply we keep at the Beach, or juiced up directly from our generators via a long cable. The entire apparatus lies hidden beneath a scavenged military net colored in desert camouflage and wired with radar jamming sensors. The only way to see the device from the sky is when it's uncovered.

La Mer glances over as we drive up. A panel he's removed from the base lies next to him and he sits on the hard-packed earth, elbow deep in wiring that bursts from within. The transceiver dish is still covered by its camouflage netting, giving him a hint of shade, but sweat streaks down the sides of his face anyway. Brady pulls the Rover up and we all climb out.

"So what is this, Eleanor? It sounded like you were going to make me swear over the life of my firstborn not to tell anyone about it before you brought me up here. But I have to admit, it doesn't look like much," Rob says, grinning crookedly.

Brady begins circling the dish, untying the netting from stakes in the ground. When they're all loose, he motions to me to take one side while he grabs the other. With a yank, the netting slides into the dirt at our feet.

"Rob, we've built a transceiver that sends and receives in real time using satellites." Vitruzzi explains. "We'll be able to talk to you or anyone else we want outside of our orbit now with no lag. La Mer's been helping us build it, but we'd like your help to test it."

"Brilliant! Yeah, I'll help. Definitely. But"—his forehead furrows in skepticism—"did you build yourselves a satellite network, too? The Admin is a little stingy with theirs, which you know."

There's a quick pause and he understands immediately what's not being said. "Oh. You figured out a way to hijack Admin tooders."

"Now you see why we've kept it under wraps," Brady responds.

"Okaaayyy." He draws the word out, then stays silent for a minute, considering what he's agreeing to. I watch him closely, trying to read what he's thinking. Finally, he continues, his voice tight but sincere, "Sure, I can help you test it. But first you have to be honest with me, what kind of safeguards do you have in place so they won't be able to either detect a hack, or trace it if they do? No offense, but I'm not sure it's worth my ship, or jail time, if you're not a hundred percent it'll work. I'd be out more than just a few contracts."

"You've got nothing to worry about," La Mer answers. "You'll just be picking up the signal. No harm in that. We'll use the *Sphynx* to transmit back to the Beach, which is the only way the Admin could trace it. But I know their systems, and they aren't going to know a thing."

"Yeah? How could you know their systems?"

La Mer is, as always, reluctant to talk about himself. The fact that he'd managed to stay hidden from the Admin for six years can be attributed to his tight-lipped style. "It's a specialty of mine," is his short reply.

"Okay, man. Just asking." Cross walks over to the dish and gazes up into his reflection in the steel bowl. Without turning around, he asks, "When's the test?"

Vitruzzi and Brady exchange a glance and I read uncertainty in their eyes. We've just put the Beach and every settlers' freedom on the line on a bet that Cross, citizen or not, friend or not, won't find a reason to turn us in. Paranoia once again bristles along my skin like a rash and I find myself wondering just where he got the funds to buy such a nice ship, but I throttle the thought before it can dig in.

Vitruzzi answers him. "The parts you brought us yesterday are the last ones we needed. Bodie and La Mer should be done putting it together . . . when?" She raises her eyebrows and looks at La Mer.

"Tomorrow maybe. Definitely the next day if not." He's still looking at Cross, his face neutral. I can't say why, but I get the impression he doesn't like Rob.

Cross turns around and asks, "Is there anything I can help with?" The calm sincerity in his voice instantly shuts down the voice in my head that keeps questioning his reliability. What's my problem? He's just a guy, an old friend. Trusting people has never been my style, but being betrayed by Rajcik must have affected me deeper than I realized.

"This is handled," Brady answers. "But you and your crew could help us move some equipment in the mine. It'll only take an hour or so."

"Sure. Anything you need."

"One more thing, Rob," Vitruzzi says, "we think it's best if you don't mention this to the rest of your crew."

"Of course, don't even worry about it." He flashes another winning grin, then looks over at me. "You know you can rely on me."

IT'S LATE AFTERNOON AND still no Karl. After finishing the day off in the vault with Desto, I grab a quick dry-shower in the mine's lavatory to blast the grit and carbon off my skin, then hop on my bike to head to Venus's. As I drive past the *Red Horizon*, the only thing on my mind is food, but I spot two of Cross's crewmembers—Sims and Montoya—standing atop their left engine housing, struggling to keep solid footing while they work inside the engine compartment.

Stopping, I shout up at them, "Hey, you guys want a better platform? I can drive the airstairs out here for you."

They both glance down at me and quickly decline with a short "no thanks." Shrugging, I keep going. On my way out, my VDU vibrates as David buzzes me.

"Hey Aly. Come by Bodie's and my place. Rob's coming over for some chow and to catch up on more old times."

I've already decided to have a quickie dinner and then track Karl down, having grown both irritated and concerned over his no-show all day. "No thanks. I'm beat. I'm just going to call it a night."

"Don't give me that. You get your ass over here—that's an order." His smile fills the VDU screen, punting my resolve aside like a deflated ball, and I can't help but react to the challenge in his voice. He'd laugh at me if I told him my concerns about Karl, and I can't have my big brother giving me shit. Besides, if I don't find Karl, what am I going to do? Sit around Venus's like a heartbroken teenager?

"Fine. Be there in five."

SIX

Bodie and David are more like an old married couple than room-mates—an old married couple who specialize in gourmet cooking—and put on an excellent feast of fresh vegetables and spice-enhanced protein concentrate that tastes almost *better* than a steak. I can't believe I almost didn't come. To top off the delicious meal, Rob has brought along several bottles of contraband wine that he says he keeps in its own secret stash room on the *'Rize*. The settlement only has enough room to grow foods for their nutritional value with nothing being wasted on fermentable grains and fruits. Consequently, we rarely see booze, and it isn't long into the evening before I'm feeling as relaxed and boneless as a drunk amoeba.

We're all lounging on a deck Bodie and David built from broken crates and spare hardware, feeling the night drop its pleasant breeze over us like a cool sheet. David takes a sip of his wine and comments, "I never had it this good, even before I joined the Corps. You know, being a citizen had its perks but there wasn't any adventure in it. It's like your life was a book that you read when you were a kid. Too simple, no surprises. Rob, I don't know how you stand it."

Rob chuckles, not offended. "It's not that bad. There are surprises, especially when you're a transport contractor like me. There are plenty of days when I don't know exactly what to expect. Take yesterday for example—who would have ever suspected I'd run into the two of you? Besides, nothing I do is routine. Running down illegal goods for folks like Eleanor and Brady isn't the stuff of a mundanity. And some of the things you've asked for, Bodie—sometimes I almost need a planetary engineer to tell me what they are before I even know where to look."

David chuckles, "Yeah, I see what you mean."

"Rob, you always seemed pretty content with life in the Corps, what made you give it up and become a citizen?" I ask.

He thinks about it for a minute before answering. "To be honest, a lot of it has to do with some of the things you talked about when we were still on the *Hammer*. You know, things about how we were being used, not having real freedom, the lies—however you put it. I don't know what I thought of it then, but I started to believe it after the Rebellion."

I turn to look at him, surprised. He's looking back at me frankly and the fading daylight casts deep shadows around his eyes, leaving just a wink of light reflecting from them. "That, and I'd finally had enough of being pushed around. The Soldier's Rebellion changed everything, for everyone. It got tough in the ranks after that; everyone was suspected of being complicit with the rebels, always monitored and scrutinized. My unit was tasked with hunting down deserters, and that's when it really came to a head for me. It was one thing to hunt down criminals who were legitimately dangerous, but some of the men and women we had to pick up were people we'd served with. *Good* people. And we knew they were as good as dead." His voice grows thicker and he pauses for a long moment. "So when my enlistment came up, I took the out." He flashes me a sad smile and takes a long drink from his cup.

"What about your crew? Did you serve with any of them?" Sims, Montoya, and Baker aren't here tonight. Curious.

"You can tell they're former Corps, huh? It's hard to shake off all that training. But no, I didn't know any of them before, uh, before I hired them. Baker and Montoya started working with me about six months ago, and Sims about four. Met them all in Tunis City."

I'm about to ask more questions, wanting a clear picture of his life since leaving the Corps, but Bodie stands up and stretches, letting out a ratcheting belch that would make a bullfrog proud. "Kids, La Mer and I are heading up to the dish early tomorrow before it gets too hot, so I'm going to leave you to your reminiscing. But I have to tell you, you sound like a bunch of grumpy old vets whose only pleasure comes from rehashing their glory days together."

We laugh and say good night. I stand up to leave as well, not wanting to be a nuisance to Bodie, and have to put a hand out on the building's wall to steady myself. Rob jumps up with me. "Aly, would you mind giving me a ride back to my ship?"

The question comes out awkwardly, like he's asking me to do something mildly indecent. Before answering, I catch David's eye and read a hint of both amusement and interest in them. I can't think of a reason to say no and don't even know why I want to. "Sure. Come on."

It takes us less than ten minutes to get back to the mine entrance. I switch off the engine and Rob lets go of my waist and jumps off.

"Almost like old times," he says, smiling, his body close to mine.

"In what way?" The cooler night air washed away some of my dizziness, but looking into his dark eyes brings it back, and for a moment, I'm lightheaded.

"Okay, you're right. Nothing like old times, really. But I want you to know that I meant it when I told you how good it is to see you again. I missed you."

I know he's not intentionally making me uncomfortable, but I feel a very strong urge to peel out and speed away as fast as I can. Instead, I try to deflect, "Look Rob, that was a long time ago. I have a new life here. I've put the Corps and everything else behind me."

"I completely understand that. I, you know, I just didn't realize . . . I mean, until I saw you yesterday, I had almost forgotten what things were like when we were together. That's what I mean when I say it's good to see you. It's good to see you happy. You're doing well here, and that's what I always wanted for you. The way things were in the Corps, before the Rebellion . . . and then when we lost touch. I was afraid you were dead, and that was hard for me."

I know I shouldn't say anything, should let sleeping dogs lie, but the world is so quiet, the binary suns' scorching light muted for the night—this moment seems to exist outside of time and may be the only chance I get for answers I've wanted since he stepped out of my life. "When you were reassigned, why didn't you keep in contact? If I meant *so much* to you."

He looks away from me and takes the tiniest step backward. I know that no matter what he says next, no matter how sincerely he believes it, the truth will always be that back then we were still too young to know what we wanted, or to appreciate what we had. It wouldn't have been hard for me to find Rob, if I'd really wanted to. Just as easy as it would have been for him to find me.

"I don't really know. I guess I took too much for granted." He sighs as if he's trying to decide if he should tell me something, but the rasping click of a sandbike as it downshifts echoes throughout the mine tunnel, cutting him off. We both look toward the entrance and see Karl emerging. He sees us too and looks like he might drive past us for a second before pulling up.

I haven't done anything wrong, but suddenly I feel unaccountably guilty and catch myself glance at Rob. Out of the corner of my eye, I see Karl's expression turn sour.

Not sure what to say, I finally break the silence: "You're working late."

"Yeah," he replies curtly, then shifts his gaze toward Rob and nods in a manner that borders on unfriendly. "Cross."

"Strahan."

"I've been wondering where you were all day."

"Busy. Working. We've got a lot to finish up before the transceiver's operational."

"I know, but . . ." I stop myself. I'm not going to get into this with him here. "Tomorrow should be just as busy. I should get going."

I haven't left the saddle of the sandbike and a flick of the engine switch brings it purring to life.

"Good night, Aly," Rob says as I roll forward.

I nod at him and turn the bike around as I approach Karl. Stopping in front of him, I ask, "Do you want to ride together?"

He gives me a noncommittal shrug and restarts his bike. Within seconds, we're clear of the mine and riding beneath the not-quite-black night sky toward his place. Once we arrive, he pulls around to the back and parks next to Desto's assault motorcycle, its huge faring and projecting rifle barrels giving it the look of a monstrous insect in the starlight. I stop next to him and kill the engine.

Stepping off, I stand squarely in front of him. "Karl, what's going on? Something's bothering you. Why don't you just tell me what it is so I don't have to guess."

Avoiding my eyes, he lights up a smoke and says nothing for a few seconds. Long enough to frustrate me. Then: "Look, Aly. I realize you've got a history that I don't really know much about. There're things in my own past you probably wouldn't care to hear about. But it's not easy when—"

I cut him off, "Karl, Cross is someone I knew in another lifetime. What he said at Vitruzzi's last night, and whatever he may have said when he was over here playing cards, that's all history. It has nothing to do with . . . with us." I almost said, *It has nothing to do with how I feel about you,* but something stopped me. It's never come naturally for me to talk about my feelings; for soldiers, emotions don't factor it to how we operate. I'd been in the Academy and then the Corps since I was fourteen and become a person of actions, not words. Talking things out doesn't give me the instant resolve that I'm used to. Maybe I've never learned how to express myself, but so far, Karl has seemed to understand me just fine. What's changed?

He stamps out the cigarette and puts the butt in a container sitting next to his dwelling's adobe walls. Standing there with his arms at his sides, his back straight, he looks almost like the mien of some primeval ruler about to pass judgment. At times, that immobile stance makes me feel safe, protected, like I have someone solid to rely on when things get tough. Other times, like now, his way of looming silently, almost stonewalling me, infuriates me to the point that I want to shake him.

"How are things between us, Aly?"

The question hits me like an unexpected backhand and I wince, knowing Karl sees it. Immediately, I want to explain myself, to tell him that it's only surprise that makes me react in that way. But I can't do that. Don't even know how. What could I say to him that he doesn't already know? How can I tell him my feelings for him without it sounding awkward and insincere, or worse, like a lie?

So, instead of telling him the truth—that I would die for him if necessary, that since meeting him, I've learned what it means to actually live, what it's like to share everything that matters with another person in a completely selfless way—I say, "You tell me." Because I need to hear it before I can say it. I need to know that if I go out on a limb and leave myself naked and vulnerable, I won't be out there alone.

There's a subtle shift in his expression, something more felt than seen, and I know I've stung him. If only he would understand that I can't expose myself like that no matter how bad I want to. I can't let myself get hurt.

He looks away over my shoulder and sighs. "I'm not sure I even know. Good night." Then he walks inside, leaving me standing alone in the night.

SEVEN

The next day begins the same as the one before, and every one before that during these past few months. Bodie and La Mer ask me out to the dish for a couple of hours—my petite hands make it easier to fit together some of the smaller components—and after I've done what I can to help them, I head out to the firing range with Desto to test some weapons. I don't bother lying to myself that mostly what I'm doing is finding ways to avoid Karl this time, wanting to drown with distractions the panicked feeling that had started the minute he'd closed the door on me last night.

Avoiding the thoughts rolling around my head like loose cannonballs on a ship's deck anytime I'm not busy is priority—so I stay busy. While Desto and I practice until we've sweat through every fiber of our clothes on the range, we get word that they've finished wiring the final pieces to the transceiver. The test will be tonight and Karl, Vitruzzi, and Venus take the *Sphynx* off-world toward Spectra 4, preparing to wait for the transmission scheduled to be sent at 2030 hours. Less than five minutes after hearing this, Mason pings us both simultaneously.

"What now?" Desto wonders, cueing the go button on his VDU.

"You two, we were just hailed by an Admin security ship. They're landing in less than ten minutes. Get your asses to the mine on the double."

We drop the rifles we'd brought into a crate and cover it with a tarp, hoping no one bothers to come out here and take a look. Scrambling onto the back of Desto's bike, I grip his waist as he guns it. We jump onto the dirt track leading to the Beach too fast and the front wheel starts to skid off the edge of a brief incline, spraying rocks and pebbles behind us and guaranteeing us a more than a few abrasions if we go down. In a synchronous movement that would seem graceful if the stakes weren't so high, we lean together to regain a balanced center of gravity and the wheel rights itself.

We reach the mine where the settlers inside are working in a frenzied but orderly burst. There are plenty of items littering the cavern that a destitute group of non-cits can't easily justify having, and tucking them away or making them appear more derelict than they are is top priority. Admin security never travels out this far, so we've been surprisingly lax about keeping things that might be suspicious under lock and key. It's much too late now, but the realization of how incredibly stupid we've all been is drilling into my skull. More than stupid, we've been *crazy* not to take better precautions. Yet the reality is that there is *no* reason for Admin security to be here. They only handle civilian centers. Anything criminal or suspected of being criminal on the Spectras gets automatically dished out to the Capital Military Corps.

Vitruzzi, Bodie, and Karl are loping from the *Sphynx*'s hold as a blast of air wafts down the tunnel from the mine entrance. It can only be one thing—a ship landing. Spotting us, Vitruzzi says, "Desto, get the vault squared away and hide. Take them with you." She waves a hand toward David and La Mer—just pulling their sandbikes in after having come from the transceiver—and I.

Desto breaks into a trot, slapping La Mer on the shoulder as he goes by in a manner that says *follow me*. David turns to go after them, but I stand beside Bodie.

"What do you have in the control room that we need to do something about?" His deep-set blue eyes widen for second, and he glances at Vitruzzi as if wondering if she knows why I'd be crazy enough not to get out of sight. "Bodie! What's in there that could tip them off about the security worm or the transceiver?"

Finally realizing what I'm getting at, he grasps my forearm, saying to Vitruzzi, "Com room. You have to scramble the last day's outgoing transmissions," and starts to pull me along as he makes for the control room.

"There's a safe-box dug into the floor beneath the holodisc reader. We need to throw in some of the terminals Jeremy and I used to track and crack the satellite programs. Most of the other equipment doesn't matter; they can't prove what's stolen and what's not."

He sounds as if he really thinks that matters, but I keep my mouth shut and run along beside him. The noise of a large vehicle echoes from the mouth of the tunnel as I pull the control room doors shut behind us. Not much time.

Doug Mason sits at the monitoring station and jumps to his feet as we enter. "What are you doing here, Erikson? They're right outside, for God's sake."

Neither of us answer as Bodie runs toward the central bank of computers lining the far wall and starts pulling datablocks from their connectors. "Keep an eye outside, Aly. Let me know if they're coming in. Doug, help me out with these. We need to cover all the evidence of the satellite hack."

I press up against the door and stare through the shatterproof window. My Derg is in my hand, though I don't remember reaching for it. Hard to see outside through the thick, nearly translucent material. People look like wavering ghosts as they hustle about and the *Sphynx* and *Red Horizon* are large gray beasts taking up the cavern's bulk.

A track–propelled transport vehicle rolls into my limited field of view and stops about ten meters outside of the control room. "Hurry it up, Bodie," I whisper. "They are right outside." He curses, then grunts as he shoves the holodisc reader aside.

The mechanical sound of an electric motor hums through the air as the hatch to the safe-box opens—I hadn't even known the thing was there. A quick glance over my shoulder catches him tossing the datablocks inside hastily, then clicking a button on the remote in his hand to close the hatch again. Pushing the disc reader back, he tucks the remote inside a storage drawer and grins. "We're good."

Appraising him calmly, I ask, "Any other handy nooks where a person my size might fit?"

His grin fades like chalk in a rainstorm. "Maybe they won't—"

"Shh!" I hush him with a sharp chop of my hand. Four security personnel have emerged from the interior of the transport and stand a few meters away. The control room doors are thick, but I don't want to chance anything drawing their attention to us. Bodie steps up beside me and activates the door's electronic lock.

Brady walks into view outside, his gait fast and aggressive. I glimpse him run his hand over his VDU and it gives me an idea. Moving the Derg into my left hand, I unlatch the tiny earpiece housed along the edge of my own VDU and insert it into my ear. Then I turn the unit on, already set to the channel the regular *Sphynx* crewmembers use.

Brady's voice comes through clearly. "What are you doing here?" Not the warmest greeting I've ever heard.

A member of the security team steps forward. It's difficult to make out her rank or features, but her voice carries through Brady's VDU with authority. "Are you in charge here?"

"This is a free settlement. There's nobody in charge." The officer who'd spoken stiffens. Brady continues, "Why's an Admin security team here?"

"The Political and Capital Administration is undertaking a census of all the primarily non-citizen settlements and colonies on the Spectra planets. Your cooperation, or lack of it, will be noted."

Bodie and Doug have pressed in next to me to watch through the window. At the officer's words, we exchange a brief, troubled glance.

"A census? Why?"

"Sir, that information is relevant to neither our mission nor to you. Now, is there any population accounting or tracking system here that we can look at, or will we need to do a walk-through of the settlement and take count ourselves?" The way her voice drops at the last part makes it clear that if the Admin team is forced to do a head count, it won't be fun. For anyone.

Brady stands in obstinate silence, staring her down. After a few seconds, he says flatly, "There are 125 people in Agate Beach."

"And do you have a list of their names, ages, and citizen status?" Her response is quick and nearly as toneless as Brady's. She's been doing this for a while and has probably dealt with worse hostility than his.

I can almost hear Brady's thoughts. His detestation for the Admin is part of his physical being; when the subject of the Obals-based government comes up, it's nearly as visible as a malignant growth would be. He'd probably like nothing better than to reach out for the officer's handgun and use it to pummel her self-important face to the other side of her head. Of course, that wouldn't do much good for him or for the larger goal of getting the Admin crew well and away from Agate Beach. He says, "Wait here." Giving them a list of the settlers is the quickest means of making them disappear.

His figure moves out of view and the officer turns to the other three personnel standing behind her. Only a faint murmur of their voices passes through the thick divider between us and we can't tell what's being said. Two of the security team crew set off deeper into the mine, apparently sent on some kind of reconnoitering mission. The officer and the remaining crewmember begin walking toward the control room.

We all lean away from the window instinctively but there's no way to see in. The room is much dimmer than the cavern and the window is too thick and mottled for visibility from their side.

"If they come in, Aly, you hide inside one of the equipment lockers. You'll fit," Mason growls in my ear.

I'd rather throw myself into the engine housing of an MCACS—being stuck in small spaces makes me feel like I'm napping in my own coffin—but I keep calm by telling myself they won't be able to get in.

The officer reaches the door and tugs against the handle. Her face is centimeters from the window and I peek through. The insignia on her uniform shows she's a Chief Class II from the Obal 8 Security Squadron. They're a long way away from home. What the hell could the Admin be doing a census for anyway?

She tries tugging the outer handle first left then right to open the door, but it's not moving. She puts her face up against the window and the three of us withdraw quickly. Her voice is faint but clear as she says to her subordinate, "Locked. We may want to take a look inside here when that Spectre comes back."

"Chief," another crewmember says, approaching the door. "We just received a message from headquarters."

"What's the gist, Corporal?"

"An Obal 5 security crew has taken casualties due to an uprising of prisoners they were transporting to Keum Libre. They want us to reinforce that crew and help neutralize the prisoners."

"They want us to aid a prisoner transport crew?" The officer sounds about as happy as if she'd just heard she'd be mopping up sewage spills with a hankie for her next mission. "Don't they have anyone closer?"

The corporal instinctively remains silent.

The chief continues, "It can't be any worse than leapfrogging around the Spectras dealing with a bunch of backward primitives. We'll get that list from the local honcho and head out. Shouldn't be more than twenty minutes from now. Corporal, send headquarters our ETA to rendezvous with Obal 5's crew."

"What about checking this room, Chief?"

"Forget it. By the look of that transport ship and this Eleanor Vitruzzi's contracting status, they have plenty of things in there that they shouldn't, but that isn't our problem. We'll ping HQ, let them figure out what to do about it. Maybe send a Corps squad down to clean up."

"Roger, Chief."

As we wait behind the control room door, it occurs to me to wonder if David and La Mer had had time to cover the transceiver. What better piece of equipment for drawing *very* unwanted attention? The three security personnel turn and walk back around the far side of the transport vehicle, causing us to lose visibility. I take a breath of relief as Brady returns and hands the officer a small disc.

Without even a nod of thanks, she motions her team to load the transport and climbs aboard last. The transport executes a six-point turn to pull headfirst out of the mine. When the sound of its engine has faded to a dull growl, I push through the control room door and jog up to Brady.

"What the hell was *that* about?" I ask.

His eyes don't waver from the retreating vehicle as he says, "Something is very wrong."

IT'S LATE EVENING BY the time everyone is back at the Beach, and we all meet in the main cavern so La Mer and Bodie can fill us in on the transceiver's status. The entire population of the settlement has maneuvered their way into the subterranean hanger, a hundred-plus warm bodies barely making a dent in the vast space. Rob has taken the *'Rize* up ostensibly on a test flight to check out their patch job on the broken reversals. They should be in orbit somewhere near the southern pole of the planet and outside of regular communication range waiting to hear from the Beach.

With so much going on, the crew hadn't had a chance to re-group and speculate on why the Admin would be taking a census of the Beach and other settlements like it. Vitruzzi and Brady had been AWOL since the security team left.

The crowd is restless; most of the people here have marginal interest in the transceiver and the effort it took to build it. They have little to do with the other planets and don't crave any connection, especially at the risk of Admin retaliation. But they also see the benefits of having people like Vitruzzi with her Admin connections and Bodie with his in-depth scientific background to help keep the colony afloat and healthy. They grudgingly accept the transceiver as a necessary means to ensure their continuity. They know only too well that if you live outside the law, you still have to be prepared for it to find you.

As I look over the group, I don't see in them many similarities to me—I'm the outsider here. Most of these people have never experienced the benefits of citizenship. The majority were born in non-cit colonies on the Spectras or their moons and have never set foot on a planet with clean air or organized development. Some are miners that were either abandoned when their mines ran dry or escaped Admin conscription, having been forced into labor on planets too harsh for softer citizens to inhabit, much less tame. A handful are like Vitruzzi and Bodie—citizens who found life under the Admin's thumb even less appealing than the hardships that come with being out here on the fringes. And then there are Desto, David, La Mer, and I—the only deserters in the bunch. We share an intimate familiarity of the costs of citizenship with the other citizens or former citizens here but have lived our lives on a tangent far removed from those who'd suffered since the day they were born. I've always thought of myself as tough, but I've never had to fight the very elements of the planet I live on for the sake of basic survival. The people here have taught me what it really means to be strong, and how to not only survive, but to thrive, without the Admin pulling my strings. It's made me realize that the years I spent with Rajcik may have gained me some coin, but they cost me nearly as much as if I'd stayed in the Corps.

Brady, back from whatever brainstorming he'd been doing with Vitruzzi, stands up on a cargo box and asks people to quiet down. He says a few words, thanking the settlers for the help they all provided in getting the dish built, recognizes La Mer and Bodie specifically for their contribution, and comments about the success and independence of Agate Beach and the example it sets as an alternative to the Admin's special brand of control. I feel an inadvertent swelling of pride in our accomplishment, reminding me of the way I used to respond to these kinds of motivational speeches from the high-ranking leaders I'd admired when I first enlisted at the Academy. I stifle the feeling quickly, my cynicism warning me not to get too wrapped up in minor successes that ultimately don't mean much.

When he's said everything he intends to, he steps onto the lift to the communication room where Desto and Bodie are already waiting. At the last minute, he motions to David and me. I'm a bit surprised that Brady would want to include me, with our endless disagreements, but don't hesitate to join them. When we enter the small room, La Mer already sits in front of main com console, a set of earphones clamped around his head, testing various relays and switches. He looks as if he's concentrating intensely and bites reflexively on his lower lip. He's not the only one feeling a case of nerves. We all know that his programming—the key to the entire experiment—will do one of three things: fail completely, work enough to hijack the Admin satellites but not enough to hide our pirated use of their system, or be a success.

The room is barely big enough to hold all of us and we wedge ourselves uncomfortably around the console. "Ready to go, La Mer?" Brady asks.

He clears his throat, brightens the resolution of the central VDU, and says, "It all seems ready."

His apprehensiveness is not reassuring, but I clamp my mouth shut against the question: *Are you sure this is going to work?* If La Mer is as good as he says he is—and if what he'd done with the Corps personnel database before the Rebellion is any indication, he is—this kind of job is routine.

"The satellites we're using are all operational. One minute until transmission. Bodie, you're up."

Bodie takes a seat next to La Mer and turns on a speaker channel. All our eyes are on the countdown, and as soon as it says 2030, Bodie depresses the comlink and says, "This is central hailing the flightline. Do you read?" The transmission was planned so no specific names or locations would be used—a precautionary measure, though the most damning breach will be if the Admin detects La Mer's security bypass.

The seconds seem to draw out too long, then finally, Vitruzzi's voice: "This is Orbiter One. We hear you loud and clear." Followed by: "Orbiter 2. That's a copy. Congratulations!" Rob had decided to transmit after all, despite the risk.

La Mer and Bodie turn to each other, grinning so widely their lips seem to have stretched halfway around their heads. David gives Brady an enthusiastic slap on the back, and Desto puts a hand on La Mer's shoulder, saying, "Never had a doubt, brother."

"Central, I think—" but Vitruzzi's voice suddenly cuts out as if it's been chopped in half.

"What the hell?" Bodie ask, then a light on the console begins to flash ominously.

La Mer looks confused, then cries, "It's the sensor on the dish. Something's wrong!"

The two of them bullet from their seats and race to the lift, followed by Desto and Brady. David and I barely get on before it starts descending at full speed, the ratchets on the cable clanking ferociously. Once at the bottom, they rush for the Rover and David and I jump on our bikes, speeding past the settlers' confused faces to the dish.

From the outside, nothing seems to be wrong with the device. La Mer and Bodie attack one of the housing panels at the base with screwdrivers, and as they yank it off, a thick balloon of gray smoke wafts out. "Shit, dammit, come on, shit . . ." Bodie intones, a mantra of disgust.

Brady brings an extinguisher into action and douses the inner compartment until it vomits foam. The smoke disappears and we all stand by silently, held rapt with disappointment. Bodie shakes his head, his face a volatile mix of anger and dismay.

"It was the goddamn relay capacitor. It was too small for the juice we sent through it. That's got to be what happened. It's fried and who knows what else in there is fucked." He stands with his shoulders hunched, speaking to the ground, looking like a defeated Pamplona bull.

"Don't worry, man. It's fixable. The damn thing works and that's the good news." Desto tries to console him.

The rest of us stand mute, feelings that crested in excitement moments before now ebbing in frustration. It might be months before we can reassemble the parts needed to repair it. Brady scans the sky thoughtfully and I guess what he is thinking: Did it really work, or is the Corps on the way to arrest us right now?

He turns back to the group. "There's nothing we can do until the fire retardant dries out and we get a better look inside. Let's get back to the mine and let everyone know what happened."

Bodie paces back and forth in front of the opened panel, each footfall hammering down like he means to hurt the ground. "I'm going to stick around for a while, see if I can do anything. You all go ahead."

Brady shrugs, letting him brood. I leave him my bike and catch a ride back on the Rover.

EIGHT

On watch in the control room the next morning, my eyes stay glued to the radar screens and cameras we have surrounding the Beach to alert us of unexpected company. I'm more than a little anxious, wondering if we'll have any unwelcome visitors.

At close to 1200 hours, when my shift is almost over, the walls of the control room begin to vibrate in a familiar way, announcing an incoming ship. Cross had radioed in a few minutes ago to get clearance, so I switch to the video-link inside the mine and see the *'Rize* settling smoothly into place on the rock floor. Hydraulic shocks on the landing tripod vent pressurized air in a high-pitched whistle, and the engines reduce speed in a cyclic hum. It's been a tense morning. I'm anxious for Mason to come and replace me, but it's Rob who enters the control room.

"I have to hand it to your crew, Aly. That was some piece of work to get that transceiver going."

"It was only partly successful."

"I know. I heard. Vitruzzi buzzed me when we got back into radio range and told me there was a fire."

He comes up beside me and leans over, placing one hand on my shoulder and one on the counter, getting a closer view of the monitors. His proximity doesn't seem casual; I get the feeling that he's trying to be near me without it being obvious, and surprisingly, it doesn't bother me. Heat from his palm radiates through the light fabric of my shirt. Inadvertently, I'm reminded of the way the rest of his body used to feel, naked and pressed against mine like a second skin. A new heat rises, flushing my cheeks.

"Looks like the *Sphynx* is here," he says, jolting me.

We watch the internal feed as Venus floats the ship into the mine as gracefully as a hawk riding a thermal and sets it down. His hand is still on my shoulder when the control room door opens and Karl and Mason step inside. Rob straightens and lets his arm fall away as I swivel my chair around quickly. I hadn't been doing anything wrong, but there's a residual blush creeping up from the neck of my shirt that implies otherwise.

Karl immediately turns and jets from the room. Mason walks up to the consoles and examines them, completely ignoring Rob. "I'm all set, Aly. Anything I need to know?"

I shake my head, already off my seat and heading toward the door to catch Karl. He's kicking up the balancer on his sandbike, which is parked among a group of them near the end of the tunnel, before I reach him.

"Hey, wait a minute." I reach a hand out to take hold of the handlebar, not letting him run from me.

"For what?" His voice echoes loudly inside the cavern, and I see the flash burn of fury in his sepia eyes.

"What are you doing?" It's such a simple question on the surface, but what I'm asking is so much deeper.

His jaw clenches until the striations of his masseter are clearly defined, then: "What are *you* doing?"

Instantly defensive, I counter, "What did it look like I was doing? Watching out for the goddamn colony!" *Calm down, Aly, don't let this get out of hand.* I take a deep breath, trying to make it clear that I'm interested in talking, not fighting. "Look, I can see that having Cross here is upsetting you, but I haven't done anything wrong."

My tactic has no effect and it's clear that he's experiencing some sort of misguided jealous hemorrhage. His sparking eyes bore into my face like an auger. I've seen him enraged before but never directed at me. It catches me off guard, so unexpected and undeserved, but I meet his rage with implacability. I *haven't* done anything wrong. Finally, he responds, his voice almost drowning in his chaotic emotions, "You're free to do whatever you like. I don't control you, and you don't owe me anything."

I feel his words like a fist to the stomach. "What are you talking about?"

"Since he's been here, you and Cross have been like fucking Siamese twins." I start to interrupt, getting angry now myself, but he keeps going, "You've never been happy at the Beach with us lowly non-cits and Admin goose-stepping contractors. Your life's not flash anymore and you don't get to be a hotshot thief, sticking it to the Admin with every take. You're bored, and Cross is living the life that you had before you got stuck with us small timers. If you want to go back to that, do it. I'm not going to stop you."

I'm completely floored by his accusations and presumptions, unable to argue or even speak. Where did he get such bullshit ideas? I'm at a complete loss and stare at him like I've never seen him before. He doesn't wait for me to figure out how to respond and drives off much too fast, leaving me standing in the mine like so much discarded rubbish.

Feeling numb, I turn around and find David behind me, looking at me with a mixture of bafflement and sympathy. "You didn't deserve that."

The muscles in my throat are contracting spasmodically, but I'm not sure if I'm about to scream, vomit, or cry. I look over his shoulder and see a few other people scattered within earshot, their faces reflecting David's surprise, and I feel an acute need to get the hell out of here. I turn, jump on my bike—much the way Karl just had—and switch it on. I hear David say my name, but I speed off, not wanting sympathy or anything else.

NINE

The silence of nighttime in the cool desert has become an ambient cocoon by the time I roll back into the Beach, wrapping me in a fragile, but blissfully detached, bubble. The suns will begin to rise in a couple of hours, but with most people asleep, for now the settlement is quiet. I am alone, free of obligation, connection, or direction. The things I deny craving the most.

The bike's quiet engine barely disturbs the stillness as I drive into the mine. The *Horizon* is docked as before with its ramp down, but this time lights from inside spill into the night. For no reason I care to ponder, I park the bike and walk aboard.

I haven't been inside this model before and find myself on the bottom level of a two-story cargo hold. The space is huge, its size emphasized by the lack of any shipment to fill it. The ceiling is segmented and looks as if it can be retracted, opening up the hold to make room for bigger machinery, possibly even small inter-atmospheric ships.

"Hello? Rob?" *Don't do this, Aly,* I tell myself. *If you need someone to talk to, go wake up David.* But it's too late, the hatchway across the hold is opening and Montoya steps out.

"What are you doing in here?" His question is blunt, almost aggressive. He doesn't appear to be armed, but the angry set of his face shows that doesn't mean he's not ready to fight. I, however, never go anywhere without the Derg strapped to my calf, hidden inside the material of my pants, and wonder if I'm actually going to have to reach for it.

"If you didn't want visitors, you shouldn't have left the ramp down."

"Relax, Montoya. It's fine. Aly is a guest." Rob enters the space and walks up beside Montoya, facing him with a stern expression that doesn't invite argument.

Montoya turns and scowls at Rob, then hunches from the hold. The exchange surprises me; I've never seen anyone react to Rob with such obvious animosity before.

Rob crosses the hold and I meet him in the middle. "Hey, it's good to see you. How are you doing?" It's clear from his concern that he'd seen, or at least heard, the altercation between Karl and I.

"Fine. Friendly crew you have."

"Yeah, well, they're not happy with me right now. I'm their captain. I'm supposed to be looking for new jobs so we can make some money, not taking a holiday on a non-cit planet so I can catch up with old friends. You know, some people just have a hard time sitting still."

"Yeah." I pause, not really sure what else to say, or even why I'm here. Finally: "Do you have anything to drink?"

He smiles, pleased to be able to help. "Right this way. I've got more of that quality claret we were drinking last night, but if you're more in the mood for some stronger hooch, I've got that too. Come on." He begins walking back through the hold and I follow. His unquestioning easiness makes me feel better about having come in the first place.

Beyond the hold's hatchway, we enter a wide corridor with large reinforced walls and access tunnels extending horizontally in both directions. The design is common enough for me to know without needing to see a structural schematic that the steering engine harnesses are attached at the ends of each tunnel, and that we're standing midship, the nexus of the structure and strongest section of hull. Beyond the access tunnels, the corridor is lined with smaller doorways, probably leading to various elements of the craft infrastructure and control: the dual emergency shuttles, avionics, propulsion controls, guidance and attitude sensors, life support, et cetera. As we make our way to the end of the corridor, he eventually stops in front of an open doorway to our right. There's nothing securing the door and no locking mechanism besides the regular airlock hatch, but it's what's inside that draws my attention.

"You don't leave those in there when you're in the Obals do you?"

Crates of contraband sit in organized boxes along shelves that fill an entire wall of the small room. Cigarettes, liquor, small arms, medical supplies—luxury items most average people desire but no one is allowed to own.

Cross smiles like a cream-drunk cat. "Yeah, actually, we do."

I hesitate, certain that I must be missing something, and he continues, "Watch this."

He squats down in front of the open door and removes a small metal panel from the floor, revealing a dark niche. A moment after he reaches inside, the doorway completely disappears. The metal wall of the corridor suddenly seems to grow right over the top of it, like a flap of skin that heals instantly and leaves no scar. It looks as if there had never been any doorway at all.

I take a sharp step back. "What did you do?"

"A buddy of mine who works in the Ministry of Security R&D Division needed a quick—and discreet—transport job. He traded me this little magic-maker for it." His smile grows as he explains this, apparently enjoying my disbelief. Leaning over again, he reaches back into the small compartment and pulls free a radio-sized tubular device with a liquid plasma display along the body and a crystalline projector emitting from one end. As he draws it out, the fake wall wavers like radar interference on a VDU.

"It's a holographic imaging device. You can take an image of anything you want, say a cargo hold wall, and then project the holograph onto a solid object—or even just empty space. Its internal processor will analyze whatever you're projecting onto and re-pixelate the holo to make it look like it's part of the object."

Impressed, I take hold of the device. It's heavier than it looks, due to the crystal projector, but compact. As I swing it slowly around, the image of the wall moves to wherever the projector is aimed. "Can it hide anything?"

"The technology can—anything that's stationary that is. It doesn't have enough processor power to replicate something that's moving. This particular device will only cloak about ten square meters. It's called a *cloak*, by the way. It's been a lot of fun to have around." He reaches for it and replaces it in the floor compartment. "About that drink."

We walk through the fake wall and he pulls a box containing a variety of clear plastic containers from the center of a shelf. Gripping the neck of one, he pulls out a bottle holding a dark blue liquid almost the color of antifreeze. "Should do us nicely. There are glasses in the galley."

The corridor ends in a teardrop shaped alcove with an elevator at the far end. We take it up to the second level where it opens out into a round galley with several chairs and small round tables arranged throughout a dining room. The right side of the room is dominated by the basic appliances needed to cook and clean more than simple traveling food and a walk-in that contains most of the ship's perishables.

As he looks for glasses, I comment, "You have a nice ship here, Rob. Looks like you have room for quite a few more crew-members."

"That would mean less of a split. No, we do fine. It's usually the deliveree who gets to unload the cargo. We just transport the goods."

He pulls out a metal chair, spins it around backward, and sits at one of the small tables. As I follow suit, he pours us out two full glasses of the peculiar liquid. "I'm just going to come right out and say it—here's to us. Old friends. Let's not lose touch again." He tips the glass in my direction, then belts the drink down.

"To old friends," I say and swallow mine. The liquid is both spicy and sweet, running down my throat smoothly. "Not bad."

"Agreed. This is probably the best hooch you can get. A friend of mine makes it on her cruiser. She won't divulge the secret ingre-dients, but that doesn't stop me from trying to charm it out of her."

I refill our glasses and we drink amiably for a few minutes. "You're up late. I didn't expect to find anyone around."

"Clients on Obal 10 sent me a wave that just came in—a job—so I was just doing the research on that. Still adjusting to Spectra 6 time, too."

"What kind of job?"

He hesitates before replying. "Oh, just a quick pick-up and de-livery from one of the Spectras. Nothing too exciting." *Then why the need for a lot of research?* "How about you, are you always out and about this time of night?"

It's my turn to hesitate. "Just having trouble sleeping. It was a long day."

"Lots on your mind, right?" His eyebrows rise sympatheti-cally. It makes me uncomfortable, but also makes me want to spill it—to just say what's bothering me, to talk to someone. But that would be too awkward. Cross is the reason for Karl's behavior and accusations. What would be the point?

He seems to pick up on my reluctance. "Hey, no problem. You've never been one to spend a lot of time talking about your-self. If you change your mind, I'm happy to listen, okay?"

There's something reassuring in his familiarity, the way he talks about me as if he's known me for years. He still remembers so much about the person I was back in the Corps, and it makes me realize that, despite the Rebellion, the years of smuggling, and all the shit that's happened since the last time we spoke, I still am the same person, deep down.

He refills my glass and I slug it down. Letting impulse take control, I stand up and walk around the table. Taking Rob by the sleeve of his shirt, I pull him toward me and he gives no resistance, as if he'd been waiting for this very thing. Our lips connect and it feels the same as it had eight years ago. His mouth is soft, warm, inviting—so different than Karl's strong, urgent kiss. Not better, just different. Rob lets the kiss linger, and I force myself to stop comparing them and just let the moment sweep me away—from myself, from my fears. From my guilt.

TEN

Waking up in Rob's bunk is like getting a glass of cold water in the face. I had not expected to stay—or to fall sleep—and when an abrupt buzzing sound jerks open my eyelids, I'm disoriented by the unfamiliar room.

Rob leans over and presses a button on the com console next to his bed. "Yeah." His voice is rough and throaty from being woken up.

"Message in from Obal 10."

"Roger that. I'll be down in a minute." He lies back and the sheet crumples at his waist, leaving his chest bare.

The darkness of the room is illuminated only by a faint red glow from the clock on the com console display, showing 0730. I stir, ready to leave and feeling foolish and out of place. I refuse to let my mind jump to the day ahead or what people seeing me leave Rob's ship might think. The mine is a busy place and it'll already be populated with early morning crews starting their daily work. As I lean forward, Rob reaches up and turns on a soft light.

"Good morning, beautiful."

I look down at him, and he beams a smile at me that could melt the ice core of an asteroid. His body hasn't changed much. The galaxy of small scars that he'd received from the shrapnel spray of a cluster bomb still trail down his right side in a scattershot pattern. Their intense pinkness has faded to a paler hue and they've flattened out some. He's just as muscular as ever, and his olive skin has not lost any of its rich, sun-loving hue.

"I have to get going," I mutter. The bunk is wider than those aboard the *Sphynx*—another example of his flushness—but still built against the wall, forcing me to stretch over the top of him to get up. He doesn't reach out to stop me. I put my feet on the cold floor and gather up my clothes, first replacing the Derg, followed by my pants. My back is to him, but I can feel him watching me. As I pull on my shirt, I feel his fingers trace lightly along my skin and linger on the ten-centimeter scar midway down my right side— Rajcik's parting memento.

"This is recent. Looks like it was bad. What happened?"

"A goodbye gift from my former boss." I slip the shirt over my head and follow it up with my jacket.

"Jesus, Aly. What kind of people did you work with?"

"The wrong kind. Smugglers. It was a mistake, but I didn't have a better plan after I deserted." My boots are the last thing I put on. Buckles tight, I stand up, preparing to go.

"Hey," Rob gets out of bed, pulling the sheet around his waist, and stands close. He's taller than me by a head and a half, lean in the hips and broad in the shoulders. I fit in his shadow when he's close. "I know you have to rush off, but can I get you breakfast first? Coffee, at least?"

"I have to go," I say again, reflexively, wanting to make my exit as quickly as possible. This time he does reach out, brushing the back of his hand against my cheek, then cupping it around the back of my head. He leans forward to kiss me, but I step back, gently releasing myself from his arm. "I'm sorry, I just have to go, okay. It's nothing personal. I'll see you later." I don't rush from the room, but I don't linger either. Rob has been good to me. I don't want to leave him with the impression that I don't care, but right now I need space, time to think.

As I pass through the galley, his three crewmembers are seated, eating breakfast. They all stare at me, their faces clamped in expressions of practiced neutrality. Except for Baker, whose scowl could peel paint. I don't avoid their looks, but continue to the hold and down the ramp without stopping.

At the bottom, the tightness in my chest begins to relax and I breathe deeply, hoping for a quiet day. My plan is to find La Mer or Bodie and see if there's any work I can do on the transceiver. At least that's one place I'm unlikely to see Karl and have to cope with the wreckage that meeting will bring.

I'm not watching where I'm going and step sharply off the ramp, straight in front of a sandbike. "Aly!" I jump back and Bodie swerves and comes to a stop, fortunately going slow enough that he's able to react before smashing into me. At first, surprise is etched on his face. "What are you—?" Then, realization of what I must be doing here strikes and he cuts himself off, having enough tact not to ask.

"Shit, sorry about that, Bodie."

"You okay?" He glances up the *Horizon*'s ramp, a troubled look on his face.

"Yeah, fine." Bodie and Karl are close, nearly as tight as brothers. I can imagine what he's thinking right now, the kinds of questions he must have, and decide it's time to channel the conversation into the day ahead. "What's the status on the transceiver? What can I do to help get it fixed?"

His eyes snap back to my face and his lips are tight, but he seems relieved to have something else to focus on. "There's not much left. Fortunately, it's only the main capacitor that needs to be replaced and some rewiring. We could use your help on that, like before. Vitruzzi is taking the *Sphynx* to Hell's Gate today to see if any locals or off-world traders are around that have the component we need. If they do, we'll be up again tomorrow."

There's a noise from inside the *Horizon*'s hold and I glance back over my shoulder nervously. It's time to get out of here. "That's fantastic news. When should I get up there?"

"You could get started right away. I think La Mer's already there."

"Sounds good. See you later."

When I arrive at Venus's, she is on her way out. "There you are! Karl came by this morning looking for you. Told him you probably crashed on the *Sphynx*. Heard you two had a row. Hope you're okay. Did Karl find you?" Her monologue crashes into me at a hundred miles an hour, almost too fast for my mind to grasp all at once.

"Did you say Karl was here?"

"Yeah, 'bout an hour ago. Didn't he—?"

"Did he say what he wanted?"

"I don't know. No, I mean. I think he was going to apologize. You know, for what he said. I heard about that! He's just a hothead. You know that. Karl's just Karl, always ready to boil over the rim. Want to come with me? He's riding along to Hell's Gate this morning, to get new parts for the transceiver. Isn't it great? It works!"

Shit, what did I do? The temptation to go with Venus and confront Karl is strong—who knows what conclusions he's drawn? Then I realize that the worse conclusion he could draw is true. I'm not prepared to face the brute force of his accusations again, even though I'll be forced to eventually. "No thanks, Venus. I'll stay back today and help La Mer and Bodie out. Let us know if things pan out at Hell's Gate."

"You got it. See ya!"

ELEVEN

It's noon and the twin Algols blaze on us like God's judgment. We've staked the transceiver's netting out in a makeshift awning over the open side of the housing assembly for some relief, but the temps are at least in the 40-degree Celsius range.

"Do you see that capacitor?"

Inside the box, where the upper half of my body is jammed, flashlight in mouth and sweat pouring from my face and neck in streams, it's even hotter. "Yeah, it looks like it's cooked."

"Can you get it free?"

Grunting, "One sec," I have a moment to think that La Mer had better be grateful for the luxury of not being inside this oven. They'd done most of the original wiring before mounting the dish and hadn't had to perform this kind of jack-in-the-box contortion act. I finally get my right hand on the crisped capacitor and yank, banging my elbow on a corner of metal in the process. "Goddammit!"

"Get it?"

I squirm my way backward and take a deep breath, showing them the damaged piece. It had smelled like overcooked plasterine in there. "I know how important this dish is, but if I have to go back in there to put in the new—"

Sand starts kicking up in a frenzied wind from the side of the hill, and a second later a shuttle I've never seen suddenly rises silently over the rim as if it bounced off the valley floor. David, who'd come up with me, has his rifle at the ready almost before any of us realize what it is, pointing it toward the cockpit screen. Like an idiot, I'd left all my hardware except the Derg behind in the *Sphynx*.

The shuttle comes to rest on the slope leading away from the dish toward the Flats, but the engine stays hot. The three of us stand still, not knowing what to expect but seeing no point in trying to run. It's a Speeder model with a center-hung gyroscopic fuselage that links to long, planed jets optimized for minimal air resistance on both sides. The fuel cell engine is mounted on a crossbeam between the two jets at the rear of the fuselage, and the entire shuttle, minus the retractable landing gear, is no taller than a seated man. There's no running from something that fast.

As we watch, the cockpit screen slides backward, opening the fuselage to reveal the pilot's controls and six passenger seats. Rob sits at the controls.

"You all need to come with me quick!" The urgency in his voice is unmistakable and even more alarming than the unexpected shuttle's appearance.

"Rob, what the hell—?" David begins, but Rob cuts him off.

"Don't argue, just get in. You've got Corps landing in the Beach!"

It's like being touched with a live wire, and I'm instantly galvanized by a surge of adrenalin and fear. "Jesus, we gotta get back there."

"Forget it, there are too many. They've got a least one gun ship and a transport. If you go in there fighting, you'll just be killed. Vitruzzi and the others are still at Hell's Gate. We'll regroup with them later, when there's a chance. But right now, we have to get you out of here. Move!"

La Mer is already hoisting his long body up the mounting rungs embedded along the fuselage. David breaks and is up next, pulling me in. Rob immediately accelerates and we speed south, staying low.

"What do you know, Rob? What's the Corps doing here and why didn't the Beach warn us? How did you know they were here?" David bombards him with questions the second the screen closes.

"Look, all I know is we took the *'Rize* up into atmo to check the modifications we've been doing on our backflow valves, and we picked up two ships on radar coming in too low for the Beach's systems to track."

Just like Rob did a few days ago. It's a weakness in the Beach's tracking, another issue that could be resolved with the transceiver functioning as it should.

"I told my crew to keep the *'Rize* in orbit so I could come pick you up. Maybe it's routine, I don't know. But none of you are legal and neither is that dish. I figured I'd get you out of there before they found you."

It takes less than an hour to rendezvous with the *Red Horizon*. I contact Vitruzzi en route to tell her what had happened, and she and the crew with her leave Hell's Gate immediately. Vitruzzi is legally contracted with the Admin, and no other Beacher besides us deserters have any outstanding warrants. Why the Admin would send Corps—with a gunship—to the settlement is anyone's guess, but if there's a way to smooth things out, Vitruzzi is the one to do it. While we wait to hear back from her, we congregate on the Horizon's flight deck where Sims is at the helm. Rob says his record is clean, and if the Corps detains him, he can hide us.

I get antsy waiting and lift my VDU to contact Vitruzzi for an update. Just as I do, both my and David's devices buzz to life and I take a quick, relieved breath, expecting it to be Vitruzzi. Instead, Bodie's face, panic-stricken and fervent, fills our screens.

"We're in deep shit here. The Corps landed about fifteen minutes ago and they're arresting everyone. Repeat, they're arresting the entire settlement. I've locked myself in the mine's control room, but it's only a matter of time. V, Brady, if you're reading this, get the hell off world. They're—"

A teeth-rattling thud rips through the room, and the image on my VDU shifts wildly as Bodie swings his arms, trying to cover his face from flying debris. Dust fills the screen for a moment, and David and I exchange alarmed glances, both of us holding our breath. I start to depress the transmission key when Baker violently yanks my hand back. "Don't do that, they'll trace the signal."

"Goddammit that's my friend in there!" I holler, yanking my arm free.

"No, Aly, she's right. There's nothing you can do," Rob says.

Before I can argue, another voice comes through the device.

"This is Major Stanford of the Capital Military Corps. You are under arrest. Lay down any weapons you have and walk forward with your hands visible. If you do not comply in ten seconds, you will be forcibly taken."

My eyes are fixed to the screen.

"You have no reason to arrest anyone. We're an independent settlement." We can hear Bodie's voice, but the image on his screen has changed. He must have tossed the unit under a desk or chair with the transmit button locked on; all we see is a fragment of counter and ceiling.

"Don't try to resist. Step out." The same commanding voice as before.

"By whose orders? What authority do you have?"

There's a pause, and then: "By order of Director Kurosawa T'Kai of the Ministry of Science and Engineering. This unauthorized colony has been implicated and found guilty of high treason. All non-citizens found on site will be immediately moved to the prisoner settlement on Keum Libre for sentencing. This is your last opportunity to surrender."

All of us stare transfixed at my VDU, listening to Bodie's deep breathing, sounding almost as if he's sleeping. David suddenly grabs both of my hands, and I realize they'd been shaking from a mixture of fury and fear for Bodie.

Bodie's voice: "V, Karl, if you're hearing this, you can't let these bastards get away with this."

"What's he—?" I start, but I'm cut off sharply by the blunt sound of guns firing, at least three automatics opening up. Gasping, I feel myself coming apart at the seams as I listen to the barrage, knowing that Bodie had fired first, knowing that he would rather die than be taken captive. "No, Bodie, no, no . . ." The words echo through my head, *no no no*, but it's all over in seconds. More dust rains down on the VDU he'd left, then clears. At the screen's rounded edge a few meters distant, Bodie lies still, his blond hair filled with dirt and blood. In a few seconds, we hear the gritty sound of boots stepping into the room.

"Bag that body. See if you can find ID but don't spend much time. We need to hit that other cesspool west of here today. Get a team in here to catalogue this equipment. These non-cits were doing more than growing vegetables."

"Should we bring any of the equipment with us, sir?"

"Not at this time. We'll leave a squad behind to secure it and come back once we transfer the prisoners to the fleet for disposal on Keum Libre."

"Yes, sir."

The room grows still at the sound of the soldier retreating. I want to stop watching but can't tear my eyes from the screen. As long as there's something to see it feels like Bodie is still there, still communicating. A pair of military-issue boots moves into visibility and the man standing in them leans over the counter above the VDU, presumably looking over the equipment lying there.

"Sir—"

At the sound of his voice, the officer turns around and one foot stomps down on top of the device, killing the transmission.

I look up into David's face and see my own horror and sadness reflected in his wide eyes and downward-curling mouth. "Those murdering fucks," he says and falls heavily into the wall behind him, shaking with shock and rage.

"Cross, we got issues." Sims is staring at a console, the bluish light reflecting off the whites of his narrowed eyes. "We need to get ourselves the fuck outta here immediately."

I turn, ready to argue—David and I have to get to the *Sphynx,* talk to Vitruzzi. I know that at least Brady, Venus, Desto, and Karl are all with her, and David, La Mer, and I are here with Rob, but that still leaves about 125 people—124 without Bodie—who are being rounded up like sheep as we speak. We'd planned for a lot of possible scenarios after we'd done what we had on the Fortress, but never something as horrific as this. I suspect I know what Vitruzzi will want to do, the same as what I want to do, but the first thing we *have* to do is regroup. Rounding on Cross, I say, "You can't go anywhere until you get us to the *Sphynx.*"

"You don't tell us—" Baker growls, standing close to me like she's going to swing.

Facing her, more than ready to take this to the next level, the muscles in my arms and back tense. *Do it, Baker. Push me just a little bit more. Give me a reason to unleash this horrible rage before it poisons me to death.*

Rob chimes in before that happens. "Bodie was a good man. I don't know what the hell the Admin would want to do this for but I'll do what I can to help." Montoya, Sims, and Baker stiffen, ready to protest, but he continues, "Within *reason.* We have to be careful but we'll get you back to your crew."

La Mer remains standing to the side, quietly, fading into the background, but the despondency in his face shows how hard it's hitting him. I don't know what I can say to help him, but I do know that the Admin and the Corps are going to pay for this.

David says, "Rob, you don't have to do this. Just put us down in the Flats and leave. You don't need to be part of the shit storm that's coming."

I twist around and glare at David, furious with him for letting Rob off the hook, but he gives me a look that convinces me to drop it for now.

"Erickson, are you there?" It's Vitruzzi. I jump a little at the unexpected transmission and hold my VDU up. Her face is a mask of pain.

"Here."

"You saw?"

My throat feels like it's filled with dirt, dry as dust, and I have to swallow before I can speak again. "Yeah."

"What's your status? Has the Corps made contact with Rob?" She's already thinking ahead, trying to figure out what happens next, and her deliberate response helps me get back on track.

"No. We're clear for now. He's going to bring us to you. Where should we rendezvous?"

Vitruzzi is silent for a moment and I wonder if I failed to transmit. Then she says, "Let me talk to Rob."

I hold my arm up so the screen faces him. He reaches out and holds the transmit button. "Eleanor, I'm really sorry."

"Thanks." Lines around her eyes show she's suffering, but she controls it with granite resolve. "Look, we can't go near the Beach. How far are you willing to take the three of them?"

"What do you have in mind?"

"We're planning to make for R'Kadia."

Rob considers it for a moment. R'Kadia is a little more than a day away, and that's if we can fly straight to it without having to evade pursuit by Corps ships. Every decision he makes from now until he cuts us loose is overshadowed by one major complication: he's harboring wanted fugitives. He, and his crew, are in jeopardy until that's no longer the case. If I were him, I'd hesitate before agreeing to Vitruzzi's proposal.

"We can do that," he replies, and I feel a touch of the tension in my shoulders let go.

His three crewmembers respond with surprising restraint. Whatever their history together, this crew has shown that it regards the rule of unquestioned loyalty to their captain as a trifling inconvenience at best and an outright joke at worst. But no one protests.

Vitruzzi sounds relieved. "You have our thanks once again. I'm sending coordinates for a rendezvous point. We hope to be there within thirty-eight hours if things go well. Let us know if you have any trouble. We'll do the same."

Rob turns to the navigator. "Baker, set our course. We'll see you soon, Eleanor." My VDU darkens as she cuts the transmission.

"Rob, are you sure you want to do this?" David asks.

"Yeah. It's fine. We'll get you there. Don't worry, man." Even as he says this, wrinkles of anxiety settle across his forehead and convert the laugh lines around his eyes into something much less whimsical. "Sims, Montoya, find them somewhere comfortable to stay for the next few hours." He turns to us. "In case you want to catch a nap . . . or something."

TWELVE

Only six hours pass before a Corps scout ship catches up to us. David, La Mer, and I sit morosely in the galley, sipping food supplement mixes and not saying much, wondering how things could have gone so wrong so fast. The craving for one of Rob's illicit cocktail mixes is strong, and I struggle to keep myself from finding the contraband room and drinking myself comatose. When Rob said Bodie was a good man, he couldn't know the half of it. Bodie was more than that; he was a friend. Despite our first inauspicious meeting, what we'd been through together—the rescue mission on the Fortress, the way he made me laugh and brought me freshly grown fruits during my recovery after Rajcik shot me, and the way he brought a sense of calm and serenity to every situation—had made him more like family, nearly as close to me as David. Thinking about a day passing in the grow rooms without seeing his wide, welcoming smile and laughing blue eyes makes tears sting my eyes, but I force them back. This isn't the time for sorrow. The Corps—vile, murdering animals that they are—ruthlessly killed one of the best men I'd ever known. And they will answer for it.

David and La Mer sit in silence battling their own pain. Despite the fragile quiet, none of us let our guard down, and no one is surprised when Rob enters the galley—not exactly running, but definitely not doddering.

Rising to his feet, David asks, "What's going on?"

"Corps-security patrol ship. They're demanding to board for a routine contraband search. Come with me. We can stash you in the swag room."

"Are you crazy? You want us to hide behind a holo?" There's no way in hell I'm going to hide in a place where the only thing between me and armed soldiers out for blood is a fragile electronic fakeout."

"Do you have a better idea?"

"You're a smuggler for fuck's sake. Don't you have a *real* hiding place?"

"Sure, if you can shrink yourself down to half a cubic meter, I've got just the place for you."

"Aly, we don't have time to argue," La Mer says, not realizing what he's in for.

To punctuate Rob's point, Montoya's voice comes through the intercom. "Cross, they're linked and engaging the airlock." Cross cocks an eyebrow at us, and with a sinking feeling in my stomach, we all sprint to the room where his illegal cache of goods are stored. In plain sight.

He activates the holographic deflector and the false wall materializes in front of us. "Keep it quiet. This always works."

"Just get rid of them," David growls.

He begins walking back up the corridor just as we hear the leader of the security squad step out of the cargo bay.

A woman's voice comes down the corridor. "You must be Captain Cross."

"That's right, Major. What's this about?"

"Under Admin authority code six-zero-six, we have the legal imperative to search your ship, and that includes seeing your identity registrations. We'll ask for them one by one. Your full cooperation is required and expected."

The voice clangs off the corridor walls, sounding full of bloated self-worth. David and I look at each other and his lips pull back in an infuriated snarl, the strange inner luminescence of the holowall giving his teeth a silvery cast. I hadn't thought what it would be like to be on this side of it, but the fact that we can't see through the wall—as if it were actually real and solid—does nothing to improve my confidence.

"Yes, ma'am. You're aware that I'm legally contracted to be in this quadrant. My contract is current, granted by the Ministry of S&E."

"Yes we are, Captain Cross. There have been activities in the area that have necessitated tightened security measures."

"Well, if you could hurry it up. We're on our way back to the Obals and most clients aren't very understanding when they're contractors are late. You understand."

There's no response as their footsteps echo past us toward the bow end of the corridor. None of us look at each other. We're all staring at the fake wall fervently, as if concentrating on it will make it more real, more *solid*.

Forty-five minutes pass before the sound of people returning echoes toward us. We all tense, counting their steps until the go by and back into the cargo hold. A few minutes later, we hear the airlock engage and a hollow sound as the outer airlock opens, releasing our uninvited Corps guests. Rob returns and shuts down the projector.

"You're in the clear. They're already outside of visual range. No worries. Just routine, like they said."

La Mer is visibly relieved and David takes a deep breath. "Nice one," he comments. "Now if you don't mind telling me what the hell that thing is . . ."

THIRTEEN

The *'Rize* settles onto the dusty landscape of R'Kadia with the fluid grace of luxury cruiser-class engines. My only other visit to this desolate Spectra 5 moon was shortly after meeting Vitruzzi and her crew—if you can call being kidnapped *meeting*. She'd recruited me to help ensure a smuggling exchange arranged with a local band of brigands went down smoothly. It hadn't, and our scramble out of the abandoned mine that served as their hideout had not been bloodless. Still, we'd taken what we'd gone for—a significant pay-load of solar amalgam seeds that will serve to keep the *Sphynx* powered long after we're all dead. Thinking back on that confrontation now, I realize Vitruzzi had been testing me to see just how far I could be trusted. That decision was a huge gamble, but she and her crew had been desperate. So had I. The irony that the situation this time is practically interchangeable does nothing to lift my spirits.

La Mer, David, and I stand in the cargo hold listening for the hydraulic landing tripod to lockout and give us clearance to open the port door. The *Sphynx* is already here, sitting silently in the dirt with her landing ramp open. We walk aboard, anxious to hear what Vitruzzi has in mind.

The rest of the crew await us in the open cargo hold, the compartment seeming small and outmoded after the last few hours spent aboard the newer and grander *Red Horizon.* I meet Karl's eyes as we approach and he holds my gaze. So much has happened since our argument two days ago that it's impossible to guess what he's feeling. Or what I am, for that matter.

Vitruzzi begins to speak, but Venus suddenly runs to La Mer and grasps him in an embrace that nearly knocks the wind out of him. They hold each other in silence, the rest of us taking some vicarious comfort in their relief.

After a few seconds, Vitruzzi says, "We're glad to see you're all safe."

David responds, "We were lucky Rob picked us up. Otherwise . . ." He trails off. At the mention of Rob, Karl finally drops my eyes, lines deepening on his forehead.

We're standing at the rear of the hold in a group. The *Sphynx* had not been stocked for a long excursion before last leaving Agate Beach and the only thing occupying the compartment right now is the Rover. No one seems to know what else to say, but a look I can't read passes between Vitruzzi and David. Something about it is unsettling.

"Okay," Vitruzzi says and swallows like she has something in her throat. "The reason I wanted to regroup on R'Kadia—"

Before she finishes, her eyes drift over my shoulder as someone else climbs the ramp.

"I didn't think I'd be seeing you people again so soon."

I swing around in a smooth, liquid turn, right hand already drawing my Mini-Derg from my calf holster.

Rajcik.

His voice vibrates nerves deep inside my core like a shockwave, triggering reflexes that come from a dark place, a place where the worst things a person is capable of come from. As I pull the trigger, an arm sweeps down and knocks my wrist aside, forcing the cutting beam of the laser to streak across the floor, its silence punctuating my furious rage. I turn, instinctively raising my other arm to strike my assailant.

"Aly, hold up!" Karl yells into my face, but it's like he's speaking another language. I swore I'd kill Rajcik if he ever crossed my path again . . . and what the fuck is he doing here now?

"Let go of me!"

"No, wait, just hold it a sec. He's working for us. Hear me?"

I hear him, but I simply can't believe it. I yank hard, trying to get him to release my arm, but his grip doesn't loosen. I'm about to strike him with my free arm, but Rajcik speaks again, freezing me.

"You don't seem to have expected me, Aly." The last time I looked into that malevolent face was while he leaned over my broken, helpless body and threatened to murder David and the crew. I almost can't believe my eyes as I run them over his swarthy features, trying to make sense of something that can't possibly be happening. He gives Vitruzzi a disgusted look. "You didn't tell her our deal?"

"Tell me what? What the fuck is going on here, Vitruzzi?" I whirl on her and the rest of the crew, my voice shrill. This time when I pull, Karl releases my arm.

"Erikson, you need to calm down until you understand the situation." Her voice is cool, placating, but with a hard steel edge.

I've gone mute, struck dumb by what I'm hearing. But fury quickly burns through my paralysis. "Understand what situation?

You cut a deal? With *him*!" My voice cracks and my stomach clenches involuntarily as if the wind has been knocked out of me. "Do I have to remind you people that he's the reason every one of us nearly died out there? He betrayed everyone in this room, some of us more than once, and now you've cut a fucking deal? Are you nuts?"

The more I speak, witnessing the careful neutrality in their faces, the more the reality hits home. Of the six people standing in front of me, La Mer is the only one who seems slightly confused, his glance bouncing to Rajcik, to the crew, to me, and back to Rajcik as he tries to piece together a connection he knows nothing about. A new thought floats into my mind like a dead and bloated thing. *David knew about this.* My own brother. The blood drains from my face and my limbs go slack. Turning back to face Rajcik, I feel my hand still holding the Derg begin to rise again on its own. His lips curl back in a snarl, then David's voice stops me.

"Aly, don't." My eyes snap to his face and I see his guilt. He betrayed me. All of them had.

Without another word, I drop my arm and careen past them through the airlock and into the passageway leading to the crew quarters. My only thought is to take what's mine and get the fuck out of here.

FOURTEEN

I can pay you. I've got cash, I just need your help getting it. Will you do it?" I'm sitting on the *'Rize*'s flight deck proposing a deal to Rob. I need a ride off of R'Kadia. If he can take me as far as the moon Kai Lum that orbits Spectra 4, I'll cut him in on a third of the money David and I have stashed over the last few years—our own insurance policy. If Rajcik hasn't gotten to it first, that is.

"Yeah, of course I'll take you. But, Aly, you're clearly pissed about something. I think you should tell me what's going on before I agree." He puts a reassuring hand on my shoulder.

"I wish I could." His hand slips from my shoulder as I begin pacing. His hesitancy makes it apparent that my decision to abandon the crew, brash as it is, is going to require some careful negotiation. The irony in the whole fucked-up situation is enough to make me want to scream. I'm forced to rely on Rob to get me gone, despite the fact that relying on others is what got me here in the first place. How could they do this? They *knew* Rajcik was alive. The *knew* it, and even worse, they forged some sort of arrangement, some sort of fucking contract with him. *With Rajcik!* Their decision compromises everything we'd fought together for. Why would they do it? Desperation? Ignorance? Necessity? I don't care. My brother, even Karl, betrayed me. It shakes me more than seeing Rajcik again in the first place has. What else are they hiding from me? Why didn't they tell me? Were they trying to spare me this rage, this disbelief? Does it matter? No. Whatever their reasons were, they still betrayed to me.

I can't explain all that to Rob, there's no time. "You just have to trust me. It's better for you and your crew if we get the hell off this rock ASAP. I'll explain on the way."

He regards me with a distant consideration that I'm not used to. "And what about David? Is he coming?"

"No, I'm not."

We both turn, surprised to see him standing in the galley's doorway. Before he tries to speak, I cut in, "Whatever you have to say, you can choke on it."

"Aly, come on. You need to just listen to this."

"Listen to what, David? That lunatic tries to kill you, and you, what? Ask him to be part of your crew?"

"It's not what you think—"

"You're my fucking brother! I'm supposed to be able to trust you!"

He's also getting angry now. Redness only slightly darker than his hair creeps out of his shirt collar and up his neck. "Dammit, Aly. Look at the way you're reacting. Are you surprised we didn't tell you? You probably would have tried to fly up here and kill him yourself like some kind of goddamn merc."

"You're damn right I would have! And so would you if you were thinking straight."

"Do either of you want to tell me what this is about?" Rob speaks quietly, leaving the request optional.

Taking a deep breath to calm himself, David continues, "Look, I know we should have told you, but this wasn't supposed to happen. Working with Rajcik was supposed to be a last chance option, a backup contingency. There was never any need to tell you because we—*I*—knew you wouldn't understand."

"Wait a minute," Rob cuts in. "Are you talking about János Rajcik? The arms smuggler?"

The urgency in his tone derails our argument and we both turn to him. His usual warm tan has gone the color of off milk and his brown eyes are wide. "Do either of you realize what kind of trouble working with him can get you into? The Admin has dedicated patrols looking for him system-wide—he's basically considered the antichrist."

"Which is why we need to get out of here."

"No, listen, both of you. Aly, just shut up for a minute." The hard set of David's jaw tells me what I know all too well; he's past the point of arguing. Pinning me to the spot with eyes as ferocious as a pouncing lion's, he forces me to listen to his explanation. "Rajcik came to Vitruzzi a couple of weeks after the Fortress. He was injured in the explosion and the *Temptation* was damaged, and they made a deal. He'd leave the Beach alone if she gave him the aid he needed."

"And you believed him—" I start to interrupt, but he doesn't let me get far.

"Vitruzzi didn't just say yes without thinking it through. She had us strip the *Temptation* of its weapons and most of its fuel and strand Rajcik out here on R'Kadia."

"Why? Why not just kill him? After what he did to us—"

"There's more. He's been helping get some of the stuff the Beach needs through his old contacts—Chisolm, Howard, the Spectre Triad. And this is the part you need to pay attention to. Rajcik had something to barter with, something we thought we might need. We assumed we could use it to keep the Admin and the Corps off our backs if they ever pieced together what happened at the Fortress."

I fall into a chair, still angry, but also intrigued enough to hold my tongue for a few minutes. Rob remains standing resolutely beside me, his sinewy frame tensed in anticipation of where David's story will lead.

"What is it, David?" he asks.

"It better be good," I add.

He tries to wither me with an exasperated look and continues, "He recorded all of the communications he had with T'Kai. And Aly, this is going to be hard to hear, but their deal was never even about stealing the Nova. T'Kai hired Rajcik to detonate it and *destroy* the Fortress. That's what the payoff was for. Rajcik lied to us. He made up the story about blackmailing the Admin so we'd help him get the Nova for himself."

"Are you saying that you two were involved with that space station? That Rajcik is your old boss?" The look on Rob's face is perfect incredulity. "I can't believe what I'm hearing."

My brain is reeling, too much unexpected news all at once, too many surprises. Plotting. Scheming. It's like being in the Corps again. I thought I'd left that world behind, thought I was in a place where I could trust the people I was with, believe in what they stood for. I should know better by now.

David's eyes feel heavy on my face as he examines it, preparing for what I might do. For the time being, I'm frozen to my seat, unable to react. He turns to Rob to explain, "There wasn't much time for planning. Neither of us was prepared for life outside the Corps. We just fell in with Rajcik by chance."

"Do you have any idea how many deaths he's responsible for?"

There's a subtle change in Rob's tone, no longer simple disbelief but moving toward something closer to anger. The hair on my arms stirs and I glance toward David, seeing the same apprehension settling over him.

"Rob, you know we wouldn't be part of something like that." David faces Rob, toe-to-toe, only taller by one or two centimeters. "But if you knew what the Admin was doing on that space station, you may not think it was such a bad thing that Rajcik blew it up. You see what they did to my fucking eyes. And what they did to Bodie. This shit needs to stop. It *has* to stop."

Rob turns around and moves toward the pilot's console, putting it between him and David. David and I look at each other, sharing a sudden realization that we may have underestimated his loyalty to the Admin. We're allies again, at least for the moment, and wondering what the hell we're going to do if that's the case. Rob leans forward on his hands, staring absently at the screen, keeping his thoughts to himself.

I should say something. "Look, Rob. This isn't your fight."

He takes a long breath before answering. "No, forget it. As hard as it is to believe what you're telling me, I guess I do."

"Then you'll still take me to Kai Lum?"

"Aly—" David starts to protest, but Rob cuts him off.

"It's not that simple anymore."

The wills of two soldiers start fighting inside me, one trying to tell me to just shoot Rob and stop him from making the mistake I'm afraid he's about to, the other not wanting to jump to conclusions. "What do you mean?"

"János Rajcik is worth a lot of money."

"Wait a minute, Rob. You can't turn him in. We need him."

I whirl on David. "Why?"

"He's the only person we know with information about Keum Libre. He can help us get to the Beachers, maybe get them out of there."

"He'll never help us."

"He doesn't have a choice."

"He'll never help us, David, and if I see him again, I swear to God I'll kill him."

"Just try to be rational, Aly. You've got friends that are being held in prison for no other reason than that they were trying to live their lives. You have to start caring about more than yourself." He hovers over me, trying to intimidate me, but we've been siblings too long and it doesn't work anymore. Despite the impatience growing in his own eyes, I don't drop mine, letting the fury there speak for itself. He stares back for a moment, then turns around and walks a few steps away, running his hand through his overly long hair in distress. "Did you really think what we had at the Beach was going to last? You were so caught up with the idea of things being normal, you and Karl living some fantasy happily-ever-after story, you forgot what was really going on. We're *deserters*, little sis. As far as the Admin is concerned, we're their number one problem, and they're not going to forget about us."

My eyes jerk guiltily toward Rob at the mention of Karl, but his face is stern, lines of agitation forming deep furrows around his mouth and narrowed eyes. David is studying my face with increasing intensity, but I say nothing. What else can I say? It's the truth. I wanted to forget about the control the Admin has over us, over our lives. I'd let creature comforts and a façade of freedom take the place of the more practical side of me, the side that's always ready for trouble and always running from it.

Taking my silence for agreement, David turns to Rob. "Look, I understand the dilemma this creates for you. You didn't expect to get caught up with something like this when you brought us those parts for the transceiver, and you couldn't have known what we were involved in. But"—he sighs exasperatedly, glancing back at me—"I'd almost be willing to drop the Nova on the Admin myself for what they did to Bodie. If getting justice for him means working with Rajcik, at least I'll be able to sleep at night. I don't care about anything else."

Rob says, "I understand. I do. But if I just walk away and forget that I know Rajcik is here, I stand to lose a lot more than my ship."

Neither of us respond. Finally David says, "It's not too late, Rob. If you left now, no one would ever know."

He sighs. "I need a little while. I have to think this through." Looking at me, eyebrows arched in worry and uncertainty, he says, "I'm sorry, Aly."

"There isn't much time, Rob," David warns.

"I know that," he answers sharply. Then continues more calmly, "Just give me a couple of hours." His eyes shift toward the flight deck hatch in a request that we leave.

I hesitate, wanting to press Rob into a decision, but stop myself. He has to decide this on his own.

Following my brother off the flight deck, we only get a few steps down the corridor before he grabs my arm above the elbow, pulling me to a stop. "Look, Aly, I'm sorry. I didn't know how to tell you."

I want to accuse him, yell at him, continue the battle until he's bruised and beaten, but what good would it do? The fight has finally gone out of me. Rob was my only chance of getting out of here and he has his own agenda. Where would I go anyway? The realization that I'm involved in circumstances I'm powerless to control holds me in check. If I killed Rajcik now, who would benefit and who would lose? The answer to that is not as clear as I'd imagined it would be before today. The settlers have given me more than I can ever repay. If Rajcik can help us free them, don't I owe them that? David and the crew betrayed me, yet I have no other choice than to come to terms with it.

"You know we have to watch him every second," I finally say, giving in completely. "He'll tell us what we want to hear, but you can bet your life that he has plans of his own. Oh right—you already have bet your life, *our* lives." My last statement wilts as soon as it hits the air, resignation making it toneless.

He looks me over, relieved that I'm dropping it. "You know Vitruzzi won't leave anything to chance. Rajcik is bugged, just like the rest of us are. We can keep tabs on him."

"That'll be a huge comfort when he does something like turn us over to the Admin."

His head bows and his chest expands in a deep sigh. "We owe it to Bodie."

For the first time, I realize how much he's suffering over what has happened. I've been too self-absorbed to realize I'm not the only one. Bodie meant a lot to all of us. I reach out to put a hand on his shoulder and he grabs me, drawing me into a hug. With my face pressed against his chest, I whisper, "We're all going to miss him." Tears are close, but I smother them with a promise—Bodie's death will be avenged.

We embrace for a minute, then David drops his arms. "The crew is waiting for us. And there's one more thing, Aly. I promise you, no more surprises. But you should know . . . Thompson is still with Rajcik."

Fuller Thompson. Rajcik's sadistic shadow. A man who hates me almost as much as I hate him.

"Jesus, what have we gotten into?"

FIFTEEN

Right now we have two imperatives: get our people off Keum Libre, and do whatever it takes to stop T'Kai." Brady stands next to the *Sphynx*'s galley doorway, addressing the crew and Rajcik. "We all agree that the Admin is dangerous and forces its rule too far, but it's T'Kai, and others like him, that are pushing the buttons. We'll never get any peace until he's brought down. And we have what we need to do it."

"You're talking about blackmail," David states. He looks around at the rest of the crew, then continues, "We were only building the transceiver in case the Admin got too close. If we change the plan and go after T'Kai, I mean actively, that will push things a lot further. Maybe too far."

Venus stands near the cabinets next to La Mer. She holds a tube of food in one hand and methodically squeezes the contents from one end to the other. The pressure she exerts is just enough to make the end of the tube bulge with each squeeze, barely short of popping it and spraying orange goo all over the room. I have to force myself not to take it away from her as she speaks. "But why does he have to know about us at all? Won't the Ministry of S&E come after us if we threaten T'Kai? We can't fight the whole Corps."

Rajcik makes a disgusted sound, and Venus, looking shaken, glances around the room, hoping to see some sign of agreement from any of us. But the crew's certainty that we're on a collision course with the director of the Ministry of Science and Engineering, and the Admin in general, is unanimous. No one will meet her eyes except La Mer, who gives her a small reassuring smile. Whatever happens in the days ahead, they'll still have each other. But for how long? The thought nearly makes me shudder.

"I don't need to tell anyone how dire the situation is," Vitruzzi says. "We need to agree just how far we're willing to go, how much we're willing to risk, to get justice for Bodie and get our people safe."

"What I want to know is why the Admin did this? Did they know about the transceiver? How did they find out?" La Mer is spooked. Not being able to identify how, or even if, his programming was detected tears at the core of his confidence, but no one has an answer for him.

"Even if we can rescue the settlers, we can't go back to the Beach," Brady states. Hearing it said aloud brings it home. To all of us. Our lives aren't just changed, they've been turned upside down, ruined. What difference does it even make if we can rescue the settlers? Where can any of us go now and not be hunted as fugitives? Just like that, the Admin completely destroyed the tenuous peace we'd managed to carve out of nothing.

Looking around, I see the same fear on everyone's faces. Everyone except Rajcik. Like an animal, he has learned the law of the jungle. Hunt or be hunted. Kill or be killed. He's not afraid of losing anything, because he has nothing to lose. Just another non-cit lowlife scum with a life story that was written before he was born, and he plays the role with perfect, even serene, ease.

"We can't leave them there," says Mason, his voice thick.

"No. We're not going to," Vitruzzi answers.

"Then we do whatever it takes." His nutmeg eyes gaze fiercely into everyone's faces, and the heavy wrinkles spanning his forehead add to his serious, not-to-be-fucked-with gravitas. Mason, as a rule, is usually quiet and brooding, and when he does have something to say, everyone listens.

"All right, so what's the plan?" David's tone is all practicality.

No one has said a word to me about earlier. When I look at Vitruzzi, she meets my eyes with stoic resoluteness, not a shred of guilt or apology about having hidden Rajcik's whereabouts from me. It's exactly the kind of reaction I'd expect from her. If Vitruzzi has any weakness, it remains as invisible to me as the day we'd met.

Rajcik sits across the galley opposite me, near the exit. His presence alone makes my stomach churn, but knowing it's my choice to be here—and let him live—ignites bile in a rancid torrent. Every time his black eyes slide toward me, I want to gag and go for my gun. Reminding myself of the reasons to let him live only makes it worse. If this is what pure hate feels like, it must only be one step short of total madness.

Brady leans against the wall near me with his arms folded. "With the data we took from the Fortress and Rajcik's recordings, we have enough leverage to make T'Kai pay attention. If it gets out to the public and the right people in the Directorate, he'll never be able to refute it. It may be enough of a bargaining chip for him to let the settlers go, maybe even leave the Beach alone for good."

I wrap my hands around the back of a chair and lean toward Vitruzzi and Brady. "But the transceiver's not fixed and the Corps has the Beach secured, probably even under surveillance. We don't have a way to wavecast it. T'Kai will know that. And there's no way we can just send a copy to the Directorate and hope they'll do something about it—except silence us. It's their job to protect the Admin's image and maintain control." My words may sound harsh and unproductive, but they are the truth.

Without raising his eyes from where he stares at the floor, La Mer responds, "Well, the transceiver's just a device. It's the programming I did that makes it useful. The security worm hijacks the TDRSs and allows us to boost their waves."

This grabs Vitruzzi's attention, "You mean you could send from any transceiver, as long as it was powerful enough to transmit to a satellite?"

"Basically, yeah."

Brady says, "So we could get the message to T'Kai—the Beachers go free or we bring him down—and find a transceiver that can carry out our threat if he doesn't."

"What's our insurance?" Desto asks. "Even if he releases them, it won't be long until he decides to shut us up for good."

It's Rajcik who responds, "So we bring T'Kai down anyway." He rises from his seat and regards the crew with wicked earnestness. My hand immediately reaches for my 'Bad, but the warning does nothing to deter him. "You all know that it's only a matter of time before he completely obliterates your little settlement and every person who can tie him to the Fortress. You're already living on borrowed time. Your choices are either to go all the way, or go cower in your hole and wait for him to find you." His speech elicits frowns from everyone, but no arguments. Scowling, he finishes, "Captain Vitruzzi, your friends don't have long. I suggest you make a decision soon. You know where to find me."

"Where do you think you're going?" The sound of my pistol being drawn stops him.

Instead of answering, he turns, raising an eyebrow as he looks toward Vitruzzi. "Let him go, Aly," she commands.

Arguing is pointless. It's like they've all lost their memories. Do they really believe he's not planning to double cross us again while we stand here and argue about plans for our own funeral?

"So what do we do?" Karl picks up the thread.

Vitruzzi responds, "We should consider Venus's suggestion. If there's any way to get the Beachers off of Keum Libre without drawing the Admin's eye, our chances will be much better."

"Assuming everyone is still alive, that's 125 people." Several of us wince at Brady's statement. "The *Sphynx* can carry them, but it might be better to separate, use two ships."

"What about the *Temptation*?" David asks.

"We shouldn't consider anything of Rajcik's an asset," I comment, glaring at David. "He's a tool with limited usefulness."

"We can't use the *Temptation* anyway; it's compromised," Vitruzzi continues. "Anyone flying on it is a target, and we can't put the Beachers in that kind of jeopardy."

"Can we buy another ship?" Karl asks.

"I don't know what with. Most of our assets have been seized."

"So we go back to the Beach and wipe out the security squad guarding it. We have to get supplies and weapons, anyway."

"What about Cross? Would he help us?" Desto asks.

"No way, he's Admin, and he's not part of this crew," Karl responds, animosity curdling his voice.

"He's still a friend," David says, defensively.

"He has nothing to gain. Why would he put himself at risk? He already knows enough to—to have us arrested," Karl says.

Startled by what he's implying, I say, "It's thanks to Rob that the three of us got out before the Corps could catch us. What more reason do you need to trust him?"

"Why do you feel like you have to defend him?" he spits back.

"Both of you drop it," Brady orders, his impatience sparking like a loose wire. "We can't ask Cross to help us. We're in this on our own. But we do have to get him out of here. We're a liability for him, and the longer he sticks around, the more of a liability he becomes to us."

David and I exchange a dark look. "It may not be that easy."

Everyone turns to my brother. "He knows about Rajcik and . . . shit, he may want to turn him in."

"Well he can't do that," Venus says, distress making her voice flat and winded, like she's been running.

Brady slowly straightens, his accusatory stare igniting the air between him and I. "How the fuck does he know about Rajcik?"

I feel hot blood rushing through my veins, threatening to bubble over. "Don't kid yourself. I'm not the problem. You're the ones who involved that sonofabitch in the first place."

He speaks slowly at first, but his words gain momentum as his anger starts to get loose. "Your goddamn vendetta is going to get people killed. Damn you, Erikson, is that what you want?"

"Stop." Vitruzzi steps up next to Brady and slaps her palm loudly against a table. She turns to me, her eyes strangely kind. "We have enough problems to deal with right now. Rajcik isn't anyone's favorite option, and if we had any choice, he'd never factor into this. But that's not reality." She scans the room with a commanding gaze. "We're going to get our friends off that prison rock, whether that means taking T'Kai down or not. But the first thing we have to do is get our assets in order, and Aly's right, that means a trip to the Beach."

SIXTEEN

A set of military-issue leg sheaths with built-in kneepads fits perfectly over my pants and zips around the lip of my combat boots. Their lightweight plating is almost as adept at repelling low-caliber bullets as the body armor I wear over my torso, but more importantly, they provide stellar soft-tissue protection in high-impact activities—perfect for an assault on the Beach. I finish gearing up inside the cramped passenger cabin of the *Sphynx*'s shuttle while Doug Mason and Desto do the same beside me.

Almost four days have passed since Bodie's death. After our conversation aboard the *Sphynx,* the crew roughed together a sketchy plan for gathering the supplies we'll need from the Beach, and now Karl lowers the shuttle into the labyrinthine canyons of Mecca Flats, carefully picking his way through sharply twisting spires and gullies. We do a final gear and weapons check before we land, the three of us preparing to jump out and sneak quietly into the settlement on foot in order to recon the security squad's position and find their vulnerabilities.

"Karl, we're in position. What's your status?" Vitruzzi checks in from a low-orbit holding pattern. The *Sphynx* did a sweep for other Corps ships in the area and is ready to back us up if we need it.

"We're almost at the drop point." Karl turns around from the pilot's seat and draws a circle in the air with his index finger pointing toward the ceiling, our signal to get ready to land.

Desto stands by the shuttle hatch, ready to slide it open. Karl eases us down while I watch the rusty sand walls, no more than a couple meters distant, rising up through the porthole window. The canyon is deep enough that we descend beyond where the suns' rays are able to penetrate and the walls are cast in deep shadows that serve to conceal points where the large, ratlike rodents living in Mecca Flats hide. Even though they are mammals, they're covered in scales, and they brandish retractable claws like a cat's, only several centimeters longer and as hard as petrified wood. When walking on all fours, their bullet-shaped heads, with jaws containing rows of long, sharp teeth, reach about midthigh on a person my height, slightly more than one and a half meters. Instead of ears, they have highly perceptive auditory organs that form ridges of concentric circles of flesh that taper toward the base of their skulls, an occasional wiry hair sprouting here and there. Like radars, they can pick up sounds several kilometers distant. The noise made by a ship is usually loud enough to scatter them and send them hiding in their caves, but the shuttle is much quieter. We'll have to be extremely cautious as we pick our way over the last couple kilometers to the Beach. These ugly beasts are meat eaters, and they'll be eager for an easy lunch.

The shuttle rises a few centimeters as the reverse thrusters activate and then drops to the ground with a thud. We waste no time getting outside and I take point. Mason and Desto fan out behind me, the three of us moving rapidly as a single unit through the canyon that eventually feeds out into a half-kilometer flat plain south of the Beach. That will be our longest sprint with no cover, but we timed our landing so the noon sunlight will be beating directly down and heat shimmers will help camouflage us from naked eyes. At least, that's the plan.

My breathing and footsteps beat a dull and persistent pattern in my ears as we run, and my eyes move ceaselessly over the top of my raised carbine, picking out shadows ahead of me that mean a blind corner or crack in the walls. The air is cool this far below the tops of the canyon walls, and the run would be pleasant if circumstances were different.

A sound catches my attention, and I pivot my eyes to the right where small pebbles tumble down the sloping wall. Jerking my head up, I catch just a glimpse of a Flat Rat's tail as it runs along a horizontal off-width a few meters up and disappears from sight. With a quick hand gesture, I make Desto and Mason aware of it.

Two kilometers later, we're almost to the edge of the canyon. I round the final bend, feeling the heat from the plains already beginning to push into the shadows. There's a clicking noise that my body reacts to before I realize I'd heard anything. A remote sentry, either motion or noise activated. But we've been *so* quiet! I fling myself back behind the edge of the wall and the others respond immediately by finding cover of their own. It's a flying mechanical device about the size and shape of a human head; its job is to provide surveillance in areas that aren't patrolled by ground troops and deliver our coordinates, capabilities, and numbers to a response squad. If it sees us, our cover and surprise advantage are blown.

It buzzes just barely within auditory range, moving slowly around the corner of the wall, seeking us. Even if we destroy the unit, any malfunction will alert responders. We need a diversion so we can pass by unnoticed. As I contemplate options, pellets of dirt rain down on me, and I feel a warm droplet of something land on my cheek. My head tips back in time to see two Flat Rats descending in leaps down the nearly vertical wall, their black lips drawn back and yellowed monster teeth revealed in ferocious grimaces. The closest is already in midair, its thirty kilos of predatory malevolence moments from crashing into me as I drop to a crouch and pull my knife free from my utility vest. Swinging almost wildly, I stab the blade into its side as it hits me, its weight flattening me to the ground. Wounded, it shrieks madly in my ear as its head lunges for my vulnerable neck.

Before it can clamp down, the other rat smashes down on top of us both, the smell of its wounded compatriot's blood already driving it into a voracious frenzy. Their combined weight and chaotic scrabbling is impossible to fight, and I know that I am seconds from being shredded to pieces. My arm is pinned to my chest; I can't get it free to stab again. Screaming for help will bring the sentry on us in seconds, but panic is beginning to replace my reason. Before I start shrieking, I draw my knees into my chest, hoping to protect my vital organs, and also hoping Desto or Mason gets to me before it's too late.

Suddenly one of the rats quits squirming and rises up on its haunches, hissing and baring its teeth. Mason runs toward me and kicks the rodent squarely in the ribs, sending it flying into the opening in the canyon wall. The wounded one is still on top of me but its strength is quickly ebbing. Deep lacerations caused by the other rat and a severed artery from my knife have mortally wounded it, and its life is leaking out all over me. The smell of its blood is a sickly sweet combination of rotten meat and carnivore viscera, making me gag. Mason grabs one of my arms and pulls me to my feet, letting the wounded rat fall. At the same time, we hear the remote sentry buzzing around the corner and we both freeze, pressed against the wall. The rat he kicked also sees it and picks itself up, limping off in a furious trot back toward the darkness and safety of the inner canyon. The sentry locks onto its movement and follows, unable to tell an actual threat from a random animal.

Mason steps back and looks me over with raised eyebrows. A quick mental self-scan reveals that I'm not badly hurt; my body armor and the durable material of my long-sleeved jacket protected me from any deep gouges, and a small scratch on the left side of my head has already stopped bleeding. I give him a thumbs-up, wishing I could take a few extra seconds to catch my breath, but this is the chance we need to get out of the canyon without being detected, and we move out at top speed. We reach the plains in a couple of minutes—our timing perfect. The only signs of Agate Beach through the shimmering haze are darker spots that might be the shadows of the settlement's squat buildings. Half a kilometer to the north stands the hillside outcropping that houses the mine. More remote sentries will be emplaced amid the dwellings, but the security force is probably inside the mine itself. If there's anything we haven't thought of, we'll know in less than four minutes.

We move in fast, low lunges and Desto reaches the settlement first. Despite the weight of his Thresher M-2209, his long, pistonlike legs never seem to get tired. Heaving himself onto the flat roof of Venus's outlying dwelling and dropping into a prone position, he provides perimeter coverage from the west while Mason takes the same position on another dwelling a hundred meters to the east. My job is to be the bait. Slinging my carbine onto my back and slowing to a walk, I head straight into the settlement's center.

Three sentries are on me within seconds, hovering at head level with their glistening camera lenses protruding in a ring around their centers like insectile eyestalks. A message from their internal transmitters plays in sync.

"You are under arrest. Stop immediately and place your hands on top of your head. You are under arrest. Shoot authority is granted if you attempt to run. You are under arrest . . ." Repeat.

The metallic taste of adrenalin coats the inside of my mouth as I comply. Five, four, three, two . . . the security force personnel don't disappoint. A heavily armored vehicle rolls nimbly across the packed earth and comes to a stop five meters in front of me. The base of its troop hold sits waist high above the ground, balanced over all-terrain tires covered by armor-plate shields. It takes a few seconds before the doors open. They're probably analyzing the sentries' video feeds, making sure I'm not hiding any surprises. Finally, the door opens and three soldiers jump down and surround me, weapons aimed at my chest.

"You are in a quarantined area. Let's see some ID and your authorization to be armed," the corporal in charge says, his voice resonating with a metal tininess through his helmet and breathing apparatus. I still wear the nostril filter Venus had given me the first day I'd set foot on Spectra 6, having grown enough used to it that I no longer even notice the soft pressure inside my alar sidewall.

"I don't have any."

"Ansen, relieve her of those guns."

The soldier to my right approaches me, his steps light and quick and his posture betraying a nonchalant casualness that will be his downfall. "Turn around and keep your hands on your head."

I do as he says and feel him grab the buckle of my carbine strap, preparing to remove it. Big mistake. He should have taken my Sinbad first. As I feel the carbine come loose, I drop to a crouch and draw the pistol from my left hip holster. Five shots split the air above me, dropping the other two soldiers and the sentries, and I spin around and press the pistol into the man's chin and pull the trigger. The inside of his helmet explodes in a red gush, but the bullet doesn't exit. Corps armor is tough, the best.

Before his body hits the ground, I sprint into the troop carrier hold. Thankfully, it's empty. The driver engages the partition that divides the cab from the hold but it's too slow. I'm able to fire through three times before it shuts, and his body folds forward over the steering wheel. Within seconds, Desto and Mason have joined me and Desto frantically works at the keypad that will reopen the partition, hoping to short it. We need the vehicle; it's our best way inside the mine.

"Should we call in the *Sphynx?*" I ask.

"No, not yet," Mason says. "If they're detected, the security force will call for backup and we'll have more than we can deal with."

Which means it's three of us against approximately seven. The inside of the mine serves as an excellent stronghold to counter a siege by three people or thirty. The settlers engineered it that way, which had been a smart decision when they were the mine's occupiers. Now that we're the ones laying siege, I can only wish it weren't so damn secure.

Still fighting the hatch mechanism, Desto finally gives up on shorting it when we hear the voice of their squad leader calling for a SITREP. Desto jumps out and runs to the passenger side of the cab, which is, except for the doors, a seamless bubble of bullet-proof resin. After sticking a ball of E-10 wax about the size of a rifle scope lens on the bubble, he lets it cook for a few seconds, then fires a shot from the 2209 into the middle of the wax. The entire shell fractures instantly, crashing inside the cabin and leaving a jagged ring around the rim.

"Aly, put on that uniform and be our driver."

Desto and I yank the body from the cab. Fortunately, my point-blank shots had been enough to pierce his uniform and body armor, but didn't penetrate all the way through. Only the back of his jacket shows obvious damage. I strip off my own, bloody and shredded from the rats, and put his on, followed by the helmet, first smashing one side of it against a rock to damage the com system, making it appear as if the driver couldn't hear the SITREP request. As I dress, the other two haul the dead soldiers into the troop van. The light-colored uniform for soldiers in this quadrant of the system are close enough to the color of my own aged and faded pants that I don't bother trading up. Finally, I belt on the dead man's sidearm holster but sheathe my own 'Bad. His assault rifle is still locked in its cradle, and I place mine out of sight but within quick reach next to me. "Let's go!"

We've lost a precious five minutes but no one's emerged to check on the doomed group. Our plan is developing as we go along, and Mason fills me in on why they loaded the bodies. I need to draw as many of their remaining security squad to the vehicle as I can once we get inside by signaling that the dead soldiers need urgent medical aid. They'll be using a portable transceiver to communicate with their airborne commander and we'll have to take that out ASAP. Once Corps command realizes there's a problem it will be an estimated fifteen hours maximum before help will arrive, if their nearest battle cruiser is within the quadrant. However, if they have a shorter range QRF ship on standby, like the one that had boarded Rob's ship on the way to R'Kadia, our time will be considerably compressed. We'll have no more than four or five hours to get the *Sphynx* in, loaded, and back out. But first, we have to settle the immediate problem.

I drive through the lead-in tunnel faster than safety dictates, but I have to make the situation appear life or death. Of course, the risk is that they'll shoot me as soon as I clear the tunnel. The thought makes sweat drip from my brow line, stinging my eyes. Why can't the Admin develop helmets with better ventilation?

Hardly slowing as I exit the tunnel mouth into the vast inner chamber, a quick look around confirms what I'd expected—the

Corps has been busy organizing and separating all the settlement's equipment and belongings into easily wrapped, transport-ready piles. Even as I notice this, I spot two rifle barrels trained toward us from behind a section of earthmoving equipment and another pointing out from behind the tunnel branch leading to the infirmary rooms. I hit the brakes a little too hard and hear a loud thump as someone is thrown against the inside of the transport's hold. Immediately, I raise my arms to where the soldiers can see my empty hands, and then start waving frantically toward the back of the transport.

"McMillan, what is your situation? Why aren't you responding to your coms?" someone yells, presumably at me. I can't answer verbally without giving away that I'm not McMillan, so I do as I'd planned and point exaggeratedly at my helmet, then back toward the rear.

No one moves. Shit!

There's a scrape as Desto or Mason pulls open the transport door, and I prepare to take cover underneath the steering column inside the cab, then Mason shouts, "Riordan and Chin are down! We need a medic back here!"

Somehow the authority in his voice, with the help of catching sight of the dead men's bodies, galvanizes the other soldiers. Four of them break cover—the three I'd already spotted and another from inside the tunnel mouth—and run toward the vehicle. As they approach, I jump from the cab, AK-80 in tow. They converge as a group on the transport's hatch and the first one begins climbing the ladder welded to the side.

"Hey!" he has enough time to yell before Mason shoots him dead in the chest. His body whips around backward before he falls from the ladder, and I see the shock that will forever be stamped on his face. The other three respond immediately, diving beneath the vehicle before Mason can fire again. Sprinting in the opposite direction, I'm able to reach the cover of the earthmoving equipment that they'd recently vacated. The firing stops, but my nerves don't cease dancing like an electrocution victim. The others could be calling for backup at this moment.

The mine goes quiet. Desto and Mason are safe inside the transport thanks to its full-shell armor designed to protect the troops from bullets and buried explosives, but I have no vantage on the soldiers hiding beneath it. The brain bucket has become constricting and is no longer serving the purpose of hiding my identity, so I ditch it and try scaring them out.

"Soldiers under the truck, you're surrounded. If you come out, we won't kill you." I fully intend to kill them, but they don't need to know that.

There's no response for several seconds, then one of them yells, "You won't get away with this."

Asshole. "I'm giving you to the count of ten."

"We've already got backup on the—"

Before he finishes the sentence, several shots ring out overhead from the direction of the communication room. Instinctively, I duck down before I can zero on exactly where they came from. Then Karl's voice echoes against the walls, "Two down up here, and their coms are destroyed."

I barely believe it. He was supposed to stay with the shuttle in the canyon until we secured the site. Obviously, he decided to take matters into his own hands. He must have crawled down from the airshaft that leads to the upper lookout and taken the personnel positioned in the com room by surprise. His initiative probably saved all of us.

"Karl," I yell, "do you know if they were able to call out?"

"Don't think so. I'm contacting the *Sphynx* now."

"You hear that? You're cooked. Throw out your weapons and get your asses out from under this truck." Desto's voice is thick with menace.

We'd hit four soldiers outside, Mason killed one trying to climb into the truck, three remain beneath it, and Karl says he's shot two others. Typical security squad size is ten troops, so it's probable we've neutralized the full threat. Still, I'm not going to take the chance that there's a rogue we haven't spotted and stay covered behind the equipment. The noise of the lift descending draws my attention and I peer around a 'dozer's corner to see Karl coming down. He doesn't share my concern apparently. The lift stops half a meter short of the floor, enough gap that the soldiers under the truck won't be able to get a shot at him without exposing themselves to me.

Desto drops the cap of a grenade over the edge of the truck as a warning. "We're not going to ask you again. Move out now, or they'll be picking your teeth out of the engine block."

Rifles scrape along the dry concrete of the mine floor as the trapped soldiers give in to their fate. As they drag themselves out and stand up, I move out from behind the equipment, my carbine level to my shoulder, ready to dispatch them. They stand in front of the open door of the vehicle, hands locked on top of their heads. Karl stays in the lift, keeping an eye on things.

Mason places the barrel of his rifle against the base of the middle soldier's helmet and asks, "How many Corps are on site?"

The solider answers quickly, "There are—were—ten of us."

"When is your relief scheduled to arrive?"

"We just got here this morning. There isn't another rotation for a week."

"You sure?" He jabs hard with the barrel, causing the man's head to jerk forward.

"Yeah! We're it. Just don't shoot us."

I flick my gaze up, look into Mason's eyes briefly, and settle the carbine's barrel firmly against my shoulder. Training the sight on the man farthest to the left, I start to squeeze the trigger.

"Aly, stop!" Karl yells. I turn to look at him, the insistence in his tone catching my attention. He's loping across the cavern toward me. "You can't do that."

I'm surprised, thinking I must have misunderstood him, but his expression makes it clear; he's not going to let me shoot them.

"Karl, don't be ridiculous. These guys killed Bodie. They deserve what they're about to get."

"We aren't going to get anything out of killing them. Doug, let's tie them up. We can lock them in the com room when we leave."

"Karl! What's your problem? What about Bodie? Who's going to pay for that?" My strained tone echoes against the walls, eliciting concerned stares from Mason and Desto.

Karl turns around and steps up closer to me, laying a warm and callused hand on my shoulder. His gaze is unwavering, but there is a gentleness that I rarely see hidden behind the hard shine of his pupils. "Do you really want their blood on your hands? Killing them won't make any of us feel better. It won't change anything."

Slowly, I lower my barrel and take a deep breath that turns into a tremble. It's hard to look at him, and my eyes fall to his chest. I want to press myself against him and let this all be over, but he turns away and starts walking toward the prisoners, leaving me feeling empty and defeated.

"Let's get these men secured and start moving supplies out," Desto says. "V and the crew should be here in half an hour."

SEVENTEEN

The remaining security squad are locked down in the disabled troop carrier, and Desto waits on the observation platform for the crew to arrive. The rest of us divide up and begin collecting the supplies we'll need for an extended trip.

I take the control room. Inside, the lingering signs of a gun-fight exhibit themselves through broken equipment, and dirt and gravel from the rock walls lie in blasted chunks everywhere. There's a grit-flecked mahogany smear on the floor near the main bank of monitors that must have been where Bodie had fallen. My eyeballs feel overheated and coated in tears as thick as motor oil as I go through the room. The Corps had taken his body somewhere, but that only makes the impact of losing him harder. How dare they? It wasn't enough to murder him, but they also took him from us. There can be no funeral, no lasting gravestone in his honor. Just that red stain and our memories.

Once the *Sphynx* arrives, the crew moves with calibrated quickness, making certain that nothing of potential use is left behind. The *Sphynx* is crammed full, floor to ceiling and wall to wall. Contraband, weapons, and stolen Admin supplies lie everywhere, with no way to conceal them. It's not important. If the Admin comes after us, the only thing we can do is run.

The last items we go after are the settlers' personal belongings, things we know of that are important to them, but there's no way we can sort through everything. With limited time and space aboard the ship, we don't bring much. Going through the dwellings shows how busy the Corps has been in the last few days sanitizing the settlement of anything valuable or dangerous. Everything of use has been collected and brought to the mine to be sorted and hauled off. With a mixture of relief and uncertainty, we find no bodies or graves. If anyone besides Bodie had been harmed, the Corps didn't leave behind any clues.

Eight hours later, I watch Spectra 6 fall away like a particle of dust through the *Sphynx*'s nav-system's local display grid. And it hits me. A drop in my stomach, like the bottom of everything is falling loose. Will I ever see the Beach again? Will I ever know what it feels like to belong somewhere again? My last sight of the mine cavern was a mess of plundered, nonessential items scattered haphazardly around like discarded junk. But it had been our home, and I'm blindsided by a sense of plummeting sadness. I never expected to become so attached. Now that the strings are being severed, I finally understand what it really meant to me.

Once we've broken out of atmosphere and our coordinates are set, I leave the flight deck. Neither Vitruzzi or Venus meets my eyes as I excuse myself and head to my bunk to be alone, but as soon as I lie down, there's a knock on my door.

"It's open."

Karl steps through the doorway and I sit up. Our eyes lock for a moment, his serene brown and mine sapphire blue. "Hey," he finally says.

"Hey."

"Mind if I come in?"

I shake my head, indicating it's okay.

He sits on the bench that doubles as a storage locker across from my bunk, the space so narrow that his knees nearly touch the bed. He leans on his elbows, looking at the floor for a minute, and my senses are flooded with him: his smell, cinnamon and leather; his countenance, stern, sad; and his presence, solid, determined, unyielding. That feeling of coming undone begins to fade instantly as I realize, without a shred of uncertainty, that he is my home.

"Look, Aly—"

"I want—"

We both stop and I wait for him to go on. "This is hard for me," he continues after a second. "I think you know how I feel about you. It was a mistake to keep our collaboration with Rajcik a secret. But you have to believe me when I say that it wasn't meant to hurt you. I didn't want to lie to you, no one did. I think, maybe . . . I *thought* that I was protecting you." He waits for a second before continuing, hoping I'll make it easy for him, but I keep my silence. That wound still gapes, raw and hot. "You have to realize we're only working with him because it is, or was, the best thing for the settlement."

Was it? I consider asking, but bottle it.

"We really need you behind us on this one. You and David are part of this crew, and we shouldn't have left you in the dark. I know that. I'm sorry." He slides forward on the bench and wraps both of my hands in his, drawing me closer to him. "And I don't want to lose you."

My skin absorbs the warmth from his palms like a desiccated flower finally being given water. The sorrow in his eyes is clear, devoid of any masked accusations or machismo. Is my return silence just me being stubborn and unreasonable, some kind of punishment for the things he said? The argument we had in the mine was bad, his explosion hurtful and unnecessary, but what good does it do me at this point to hold on to my anger? If I let it go, we may have a chance at working things out.

He looks into my face, and whatever he sees there seems to encourage him. His mouth wrinkles to one side in a half grin. "Why don't you say something?"

I consider for only a moment, then say, "I'm sorry about what happened with Rob."

Apparently that was not what he was expecting to hear. Though his expression doesn't change, the muscles holding his smile twitch. "What do you mean?"

And it hits me. He doesn't know about the night I'd spent with Rob. How stupid can I be? "I thought you didn't care, Karl. The things you said . . . I was hurt."

Clenching his jaw, he drops my hands and leans back, his torso becoming as straight and rigid as a plinth. "So you fucked your old boyfriend?"

I wince. "Isn't that what you were accusing me of? What did you think? You can't treat me like that and not expect me to—" I stop myself. What I was about to say is *get even*, but is that what sleeping with Rob had been about? No. It's time to start being honest. I won't lie to Karl, and I'm done lying to myself. I slept with Rob because it was easier than trying to explain my feelings or make myself vulnerable. But I'm tired of this combat, both with myself and with Karl.

Leaning toward him, trying to take one of his hands, I continue, "Karl, I can't keep doing this with you. I—" *love you*. But it's too late. He stands up and charges from the room, nearly running.

For a minute, I forget to breathe. When I start again, my chest convulses violently, like it's being crushed under hundreds of pounds of stone, like I'm being buried alive. I fall back onto my bunk, the leaden mass of my loss pushing me against the mat like a tombstone. I'm too empty to resist. Whatever happens now hardly matters. Rescuing the settlers will be the end for me. The Beach is gone, Karl's gone, and everything that matters—gone. There's no reason left to run. And nothing left to run to.

EIGHTEEN

"Rob's agreed to help us," Vitruzzi announces while standing in the *Sphynx*'s galley, where she'd called us all. We're five hours out from landing back on R'Kadia and moving into the next, and most crucial, phase of our plan to rescue the settlers from Keum Libre. "He's going to smuggle La Mer and a couple more of us into Tunis City, and then go on his way. The risks for him are minimal and Tunis is his next stop anyway."

Our heads all turn to La Mer, none of us yet understanding why he'd sign up to go to Tunis, the most unlikely place in the system to hide. He begins to explain, but his eyes are on Venus, as if trying to make her understand. "I know people, other wire-rats, on Obal 10, who can help us access the Admin satellites. If I can get back there—without getting caught—we can provide the cover the rest of you will need to get to Keum Libre and save the Beachers. We can call in the threat to T'Kai and show him what we've got. Maybe create enough of a distraction."

So that's it—keep one of the Hydra's three heads busy while the rest of the crew slips past. That still leaves the Corps and whatever security exists on Keum Libre. I glance at the others, seeing the same thoughtful look on all of their faces. La Mer's newness to the crew and the Beach should be enough to ensure his plan is automatically regarded with skepticism. Yet somehow Venus's devotion and his total absence of guile have endeared La Mer to all of us quickly and thoroughly. I still have to work to convince some of the crew, mostly Brady, that I can be counted on, but La Mer has fit in with ease since almost the beginning.

"These wire-rats—why would they help? It would be crazy for anyone else to volunteer to get involved in this," Karl says.

La Mer looks away from Venus for the first time, and I catch the glow of fear behind his eyes. He's well aware of the risks in what he's proposing. "I know. And they know it, too. But this is a network that has been working against the Admin in secrecy for years. Their goal is to change the system, to erode the Admin's power any way they can. Once I talk to them and explain what we've got, they'll help us."

"What will they want in return?" I ask.

"If we can expose the corruption in even one of the Ministries, that'll be reward enough. And if not"—he shrugs—"we may have to write them an IOU."

With no one else prepared to offer up a better idea, there's a pause in the discussion. Eventually Desto breaks the silence: "Sounds shaky, but it's all we've got right now. V, how do you want to divide up?"

"I'm going with Jeremy," Venus states.

I don't miss the way Vitruzzi winces, as if slapped. She says, "Venus, we need you to fly the *Sphynx*."

Venus's already pale skin becomes nearly translucent as the blood drains from it. "Karl or Doug can fly it just fine. I'm not going to be separated from him." She reaches out and grasps one of La Mer's hands hard enough to make her fragile blue veins stand out.

Vitruzzi's voice becomes very quiet, a tone that would be soothing under normal circumstances. "Yeah, they can, but what if we get into trouble? No one can make the *Sphynx* fly the way you can. The Beachers need you. Jeremy can handle things on Obal 10, and he won't be alone."

"I'll be keeping you safe, love," he says, staring into Venus's frightened green eyes.

She looks around at the rest of us, searching our faces, and I know I'm not the only one who has trouble meeting her gaze. Her voice tremors at the realization that the decision isn't hers. "After you send the transmission, how are you going to get off of Obal 10?"

"Don't worry about that yet. Eleanor is right, you'll be helping more people if you go to Keum Libre," Brady says, trying to soothe her, but his words have the opposite effect.

"I don't care about that!"

"Venus . . ." La Mer says.

She whirls around without releasing his hand and sweeps her bulging, phosphorescent eyes over the crew. "They're going to wipe us out. You all know it. What's the point? They'll just keep coming until they kill all of us. Like Bodie! Like my parents!"

This time my glance drops to the floor. I can't help feeling guilty and I don't know why. She's probably right. It feels like a lie to try and convince her otherwise.

La Mer wraps her in a hug, folding his long arms around her petite form like a cape. She stands stiffly in his embrace for several seconds but she doesn't cry. Like the rest of us, she's been too hardened by a life that's already seen too much loss to waste any more tears. After a few seconds, she steps back and says in a husky voice, "I'll be in the cockpit."

The galley is quiet for several seconds after she leaves. Each of us contemplate her outburst, the words like a shroud threatening to suffocate our resolve.

Finally, Vitruzzi says, "We only need to send one or two others with La Mer. Think about it and decide for yourselves who'll go. I've already transmitted the plan to Rajcik. We'll pick him up and leave for Keum Libre at first light tomorrow."

NINETEEN

Venus plants the *Sphynx* like a lawn dart outside the mine entrance where Rajcik has taken up residence. Unlike her normal, floating descents, the haphazard way she ratchets the ship between the canyon walls feels like we're descending on a broken elevator whose cables snap and catch. One second we're dropping much too fast, the next she's opening up the reverse thrusters with maximum torque, effectively braking us with the force of a crashing tidal wave. I have to grab the handrail of the galley stairs to keep from breaking my neck, and there's a crashing sound somewhere inside the ship as unsecured cargo topples. Brady curses in the galley behind me.

Vitruzzi transmitted Rob the coordinates and asked him to move the *'Rize* to as near the cave entrance as possible. Two ships the sizes of the *Sphynx* and the *Horizon* docked together on this stripped moon will quickly attract any scout ships in the quadrant, so we plan to keep the stop short and to the point. La Mer and the crew going with Rob will load weapons and the equipment they'll need on Obal 10 aboard the *Horizon* right after meeting with Rajcik and depart immediately. Everyone else will board the *Sphynx* and should be back in the air and on the way to Keum Libre early tomorrow morning.

The crew's been too busy to discuss who'll go with La Mer, but I've already decided to put in my ticket. Karl has moved around the ship like a ghost since our last encounter, confirming my grim fear that anything we had is over. I'm certain Vitruzzi will want him to stay with Venus and be her backup, and getting as far away from him as I can is the only way I can cope with his anger and my own feelings of betrayal. I can still aid the settlers and give him what he wants by taking the trip to Obal 10. Everyone wins.

The cargo hold ramp lowers and the rest of the crew disembarks while I hang back to gather a few extra magazines and clips for my carbine and 'Bad. As I pry the lid off a case of ammunition, David walks up behind me.

"You're going with Rob." He doesn't have to ask.

I acknowledge the statement with a quick nod and shove as many magazines for my AK-80 into my duffel as it can hold. He watches me quietly for a minute and then sighs. "All right, me too then."

I pause, feeling both relieved and touched—and slightly embarrassed about it. "You don't have to do that."

"Yeah I do, Twig."

There's a familiar vibration in the air. I zip up the duffel and we step out into the shifting sand-colored haze of the R'Kadian evening to watch the *Horizon* settle onto a flat plateau above the mine's entrance. Everyone else has already gone underground, but David and I wait for Rob. He, Baker, and Montoya drive sandbikes down a narrow trail that twines its way into the canyon between boulders and spires, finally reaching us at the base within a few short minutes.

Rob stops beside us and David asks, "You ready for this?"

Apprehension ripples across Rob's face for a second, then it's gone. "Ready for anything, brother. Just another job. Maybe a tiny bit more, uh, interesting."

He smiles and asks Baker and Montoya to double-up on one bike so David and I can take the other. As our group enters the mine tunnel, the bikes' low-watt headlights are barely powerful enough to illuminate our path. The mine has been out of commission for a long time, and none of the original fixtures mounted along the tunnel's high ceiling still work. There's a dry, desiccated smell to the air as if nothing has lived inside for years. As we approach the central cavern, a dull yellow glow creeps along the walls toward us. At least one generator must be running, but the air is so full of floating dust and dirt from the Rover and sandbikes that it's hard to just make out the tunnel corridor, much less gauge distance.

We reach the end and the walls rise at precise right angles ten meters above our heads to the ceiling. Sitting on one side and filling half the cave is the *Temptation*, safely docked under millions of tons of rock and earth where no Corps scanning system can detect it. As soon as I see it, my guts do a nauseating flip-flop and my palms grow slick as a combustible mix of fury and revulsion begin seeping from my pores in a feral sweat—a poisonous biochemical reminder of my hate for the Admin and what they'd taken from us and for Rajcik for what he'd nearly taken from me. We made the wrong decision, I know it. I *feel* it in the way my stomach clenches and my skin leaks a layer of oily dampness. Counting on Rajcik to help us is a mistake, the biggest mistake any of us will ever make. And if Venus is right, none of us will get a chance to make another one.

Dismounting the bike, David catches me staring at the ship and nudges me forward with his elbow. "Hey, they're over there. Come on."

It takes an effort to pull my eyes from the *Temptation*. "David," I warn, "this can't end well."

"It will. We just have to stay together, little sis." He gives me a smile that's supposed to be reassuring, and we move to catch up with the others.

Everyone is gathered in a circle near the freight elevator. The hole Desto had punched with grenades into the nearby wall during my first visit to this rock has a fresh scar of blocks and mortar plugging it, but it's the man standing next to it that draws my stare. The vulpine, brown-stubbled face of Fuller Thompson evokes as much disgust in me now as it always has. He stares back at me, our mutual animosity eliciting the same reaction in both. He's grown thinner, as has Rajcik, but neither are any less menacing, like a pair of sharpened axes dangling over us by the thinnest of threads.

Vitruzzi sees us approaching and says, "Now that we're all here—"

Nobody expects the way Karl spins around and leaps at Rob, one fist balled and swinging through the air in a precise trajectory directly into Rob's chin. It's a sucker punch, and Rob is as surprised as everyone else. His head jerks backward, snapping to a stop as his neck catches, his body following. Staggering, he still somehow deflects a second blow coming from Karl, and by then everyone is jumping in to stop him. Desto and Mason race to Karl's side, each of them taking hold of an arm as he strains forward, looking as if he wants to tear Rob's heart out. To my surprise, both Baker and Montoya have drawn small handguns like my own Mini-Derg, aiming them directly at Karl's chest, their mutual expressions of detached alertness almost an exact match.

"Karl!" I yell, but his attention stays on Rob, who quickly regains his footing.

Rubbing his bruised chin, Rob's eyes contract into wounded, watering slits. He's not badly hurt, and the fury radiating from him almost heats the air around us. "What the fuck do you think you're doing, Strahan?"

Karl acts like hasn't even heard him. He jerks against Desto and Mason, but the two men hold on like plow oxen, solid and unyielding.

Brady steps between them and leans toward Karl so their chins are centimeters apart. "Dammit, Karl, we don't have time for this."

Finally, Karl shifts his gaze to Brady, and a battle of wills is fought between their locked eyes. After a few more seconds, he relaxes his shoulders, letting his balled fists drop to his sides. Mason and Desto exchange a glance, then release Karl's arms, but don't move away in case he erupts again. The fire stanched for now, Brady turns away from Karl and abrades me with a look of exasperation and frustration. "The same goes for everyone here. Whatever petty bullshit you're holding against each other, it doesn't matter anymore. There are lives at stake, and not just the settlers'. Every one of us is in the Admin's crosshairs. We've all lost people we care about, and it's time to stop fucking around and start working together."

His eyes land on me once again during his last statement, infuriating me, then he turns to Rob. "Cross?"

Rob's attention is still on Karl, both wary and furious, but he waves a hand toward Baker and Montoya, who sheathe their pistols inside their jackets. I don't like the way they reacted to the fight, like fixers who will clean up whatever mess inconveniences them. Rob I can, if not trust, at least understand, but his crew is another story. In the days ahead, something tells me I better pay close attention to them.

Rajcik clears his throat with a guttural flourish and says, "Are we ready to get on with business? Vitruzzi, I thought you had better control of your crew." His callousness is typical—Rajcik isn't concerned with making new friends.

Vitruzzi lets his statement slide, the familiar vein pulsing prominently between her eyebrows giving the only indication that she's having to work to control her anger. Walking into the center of the group, she lays the plan out.

"This is how things will go down. Rajcik, you'll fly with the crew on the *Sphynx* and take them to KL. La Mer, me, and . . ." She pauses, looking around to see who's decided to go to Obal 10. I can't look at Karl and witness the expression on his face as I step forward, David right next to me. Vitruzzi nods and continues, "Aly and David will go with Cross to Tunis City. We'll contact La Mer's sources and set up the security worm, then we'll send a warning shot to T'Kai. The *Sphynx* will stay in a holding pattern, either within safe distance of KL or on the rock itself, until we confirm we've succeeded—"

Rajcik cuts her off, "And if you don't succeed?"

"We still go after the settlers," Brady answers.

"With your one ship? You people really are suicidal," Thompson grunts.

Vitruzzi looks Rajcik and Thompson over, gauging their dubious commitment to this mission. Her eyes flick to Rob, then fix on Rajcik. "I'm sure it's occurred to you that we may already have all we need to bargain with T'Kai for the settler's freedom."

I'm reminded of just how relentless, grim even, she can be, and my admiration for her swells again as she implies that we could exchange Rajcik for the settlers.

"The only thing I can't figure out is why we haven't already done it," I blurt out.

Thompson's hate-filled stare burns like two hot coins laid on the skin of my face.

Vitruzzi continues, ignoring my comment, "But we already have a deal, Rajcik. And we intend to uphold our end of it. As long as we think you'll uphold yours."

"I'm as trustworthy as you," he says, and it's my turn to grunt in disgust.

"Fine. How long do you expect it to take to reach KL?"

"No more than fifteen days, provided we avoid any patrols."

"And Rob, it should take you approximately ten days to reach Obal 10. Is there any way you can shave that time?"

"The best we can do is about eight." Since recovering from Karl's attack, Rob hasn't taken his eyes off of Rajcik. I'm sure he's thinking the same thing Vitruzzi had threatened, and Vitruzzi's glance a few seconds ago tells me she knows it. Rajcik is worth a lot of money to the Admin. The gamble is tremendous; all sides but ours have more to gain by following their own agenda instead of the one she's laying out. For Rajcik, this operation is a plot to get even with T'Kai for reneging on their deal, and it's only a matter of time before he does something unlooked for that could help him do that. Whatever it is, it's certain to jeopardize the rest of us. For Rob, the only thing that's stopping him from apprehending Rajcik, or at least leading a Corps security patrol to his doorstep, is a sense of loyalty to Vitruzzi and the crew, maybe even to me. The question is: What would it take for that loyalty to expire? The *Red*

Horizon is a nice piece of machinery, advanced, expensive. Maybe all it would take for Rob to switch sides is money. How much is anyone's guess.

It's a dark thought, but the kind of thought that's kept me alive this along. *You're just being paranoid*, I tell myself. But looking at Montoya and Baker, I wonder if that's true. They've been standoffish, even outright hostile, toward the crew since coming to the Beach. Even if Rob is on board with our plan, what's going to keep them in check?

"When do we leave?" Rajcik wants to know.

"First thing in the morning. Pack your gear aboard the *Sphynx* tonight."

He nods, then says, "One final thing, Vitruzzi. I have interests to protect. Thompson goes with you to Tunis."

TWENTY

As if stage directions have been given, the group breaks up, everyone jumping onto their respective transportation and heading to the ships to prepare. I'm already packed and deliberate about staying behind to keep tabs on Rajcik and Thompson. If they have plans to jam us up, this is the best opportunity to put an end to them. I know as certainly as I know that I'll never taste squash as good as Bodie's again that they're operating from an alternative agenda, and it will most likely come into play when it's least looked for and most damaging. But Rajcik is much too shrewd to be caught off guard this early in the game. He and Thompson loiter around the cargo bins where we'd met, their nonchalance seeming to mock my paranoid hypervigilance, and reluctantly, I jump on the bike with David and follow the rest of the crew to the *Sphynx*.

Low clouds, tinted a sickly grayish-red like festering flesh, drape heavily over the landscape and along the horizon. Compared to the relatively clear and sunny atmosphere of Spectra 6, evening here is dim and oppressive, and I look forward to getting off this rock as soon as possible.

Hanging back outside the ship's opened cargo bay ramp, I wait for David and Vitruzzi to collect their weapons, supplies, and sundries, and I have time to think over the plan we've discussed. We have enough food for the duration we expect to be on Obal 10—around a week, two at the most—and we'll be relying on La Mer and Vitruzzi's familiarity with Tunis City to find a place to hide and set up the security-override worm. Despite how direct and simple the plan is, a deep, foreboding gloom clings to me. I wonder if this will be the last time I ever see the *Sphynx* and the crew.

Squatting at the edge of one of the landing legs, I draw bored circles in the sand with my index finger, anxiously awaiting our mobilization. This is the hard part, the anticipation of what's coming. The sound of a motor catches my attention, and I look up as Rajcik approaches on a bike. Knots of tension cinch tightly around my muscles as I jump to my feet, surprised that he's arrived so quickly. The prospect of a one-on-one encounter with him makes me feel like an overpressurized oxygen tank next to a lit torch. Before I can do more than draw my Sinbad and glance down the sight in a reflexive check, he pulls up to an idle a short distance away, remaining astride the bike. Temptation to put a bullet through his forehead shakes my reason, but my gun hand remains steady and straight.

Letting the engine rumble in a synchronous thump, he stares at me. "We have some past business to put behind us."

I let the words hang in the air for a few seconds, trying to get my snarl of emotions under control. Finally, I spit out, "Why would you help us, Rajcik? What are you planning to get out of this?"

"I have my reasons." The words thrum from his tattooed throat like a slow-burning fuse.

"I know, and you better tell me what they are or I swear I'll kill you where you stand."

Laughing, he replies, "Maybe this is my idea of atonement for betraying you. What? You don't think I'm capable of remorse?"

"You're no more capable of remorse than I am of believing you. I know you, Rajcik." The words come out slowly, deliberately. "I find out whatever you're hiding on my own, it's not going to go half as well for you as you're expecting."

A dangerous look dances behind the dark sheen of his pupils. "I'd be more careful about making idle threats, Aly. You never know when someone will take you seriously." Engaging the bike's tripod, he slowly dismounts and steps into a more conversational range. He's not wearing a jacket, and for the first time I notice a long, still-red and puffy scar emerging from the outside of his right sleeve and curving down to the back of his arm, nearly to his elbow. The depth of the gash is wicked, showing that whatever had caused it had bitten deep, probably to the bone. He's lucky not to have lost the arm.

So, that's what had made him desperate enough to call on Vitruzzi.

"But you want an answer, here it is. T'Kai fucked me. It's time to pay him back. I know you, of all people, can understand that." Coming even closer, he leans forward, carefully ensuring his hands remain visible. "You know what I'm talking about. You felt that bitter hatred worming its way through your guts when I betrayed you. Treachery, like a poison, working itself deep. And it will stay there, cooking you from inside until you have your revenge. That's what you live for." He draws back and looks at me candidly, holding my unwavering blue eyes with his cave-black ones, and the savagery lurking in them makes me almost pity T'Kai.

I finally look away, repelled by the intensity of his hate. "I'm just trying to help the settlers." But is that true? The memory of my intention to kill the defeated soldiers at the Beach, and how Karl had had to stop me, bobs to the surface of my brain. That had been pure darkness, bloodlust. A demon of revenge, as insidious as Rajcik just described. Was the look in my eyes then the same as his now? No. I won't believe that. "Whatever your sick reasons," I say, trying to cover my unease, "just make sure you stick to the plan. You'll get your chance, but we're all in this together this time. If any one of us fucks up, we're all going to die."

"There are worse things than dying."

"What do you mean—"

He turns away and begins untying a bag from his bike, cutting me off. "Aly, you're such an idealist. That's what I used to find interesting about you. But you still haven't learned that idealism means nothing unless you're willing to take action. You and your brother were only content to run from the Admin, hide in a hole like scared rodents. You never had enough guts to do anything that mattered."

His tone grates my nerve endings raw. I should turn around right now and walk back aboard the *Sphynx* before one of us does something that will endanger the mission. Instead, I counter, "You're talking about conviction, János, and we have more than enough of that. We just knew better than to inflict our 'idealism' on innocent people. All you believe in is murdering for profit. You aren't fooling me—you're just as demented as T'Kai and people like him."

As soon as the words leave my mouth, I realize they're a mistake. He's on me too quickly for my eyes to register, spinning me around and wrenching my right arm behind my back, forcing the Sinbad to fall uselessly into the sand. He slams me face down against the ramp, and I feel his weight come down on me, pinning me to the spot.

"Get off me!" I manage to grunt, immediately wishing I could get the air back as his heft compresses my lungs.

"Step the fuck back!" Desto yells, and two sets of booted feet run down the ramp toward us. Rajcik is off me instantly.

"Just discussing the plan," he says, as if that truly is all that we've been doing.

I roll over, sucking in a deep breath. His face looms just above me, his expression calm and implacable, barely seeming to notice Desto and Mason. It's almost as if Rajcik is somewhere else, the people around him not even present, and I realize that, in a way, he's *not* here; his interests have nothing to do with me, with the settlers, or with the crew. For the first time, I'm really seeing who Rajcik is, what drives him. He's not moved by petty feelings or interests the way normal people are. He doesn't feel a sense of attachment or concern for the mundane humdrum of typical lives and can't be distracted by things that don't move him toward achieving his purpose, no matter how sociopathic and twisted that purpose is. Until he resolves his issue with T'Kai, nothing else will factor in. The realization that he feels nothing toward me or about what he did to me, one way or another, completely sucks away any satisfaction I might have had in getting even with him. What good is killing a ghost? He has no more interest in my selfish, vengeful hatred than he had in my loyalty.

"You okay?" Desto helps me up with one hand, pointing a modified Bhishma pistol the size of my forearm at Rajcik's chest with the other.

"Fine." As I brush the sand from my clothes, the need to confront Rajcik and make him suffer for what he'd done fades like a carcass washed off a beach, pulled away by the tide. I'm beginning to understand David's perspective, how he'd been able to move beyond Rajcik's betrayal and get to the point where he can see him as an asset instead of an enemy. "I'm fine. Let him be."

Desto stares at me for a few seconds, surprised at my quick forgiveness, then holsters the Bhishma and says to Rajcik, "Come on. I'll show you where you're bunking."

Mason starts an inspection of the ramp hydraulics as Rajcik unloads his belongings and follows Desto inside—to my old bunk. The place I'd called home on many nights for the last three months is now Rajcik's, another rude slap symbolizing just how dire and desperate things have become. Lending Mason a hand helps pass the time, and a short while later David emerges, soon followed by Vitruzzi and Brady, their hands held tight. I can only imagine what the doc is feeling at this moment. She's already lost one husband to the Admin. How can she be so calm and resolute, knowing that the chances of reuniting with Brady again are so small? A knot rises in my throat, realizing that the same is true of Karl and I. Hopelessly, I wait for him to come out, at least to say goodbye.

La Mer and Venus are the last to join us, Venus's eyes and nose red from crying, and La Mer seems unable to quit wiping his own eyes with his sleeve.

"I'm going to tell you one last time, I wish you'd let me go to Obal 10 instead of you, Eleanor." Brady's face, usually ruddy anyway, has hectic patches of red on the cheeks, making his scar stand out starkly. There's no doubting the distress he's feeling, though he's trying, like the rest of us, to keep it together.

"I know you do," she replies, and brushes a kiss across one of his cheeks. "Someone has to negotiate with T'Kai, and I'm better at it."

He grabs her in a tight hug and I hear her whisper, "The Sphynx is yours now. Take care of it. I love you." When he lets her go, water threatens to break over his lower eyelids, and for the first time, I see softness in Brady.

"You be safe," he says and shakes David's and La Mer's hands. When he turns to me, that same softness is still there. "You too, Aly."

His gentleness hits me like a soft blow, driving home more than anything else the possibility that this may be the last time the crew will ever be together. My voice is tight as I respond, "You all be careful, too."

The rest of us say our goodbyes, Desto nearly squeezing me lifeless in a farewell hug, and we make ridiculous promises to be seeing each other again soon. Then the three of us going with Rob mount sandbikes and trace our way up the canyon walls. I look back one more time before boarding the *Horizon*, but Karl is nowhere to be seen.

TWENTY-ONE

"Stay off the bridge," Montoya says, backing me through the doorway. He towers over me, his brick-shaped jaw only centimeters from my forehead. His face tilts down as he enters the door code, his hostility emphasized by the deep, oversized pores running along his cheek and nose as he promptly seals me out.

I've been walking around the ship, taking in its design and layout in case the need for a quick evacuation or disappearance comes around, laboring valiantly to keep my thoughts strictly on the mission ahead. Most of the doors inside the main hull are locked, and the ones that aren't lead to insignificant storage rooms and empty berths. Besides our quick flight to R'Kadia, I haven't been aboard a ship this size since the Corps and find its roominess a little disconcerting. The beauty of these long-haul cargo carriers is their self-sufficient handling. It's easy for Rob to run a skeleton crew with the ship's advanced piloting functions. Besides handling takeoffs and landings, the only essential functions to fulfill are setting the coordinates and fixing anything that breaks. Even so, I bet Venus could make it dance like a ballerina if she had a chance to bump it off auto.

After my sweep, I came to the bridge looking for Rob. The moment I entered the flight deck's open hatch, Montoya shut me down, jumping from his seat and letting me know in no uncertain terms that the bridge is now off-limits. What are they afraid I'll do? We're all headed to the same place. So maybe it's not what I'm doing that's of concern, but what *they're* doing. Montoya's behavior is just another example of their odd behavior, and nothing about the crew has put my mind at ease since they landed at the Beach.

Jesus, has it already been over a week?

I'd gotten just enough of a glimpse onto the flight deck to see that Rob isn't there, but it's time to track him down and get some answers, so I head straight to his cabin. When my knock is answered, I find both him and David inside, sitting at a table and talking.

"Pull up a seat. I've been wondering what you're up to," Rob says.

I sit down. "Why aren't we allowed on the bridge?"

There's a slight blue tinge to his jaw where Karl had struck him, almost lost in the shadow of a day and a half's growth of dark beard. "Just trying to keep things as under control as possible, Aly. My crew isn't exactly celebrating the fact that I've agreed to help out on this mission—"

"And why are you helping us? You said yourself that you stand to lose a hell of a lot if it comes out that you're involved in anything that happens in the next few weeks."

Rob hesitates before answering, thinking about his words carefully. His eyes search my face, as if picking out a bottle of Bordeaux. David leans back on two legs of the chair and remains diplomatically quiet, knowing that it's better for me to get my questions answered now, regardless of my own lack of tact, than to leave me guessing.

"The Admin went too far. The settlers at the Beach are peaceful people. They shouldn't be treated like this." There's nothing in his dark brown eyes but calm sincerity as Rob continues, "Besides, hundreds of ships go in and out of Tunis City every day. Mine will be just another entry in the dock logs, and no one will be able to connect whatever happens to me."

"So that's it? You just want to help?" I'm not that easily convinced. "What about the money you could make by turning Rajcik in?"

A worried shadow passes over his features, then it's gone. "If your crew needs him as much as it sounds like, I'd be doing more harm than good by turning him in." His glance jumps between David and me. "You know, I'm more than a little curious about this footage you say Rajcik has. I mean, information that could implicate Kurosawa T'Kai—that's heavy. Any chance I could see it?"

"*I* haven't even seen it," I comment caustically.

Changing the subject, David asks, "What about your crew? How did you get them to agree to this?"

Rob cocks one eyebrow in an expression I can't read. "They'll do as they're told. They're citizens, but they're also ambitious enough. If they think there's a payoff, they won't question too much."

"Rob, there's no payoff in this deal."

"Yeah, but they don't know that." His mischievous grin is tired, and he sighs. "I've thought of something to keep them off your backs. Leave that to me."

"Look, Rob, I wish this didn't have to involve you. You realize that, right?" David says, his face drawn. "Old friends or not, you've got more at stake here than we do. If there was any other way, we wouldn't have asked for your help." My brother the peacemaker. He didn't get my temper, which is a surprise. It was David's father who was always the angry one, the guy who'd jump off the handle if you said anything disrespectful or sarcastic. David's father, not mine. We only had the same mother, and David tells me she was always more passive, docile even, before she split.

"After the shit we've been through together, brother? This is nothing. You'd do the same for me." Rob seems to relax a little, and his charismatic grin returns.

We fall silent for a minute, then David pushes back from the table and stands up. "I'm going to get something to eat. Anyone else hungry?"

Neither of us are, and David drops a teasing wink at me before heading toward the galley.

Rob leans forward and lays a hand on my leg. "So how are you holding up?"

I have to think about that for a second, but thinking makes me worried, and worry makes me feel helpless. I answer stonily. "I really don't know. How would you be doing in this kind of situation?"

"Yeah, I hear you."

Our eyes stay locked. "I'm sorry about Karl . . ." I trail off, not really knowing how to apologize for something like that.

Anger flashes behind his pupils, but he shrugs. "Yeah, well, I'll live. But your boyfriend better not try that again. It could get messy."

His comment strikes a painful chord, and I look away, letting the conversation lull. Rob leans back on his chair and takes his hand off my leg. After a few seconds, I start to stand up to leave but am stopped by his muffled chuckle, as if I'd said something mildly amusing. "Look, Aly, it's obvious that you're in love with him. So why don't you just tell him—go and be with him? I mean, I know I have my appeal"—he smirks a little—"but what are you doing with me?"

"I don't know."

"Come on, give me a real answer."

Tearing my eyes away from the table and looking into his face is harder than it should be, but I'd made a deal with myself to start being honest. So I answer with the truth. "Being with you—it's just easier. You seem like a better alternative."

He stares at me blankly for a second, then his lips wrinkle back in a cynical smile. "I'm an *alternative*. Alternative to what? Forgive me for sounding like an asshole, Aly, but that's exactly what you just sounded like." He chuckles again, like an exhalation. "You're still so much like that kid you were a few years ago. I have to admit, I'm a little surprised."

I want to be angry at him, but I just don't I have the energy. In fact, more than anything, I feel tired. Depressed. Like I lost something I should have fought for much, much harder. He must sense the way my mood is spiraling because he stands up and puts his arms around me tightly, almost protectively. "Hey, sorry. You'll be all right. You just have to quit worrying about it, you know. Things will work out the way they're supposed to. 'Cause look, it's not hard to tell he feels the same way about you. You both just have to relax long enough to tell each other the truth."

I pull away, not liking the way he's lecturing at me, as if to a child. "What do you know, Rob? You're not exactly an expert on relationships. You want to talk about honesty? Do you really think I believe there's nothing going on between you and Baker? And back in the Corps, when your detachment got reassigned, what happened there? Did you even try to keep in touch?"

Instead of biting at my hotheaded bait, he walks away and sits down on the bunk. "Yeah, I noticed the waves pouring in from you."

Ouch. Nothing like pointing out someone's hypocrisy to douse whatever self-righteous fire they were starting to whip up. Instead of getting pissed off and storming out of his cabin, I'm back to feeling the same empty sadness that's begun to take up permanent residence in the pit of my stomach. "Yeah, well, I was still a kid. Like you said."

Before I can walk out, he comes up behind me and gently takes hold of one of my wrists. "Come on, don't be like that. We have too much happening to start fighting over old news." The sincerity in his face is enough to melt through some of the frost starting to form between us. "I'm sorry, okay? We're good, right?"

"Yeah. We're good." My eyes are pinned to the ground, and I start to speak before I realize what I'm going to say. He's always had this kind of effect on me, made me feel like it's safe to talk to him. "It's really not as easy as you think it is, though. Karl and I are through. And once this job is over, once we get the settlers free, I can't go back to the Beach. I don't know what I'm going to do."

He's silent and I begin to feel a little foolish. It's not like me to be so forthcoming.

"You could become a citizen."

There's no need to tell him how crazy I think he is; the expression on my face makes that clear enough.

"I mean it. You said you had money—it's not that hard to buy an identity. You know? Your records were destroyed in the Rebellion, right? And you haven't been arrested and IDed since you deserted, right?

"That's right."

"I know people who could make you a real person, fabricate an entire life history for you, and get you back on the Admin registry. It could be a fresh start for you."

"And what would I do?"

"You could come work for me."

I say nothing.

"Okay, okay. Whatever you want. That's my point, though. You can start over and do anything you want."

Before I can even think of how to respond, Sims comes through on Rob's wrist VDU. "Captain, you need to get up in the flight deck. There's some trouble with one of the, uh, passengers, the one that works with the smuggler."

"What kind of trouble? You were supposed to be watching him!" Rob answers while reaching inside his closet to retrieve a handgun, instantly transformed into the no-nonsense platoon sergeant I remember from the Corps.

"He's a sneaky sonofabitch. Slipped out of the galley while I was eating. Montoya says he bypassed the code somehow and just walked on deck. He's under control now."

I follow Rob out of the cabin during Sims's explanation, and we move out at a good clip toward the flight deck. I'm not in the least surprised Thompson pulled this kind of maneuver; he isn't one to stand by meekly and do what he's told, unless Rajcik is doing the telling. Halfway down the crew quarters corridor, Rob stops at the elevator and uses a personal code to open the door. It puts us one story up, directly onto the flight deck. When the doors open, we're staring into a wall of streaked blackness. The observation shields are open and the entire front surface gives us a view into nothingness as we cruise through hyperspace.

Thompson sits stiffly in a seat near the door with his lower lip split and bleeding. Montoya stands nearby shaking one fist limply, letting the sting in his knuckles diminish, and pointing a pistol at Thompson with the other hand.

Rob turns to Sims, who stands just on the other side of the main entryway working with a set of dangling wires extruding from a missing panel where the entry keypad belongs. "Damn it, Sims. How hard can watching one guy be?"

Sims glares back. He's taller than Rob by a few centimeters, but lanky and long limbed and closer to my age. His frosted blue eyes rest on Rob angrily, obviously resentful of the criticism, but he keeps his mouth shut.

"Captain, he used this to get through the door. And I took this from him," Baker informs Rob, handing him a portable electronics board with various leads hanging from it and a pistol. "He wanted our client's name and clearance codes for Tunis."

Scowling at Thompson, Rob says, "Who our clients are is not your problem. You're just a passenger on this trip and you either follow the rules, or you'll have to deal with the consequences."

"I'm just making sure you aren't flying us straight into an Admin security station." Thompson's angular face and crooked, jack-o-lantern eyebrows always make him appear to be sneering. The expression is more pronounced with Montoya's pistol pointed at him.

"Even if we were, there's not a goddamn thing you can do about it," Baker says.

The look on Thompson's face makes it clear that Montoya's pistol is the only thing keeping him from leaping at her. "Fuck you, bitch."

"Quiet. We've got a few days to go. Everyone here needs to keep their mouths shut and stay where they belong." Rob sweeps the crew, Thompson, and me with a hard stare. "Thompson, you're just going to have to take it on faith that we're doing exactly what we promised Vitruzzi we'd do. Since that doesn't seem to be easy for you, you'll stay in your bunk until we get there."

"Try it," he mutters, but not loud enough for Rob to have to do anything about it.

"Montoya, put him and his gear in twelve," he waves the by-pass board at the crewman, "and double-check that there's nothing in there he can use to short out the lock."

"I can take him," I volunteer. This is a good opportunity for me to make it crystal clear to Thompson what will happen to him and Rajcik if they fuck this operation up.

"No way," Baker instantly says.

"It's fine," Rob jumps in. "Go ahead, Aly. You know where it is?"

"Captain—" Baker continues to argue.

"It's *fine*." He turns and faces her, his stance rigid and irritated. She holds his eyes for a few seconds, then turns angrily back to the navigator console.

Putting my hand on my Sinbad, I jerk my eyes toward the exit to get Thompson moving. He does it with a last scathing look at the crew.

When we've walked too far from the bridge to be overheard, he says, "That crew is Corps."

"Don't be an idiot." He stops and turns to face me, prompting me to pull out my 'Bad. His long figure and wide shoulders create a barrier directly in front of me, but the corridor is plenty wide enough to dodge if he lunges. "Keep moving."

"What? Are you blind? Living on that rock made you stupid, Erikson. You used to be able to smell Corps coming before they were in atmo."

"Listen to me, Thompson. I know you and Rajcik are planning something, but you're not going to distract me with accusations about Rob's crew being Corps. I'm warning you now, and it's the only time I'm going to do it, David and I will be watching you like a germ under a microscope. If you do *anything* I don't like, you know it won't bother me to kill you. I might even enjoy it."

"Stupid cunt, wake up! They're *Corps*."

"*Move!*" This time I swing the pistol up and point the barrel at his stomach. This gets him turned around.

David meets me at the bunk where Thompson will be deposited, keeping watch over the smuggler while I sweep the small room and his gear for any objects that can be used to his advantage. By Rob's orders, Thompson's weapons have been locked up, and the rest of us keep ours only because of his heavy-handed dispatching of his crew's protests. There's no reason for Montoya, Sims, and

Baker to distrust us as much as they do, but their survival is being gambled. I can understand their concerns about getting pinched by Admin security, but Rob trusts us. That should be enough for his crew.

Once Thompson is secure, David and I walk back toward the cargo hold with a vague plan to re-inventory the equipment we'd brought from Agate Beach, but his statement, and his sincerity, worms through my brain. *They're Corps.* Why would he say that? Is it just paranoia, the result of living most of his life as a thief and a hood? They *were* Corps, yeah, I can see that much. But Rob had assured me that they were citizens he'd contracted as his crew. My instincts are usually good, but they aren't coming through as clearly or loudly on this one as they usually are. If we're being set up, how could Rob possibly sound so sincere?

Forget it. This is just the result of the past couple of weeks' insanity fucking with me. Anyone would be a little insecure, a little strung out, after what had gone down. The best thing to do is stay alert and come to my own conclusions. Hopefully, not too late.

Vitruzzi and La Mer are also in the hold, loitering in a convex extension of the main cargo area where most of our gear is stored. Our footfalls are quiet, but they notice us anyway, proving everyone's nerves are on high alert. Vitruzzi would at least be considering the possibility of Rob's crew being Corps if it were even remotely possible, and she hasn't said a word. Obviously just part of Thompson's gambit to keep us on edge.

She looks over and nods a welcome, but La Mer, sitting cross-legged inside a helter-skelter ring of parts, doesn't look up. The components are spread around him like the blast pattern of the world's strangest frag grenade, the frags in this case being wires, transistors, capacitors, electrical boards, levers, and assorted metal and plastic miscellany.

"What's up?" David asks as we approach, but his tone and the way one of his eyebrows rises suggest that what he's really asking is, *Has La Mer gone off the deep end?*

La Mer halfheartedly tosses a part back into the pile and says, "We should have brought some receiver plates. They're lightweight enough; we'd just need a transport. They break so easily, we may have a hard time finding extras."

"Why would we need any? Do you think we'll have to build a new transceiver?" I walk over and lean against a table next to Vitruzzi.

"I want to put together a prototype, something small that I can use to do some regression tests. I know most of the Admin protocols well enough to set up temporary barriers, I just want to make sure I'm not missing anything."

I'm anxious to pass Rob's suggestion about becoming a citizen by David, get his take on the idea, but don't want to do it now while La Mer and Vitruzzi are here. Neither of them could easily entertain the same option, and hearing it may be more demoralizing than hopeful. Vitruzzi's been calm and focused since the Corps assaulted the Beach, despite the fact that they'd killed Bodie. It's hard to say how she's taking it, the way she bottles everything. Even now, she's methodical as she inventories her medkit, the one she carries anytime she's on the job. Its contents lie spread across the table. Beyond the basics we all carry—bandages, antibiotics, skin glue, a retractable splint, and rehydration tablets—hers contains a variety of drugs in syringes, liquids, and pill form that serve not only to dull pain and inhibit fluid buildup in soft tissues, but, when mixed properly, can make even a mute whisper the contents of their soul.

She shared this with me one day back on Agate Beach while I was still recovering in the colony's sick bay. If she'd carried the specific drug cocktail at the time, she could have used them on the commander of the MCACS we'd hijacked to get to the Fortress when he'd refused to tell us the station's coordinates. She'd ordered his execution as incentive to make his XO talk, and it had worked like magic. I've never faulted her decision, but it seems to bother her.

Shifting my attention back to La Mer, I comment, "I thought you already tested it before we tried the first time."

"Yeah, I did. But they found us. I must have missed something."

"We don't really know if the Admin caught on to the satellite hijack," David says, attempting to pull La Mer out of his brooding. "They could have been tipped off about a smuggling job the crew pulled or even noticed discrepancies in some of the *Sphynx*'s contract manifests. Who knows?"

La Mer's shoulders are hunched, and he won't meet David's eyes. "Or maybe it's my fault."

David squats down to get his attention. "Look, don't beat yourself up. I don't think you should take the blame for something like this. We all knew there were risks. Everyone was behind it, and we still are." He glances at Vitruzzi and me for confirmation, and we dip our heads in agreement. "The important thing is to keep our focus and figure this out."

La Mer sighs heavily, then nods, looking moderately less beaten. It's not a good time, but it seems important to mention it anyway. "Thompson thinks Rob's crew is Corps."

"Did he say why?" Vitruzzi asks.

"I think it's just a guess, or maybe part of some alternate plan of his and Rajcik's, but he sounded pretty sure."

La Mer's response surprises me. "There's something . . . off about all of them. No offense, I know you two and Cross go back, but I don't trust him."

I can't easily dismiss La Mer's suspicions. His instincts are solid. After all, it took the Admin over six years to catch him. When they want someone as bad as they want him and the group responsible for destroying the Corps records, it isn't a simple matter of staying off the grid. Like every Corps deserter who still draws free breath, La Mer had to develop a sixth sense for danger. Still, the idea of Rob being an Admin sympathizer sounds absurd. Even when he was Corps, it was just his way of filling a need for adventure and direction. Yeah, he has his faults—his unnerving capacity to be simultaneously sincere and manipulative, well-meaning and self-serving, loving and licentious. But treacherous? I just can't see it.

Trying to deflect the insidious fear and paranoia beginning to sweep over us like a polar crosswind, I say in a voice that carries no farther than their ears, "We're going to have to stay sharp and not let our guards down. I know Cross isn't going to turn us in, but that doesn't mean we can afford to take it easy. His crew makes me nervous, too." Admitting this out loud finally brings it home to me, centering the weight of my suspicions like a heavy lead ball in my chest cavity. "And I—"

"What are you doing?" None of us heard Baker enter the hold. Her stealthy approach, intentional or not, and the accusatory note buzzing in her tone, increases my swelling apprehension. She stands just inside the entry to the main passenger section, her frame as rigid and challenging as a wolf's circling for a fight.

David stands up and turns toward her slowly, his deliberate movements announcing his irritation. "What does it look like?" he responds angrily, making it clear that he doesn't appreciate having to explain himself to her.

She squints, her icy blue eyes chilling the air between them a few degrees before traveling over the rest of us like a fly across a horse's flank. "You need to stay out of the hold. Your bunks or the galley are the only places you're allowed."

"Is that your captain's order?" I challenge.

"I'm part of the crew, you're just passengers. You do what we say, when we say it. Do you get me?"

I don't see what she stands to gain by provoking us, but her tone is jarring and my patience lacks the endurance it would take to ignore her. "Whatever you're trying to prove, you can put the fucking brakes on right now, Baker. You have zero authority over us."

She squints angrily and steps farther into the hold, closing the gap between us and reducing firing range. Her right hand goes inside her jacket. I can't see a weapon, but I read the movement as clearly as the page of a book. The fact that this citizen crew carries weapons is another of the many discrepancies about them that feeds my doubt, and I realize Thompson must have clued in on it as well.

"Baker, what's your position?" Rob's voice comes through the fabric of her jacket. She has to withdraw her hand to access her wrist VDU, but her weapon stays put.

"In the hold." Her eyes don't drop from us.

"Is Thompson secure?"

"Roger."

"Then why aren't you back on station?"

"The passengers are in here messing around with the cargo."

There's a long pause, then Rob responds, "And?" Then my own VDU pings. "Aly, everything all right?"

"Baker seems to think our access is restricted to the galley or our bunks."

There's another long pause, then he speaks to all of us. "Would the four of you mind meeting me in the galley? We've got some things we need to discuss." Then we hear his voice clearly from Baker's receiver. "Baker, get your ass back on the bridge. Now. Out."

Vitruzzi quickly repacks her medkit, and we walk out together. Baker doesn't move and stands like a sentry at the door until we pass her. I'm the last one out, and she steps in my way before I can exit.

"You and I are going to have to work some things out before long." She has a few centimeters in height advantage, but otherwise, we're similar in size and shape.

"Let's work it out now."

Before either of us move, David steps around her and puts a hand on my back, gently pushing me forward. "Enough. Come on."

Neither she nor I move. My breathing and heartbeat are slow and steady, a subdued physiological state that years of danger have trained my body to assume before combat. Baker's hate for me is like a cloud of mustard gas. I can only assume that she's jealous of what's going on between Rob and I, but I feel no sense of guilt or remorse. Fucking your CO is never a good idea, and if Rob's chosen to break it off with her, it's not my problem, or my fault. She's dangerous, I can see that in her fluid, stealthy movements and taciturn threats. She isn't scared and nervous like someone who's reacting out of emotion, but calm and steady, like someone who's accustomed to carrying out her threats. With an implicit promise for more trouble, she finally turns abruptly around and strides toward the stairs leading up to the flight deck level.

"Probably shouldn't have hooked up with Rob again, Aly. It doesn't look like the natives are friendly," David quips.

I give him a disgusted look, and he leads the way to the galley with a chuckle.

"WE CAN'T LET YOU PUT yourself in that kind of danger. You've already done enough. Maybe too much," Vitruzzi says.

Rob stands by the galley's rear door with his back to it, but he keeps glancing into the hallway as if expecting someone. Vitruzzi is the first to recover her voice after what he's suggested, but the rest of us still can't believe it.

"Don't worry about it," he responds, throwing another glance outside. "Flying you off Obal 10 after you shake things up with T'Kai is all contingent on things going smoothly. If you all get into serious trouble . . ." He lets the statement hang. "But I can help out as a transport."

"Rob, you'd never be able to fly again if they suspect your ship of harboring fugees," David says.

"Believe me, I know. The *'Rize* has a reputation for being squeaky clean, and that hasn't been easy. But I've got another ship, an unregistered ship. Anonymous and fast enough for our needs." He looks around at us, and continues, "Who better to get you out of there? Have you even thought about how you're going to do that?"

No. At the moment, it's more expedient to keep our thoughts on what we know and what we can control. Figuring out the next part of the plan is being shelved until the first part is complete. But . . . but if we agree to let Rob join us, we'd have one of our many problems already solved. Looking around the room, I see expressions of careful neutrality on everyone's faces. No one wants to hope for that much good luck.

Seeing our hesitancy, he leans casually against the wall and holds his hands out in a gesture that's both generous and oddly contrived. "Look, I'm not the kind of guy who just turns their back on friends when things get heavy. I'm not doing this as a favor, I'm doing it because"—he glances in my direction—"I care about what happens to all of you. We've been in business for a while. David and Aly and I go way back. I don't think I could sleep if I left you hanging, you know?"

TWENTY-TWO

Streamers of steaming exhaust billow out from the pipes and turrets of the industrial complex surrounding us like a post-apocalyptic graveyard. The air glides slickly into my nostrils and down my throat, tasting more like a chemical vapor than oxygen, which is perfect. We all still wear our nostril-implanted air filters to protect our lungs, but no one else wants to come near an urban junkyard where ragged and dangerous dregs of people mix like rotting vegetables with the toxic soup that stands in for the environment.

Tunis City, despite being located on the most populated Obal planet, still has its industrial blights. Once they outsourced dangerous manufacturing jobs to the already hazardous Spectras and smaller moons, these dilapidated factories were simply abandoned, one by one. Over time, they've been picked bare by vagabonds and skulkers looking for materials that can buy them a meal or a fix. The only thing left is the sludge and pollutants that were never cleaned out, slowly aging and festering like wounds and occasionally spewing out their noxious residue. Like I said—for a quiet, witness-free location, it's perfect.

Rob put us down two days ago on a busy resource shipping dock, and we'd gotten off the *Horizon* with almost unbelievable ease. Most of the transports in the area were older and bigger, beaten from traveling to and from the Spectras carrying heavy loads of metals, minerals, and ore, making the *Red Horizon* almost conspicuous in its newer, shinier state. Rob procured a small land transport and snuck us aboard while the dock controllers read the *'Rize'*s manifest and checked his crew's IDs. Lying in back of the transport, I could smell smoke and hear shouting and alarms as the engines of a nearby ship went to shit. The airspace around was crowded and getting worse by the minute thanks to the grounded ship, and the controllers moved on without hesitation. With Rob at the wheel, we merged with the general din of road traffic and traveled quickly to this section of town, more a satellite district of Tunis than part of it. And the wait for La Mer to track down contacts from his past to aid us began.

Though it's dark inside the old factory, the gloom is still more inviting than the penetrating fog barely held at bay outside. The last forty-eight hours have ticked by with the painful slowness of waterboarding while La Mer sends out queries. If there is a bright side, it's Rob's assurance that he can get us off-world when the time comes. Maybe we'd accepted his help a little too fast, but without him here, Brady's tendency to painstakingly consider every option before making a call got dropped. If our choice was too brash, there's only one way we're going to find out.

It's almost my watch on the rooftop, and I glance at La Mer on the way up. He's been monitoring his netwave console almost constantly, barely leaving to sleep or eat, but he's not looking too worse for the wear. A few anonymous wire-rats have responded to his queries, and they keep a running conversation, speaking in a lingo that seems to be universally understood by their type but is basically indecipherable to me—quantum process transmogrifications this and transduction referrals that. I put enough effort into trying to make sense of their communications to make sure La Mer isn't giving anything away that could get us caught, but stay out of his way outside of that.

He's talked to some about the security worm, keeping the details of how it'll be used as ambiguous as possible, and refining things based on their recommendations and questions. One mobile console stays with him at all times, its screen filled with code that shifts and changes regularly as he makes minor tweaks. In many ways, the fewer changes he makes to the bypass program, the more relief I feel, and I'm guessing the same is true for the others. La Mer's code is good, at least good enough to deal with the Admin security he knows about. The question is: What if there are things he doesn't know about? Detection programs, tracking programs, new technology that's been deployed since the Soldier's Rebellion? It's all too easy to think something like one of these led to the discovery of our first test at the Beach and the subsequent invasion by the Corps. What else can we do though, besides take our chances?

On the 'Rize, when La Mer'd copped to the fear that it was his fault the Corps found us and killed Bodie, I had worried he wouldn't be able to gain enough objectivity to keep working on the worm once we reached Tunis. Even now, I can't imagine the pressure he must be feeling. Despite what's at stake, his attitude is shifting slightly, and his confidence in the worm, and himself, is building. The heavy-hearted gloom he's carried since the Beach is lifting, incrementally being replaced by infectious optimism, and we've all started to share it to a degree. It helps make the passage of time more bearable, even as our fears for the *Sphynx* crew and the settlers grows stronger.

The shifting dark of our second night here wraps around me as I step onto the roof. David leans against the south lip of a half wall, gazing into a puzzle of thick, curdling fumes and fog. He looks deep in thought, his forehead wrinkled in frustration and that omnipresent feeling of impotence that we all loathe. His thoughts probably aren't far from mine: with so many lives depending on us, it's excruciating to have to find and rely on a group of unknown wire-rats to make our plan operational.

"My turn to watch the toxic waste bubble."

I move up beside him and he half turns his head, nodding an acknowledgement, but makes no move to go back inside. Leaning up against the wall next to him, I raise my AK-80 to the rim and settle it on its self-mounted tripod. The scope's dark eyepiece stares back at me, seeming to ask where its next target is. The rifle is short and compact with a built in scope and tracking light, yet still weighs less than its cousin, the Corps-issue CCIX-2655. The effective range is slightly less, approximately 550 meters with night-vision scope or 720 meters on a clear day, but when the bulky CCIX and its ammo weigh a soldier down too much, I'll still be firing up the night with my lighter extra magazines.

He rubs a hand along his jaw, the scruff of a new auburn beard scratching a whisper as he does. "Yeah, but there's nothing going on in there. La Mer's got it under control, and I hate just sitting there watching. I feel less than useless. V can keep an eye on Thompson. Mind if I just hang with you up here?"

I shrug, happy to have the company.

After a while he says, "What do you think of our chances, little sis?"

"Honestly, I think the best thing we can realistically hope for is to keep ourselves alive for a few months until T'Kai sics every last soldier in the system on us."

"Not very optimistic."

"Do you think otherwise?"

"I don't know. But if I didn't think we had any chance, I wouldn't be here."

We fall silent, listening to the sounds of decaying buildings settling around their bones. Eventually, I say it, letting the fog soak up my words. "David, I'm getting out."

He turns toward me, eyebrows raised.

"Rob knows people that can forge citizenship registration papers, create a fake history. He can get me back in the system as a new person."

"You really think you could go back to that life?"

"There's nothing else left. They'll catch up to us eventually, even if we succeed in bringing down T'Kai. But if we're not criminals, just regular people doing what regular people do, with real lives . . ." I pause, not ready to look into his face and read his reaction, then continue, "We can just buy them—new lives, new identities. Start off working for Rob, then set ourselves up with our own ship, or even live on one of the Obals, maybe here in Tunis City. You'd be crazy not to come with me."

Finally I face him, and I don't like the way his blue-green eyes peer into mine, as if trying to brand his disapproval on my brain.

"Aly, what about our friends? What about Karl?"

"He left me, David. He doesn't care about me. Our friends are probably dead already. What do we have to go back to if we live through this? Any of us?"

Holding back a response, he looks out into the night. I want to keep trying to convince him, argue the point until he agrees with me, but don't. Eventually he'll either come to the same conclusion, or he won't. He's always been the more thoughtful of the two of us, even-keeled and deliberate. He knows as well as I do that things will probably never be easy again. Neither one of us are martyrs, all we can do now is pick the path with the least exposure. Or Corps.

TWENTY-THREE

Which one of you wants to go to the docks and get a read on Cross's ship?"

Before the sentence is out of Vitruzzi's mouth, David and I are both on our feet, the game of Pussers Bones we've been playing for the last four hours instantly forgotten. A hint of a grin lifts one side of her lips, but she says, "Just one."

This time, a game of Bear, Ninja, Cowboy resolves the issue, and David exits back up to the roof in disgust to keep watch both with and on Thompson.

"Rob sent me the location of the warehouse where he's storing his planet-hop, and I want someone to take a look around to get the lay of the land. Keep your eyes open for regular security patrols in the area, who's coming and going, and how likely it is we'll be noticed if we have to get out of here fast. Keep your face covered and don't, whatever you do, get out of the land trans." I'm nodding as she speaks, impatient at being told what I already know, but Vitruzzi is going to say it anyway. "Just look around and then turn around. Read me?"

"Loud and clear."

As I sling my carbine strap over my shoulder, she says, "You're not taking those." Her eyes drift between the AK-80 and my Sinbad pistol, then stare straight into mine. "And the Derg stays, too."

"What if there's trouble?" Surprise and irritation fight for control over my tone.

"Then handle it, but no shooting. You'll be dead before your rounds hit the target if you fire a weapon. This isn't a Spectra. Security teams are all over the place." She throws me my watch cap. "Be careful."

I hate that she's right, but I deposit the guns on the table next to La Mer's consoles. She and I walk into the warehouse's garage, and I jump in behind the beaten-up transport's driver console. The electric engine chugs unevenly as she raises the garage door for me to drive out. In a few minutes, the industrial complex fades from the cracked rearview display, and it takes another thirty before I get to the shipping docks where we'd parted ways with the *Horizon*.

The Uhr River, meandering thousands of kilometers down from the northern border of Obal 10's largest continent, spreads wide and deep on the western edge of Tunis City. It serves as an economic divider separating the city, with all its controlled cleanliness and orderly development, from the shipping and manufacturing operations. The river grows wider and fatter over the distance of several kilometers, leveling into a bloated estuary before rolling into Voltendar Bay. The bay is easily a half-day trip by boat from north to south and varies in width from east to west before it feeds into the Gemenez Ocean through the Strait of Ruiz.

Docking platforms and piers for water-capable craft line every grid of earth along the bay's western and southern banks. Where each ship is docked depends on what they're delivering and to whom, and less important clients or ships peddling unsought goods are more likely to be directed to the docks along the bank's southern stretch. Dock access is a mark of status, and those that can't pay or don't have something the Admin wants don't get any favors. The south bay docks are the cheapest and least regulated, and the security teams roving along them are often more corrupt than some of the privateers that frequent them. This opens the area up for more people like us: questionable, crooked, and, more often than the Admin finds it convenient to notice, criminal.

But the area is still monitored, and security forces still have all the authority they need to hold and question anyone that could be on their wanted lists, or who just pisses them off. If you're not paying a bribe, and sometimes even if you are, the rule is to keep your head down. A skill I've practiced to an art.

Once at the bay, I drive cautiously through the sprawl that's grown up to accommodate incoming and outgoing ships, the road made even more congested by off-loaded shipments from other planets that are waiting to be either hauled off or paid for. More than once, irate drivers in transports bigger than mine pass me, their scowling faces looming down as they go by. The need to avoid any ill-timed confrontation, or worse, a wreck, compels me to keep my speed steady, hoping not to draw too much attention.

I drive along the main road feeding into the line of docks until I reach a T-intersection snarled with traffic branching east and west along the bank. The location Rob had given us is west, so I wait for a gap and hang a left. As I pull into the milieu, gridlock quickly forces a standstill, wedging me between two larger transports with no room for escape. The stoppage is caused by a parade of haulers waiting for loads a few docking platforms down.

Time on these docks truly is money, and the traders exhibit very little patience at the inconvenient slowdown. Rude shouts and pounded-on horns signal their disgust. The ship most responsible for the delay is some kind of contractor-owned piecemeal conglomeration of a decommissioned Admin cargo carrier and private sector model. It's being guarded by tough-looking pirates planted strategically around the hold while others unload it. Their matching grimaces and bulldog statures indicate they can handle any trouble people decide to shove their way and do it without breaking a sweat.

The longer we sit, the more tangled the congestion becomes, and each additional vehicle piling up behind is like another brick piling on top of me until I'm nearly squirming from claustrophobia. There's no way to drive free of this mess, and if any security comes by and decides to kill time by checking IDs, I may as well have a target drawn on my forehead.

After five minutes of waiting, the situation goes from annoying to incendiary. A twelve-ton transport with a double trailer is attempting a wide turn that cuts through the full width of the road when a sizzling arc of electricity suddenly blazes through the cab, instantly turning the driver into a smoking husk of meat and leaving the hauler equally dead. Realization that no one is going anywhere for a while sweeps through the crowd of stalled transports like the scent of fire on the wind. People start to exit their vehicles and enter the street, some carrying crowbars and other tools. The warm day and mounting hostility over the delay gives the crowd a sharp, sweaty odor, like a cornered beast. No one acts in the least concerned about the dead trucker, instead converging like a hellish ant hive on the line of transports still being loaded. Security teams start signaling each other, preparing to close in and circumvent the looming brawl.

Goddammit, this is *not* what I want to be happening. Time to fade out of the scene. If I stay with the transport, I'm sure to get pinched. Abandoning it is the only way I'm getting out of this clusterfuck. I'll have to figure out another way to get back to basecamp later when things cool down.

A quick sweep of the cab unearths a bent metal rod about the length of my arm. It's thin but has some heft. Might come in handy. As I pull on the door handle to get out, a column of the dock security crew leapfrogging their way up between the line of stopped vehicles shows up in the rearview display. Shit, shit, *fuck*. They're working in pairs, one scanning each vehicle's cargo, and the other shoving handheld ID scanners at the drivers. If I get out of my trans, they'll see me, and if I run, they'll chase me.

Pressing back into the seat, I force myself to calm down and plan an escape. Many of the stalled transports are bumper to bumper, so I can't run through them without scrambling over hoods and tailgates. No good. That will just slow me down and make me an excellent target. I'll have to run straight up the line and look for a break, try to get to the warehouses opposite the docks. The teams will see me if I try to run, but maybe I can lose them amid the buildings.

The nearest man is still about ten meters behind my truck. Using my shoulder to shove the door free of its warped frame, it swings open with a teeth-clenching squeal that makes me curse darkly. Sliding from the seat to the ground, metal rod hidden against my leg, I leave the door open to provide some cover to my rear and start walking casually up the line.

Two steps forward and I hear: "You in the black hat! Stop where you are!"

No, no, no, this *can't* be happening. It suddenly hits me that I hadn't called in the situation to Vitruzzi and David. Too late now.

Opening up my stride, I hurtle forward, increasing the gap quickly, praying no one opens their door to find out why dock security is going ballistic. A shot rings out, and heads inside the cabs drop behind their steering consoles, everyone having the same automatic reaction to the sound of a firing weapon. The bullet whips by me, embedding itself in the rear bumper of a hauler a few meters ahead. Thank dumb luck that they're not using seekers. Too many potential targets in the crowded street.

In moments, I reach the crowd, five or six people deep, that forms a semicircle around the stalled hauler and smoking driver. Up ahead and to my left, there's an alleyway passing between two warehouses. That's my opening. A quick look over my shoulder shows the squad closing the distance between us, their faces hidden behind black helmets and lowered face shields. Renewing my effort, I shove through the crowd, putting the full force of my shoulders and elbows into people. Most are too surprised to stop me, but one or two shove back. Doesn't matter, I'm getting closer to the edge near the warehouses. Another look back shows the security squad yelling at the crowd, forcing a hole by waving and pointing their weapons. People turn to find out what's going on and start dropping to their knees around me. No, dammit! I need cover!

With a final shove, I try pushing by two of the thugs guarding the cargo ship, but their combined mass is solid and unmoving. One grabs the meaty part of my arm to stop me, jerking me backward, probably thinking he can turn me in to the security team for a reward. I snap like a rubber band at the end of his yank and bring my metal bar up, using momentum to double my own strength. The bar connects with a chunky slap against his cheekbone, opening it up and whacking his head to the side. He releases me immediately and I squeeze past, sprinting into the alleyway.

My excitement evaporates instantly as I realize the end of the alley is completely blockaded by a wall, easily ten meters tall, all smooth concrete. No way to scale it. Panic starts to bubble like acid in my throat. Looking side to side for a way out—a door, a fire escape, fuck, I'd take a trampoline—reveals nothing but five or six stories of featureless walls. I start to turn around and go back the way I came with a hopeless goal of somehow getting lost in the throng, but a darker depression to one side of the barrier catches my eye. It looked like a shadow at first, but maybe it's something else. Maybe a doorway. I reach it in a few quick strides and yes! It *is* a doorway, with a heavy steel door. Locked, of course.

As I strike the handle hard with the bar, wicked pain reverberates through the bones of my hands and up my arms to my shoulders at the force of the blow. They go numb, almost making me lose my grip on the bar. Regardless, I raise it again and swing it hard—but the door opens on its own and I tumble into pitch-blackness. Spreading out my arms to catch myself, I end up face down on the ground, my knees and palms stinging, and the bar tumbles off somewhere ahead, clanking against the concrete floor. Before I can get up, someone has a grip on my arms and pulls them cruelly behind my back. Panicked now, I begin bucking, trying to flip myself over and get some leverage with my feet, but the assailant straddles me, his weight like a tank on my back. He binds my wrists quickly, expertly, and I hear the door pushed closed and locked. A rag is stuffed into my mouth as I try to yell, and then a bag is pulled over my head. Thrashing and kicking nets me nothing but bruises and at least two different voices cursing at me, but they have my legs also bound in seconds, trussing me like a turkey.

Helpless.

Someone starts banging on the door from the other side and muffled, indistinct voices demand it be opened. The words "security" and "violation" come through loud and clear, making me realize that whoever has me is *not* the security team that had been pursuing me. I am in deeper shit than I thought.

The voices on the other side of the door continue to yell as I'm lifted off the floor, none too gently, and carried away.

To where?

TWENTY-FOUR

The bag is yanked off my head, pulling my watch cap and a few errant hairs with it.

"You a merc? Or just popular."

A man stands in front of me arm's length away, looking at me flatly as if examining something he finds slightly objectionable. He has dark hair and dark eyes set into a flushed face that's oblong and squat, like a melon thrown against a wall. He's not very tall, about Doug Mason's height, stringier, with arms crossed, and wide, slightly hunched shoulders.

So this is my abductor. The latest in a string of them.

"Who. Are. You?" Things have to unfold a little more before I'll know how much danger I'm in, but the sound of a gun being cocked behind me is proof that it's enough.

"You can call me Quantum. And you are Aly." His arms open and he holds my VDU up in one hand. "Associate of David, Vitruzzi, and"—he pauses for a long second—"La Mer." Returning the device to the pocket of his cargo jacket and recrossing his arms, he finishes, "And who else?"

My team must have been calling me, trying to find out what's been going on. I take a minute to look around, letting him wait. The room is deep and long, several computer and equipment consoles lined up in neat rows filling the space. I've been their captive for over two hours at this point, but we only arrived in this location a few minutes ago. After I'd been gagged and hooded, they'd made me sweat it out in some sort of tiny burrow in the warehouse that had been barely big enough to lie lengthwise in. Something thick had been lowered over the space, and I'd been left trapped underneath for a long, cramped hour. Panicked claustrophobia had me nearly screaming to be let out, but somehow my rational mind had held it in check, knowing that I'd be beyond help if the Admin security team found me. They'd finally pulled me out, and with no explanation, driven me to this place. Saying that I'm angry and frightened enough to kill someone right now is like calling a bullet hole in the stomach a minor annoyance.

Keeping my fury in check until I can suss out the situation, I ask, "Why should I tell you?"

He takes a sliding step forward and backhands me across the cheekbone. It stings, but it isn't hard enough to bruise. He's trying to scare me.

My cold stare is enough to make it clear that I'm not easily intimidated. He gives me another few seconds, then tries a new question.

"What are you doing on Obal 10?"

Recollection suddenly pierces through my anger like a shard of ice. Quantum—he said I can call him Quantum, and it's a name I've heard before. One of the wire-rats La Mer's been trying to reach—he'd called the guy our best chance. "Looking for you," I answer.

He reaches back inside his jacket. When it comes out, he's holding a very long, very sharp-looking knife. He steps forward and leans over me, pressing its needlepoint tip into my throat, just to the left of my windpipe. His other hand comes to rest on my thigh, its warmth oppressive through my pants.

"Toying with me will not make this easy for you." His teeth are jagged, like an animal's, fierce and feral. The knife tip presses deeply into the fragile skin of my neck, so sharp it almost doesn't hurt, but I reflexively try to draw away. "You have only this chance before I decide you're not worth my effort. How many people have you brought to Tunis City, and which one of them is Axone?"

La Mer hadn't mentioned anything about what kind of man Quantum would be. I assumed—wrongly—all these types were unprepossessing, noncombative punks who would run at the first sight of trouble. Not bring trouble *to* us.

"If you pull that blade out of my throat, I'll start talking." I need to swallow, but the knife has started to pierce. Swallowing will make it bite deeper.

He removes the point, but keeps the edge against my throat. I never thought I'd be the one negotiating for help from some wire-rats, and I try to imagine what approach Vitruzzi would take. Unfortunately, my reactionary personality is nothing like her natural composure. It seems likely that what I come up with will barely scratch the surface of how she'd have chosen to handle this situation. So be it. I decide to proceed with my usual tactic—the forward assault. "We're going to blackmail the director of the Ministry of Science and Engineering, and we need your transceiver."

Without backing up, he laughs, his breath exploding against my face. When he does, his lips roll back to show his teeth have the same ragged sharpness all the way to his molars. "You're going to blackmail Kurosawa T'Kai? That is really funny. Please, tell me more, merc." He shifts backward and the knife is finally withdrawn.

I don't usually underestimate people, and I won't make that mistake with him again. But I have to give him something that shows we mean business. "You sound like you don't think we can do it. Believe me, T'Kai will take us seriously after what we did to the Fortress. And we're not mercs."

He stops laughing, the cold sincerity in my voice freezing his febrile humor, and studies me closely. "You are trying to tell me you had something to do with that biowarfare laboratory?"

"More than something—*I* destroyed it." His expression doesn't change, but I recognize the effort it takes to keep it that way. "You wouldn't find it so funny if you knew what we have on T'Kai."

He looks over my shoulder and nods his head at someone behind me. One of the other men pushes the end of a gun against the back of my head. I press my body tightly against the seat, using its stability to provide the leverage I'll need if I'm forced to lunge. Keeping my eyes on Quantum, not sure what I'm going to say, but knowing that I better say something fast or I'm going to be treated to something decidedly more painful than a slap on the cheek, I start to bargain. "Now look, Quantum, let me talk. I think you'll see—"

Before I can tell him what exactly it is he'll see, he leans forward again and takes hold of my left hand, pressing the knife through the skin of my palm and downward in a diagonal line. The pain is like fire, streaking up my arm, bursting into my elbow, and continuing until it dissipates at my shoulder. I cry out, the pain and fear of a bird caught in a net, and the knife is withdrawn. He leans close, putting his face centimeters from mine. "You are arrogant and foolish. To throw words at me like the Fortress. What does an Admin spy know of the Fortress? It's only a superstition made up by simpleton non-cits who think there is government conspiracy everywhere."

Now I'm a spy instead of a merc. It must be a trick, an attempt to manipulate me into giving up my cover—a cover I don't even have. It would be my turn to be amused if I weren't fairly certain that I'm about to be carved up like a whittling stick.

I stare directly into his face, unflinching and calm. "I'm not a spy and you know it. I'm a deserter. And a friend of Axone's. He's a wire-rat who helped destroy the Corps records database during the Soldier's Rebellion. The Admin sent him to become a test subject at the Fortress. My team intercepted the prisoner transport he was on, and he's been working with us since then."

"He was arrested?"

"Why else would he be on a prisoner transport?"

That comment gets me another backhand, this time across the other cheek. And this time, a lot harder. But he leans back away, giving me hope that he'd seen what I wanted him to see in my face—the truth. I take hold of my injured hand and hold it up and away from my body. Blood streams down my palm and forearm and begins dripping onto the floor. I wiggle my fingers. No tendon damage, not that deep, and—most importantly—not my primary firing hand.

"How much does the Admin know about the people that destroyed the database?"

"Nothing. La Mer—Axone—didn't tell them anything. They sent him to the Fortress to spill it, I guess, but according to him, everyone else is already dead."

"Everyone." He says the word in a peculiar flat way.

"Yeah. Dead."

"What do you have that will force T'Kai to cooperate?"

My whole world has become Quantum's unwavering eyes, their irises deep brown and flecked with hints of gold like glitter. I stay silent. It's turning out that he's more of a free agent than any of us had anticipated. The way he's strong-arming me and his focused, intent questions make me wonder if he's planning to try and take over the show. Maybe use me as a bargaining chip of his own to get the footage Rajcik had collected. He must have friends, a network he can rally to go after T'Kai. If he gets that footage, he won't keep us around, a bunch of non-cits and deserters. The fact that he's only asked me *what* we have that would impact T'Kai, and not *why* we'd want to go to such outrageous lengths, concerns me the most.

That, and how he'd found me in the first place.

He lets me hesitate for a few seconds, then grips my shirt in his fist and pulls me up. My nose comes to his chin, and there's still a gun pointed at my head. I'm pushed to a bank of monitors and he switches them on, saying casually, "Your friends will not be able to help you."

The monitors hum to life and focus on images of Vitruzzi, Rob, David, and Thompson scattered throughout a stairwell.

"They are outside, not far from us, but they cannot go anywhere. I've activated the firewalls and sealed the stairwell. It would be easy for me to gas them, or pull out all of the oxygen, whatever I choose. Do you finally understand what the stakes are?"

They must have found me using the tracker Vitruzzi implanted in my arm. The building is at least a few stories tall. When they'd brought me in, we'd descended three levels in an elevator and the lack of noise or windows makes me think we're underground. With the amount of equipment in here and the promise in Quantum's voice, I have no doubt that he can do exactly what he's threatening to. Through the monitors, I can see the words Sublevel 1 painted on the wall behind Thompson and David, and Sublevel 2 painted near Rob and Vitruzzi. They're spread out. How long have they been here? I can see on their faces that they know they've been barricaded in.

But I'm not ready to surrender or give him the satisfaction of believing he has the upper hand. Without turning, I warn, "Maybe *you* should consider your options. They're here, and they're not going to leave without me. Besides, what do you gain by killing us?"

Before I finish speaking, the monitors are suddenly filled with an explosion of white, then blank out in quick succession. There's a loud *bong* from outside of the room, and the window in the stairwell door is shattered. Everyone ducks instinctively. Immediately, the air is suffused by a fizzing sound, as if a steam pipe has broken, and moments later the heavy, garlicky-smelling smoke of a phosphorous device begins to fill the space.

The man with the gun yanks me backward by the shirt. This is my moment, while they're distracted. I leap forward, breaking out of his grasp easily, and dart past the equipment, grabbing a handheld radio as I divert behind a bank of tables and hit the deck.

"Hirota, get her!"

The overhead lights cast a yellow pall that barely penetrates the thick smoke. I pull my shirt over my nose and try not to breathe heavily, relying on my nasal filters to help protect my lungs. I can see the stairwell door at the end of the room. The man called Hirota is moving around nearby, and he'll be on me in a second. As he approaches, I crouch and wait until the moment I know he'll have to come around the desk's edge, hopefully with his gun held in front of him where I'll be able to knock it free.

My eyes grow teary, blurring my vision just as I start to lunge, but someone has come up behind me and grabs me by the hair, pulling me to my feet. I swing the radio like a hammer at his face and strike him in the chin. He curses loudly, and his grip comes loose enough for me to pull away, but Hirota is right here, a laser pistol pointed at my chest. Frantic, I glance behind me toward the stairwell opening, and my last hopes are dashed. It remains closed.

Blood is dripping from a deep gash along Quantum's jaw. I have a moment to savor the fact that I'd injured him in return before he walks in front of me and plugs his fist into my stomach, doubling me over and leaving me completely breathless.

"You should not have done that."

Water pours out of my eyes as my chest hitches for air. He glowers over me like an enraged dog, all snarling teeth and fierce eyes. "What are you going to do now?" I manage to gasp.

Before he answers, the sound of Vitruzzi's voice comes from his pocket. My VDU. "Aly, what's your status?"

I straighten up and feel the barrel of Hirota's pistol poke against my spine, just beneath my cervical vertebrae. Quantum looks thoughtful for a moment, then walks a short distance away, pulls the VDU out, and activates the screen.

"She is fine for the moment."

There's a pause, then Vitruzzi again. "Whom am I speaking to?"

"Enough games. Your friend has managed to put a bad taste in my mouth, and now I will tell you what is going to happen." As he speaks, he motions Hirota to push me into a chair and places my VDU on a desk, where he links it to a console. Vitruzzi's face comes up on the attached monitor. "She mentions that you have some very important plans for a very important man. You have some information that will convince this man to meet your terms. I want to see this information."

"There's no way."

Quantum looks over at me and a drop of blood falls from his chin, splashing onto the console. He turns back and says, "That's a rash decision. How much do you want to see this woman again?"

David breaks into the conversation and his face appears in another square on the monitor. "You should be careful who you threaten, whoever the fuck you are."

"Uh-huh. So, Vitruzzi, this information?"

"Let me speak to Aly."

Quantum nods and Hirota walks me over to the console. I pick up the VDU. "I'm okay, V."

"What's going on?"

Quantum nods at my questioning look and I reply, "I'm, um, with Quantum, the wire-rat La Mer's been trying to contact, and a couple of his friends. I don't know how they found me, but they picked me up on the docks."

"Tell us exactly what happened, Aly. Are we compromised?"

Compromised? That's not so easy to answer. I'm fairly certain the Admin security teams on the docks hadn't IDed me, and right now, they're a minor issue. Mainly because I'm feeling majorly fucking compromised by Quantum and his thugs. I'll just go with a simple response. "There was some trouble and I lost the truck, but I'm certain we're still clear of the Admin."

While we speak, the third man working with Quantum goes to a control box on one wall and triggers the ventilation system. The room begins to clear.

"What do they want?"

I glance at Quantum and answer, "You'll have to ask them that."

Quantum retrieves the VDU and pushes me back. "Vitruzzi. Your associate tells me that you have some means in which you intend to blackmail Director T'Kai, and that you need my transceiver to do so. This tells me that your information is digital, perhaps video." He pauses, assessing Vitruzzi's reaction.

"Continue," she replies.

"We have some common interests, but it doesn't matter to me if the Admin discovers your scheme and obliterates you. And they will. If you have any sense, you will leave something of worth, like this information, behind, where it can be leveraged effectively. Which I have the means to do. And I also have your friend."

Vitruzzi closes the connection and my VDU darkens for several seconds. Quantum quickly grows impatient and forces me to open a link to her. "I don't think you understand the urgency of this situation. Your tactics to get my attention lacked subtlety, and now that you have damaged the firewalls, maintenance will be coming. I'm sure you didn't fail to notice that we are in an Admin structure. When they get here and find you loitering in the stairwell—illegally armed—we will already be gone. And they will find your friend's body in the bay."

She responds this time. "If you let us use the transceiver, you can have our information after that. That's the deal." The edge in her voice is cool but frustrated.

"I must see it to make this deal. Is it with you?"

"Yes. But I won't show it to you over the com." There's no give in her voice, and Quantum's tight mouth curls at the edges, looking almost pleased. He walks to a console near the elevator and manages a series of switches and buttons, presumably retracting what remains of the fire barriers and unlocking the stairwell door.

The third man takes a position near the door and yells in an accent that sounds far-Obal, "Place your weapons down on the floor in front of you. Now turn and walk to the back wall. Put your hands on it. Stay there." He opens the door and he and Quantum quickly gather their guns.

Once the team's inside, excitement and relief flood my overly taut nerves, quenching some of the anticipation that's been burning through them for the last several hours. Seeing Rob here helping the crew gives rise to a complicated set of emotions: guilt for putting him back in danger, and a heavy and awkward jolt of relief that he's willing to take a risk—again—to come to our aid. To come to *my* aid.

"You okay?" David catches my eye and checks in.

"As good as can be with a pistol in my back."

"Your hand?"

Blood has soaked through the material I'd wrapped it in, but it's not leaking. Judging by how heavily it throbs with each heartbeat, my heart must be the size of a whale's. I nod to let him know it's not a concern at the moment. I can still shoot, provided I get my hand on a weapon.

Quantum looks them over like a scientist examining something new at the bottom of a lab petri dish. "None of you are the wire-rat she has called La Mer."

His sharpness exceeds his people skills, that's a given.

"He's keeping an eye on our basecamp," Vitruzzi responds.

"I see. I'd very much like to meet the *last man alive* who was responsible for bringing the Admin as close to its knees as it has ever come."

"You'll get your chance."

Quantum looks at her sharply and the corners of his mouth retract into a snarl as he realizes she's been playing him.

Vitruzzi continues, "You're going to have to take us back there to see the footage."

She drops her hands from her shoulders and the others follow. Quantum's men don't react. The tide has shifted.

"Look, your fucking game is as tiring to us as it is to you," she says. "You'll see the footage, but first we have to come to an understanding. You're not going to kill us or throw Aly in the bay. And you're not going to continue this pointless charade of yours. You're just a pretender, dicking around on jacked satlinks. Not some of kind of antigovernment subversive." There's a faint sheen of sweat on her forehead, so thin you might think it was just glare from the lights. But she keeps her cool. So cool I can almost see the air condensing around her breath, as if her lungs were made of the same frosty material as her composure. "If you want to step up and do it for real, this is your chance. We're going to bring T'Kai down. Either he's going to agree to our terms—which you don't need to worry about—or we're going to show the entire population of the system what our government is doing to people behind closed doors. We have the power. *We have* the leverage. We just need a goddamn transceiver and someone with enough balls to give us access to it."

One thing is clear, she's completely shed the last vestige of herself that was ever Admin. She sides with non-cits now. Anyone who hedges their bets by playing the Admin's game is nothing but a tool to her, or an impediment.

Quantum's face turns red. This is the first time he's been at a disadvantage since abducting me on the docks, and he doesn't like the situation. He points a small-caliber pistol with a silencing barrel at Vitruzzi. She and the other three have spread out at arm's length, blocking the stairwell and keeping them covered a few meters away from where Hirota holds me at gunpoint. If shooting starts, there's enough equipment in the room that at least David and Rob, who stand on the ends, may be able to dive under cover out of the line of fire. Quantum's third man stands behind them, right where he's most likely to get picked off by Quantum or Hirota's crossfire, so Vitruzzi and Thompson have a better than average chance of not dying if they duck in time. Still, I've had odds I liked a lot better.

Anticipation, fear, and anger mix with every breath taken and exhaled, making the air so dense I could choke on it. No one speaks. Several monitors still feed live footage from cameras placed in various parts of the building, and movement in one of them catches my eye. A municipal emergency truck is pulling into the garage above us and maintenance workers begin to disembark. They'll be here in minutes.

Turning to Quantum, I ask, "So how do you want to do this?"

TWENTY-FIVE

When we enter the warehouse, it's hard to tell if La Mer's nervousness has more to do with the fact that he's meeting Quantum in person or the fact that our group has nearly doubled—and all of us, including Quantum and his compatriots, carry weapons. When the impasse downtown had tilted in our favor, Vitruzzi had gambled they wouldn't be dumb enough to shoot us and expose themselves, so we hadn't disarmed them. If we'd been stopped by Admin security before getting back to the industrial district, this mission would have been over. We're in the middle of the hornet's nest where even the tiniest shake will cause the entire hive to erupt.

After Vitruzzi helped Quantum adjust his perspective, he and his men must have liked the odds less than I did. As the maintenance team descended the stairwell, Quantum led us out of the room through a service tunnel filled with banks of power-storage units serving the downtown area, out through a storage closet for the city's zip-rail line, and topside through the zip-rail station. Without citizen ID, none of us from Agate Beach could take the underground transportation, but Quantum and Rob were able to return to the garage and retrieve their vehicles, just as if they were average citizens on their way home after a day of work. The rest of us waited at a bench outside the station, sheathed in cold sweat and feeling completely naked. All of us but Vitruzzi have been criminals for too long to be at ease standing on the street corner of one of the settled planets, knowing that everyone around us has implicit or explicit authority to detain us, place us under arrest, or if they're security, outright shoot us. V appeared much calmer than I felt, and I couldn't tell what was going on inside her thoughts. I'm not really sure I would have wanted to. In less than half an hour, they returned with both vehicles, and we mixed our teams and drove back here to the decrepit factory.

While La Mer sets up the video feed with Rajcik's footage, I pull Rob aside and ask quietly, not wanting to draw the others' attention, "What are you doing here? You weren't supposed to get involved until we were ready for an outbound ship."

Basking me in a fawning smile, he answers, "Involved? Is that what I am?"

I stare at him blankly, knowing he's misinterpreting my reason for asking. After a pause, he says, "Yeah, I guess that's what I am.

Vitruzzi pinged me and said you needed my help. What was I supposed to do?"

"We can't trust these wire-rats. They could turn you in." I don't add the fact that I'm relying on him to stay in the clear in order for David and I to get new identities. "I know you know that, so . . ."

His smile tightens as he realizes that what I'm really trying to figure out is his angle. What's he getting out of this?

"Losing you again would be worse than getting compromised, " he says. He catches the way I wince and continues, growing defensive, "Jesus, Aly, why are you still pushing me out? Don't you trust me?"

"Okay. I get it. I just . . . I just don't want to be responsible for what could happen." That came out wrong. "I mean to you," I add hastily.

With a derisive shake of the head, he walks past me, not bothering to respond. Dammit, I really have a way with people. I hadn't meant to . . . to what? Hurt his feelings? I'm too raw, still aching from Karl and the way things had ended. Whatever feelings I'd once had for Rob are part of the past. Right now, all I want is a clean break, a new life, and an escape.

La Mer has set up a monitor for viewing Rajcik's footage and Rob joins the others around it. Thompson is the only man absent, keeping watch on the roof. Night has fallen around us now, the darkness close and dangerous, more like the walls of a prison than a cloak of anonymity. I see David lean toward him and say something, and Rob responds with a sharp shrug. Feeling small and mean, like child who has cruelly pulled the wings off a butterfly, I stay where I am, keeping my distance.

"Aly, will you make sure all the window and door covers are tight?" La Mer asks. "We don't want any sound to carry outside and draw attention."

I make a circuit around the small room—once used as an office or file room—checking on the panels we'd placed over all the openings, then give La Mer a nod to let him know things are good to go.

He stares at the screen as he places a disc in the connected console. "T'Kai made the transmissions using digital blocking codes, but Rajcik recorded everything with a nonlinked camera disguised inside part of his ship's nav console housing." His tone is neutral, but the shake in his hands shows he's grappling with a bad case of nerves. He actions the video and the monitor switches to life, showing us an image of T'Kai's face staring out of the communication display in the *Temptation*'s cockpit. The camera's perspective is odd, capturing the scene from below and slightly to the side, turning T'Kai's tan features and narrow, almond-shaped eyes into a hatchet's profile. This is the first time I've seen the man, and though his skin is flawless, the rigid, distinguished posture and wash of gray in his eyebrows suggest he's an older man, maybe early seventies, but it's hard to know for sure.

The video plays.

T'Kai: "I want the entire place destroyed. You'll have entry access near the weapons labs, hangar zero-one. There will be plenty of items there that can accomplish this task."

Rajcik: "Is that where I'll find the Nova?"

T'Kai: "The Nova and any number of other useful pieces of equipment you can turn into profit. Just remember that your first directive is to destroy the Fortress. Concentrate on that or you'll see no reward. Understand?"

The camera never captures Rajcik's face, but the low-pitched growl in his voice makes his disgust of T'Kai clear. "What will it take to override the airlocks?"

"I have a man on the inside. Command Major Sydney. He'll be at the helm when you arrive to grant you access and open the airlocks. However, he specifically will need to be disposed of once his usefulness to you is complete. I assume that won't be an issue."

Rajcik doesn't bother to respond other than to say, "Send me his direct link." He pauses, and we can see T'Kai's hand moving to cut the transmission, but Rajcik halts him with another question. "This is more than we originally agreed on. I'll assume this replaces your claim to anything I make."

T'Kai: "Yes, you can assume that. The Fortress has become an unexpected liability. It's costing me too much to keep the personnel quiet and I have intelligence that there may be an attempt to expose the cause of the Soldier's Rebellion. Experimentation on our fine military was, perhaps, an overly ambitious enterprise. Three weeks, Rajcik. If you haven't completed the mission by then, you can also make the assumption that our deal is null and void."

The image on Rajcik's monitor flicks off and La Mer disengages the disc.

"Motherfuh . . ." Rob's voice fades out. Besides him, I'm the only one who hasn't seen this footage, and I'm just as speechless. I thought I'd stopped Rajcik by forcing him to detonate the Nova inside the Fortress. I'd been happy to see the station destroyed, but knowing that had been T'Kai's intent all along sucks all the joy out of the event.

I feel sick. The Soldier's Rebellion was rumored to have been started because of an Admin-created virus, the Crowers Croup. People said it got loose and the Admin didn't do enough to control it or to protect the soldiers whose job it was to quarantine its victims. What T'Kai just said proves that those rumors were partly true, but that the whole truth is much, much worse. The virus had come out of Admin labs, and they'd been using it, and probably other biological experiments like it, on soldiers from the very beginning. Vitruzzi's daughter and husband had died because of T'Kai's god complex. Human experimentation, not only on non-cits, the supposed waste and by-products of the species, but the soldiers who *volunteered* their lives for the Admin and the Corps. Used like lab rats, and for what? Did T'Kai hope to achieve some kind of bug-resistant soldier, or was he merely using them for his own demented scientific curiosity? The more I learn of the Admin's schemes, the more I start to believe that even the best in humanity can never hold a candle to the worst in us. Does power make you lose perspective the way T'Kai and those monsters posing as scientists did?

Vitruzzi catches my eye and says, "Now you see why we kept Rajcik close. This is big, bigger than the data we got from the Fortress. This paints the full picture and gives us what we need to settle the score."

I'm not sure if it's the slight catch in her voice or the way her eyes jerk away from me as she says this, but I can see that she doesn't just mean settling the score for the Beachers. She's talking *personally*, settling the score for herself and her dead family. She'll never admit it, but this time, it's about revenge.

And I'm all for it. Working with Rajcik is dangerous and unpredictable, but no more dangerous and unpredictable than letting a murderer like T'Kai, a murderer with the power of the entire government backing him up, run loose. It's gone beyond simply wanting to be left alone. At this point we *have* to do something to try and restore some fairy tale of balance to the social order of the system, at least make T'Kai accountable for what he's done. That, and only that, is the mission.

"What's it going to be Quantum? Is this information *worthy* of your help?" Vitruzzi asks. I can tell she's rattled; it's unusual for Vitruzzi to use sarcasm to make her point.

The wire-rat looks more off center than I've seen yet, but there's also a subtle look of sly contemplation shrink-wrapping his features and pulling his eyes into slits. He's thinking hard about how to play this and about what he can manipulate to his own advantage. Finally, he says, "Is this all you have?"

His flippant dismissal of the video's potential impact surprises me. "All we have? What more could we possibly need? We've got a Ministry director on video admitting to using soldiers for human experimentation and paying off scientists to keep their mouths shut about it." David gives me a look, warning me to calm down, but I ignore him. "He caused the goddamn Soldier's Rebellion for chrissakes! This is enough for the Admin to burn him at the stake!"

Quantum gives me a look of mild contempt. "The Admin will not punish him." He walks toward the back of the room, his shoulders slightly hunched and his head down, as if deep in thought. "They will do nothing except shield him and alter the story for citizens to make this all appear to be nothing but a hoax, a terrorist attempt to launch another rebellion. The Admin will be quick to point out that it was a rogue virus that decimated so many citizens before the Rebellion, that it spread too fast to contain, but that their quick quarantine response saved millions of lives. They will repeat the rhetoric that the soldiers who died were a regrettable loss, but they were good men and women who died for everyone's safety.

"Then they will say that those noble heroes' dignity and honor are being sullied by you malcontents who have bobbed up from the muck of the far-flung backwater Spectras—that you were given a chance at a better life but chose to spit on it." He faces us again, his eyes blazing with dreadful intelligence. "They covered the Rebellion up too perfectly when it occurred, and now they hold that possibility as a threat over the heads of the citizens as a representation of how easily all of our rights and safeties can be taken away if these kinds of antisocial actions are allowed to flourish. They will show that your supposed proof of T'Kai's treason is nothing but a false rendering by deserters that have not yet been caught. And then—then they will find you and squash you until you are nothing but a stain on a lab table."

"Then what, Quantum? You don't think we should blackmail T'Kai?" La Mer asks.

"You'll be wasting your time."

"There's more," Vitruzzi says.

He looks at her, raising one eyebrow.

"We have several drives of data on the experiments they were running. Tests, results, types of viruses, strains of disease—we have the proof to backup his admission. The digital signatures tie it all directly to the Admin."

"And you want to go to T'Kai with it, use it to threaten him into releasing your friends. And then what will you do? Go back to living on the rock you came from?"

She doesn't respond.

"You don't get it. You don't know, do you?" Seeing our confused looks, Quantum shakes his head. "All you Spectres are nothing but ghosts anyway. You're already dead."

TWENTY-SIX

The next half hour is a surreal nightmare of information overload as Quantum launches into an explanation of what the Cabinet of Directorates of the Political and Capital Administration of the Advanced Worlds has been discussing—vehemently and thoroughly—for the last three months.

Quantum wasn't merely theorizing when he said the Admin will have no problem selling the public on the idea that deserters and malcontents are flourishing and threatening everyone's safety; they've kept that message on slow-drip through the media for some time now, every new "catastrophe" instigated by non-cits feeding the public's fears, slowly building their resentment, indifference, and intolerance toward the inhabitants of the Spectras, commonly called Spectres. First the Soldier's Rebellion and now the destruction of the Fortress have rattled the Admin much more than we knew, and their decision to rescind transport contracts and limit travel into and out of Obal airspace is a strategy to serve a more sinister purpose than simply controlling criminal activity.

They plan to completely wipe out the populations of non-cits living on the Spectras.

Quantum's network of wire-rats have had spy-hacking ears and eyes on the Admin since before the Rebellion; he says that it's become clear that the Admin has been prepping for a showdown and just waiting for an excuse for carte blanche freedom to implement total dominion over the system. According to Quantum, their plans focus specifically on the Spectras for the simple reason that non-cits are harder to track and control. Then he brought up something that surprised us all. The Admin has the perfect weapon for the job: the soil amendment compound.

As Quantum lays out the puzzle pieces, I know I'm not the only person in the room whose stomach does flip-flops at his description of the soil compound. The missing piece that Bodie needed would have killed us. Originally called the "C-virus," the compound is a terraforming additive that, indeed, converts marginal soil into a more fecund, life-sustaining earth, but it's first phase is pure poison that kills everything it comes into contact with. It takes between five to ten years for it to become totally inert, during which time the chemical process slowly alters the soil, supercharging it for new growth. The Admin can effectively kill two birds with one stone if they deploy it on the Spectras; clean out the troublesome settlers and provide fertile new grounds for food production and resource development.

Quantum gives us a few minutes to digest all of this, then says, "What if I told you that I know a better way to use this information you acquired from the Fortress?"

"It's our show, Quantum. We just need your transceiver." Vitruzzi's face is an iron mask, inflexible and resolute. Quantum could tell her he is the Messiah in the flesh, but she is finished listening to his stories and machinations. Despite the feeling in my gut that he's not lying, I still try to convince myself he is, and I think she's doing the same thing. He's perceptive enough to realize it and shakes his head slightly, but presses on.

"Can you think of another reason the Admin would be taking a census of Spectra settlements?" He pauses, letting the question taint the air with its obvious implications. "They need to know the numbers they're dealing with, of course. In order to prepare."

I turn to Rob. "You've been working as a contractor for a few years, Rob. Does any of this sound real to you? Have you heard anything about it?"

Rob looks like I feel, sick and angry. "I'm just a contractor, Aly, what could I possibly know?"

Quantum continues, "There are others who want to see an end to this kind of tyranny. If you can truly tie T'Kai to this information, this data, enough people could be convinced of the Administration's duplicity to force the entire regime to its knees. There are many that want this . . . revolution."

"You're saying there are people looking for a reason to overthrow the Admin?" David asks.

"Not just a reason. The reasons exist all around us. No, people need proof. Maybe this is the proof."

I'm trying to hold back my bitter laughter at his absurd idea. "Do we have to remind you that they're the ones with most the guns? How can you realistically imagine trying to fight them?" I look at Vitruzzi for confirmation that this guy is nuts, but her expression is surprisingly contemplative. She holds Quantum's eyes with her own, and I get the sense they're communicating on a level I can't quite grasp. "V?"

"How many are there?" she asks.

"Many." He doesn't drop her eyes.

The rest of us are silent, watching this exchange. Hirota, thin and wiry, and the other man, finally identified as Faisal, bigger and mugging like an angry rhino, scan us with busy eyes, though they don't move. "V, you're not seriously—"

"Quiet." She looks at me sideways, speaking sharply. Her attitude *is* serious, as serious as I've ever seen it. It's enough to make me shut up, at least for now. David and I exchange a glance, his expression mirroring my own wary curiosity.

Vitruzzi continues, "Let's say, for the sake of conversation, there was a possibility of starting a rebellion, something substantial, organized, equipped. You say you know of others, but what do you know *about* them? I've seen from the experience here with La Mer that your type wouldn't know each other if you met on the street. With that being the case, how would you mobilize? What would be your plan of attack? How would you initiate this rebellion?"

Before responding, the wire-rat sweeps the room with a paranoid glare. "We can discuss that at another time."

"We don't have time."

"No, Vitruzzi. All you *do* have is time."

Her jaw clenches, but there's no intimidating him. Right now, we have nothing to offer him in exchange. Did we really expect him to give us access to his hardware out of the goodness of his heart? La Mer believed he would, but La Mer's been on the run since the Rebellion, and things have changed for people living outside the Admin's laws. No one who doesn't want next week's newcast to include their obituary would risk what we're asking for the simple satisfaction of making trouble for the Admin. And Quantum has made his price clear.

"We already have a deal. The use of your transceiver for our information. In that order," Vitruzzi says, staring at him with acetone intensity.

Quantum faces her with squared shoulders and an unwavering glare, matching her intensity. Then, for the first time, his lips curl up into a grin that's almost frightening in its ferocity. "As you wish. We have to go to Obal 6." And in a final surreal act, he reaches out to shake hands, sealing a contract that could—if not for the complete insanity of the idea—potentially bring on the downfall of the Admin.

TWENTY-SEVEN

"We're going to have to get a bigger ship." David's voice tickles my ear as his elbow jabs me in the ribs. The half sleep, half daze I've been fading in and out of like a faulty radio transmission for the last six hours comes to an annoying halt. He laughs at my disgusted look and stands up to go to the head.

He's right; this boat is not built for eight people. In the forty-plus hours since we broke through Obal 10's atmosphere and slipped into the general din of interplanetary traders and traffic, I've become more in touch with my kneecaps than I ever really wanted to be. With a hull that is merely a dual row of jumpseats, a toilet, overhead storage cabinets, and a single sleeping bench at the rear of the passenger cabin, moving around isn't an option. The only place tall enough for a person to stand at their full height is the narrow space in the aisle between the overhead lockers that crowd the ceiling. David, Vitruzzi, La Mer, and I, along with Quantum and Hirota, fill up the jumpseats while Rob and Thompson, the only other pilot among us, rotate at the helm. Quantum had left his third man behind, and I almost wish Vitruzzi would have asked me to stay back on Obal 10, too—I've kept my claustrophobia at bay by trying to stay asleep, but a person can only sleep so long. The hop was never intended to support so many people on any kind of lengthy journey, and it's starting to feel like we're attempting to fly to Saturn in an iron maiden.

We have enough water and a solid enough capture-and-recycle system to make it for at least two weeks, provided no one gets attached to the idea of regular showers, but food is tight. We're small enough not to be noticed by most patrol ships in the Obals—being basically nothing but a personal vehicle for jumping between local planets and moons. Usually these types of hops are owned by wealthy travelers jumping between part-time homes or as transports for business stakeholders to get to and from franchise hubs. But if anyone locks on our flight path and does a quick analysis, they'll catch on pretty quickly that we're neither one of those.

Then there's the ship itself. I don't know where Rob picked up such a run-down piece of junk, but I'm a little surprised, and more than a little grateful, that we're still in flight. The interior has been scoured of unnecessary bells and whistles—like seat pads, sound dampeners, or up to code ventilation—making the ride a little like being stuck inside a tin can being flushed through a galactic sewer. The outer hull isn't much better and looks like the ship's been used by a flock of birds as a shithouse for the last three hundred years or so. When we loaded up at the Tunis City docks, the engine housing was so encrusted with grit and droppings that I wasn't sure it would be able to overcome the cross friction gumming up its RPMs enough to break through atmo. Yet, despite its complete derelict façade and torture chamber fuselage, the ship has flown smoothly, and it's obvious Rob has kept this hunk of metal around for a scenario such as this.

Our time aboard has not been wasted. After getting clear of Obal 10, Quantum made it clear that nothing would be sent using his transceiver that wasn't first run by him, so he and La Mer immediately went to work on portable consoles looking for any kinks in La Mer's transmitting worm. After examining it, Quantum came down on him hard for not building redundancy into the signal rerouting piece of the program. Worse, he'd claimed that the transmission's origination source will be easy to find if the satellite administrators are looking. David and Thompson had barely jumped between the two of them in time before La Mer—interpreting the statement as an accusation that he'd been responsible for the Corps coming to Agate Beach and rounding up the settlers—did something we'd all regret.

Why anyone would be looking is the real question. If the worm works the way La Mer built it, no one should know the satellites are being hacked. Besides, it's hardly an issue at this point—we don't plan on staying in one place long enough to give the Admin time to catch up to us. The bigger problem now is managing two-way communication. If we send a message to T'Kai with the expectation that he'll reply, we have to give him a coordinate to reply to, and triangulating our location will be easy from there.

Or so I assume. We're only ten hours out from Obal 6's orbit and Thompson is at the helm, giving Rob time to catch some sleep before the next phase of our mission. Quantum stands up to stretch his legs and Vitruzzi asks, "Why Obal 6? Why not put the transceiver on one of the Spectras?"

"Because Bi Schtum is one of its moons," he responds matter-of-factly, "and home to enough citizen-owned satellites to mask transmissions sent from Obal 6 for a while. We can stay until we hear back from T'Kai. Then we'll have to move."

"What do citizen satellites matter? I thought the whole point of this worm was to use Admin TDRSs," David says from the rear of the fuselage, yelling to be heard over the engines.

Quantum leans back against the wall next to the cockpit hatch, the expression on his face asking, *Why do I have to deal with such morons?* He levels a flat, lizardlike gaze on David for a few seconds before replying. "There are people working from inside— Admin personnel—who are helping us. They forward things that are useful, but for reasons I hope I don't have to illustrate, we cannot let these be sent to us directly. Some of the satellites work as our hubs. They receive and bounce incoming transmissions, but they filter the messages through scramblers that hide their final coordinates. I will contact our allies who have hardware around Bi Schtum and the neighboring planets. Any messages we receive will only be traceable within this quadrant. The Admin may come in and block or destroy the satellites, but unless they are very, very lucky, they will not isolate those that we'll be using right away." He lets this information soak in and then looks around for comprehension. My face reflects the same confusion on everyone else's.

He continues, disdain thick in his voice. "If T'Kai responds, he will use digitally encoded transmissions that cannot be unscrambled by Admin satellite programs. Only Corps and non-Admin satellites will transmit encoded messages, and T'Kai will know—or think he knows—that we don't have a receiver that can pick up Corps transmissions. It is not legal to own receiver codes for those frequencies, and difficult to build one that isn't traceable. Of course, my transceiver *can* pick up Corps transmissions, but that is beside the point." Quantum smiles, pleased with himself. "If he wants to ensure his message will get through, and stay untraceable by any unwelcome Admin ears, he'll have to use alternative satellites. Satellites controlled by *my* allies. With the program Axone has written, he will not be able to figure out where the signal is coming from, but to respond, we will have to point him toward the haystack we are hiding in."

"It sounds like you've been planning something like this for a while," Vitruzzi says.

"We will only have a single opportunity of this nature, and we have been waiting for it. Why would we not be prepared?"

"I'd like to know more about who this 'we' is."

Quantum doesn't respond, but his eyes stray to the opposite side of the fuselage, and after a moment, I realize they've settled on Rob.

QUANTUM'S TRANSCEIVER SITS on the roof of a warehouse inside a pocket of indistinct buildings near the small down of Rej on Obal 6. Like the majority of planets in this quadrant, this one is mainly water with several landmasses, mostly small habitable continents. With the abundance of water, many of the local populace's re-sources—steel, iron, other metals—are shipped in, and what isn't comes from oceanic drilling. The surplus is stored in these struc-tures and most of the area's activity consists of roving drones used to keep an eye on the place. There aren't many people, and the few we saw as we came in were civilians minding their own business, busy at work.

Quantum directs the hop into a warehouse, which he opens us-ing a remote transmission key. I'm so happy to be out of confine-ment that I want to run laps around the area just to stretch my legs and move my body again. Instead, we convene inside a cramped com room after being warned to stay inside and keep quiet. It's clear from Quantum's face that I don't have a choice in the matter, but I refuse to sit down a minute longer, broadcasting my decision by leaning grumpily against the wall.

Everyone busies themselves with getting blood back into their limbs while Quantum contacts his resources and arranges for coop-eration with the satellite transmissions. Before I'm really prepared, he turns to Vitruzzi.

"Ready to begin your show."

She doesn't hesitate. "Is it on the right channel?"

"Your transmission will be sent directly to the official fre-quency belonging to T'Kai's office in the Ministry. It will be re-viewed and, if you are convincing enough, brought directly to his attention."

She straightens up so that she's poised on the very edge of her seat. The building is deep and long with no windows, making it dark inside, with only dim green LEDs dotting the ceiling and cast-ing a swampy glow over us. As she looks down at the com unit, lines of deadly seriousness create deep, shadowed grooves across her forehead and beside her mouth.

The sound of the mic activating reminds me of a trigger. "This is Captain Eleanor Vitruzzi of the *Sphynx* ISPS, registration ID N295831, formerly a legally contracted arms and cargo transporter for the Ministry of S&E. I'm a resident of the non-citizen settlement known as Agate Beach on the southern hemisphere of Spectra 6. Recently, the majority of the population of our settlement was illegally arrested and one member murdered by Corps soldiers. The remainder were transported to the prisoner colony on Keum Libre without cause. All of these events occurred by order of Director Kurosawa T'Kai. I demand these people be set free and our settlement reestablished with a guarantee of no further Admin or Corps interference.

"I am in a unique position to make these kinds of demands. If you doubt me, I urge you to review the flight logs of the MCACS PCA *Bellerophon*, which was lost en route to the Admin space station known as the Fortress. You'll find the derelict in Beta Delta, where we left it after using it to infiltrate the station and destroy it. You have five hours to respond using the frequency uplink we send." The glowing console of the com unit fades out as she releases the transmit button and hands it back to Quantum to input the freq.

"What if he doesn't respond?" David asks, his question not aimed at anyone in particular.

Unexpectedly, Quantum answers, "Then you give the assets to me and my network. We will take it from there."

I inquire, "And what about our friends on Keum Libre?"

"There are martyrs in every revolution."

It's the flat, uncaring tone in his voice that gets to me. "Fuck that, Quantum. You've helped us out some, but you don't get to decide if our friends live or die."

"I am not deciding. All of you made that decision for them."

His statement smacks me into silence—because it's true. Whatever would have happened, by threatening T'Kai, we're no longer an anonymous annoyance but identified enemies, and our friends are his collateral.

Rob speaks up. "What would be the point of wavecasting the fact that T'Kai is some kind of villain, anyway? What can it possibly achieve?" He sits forward on his seat in the same alert position as Vitruzzi and focuses on each of us in turn. "At best, you'll make a lot of people in the system upset, or angry. But that won't make most of them want to automatically give up their entire way of life. T'Kai's just one man, he doesn't speak for the whole government, who, in case you've all forgotten, wasn't completely aware of what he was up to in the first place."

"But they're just as complicit, Rob," I respond. "Don't you remember all the shit we did in the Corps? The people, mostly innocent people, we were ordered to 'suppress'? That wasn't just a Corps decision; those directives came from the Admin. From the government. And now, this chemical they have that will wipe out the Spectras—" Why is he playing devil's advocate? It's too late for that.

"*Some* of those decisions were Admin, but they had their reasons. They mostly take care of people—healthcare, stability, safe planets for people to live on. And you don't know if this wire-rat is even telling the truth about that soil compound!"

"It's right for people to know," David interjects. "We should tell them what T'Kai is doing anyway. Let people decide for themselves."

"You're just going to introduce instability, and like Quantum says, they'll discount the information as fraudulent the minute it gets out. You'll get nowhere. If T'Kai doesn't cooperate with you, you'll gain nothing by implicating him anonymously."

"Do you think we should just let him get away with it?" I ask.

"That's not what—"

I don't let him finish. "I can't believe I'm saying this, but I agree with Rajcik. T'Kai has to be brought to justice for the things he's done, the people he's hurt."

"But Aly, we're hardly in a position to—"

"*We are in a position.*" Quantum glares at Rob, anger blooming in red stripes along his cheekbones. "You are not listening to me."

"You mean you have enough allies to go to war? With the Admin?" Rob bites the end off his words, his own anger bleeding through. "Then what are you waiting for? If there are that many people who want to overthrow them, there must be a reason. They don't need this information, or *evidence,* that a single member of the Directorate is crooked. If all these people you're talking about want to revolt, they must already believe the Cabinet is corrupt."

"This is the type of evidence citizens should see in order to help them decide which side to take," Quantum responds, eyes spitting defiance.

"I'm with these guys," Thompson chimes in. "Everyone knows the Admin is fucking them over. They just need a reason to do something about it, something to set them off. If knowing the Admin is using its own as bags of test meat doesn't wake people up, let 'em fuckin' die. Let 'em drown in their own rotting guts."

As crude as his words are, no one disagrees, not even Rob. I lean toward him and remind him as gently as I can, "You came with us by choice, Rob. You knew it could come to this."

He holds my eyes for a few seconds, his eyebrows still raised and causing wrinkles to ladder up his forehead. Then he sighs and leans back in his chair. "Yeah, I did, didn't I?"

Vitruzzi reaches for the com unit Quantum still holds. "I want to send a message to the *Sphynx.* Can you give them the same transmission coordinates to respond to?"

AFTER VITRUZZI SENDS WORD to the *Sphynx,* the rest of us spread out inside the warehouse, killing time as we wait for T'Kai to make his move. We're all edgy and eager to hear back from our crew. Another advantage of Bi Schtum is its proximity to Keum Libre, approximately four flight days away. If there's any such thing as luck, they've already been able to suss out the prison rock and are waiting for us somewhere between here and there. Rob's hop will make it possible to rendezvous with the ship, and we'll be able to execute the next part of the plan as one team again. If I weren't completely mentally and physically wrung out from everything that's happened since the Corps assaulted the Beach, I'd be anxious and uneasy about being back on board the ship with Karl. Only a couple short weeks have passed since things fell apart between us, but they may as well be years, the distance between us galaxies. I don't even know what I'd say to him at this point.

TWENTY-EIGHT

It's time I tell Rob that I plan on taking him up on his offer.

The warehouse contains orderly stacks of cargo crates almost the size of Rob's hop, and I wander around for a while trying to find him. I don't have any luck, so I nudge David, who's fallen asleep leaning back against a crate. Payback. Irritably, he grunts that Rob's gone back to his ship.

Rob is also probably trying to stockpile some shut-eye, but this is important and I don't know when I'll get another chance to talk to him. The hatch is pulled closed but not latched and I enter quietly, surprised when I don't see him lying on the bench in the fuselage's rear. Except for the light emitting from the cockpit, the interior is dark. The back of his head is just visible over the headrest of the pilot's seat, and I walk up and lean casually against the wall.

"Hi."

He jumps and spins the seat around quickly, his eyes wide. "Jesus! You scared me. How long have you been standing there?"

"I just walked in. What are you doing?"

"Just going through the works, making sure things are all good to go. I don't exactly trust Thompson, so I thought a systems check wouldn't hurt." He runs a finger along the com console control bar to shut it down.

"That's probably a good idea."

"What's up? Have we heard back from anyone?"

"No, not yet." I pause and take a deep breath, as if I'm about to jump in over my head, then let the words tumble out. "I've been thinking about what we talked about, about buying myself a new identity and becoming a citizen, and I want to do it."

The look of relief that springs to his face is oddly surprising. "I'm really happy to hear you say that, Aly. Really happy. I think it's the best choice you could possibly make."

"Yeah. That is, if we live through this."

"We will. I know we will. This deal with T'Kai is insane, and to be honest, I don't know what Vitruzzi thinks will happen. I want to help the Beachers, but I mean it when I say that I'm not going to die for this mission." The laugh lines that groove the edges of his mouth pull down sternly, stretching his lips to thin, bloodless stripes. I'm not sure how to respond. If T'Kai comes after us, dying is the best thing that could happen. Rob must know that.

"Hey," David says, leaning into the fuselage door, out of breath. "We just got word back from Brady. Come on."

We can't get back to the com room fast enough. It's been less than an hour since Vitruzzi sent the transmission to the *Sphynx*. For them to be able to respond so quickly means they must be close, probably in the same quadrant, and able to make use of the higher density of uncontrolled citizen satellites. Nearly shaking with impatience, Vitruzzi waits for everyone to settle, then plays the message.

Patrick is seated at the console in the *Sphynx*'s communication room. He looks tired and worn, with dark circles embedded in the skin under his eyes, but he's smiling. "Your message just came in, and I can't tell you how happy we all are to hear that you're safe. Everyone here is fine. Here's the rundown on what's been going on.

"When we left R'Kadia, we set a direct course to KL with bypasses around Corps security substations between here and there. It worked; we haven't been in contact with any of their ships so far, and we arrived in KL orbit three days ago. There's no security outside of the moon's atmosphere, so we went down for a better look. The only patrols we've seen are done by remote sentries, all below atmo, and only around the penal colony. They don't seem concerned about anyone showing up here, and Venus has been able to maneuver around all of the drones.

"We were able to do a planet-wide sweep. It's mostly water with five land masses big enough to support a colony or more. The prison island was covered by fog and low clouds when we were in range, so we couldn't get a good look at anything. The climate sensors picked up some weak signs of civilization, but there aren't a lot of people there, that's for sure. The other islands were completely devoid of infrastructure.

"There's an Admin structure, some kind of oceanic command station, with a good-sized landing platform about six klicks from the prisoner's island. From what we saw, it's the only place a ship as big as the *Sphynx* will be able to set down, at least to get access to the prison compound. From what we could pick up from the scanners, the island is just a jungle, either tree-covered or marshy, with no clearings. If it's anything like the other islands we flew over, it'll be a nightmare trying to get in there. Rajcik says it's all changed from when he was a prisoner here, says the place use to be mostly tundra with no forest or jungle, but Venus assures us the scanners are right. So, the Admin platform is the chokepoint. I'll send you the digitals we took after this message so you can see for yourself.

"Nothing we saw could help us confirm the Beachers' status, or if they're even there, but it started getting too risky to stay in KL's airspace. More Corps ships arrived yesterday, flying live patrols over the penal colony. I don't know if there's something going on down there, but we boogied. It's gotten too busy up here for our taste. We're en route to your quadrant now and will wait for word from you there. I don't know what, but we're going to have to come up with a diversion if we're going to get access to that landing platform. We're putting our heads together on it, you do the same. And don't wait long to send word." Brady reaches out toward the screen and gently touches it. "I love you, Eleanor. *Sphynx* out."

The barometer of collective anticipation and anxiety drops for everyone in the room. I draw my first almost-relaxed breath in days, yet we're all still feeling strung out on fear, worry, grief, and fury, the mixture creating a volatile explosive that could ignite at any trigger. Looking around at their faces, I realize the haggardness I saw in Brady's is no different than the rest of us. Rob's the only one who's still cool thanks to the emotional distance he has from the stakes—no one else has that luxury. Quantum and Hirota are the freshest of all of us, still vying for an angle that will bring them out on top. Even so, Quantum has basically claimed that their ultimate goal is something akin to a sparking civil war, and nobody can look forward to something like that without feeling the weight of future destruction trampling them down into their own version of hell.

"T'Kai has under three hours left to reply. Eleanor, we need to make ready to rendezvous with the *Sphynx* if he doesn't. I don't like saying it, but this mission could end right here." Rob's voice is calm, and though no one else likes what he's saying either, we've all been thinking it.

"You seem in a hurry to give up," Quantum replies.

Animosity between the two men sparks like flint and stone. Rob's jaw tightens for a minute as he tries to bite back his words, but it doesn't work. "What do you think is going to happen here? All of you? T'Kai's just going to bend over and take this? He's already shown you how far he'll go to shut up anyone who crosses him. He was willing to blow up an entire goddamn space station. And he's well-enough protected that he got away with it."

Quantum looks him over, derision turning his features stony. Thompson stiffens beside me, and I glance down to see that he's drawn his sidearm, letting it dangle by his thigh. Alarm floods my nerves.

Thompson says, "Quantum's right, Cross. You're pretty eager to give up, and you seem to know a lot about T'Kai."

Rob's seen enough combat to know when things are verging on the edge of chaos, and his face stretches into a sneer as he responds, "Any moron can tell you exactly the same thing I just did." He looks around at the rest of us. "And if you're implying what I think you are, let me ask this: Can someone tell me what the hell he's doing here anyway? If memory serves, he and his boss already made a deal with T'Kai once. If anyone should know what kind of man T'Kai is, Thompson, it's you."

"Fuck you—" Thompson begins to rise from his seat, bringing his pistol up, but stops with a jerk when he feels the barrel of my Sinbad pressed into his rib cage.

"I think everyone should calm down," I say.

Vitruzzi's face has gone the color of a corpse, but she's not looking at us, her eyes are on the com console, fixed on a green indicator that blinks languidly. A transmission is coming in, and it's live.

"Quantum." Her voice is hushed, almost reverent. She *wants* something to go down with T'Kai, and realizing that makes my arms dimple with goose bumps.

The wire-rat moves toward a selector on the console to play the transmission, but Vitruzzi stops him. "No, open up a video link. I want to see him."

He sets it up and Vitruzzi, still standing, stares into the transmitter's feed and clicks it on. The com monitor is almost as long as my torso and mounted on the wall. T'Kai's face fills the oversized screen.

TWENTY-NINE

"Ah, Dr. Vitruzzi. A pleasure." The image is much better resolution than Rajcik's makeshift recording, and my attention is instantly captured by the man's eyes—one a limpid brown and the other an unsettling, almost cataract blue. He's sitting cross-legged behind a table made of unusual wood that glints with an oily burnish. The room he's in is devoid of any furnishings except a giant warrior mask taking up most of the wall behind him. His business-class suit and the carpet are both a crisp and impeccable white. "We've been keeping an eye on you for a long time. No, don't look so surprised—a mind as talented as yours is not an easy loss for the Administration. There was that . . . unfortunate situation with your family, so we of course understood your decision to leave the Medical Directorate. But don't think that your whereabouts and your activities have gone unnoticed." He smiles a perfect smile, his teeth even and as white as his flawless suit. He speaks to her as if they've known each other for years, maybe shared formal meals at posh restaurants or drank cognac together in a mutual friend's living room. "We did hope you would find your way back to the Administration, but we never expected it to be in this manner."

Vitruzzi stands motionlessly, her face still drained of blood. She opens her mouth to say something, but T'Kai cuts her off. "No, no need to respond. We are quite aware of the accouterments of the lifestyle you and your fellow, ah, villagers have collected. You should know that you have nothing that the Admin would miss overmuch. There are the weapons, of course, but the fact is you could do very little damage with what you've managed to appropriate." He sits rigidly behind the desk, never moving. His hands lie placidly on his knees, and only his gleaming eyes and his mouth give any indication he's not some type of robot or statue. "Despite your Protean personality, Eleanor—if I may—your brilliance in your field has remained almost unmatched. We consider the things you've stolen to be a small severance for your contributions to the advancement of biomedics and engineering. Your husband was a good scientist, not the greatest, but good. Still, his abilities could never compare to yours. It was a blow when you left us. Unfortunately, it's now too late to reconsider."

The rest of us sit at an angle that inhibits T'Kai from seeing us and I'm oddly relieved. There's something so inhuman and cold in his mismatched eyes that I don't want them on me. I can't tell if he's trying to ingratiate himself with Vitruzzi or piss her off. Men like him are so used to speaking obliquely, you wonder if they even know what they're trying to express. In any case, it's clear he's done his research and his patronizing speech is having an effect on Vitruzzi. I haven't seen that look on her face since she asked Karl to kill the captain of the MCACS we'd stolen to break into the Fortress. There's no mercy in that look, no hesitation; it's as stern and set as a tribal chieftain ordering a sacrifice to the slaughter. If T'Kai were here, I'd recommend he start writing his own obituary.

"You know why we contacted you, T'Kai."

"On the contrary. You've placed demands, ones that are so completely outside the realm of reasonable that, if you were still at your post in the Ministry, I would have no choice but to initiate a formal inquiry into your judgment."

"But you're responding, which means you must have found the *Bellerophon*. And you know we've been to the Fortress. You can guess what we brought back with us."

Like a shape-shifting necromancer, his friendly smile suddenly morphs into the toothy sneer of a barracuda. "Already I tire of your facile and indirect threats. They annoy me. Tell me something interesting before I regret having let my admiration for the work you've done expose me to petty extortion. If there's anything that I find more pathetic than a shining star that's lost its luster, it's seeing that same star forget its place in the univer—"

"Shut the fuck up and listen, T'Kai. We have proof of what was happening on the Fortress. We could bring you and the entire Ministry of S&E to its knees if we wanted to." Vitruzzi matches his ferocity with icy determination and cold, cold words. "But that's not what we want. My terms were clear in the first transmission you received. Free the Agate Beach settlers, let them return to Spectra 6, and keep the Corps off their backs for good. If you do, Rajcik's footage of your discussion of the Nova and destroying the Fortress, and the data of the biowarf testing being done on non-citizens *and soldiers* will be returned to you. Otherwise, we'll wavecast it to every human being in the system. Your choice."

T'Kai's face has gone the same color as Vitruzzi's and his words are like short, brutal jabs thrown in a bar fight. "János Rajcik was killed during his terrorist activities that resulted in the destruction of that space station. I have never been in contact with that criminal—"

"Shut up," she cuts him off again, her patience for bullshit snuffed. She leans forward and places her hands on the com console, her face centimeters from the monitor. If T'Kai were actually here, she'd be in range to kiss him. "Listen to me, T'Kai, I'm not playing games here. You think you know me? Then you know how determined I am. You know that I'm not going to quit just because you flatter or threaten me. This is how it's going to be. You either do what I ask, set the Beachers free, or I will bring you and every minister in the Cabinet down. Think it over. You have an hour."

She severs the link and the monitor fades into a dull gray that mixes with the green overhead lights, leaving the room as dim as a subterranean tomb.

David says, "What do you think he'll do?"

She's hunched over the console, the ends of her long, curly hair brushing against the controls. She stays there for a minute before answering. "He isn't going to negotiate. I didn't think he would, but I had to see him to find out." She goes silent, not looking at anyone. Finally, she turns around and says, "Quantum, do you have the equipment here to make copies of everything? I'm leaving it with you. The rest of us will rendezvous with the *Sphynx* to try and free the settlers on our own."

"Whoa—hold on," Thompson says. "What are you talking about? You can't leave the footage here with this wire-rat. The deal was to bring T'Kai down."

She ignores him, still speaking to Quantum. "You're our insurance. Give us seven days and then you do whatever you want with that footage. Tell the whole system, I don't care. We're done here."

Thompson jumps up and grabs Vitruzzi by one wrist, towering over her by more than a head, and spins her around to force her to look at him. She's quicker than he expects and faces him with the barrel of one of her pistols pointing into his teeth. "You don't call it, Thompson. *I* call it. You're here because *I* made a deal with Rajcik—now that deal involves him."

Thompson barely breathes, wincing at her like a snake about to strike. Unwilling to carry the confrontation further, she backs away and lowers her weapon. He isn't stupid. He knows the second his hand goes for his gun he'll be target practice for the rest of us.

Rage makes his jaw clench and his hollow cheeks flush, but he says nothing.

Vitruzzi looks back at Quantum. "You're prepared to do what you said you'd do?"

He nods.

She looks at Thompson. "Then T'Kai is handled. Now, everyone get out. Take a break. It may be a while before any of us sleep again. I'm calling the *Sphynx*."

"V," I start, but don't get far.

"I'm not arguing. This is not a negotiation. This is done." Her eyes blaze with something that isn't quite anger and isn't quite fear, and I see how close to the edge she is. Something in T'Kai's transmission has hit her deep in the soul, like a pry bar wrenching on the lid of a coffin, and it's hard to say what might be underneath.

THOMPSON SKULKS AWAY INTO the far corner of the warehouse and throws a crate against the floor, making a lot of harmless noise. Watching him from the corner of my eye, I wait just outside the com room for Vitruzzi and Quantum, who's stayed with her presumably to copy the footage and data. Hirota sits a few meters away on a crate by himself, and La Mer and David keep me company while Rob heads back toward the hop.

David leans against the wall next to the com room door. "What do you think, little sis? Is she going off the deep end?"

I think about it for a minute before answering. "She's definitely closer than I've ever seen her."

"Yeah." He slides down the wall until he's seated and looks out into the dark warehouse. Outside, it's daytime, but the walls block any light from shining in, reinforcing the feeling that we're trapped in a cave. The sound of a distant track vehicle trundling through the area is the only thing breaking the stillness. "You know the chances of us saving the Beachers is just about zero."

Out of the two of us, David is the optimist. It's rare for him to lose heart, and seeing it happening now triggers a primeval fear that tremors up my spine like the aftershocks of an earthquake. "Hey, you forget that we're the same people that destroyed the Admin's most heavily armed space station. If we can do that, saving a few prisoners from a rock that's guarded by nothing but drones won't be hard."

That gets a grin out of him, but it's halfhearted. La Mer and I both sit down beside him and I lean back and close my eyes. It's a futile effort, I know, but there's nothing else I can do for now. No one is talking, and I hear a soft whisper coming from the walls to our left, probably rats or mice looking for nest-building material. After a few minutes, Quantum and Vitruzzi emerge from the com room.

The three of us are on our feet immediately. She looks at us flatly. "Let's get going."

THIRTY

Rob trades off the pilot seat with Thompson and takes a seat next to me on the rear bench. A heavy frown furrows its way down his brow while he stares at the floor distractedly.

"What's the matter?" I ask.

"What?"

"You look like something's wrong." I raise my voice against the engine noise.

"Oh. It's probably not a big deal. There's something wrong with the communication system. I can't transmit. Maybe just a loose circuit board or something."

"Who were you trying to transmit to?"

"Just bouncing some queries around, trying to see who's in the area. I'd like to avoid any Corps ships if we can."

I nod, dropping it. Trying to compete against the hop's rattles and revving is more trouble than it's worth. Everyone else lounges with their eyes closed, probably wishing they could catch some real sleep. The last three days have collapsed together like a waking nightmare, hopping from Tunis City to Obal 6, and now to meet the *Sphynx* on the moon Letum Uti, near Obal 5. From there, Keum Libre is only another day-and-a-half flight time.

We've been in the air thirteen hours with another five to go. Rob has been steadfast at the helm, not taking a break until now. I'm not sure how he's going to hold up once we get aboard the *Sphynx*, but I'm hoping that we'll all be able to take a few hours down time in the relative comfort of the bigger ship. I miss the *Sphynx*. Not just because it has more space to spread out and get some real shut-eye, but because it and the colony of Agate Beach were home to me for the last three months. More home than any-place has felt in a lot of years, and I've grown attached, despite my own rules against it.

We left Quantum and Hirota behind with basic instructions; give us seven days, then do whatever they want with the footage and data. They have almost no incentive to follow these directions, but Vitruzzi must think they'll comply—or maybe she doesn't see any drawbacks if they don't. Quantum agreed to forward any message that came from T'Kai on to the *Sphynx*, but Vitruzzi made it clear she doesn't expect one. As far as she's concerned, we're on our own and whatever happens to T'Kai is now in the hands of fate.

Based on the intel from Brady, we're gambling on Keum Libre staying minimally guarded. T'Kai may suspect we'll try and rescue the Beachers, but he may not expect our attempt to come so soon. Even though Vitruzzi had given him an hour to respond to her demands, we'd left before he had a chance. He'll expect us to be on the move, so it won't surprise him if we don't have a live-feed link with him next time he tries to contact us. If we have any luck, he'll be able to trace the transmissions to Bi Schtum and look for us there first. Whatever we do, the mission's success hinges on us making our moves before they make theirs.

Which is exactly what Vitruzzi is thinking. I glance at her and realize she's not sleeping. She sits back in the jump seat, her eyes fixed on a spot in the fuselage wall across from her. She's holding something in her hand and every now and then her thumb rubs along the edge of it. A photograph. It doesn't take much guesswork to figure out who it's of. Probably her dead daughter, maybe also her dead husband. Dead because of T'Kai. His experiments, his fault.

David and I were aboard the PCA *Thor's Hammer* patrolling the Spectras when the Crowers Croup broke out. The Admin kept it quiet for as long as they could after the virus got loose. But soon, word about the Corps being sent in to quarantine masses of citizens in the Obals and rumors that the dead were being burned started to spread. Fast. The Soldier's Rebellion erupted like a gas torch, chaos sweeping through the ranks too swiftly to contain. There was too much happening to be certain of anything, and David and I lost track of distant friends in the Corps who were assigned to the Obals. After the flash fire that launched the Rebellion burned up its fuel, the Admin went to work hunting down those responsible for it, and David and I kept our heads down and kept moving. There was no way to find out if we'd lost any friends, and no point in looking anyway.

For people like Vitruzzi, people who'd shaken hands with the deadly virus and seen their own families destroyed by it, there was no clean break, no easy excuse to forget the past. I can't imagine how much pain she's in, having just been face-to-face with the man who caused the obliteration of her whole world. And who's doing the same thing to her new life a second time. I was closer to completely losing my shit than I care to remember when I thought I'd lost David, but she seems to be staying calm and collected. At least on the surface. If she does lose it, there's no telling what she'll do.

THE HOP DOESN'T HAVE a ship-to-ship airlock seal, so once we arrive in Letum Uti we set it down in a field outside a scratch of a town and wait for the *Sphynx*. The hop's transmitter is still blown, but Vitruzzi had prearranged the pickup with Brady. The shuttle has already arrived by the time we land, and the six of us load up.

Karl is flying the shuttle and turns around with a grin to greet Vitruzzi as we settle into our seats. "It's good to see you again, Captain."

"Same to you."

He nods at La Mer and David, who've taken the seats directly behind the cockpit, and then lets his eyes find mine. "Aly."

"Karl."

"Can we get the fuck out here before some farmer decides to come see why we planted a hop in their field?" Thompson asks.

The ramp door closes and we get airborne.

"RADAR PICKED UP TWO gunships from inside atmo before we left KL, at least that's what we think they were. We couldn't get a positive read, but we didn't want to be IDed, so we kept our distance. We weren't followed." The crew has gathered inside the *Sphynx*'s galley for Brady to lay out what they'd discovered on the prison-rock recon.

"You sure?" Vitruzzi asks from her seat next to him.

"Hundred percent sure, Captain," Venus responds over the intercom from the cockpit.

"Maybe they were bringing in more prisoners," Rob says.

He and Karl stand at opposite ends of the room and do everything in their power to keep from looking in each other's direction. It's been two weeks since I've seen Karl. What will he think of my decision to join Rob and buy back a citizen's life? Am I lying to myself if I think he'll even care?

"We thought of that, and if it's the case, they'll have to drop them on the offshore rig. Maybe it's a failsafe so the prisoners already on the rock can't attempt a takeover or hijack a ship. It's too long to swim to the platform, so we have to assume the only way out of the colony is by boat. The colony itself is spread out along the top of a bluff about three hundred meters above the ocean's surface," Brady continues, outlining the buildings with his index finger on the scans spread across the table. "There's a desalination plant at the cliff's edge that has a pipe dropping down to the sea, and a cargo elevator runs along it, terminating at a dock."

"Which means to get there we'll have to take a boat from the platform," Doug Mason states.

"Right, and first we'll have to disarm whatever security runs it," Brady finishes.

"I can't believe there's *nowhere* to ground a ship on land." I'm seated at one of the galley tables with a plate of food in front of me. I'm not really hungry, but there's no telling when I'll get another chance for a meal. If you live on the run, you don't hesitate to take advantage of opportunities as soon as they present themselves. "They had to set up at least a temporary building site at some point to even get the platform and desal plant built."

"There used to be," Rajcik announces, his voice a marauding whisper that kills all other sound. "When I got out of there, it was just grass and dirt. No trees, barely even any bushes. There were two landing zones near the colony and half a dozen buildings. "Now"—he stares at the scans—"this. Nothing but jungle."

David and Vitruzzi exchange a glance and he says, "There's something you should know. Something the wire-rat told us."

He gives a brief explanation of the soil compound and its dangers, finishing up with: "It looks like KL may have been one of their original testing grounds for whatever that stuff is. We may even be looking at a dead world." His expression blanches uncertainly for a moment. "I mean, dead in terms of the prison population."

No one likes the sound of that, but Brady says, "No. That isn't the case. We picked up signs of life—of people—when we did the recon. Besides, we all heard the security squad that killed Bodie say they were bringing the settlers here."

The room is silent for a minute as everyone contemplates the possibility that we may be on a wild goose chase. It doesn't go on long before David continues, sounding as if no one is even vaguely entertaining any doubts, "It doesn't look like we could get anything bigger than a shuttle under that canopy, but if we wait for those Corps ships to leave, we can probably access the platform. Do we know what kind of security they have on site?"

"Nothing above decks that we could make out through long-range images," Brady responds. "We couldn't get too close, but the main part of the platform is just open landing tarmac and a small building, probably the command center. Looks like most of the structure is underwater, which makes it that much harder to get to."

"And then there are the drones in the air," Desto adds.

"If we can get the *Sphynx* in range, I think I can neutralize the drones' sentry-net by modifying the trans-worm I built for the satellites. They'll still be out there and they'll still be weaponized, but they won't have the capacity to fire on us," La Mer says.

"How would that work?" Rob asks.

"It's a matter of scrambling their priority matrix." He takes a deep swallow from his cup, obviously secure in his topic, and continues, "Basically, we short-circuit their decision systems; they'll see us, but the AI won't be able to decide on a direct course of action. Their routine patrol programs will stay the same, so they'll move in the right direction, they just won't be able to identify us as a threat."

"This ship has an armed shuttle. Why not just blow them out of the sky?" Thompson asks.

"No, this is better than shutting them down completely because the personnel on the platform will be less suspicious. See, the sentries will still be active, just not reactive. Admin teams won't know they're not doing what they're supposed to."

Finally, something that might actually work in our favor. Heads nod enthusiastically. Brady asks, "You sure you can do it?"

"Yes, definitely. Quantum showed me a few things that will help. I'm not sure how, but he's been inside some of the Admin security programs. He's . . ." He pauses, a look of concern washing over his features, and his eyes shift around the room, then drop to the floor. "I don't know. He's the best wire-rat I've ever seen."

Desto picks up the thread. "Okay, sounds like we've got a way in. Time it so there's no Corps gunships in the area, cut off the drones, get on the platform. There can't be more than a few security personnel. Maybe we don't even have to engage. We just lock them in and shake our asses on over to the colony."

"That's a good idea," Karl says, "but they'll probably have submersibles. We won't even see them coming if they launch."

"The *Sphynx* has enough surprises on board to handle that," Desto responds.

Shaking his head, Karl says, "Yeah, but not if they're firing torpedoes. We'd never know what hit us."

Desto, out of ideas for the moment, gives him a disgusted look.

"So, we'll probably have to neutralize whoever's in the structure," Brady cuts in. "Control them enough to be able to make a trip over to the penal colony and get the settlers out."

"We'll have a better chance if we keep the element of surprise," Karl says.

Rajcik's hasn't said anything in a while and I turn to look at him, not trusting his silence any more than I trust his words. His face is tight with contempt and it sets my teeth on edge. He catches me looking and brings his dark eyes to bear on mine, silently daring me to call him out.

"What do you think, Rajcik?" I ask. "Have you been inside that structure?"

He hesitates before answering. "For inprocessing, yeah. When I was eighteen."

"What can you tell us about it?" Vitruzzi asks.

"Nothing useful, sweetheart." He tries to get off without saying anything, but the weight of a room full of cold stares compels him. "It's been twenty years since I was down there and I only saw one area—where they tag and outfit new prisoners."

"Any suggestions for hobbling their security?"

He sweeps us with a flat, death-mask glare. "Kill everyone you see."

"That's great," Rob replies. "Do you have anything constructive to add?"

He acts like he didn't hear Rob and begins twisting his head, first left than right. His neck bones crack hideously. Finally, he brings his attention back to the room. "You want constructive? Here's my advice—forget about your friends. You'll die trying to infiltrate that rock, and they're most definitely worm food. Your issue—*the* issue—is T'Kai, and from what Thompson tells me, you've let that one slide through your fingers. As far as I'm concerned, I've done what I can to help you people, and every minute I spend listening to your bullshit is a minute wasted."

I lean across the table until my eyes are level with his and seethe. "No one's stopping you, János. You can walk out of that hold any time you want." Straight into emptiness.

His jaw clenches, but he clamps down on his building fury and leers at me instead. "Your charm, Aly, is that you always say what you're thinking."

"This isn't getting us anywhere," Vitruzzi interrupts. "The fact of the matter is we've done what we can about T'Kai. Quantum will wavecast everything in another couple of days, and it will be up to anyone who sees it to deal with T'Kai. He can't suppress the information once it's out, and we can't attack the entire Admin. This is the only way to help the settlers and bring T'Kai to some kind of justice."

"Justice?" Rajcik says. "I'm a little confused about your idea of justice, Vitruzzi. Leaving to chance what a single bullet could accomplish is a coward's way out. I expected your team to face T'Kai, not run away and let a wire-rat do your work."

"Shut up, Rajcik." My patience is getting close to snapping.

Rajcik knows it and taunts me, "Or what, Aly?"

A dark look from Vitruzzi convinces me to drop it. I glare at Rajcik, daring him to keep going, but he seems content to resume ignoring me. It's Thompson who quietly returns my stare, his eyes eerily similar to the beady, ferocious gaze of a Flat Rat.

"How many levels are there, Rajcik? Do you know anything at all about the structural design?" Vitruzzi presses.

With a final contemptuous grunt, he spills it. "It's basic. Key-pad door locks, security screening at all corridor junctions, hermetic seals on all doors. If I had to guess, I'd say three levels, but I've never been below the first. Could be more, could just be the one."

"But if it's underwater, there's only one path of attack. They can't call for backup from outside. That should make it easier to create a bottleneck and hold their security in check," Karl says.

"To keep them in check, we may have to divide into two teams," I insert. "One to hold the platform, the other to get on land."

"Some of the settlers still have their embedded trackers—Zeta, Jade, Fowler, a few others. We can trace them, and they should be able to lead us to the rest," Venus adds over the com.

Everyone puts in his or her piece as we continue constructing the plan. Hearing it spoken aloud helps us feel like we have control, like our actions will bring about the results we expect. A team's faith in a good plan is as important as their ability to carry it out, and we have plenty of both. What we don't have is any guarantee Quantum will transmit the footage, or even live to try.

THIRTY-ONE

Sleep is impossible. I lay in my old bunk like a petrified log, every muscle rigid, hypersensitive to the rhythms of the air exchanger and the ship's familiar hums, dings, and creaks. Venus and Bodie take—*took*—care of her better than most parents care for their kids, but she's still older than a lot of the ships that have seen the AUs the *Sphynx* has. My mind races over the plan, looking for holes and alternatives should anything happen that we don't expect—and we can be sure something will. But years in the business of crime and Corps have taught me that you can still prepare for it, even if you can't know what's coming.

After an hour or so of useless tossing and turning, I get up, get dressed, and head for the galley.

"I absolutely think you did the right thing, Jeremy. No question."

Desto is talking to La Mer as I enter, and Karl and David sit around the table they all share.

"What's the right thing?" I ask, returning David and Karl's nods.

"Have a seat, sweet thing," Desto says. His suggestive tone helps calm my frantic thoughts, and it hits me how much I'm going to miss this kind of camaraderie. It's this familiarity and comfort with each other that have made this crew my family and Agate Beach my home. My stomach twists a little. Eventually, I'll have to face the fact that I may never see any of them again.

"What's the matter, babe? You look a little pale," he asks.

I shake it off, not ready to admit my decision to leave. David's eyes follow me as I pull a seat from under the table. "Nothing, just can't sleep. Looks like I'm not the only one."

The chair I take is directly across from Karl. His scrunched brow overshadows his eyes as they bounce from me to the table and back. His naturally stoic composure rarely cracks, and seeing him looking uncertain gives me a momentary, irrational spark of hope. Can he still care about me?

To hide it, I repeat my question, "What did you do, La Mer?"

The way he hesitates before answering has me even more interested, but he eventually spills it. "I shorted the com transmitter on Cross's hop before we left Obal 6."

"What? Why?"

"I just . . . just thought it was a good idea. It seemed better to make sure no one could, uh, inadvertently send any information that could endanger us."

"You mean you don't trust Cross." I don't have to ask; the answer has been clear since the day the *Red Horizon* landed at the Beach. And I have to hand it to him, he's smart and thinks on his feet. Besides, it's done, no point in arguing.

The room is quiet for a few seconds, then David pushes back from the table abruptly. "So Desto, let's you and me walk through the armory. I want to make sure I know what's in stock in case we need it."

"Dave, you know what's in there as well as . . . oh, yeah, sure. Let's go."

La Mer gets up too and follows them out, and like that, Karl and I are alone.

We're strangers again, neither of us knowing what to say to the other. I fumble to come up with something. "What do you think of the plan?"

His eyes settle on me and he responds, sounding relieved to have a neutral topic, "It's thinner than the atmosphere on Nexon, but that's as good as we're going to get. If any team can do it, it'll be us."

Scanning his face as he speaks, I don't really hear his words. I know how thin the plan is, but what I'm really asking is what he feels not what he thinks. He doesn't continue, so I finally respond, trying to dredge up something to keep the conversation going. "Have you talked to Vitruzzi about T'Kai? It seems like he really got to her, the way he brought up her family . . ."

"Why would I?"

He doesn't ask in a confrontational way. He sounds curious, reminding me how clueless he can be when it comes to people's feelings. I almost say something about it, but stop myself. It would only start an argument. Besides, what do I know? Haven't I been just as clueless, made the same mistakes?

"I just mean, you're the only one here who's known her that long. It might help if she had someone to talk to, you know? She seemed upset."

He sighs and looks at the bottle he holds in one hand. "She's strong. She'll cope. Like the rest of us."

"I just thought—"

"So you're going to go back to the life," he cuts me off, finally looking up, his eyes boring into my face.

"How . . . did David tell you that?" It's hard to find my voice, torn between being surprised and defensive. Damn my brother. Doesn't he understand privacy? But I get why he told Karl; he knows I'd never do it on my own. I'd let Karl find out when I was thousands of miles and a new identity away. There's no reason to deny it. "Yeah."

"You may not believe it, Aly." He stands up and walks toward the exit with his shoulders set like iron bands. The tension in them makes his shirt taut, and he takes a deep swallow of his drink before continuing, but his voice is thick anyway as he says, "But I really hope things go well for you."

The words sting in a surprising way. I never would have expected such total and unquestioning acceptance. But what *did* I expect? That he beg me to stay? That he scream at me, or curse at me, or cry? He's a realist, I'll give him that. He knows me well enough to know that when my mind's made up, it's as rigid as his locked shoulders.

I take a deep breath and almost choke on it. "Thanks."

He doesn't look back and leaves the galley, deserting me. Moments later, Rajcik enters through the same door. The hollowness inside me instantly begins to compress as rage wraps itself around my torso like a vice. But this time, it's not about Rajcik.

He pauses and looks me over before coming in, blatantly measuring how much trouble I might be, then walks toward the cupboards.

But talking to Karl has taken the fight out of me. I don't feel like moving, but I can't just sit here and say nothing. "I'm surprised Vitruzzi lets you walk around without a shadow."

He hears the strain in my voice and looks at me again, disquieting interest sparkling in his eyes.

"I guess she trusts her crew to handle me if I do something unwise," he says dismissively, rifling through the cupboards.

He's wearing a thin shirt, the same plain gray color of everything that's been laundered through the cleaning system over and over. The sleeves are tight and ride up on his thick arms as he lifts them to dig past things on the shelf, looking for something edible. I see the scar again, cutting a deep groove between his muscles.

"You almost lost it didn't you?"

He finally grabs a couple of nutrition bricks wrapped in plastic, rips one open with his teeth, and sits across from me in the same seat Karl had just vacated. He knows what I'm talking about, but before responding, he throws the unopened bar on the table and swallows the other in two large bites, then rubs his hands together to shake off any crumbs. My own curiosity keeps my frustration at his stalling at bay. Finished, he leans back and extends his right arm to his side. Once his forearm swings in front of him about half of its full range, it stops, the triceps unable to extend completely.

"I'll never do another push up," he says, looking disgustedly at his arm. "Not unless Vitruzzi decides to work some fancier magic. But she doesn't have the resources she'd need for that. Maybe I'll be able to get them for her once I get the *Temptation* back up and running."

A chuckle escapes me. "That's not likely to happen."

He raises one eyebrow. "You don't think I will?"

"Why would Vitruzzi give you that much freedom? I don't care how much you've tried to help us get the Beachers back; you're still a criminal. And a liar."

He smirks. "Same thing, right? Besides, Vitruzzi still owes me. She helped me by fixing me up. I gave her the video of T'Kai. Now I'm helping you get your friends out of the shank. Don't you think that deserves some payback?"

"She doesn't owe you a damn thing. None of us do. After what you pulled."

"We'll see, Aly. We'll see."

"In any case, you're not much help to us. You said yourself that you don't know the layout or how to infiltrate the platform on KL."

"I'm still a hired gun."

I stand up, no longer able to stomach bandying words with him. "When the shooting starts, Rajcik, we'll see where your gun is pointing. Something tells me you've got other targets besides the Corps in mind. And you can rest assured that theirs won't be the only ones pointing at you. All I need is a reason."

"Sit. Down."

His tone surprises me. He hasn't been my boss in months, but the undeniable command in his voice still gets an automatic reaction out of me. I start to lower myself back into my chair before I even realize it, but catch myself.

"No. You don't get it." I smile grimly. "You're not in charge anymore."

He reaches out and grasps my wrist as quickly as a striking cobra. "There's something I have to explain to you. So sit down."

He doesn't get up, doesn't pull me. He just holds my arm, giving me the chance to decide if I want to listen or not. After hesitating a second, I sit. His grip releases, leaving white bands around my wrist.

"You're smart, Aly, but you're wrong about something. You think I'm some kind of monster, a big bad wolf. But I'm not the one you have to worry about here."

"Bull—"

He cuts me off. "Just fucking listen. T'Kai is more dangerous than you realize. He's in it for blood. My blood, your blood, your whole crew's blood. The only way to stop him is to kill him. That's why I'm here. That's the only reason I'm here. I don't give a damn about you and your brother."

"And you took a job from him." Acid contempt bubbles in my throat.

"I've been working for him since I was eighteen, three years after they sent me to that shithole on Keum Libre. In fact, you've been working for him, too."

It's as if he's just thrown a bucket of cold water in my face and I nearly gasp. "What are you talking about?"

"How do you think we managed to keep clear of the Corps for so long? After all those jobs?" He has my attention, and he knows how to keep it. "T'Kai's been bankrolling me since I was a prisoner on KL. He picked me to be his personal thief. The first cache of weapons I stole paid for his vote of confidence, and everything after that we split fifty-fifty. When you and your brother were on my crew, nearly every heist we pulled was for T'Kai. We made him rich. It was a perfect arrangement, until he got too greedy."

My mouth opens, but nothing comes out. I'm reeling, not wanting to believe a word, but unable to stop myself. It's so obvious, it has to be true. We were lucky, too lucky, for a long time. The *Temptation* was a wanted ship; we'd seen it come up in plenty of newswave bulletins, and Rajcik's identity has been known throughout the system for almost as long as his reputation has. We were always so careful, so methodical. The truth cuts deeply now, but it never occurred to me that we weren't as good at stealing and selling illegal weapons as I thought we were.

And something else—Rajcik had always handled the arms sales on his own. He kept the crew in the dark, so we didn't know how much he was really making from the deals, and our cuts were always enough to keep us quiet. That and fear of what Rajcik would do to us if he suspected we would turn on him. All that time, half the money had been going back to T'Kai. My skin goes cold as I realize how naïve, how utterly and completely oblivious, I'd been.

"Want to know the best part?" he continues. "Half the shit they blamed on me wasn't even me. That Corps ship I got away in when I escaped from KL, where the crew was slaughtered? I would have gotten out of there without anyone knowing, but T'Kai tipped them off that I was a stowaway. He was testing me, trying to see if I could do the job. I had no choice but to kill them. And New Sweden"—he chuckles coldly—"those stupid colonists were just patsies that T'Kai hired to guard the arms until we got there. They were fine when we left. It was T'Kai who had them wiped out. Now I realize that he was covering his tracks, making sure that anyone who knew I was working for him was gone. Because he wanted *me* gone."

"Why didn't you tell us the truth?"

"Why would I? You all got what you wanted. Don't forget, Aly, you and David were there by your own choice. You could have walked any time you wanted to, but you didn't." His black eyes shine with an evil mirth. He's actually enjoying watching the effect his story is having on me. "I'd already figured out T'Kai was going to try and have me ghosted after the Fortress. In a way, I did you two a favor when I cut you loose. Things might have turned out differently—maybe no one would have escaped."

It's my turn to laugh, and it burns like bile in my throat. "If he wanted you dead, how the hell did you get away?"

He sly smirk makes me want to squirm out of its range. "You're going to like this. You helped. Nothing happened the way it was supposed to on that station. T'Kai didn't have enough security, and the ones he did have weren't prepared for the shit-storm you and your new friends created. When the place blew, the soldiers acted like frightened little ants and scattered. After we launched, only one gunship came after us. That bastard was lucky enough to hit us." He reaches around and rubs the long scar.

I'm scrambling, just trying to keep up with everything he's saying. Through a mouth lined by felt, I ask, "Why didn't it finish you off?"

He arches a speculative eyebrow. "Orders, probably. Their priority must have been to help their distressed comrades." That cold chuckle again. "If T'Kai ever reads that commander's flight logs, I imagine the stupid sap will die choking on his own screams."

My confidence is so badly shaken that it's a long time before I can muster any kind of coherent response. Rajcik has gotten the better of me, far, far beyond what I'd imagined, at every single turn. For the last six years, I thought I had it under control, my life in my own hands, but I'd been wrong. The Corps was everything to me before I woke up to the fact that I was nothing but its puppet, and it had eaten me up inside until I'd escaped. I'd sought out Rajcik as a way of rebelling against the sick corruption of the Admin. But I realize now that I'd merely gone from being a knowing tool of that corruption to an unknowing one of Rajcik's own special variety. I want to scream my lungs out and strangle Rajcik and all his smug contempt to death, but don't. If I'd paid attention, I would have seen the truth a long time ago. Had I wanted to be blind? Is there some terrified, weak part of me that's afraid to be free? Is that what's driving my decision to follow Rob and become a citizen again?

He stands up fluidly, like a coiled spring. "Don't look so surprised. It's just the way they work. And you think I'm evil and corrupt. Now you know the truth. The only reason I haven't killed T'Kai already is because I've never been close enough to him to do it. But that will change, soon. Something tells me that we haven't heard the last from him."

He walks past me out of the galley.

I look down at the table and see the nutrition bar he left behind. Picking it up, I hurl it as hard as I can against the wall, completely unsatisfied by the soft crunch it makes. *Goddammit!* I've never been so gullible, so duped, so deceived. And I swear, it will never happen again.

Does David know about this? I need to talk to him, if only to make the news less difficult to swallow. But first, the com room, find out how far out we are. The sooner this mission is over, the sooner I can put all of it behind me. Forget the past and start completely over from scratch. Nothing has ever sounded so good.

When I get to the com room, La Mer is hunched over the main console that links with the ship's central computer. His long, ropy hair hangs down across his cheeks, and he squints as he types intently on the keyboard. He looks up when I come in, his eyes still far away for a few seconds before focusing on me.

"How's that security program going?" I ask, leaning against the wall beside him.

He looks back at the screen for a few seconds before answering. "If what Quantum told me about their protocols is right, it's basically done. Once we send a signal burst that the drones pick up, they'll analyze it, and that'll be all she wrote. It's like scrambling an egg. All the components in their brains will still be there, but they won't be put together the same way. We'll be able to fly right past. Some of them may retain enough of their programmed protocols to follow us, but that's about all they'll be capable of. It may be a little nerve-racking, but if it gets to be too much, Venus can always shake them. They're intra-atmospheric, so their range will be limited."

His confidence is reassuring, and the conversation helps redirect my scorched thoughts away from Rajcik. "How do you feel about things after we get on the platform?" La Mer is a thinker, not the kind of combat soldier that most of us are. He can hold a gun and point it in the right direction, but his instincts are evasion not engagement.

His eyes shift toward the floor before he answers, the confidence of a moment ago blown away as if on a sudden gust of wind. "I guess I'm just hoping that we won't see much fighting. They aren't prepped like they expect an attack. Why would anyone attack a penal colony guardhouse? Maybe they'll just have a couple of personnel . . ."

"We can hope, right? But just in case, maybe you should stay on ship with Venus. No one else can do what you can. You'll probably be the most help to us on the move and with access to the ship's com equipment."

He looks at me sideways, his large eyes limned with emotion, either gratitude or relief. Or both. Then he says, "About Cross . . ."

"Doesn't matter," I cut in. "You did what made sense to you, and that's a good way to stay not dead. No harm done."

A knock pings against the hatch, and I look over to see Vitruzzi. She opens the door and comments, "We're only ten hours from KL. What's the status on the drone override?"

"I'm there. Just point the transponder in the right direction and give it a boost. Everything within a couple hundred klicks will get zapped. We should try to get as close to the platform as possible in order to hit anything they have on reserve down there. Nothing outside that range should be picking us up anyway, so they'll all continue their normal routines without ever knowing we've been there."

She nods and manages to look almost pleased. "That's excellent. Good job, Jeremy."

"V," La Mer says, "I'm wondering where you want me when you go down into the substructure."

She sees the fear in his eyes and smiles at him softly. "We need you here, on the *Sphynx*. In fact"—she looks at me—"the ship's never going to sit down. We'll take the shuttle in. I've already told Venus to cover us while we make the descent. Once we hit the platform, she'll stay in flight until she hears from me or Brady. We don't know what might happen down there, but if the ship gets locked down, we're all fucked. You two can manage the ship and keep the drones under control from a reasonable distance."

It's a good plan, even though we'll be sitting on each other's laps inside the shuttle until we hit ground. I ask, "How close do we need to be to the colony until you can read the Beachers' tracking implants?"

I don't need to say it aloud, but if none of the devices are transmitting, it's either because the colonists aren't there or their bodies aren't outputting enough energy to keep the devices active. Because they're dead.

"They have a fifty-K range."

I nod. "Any word from Quantum or T'Kai?"

"Nothing," she answers, her voice clipped. She turns back to La Mer. "Do what you have to to make sure that program works, then try and get some sleep. This is it."

This is it.

THIRTY-TWO

"Where the fuck did it come from?!" David yells as Venus forces the ship into a hard left bank and starts to climb.

"I don't know, but it's not a drone," Karl says, his eyes not wavering from the command camera feed linked to his VDU.

I watch mine just as intently as I grip the crisscrossing bars along the armory door a level down from David, my body tensing in anticipation of the next shearing turn. The Corps ship chasing us had come out of nowhere after we broke through KL's atmosphere; our radar never even picked it up. The drone program worked just as La Mer had said it would, and we were minutes outside of reaching the oceanic landing platform, planning on doing a NAP of the earth flyover of the island colony before setting down. Venus began evasive maneuvering the second the *Sphynx*'s secondary sonic pressure wave sensors detected a higher than normal reading coming from above us, but none of us were ready for it.

The ship may have followed us from orbit, or it may have picked us up from somewhere else on the planet. Either way, it came at us so suddenly that no one had a chance to get to the lockdown seats. We'd all been in the cargo bay, getting ready to deploy, when Venus's reflexes thrust the ship into instant pandemonium. As far as I can tell, no one is injured, but we've been thrown around like loose cannonballs. Vitruzzi and Brady made for the cockpit as fast as they could while the rest of us try to get our bearings in the hold.

"Desto, what's going on in the fire control room?" Brady asks, using the onboard com system.

"I'm in position, but I can't get a lock with the way Venus is juggling sky. Can we get on a straight path for a minute?" His voice is calm, almost detached, a freakish counterpoint to the danger.

I look around and see Rob inching for the shuttle's hatch. He has a good idea; we need to be prepared to detach at a moment's notice. The shuttle can't go anywhere while the ship is flying this erratically, but there's a chance Venus can get enough of a lead to let us deploy.

"It's locked on. If I stop for a second, it'll have its chance. Can't let that happen." Venus responds. And then, as an afterthought: "Everyone okay down there?"

Karl lets her know we're all in the green, and the ship goes down in a hard dive that makes my stomach shoot into my mouth and my feet leave the floor.

"Fuck!"

"Get in the shuttle, everyone!" Rob yells. He's at the shuttle airlock but can't activate the hatch without the keycode.

The ship's crazy gyrations halt long enough for me to let go of the armory door and start making my way along the wall toward him, using everything I can get my hands on as a life preserver. David and Karl do the same.

"Desto," I try to warn him, "we're getting inside the shuttle. Can you—?" The target lock siren begins to blare, overriding my voice.

"Brace yourselves! Brace for impact!" Venus screams, and the ship veers sharply.

The missile doesn't impact, but explodes close enough to our port side that I can feel the entire ship suddenly shift laterally through the sky, as if on rails. The alarm continues and the craft shudders violently. I fall flat against the floor and feel every vibration through my skin, rattling my bones, my organs, even my eyeballs. I pull my wrist VDU up against my mouth and try to call for a damage report, but my throat has locked tight against the hammering tremors. My heartbeat is an electric hum inside my chest, and I pray that it doesn't get into lockstep rhythm with the ship and burst through my ribcage.

"Stupid-sons-a-scumbag-bastards, they didn't even hail us! Just started firing. Come here, boys, I'll give you a show you'll never forget." Venus doesn't realize she's broadcasting, but it helps us prepare for another bone-crushing maneuver. The hull's vibrations abruptly fade away, and we start climbing at an impossibly acute right bank. If there is damage, it hasn't hindered the *Sphynx*'s maneuvering capabilities.

The climb goes on and on and my fingers are losing their hold in the deck. The floor starts to slope away steeply over my shoulder. We're moving too erratically for the grav stabilizer to keep up. If my grip fails, I'll slide into the opposite wall, sixty meters away, at a speed that is guaranteed to splinter at least my legs and maybe everything. The angle grows sharper and my full weight hangs on the last joints of my fingers. I can't let go to grab the tie-down anchors that line the walls. My fingers shriek in pain as I crimp them harder, and then the ship suddenly arcs forward and settles into a relatively flat plane. It happens so quickly that my body is momentarily suspended a few centimeters above the floor, the sudden change in direction doing what the climb couldn't and popping my fingers free of the deck. There's still enough angle that I begin to skid anyway, flipping over to try and get my feet in front of me. My hand is suddenly grabbed, and Karl pulls me up off the floor to the safety of the wall.

"You okay?" he yells into my ear, his voice echoing the chaos around us.

After a pause to catch my breath, I reply, "Yeah, I'm okay." His arm circles my waist and he holds me tightly against him. I turn my head, and our faces are centimeters apart. His eyes drill into mine, and the feelings I thought he'd lost spill out as if his soul had cracked apart.

"I'm okay, you can let me go," I whisper.

Instead, his grip tightens for a moment. "I'll never let you go, Aly. Not again. I'm going to make sure you're safe." Then he releases his hold and staggers toward the shuttle's airlock.

"Where are you going?" I ask, getting a death grip on the wall as Venus makes another sudden evasion.

Karl white knuckles a pipe running next to the airlock and opens the hatch. "I'm going to get rid of them. This is the only way." He opens all channels on his VDU. "Desto, I'm taking the shuttle. Give me some cover. Venus, get us level for a few seconds. I'll release and draw him off. Climb out of range and drop down behind him. Then blow that motherfucker to pieces. Do you copy?"

Without waiting for an answer, he pushes by Rob and jumps into the shuttle. The hatch closes before anyone can move to help him, or stop him.

Vitruzzi's voice comes over the com: "Karl, don't be crazy. We need the shuttle."

"It won't do anyone any good if we all go down. If I can divert him off our tail, you'll be able to get some distance and surprise him. I'll have a better chance of evading him in the shuttle, and we can rendezvous at the platform after you punch his ticket. Venus, try to keep her flat for release—in five . . . four . . . three . . . two . . . release."

I let go of the wall as he breaks free and let the ship's momentum carry me to the cargo deck porthole. Pressing my forehead against it, I catch sight of the shuttle as it drops back. Karl engages the forward thrusters and elevates directly into the path of the ship chasing us. It's a Corps skiff, used for high-speed stealth reconnaissance. They aren't often deployed for enemy engagement, so its weapons payload will be minimal. They move fast and cover a lot of ground, making them unlikely to be seen on radar. But this one's seen us, and now we have to deal with the likelihood that reinforcements have been called. How long until they get here?

Venus glides the *Sphynx* up into another steep climb, letting Karl pass below us. I'm pushed against the rear hatch with what feels like the weight of an elephant on my back, but not before seeing the skiff take the bait. As far as it knows, we're not armed, and if we're hiding something, we'd likely have jettisoned it in our shuttle. I lose sight of them quickly as the *Sphynx* rises above the clouds, levels off, and decelerates.

"Venus, get back down there! Follow him!" I yell through my VDU. I should be trying to stay calm, but gut-wrenching helplessness turns my voice into a strained warble.

She doesn't respond, but the ship begins to slide smoothly through the air in a controlled descent. "Desto, get ready. You're on," Venus says. The command feed coming through my VDU is scratchy with interference from the skiff's backdraft.

"Missile released," Desto says.

Flames engulf the VDU screen in a high intensity wash of red, yellow, and green, and Desto shouts in victory. Venus rocks the ship carefully, skimming around debris, then comes back to bear on the same trajectory the shuttle had taken. I hold my breath waiting for Karl to transmit his status. In a second, we catch his tail, but something is drastically wrong. The shuttle cants at a dangerous left angle, the thrusters spurting erratic jets of fire. I can't tell if he was fragged by the skiff's wreckage or took a hit. As we approach, the shuttle begins descending in a steep arc straight for the unforgiving surface of the ocean.

Scrambling for the hold's transmitter, I say, "Karl, pull up, you're coming in too hot. The shuttle can't maintain that rate of descent. Do you read?" If he keeps diving like that, there won't be time for the reverse thrusters to slow him down enough to avoid a catastrophic collision. I don't let myself think about the possibility that he might have no control over the thrusters anyway.

There's no response and no change in the shuttle's course. Venus starts to ease the *Sphynx* off for the same reason Karl should be slowing the shuttle. The *Sphynx* will need more time to decelerate, and in a few more seconds we'll lose visual contact. I try again. "Karl, do you read? You need to pull back. Over."

Still nothing. Panic sinks ice cold fangs into my heart. "Strahan! Goddammit, acknowledge. Slow your rate of descent. At least try!" The ship melts into a cloudbank and disappears with no sign of a course change. Frantic, I yell, "Venus, keep on his ass! Do not lose him!"

"Aly, we can't—" Rob says as he comes up beside me.

I cut him off. "I know we have to pull back, but we can keep him in range. I want to know where he hits."

The *Sphynx* floats through the clouds, Venus gradually cutting her speed until we're only about a klick above deck. We come out of the cloudbank looking into a grayish-green expanse of water, small whitecaps dotting the horizon to the edge of my sight. A speck that can only be the shuttle is a short distance away, still hurtling toward the water like a dart. In no time, its silhouette blends into the spray below it.

"Strahan! Karl! Acknowledge!" I'm screaming into the transmitter.

We approach out of the north and are greeted by a thick cloud of curdled steam being greedily snatched up by a crosswind where the shuttle went down. My mouth dries up. Venus drops us into a slow glide. Everything around me seems to freeze solid, even the passage of time. Finally, she brings us in range, and I see what I most feared. The ship fell hard, slamming into the water and fracturing into debris on impact. Sheered metal and parts scatter over the surface, sinking fast. Jets of fire can be seen underwater, components still exploding inside the wreck.

Through a fog, I hear Vitruzzi over the VDU. "Pull us up closer and skim slowly over the surface in the immediate area. We need a better look."

"Vitruzzi, if you plan on doing anything else today, it would be wise to get to the platform ASAP." Rajcik says over the intercom. "That skiff made us. It's only a matter of time before more Corps arrive. Besides, your shuttle looks like a total loss."

I feel my body in motion before any conscious thought happens. We're hovering about five meters over the wreck and the metal hull is still visible suspended beneath the surface. Swinging my carbine strap over my back, I reach out and grasp the hatch's handle, torque it open hard, and hurl myself out. Instead of falling, I'm grabbed by my equipment belt, yanked backward, and shoved against the wall.

"Aly! Don't be insane! You can't do anything for him." Rob, his eyes wide and alarmed, uses his weight to keep me pinned.

"Let go of me! We have to help!" I struggle with him, but he holds my arms rigidly against my body in a bear hug.

Burning, chemical-tasting air rushes into the cargo hold. "Someone get the door!" he yells, and the sharp reek is choked off as Mason pulls the hatch to.

I struggle against Rob, straining to get free, but the ship suddenly banks hard. Gravity shifts direction, pulling us to the floor while Mason grasps whatever's nearest to avoid being thrown through the hold.

"Venus is taking us back to the platform. There's nothing we can do for him." Vitruzzi's voice comes through the com system, defeated and dead sounding.

I yank an arm free and scream into my VDU, "No! What does his tracker say?"

There's a pause, long enough to give me hope. Then: "There's nothing."

Disbelief pummels me in the stomach, making me nauseous and shaky.

Rob pulls himself into a sitting position and lets go of me. "You'll get yourself killed too if you jump out there. You know he couldn't have survived that impact." He pauses, gauging the effect hearing the hard truth will have on me. When I don't flinch, he continues, "I'm sorry, Aly. I'm really sorry."

My eyes fall closed, as if darkness will hide the despair scrabbling through my soul.

THIRTY-THREE

A quick aerial sweep of the area confirms that we're alone for now, and Venus sets us down on the platform. Three drones locked on us after the skiff was destroyed, but none followed for more than a couple kilometers, their programming irrevocably scrambled. It's only a matter of a few hours, maybe less, before Corps ships arrive. Every second counts.

The ramp lowers and we move out in sweep positions, running in formation for the platform's only building, which must serve as an access point to the underwater structure. La Mer and Venus wait for us to get inside. They'll relaunch and stay airborne while we take care of business on the station, the plan unchanged except for the loss of the shuttle. I take right flank and run hunkered low, my mind blank and shut down to anything that's not going to keep me alive. Desto and Mason take right and left rear and David takes point with Rob near his right shoulder. Vitruzzi and Brady spread out in front of Mason, and Thompson and Rajcik are in front of me.

Gritty wisps of sea spray blow over the edges of the platform, cold against my bare cheeks. We're at least ten meters above the ocean's surface and the platform is stable against heavy seas and storms. The platform spreads north to south about the same length as the main cavern of Agate Beach's mine, and east to west about twice that distance. Venus landed within a short run from the access hut, and we're able to get out of the open quickly.

David reaches the entryway first, where a small alcove protects the door from the wind. The stock of his rifle remains planted against his shoulder as he takes a quick look around the corner, scanning for guards. When he determines it's all clear, he gives the signal to take a knee while he runs a keypad bypass to get us inside. I'm more than a little nervous about all of us being stuck on the same elevator to get below the surface, and I know I'm not the only one. But from what we can see, it's the only way in or out. If the elevator is destroyed, the station would be cut off from the surface for who knows how long, possibly even at risk of being breached by the relentless ocean. Knowing T'Kai's history of sacrificing whatever is necessary for his own benefit, the hope that anyone not wanting us here wouldn't dare destroy the elevator seems empty.

It's been too long. What's the hold up? As soon as I start to get up to find out, David leans back and waves us up. It only takes seconds for the crew to reach the entrance and pile through to the room inside, leaving Mason to stay back and keep a visual on the platform. No guards are in the access room, and David and I exchange a worried look. Where is everyone?

The room is large and utilitarian. One wall is lined with communication consoles and monitors, all dark and powered down, and a thick steel sub-bay gate above the elevator shaft covers a wide section of the floor. The gate looks strong enough to resist anything from a small nuclear explosion to a minor volcanic eruption— probably designed to guard against an accident or explosion below the surface from traveling up the shaft and decimating the control room. David and Brady immediately get busy on the consoles figuring out how to operate the elevator.

Outwardly, I'm nervous and unsettled, but something worse than mission anxiety looms just behind it. Something frightening and deadly that's creeping up on me like a tsunami on the distant ocean, a huge wave that's traveling too fast to run from. *Karl's dead.* I haven't allowed the thought to creep into my consciousness, but it lies in wait within that wave. When it reaches me, I'll be crushed and I'll drown.

I glance toward Rob. He stands by the entryway keeping an eye on the outside with Mason until we can get the elevator running. For a split second, a barely containable urge to aim my carbine at his skull and blow it off surges through me. Jesus, what's wrong with me? Nothing that's happened is his fault. The only one I can blame is me.

"What's the problem?" Thompson asks David, his tone tight and abrupt. Judging from the rising level of tension in the room, the lid could blow off any minute. Why isn't there any security? Everyone's eyes are lit up with hot intensity. Death and danger are nothing new to us, and no one has any false illusions about the probable outcome of this mission. The deaths of both Karl and Bodie just bring everyone that much closer to bursting apart at the seams.

There's a clicking sound followed by a deep vibrating hum beneath our feet that makes me jump.

"It's on its way," David informs us.

We take firing positions, bracing for a security crew to greet us. Hydraulic safety bars open around the gate perimeter, coming to rest vertically like teeth. Finally, the humming stops and yellow lights begin flashing on the corners of the railing surrounding the gate as it slides open. We're looking down at the roof of the elevator, thick and solid. When it's clear, the elevator rises all the way and comes to rest at floor level. There's no sound inside the control room.

"Open it," Brady directs.

David activates something on the console and the doors slide open. Exposing emptiness.

I glance at David again and we both shrug at the same time.

"What the fuck is going on?" Thompson asks no one in particular.

"Maybe they have it rigged to gas us when we get inside," Desto offers, and I throw him a dark look.

"Rajcik, any ideas?" Vitruzzi asks.

He turns toward her, his face expressionless, and shakes his head slowly. Vitruzzi hesitates and exchanges a look with Brady. None of us are in a hurry to get inside. It's nothing but a box with no way out once it starts to descend.

"Shit," Brady mutters. "Okay, everyone inside except Mason and Thompson. You two keep watch. Monitor topside coms, and get down there if we call you."

"I'm not staying up here," Thompson says.

He glares at him. "Yes. You are."

Thompson scowls and looks toward Rajcik, who gestures for him to sit tight. He hunches out toward the entrance and joins Mason.

"Let's go," Vitruzzi says and steps aboard.

It's hot inside the elevator, but there's more than enough room for all of us and we spread out. A touch screen is mounted on one wall, and David steps up and slides his fingers along the activation bar. The doors close and a basic structural schematic showing three levels flashes onto the screen. The first is labeled "Vessel Dock," the next is "In-processing," and the final is labeled "Research." A shudder runs through me. A lab, here, at a penal colony. I don't have to wonder what that means.

"Take us to the bottom," Brady says, his voice thick with either rage or something close to derangement as he reacts to the schematic.

David swipes the screen and a female voice says, "Enter the security clearance code."

He turns around, eyes wide and uncertain. "I'm not sure how to override this. I thought I had it at the control console."

Vitruzzi activates her VDU. "La Mer, do you copy?"

A few seconds later, La Mer's voice comes through, but it's choppy. " . . . here . . . every . . . okay . . . over."

"Must be distance," Desto says.

Vitruzzi grimaces and tries another tactic, this time using the elevator intercom. "Doug, come in."

Mason responds immediately, "Mason here."

"Get in touch with La Mer. Ask him if Quantum gave him anything that might be an elevator control code."

"Roger. Wait one."

The seven of us wait tensely as the minutes pass by, pressure building with all the force of tectonic plates in a subduction zone. The schematic fades from the screen after a few seconds, but it might as well be burned onto my retinas. Desto stands in front of me and sweat begins to bead up on his thick neck and run down between his shoulders beneath his heavy body armor. I wipe my hands against my pant leg; I don't want them to be slippery if shooting starts. The wind outside blew my hair helter-skelter and I brush the tangles out of my eyes, feeling bits of damp spray still clinging to them. The waiting becomes interminable.

"V, do you copy?" Mason, finally.

"Go ahead."

"He said he found a master security code, but he's not sure it'll work for the elevator."

"We'll take it."

"Okay, here it is." As he reads it off, David reengages the touch screen and repeats the string of numbers and letters into the voice console. I pull a marker out of my equipment vest and hastily write the code on the inside of my wrist. When he's done, he asks Vitruzzi, "Which level?"

Before anyone answers, Mason clicks back on. "Hey!" His voice is more excited than I've ever heard it. "Venus says she picked up active tracker feeds."

"Hallel-goddamn-ujah," Desto says. "That kid is a genius."

Breathlessly, Vitruzzi cries, "How many?"

"She says it looks like everyone. All of them."

"Take us to the docks. Now," Brady orders.

Finally, some good news. David makes the pick and the clicking sound we'd heard earlier repeats, this time much louder. The lift starts down.

In less than a minute, we come to a smooth stop. Before David opens the doors, Vitruzzi says, "Okay. Keep low, move fast. Don't make yourself a target. We can't get locked down in here. Aly and Rajcik, take point."

Suddenly I remember something. "Wait, don't open it yet."

David's nerves sizzle almost audibly, and he responds with a short, "What?"

I reach into another pouch on my vest and show them what I have.

"What the . . . Aly, did you take that from the *'Rize*?" Rob knows immediately what's in my hand.

I don't look directly at him, feeling a touch of embarrassment at my thievery, but it turns out it was a good idea. "This is a holographic imager," I explain to the others. "It can hide us behind a fake projection of the inside of the elevator when the doors open. Whoever's in there won't be able to see us through the image, and we can get a fix on the room. Then surprise them."

Rob is annoyed, but the others are quick to adopt the plan and we set up the cloak.

When it's ready, Rajcik and I move up against the opposite side of the doors, our actions coordinated from long practice. As much as we've come to hate each other, we still retain the survival instincts that once made us a good team. Before he tried to kill me. For a second, he looks me in the eye as the doors slide open: *Are you ready*? I nod.

The doors stop. And—nothing. Just more silence. Simultaneously, we lean out to get a snapshot of what lies outside.

We've arrived at a belowdecks boathouse underneath the main platform. A dock extends directly from the elevator over placid water, one side flanked by a squat, flat, open-top cargo carrier with a covered steering booth and not much else. The other side of the dock is empty.

The rest of the bay is dark, but there are no other visible structures or watercraft. "Looks clear," I comment, stepping forward.

The rest file out, Rob hesitating long enough to pocket his projector. The local personnel must use the cargo ships to transport people to and from land. Thick walls drop from the edges of the platform overhead and disappear below the surface of the water at some depth we can't make out. The entire space is barely illuminated; the only light coming from inset lighting tracks that extend to the end of the dock and from within the elevator itself. I move at a jog to the end of the pier to get a better idea of what there is and Rob follows at an interval behind me. We arrive at the end without incident, no spotlights flashing on or gunfire breaking the silence. The boat bay is just as uninhabited as topside. Brady and Rajcik climb cautiously aboard the carrier and do a quick pass. They locate the hold controls and open it up. No one's below.

Confused, nervous, and ready for a more complete picture of the space, I turn on my scope light and sweep it around.

"Hey, Rob. A submersible." I wave my light over the craft's sleek hull where it floats at the dock's terminus, its hatch a few steps down a short ladder.

He gives it a quick look and says, "No, too small. Looks like a recon or scout sub. We couldn't get everyone aboard."

"True, but—"

Before I finish the thought, Vitruzzi uses the elevator intercom to call Mason and ask him to find the controls to open the launch-bay doors, then grab Thompson and meet us down here. We need them on the island more than guarding the platform. Within a minute, the giant bay doors rumble open and suffuse the chamber with outside light. The elevator disappears, returning with Thompson and Mason.

As we wait, Brady tells the rest of us, "We'll take the carrier to the penal colony. We should be able to find the settlers quickly and get back here and off this rock."

"Did they evacuate the whole complex because they saw us coming?" Thompson wonders aloud. "That could mean they're waiting for us on land. Or, who knows, maybe they went over there to pick up some fresh meat." He must have read the levels schematic, too.

"We'll know soon enough," David says.

Rajcik had sketched out what else he knew about the prisoner colony on our way from Letum Uti. When he was here, there were two main housing barracks, each six stories tall with plumbing and electricity. They desalination plant also fed a turbine generator that provided power. The prisoners mostly stayed within the complex, but with almost no security oversight or controls, many had ranged afield and set up pseudo-tribal factions that vied against each other for whatever they could get. There had been around six hundred other inmates on the island, the most hardened and violent men and women the system had produced. Problem is, like Rajcik said, it's been twenty years since he was a prisoner here. The hard truth is, we have no idea how many people besides the Beachers we can expect to encounter on the rock. The more of us there are, and the more hardware we bring, the less interference we should encounter while we search.

But there is something else I have to do.

As the crew loads aboard the carrier, I lag behind. Rob, sensing my hesitation, turns to me, his eyebrows steepled questioningly. "We better get going," he says.

"I'm not coming."

He snorts with a tinge of irritation. "What do you mean?"

The others turn to look at me, surprised.

"It's only been forty-five minutes since the shuttle went down. He could still be out there. I have to know," I try to explain, but I can see that I don't have to. Not to them.

Rob walks back onto the dock, his deep brown eyes filled with concern. "Aly, look. I get it. You were in love with him"—he puts a hand on my elbow, exerting the slightest pull—"but there's no way he survived."

I take a small step back and let his hand slide off my arm. "You're right, Rob. I did love him. And I still do. I'm taking the sub. Please, just let me go."

His mouth curls downward in a frown, and he glances back over his shoulder at the others. Then he moves closer to me, speaking in a whisper that only I can hear, "Aly, if you go out there, I may not be able to help you."

He's so sincere that I feel like I must be misunderstanding something. Does he mean that if I choose Karl, there's no life for me as a citizen? The choice is easier than I would have expected. "It's okay. I understand."

David starts to walk toward us, and I put up a hand to stop him. "It's all right. It shouldn't take me long. I'll meet you at the colony dock."

"Can we get the hell out of here?" Thompson asks.

Rob doesn't say another word, but I see the dark flames of anger burning behind his eyes. He turns around and steps aboard the carrier.

THIRTY-FOUR

As the engine powers up, I load the shuttle's crash coordinates into the sub's nav-system. The sub cycles through a maintenance and safety checklist and prompts me to activate detachment when all readouts are green. There are no portholes to see into the water outside, but the front half of the cockpit is embedded with screens video-linked to exterior cameras, every image enhanced to achieve perfect clarity. After diving a short distance, it begins to propel backward toward the crash site, its design negating any need to turn around.

Sub training is part of every Academy student's routine, but it's been at least ten years since I'd been in one and I'd forgotten the feeling of being underwater in a tiny tin can. Human perceptions aren't developed enough to detect the difference between pressurized, climate-controlled interstellar versus underwater crafts, yet my senses are alight with anxiety, my innate fear of tight places making even my skin feel as if it's shrinking over my muscles, choking me. I'd rather not know it, but even the smallest breach of the hull will quickly lead to an implosion, letting billions of gallons of crushing water obliterate me. Something about that sounds much worse than having my blood boil out of my pores in the middle of space.

The sub moves as soundlessly and smoothly as a ray and I arrive at the wreckage site in under twenty minutes. The video-link shows nothing but black empty water. I raise it above deck and activate the long-range radar, searching the area for anything still above water, hoping Karl was able to get free of the shuttle and find something to float on while waiting for a rescue. The scan shows nothing. I force the craft into a steep dive until the pressure gauge blinks a warning and auto-adjusts the speed to keep me from descending too fast. Within moments, it comes to a stop and a voice from the console tells me I'll have to don the onboard pressure-control suit if I want to continue. Frustrated, I quickly slide into the suit. It's stiff and much too bulky to allow optimal freedom of movement, and I won't be able to grasp my carbine—not that I'd want to shoot anything down here.

Another three thousand meters and the video-link scans the ocean floor, but I'm no longer looking. Karl is dead. There's no sign of the wreckage; underwater currents must have swept it away.

It's useless to search. Even if he survived the crash but was stuck inside, he'd have died long before he got this deep. Tears burn my eyes and slide down my cheeks, a flood of pain and anguished guilt. Why had I been so stubborn? Why hadn't I ever told him how I felt? What the fuck is wrong with me?

Staring unseeing at the control panel, I cry until my eyes feel like overheated ball bearings, until they go dry and rub my sockets raw. The suit holds me erect, keeping my sagging body from spilling bonelessly onto the floor. Time passes, I don't know how long, and I consider what would happen to me if I took the suit off and let the sub resurface. The agony of nitrous bubbles stabbing through my blood, skin, and bones would almost be welcome as long as it could overcome the torment I feel in my soul. What had Karl felt? Was he still conscious when he hit the water? God, I hope it had been quick.

But I'm not ready to die. There are people here who can maybe still be helped. David would never forgive me. And there's T'Kai. Above all else, he's behind everything, the reason everything has gone to shit. I finally understand Rajcik's rage, and like him, it makes me want to live long enough to see T'Kai squashed and bleeding like an insect beneath my boot heel. Quantum should be transmitting in another day, if he hasn't already, and I plan to convince Vitruzzi to go back to Obal 10 and watch the Admin deconstruct from the inside.

Pulling it together, I reengage the sub's controls, letting it rise to a shallower elevation and deadhead toward the island. On the way, I set one of the console arrays to cycle through feeds from the multiple scanners installed throughout the platform and subcomplex, wanting to be warned if watercraft or aircraft arrive. It shouldn't take more than half an hour to get there, and I begin playing with the sub's transmitter to try and notify the crew I'm on my way. An image flashing on the scanner console catches my eye and makes my lungs lock around my breath. There's another ship landing on the platform, and it looks familiar. It's the *Red Horizon.*

Confused, alert, and prepared for anything, I alter course to pass closer to the platform. What the hell is the *'Rize* doing here?

Anxiously, I watch the bioreadouts on the pressure suit, itching to get out of it and back in control. As soon as I have the green light, I shed it and jack the sub's speed up a few knots, all the while keeping my eyes locked on the cycling video feed. The ship sits quietly, none of the hatches opening. And then the feed shows something else unexpected: the *Sphynx* is coming in to land, too.

What's going on? Did they find the settlers already? The fire racing through my nerve endings warns me that isn't it. I try the com console again but nothing happens. It's either broken or being jammed, and I can't pick up or send anything. I'm only a minute or two from the platform and I have to make a blind decision—get to land or find out why Venus and the *'Rize* have docked.

I reach the docking bay and kill the sub. If Venus and La Mer are in trouble, right now I might the only one who can help. Steering the sub to its magnetic anchor point, I scramble out and onto the pier. The elevator is still where we left it. Saying the code I'd written on my arm, I bring my carbine up to firing position and prepare for the doors to open topside. Fleetingly, I wish I'd taken the cloaking projector back from Rob, then let the thought fade into oblivion. It doesn't matter what I wish.

The lift comes to a stop and I open the doors. The control room is just as we'd left it. Empty. Carefully, I make my way toward the exit, listening for the sound of footsteps or a ramp opening, but I can't hear anything over the wind. A quick look outside shows both ships still sealed. Backing up into the alcove, I try to contact Venus through my VDU. Nothing but silence from her end, so I try Vitruzzi. Same issue.

Seconds tick by as I try to imagine what could be happening. There's only one reason Venus would have landed; someone from the crew hailed her. Yet, my gut and the unexpected presence of the *'Rize* tell me something else is going on, something not part of the plan. Something wrong.

The longer I hesitate, the worse the scenarios I imagine become. It comes almost as a relief when the cargo ramp on the *'Rize* opens and four sets of legs begin to descend. A second later, they're in full view standing at the bottom of the ramp.

With another glance around the edge of the alcove's protective wall, I recognize T'Kai immediately though he's shorter than I'd pictured, barely a few centimeters taller than me. He stands in front of Venus and La Mer, both standing with their hands linked behind their heads, eyes cast down. Rob's crewmember, Baker, is a few steps behind, a carbine pointing at their kidneys.

T'Kai looks in the direction of the control room and calls, his voice malicious and all business. "Come out where I can see you, Ms. Erikson. You're friends should also be along shortly."

I don't believe it. Thompson had been right. Rob's crew is Admin. We've been betrayed.

"I've got a bead on you, T'Kai. Let them go or you'll take one in the heart. I won't miss at this range."

His expression doesn't change. "Your pilot and wire-rat deserter friend will be next. You don't want to cause their deaths, do you? No, of course not. Now, I'll give you five seconds to come here. And be smart. Keep your weapons in a neutral position."

Too enraged to even speak, all I can do is what I'm told, not doubting for a second that the bitch Baker will happily fill Venus and La Mer with holes if I give her a reason. I approach holding my AK-80 and Sinbad by their barrels at arm's length.

"Very good. Soldier, take those from her," T'Kai orders Baker.

For a moment, I consider ending everything right here. All I have to do is raise the 'Bad, pull the trigger, and T'Kai is done. Then, so are my friends and I.

I reach the group and stand stiffly in front of Baker. She sneers at me, a look that reflects my own loathing for her, and motions for me to drop my weapons. I do it. She pushes them back toward the ramp with her feet without taking her eyes from mine.

T'Kai walks to my Sinbad, picking it up and turning it over in his hands thoughtfully, noting the disabled ID reader. Putting it into the waist of his pants, he leans toward me and speaks close to my ear. "You see. It's people like you that make the work I do necessary." He steps away and nods at Baker.

She demands, "Everyone, on your knees. Hands stay up."

I get down and tilt my head to Venus. Her eyes are wide and scared, but she seems to be staying calm. "Are you two okay?"

She nods.

"How did they get the *Sphynx*?"

Baker shoves her carbine's barrel sharply into my cheek. "Shut the fuck up."

Rage surges through my veins, and I have to clench my fists into tight balls and dig my nails into my palms to keep from jumping up and strangling her.

"Ah, here they come," T'Kai says.

The rest of my crew is filing out of the control room, their weapons held in the same manner as mine. No one is with them forcing them to surrender, but they know if they don't, Venus, La Mer, and I are dead. As they approach, I hear footsteps coming down the *'Rize'*s ramp behind me. Montoya and Sims?

T'Kai continues talking. "Come, join your comrades. That's right, down on your knees."

"What kind of rotten fuck salad is this?" Desto asks as he drops down beside me.

I catch David's eyes. He doesn't have to say anything; I know what he's thinking. There are only three of them, plus T'Kai. How many more on the *Sphynx*?

We're forced into a semicircle at T'Kai's feet, but Rajcik refuses to kneel. He stands a little in front of us, towering over the director, his bulkiness shielding the smaller man almost completely from sight. The muscles in Rajcik's shoulders bulge through his shirt, tension and rage making him seem even larger.

"Here I am, T'Kai."

The director's eyes crease into slits, Rajcik's insolence and complete lack of fear souring his brute disdain. It only lasts for a moment. Then he smiles, his lips splitting apart grotesquely, like the skin of an overripe tomato.

"Yes. So clever of you to have evaded me this long, János." He takes a sliding step backward, and Sims moves up beside him with his gun leveled at Rajcik's stomach. "I've been very curious how you figured out that I would no longer be needing your services."

"You mean how I figured out you were going to kill me?" Rajcik grunts derisively. "It's what I would have done."

T'Kai blows air through his nose in an expression that suggests he laments having to speak to a simpleton. "You've wasted a great deal of my time, Rajcik. Can you possibly not understand that the resources at my disposal are *unlimited*? I *am* the Admin, or all of it that matters. And you—nothing but a speck of dust. *You* betrayed *me* when you stole the Nova, and the punishment you're about to receive is justly deserved."

The inside of my throat turns to sand at T'Kai's words. Did he say Rajcik had stolen the Nova? Stricken disbelief causes me to blurt without thinking, "The Nova's been destroyed. Rajcik detonated it inside the Fortress and blew the whole place apart."

The director nods at Montoya, who stands to the side of the group. He walks up and jams the butt of his rifle into the back of Rajcik's right thigh. The smuggler's leg buckles, sending him to one knee with a snarl.

T'Kai's eyes shift to me, their strange colors unnerving. "The remains of the space station showed only nuclear residue. I've no doubt you detonated something"—they slide back to Rajcik—"but it was not the Nova. You covered your tracks very, very well. However, it was your former crewmember, Ms. Erikson, that led me straight to you at R'Kadia, and I was able to recover the weapon."

Rajcik looks to where I kneel, his lips drawn back in a predatory grimace, but I return the stare with nothing but confusion. "I don't know what you're talking about," I say. "I didn't even know he was alive."

"You didn't have to know to still be of use. Our mutual friend brought us all together. And that, Ms. Erikson, is how you led me to Rajcik." His leathery skin wrinkles around his mouth and eyes in a reptilian smile, but I'm no longer paying attention to him. The only mutual "friend" he could be talking about . . .

My body jerks around, looking for Rob, but he's no longer seated behind me. He stands next to Montoya, a pistol in his right hand. From the corner of my eye, I see David's face contort into a kind of anguished spasm. It was *him* who had betrayed us. It was Rob all along. The word *sonofabitch* drop from David's lips like a blood spatter.

"Rob?" My throat contracts and turns my voice into a squeak. "What the hell is going on?"

His eyes barely meet mine before skittering away again and he says, "C'mon, Aly. You know I only gamble on winners."

"You motherfuck—" Thompson begins, rising from his knees, but the flat of Montoya's rifle butt against his teeth ends it.

I'm stunned, shaking with anger and something else, a deep, writhing feeling in the pit of my stomach. I wouldn't, *couldn't*, have ever believed he'd be capable of this. I whisper, "You turned us in," needing to hear it aloud for confirmation,

Bored with the spectacle, T'Kai turns and waves at the cockpit of the *Sphynx*. Shortly afterward, two more men walk down the ramp and join the others. Rob walks around and stands next to the director. The carefree grin he's always worn is scoured from his face, replaced with carefully crafted neutrality, like an automaton.

Rajcik spits, disgusted, but also amused. "Even I'm impressed, Cross. You had everyone fooled. I can see Aly being blinded by her own gullibility, but I don't know how you sold her brother on your bullshit. Bravo."

"I'm happy you're so impressed. Now shut the hell up."

"Right, or you'll shoot me, is that it?" The two men lock eyes, neither flinching.

For the first time, Vitruzzi speaks: "T'Kai, you have us. Arrest us, do what you want. But the settlers having nothing to do with any of this. Just let them go."

"Dr. Vitruzzi, surely you realize by now that there is nowhere left for them *to* go." He stares at her quietly for a moment, waiting for a comeback, but Vitruzzi falls silent.

"Where do you want them?" Baker asks.

T'Kai nods in the direction of the platform's edge. "Over there. Let them fall into the water and the tides will clean up. Mr. Cross"—he turns to face the Judas—"please prep your ship for takeoff. We'll be returning to Tunis. And notify my private dock of our estimated arrival on"—he looks at a display on his wrist—"Wednesday."

Rob climbs the *'Rize*'s ramp. Before he reaches the top, I yell, "You made the biggest mistake of your life, Rob! You'll pay for this!"

He stops for a second but doesn't turn around, then disappears inside.

"Get up," Baker grunts, jerking me by the collar and trying to push me toward the edge. I don't budge, and she jams her rifle butt into my kidney. The pain is sharp and immediate, helping to redirect my fury back to the here and now.

We're prodded and jostled and finally lined up along the edge of the platform. There is no railing. I glance down into the water before being spun around to face our captors. It's far, probably far enough to break my neck. Is a bullet preferable?

In a tone that's nearly pleasant, as if she's explaining a minor surgical procedure to a patient, Vitruzzi says, "T'Kai, you may kill us, but you'll still go down."

He and the five shooters are lined up in front of us, the salty wind whipping everyone's hair and clothes. "You're referring to those wire-rats, aren't you? Cross filled us in, and we wiped that slate clean a couple of days ago. Such wasted talent. But then, the damage sending that information to the public would have caused—it might have had a highly negative impact on the Administration. Dr. Vitruzzi, you have no idea how important the work I do is. One would think that a scientist of your caliber . . . but I understand. Some minds are simply not capable of thinking beyond a very narrow set of parameters."

They'd gotten to Quantum. Just like that, my last bit of strength collapses, a desperate sense of defeat pushing my heart to the verge of quitting. The last hope we'd had, smashed in a firestorm by a maniacal psychopath with a God complex. I look down into the water and imagine how it will feel. A burst of pain, freezing cold; then, thank Christ, it will be all over.

Rajcik takes a slow step forward from the line until he's standing directly in front of T'Kai. Three guns swivel toward him instantly but have no effect on his smug grin. He levels his gleaming black eyes on the director.

Without turning around, he says, "Vitruzzi, my business with your crew is finished."

So quickly no one has a chance to react, he lunges toward T'Kai—and the world fills with the sound of gunfire. I drop down and hurl myself forward toward Baker, the will to survive still ruling me. She jumps back and I yank free my Mini-Derg—they hadn't searched us—firing at her, but she's too fast and I miss. Movement erupts in every direction; Mason and David charge Montoya. while Rajcik grapples with T'Kai, and Vitruzzi and Brady hurtle toward Sims and one of the other men from the *Sphynx.* Venus sinks her teeth into a soldier's arm, and La Mer is punching another one in the face furiously, trying to keep the man from aiming his carbine.

Baker lunges away and trips, landing on her back. I pounce, reaching for her weapon and getting a grip on its strap. I yank as hard as I can, but she's already lost her hold and it comes away much too freely, flying off over the platform's side and into the water. She jumps to her feet, dashing frantically toward the *'Rize*. I fire the Derg, missing her again. It's out of juice and useless now, and I throw it after her carbine in disgust.

As I push myself to my feet, something solid connects with my ear, and I immediately fall back. My eyes blur with water, a distant ringing beginning in my head. Pain radiates down my face, into my teeth, and deep into my jaw as I roll to my side. In the panicked melee, I can't tell who hit me. I put a hand down to get some purchase to push myself up again, and it slides through a wet, warm puddle, the coppery smell of blood bursting into my nostrils. A cavalcade of pistol shots ring out so close that I have to cover my ears. Then, it's quiet.

"Hey, Aly, you okay?" I look up into David's face as he reaches down and grabs my shirt, pulling me to my feet. He's bleeding from his bottom lip, and a dark red bruise sweeps across one cheekbone.

"Yeah. Okay. Baker took off, she's heading toward the *'Rize.'*" I pull myself to my feet and look around. Montoya is definitely dead. He's down on his stomach with his neck twisted at an angle that isn't natural. Two other soldiers also lie prone, with Desto standing above them holding his own recovered rifle. There's blood splashed around us like a slaughterhouse. But it's Rajcik that draws my attention.

He stands over T'Kai's still frame, his back to everyone. A thin trail of blood leaks into his shirt from a gash on his neck. The wound looks superficial, but the pool of blood growing beneath his feet tells a different story. He must have been struck by at least three or four bullets when he'd jumped T'Kai. He can't last long with the amount of blood he's losing.

I glance down at T'Kai's body, quickly looking away as my stomach does a nauseating flip. There is nothing left of his face but shredded bits of bone and oozing brain matter sticking out of his shirt collar. Rajcik had grabbed my 'Bad from T'Kai's belt and shot him over and over in the face, no doubt getting exactly the kind of revenge he'd planned and imagined. For better or worse, T'Kai has ceased to be an issue for us.

"Baker and Sims ran back to the *'Rize,*" David says, his breathing quick. "Rob's in there, too. We have to stop them from taking off."

Vitruzzi waves her arms at the two wounded soldiers. "Mason, tie them up. Watch them. Everyone else, let's go." She takes a step forward and then stops suddenly, bending over and gripping her side.

"Eleanor!" Brady grabs her gently, his face terror-filled.

She sucks air through her teeth. "It's okay, went through. Just hurts like a sonofabitch. Hand me my bag."

I bend down and pick it up. "What do you need?"

"You go get Cross. Venus, help me with this."

I exchange a look with Brady; it's clear that he's not leaving her side, so I nod at Mason, who joins the rest of us as we start a cautious ascent into the *'Rize*'s hold, picking up weapons as we go. Desto and Mason take a flight of stairs for the upper deck while David, Thompson, and I split up to cover the larger lower deck. I take a look back before going in and see Rajcik still standing like a gravestone over T'Kai's body. He doesn't budge.

THIRTY-FIVE

My first sweep takes me through an outer corridor that runs along the ship's left flank, serving mainly as a service tunnel for the engines and life-support components. As I cover the distance, I pass three or four narrow doorways and several service panels that are big enough for a person to fit inside. Cautiously, I flip open every one, listening for movement or breathing to verify if they're empty. When I find no one, I'm not surprised; Baker doesn't seem like the type who'll hide.

The corridor dead ends at a ladder leading to a ceiling hatch near the bow. I decide to turn back toward the hold instead of climbing it, hoping to meet up with another one of my crew. Whatever T'Kai's people had done to jam our VDU's, it's still in effect. The jammer must be aboard the 'Rize, probably somewhere on the flight control deck. Except for my footsteps, it's completely silent. Rob hasn't been able to start the engines yet. He must have heard the firefight outside and is lying low, setting up an ambush, planning to pick us off one by one instead of en masse.

My guts tighten up more each time the thought of his betrayal fires through my brain. How could he do this? He'd never been deceptive or malicious, never been the kind of person who'd sell his soul for profit or make a compromise that would fuck over his friends. He and David had practically been brothers. And he and I . . . I'd believed he cared about me. There had to be something, T'Kai must have threatened him . . . I don't know. And it doesn't matter, the results are the same. Rob betrayed me, betrayed *us*. There's only one way to resolve it.

I reach the door to the hold. Closed. I thought I'd left it open. Using the activation keypad, I try to open it, but nothing happens. I hit the button again and again, frustrated by its failure to cooperate, and finally give up. Shouldering my '80 on its strap, I grab the manual crank and begin pulling with all of my strength. The thing's locked up tighter than a hangman's noose. Grunting with the effort, it still doesn't move, and I begin to think I'll have to go back down to the ceiling hatch, when out of nowhere, it starts spinning. I jerk my hands out of the way just in time to keep them from getting ripped off inside the mechanism. The hatch opens and I careen off balance into the hold like a drunk, catching myself just before hitting the floor. Quickly sweeping my carbine off my shoulder, I try to look into every corner and angle at once.

A rustling noise makes me jerk my head left just in time for a fist to land squarely on my cheek. As my head bounces back, my attacker strikes my right arm hard, just above the elbow, making it fall momentarily numb. My carbine sling slips from my shoulder, and the gun drops from my grasp. I hadn't seen the attacker, but reflex takes over and I close the gap between us in one quick lunge.

Water pours from my eye again—the same goddamn side as last time—but I can see fine from the other. Baker stands near the wall, poised and ready to fight. She feints to her right and then jumps forward with a flat hand aimed at my throat. Barely in time, I block her arm and let the momentum spin me into a roundhouse kick that catches her in the ribcage and sends her sprawling sideways. Lightning fast, she's back on her feet before I can close in and finish the job. She lunges in low, blocking the next kick, and sending me backward off balance. She follows through—*so fucking fast*—and lands a kick of her own directly into my side. Air explodes out of my lungs and I crumple sideways, my back exposed for another kick, which I know instinctively is coming. Instead of giving her space for a windup, I roll back toward her and scrabble to grab her booted foot as it swings toward me. I catch it as she tries to jump over me and send her smashing into the wall. I have no breath and struggle to unlock my lungs as I roll away this time, blinking and trying to get to my feet. She spins around, blood dripping from a cut above her right eye where she'd hit the wall.

"I'm going to fucking kill you, Erickson."

"Try it," I wheeze, finally pulling in snatches of oxygen as my chest opens up.

We circle, both looking for an opportunity to tear the other to shreds. I'd felt her animosity like a walking cancer since the first time our paths had crossed, even before my crew had become the Admin's target. The friction between us was destined to turn into flames and we're both prepared to fight this out to the death.

She snarls and picks the moment to dart forward and reach for my carbine, still lying on the floor a meter away. I leap toward her, using my body to push her past the gun, but she grabs me and pulls me over. Moving with the dexterity of a snake, she somehow gets on top of me and grabs my throat. I buck furiously and twist onto my side underneath her, forcing her hands to release. But she grabs my hair instead and jerks my head up, then slams it down against the hard floor.

Sparks erupt behind my eyes and she does it again. A warm sensation spreads down the side of my face and the sparks start to dim, as if a shade is being pulled down on the inside of my eyes. I flip my body back to flat beneath her trying to get my arms up to make her release my hair, but she's ready and smashes her fist into my nose. Ferocious, mind-splitting pain erupts inside my head, my brain stutter-stepping in a dance of agony like a hive of angry bees. I taste the blood pouring down the back of my throat, and suddenly the pain no longer matters because I'm choking on it. Gasping, coughing, gagging, I spray her with blood while I struggle to breathe.

She jumps up, her weight mercifully gone, and I'm able to roll over and get to my knees. I cough hard, nearly vomiting as I clear the blood from my throat and lungs. My vision has narrowed to two small chinks of light directly in front of my eyes. All I see is the floor beneath me and the spatters of blood from my struggle to breathe, like delicate drips of bright red paint.

"I told you I was going to kill you."

I look up and see her knees a few centimeters in front of my face and realize she's pointing my own weapon at my head. The sound of a gunshot—

Her body buckles and tumbles over backward, lolling in an unnatural sprawl as blood begins coating the floor beneath her. Nearly in shock, I spin over into a sitting position to see who's behind me and where the shot came from.

Rob stands there, his weapon lowered, and his hand reaches out to help me up. "I'm sorry, Aly. I didn't want it to go like this."

I hitch air into my lungs and stay sprawled on the floor, unable to react.

"Come on, we can still get—"

Then he's tumbling forward as a giant red flower explodes from his chest, landing on top of me. I writhe out from beneath him, pushing his body over in the effort. One of his hands clenches around my wrist and I look into his face. The pain and sorrow I see in his eyes rips at me like daggers. Then his hand grows slack and he's gone.

I turn around and find David standing a few meters away. Our eyes meet, and his aquamarine irises are as hard as obsidian, as cold as a glacier. I pull myself to my feet, unable to look back at Rob's body, and start walking toward my brother. The sound of footsteps on the ramp draws our attention.

La Mer runs up, out of breath. "Venus is on the *Sphynx* and picked up two Corps ships in the area, coming directly for us. We've got to get the hell out of here, now!"

"Desto, Mason?" I wheeze, still short of breath, my nose swollen and clogged.

"I'll get them, you just go," David says, running back into the corridor toward the bow.

Galvanized, La Mer and I run outside and board the *Sphynx*. A glance toward T'Kai's captured soldiers shows them still tied up and lying where the crew left them, alive. I'm momentarily surprised, but then, with the way things have unraveled, what difference does it make at this point if they're dead or alive? Both the Corps and the Admin know who we are; there's nothing these soldiers can tell them that isn't known already. Vitruzzi isn't bloodthirsty; she knows their deaths would be futile.

The ship's engines are already cycling up and Brady waits for us in the hold. "Where are the others?" he asks.

"David's gone to get Mason and Desto. What about the settlers?"

Brady's expression is desperate, but he merely gives his head a short, definitive shake. "We'll have to try and come back." He looks haggard and angry, but there's the same solid determination in his face that epitomizes his approach to everything.

"We'll get them, Brady. Soon." I try to be encouraging, these are his friends and family, but deep inside, I feel the bottom dropping out.

In a minute David, Desto, and Mason sprint up the ramp, Mason slamming the control and closing the hatch. Brady's on the com telling Venus to go, go, *GO!*

She launches and arcs into a steep climb, everyone in the hold grabbing onto something. We're all here except for Vitruzzi, who's in the cockpit with Venus, and—

"Where's Rajcik?" My eyes dart around, searching for him.

"He's . . ." Brady starts and trails off.

"David, did you see him on the *'Rize*?" I ask.

Instead of responding, he slams a fist into the wall. "Shit!"

Realization dawns on all of us: both Thompson and Rajcik are missing.

"T'Kai said the Nova was on that ship." My words come out flat and dull, wasted. "He was bleeding. He can't get anywhere."

Brady says, "Eleanor slowed the bleeding and gave him an IV. That ship's got to have a med-station, maybe some supplies. It's hard to say how long he'll last."

Venus's voice comes through the com: "I think we'll shake them, we've got enough lead—" She's cut off by ear-splitting feedback and then the ship starts to dive, hard, cutting through the sky like a plunging eagle chasing its prey.

"Ohfuckohfuckohfuck." I'm looking directly at La Mer as he whispers what will probably be his last words in a prayerlike litany.

The pressure changes inside the ship as we descend, and my grip on the hold's railing grows so desperate I feel as if the bones in my hand will crack. It's the only thing I can do.

Suddenly the *Sphynx* bucks hard, throwing everyone forward, and a small explosion emanates through the hold from somewhere near the belly. Mason's body hits the wall like a piece of stout furniture, and he slides to the floor unconscious and bleeding from the back of his head. Our rate of descent begins to decrease. The explosion may have been Venus engaging the reverse thrusters before our speed was slow enough, effectively destroying them, but maybe, just maybe, keeping us from hitting the deck so hard that the ship breaks into a million pieces. Maybe giving us a chance.

As soon as I have the thought, the floor beneath me begins to bounce and vibrate furiously, knocking me to my knees. Then I hear things crashing into the ship outside, banging off the hull and snapping, like we're going through trees. Venus got us over land, at least. Clenching my teeth and preparing to be flattened or blown up, I curl my body into a tight ball against the floor, one hand still clutching the rail as, finally, the ship starts to slow and drop, almost gently, to the ground.

I open my eyes, first to unexpected stillness and then frantic movement as the crew starts to pick themselves up. I hear engines outside, at least two ships buzzing us, and know that the shit is just beginning.

"David?"

"Yeah, I'm good. You?"

I hardly believe it, but aside from some bruises, I'm not hurt. "Good. Desto? Brady? La Mer?" Mason is still unconscious, but it doesn't look like he's bleeding too bad.

Brady doesn't bother to respond, but immediately takes off running for the cockpit to check on Venus and Vitruzzi. La Mer stands up shakily and follows.

"We can't stay here, we gotta move out," Desto says, grabbing Mason under one arm. "Give me a hand."

David runs over and the two of them lift up Mason's limp body. I reach into my vest and pull out a vial of chemical salts, snapping them under his nose. He groans and twists his head, then, with surprising vitality, regains his feet, yelling loudly.

"Hey, man, it's all right. We got you," Desto says.

Mason's cloudy eyes slowly focus and he asks, "Did we go down?"

"Yeah. There're still Corps ships in the area. We need to move. Can you walk?"

He nods.

"What about the others?" I ask, knowing we can't wait for them.

David says, "Let's figure out how to get out, then get a bead on things from outside."

The cargo ramp is buckled, useless, which means we won't be able to get the Rover out. The three of them start working on the man-door while I run into the armory and gather more ammunition, passing it out to them once I've collected as much as I can carry. The door is jammed and Desto melts a hole through it with the last of the ship's E-10 wax. With a short drop to the earth, we're free of the ship and in the middle of a jungle.

THIRTY-SIX

The air hits my nostrils in a frontal assault, the stench of wetness, putrescence, and rot. The entire atmosphere is hot and heavy, almost syrupy, and I have a hard time buying Rajcik's assertion it had once been arid. The ground squishes as I step across it, each footprint instantly filling with seepage that is the same greenish color as everything around me. The ship is infested with vines and foliage that broke from the canopy during our descent and were pasted against the hull like camouflage. Despite the cover, Corps ships will still spot the wreckage easily.

David holds his carbine at the ready, surveying the area around us as we all hustle toward the bow. There's a service door for the electronics bay directly underneath the communications room, the closest exit to the cockpit. It isn't open when we reach it, and Desto, the tallest of us, stretches up to bang on it, hoping to attract Brady or La Mer's attention. In a minute, we hear Brady's voice.

"Desto?"

"Yeah, is everyone okay?"

"No." There's a noise, like someone's stomping on the door, then it flies open and Brady leans out. "Venus is hurt, pretty bad. I'm going to hand her down. Grab her."

Desto and Mason position themselves below the door as David and I keep watch. I look back over my shoulder and see Venus's limp body being lowered. There's no blood or obvious injuries. Internal? Her eyes flutter as Brady releases her, but she spills into their grasp almost lifelessly. La Mer jumps down immediately and takes her, cradling her in his arms like a child.

"Where can we take her?" His eyes are wide and desperate. No one answers, and I have to turn away before he sees in my expression what we're all thinking—she probably won't make it.

As I look back toward the swathe of wreckage the ship's landing caused, I see another ship coming in low, following the broken tree line.

"Time to move!" I shout.

I turn back around to make sure they're reading me as Brady helps Vitruzzi down. She's carrying her heavy med-bag, and her face is twisted in pain. She only puts weight on one leg as she hits the deck, reaching out for help, and fresh blood that had begun to crust on her shirt from where she was shot seeps through. Brady supports her with her arm over his shoulders and we all begin running, as best we can, toward the nearest patch of heavy overgrowth. The trees are thick with ropy plants climbing them, and the ground sucks at our feet, keeping our progress slow and laborious. We make it a few dozen meters as the Corps ship sweeps overhead, dropping a stun bomb directly onto the *Sphynx*. The heavy *whoomph* sound of the payload detonating reverberates in our ears. If anyone had still been inside, they'd be down for hours.

"They didn't blow the ship. They must want to capture us alive," David remarks, fighting with the stalk of a leafy plant that's somehow become wrapped around his leg. I walk over and cut through it with my NKT bolo. Exasperated, he says, "We need to try and find the colony. They've got to have some kind of barracks or buildings. At least somewhere we can help Venus."

Vitruzzi says, "We came over it during the escape. We're probably about ten klicks away, back toward the east." Her jaw is set, cords standing out on her neck from pain.

Ten kilometers might as well be a hundred in this undergrowth, but we can't just stand here and wait to die. We have at least fifteen weapons between the eight of us, and enough ammunition to fend off or assault a small force should we encounter any. We should be all right against any hostile prisoners we come up against. The key is to move steadily, stay alert, and keep under the canopy in case the Corps comes back.

Desto and Mason make a quick run to the ship, returning with some food, water packs and purifying tablets, and a stretcher to carry Venus. Her skin, always pale, has gone the color of watery cream, the network of her veins clearly visible beneath the skin. Vitruzzi works on her briefly, trying to keep her stable and out of shock, but we don't know the extent of her injuries. After donning an inflatable splint, Vitruzzi lets us know she's ready to move out. David and Desto take the stretcher poles, and the rest of us span into a line, keeping our weapons at the ready.

The drudge is interminable, the sticky jungle floor and tangling plants making every step a battle. Trying to conserve water in the stifling humidity is a lesson in defeat as our skin seems to instantly convert every sip we take into sweat. My nose and head ache from the fight with Baker. Anti-inflammatories help curb the swelling, but the thick air still makes me feel like I'm breathing through a wet towel. The nasal filters we all wear are flexible, almost like a low-density sponge, so Baker's punch had not dislodged mine. There's no telling what else is in this atmosphere thanks to T'Kai's monstrous science experiments. Lethal pollens come to mind.

Three hours pass and eventually the ground around us begins to show signs of activity. Trees have been cut and undergrowth has been trampled or ripped away, allowing us to walk faster. We cross a wide path containing tread marks that extends to the west as far as we can see. It must serve as the main artery for this region, but we don't know where it goes. Our better judgment tells us not to follow the road, but after trudging through the odious undergrowth we can't resist the easier going it affords. Besides, we'll be able to make much better time, which is what Venus desperately needs.

About an hour into the march, we'd witnessed two Corps ships overhead, their flight paths so close it seemed as if one had been in pursuit of the other. It struck us all as unusual, but what had been stranger was the sound of an aerial explosion far south of us just after we'd lost sight of the ships. Whatever was happening is of little consequence to us now. Once they land on the ocean platform and figure out that the bloody mess lying there had been T'Kai, we're certain to see more activity out here when they come searching for us. In the meantime, all we can do is try to help Venus and continue the original mission of finding the Beachers.

A hedge of low-slung stone buildings emerges from the line of trees directly in front of us, looking derelict and abandoned. The group stays put while David and I move into the doorway of the nearest in order to find out what, or who, is inside. The door is made of iron and wood and swings inward heavily, the hinges reluctant. The walls are completely windowless, and it's pitch black in the interior. There's no sound. I flip the scope light of my carbine on and scan the room. There are about fifty bunk beds lining both sides of the walls, like a barracks, all with sheets and blankets that appear to be in reasonably good shape. There *are* people living here. The room takes up the entire floor of the building, and there's another door at the far end. David explores it and says it's a latrine and shower. Nobody's home. Cautiously, I signal to the others, and they join us inside.

Brady finds a panel on the wall and hits a switch. Naked overhead lights ping to life, showing more of the room. It's definitely lived in. Every bunk has a locker at the foot and to the side for the inmates here to keep personal belongings. It's a lot more orderly than I'd expected to see.

"Put her down over there," Vitruzzi tells La Mer and Brady, who've taken over the stretcher.

Venus's breathing is ragged and shallow, but she's holding on. La Mer kneels beside her, holding her hand and whispering something into her ear too quietly for anyone else to hear.

Vitruzzi leans against the wall next to the bunk they'd laid Venus on and says to the rest of us, keeping her voice down, "She has at least three broken ribs that have probably punctured a lung. If I open her up here, she'll get an infection, and I don't have what I need anyway. The only thing we can do is keep her completely still so the tear doesn't get worse. But she's bleeding into the pleural cavity and developing a pneumothorax, so time is getting short." She's angry, almost spitting the words out, knowing that she could save Venus if the situation was different. "Patrick, we have what I need on the *Sphynx*."

"Eleanor, we can't go back."

She stands completely still for a minute, her eyes focused hard on the wall, then hurls her med-bag against the floor. "Goddammit! Goddamn those bastards!" She lets her head fall forward, her hair obscuring her face, but not before I see the tears spilling down her cheeks. Brady puts his arms around her and they stand together in an embrace.

I turn to David and Desto, the need to keep moving making me jittery and volatile. "Let's sweep the rest of the buildings and then head to the desal plant. There may be someone who can help." I feel like an idiot for saying it, but their eyes show they're on board. Anything is better than standing here watching our friend die.

Mason elects to stay behind and help keep watch with Brady, so we move out. Four other buildings stand in the immediate vicinity, all of them squat, built of the same brown stone. Two of them are also barracks and one is a dining facility. We don't find anyone. The fifth building is newer and bigger than the rest. Like the others, there are no windows, but this one is two stories tall. Along with a standard man-door, an articulating track door rises up the wall. It's a warehouse, probably where they store all the supplies, and locked up tightly.

I turn to David. "Where do you think everyone is?"

He shrugs. "Maybe they're all at the desal plant. Or hiding. Corps ships in the area may make people antsy."

"Or maybe there's nobody here at all. Maybe they just killed everyone," Desto comments, his eyes sweeping the surrounding jungle suspiciously.

"No, that's not possible. Those barracks have been used. The DFAC's stoves are still warm."

"Well, whatever it is, it's going to be dark in another hour or so," David says. "We should make a quick run over to the plant, then head back to Brady and the rest."

We can see a silo or smokestack rising from the plant, and the road continues past the warehouse straight toward it, about fifteen hundred meters distant. Keeping close to the trees, we extend into a wide line to reduce the chance that any shooters can hit all three of us with one burst. David takes lead, I'm in the middle, and Desto is behind. The brush and trees have been hacked away to nothing several meters around the plant's perimeter, leaving a wide-open area that makes the last of my spit dry up.

When we reach the edge of the cleared area, David takes a knee and looks back at the two of us, giving us a tiny nod. I move up into a closer position to cover him as he makes the dash forward. When I'm ready, he stands up, leans forward for the sprint, and—

Someone grabs him by the collar and yanks him hard into the trees. David lets out a grunt of surprise and I see him and whoever had grabbed him rolling down a short berm, bodies entangled. I'm on my feet instantly, jumping down the berm after them. I arrive as David gets on top of his attacker and plants a knee in his chest, simultaneously pulling a pistol and pointing it into the attacker's face. His bright, wide eyes gleam through a layer of dirt, and blood leaks from his lips. Desto hurdles over the edge of the ditch and lands heavily beside me.

"Got it, it's under control," David hisses, his eyes not leaving the attacker's face. "Who the fuck are you?"

Desto hunkers down beside me, his eyes cutting back and forth between the trees and the guy on the ground, ready for more people to jump out of the bushes.

"I'm a prisoner, just a prisoner. Don't shoot me, man!"

"Why did you jump me?"

"Look, there's about thirty Corps soldiers in the plant. If you go in there, they'll cut you down." The man's breathing starts to slow, and a look comes over his face that reminds me of a rat that has just escaped a trap. "You got guns, right? How many you got? I saw your ship go down. Can you get me outta here?" Then, in a peevish voice, he asks, "Can you get offa me? I'm not gonna do nothin'."

"David," I whisper, "don't." But he doesn't need my advice.

"Shut up and listen. You're really goddamn lucky that I didn't kill you for that. Here's what's going to happen. I'm going to ask you a few questions, and I better like your answers or a busted lip is going to be the least of your worries. You get me?"

The man on the ground nods miserably.

"What are you up to out here, and where are the rest of the prisoners?"

He sucks at his lip, reluctant to give up any information. So David gives him incentive by deliberately pointing his pistol straight into the man's eyes, letting him get a good look down the barrel.

He decides to talk. "They're locked up in the plant. The Corps came in early this morning and rounded everyone up, just like they do right before they bring in a new group." He adds ominously, "Or before they take some away."

"Why didn't they round you up?"

"Not all of us live in the barracks. Some of us have been here awhile. Since before . . . before the big die off. So they don't know we're out there."

"How many?"

He starts to squirm. "Man, I told you what you want to know. Can't you just get off me?"

David grasps him by the chin and forces him to keep still. "How many?"

"Ten, man, there's ten of us."

"Okay, good. One more question. Were some new prisoners brought in a couple of weeks ago? About a hundred of them?"

"You mean those miners from Spectra 6. Yeah, they're here."

I glance over and catch the excitement on Desto's face. The settlers are here, probably still alive. Only thirty soldiers—and the entire Admin and Corps—between them and us.

"All right look," David says, "I'll let you up, but I want you to take us to your group and show us the weak spots in the plant, help us figure out how to get in there and neutralize the soldiers. Then, if we work together, we can help you and your friends get off this rock."

"You want to take on those soldiers? There's only three of you!"

David stands, keeping his pistol at the ready. "There are others, and we've got the advantage of surprise. With your group, we'll have more than enough."

I glare at David, not liking his plan at all, but I keep my mouth shut. Giving guns to a bunch of murderers and thieves is like giving them to a pack of rabid monkeys, but maybe there's enough incentive for them to help, and not turn on us, if they think we can get them out of here.

The prisoner brushes himself off exaggeratedly, though the filth ingrained in his clothing isn't coming clean without the aid of a fire hose, or possibly a fire, and then moves into the jungle without another word. We follow closely, struggling to match his pace. He's used to walking through the grasping, clinging undergrowth and adopts a dipping and diving method that is almost completely silent. We try to move with equal stealth but can't help making a little noise just trying to keep him within sight. Finally, David demands that he slow down so we don't expose ourselves. He complies, obviously disgusted, but it gives me the time I need to dig a food bar out of my pack. I don't remember the last time I ate anything and some extra energy is sorely needed. My mouth is too dry to do much more than break the material into small enough chunks to swallow, but it helps keep me going.

"Duchamp, what are you doing bringing strays out here?"

The voice comes from somewhere close by but I can't see anyone. The man called Duchamp freezes and says, "Found them trying to get into the plant. They're the ones from the ship we saw, not Corps."

Like an apparition materializing from inside the tree, a man steps into our midst. He's dirty like Duchamp, bald, and missing most of his left ear, creased shrapnel scars covering that side of his face and neck. He carries a thick, straight branch that's been sharpened to a wicked point. "Why are you people here?"

There's a rustling around us almost like a breeze, and suddenly there are several more of them. Standing in trees, under tall plants, in front and behind, all of them carrying some variation of club or spear. Desto and I close ranks and point our weapons at the nearest figures.

David thumbs his pistol to auto-fire but keeps his tone conversational. "We came to try and rescue the settlers who were brought here from Spectra 6."

"Does your ship still fly?"

"No, but with your help, we can overrun the Corps team and get out of here on one of their ships. We've been to the platform, we know their security, and we have enough weapons to do the job." David's taking a huge risk, but then, they don't know what's really going on.

The man turns his back to us and walks a few paces away, thinking. Then he spins back and says, "Let's go somewhere we can talk."

David glances toward us and I ask, keeping my voice low, "Don't you think we should try and get word to Vitruzzi and Brady?"

"We can't afford to get separated."

I tap my VDU, more out of frustration than hope, but it's still black. Nodding reluctantly, I fall in behind Desto, and the group begins walking deeper into the jungle. There's a noise by my ear, a *whzzzngg* sound that resembles a mosquito's buzz or hummingbird's wings, and the man leading the group suddenly begins clutching at his back frantically, like he's been stung. Then something metallic clicks loudly behind us. Everyone begins to run.

THIRTY-SEVEN

Rubble lies on all sides of me: broken rocks, shards of glass, bits of steel and lathe. It creates a cradle of debris that I sit amid like an invalid on a sick bed. When the occasional Corps craft does a low pass overhead, the broken roof of the building I'm in vibrates, shaking loose more dust and debris, which rains down on me. The humid air saturates the fine particles quickly, leaving me in a sticky sheet of dirt. It's easy to imagine the foliage creeping in and swallowing me completely in a short time, the jungle life around me as potent and teeming as I am drained and wretched.

I don't know where the others are, or even how many are left. The Corps assault had hit too fast and hard for me to keep track of everyone, all of us scattering to keep from getting mowed down. At first, they'd only been shooting tranquilizers, trying to round us up, but switched to live rounds as soon as they realized we were firing back. I've been lying in this ruin for the last two hours trying to decide what to do next while the prisoner I'd followed through the jungle bleeds to death beside me. The last thing he'd told me was his name, Slobadan Zand, apparently arrested twenty years ago for nothing but stealing supplies from Admin warehouses. Delirious at the end, he'd pleaded with me to find his family on Eruo Pium if I make it out of here and tell them what had happened to him. Despite the three bullets he had taken in the back, he managed to lead me to this decrepit ruin after the attack, part of the original complex built sixty years ago and long abandoned. There was nothing I could do but give him something to dull the pain as his life drained out on the ground around us. Another good person dead. I'm almost surprised I still have the energy to care.

My ears start to hum and the wall I lean on begins a slow vibration. I press into it in a primitive impulse to try and make myself smaller and less conspicuous as another ship flies over. Their passes are getting closer together as they close their search grid. An explosion echoed through the jungle some time ago, reverberating like thunder. They must have decided to blow the *Sphynx* to make sure no one could get out of here. I'm going to have to do something soon or they'll find me, but it doesn't seem worth the effort. In reality, I'm too tired, too spent, too far beyond caring anymore to move. It's over. We failed. The Admin is too strong and we're too weak. It's a simple matter of evolution. If this is what our species has become, I'll go ahead and die now.

"ALY ERICKSON. DO YOU COPY? Come in."

I scramble upright, realizing simultaneously that I'd fallen asleep and my carbine is missing. Running my hand along the ground beside me, my fingers encounter the familiar cold metal, and I take a relieved breath as I pick it up.

"Erikson. Come in. Are you there?"

It's clear that I'm starting to lose my grip. The voice can't possibly be who it sounds like, but my VDU is working again, at least the receiver. The screen is destroyed, so I can't see who's calling me, but the transmitter button is still intact.

The light faded while I slept, the blackness so dense it's an almost physical presence. How long have I been here? It's strange to be on solid ground and have a real night; I'd grown so used to the short darkness of Spectra 6. In space, it's always night, but it's different. It's an artificial, disjointed night, not in touch with natural Circadian rhythms. But here, the darkness seems prolonged; it feels like days since I've seen the sun. My bone-tired weariness blocks every other consideration out and ignoring the voice coming through my com seems like a rational choice. When have I ever been this tired?

"Do you read me? Come in, Erikson. Aly Erikson. This is Karl Strahan. Do you copy?"

I jerk fully awake again. What the fuck is going on? Karl is dead. And in a short time, I will be too. Is this some kind of joke? Does the Admin have our names? Of course they do; Rob had given them everything.

Strangely, I'm annoyed. What's the point of this game? Am I really a threat to the Admin anymore? What do they care? My crew is wiped out, probably dead, and the settlers don't have anyone else to come for them, so they'll be dead soon, too. Can't they just leave us alone, leave *me* alone, instead of playing this sick charade?

"Aly, are you out there?"

But that voice. It *sounds* like Karl, and there's an edge of desperation in it. Not an easy tone to fake. I think for a few minutes. If I'm going to die anyway, does it hurt to satisfy this last touch of curiosity?

It's hard to stand; my legs have gone to sleep and I'm dehydrated. Jamming my hands into chinks in the wall's crumbling surface, I use it to pull myself up, like scaling a rock face. The silhouette of the doorway is a lighter shade of black than the room, and I begin to stumble toward it, tripping over chunks of concrete and roots that have broken through the floor. I switch on my carbine's light, and my legs begin to tingle as the blood starts moving through them, making my steps even more faltering. Finally, I reach the doorway and lean outside, taking a deep breath of the thick, moist air. It's less stagnant at night, a cool wisp of breeze stirring it around. Almost pleasant.

The breeze picks up, whipping through the dark forest like a swath. No, not a breeze, someone is coming, several someones, moving toward me in the dark. My light is a target, and I turn it off automatically, knowing it's probably too late to do anything.

"Aly?"

The movement has stopped. I don't respond, can't respond. There's no way I can mistake that voice.

"Aly, it's Karl."

It's as if my throat has closed to the width of a pinhead, but I force a whisper, "Karl?"

A form materializes less than two meters in front of me as the dull green glow of a nightstick slowly powers up. A man stands there. It could be him, but I don't move. Finally, he pulls the night vision goggles off and I see him. Karl. Alive. I'm forced to grip the doorjamb as my legs threaten to collapse. Then he's standing beside me, holding me up, his breath blowing through my dirt- and blood-matted hair.

"Are you hurt?"

I shake my head, unable to believe what I'm seeing. "Karl, what . . .?"

"Come on. Let's get you out of here. I'll explain when we're airborne."

THIRTY-EIGHT

A doctor comes in and takes the vitals for Vitruzzi and Venus, ignoring me. He's used to me by now. His Corps uniform still makes me feel edgy and slightly unreal, like some part of me that lives in the future is looking back at the past but is unable to warn me. I want to run like hell whenever I see him or an orderly, but where could I go anyway? The ship is fleet, as Corps as his uniform, and even though I know the personnel *aren't* Corps, not anymore, I still can't shake the feeling that they're going to arrest me.

Vitruzzi and Venus are both awake listening to Karl explain what had happened between the moments we watched his shuttle go down and several hours later when he'd used our embedded trackers to locate everyone. He's already gone through the series of events twice, but even now, most of me is still in too much shock to really believe it.

The patroller that had picked up the *Sphynx* and shot Karl out of the sky had been on advance recon for T'Kai, just waiting for us to show up. After it had blown out his flight controls, Karl was able to coax just enough auxiliary power out of the shuttle to pull the nose out of its dive and cut the engines just before hitting the water, alleviating the impact enough to keep from killing him. Bruised but whole, he'd swum out and been carried more than a kilometer from the impact site by the current. Over an hour passed before a Corps drop-ship had flown over. Figuring his ticket was already punched and preferring to die dry, he'd flicked on a strobe and they'd spotted him. When they fished him out, he'd prepared a story about being aboard a cargo hauler with a malfunctioning nav-system that went down on Keum Libre, just to see how much time he could buy. Turned out, he never had to launch into the story at all. The drop-ship's captain had taken him to a long-range fleet cruiser where he met the commander, General Medina, and her associate— a wire-rat named Quantum.

Even though Vitruzzi and I have heard the story, this is the first time Venus has been awake since coming out of surgery, and Karl continues to explain. "Quantum didn't wait. He copied the information we got from Rajcik and the Fortress and sent it to a dozen other wire-rats and contacts he had in the Corps. They started lightwaving it just a few hours after you left Obal 6. Apparently, they've been planning another rebellion since the last one was squashed, and planning better. This ship's commander, Medina, is one of the, I guess you'd say, leaders. They've got seven other carrier commanders, or at least their ships, and most of the troops on Obal 5, 7, and 8 behind them. This is bigger than it was last time. They're planning a coup on the Directorate within the week."

"Quantum is alive? T'Kai said they'd killed him before the transmission was sent," Venus says. Her feet bob to-and-fro under the blanket as if she's pedaling a tiny bicycle, causing the IV tubes tangling from almost every limb to dance and jitter around her. Her voice is barely a whisper.

"T'Kai either had bad intel or he was bluffing. Quantum wasn't lying when he said they were ready for this. He's here, been on this ship since the transmission was sent. He and General Medina have been working together since the beginning. Don't ask me how a Corps fleet commander can hide the fact that she's planning a mutiny, but that just goes to show you how widespread this is."

La Mer asks, "Why did Quantum bring them to Keum Libre?"

It's a good question. Quantum never hid the fact that he didn't give a damn about us or the settlers. It was always about overthrowing the Admin.

Karl continues, "Two reasons: he knew Cross was working for the Admin, and he knew enough about what had happened between Rajcik and T'Kai to expect T'Kai to come for him. Where better for T'Kai to erase both us and Rajcik than KL? But after they picked up Rajcik on the 'Rize and interrogated the soldiers you'd left on the platform, Medina decided to try and help, if it wasn't too late. I think she's a little more humane than Quantum."

"What's the other?" I ask.

"The other reason? It's a good place to lay low. Keum Libre is outside the normal flight patterns for Corps assault and enforcement crafts. Medina can stay relatively obscure in this zone and launch battalion gunships from here to mop up Corps holdouts throughout the rest of the quadrant."

Karl puts a warm, rough hand on my neck, rubbing the skin gently. I'm sitting on a chair at the foot of Venus's bed with him beside me, and my body floods with a deluge of emotions, almost too many to manage. I feel like I might burst. Relief, fear, guilt, gratitude, shame, hope. And the deepest, most powerful, love. I sit still, letting them wash through me, not trusting myself to say anything, or even look at Karl. Not yet.

After Rajcik's suicide move on T'Kai, only one of the ships that had chased the *Sphynx* from the platform had been hostile. The other two were part of Medina's battalion, the one that had picked up Karl, and the third that had gone after the *Red Horizon*. Rajcik launched just after the *Sphynx,* knowing that he wouldn't be a target for the Corps drop-ship since the *'Rize* was supposed to be transporting T'Kai. To his extreme surprise, Medina also knew T'Kai was supposed to be aboard Rajcik's hijacked ship and had curtailed the escape with a ship-net, incapacitating the engine, and allowing Medina's carrier to bring the *'Rize* in. They'd questioned him and Thompson, learning what had happened to T'Kai and about the *Sphynx*'s dire situation, prompting Medina to send three gunships to neutralize the Corps ship looking for us, destroying it, which must have been the two ships we'd seen flying over us as we'd been hiking Venus to the colony. Finally, when things were under control, Karl led a company of new rebel soldiers to land, overtaking the detachment guarding the plant, rescuing the settlers, and then taking a search-and-rescue squad to track down the rest of his crew.

A RABBLE OF VOICES comes from the main benches of the locker room as I push through the door. All I want right now is a shower, some clean clothes, and food. I highly doubt a Corps ship has any good hooch in the galley, but I'm betting I can track down a handful of soldiers—make that *ex*-soldiers—who'll have a stash somewhere. I'll leave that for when I have more energy.

The smell of gun oil and aftershave hits me in a wave. Karl is seated on a bench with Desto and David, who turn their heads as I enter.

"Desto, you look like you were in a fight with a wildcat," I comment. The scratches covering most of his face, neck, arms, and hands from running through the jungle when the Corps attacked have finally started to fade. David looks only a little better, having been right behind Desto, who broke through most of the brush.

"Honey, I'm looking at the only wildcat I ever want to tangle with."

I can't help but laugh.

Moving past them to the shower stalls, I drop my clothes on the bench outside. The water is hot and abundant, and I linger for a while beneath it. I forgot how good this feels—one of the perks of being a soldier on a fleet cruiser my subconscious had conveniently stifled. If not for these little things, mutiny would be a much more common occurrence among the fleet. Or would have been, until the events of late.

After a few blissful minutes, I can't steal any more time or any more water from the ship's tanks and turn off the tap. All of the Beachers have been given an assigned locker and extra clothing from the ship's requisitions. I stand in front of locker 1127 and pull the familiar pieces of uniform on once more. The Corps fatigues and undershirt are soft and loose, probably a batch salvaged from recycling, and I'm grateful for their comfortable intimacy.

By the time I've slipped the shirt over my bra, pulled on the cargo pants, and cinched up my boots, the dry air of the ship has sapped most of the moisture from my hair, which is getting long and unruly. I look into the mirror hanging from the locker door as I pull it back from my face and wrap it up in an elastic band. The bruises from my fight with Baker are already faded, and my nose just has a small cut on the bridge, the swelling completely gone.

I pop the door closed and notice Karl standing at the end of the line of benches, the muted lights in the room casting a shadow over his face. I can't see his expression, but I can see the sparkle of his amber eyes.

"Aly, we need to talk."

The locker room is full of metal, but his husky voice doesn't echo. It carries to my ears like a balm made from cherished, yet painful, memories. We've been airborne for just over a week, enough time for me to catch up on my sleep and listen to the unbelievable story again and again, waiting for it to feel real. We still haven't spent much time together, and the moments we have were awkward, neither us capable of saying what we're really thinking.

"Sure. What's on your mind?" I turn back toward the locker to hang my wet towel on the protruding hook, hoping he doesn't notice the way my hand tremors.

After a pause, he comes closer and stands resolutely beside me, centimeters away. I turn to look at him, and his face is fully illuminated by the overheads. I'm almost knocked to the bench by the depths of both sorrow and hope I see in his eyes.

"Look, I know I was wrong. I owe you an apology."

"Forget it," I say quickly, my voice too thick, betraying me.

"Aly, I shouldn't have said the things I said. I . . . I fucked up. The way I treated you was—you didn't deserve that. I was just so afraid I was losing you. I didn't know what to do."

"It's all right, Karl. It's over. I'm not worried about it, okay?" I don't know how much longer I can take him standing there staring at me like that before I break down. If I let him in again, will it hurt as much as last time? Am I strong enough to try?

He doesn't say anything for a few seconds, then puts a hand on my wrist. Its warmth spreads up to my elbow like a burning brand. He takes a deep breath, searching my face, as if what he's about to say is something heavy that will take all of his strength to utter. "I'm trying to say I'm sorry. When I thought I'd lost you, it felt like someone had ripped me open. I was so afraid of what life would be like without you. For the first time, I realized what you mean to me. Aly, you're the reason I keep going. You're the only thing that makes all this shit that's happening worth it. When I thought I'd never see you again, I realized how I've failed you—"

Overwhelming emotion suddenly wells up in my throat and threatens to choke me. I raise a hand to try and put it over his mouth, but he grabs it between both of his and wraps it away like a tiny, fragile gift that he treasures too much to even chance a look. "I realized what you needed from me wasn't just for me to be around. You needed to know that I love you. I love you. I love you so much."

Salty water slips from my eyes to my lips, left, right, left, like disciplined soldiers on the march. His blazing eyes search my face for a response. Gently, I pull on my hand and he lets it slide out of his grasp. Swiping at my face, I say nothing and reach out to grab the sleeve of his jacket and lead him to my bunk.

"DON'T FORGET, MEDINA WANTS us all to meet her in the command center at 1700," Karl says as he straps on his boots. His shirt is still off, and my eyes trail along the muscles of his back, his wide shoulders, strong traps, long lats. The familiar pattern of scars on his skin is a roadmap for me in the dark, all I need to find my way to complete happiness. As he pulls his shirt over his head, I make a silent promise to myself that I'll never lose him again, never fail him again. Or myself.

"I'll be there."

He leans down and kisses me once more, then heads out the door to help Mason and Brady sort through the rest of the salvage from the *Sphynx*. Just before stepping out, he picks up his jacket from where he'd thrown it on a chair, and a scowl crosses his features. He reaches for an inside pocket and pulls out a small box.

Hesitantly, he comes back beside the bed and extends it toward me. "We found this with Cross's stuff on the *Sphynx*."

I take it from him uncertainly, not understanding why he's giving it to me until I see my name written along the top. "Thanks."

His eyes linger on my face for a second. "I love you, Aly."

I smile widely, surprised that those words can penetrate so deeply into my heart. "You too."

Once he's gone, I get dressed, leaving the box lying on the bed. Cross's betrayal had been so unexpected that I still haven't wanted to examine the full extent of the damage he'd caused. More of me wants to forget about it and never think of it again than deal with it. David hasn't spoken a word of the situation to me, and I know that he's feeling just as betrayed and hurt as I am. Cross must have known I'd never have taken him up on his offer to buy a new identity and false citizenship if I'd known what he was up to, but how could he have believed he could hide the fact that he was working for T'Kai?

The box sits there, tugging at me like a tiny black hole, its weight on my thoughts a physical burden. I break down and clean both my Sinbad and then my AK-80 before I finally give in and open it. Inside lays a small recording projector. Not completely sure I want to hear whatever Rob had wanted to tell me, I position it on the edge of the bunk with the lens pointing toward the blank wall across from me and turn it on.

The first image I see is a hand moving away from me, presumably having just turned on the device. As it recedes, I'm looking at the black-shirted chest, and finally, the face of Cross. He sits down—by brain notes that he's sitting in his cabin aboard the *Red Horizon*—and looks directly into the lens for several seconds before saying anything. The image is so sharp that he could actually be sitting there in the flesh. Goosebumps ripple up my arms.

"Well, Aly, if you're watching this, I must be dead." He almost smiles, the statement evoking some kind of cynical humor that he'd rarely displayed in life. There's a long pause, and it doesn't look like he has any idea of what he's going to say. I almost turn off the device. The man had nearly been responsible for getting everyone I know killed. But somehow, even worse, he had betrayed me. I'd been stabbed in the back by others, like Rajcik, but no double-cross could have ever surprised me, or hurt me, more than Rob's.

"Aly, I want you to understand what happened. I'm sure you believe I betrayed you, and Vitruzzi and the crew, but I never in a million years wanted that to happen." He takes a deep breath and continues, "I was busted by Admin security five months ago. They knew about my smuggling. Jesus, I thought I was so smart, but they knew everything." He runs a hand through his hair, creases appearing around his eyes and forehead as if he's in pain. Even through the medium of the image, I can see the turmoil writhing just behind his dark eyes. I want to hate him. He deserves nothing but my loathing and contempt, dead or not. But I can't.

"They offered me a deal. Keep doing what I was doing and lead them to the more dangerous procurers—the people that actually posed a threat to them, not just random non-cits looking for backup parts for rusted out derelicts. The Admin knows there are a lot of people like that out there, but they don't care about them. So I did what they wanted, informed on the people I delivered to, people like Rajcik, and I got to keep my ship and stay out of prison.

"But you and Vitruzzi's crew hit them hard when you blew up the Fortress. T'Kai fed them Rajcik as the most likely culprit. Of course, he knew it was him anyway, but it was a good way of redirecting the inquiries. T'Kai's back was against the wall. He was responsible for the Fortress's security and operations, and the Admin lost billions from the station's destruction. The only reason he wasn't held accountable was because he had enough evidence to convince them that it was Rajcik. He had security scans from the outpost on Obal 3, from when your team stole the station's disc. Goddammit, Aly, he even had scans of you and David."

I suck in a quick breath. T'Kai had been telling the truth about knowing we were part of Rajcik's team.

"After that, T'Kai changed the game. He wanted me to keep my eyes out for Rajcik and his team, gather intel from around the system, and he showed me the scans. At first, I couldn't believe it. See, I didn't know about the research they were doing on the Fortress. I just thought you and David had been part of some massive weapons-smuggling op that turned into a . . . a mistake. Back when we were in the Corps, you'd always thought the Admin was corrupt; blowing up that space station seemed like just the kind of thing you'd have done if you had the chance. And T'Kai had proof. If I'd known what he was trying to cover up . . . but I didn't. What was I supposed to do?

"I only wanted to find Rajcik. But when I landed on Spectra 6 with Vitruzzi's transceiver parts, you can't know how shocked I was to find you and David there. That was the last thing I ever expected. It wouldn't have mattered, I would never have turned you in after you led me to Rajcik, but my crew—Sims, Baker, Montoya—they're Admin, they're not mine. They were assigned to me to make sure I did my job and kept my mouth shut. I just wanted to bring Rajcik in, but now T'Kai knows about the footage and the data."

He looks at something away from the screen and his vision goes distant for a few seconds. Are there tears in his eyes? The skin of his face is tight and shiny with torment. When he made this recording, he already knew there was no way he was going to get out of this, but I can see he's still wishing he could. Still not wanting to betray anyone.

"I don't know what's going to happen, but if it goes bad, you have to know how sorry I am. If it were just me, I'd have taken the bullet for you already. But it's not. My crew . . . they know almost everything, and they're not going to stop, even if they have to kill me to carry out T'Kai's orders. The only thing I can do is try and find an angle that gets the least amount of people hurt. But shit"—that cynical smile again—"like I said: if you're seeing this . . . well, you know.

"Remember this, Aly, whatever happens, I'm not the bad guy. I never wanted to involve you or David in this. Vitruzzi, Brady, Desto, they're all my friends. It's just the way of the worlds. It's a fucking mess and the best we can do is try to survive." He leans forward and his hand approaches the recorder, preparing to turn it off. Before he does, he adds one more thing. "I'm sorry for whatever trouble I may have caused between you and Strahan, but I never met another woman like you after the Corps. You should know, Aly, I'm going to do—or I did—everything I could to keep you safe."

And he shuts it off.

I don't know how long I've been sitting on my bunk staring at the blank wall when someone knocks.

"It's open."

David comes in, gets ready to say something and then pauses, looking at me closely. "Everything okay?"

I nod, lacking any certitude that everything will ever really be okay again.

"Yeah, well this shouldn't upset you too much then—Rajcik and Thompson killed the dock control crew guarding the *Red Horizon*. They took the ship."

THIRTY-NINE

We've been gathered on the carrier's flight deck for forty-five minutes watching the reports coming in from all over the system: citizen and non-citizen station casts, Admin-controlled newswaves, even some Corps ships who are still under the Admin's control. Rajcik flew the *Red Horizon* directly to Obal 10. When we warned Medina about the Nova being on board the ship and how deeply Rajcik's anti-Admin motivations were rooted, she'd had other things on her mind and never secured it. There is no way to set up a search-and-destroy mission with the amount of fighting going on throughout the quadrant. Rajcik had slipped through all the nets, sliding by rebel ships who had more important issues to deal with than a harmless transporter, and aided by those still loyal to the Admin for being known to be contracted by, possibly even carrying, T'Kai. He'd breeched Obal 10 airspace an hour ago, using the ship's transceiver to send one final message to the Admin.

A communications tech sergeant put his broadcast on one screen set to loop, and I haven't been able to look at anything else since the first viewing. Rajcik stands in the *'Rize*'s cockpit, staring into the lens of a handheld recording device just like the one Rob had used. His opalescent teeth gleam as he talks, telling the Admin that the time has come for them to reap what they'd sown for so long. Tunis City can be seen through the ship's viewscreens as the *'Rize* approaches it in a full-tilt dive. Rajcik pans the device over the sleek body of the Nova as he explains what it is and what he's about to do with it. There's a loud explosion, and the recording jolts violently as a gunship in the area begins pursuing him, someone out there realizing he's on a collision course with the system's capital city, even if they don't know he's about to annihilate it. But the dive can't be stopped. The last thing Rajcik does before short-circuiting the ship's electrical systems and causing an electromagnetic pulse that detonates the Nova is smile his deadly, yet somehow completely sane, smile.

Tunis City is destroyed. Obal 10's atmosphere is destabilized. Millions are dead. The real war has begun.

CONTRACT OF WAR

SPECTRAS ARISE TRILOGY
BOOK 3

The whole war is a battle between these two systems; between the Empire and the Foundation; between the big and the little. ~ *Foundation,* Isaac Asimov

A great civilization is not conquered from without until it has destroyed itself from within. ~ Ariel Durant

PROLOGUE

FROM THE JOURNAL OF DOCTOR ELEANOR VITRUZZI, YEAR 2727
Yesterday marked 460 days since the system's civil war began, but sometimes I feel like I've been at war my whole life. Only eight years have passed since the Soldier's Rebellion, and in that time, I now realize, *peace* was the illusion. When I look up at a rust-red sky filled with grit and chaff from the latest strafing, the smell of burning things, burning bodies . . . on days like those I can't remember what life was like before the suffering and fighting. There's been more death since this all began than anyone will ever be able to tally. Still, how could it have been any different?

When Rajcik dropped the Richter Mini-Nova on Tunis City, the war was inevitable. Cits and non-cits predictably divided straight down the middle, but that first year was devastating for those who still called themselves citizens. They were people who'd never known the harsh realities of noncivilized worlds, never had to adapt to bad air and a shortage of food. Except for the ones who'd been soldiers or engineers, they didn't even know how to get around the DNA signatures that would enable Admin-manufactured weapons to be fired. They dropped like headstones in an earthquake, and for a while it looked like the non-cits, with the help of the former-Corps-now-anti-Admin forces, were going to overrun all the Obal planets with ease.

The soldiers fighting from inside the fleet were another story, however. With Tunis City obliterated and the acceleration of Obal 10's magnetic reversal causing mass extinction and climate disruption, most of the Admin's political and military leaders died or disappeared. Like a chicken without a head, order and discipline disintegrated, and the rest of the Corps advanced rapidly into complete self-destruction. Soldiers who had been loyal to the Admin their whole lives suddenly switched sides and started mutinies within their divisions. Others who'd always been fast and loose with their beliefs locked onto the Admin rhetoric and dug in against the mutineers with a vengeance. Battles were waged within ships and between squadrons that most often ended with the deaths of everyone involved. For the first year, the chaos unfolding within the ranks kept the Corps and their weapons and ships too busy with each other to do much about what was happening on the ground. And we stayed busy.

And what's it all been for? For years non-cits have been thrown to the wolves on the edges of the system, left defenseless and completely at the Admin's mercy—expendable. There was more than enough festering hatred built up in the hearts of the people living on the system's eight Spectra planets; when the transmission was broadcast detailing the Admin's human experimentation, their diseases and plagues, and their utter contempt for human life, it was all the spark that was needed. Non-cits and criminals teamed up on every planet, galvanized by a shared motivation for revenge, and the citizens on the Obals, who never even knew of their own complicity, were systematically, ruthlessly slaughtered.

A few levelheaded leaders have risen, people who still have the capacity for reason and compassion. But they're becoming fewer and fewer. Even Command General Medina, leader of this fleet cruiser, the *Celestial*, seems to be losing sight of the goals. We need to bring order and meaning to the lives that are left. Halt the slaughter and begin bringing others onto our side, the side that fights for freedom before all. The people who were once citizens, as I once was, who had it easy before the war and thought they were being looked after by the Admin—like children—they have to know deep inside that their lives were so simple and sedate only because they consented to well-masked tyranny. And some already have. Whether it was their wounded dignity that forced them to step over, or something deeper and more noble, something like an innate understanding that there is nothing more important than freedom and self-governance, a great number of these people have quit cowering and picked up the banner of anti-Admin sentiment.

Yet the fighting continues.

ONE

For the love of all that is holy. If they'd shut up, I could sleep.

This grating thought finally brings me fully back from the nearly comatose sleep of complete exhaustion. Two and a half days rendering round-the-clock maintenance on the *Nebula* and *Orika*, our two largest scouts, prepping them for the next retrieval and salvage run has completely done me in. Once I found time to take a break, I would have jumped to my death off Keum Libre's oceanic landing platform just to get some much-needed shut-eye if I hadn't known I'd be able to bunk up in Venus's maintenance shed before heading back to the colony. Awake once more, groggy, cranky, and covered in oil and carbon dust, I don't think I've been asleep for more than a couple of hours. But now I have to listen to whoever's outside bitching at each other?

I'll give them something to yell about. Sitting up, I have to jam my hands into the small of my back, trying to rub away the stiffness nesting there. Cramp inducing or not, the purgatory of sleeping on Venus's tucked-away cot still beats the crowded, open-bay barracks of Keum Libre's old penal colony. Until *now*. And I don't like staying alone in the one-room outbuilding Karl and I share when he's not there.

The argument that awakened me continues.

"Doctor, the only thing you are in charge of on this rock is your pointless convalescent house for the broken and dying people you treat. You don't decide for me or anyone else what goes." Quantum's voice, his usual lack of tact making it unmistakable.

"You're wrong," Vitruzzi answers. "This colony has chosen a system of leadership. And that means Brady and me."

"*Chosen.* Don't make me laugh. You mean your demagoguery and threats have made everyone your puppets."

These two again. Quantum and Vitruzzi have been going rounds lately, but I haven't been able to find out what exactly their disagreement is about. I don't care really; I just want to stay focused on making our regular salvage runs around the system and lying low. Anything to keep from being sucked back into playing medic to the injured people inhabiting the colony's makeshift field hospital—the broken and dying people Quantum's talking about—even if it means thirty-six hours as slave labor, forced to beat the dents out of our busted-up scout ships.

"Quantum, I've already told you, and I'm getting tired of doing it, that you're more than welcome to leave. I can have Erikson or Strahan drop you at any point you'd like on their next run."

"And I will. When you give me access to the soil compound."

Soil compound? What the hell?

A long pause, then Vitruzzi: "You can't just let that stuff loose anywhere you want. There are still people living on most of the planets. The compound isn't an asset; it's a poison."

Quantum responds, "A few people maybe dying is a price I'm willing to pay for the chance—"

Voice pitched low, she cuts him off. "There's been enough death; we don't need to add to it. It's time to rebuild, not continue the destruction. If you're seriously thinking about using that compound . . . you're talking about genocide."

Quantum's voice, however, hasn't lost any of its volume. "You would know," he responds.

Footsteps, only one set, recede, and then the maintenance bay's door slams shut.

The fact is that a number of quarrels and scuffles have broken out between settlers over the last few months—even among people you'd never expect to be short-tempered or malcontent. My brother David and I have talked about it a couple of times, and it seems to boil down to two things. First, simply put, people are going stir-crazy. Nothing about trying to make this tiny settlement with less than two hundred inhabitants livable and viable has been easy, and those of us who don't get off planet much are stuck with a radically reduced—everything. Space, resources, new faces, they are all in short supply on Keum Libre. Second, people are having a hard time trying to adjust to the way things are now that there's no longer anything remotely close to a central government to govern the worlds out of chaos, along with the fact that half the Obals are wastelands. It *used* to be a big system. Now we're all just the last threads of a tattered spider web still clinging to the gutter after a cataclysmic storm. Personally, though, there's not a damn thing I miss about the Admin.

It's still quiet on the other side of the maintenance shed's door. Remaining seated, I listen awhile longer, more rattled by V and Quantum's conversation than I want to admit. Venus is out on the platform, working on the damaged scout Karl, David, and I had been hopping around the quadrant in before three of its four stabilizers had gone tits up. No one else is in the shed now besides me and whoever stayed behind after their argument.

Concluding they may both be gone, I lie back down, already feeling the heaviness of craved-for sleep pressing against my eyelids. My thoughts return to the overheard discussion and the soil compound. We'd found thousands of kilograms of it stored on the bottom level of the landing platform. The Admin had engineered the stuff to chemically alter a planet's soil and make it more fertile in a matter of only a couple decades, thus giving them the power to terraform more planets and make them not only more productive, but more livable. Keum Libre had been the experiment that proved its efficacy.

And, we've learned from the survivors, its deadliness.

After synthesizing and analyzing the data stored out here on the platform, as well as what we could retrieve of the data Bodie, my old friend who'd been killed by the Admin, had taken from the Fortress over two years ago, we know phase one of the compound's cycle is to wipe out everything living. By introducing a poisonous catalyst, which is beyond my rudimentary chemistry knowledge to understand, it clears an area completely of organic life, and essentially lets newly introduced flora and fauna regrow new ecological foundations from scratch. Perfect if you move into a place ten years after the compound's deployment. Not so great if you happen to be an organic life-form that's there from inception.

It sounds like Quantum wants access to it, but what for? Keum Libre has room enough to sustain our current population, as well as plenty more for expansion. The compound is dangerous, and no one here is an expert on chemical or planetary engineering, so we don't even have a full understanding of how it works. The data on the KL data-storage blocks has shown us all we really need to know: keep it locked up and don't let anyone near it.

Despite my tiredness, the questions evoked by their argument don't let me sleep. I'm trying to shut my mind off by reciting nav-chart coordinates (a technique I'd practiced to perfection when I was still enlisted—anything to push out the constant replay of past firefights) when something starts to feel off. A slight vibration works its way up the cot's legs, then through its thin fabric and into my back. A low droning noise leaks through the walls, like a million hummingbirds' wings flapping, deepening slowly until it becomes a buzzing roar outside. They must be testing something on our broken scout, the *Nebula*, and have the engines cycling. Fantastic. Naptime is officially over.

Standing up with a groan and a rapidly devolving unzenlike attitude, I walk to the wall and pull my jacket and arms-belt from their hooks. My boots hadn't made it off my feet before I'd passed out.

I step out of the cot room and see Vitruzzi seated on a stool inside the maintenance bay, which is really nothing but the psychotically disordered interior of Venus's old dwelling at Agate Beach, increased by a factor of ten. As Queen of All Things That Fly, Venus is the unquestioned ruler out here, and when I say *disordered* I'm not being entirely honest. The bay looks like Satan's funhouse to me and every other "normal" person who dares to enter, but Venus can tell you the location of every part, piece, wire, and nut and bolt it contains, down to the centimeter. And she gets *hostile* if you move something without telling her. To her radically enhanced brain cycles, this is just an excellent storehouse for the tools of her trade. My nearly three months of living with her at the Beach have inured me somewhat to the chaos, which is my ace in the hole when I need to borrow her quiet little corner of serenity. No one else comes in here without a very specific, and very brief, need.

I nod at the doc but have to shout to make myself heard. "Everything okay, V?"

The level of weariness in her eyes is almost shocking. And—there's something deeper there. Something that reminds me, in the quieter corners of my mind, of the look I'd catch in Rajcik's eyes, my former black-market arms-smuggling boss, when he was about to do something totally insane.

She jumps a fraction—so unlike her usual unflappability—then returns my nod. "Didn't know you were in there, Aly."

She says more, but I can't hear a thing over the *Nebula*'s engines. Hand-signing that I'm heading back to the colony, I leave her behind. As mentioned, whatever the disagreement is between her and Quantum, it's none of my business. And I'm happy to keep it that way.

I run into Venus at the skiff that will take us the six kilometers from the platform to the colony. Looking like a windblown cheetah, she's shifting her weight from side to side like a little girl who has to pee as she stands at the boat's release console.

"You heading back to the mainland?" I ask, walking up beside her.

"Yep! Jer is making cake for me! My birthday dinner!"

With the addition of flecks of engine oil, dust, and salty ocean spray covering her, the violence of curls haloing her head, their shade somewhere between the inside of a cantaloupe and the red skin of an apple, only looks more ferocious and indomitable. When I'd met Venus, her hair had been clipped short almost to her scalp, but now, two years later, it's grown out to her shoulders. Or it *would* reach her shoulders, except for the nearly afro-tight curls that explode from her head as if filled with electricity. Like everything else about her, from her phosphorescent green eyes to her overcharged brain to her savant flying skills, even her hair is almost impossible to believe. Venus is basically an exclamation point on legs.

"But I thought your birthday was last month."

"It was, but now we're going to celebrate it every month. Did you try that cake he made me last time?"

"I didn't get—"

"Well, if you had, you'd understand. It tastes just like an orgasm in your mouth, Aly. Really."

"Okay, fantastic, that's all I need to know."

Jeremy La Mer, much like Venus, is full of surprises. At first, we'd all assumed he was just a highly talented wire-rat. But he's proved in these past few months that he can make just about anything sing and dance for him, including cooking and gardening. I guess when civilization takes the kind of nosedive we've just experienced, all kinds of hidden talents people didn't know they had or had never cultivated before suddenly become not just talents, but essential skills.

Venus finishes the unmooring sequence, and the bay door at the end of the docking hangar begins grinding open. We jump inside the skiff together and she takes the pilot's seat.

"It sounded like the *Nebula* was back in action," I comment.

As she double-checks the boat's systems, she nods. "She's in good shape. Goodish. We need to replace a bunch of stuff inside the controls and reactors, but she'll fly fine for now."

I don't like any sentence that ends with the words *for now*, but I have nothing to respond with. On a planet without a manufacturing plant of any sort, or even people with the skills to construct whatever components we may need, you learn to live with *for now* until . . . you can't.

"Can you get David or me a list so we can look for derelicts to take parts from on our next run?"

"Consider it done. And don't forget. You're on med-bay duty tonight after the town hall."

Town hall? Med-bay duty? "Jesus, Venus, what am I, a robot? When am I supposed to sleep?"

"Hey, Aly-oop. You volunteered, remember?"

Even the war was less exhausting.

TWO

Quantum and several others have requested they be given one of our three scout ships to join the colony called Bogotan on Obal 6."

Rumbles and the occasional epithet follow Brady's first order of town hall business. He stands in the center of the desalination plant's largest filtering room, which may be the only functioning industrial facility remaining in this quadrant, and grits his teeth. He enjoys this about as much as I do. Another town hall and more arguments, or, as I like to call it, another night of slinging bullshit.

"We only have three! Why give one up?"

"How does it help our own colony to give away our few resources?"

"We need all our ships!"

Brady lets the hollering die down before relaxing his scowl. Deep lines spread out from the edges of his mouth and eyes, making him look twenty years older than he did the short two years ago that I'd met him. He must be somewhere in his midforties, maybe late forties, and still strong. But those lines show many more years of pain and hardship than that. Too many.

"This is a town hall. I'm only going to remind everyone one time that you wait to be called on. I'm chairing tonight, which makes me in charge."

Quantum, who stands near the right front flank of the semicircle of colonists, fronts his own hard scowl on his squished, round face. I can almost read his mind. The only reason we're here right now is because of him. When the *Boelke*'s—a light bomber and transport craft we'd commandeered when we left Medina and the PCA *Celestial*—navigation sequences performed the equivalent of a programming seppuku and left us flying blind just before reaching the moon, he had fixed our radar and visuals with his almost freakish wire-rat skill set as we broke through the atmosphere, giving the engineering team the information they needed to land the cruiser without killing anyone. The *Boelke* won't ever fly again, at least not with our current limitations on engineering and mechanical materials, but the sixty passengers and crew aboard it had all survived. Why shouldn't he get his own long-range ship? The colony has three.

Narumi, a hardworking aide to Vitruzzi, raises her one hand. The other was blown off at the wrist during the war. A replacement could easily have been created for her under normal circumstances, and no one could have done a better job of it than Vitruzzi herself. But circumstances aren't normal, and Narumi gets around with only a primitive, nonrobotic prosthetic. Despite this, she gets as much done as anyone else in the colony, and maybe because of it, she's particularly empathetic with some of the other victims of disfigurement and amputations who've found their home on KL. Brady nods in her direction.

"As everyone knows, Jillian, Tomaz, and I all came from the Obal 6 colony four months ago. Why did we leave? Because they wouldn't let me stay—they said resources were in too short supply to help a cripple. Why would we give them a ship when they won't even help a woman who's missing a hand?"

Grumbles of agreement, then Dan Hoogs, another ex-Corpsmember (but aren't most of us now?), steps forward with a hand in the air. Brady nods a go-ahead and Hoogs says, "The more of our own resources we give up, and the more they get, the less secure we are. If Quantum wants to live with them, we can drop him off nearby and he can wait to be found. Our assets are limited, and we're not doing ourselves any favors if we start letting others know what we do—and don't—have."

Almost every face in the room shares expressions of agreement. I glance back toward Quantum. Someone has draped and fastened an old canvas across the wall behind where he stands with the words *Adapt or Die* carefully stenciled across it in letters a meter high. It's become the motto of our settlement, replacing "Fight or Die" now that the war is essentially over. Yet some of us have had more trouble than others embracing the newer philosophy. Looking at some of the hardened and angry faces in the room, I wonder if we ever will.

It's Quantum's turn to step forward, but he doesn't wait for Brady to approve before he speaks. "We're not suggesting we just hand over one of KL's ships. Brady"—he flicks a sneer at Brady that's pretty ballsy, given the crowd—"hasn't been clear. We would like to borrow a ship to visit Obal 6's leading city and begin negotiations for joining our two colonies in trade."

"What makes you any kind of spokes—?" someone blurts, but Brady's on it.

"No talking out of turn, dammit. Or I'll adjourn the meeting right now."

The voices of the crowd hush, but the restless and agitated fidgeting going on around me doesn't let up. These people feel more and more like they're being pushed closer to the edge on a daily basis, and it's beginning to get under their skin.

Quantum's features flatten out into what I think he must assume is a neutral expression, but it only makes him appear as calculating as I know him to be. Not really what you look for in a diplomat.

"Think about it," he says. "Bogotan has a manufacturing plant, a functioning city power grid with municipal water, and an untold number of experts in everything we lack. Right now, we fight nature just to keep the desal plant running. If we lose that, we are done. The time to form alliances is before time runs out, not when we are desperate."

"Dr. Kittinger keeps the desal plant running fine," Vitruzzi cuts in from where she stands next to Brady.

Quantum shifts his gaze to her, the same calculating expression still fixed. This isn't going well for him at all. Much as I don't like the man, though, I see his point.

Covering a yawn that threatens to split my skull in two, I start inching toward the exit. I already know this is going to end in another stalemate, and I'm too tired to give it more than a minimum of my attention. This is the third town hall in as many weeks, a brainchild of Brady's to help bring order to the colony's slowly expanding population. Obviously, he's well suited to the task after leading Agate Beach for several years, and his own mining crew somewhere on the Spectras before that. Despite few resolutions or social ordinances getting past the discussion stage, I have to admit that the spiking curve of disorder and dis-ease that's been growing among the settlers has at least leveled off because of Brady's lead-taking. Or it seemed to have, but part of me wonders if tonight's meeting portends an about-face in the relative calm of things.

Dusk is falling and some of the air's constant humid saturation is easing off. My shift in the *Andromeda*'s med-bay starts in a few minutes. We have only a few sick and wounded at the moment, so I'm hoping I'll be able to convince whoever I'm partnered with tonight to trade sleep rotations with me.

Karl and David have been out for three weeks on a salvage run—which always makes my nerves sizzle like a slow-burning fuse until I know they're safe again—and are expected back any day now. I didn't go with them this time thanks to a flare-up of what best might be termed *acute gastrointestinal distress*—of the extreme variety. A lovely side effect of using myself as a testing ground for some of the questionable salvage we find. Once that "passed" I reverted to my constant focus on staying busy, despite difficulty sleeping, just to keep my mind off all the possible things that could happen to them. Regardless, I'm about ready to fall into a walking coma, and tonight's shift is just the chance I need to catch up on sleep after the last two days on the platform doing maintenance.

Bidding an unfond adieu to the bickering, I drop to the back of the crowd, catching a suggestive wink from Desto, and start the short walk to the *Andromeda*, surprising myself with the realization that even I'm undecided about whether or not Quantum should get what he's asking for.

THREE

The Corps Loyalist cruiser is down and the last of their air forces are neutralized."

The voice belongs to Lieutenant Steward, the OIC of this operation. At first glance you wouldn't think much of the slight, pale at-one-time career Corps officer, but his mind for strategy has led to the decimation of at least half the enemy we've come across since the war started. Between him and Medina calling the shots, and strong fighters like my brother and most of the rest of the crew of our cruiser, the *Celestial*, I don't see how this war could go on much longer.

The enclave of Corps soldiers we're here on Iso Umm, a moon off Spectra 5, to mop up has dug into a substantial weapon cache hidden in an old Admin mine. It had taken almost a week to neutralize their air defenses, and another three days of constant assault on the ground to breach their bunker. David and I are here with the other 247 fighters from Ground Squadron 8, 90 percent of us former Corps.

Steward continues, "The only thing left is to deal with are the remaining Loyalists at your location. Can your unit handle that?"

The question is rhetorical. He means he'll send a transport to bring us back to the *Celestial* after, and only after, we've handled it.

David gives the affirmative, clicks off his satcom channeler, and leans his back against a black, smooth boulder, the same as the kind that makes up almost the entire surface of Iso Umm. "Fuck," he says.

"No more than another day, tops," I try to reassure him and dig through the remaining containers of liquids our platoon has piled behind our frontline berm. Pulling out one labeled Passion Fruit, I squash the urge to celebrate like I'd just won the lottery. Everyone loves this flavor and the passion fruit always disappears first. Sure, it may taste a little like someone tried to mask the flavor of sulfur with asbestos dipped in sugar, but that's just the vitamins (they tell us). Besides, the flavor is better than the rest, which taste more like toxic waste dipped in monkey piss, and I can't believe one got overlooked. I pull off the cap and take a swig, then wave it toward David. "Want a drink?"

He nods and I pass it over. Tilting his head back, he takes several deep swallows. Before he can finish the whole container, I swipe it back with a disgusted "Yeah, you're welcome. Don't mention it," then drain it and go back for a second. Monkey piss it is.

After settling down against the boulder beside him and finishing the drink, I start to nod off when he says, "Christ, what's that stench, Aly?"

"Dunno," I mumble without opening my eyes. "You'll get used to it." He's referring to the cloud of cheap-smelling cologne wafting from my body armor. Some practical joker made me their target. And they will pay.

I hear him scooting across the loose gravel to get some distance from me, then nothing for a few blissful minutes.

But that's all I'm going to get. Being a soldier in a war whose outcome matters to oneself makes sleep both a commodity and a distraction. My eyes jump open again soon, almost as if they're linked to some internal timer. The rest of our platoon, fifty or so dirty, dust-covered troops, encircle us, leaning against boulders of their own with their eyes closed, also trying to get something approximating sleep. It's the first break we've had in forty-eight hours of pushing the last of these Corps Loyalists underground. Third and Fourth Platoons group together nearby, inside perimeters of their own. David took charge of the whole company twelve hours into the ground assault after our CO, a guy from Obal 8 whom I'd liked and respected, got himself incinerated trying to take some of their fighters as captives. All of us now are just waiting for David to give us the final green light to end this operation.

"We could just starve them out," David says, his voice low enough that I can tell he's talking to himself. "They'll come out eventually if they know they're not going to get any reinforcements or supplies."

"Sure," I comment. The thing I don't mention is we're not getting any help either if we don't finish the job. But he's right, and that's the hell of it. It would really be that easy. "What do you think Medina's pushing us to attack for?"

"She wants the weapons."

"And if we leave them in there too long, they could start to sabotage them."

"Exactly." He clicks on his com and links to the other platoon leaders. "Henderliter, Joy, what's your status?"

Henderliter: "We're all green. Ready for go. Over."

Joy: "Ready on your mark, Erikson. Over."

David stands, runs his eyes and hands over his gear in a routine check that's been practiced hundreds of times, and calls out, "Second Platoon, at the ready!"

Fifty-plus soldiers get up with no hesitation. I follow, running my hands over my helmet, body armor, utility vest, ammo belt, and weapons in the same obsessive check, ensuring all straps are secure, all connections are closed.

He clicks on the com and gives the attack command. In a perfect military maneuver, our three platoons infiltrate the remaining thirty Loyalists' bunker and neutralize them in one hour-long push.

Sometimes a firefight is just that. Other times, it's a massacre.

SCRAPING THE CRUST OF dried blood and dust off my face and arms and out of my hair is going to be a full-time job tonight. By my estimate, about two hundred of us came back. But none of the Admin Loyalist soldiers are going anywhere except back into the dust—and down the drains aboard the *Celestial*.

"Hey Erikson!" someone yells, and both David and I halt our trudge toward the showers and turn. Potts, a dark-haired ex-citizen, one of the few aboard, continues, "Uh, you, David—Medina wants you on the bridge."

"Can it wait?"

"Guess you have to ask her," he says and hustles past us on some other task.

"Must be something important," David mocks.

I nod. One thing about these ex-citizens working aboard a fighting vessel, they seem to always elevate whatever task or duty they're on into some kind of overdramatic life-or-death status. As if Command General Medina would entrust anything more essential than cataloguing gear or indexing data to these militarily clueless pinheads. Sometimes we get a laugh at their self-created grandeur. Other times, like when we're covered in gore and haven't slept more than a few hours in days, we have a hard time not strangling them.

"Come on," I offer, "I'll go with you."

It's strange to be walking these pristine, gleaming passageways, which are the hallmark of a fleet cruiser. There's no dust in space, and ship environments are as hermetic as they come. Before the Soldier's Rebellion of 2719 and our subsequent desertion, when David and I had still been in the Corps, every reentry of a fleet craft after a planet-side chit included twenty-four hours of quarantine to examine soldiers for new or infectious pathogens we may have picked up. This was after the full-body scrub down, of course. For a soldier, privacy is a myth, and being turned into the focal point of multilevel tissue and cell scopes was never really a big deal—even our bones and guts got more attention from ship doctors and medical analysts than most children get from their parents. We'd been held inside a decontamination airlock until every last speck was scrubbed, sucked, or sponged from our bodies and gear—and the truth is, soldiers looked forward to the observation period simply for the time it gave us to rest.

But because reentry processing took a squad, a platoon, or sometimes a full company out of rotation for so much time, our tours planet-side tended to be as long as, and often longer than, needed. I'd gone from periods of days to months stuck on scattered rocks throughout the system, with nothing better to do than learn new ways to gamble and lose my pay, or collect new recipes from the population for cooking up whatever edible local flora and fauna were around. Populations that were friendly, that was. Which weren't all of them.

We didn't spend time patrolling backwater planets for nothing. We were there with a purpose, usually to quell potential rebellions or uprisings. Someone in the Corps monitoring stations would read suspect satellite message packets or overhear key terms while listening to planet radio coms that would send up alarms. Or an analyst would simply do math on variables such as age spectrum, resource and equipment quality or lack thereof, mortality rates of the population, and a number of other factors, and come up with a higher-than-average probability of rebellious activity, and in we'd go. Mission: keep the locals in line.

In line. There was a term of such extreme vagueness that even the most unimaginative soldier in the system—and that's saying something—could come up with some kind of plan of action or mission goal. I'd seen the words come to mean everything from helping to restore derelict factories to shooting on sight any person or group that was considered a threat.

And what exactly had we considered a threat? That all depended on who would be filtering and evaluating the after-action report. If it was an officer known for their hostility toward non-cits, a threat could be as simple as a fist shaken in anger or a warning to soldiers to leave them alone "or else." If it was an officer with a conscience, our platoon leaders had to keep it civil. We were, after all, the Capital Military Corps of the Advanced Worlds.

Advanced. The word is almost a punch line.

But the situation now is a little different. Medina hasn't quite been able to reconstruct all the prewar protocols that used to be in effect, and David and I reach the bridge without even a second glance from the onboard protocol monitors.

Activity on the bridge isn't as frenetic as I'd expect after such a large-scale assault—the annihilation of a Corps Loyalist fleet cruiser is the biggest success, and biggest operation, in our strategy—but that's how Medina commands. Order and efficiency rule everything she touches, and there are rarely any moving pieces that aren't comparable to precision clockwork. Sometimes I try to imagine what she would look like panicked, but my mind can't seem to dredge up anything that fits. The closest I get is an image of a cartoon caricature of a freaked-out cat, with its back arched, fangs bared, and fur bristling.

"Commander," David says, approaching the bridge's command booth where Medina stands in discussion with her first lieutenant.

She turns around gracefully, her face alert and slightly predatory. David's quiet approach must have surprised her. I'm again reminded of a cat. One that's about to pounce. Then her features smooth out and she says, "Erikson, thanks for coming. I know you must be ready to take a few hours off, so I'll get right to the point."

I can hear her just fine from where I linger, waiting at the rear of the bridge, another indication of how orderly and smoothly everything on the fleet ship *Celestial* runs. The fact that I'm on the bridge at all is something that would have been completely unheard of in my days in the Corps. I'd been an enlisted navigator for surface-to-orbit troop ships, but never on these cruiser-class ships. And only officers worked the bridge.

Medina runs things with more transparency, a quality that seems to have endeared her to more than an expected number of followers and fighters. The Admin's underhanded duplicity and lying is what led to the war in the first place, and I assume Medina wants to make sure no one thinks that way of operating will continue. She's fond of the phrase "unity through trust," which has been a necessary philosophy for helping blur the dividing lines between the citizens, non-citizens, and now ex-Corps soldiers who have been fighting together on the anti-Admin side. Since before people began inhabiting the Algol system, a classist mentality had typically set these three groups at odds, theoretically if not physically. Even the Capital Military Terrestrial Corps and Capital Military Stellar Corps had maintained a vibrant sense of competitive contempt for each other before this war changed everything. The Terrestrial Corps ranks, as David and I had been, called ourselves the "Fight" soldiers and the Stellar Corps the "Flight" soldiers to differentiate ourselves, taking pride in the fact that we spilled our blood in ground combat and didn't have the opportunity (or, presumably, desire) to fly away when things got sticky.

Medina's doing what she can to erase that dividedness and listens to what David has to say about our mission on Iso Umm without a hint of rank bias. As the equivalent of a company commander, and having spent a good share of his time outside the Corps participating in non-cit life and using real-world fighting tactics as a deserter, David's experience and leadership are qualities Medina highly values. His utility to her, and by extension mine, is uncomfortably reminiscent of the reasons Rajcik had hired us on after we deserted the Corps during the Soldier's Rebellion. But I don't let it keep me up nights. Given that every other week since the war began has seen fighting conditions similar to the last few days, I've continually been too overworked to let *anything* keep me up at night when I'm back in garrison.

"How did things look out there?" she asks.

David leans against the control bench. "Same as things always look on these moons. Like God bleached the color out of everything and decided it would be fun to litter the ground with rocks that rip through your clothes like razors."

That's my brother. A poet at heart.

"Did you capture any Loyalists for interrogation this time?"

"None of them seemed willing to live long enough to be taken prisoner."

She scowls at him. Intel has been the hardest commodity to get since the Admin had the Corps wipe out communications system-wide by destroying all of their satellites. *System assets have permanently lost telemetry,* as the saying goes. With the latest mission's success, we know of ten fleet cruisers that have been knocked out of the game, and, last we heard, our side still had four others working with us. But that leaves eleven unaccounted for, and of those, six Admin and Corps Loyalist fleet cruisers remain the biggest threat we face.

"David, you're one of the most experienced ground soldiers I have. Which means you know that anything you can do to get us more information will help us win this war. The sooner we win it, the sooner we can start putting the pieces back together."

"Roger."

From where I stand, Medina's scowl almost looks like it's hardening into stone. David's lack of military decorum has to be like sticking hot needles into her eyeballs, but what can she do? We're not an army, this isn't the Corps anymore, and there's no such thing as a code of military order and discipline. What chain of command we have exists because there's no other way we could keep the ship in the sky, or even survive, without some kind of functioning system. But Medina learned quickly how to toe the line with those of us who deserted after the Rebellion. We lost a taste for taking orders long before she came into the picture. And it doesn't matter that the Admin is a common enemy; David and I, and others like us, will never willingly accept a reversion to old Corps standards.

"Anything else, Medina?"

Her scowl gives way to her regularly composed, yet stern, expression. "Just a heads-up that one of our scouts has reported activity near Broon, off Spectra 6. We'll be moving in to investigate in a few hours."

Bleeding Christ, another operation in just a few hours, a day at the most? David's tone mirrors my thoughts. "Commander, my unit is wiped out. We need a few days to stitch ourselves together before another ground incursion."

"Oh, you misunderstand—of course, Erikson. I don't mean to send your company back in. I'm letting you know that you'll be staying ship-side for a few missions. You, all of you"—she turns her head toward me and dips her chin in acknowledgment—"have shown incredible aptitude and achieved fine successes out there. I know how hard it is to be fighting *against* people you once fought side by side with, and I can't promise you the worlds will ever recognize your sacrifices and courage. That being said, I want to give you some time to rest. It's the best I can do. We'll rotate your company into onboard duties in a couple of days. Until then, consider yourselves to be on R&R, for what it's worth. You'll let your people know?"

"Roger," David repeats, keeping his own face stoic, and I wonder what's going on behind his light-green eyes.

"For freedom," she finishes and turns back to Lieutenant Steward, who still waits quietly in the booth.

David skulks down the corridor to our unit's berth, and I follow along, fighting to undo a dirt-encrusted buckle on my armor's torso plate. When we reach our bay, he slams his hand into the hatch code box hard enough to make its backlights flicker briefly.

"Whoa, big brother, it's zed-zero-zed-five, not *wham!*, FYI."

"Sacrifices and courage? Aptitude and achievements? Who does she think she's talking to? This war isn't about freedom any more than she's still a Corps officer. Maybe before, but not now. If I'm going to be condescended to, she should at least stop pretending she's some kind of leader of a new-and-improved master society. She's just repeating the same fucking bullshit jackboot game that got us here."

The hatch opens and La Mer and Desto come through it. "Hey, Erikson His and Hers! You're back," La Mer quips. "You look like shit."

"And damn, Aly, what's that smell? You visit a brothel while you were playing soldier?" Desto and La Mer both break up at my body armor's odor, still front-and-center, even after the three-day-long incursion.

"This was you?" I ask, finally identifying the prankster behind this nauseating practical joke. "I can barely breathe!"

"Don't worry, Twig. Despite your stench and filthy mouth, your overwhelming beauty and charisma still have the power to turn every man into your personal twat-bot."

La Mer looks aghast. "Jesus, you guys. Gross."

"It's the language of love, baby. Aly and I have an understanding." Desto winks at me.

Rolling my eyes, I reply, "You're going to pay for this. And I told you not to call me Twig."

With a last chuckle, he calms down, and his face grows serious. "How'd it go?"

David pulls his torso piece over his head. Sand and black rock dust filter down around his feet. Pushing his matted hair out of his eyes, he replies, "Brother, all things being equal, I'm starting to wonder if we're even fighting for anything anymore."

FOUR

Another one died last night. He had an unexpected and unquenchable fever and then . . . gone. Like a magazine running dry and the world going silent with your last trigger pull. It's things like this that make me wonder if David had been right. Had we been fighting for anything?

At least it was natural causes this time, not suicide, like the last one. Thank Christ. I don't think the doc could take another one of those. Still, how natural is a death that could so easily be avoided if we had the right medical supplies? I just wish I wasn't the one who will have to tell Vitruzzi.

I step through the cruiser's pedestrian exit to get some fresh air before doing the deed. I don't like to spread news like this on the radio; it feels so—uncaring. Like someone's death doesn't rank any higher than reporting on supplies and ammunition. That's too much like combat, where a casualty count really is nothing more than a number. I'd known commanders who would curse the dead for having the gall to die midfight and leave a battle undermanned. But the fighting is over, and civilized people dignify death with a little more . . . I don't know . . . compassion? Besides, she's usually here early to make morning rounds. I'll tell her then.

This fleet cruiser, once the PCA *Andromeda*, is nothing but a five-city-block-sized steel derelict that's been planted in the midst of vines, trees, and scrubby brush outside Keum Libre's colony like a monolithic statue of a past age. It came down sometime during the war, and the crew who hadn't abandoned have assimilated smoothly into KL's colony. The thing it really is, though, is our last connection to civilization. The technology inside its structure is the only thing that sets us apart from the nomadic tribes of old Earth. One half is an armory with enough weapons and armaments to lay waste to a city, and the other half serves as a hospital for the sick, the feeble, the broken, and the dying. And the supreme god— goddess, really—that haunts its alloy and polymer halls is none other than our good doctor and former *Sphynx* captain, Eleanor Vitruzzi.

Without access to the vast energy sources required for these types of cruiser-class fleet ships to stay in the air, and with the easiest interior to keep clean and sterile, it wasn't hard to decide it should serve as the hospital for wounded fighters who somehow managed not to get turned into carbon sludge during the war. Karl and I, Vitruzzi and Brady, Desto and my brother David, Venus and Jeremy La Mer, and most of the other surviving settlers from Agate Beach put our roots down on Keum Libre as soon as the main fighting was over. Even if the outcome wasn't clear, the one thing that even the dimmest bulb knew by then was that everything was irrevocably changed. After the war, there would be no picking up the pieces and rebuilding the system based on the old model. Even the pieces were in pieces. Knowing the kind of chaos that would be coming, settling on KL was an easy decision. With the desalination plant, the mostly unsettled expanse of the planet, and limited take-off and landing points, it's ideal for hunkering down and staying out of the line of fire.

And we're doing okay here. We're already growing produce crops—La Mer and Brady's facility with cultivation coming as a surprise to more than just me—and have a small fleet of watercraft that tap the sea to keep us fed. But another purpose of our happy little home has been to provide what aid and shelter we can to the wounded we come across. Becoming an impromptu medic for the colony is never something I anticipated. But V needed help, so we all found ways to do it. I've had my hands in more wounds than I ever thought I could stomach in the last few months, and it never gets any easier. It just gets to where you can shut off your mind and treat it like a science experiment. A science experiment that some-times screams. I know more about tying off a spurting artery and stitching up a layer of torn muscle than most third-year residents, but at least we're doing more than just waiting for starvation and infection to pick us off slowly. And these days, it seems to be the only thing Vitruzzi can stay focused on.

Haggard isn't even the right word to describe her; she's grown almost too gaunt to find clothes that fit, and frequently I've had to repeat her name three or four times before getting her attention. It's like she's not even present in her own body anymore, and it's wor-rying everyone. The bad news I have for her today just seems that much worse because I'm no longer sure she's stable enough to handle it. At least she has Brady.

Sunlight reflecting off the windscreen of an approaching hover-runner draws me out of my thoughts. It pulls into the wid-ened-out area beside the cruiser and powers down, settling against the earth with a dull thud. The screen retracts, and I feel an instant sense of relief at the sight of David stepping out of the cab.

Rushing over, I reach him in time to catch his pack as he tosses it over the side. "No one told me you were back!"

He smiles, looking a little tired but happier than usual. "Yeah, we got in about twenty minutes ago. The colony's satellite seems to be on the fritz again, so we couldn't call in."

"Did it go okay? Find anything we can use?"

"Only"—he reaches into the cab and grabs a sealed metal cylinder that rattles slightly—"the jackpot. I'll tell you about it—"

The sound of the colony's heavier track vehicle drowns him out as it pulls in beside the runner. Two of the colonists jump off the back as it powers down and slide open the bars holding the cargo-bed door closed. Then Karl swings out of the cab.

Tripping over my feet with excitement—and more relief than even seeing David had elicited, which I'd never admit to my brother—I rush over and grab Karl, holding tight. "Missed you, lover," I whisper against his neck.

"Me too," he says, and we stay this way, in each other's arms.

"Don't let the rest of us disturb you," David says eventually.

Letting go of Karl, I wave my hand toward the cargo bed. "Is that the jackpot?"

David smiles at me. "Nope, that's just the first card."

Curious, I walk over and see what's inside. Hard plastic bins about the size of an ammo crate fill half the cargo space, and the remaining space contains boxes stamped with caducei and the names of hospitals or clinics that had once been on Obal 8. The extra medical supplies alone, something we rarely come across even on the longer scavenging missions, make this score better than good.

"So what's in those bins?"

David responds, "Help us unload and I'll tell you."

"IT'S ABSOLUTELY BEAUTIFUL, Karl. But I'm going to have to agree with V on this one. This is less than useless out here," Desto says, clenching his entire body to keep himself from breaking into hysterical laughter.

Vitruzzi had arrived for her morning rounds just a few minutes after David. Her subdued excitement at seeing the med supplies quickly gave way to the same curiosity I had about what the rest of the cargo contained. Because of Desto's ability to identify and defuse anything that might be rigged for bigger surprises, we'd called him up before opening anything. Once he'd inspected everything and given the all clear, we popped the bins.

No doubt, the disappointment and confusion on my face reflect the rest of theirs. A good portion of the cargo bins are full of contraband liquor, something that smells like it had probably been part engine degreaser and part something you'd find at the bottom of a rubbish bin. The stench is suspiciously close to the crud I'd drunk just before my guts jumped ship through the back door and kept me off David and Karl's last run. The rest of the containers hold a mix of more medical supplies and a strange array of sealed chemical elements. Carbon, nitrogen, sulfur, hydrogen, oxygen, and various others.

"I guess now we know why they left it out there. This stuff will make you blind faster than a sledgehammer to the brain stem," Karl responds, chuckling despite himself. "Want to run it past your more refined taste buds, Aly?"

I throw him a scowl loaded with a promise to make him pay later, and he returns it with a half-lifted eyebrow that promises to enjoy it.

Glancing at Vitruzzi, I realize her eyes haven't left the contents of the final bin since we'd broken the locks. The tendons in her neck stand out like barbed wire strained close to the breaking point. It didn't help that I'd had to tell her about the newly shipped-to-oblivion colonist. She'd taken the news with as much silent composure as always, but she didn't try to hide the sag of her shoulders or the tension that had further deepened the lines around her eyes and across her forehead. I understand her disappointment about losing someone, but now, looking at the usual cargo, she looks as if she's about ready to kill someone.

Unsettled by her expression, I try to calm her down. "We're still good, V. We have plenty of bandages in storage, and the antibiotics are lasting longer than we expected."

She snorts, and her expression goes from rage to disgust. She's like an ever-shifting storm front these days. Sometimes I want to tell her she needs to take a vacation, but I value the current arrangement of my facial features too much. Besides, she's Doc V; she's the reason so many in our colony are even still alive. If her job has caused her to lose her sense of humor, I'm sure there's no one here who doesn't think the trade-off was worth it.

"I have work to do," she says, and leaves.

The rest of us stand around the crates, feeling like a group of incompetents.

Finally, David remarks, "So the takeaway is to open the salvage before getting back to KL, next time."

"Don't worry about it," I say. "You know you don't hang around a derelict and take your time looking through everything. That's just a good way of advertising yourself as a mark."

"I think what David means is, he could have spent the last couple weeks en route getting sauced, pickled, and otherwise drunker than Cooter Brown. Missed opportunity if I ever saw one, bro," Desto says, slapping David good-naturedly on the shoulder. Then, more seriously: "Don't worry about it, man. We all know it isn't easy out there."

After a pause David tries smiling and replies, "Pickled? That shit would have turned me into something you'd put in a jar next to a two-headed calf."

"And you'd finally be with your own kind," Desto says, making us all laugh.

"Anyway," Karl puts in, "what the hell should we do with this?"

"Let's see if Venus wants it," I say. "Could be good for cleaning parts."

Everyone nods in agreement, and we spend the next half hour loading the bins back on the tracker to take over to the dock and out to Venus on the platform.

IT'S ALREADY LATE EVENING before Karl and I finally get some alone time.

"Yeah," he says after I ask about the salvage op Venus's new degreaser came from. "It was easier than we expected. The ship was just an Admin derelict hanging free outside of anyone's orbit. We got lucky. I mean it was purely random to find it out there."

Karl hands me his Kaldor 75 sidearm and starts stripping out of his equipment vest. I watch closely, hoping to get a chance to help him with the shirt and pants soon. "We took that route through the Spectras specifically to avoid coming into contact with any other ships. The number of scavs is getting worse again, just like it was right after the war started. I guess . . . I don't know. People are either getting more organized or more desperate."

"Could you tell what happened to the derelict?"

"We didn't have time to do much searching, but it looked to me like it was out of power. The hull, everything we saw, was still intact. The crew must have jet on landing skiffs and probably intended to come back for the goods." He shrugs, his features arranged in disturbed contemplation. "Guess they got sidetracked."

Out of power—same story for most of the bigger ships that are still in one piece, and the same reason the *Andromeda* will stay permanently parked on KL, even if we could repair it. We were lucky that the *Sphynx* had a solid supply of solar seeds when we hit the deck right before Rajcik went off the deep end. That surplus has kept our three scout ships in the sky for the last six months.

Speaking of sidetracked, Karl's not doing anything to stop my hands as they embark on an exploration of the lines of his abdomen and over the lower shelf of his pecs, my fingers running through his chest hair on a safari that feels weeks overdue.

"Next time you go, I'm coming with you," I inform him as I lightly tease one of his nipples.

"Like I'm going to argue," he answers, then pulls me hard against his body in a way that lets me know we're done talking.

THE RISING DAWN SLIPS through our window box, and I reach over Karl to tug the improvised sunscreen over it. There isn't much to scavenge on Keum Libre, but everything that can be stripped from the *Andromeda* has been, and enterprising builders like Karl and me have begun constructing our own private dwellings outside the main colony area. I don't sleep here when he's not around, though—too much quiet for me to be able to relax. For years in the Corps I craved privacy. But now that I have it, I can't help but get a little spooked. And then, of course, there's the coffee-cup-sized arthropods clicking around outside. A face-to-face moment with one of those one morning as I left for work was all I needed to assassinate chivalry for good. When Karl and I stay out here, I always hold the door for *him* to go out first.

"So was there anything else worth another trip on the derelict?" I ask, picking up the thread we promptly forgot about last night.

He pauses before answering, brushing his fingertips along the inside of my arm. "Yeah. I mean, maybe."

"Maybe?"

"It looked like some sort of data-storage unit, but bigger than any I've ever seen. There was a mechanical component to it too. It's hard to explain. Almost like a matter printer—you know the kind I mean?"

I nod.

"We didn't locate the ship's manifest, and it didn't look like something that had any immediate benefit to the colony, so we left it there. In any case, I'm curious. David was too."

"Even a solid-matter printer could come in handy, if we can get the right drivers and materials for it. Are you planning to talk to Brady about taking the *Orika* again?"

"It's probably a good idea. But I'm in no hurry to leave. I just got back and our love shack needs some work."

I roll my eyes at him, and he gives me a sexy half grin. "I know. Venus and Jer are working on the portable com-boxes for all the outlying dwellings that are getting put up. And they're already running an ion net for everyone to tap into power."

"All that has happened in the three weeks since I left? Wow. Those two don't sleep, do they?"

"As if you have to ask . . ."

"C'mon, lover. Let's go get some breakfast," he says and hands me my shirt.

FIVE

Being part of a good crew can get you a lot of places, but one place it will never get you is out of your own head. Mornings on Keum Libre bring that home to me more than anything else. At least, the mornings when I'm not dealing with the tragedy of another colonist's death or some other kind of emergency. In one sense, I guess we're all fortunate that those hectic and troubling mornings are growing more and more rare, but in another sense, waking up and having the time to realize—to fully comprehend—that civilization as we knew it will never exist again can really throw off a person's equilibrium. And discovering how okay with that I am, well, that's the most unbalancing thing of all.

Which explains the spike of excitement I feel when Vitruzzi walks up to our table as Karl and I eat in the *Andromeda*'s main chow hall and says, "You're leaving in thirty-six hours."

Karl splutters into his coffee. "What?"

"You said there are more med supplies on the derelict you and David found, right? It's imperative that we have them, sooner rather than later. The drug stock here is too thin already." She places a cup of coffee on the table and sits down beside me. Drops of the pounding rain, so common in KL's jungles, bead off the tips of her lank hair, emphasizing how worn down she looks.

Inwardly, I heave a sigh of relief. I'm better in the air. All this staying put makes me restless, and the constant arguing among the colonists makes anywhere else sound like paradise. Life's hard enough—without *people* making it harder.

Karl gets over the surprise quickly. Whether he admits it or not, the same jet-setter traits that made him join the Corps all those years ago in the first place still exist. "You know, V," he says, "maybe you should come with us. Jade and Sánchez can handle the infirmary for a few weeks, and we could use you on the ship to help identify things we need."

The Millar triplets of about twelve years old run up to our table, giggling and fighting at the same time, and interrupt Karl. "Mr. Strahan," the silken-black-haired girl says, putting her arm into the chest of her trailing brother to stop him, "can you take us up in one of the scouts? You promised you would when you got back."

Karl smiles at them, then glances around the mess hall, probably looking for their parents, Jennifer and Ivan. "Looks like I can't this time, kids."

"Aw, when?" one of the boys, Jens, I think, asks. Before Karl can answer, the kid stands up straighter and nods at me somberly, like a meter-and-a-half-tall CEO. "Hi, Miz Erikson. How are you?"

His sister and brother start giggling again, and he withers them with his violet glare. Or rather, he *tries* to wither them, but coming from a twelve-year-old it's about as intimidating as a puppy chewing on a sock. The giggling continues until I answer, "Good, thanks, um, Jens? Where's your folks?"

"They're still asleep," the other boy answers.

Shouldn't you be too, then? I want to ask. My facility with children is about the same as it is with kitchen or gardening tools—essentially nonexistent. I've been to dozens of planets and encountered all types of creatures and germs that make sleeping anywhere but inside a sealed room a bad idea, but children are by far the most alien.

"Look, we're heading out again on another scout run in a couple of days," Karl interjects. As their expressions begin to wilt, he goes on, "It's an exciting mission! We're rendezvousing with a mid-class transporter that's full of supplies and who knows what. If we find anything you'd like, I will definitely bring it back. Maybe we'll find some hover-skis or bikes."

"Hey kids," Vitruzzi breaks in. "We have a lot of planning to do, okay?"

"Okay, Dr. Vitruzzi," they chime in unison and take off at full throttle again, as if they'd never even slowed down.

Karl's eyes track them across the chow hall, a strangely bemused glint in them. When he looks back, he's serious again. "So what do you say, V? We could use you to pick out the necessities. I don't want to haul in a bunch of aspirin if there's something more important right there."

"No, that's not—"

"You should go. Get away for a while." Brady comes up behind us with his own tray, apparently overhearing the discussion.

"Patrick, I'm the only doctor this colony has," Vitruzzi protests, as he grabs the stool across from her and sits.

"Yeah, but you're also only human. You *need* to go. Karl is right, and you're killing yourself right now."

As if it's any less hazardous for her health to be flying through airspace that's infested with scavengers, and worse—the desperate. The rumors about what's happening in some of the more remote outposts, the lengths settlements have gone to for the sake of survival, get worse with every salvaging op we run. Some people who were only marginally civilized before the war have become outright animals, and pirates, slavers, and marauding raiders are now just part of daily life beyond KL. I don't mention this, though. Karl and Brady are both right. Vitruzzi *is* killing herself, and she's the best judge of the colony's medical needs.

She sighs, warring with her sense of duty and her sense of reality. She can't keep up the pace she's going, and if there's something else going on in her head, maybe a change of scenery will help her work it out. That's always been my best fix. And I'm completely well-adjusted.

She seems to decide and asks, "How much more cargo is there?"

"A lot more than we can take on one ship," Karl responds. "We'll probably need two. The Orika and the Nebula have the most capacity, but the *Teibo* is in the best condition. And there's this other thing we found—some kind of materials processor, but small. Pretty interesting. It may be worth hauling back and having Kittinger look over."

It hits me. "Materials," I blurt.

Brady stares at me curiously until I go on. "Like all those sealed-up chemicals that were in the haul you brought back yesterday," I tell Karl. "Maybe this thing you're talking about uses those."

"For what?" Karl asks.

I shrug, then Vitruzzi says, "I want Quantum with us."

"Why?" I ask, clamping down on a stronger protest lodged right behind my teeth. I guess you just never stop disliking someone who once kidnapped you. Unless they become your crew, that is.

"I don't want him near the soil compound."

"Look, V," I reason. "Let's just drop him off at Obal 6 like he's asking. You don't trust him, I don't like *or* trust him, and he doesn't want to be here."

"We've offered, Aly," Brady says and takes a swallow of his coffee. "But he doesn't want to go without 'assets,' as he puts it."

"Last time I looked, no one here signed a socialist charter," I respond. "Life's tough. He can either take the offer of a ride, or he can shut up, right?" If Karl were an eye roller, he'd be rolling them at me. When no one answers, I sigh. "Fine. Then I'd like Desto to come too."

"With Zeta pregnant? He's not going anywhere," Brady remarks.

"She's a good pilot; she can fly the *Teibo*. Besides, they've been wanting a honeymoon." My joke falls flat. Tough crowd.

Brady continues to argue. "She was a *commercial* pilot. Tactical flying is a different matter. I don't want to put anyone in harm's way, but especially not someone in her condition."

"Condition?" Vitruzzi asks. "Pat, she's pregnant, not dying of cancer. There's nothing stopping her from flying."

Awkward silence. Outside myself and Karl, I've never met two more stubborn people. Vitruzzi and Brady never fight, at least not that I've heard, but they *disagree* at a level that makes anyone in their orbit feel like they're being tractor beamed into a volcano.

Eventually, Karl says, "Aly, why don't we run it by them before I head out to the platform today. Thirty-six hours?" He raises an eyebrow at Vitruzzi, who nods. "Then I guess I don't need to unpack."

SIX

Spinning slowly in a vertical position, like a carousel with a dying engine, the Admin supply transporter seems to have been pinned to its section of empty space and left there to dry up and wither away. The name—PCA *Galatea*—hovers into view for a moment before disappearing with the ship's next rotation. The funny thing about out here, though, is that a hundred, two hundred, even a thousand years from now, as long as nothing barrels into the derelict or knocks it out of its orbit, it will still look pretty much the same.

Our sensors pick up no trace of electrical or other energy fields, and just as David and Karl had said in the pre-mission briefing, there's no one on board answering our hails. It's just as dead in the air as it looks.

While Venus maneuvers us onto a wide, flat surface and engages the magnetic clingers, Karl, Vitruzzi, Hoogs, and I get suited up. Vitruzzi contacts the *Teibo* and directs Desto, David, and Mason to do the same and then join us on the derelict. We'll be able to scour the transport quickly with every able body available to help. That leaves Zeta, who hadn't needed to be asked twice to join the excursion, alone on the *'Bo* with Quantum. If he's wondering why Vitruzzi wanted him along, he hasn't said anything. I wonder how he likes being left out of the search, then realize he's probably more than happy not to be floating around in space aboard a ship that could be home to hundreds of potential hazards. Quantum is not a fool.

The rest of us on the other hand . . .

After we're all gathered and tethered together at the outer man-door that served as Karl and David's entrance on their pass a couple weeks back, V tells Zeta to hang back and keep the *'Bo* on low power with cloaks on until we've had some time to get a look inside the *Galatea*, and Venus keeps the *Orika* attached and waiting. Now we just have to hope that David and Karl's luck held on and no other salvagers have come through.

We drift in one by one, but my scavenger's sense is already telling me what I need to know, and I exchange a glance with Karl. The expression on his face says exactly what I'm thinking: nobody's home, or if they are, they gave up the habit of breathing long before we arrived.

No pressure, no gravity, no air, and no lights. We flip on the high-beam LEDs attached to our face shields, then split up to start a search. Karl and I head toward the lower deck, David and Vitruzzi take a right-hand corridor, and Hoogs, Desto, and Mason go left. Usually, the need to hurry in salvage jobs like this is paramount, but today is different. We have two ships and a lot of personal fire-power, which should serve as a buffer to let us take our time going through every room. Vitruzzi's made clear that our main needs are medical supplies and, as always, weapons and food, but with the limited capacity for salvage and cargo aboard our two scout ships, we have no choice but to be selective. Still, an Admin supply ship this size out in Spectra territory is unusual; maybe we can find something on board that will explain why it was here. And just maybe it will be something we can use.

After about an hour, Hoogs contacts us. They've reached the engine room and found severe damage to the flight controls from an electrical fire. By all appearances, the original crew had managed to get the meltdown under control, but not before it had moved into the central grid for the life support systems. Since we've found no bodies or signs of a struggle, the working theory is that, once their systems went offline, they'd been forced to take their landing craft down to Eruo Pium, a moon orbiting Spectra 3, in search of parts and aid to get the ship back together. The theory is further supported when we find no landing craft in the hangar or cargo bay. We know they've already been gone for at least four weeks—between the time it took for David and Karl's scout team to return to KL after finding it and then turn around and come back—so whatever is keeping the original crew away may well be permanent. Bad for them; good for us.

There hasn't been a peep on board, and Vitruzzi lets everyone know she and David are heading toward the bridge, leaving Karl and me to go down the last corridor to where the crew quarters probably are.

"Bingo," I whisper after my first glance down the hallway. Three rooms labeled Medical are lined up in a row. I know how excited this will make Vitruzzi.

I get Karl's attention and gesture toward the first. Inside, it appears that the room has never been touched. Aside from sundry items floating around, the wall cabinets are all closed and locked, and the equipment that's strapped to the ground is in pristine condition. If the other two infirmaries are this mint, we'll be able to gather enough med supplies to stock the settlement for at least six months. Maybe it'll help get Vitruzzi out of whatever funk she's in.

Karl hovers in behind me and shoots me a gleeful grin after getting a look around. "We're in business. Vitruzzi," he says into the com's open channel, "we hit pay dirt. Looks like the medical stations are all intact and still stocked." He puts a gloved hand on the arm of my suit and nods toward the doorway. "There could be more storage nearby where they keep the extra supplies, drugs, what have you. I'll get a look down the corridor and also see what I can find in the way of containers or boxes. Get to work on these cabinet locks until the rest get here to help."

I nod affirmatively and he pulls himself back outside, then lets the others know where we are while I start dismantling the first row of cabinets, hoping to find a healthy supply of antibiotics. Infections stemming from wounds are the primary problem back on KL and cause us to use up antibiotics faster than anything else.

Both scout teams arrive and we pick the place bleached-bone clean. While the antibiotic supply isn't as big as I'd hoped for, a major bonus comes in the form of a data-mesh that lists the contents of a bunch of unlabeled boxes we'd found in the cargo hold: a holographic surgical scanner that will assist Vitruzzi with diagnosing and potentially performing surgery on the more serious patients, as well as several more containers with lab-testing assays and equipment. The manifest doesn't list where any of this stuff was to be delivered, or why the ship was way out here near the Spectras, but with this excellent haul and the good it will do for the colony on KL, it hardly matters.

We direct all of the supplies to the main hangar and stage them with the cargo bins we want to take, along with the machine Karl spoke of—the matter printer, or whatever it is. Small containers can be pushed through the hull breach Karl and David's crew created last time, and someone on the outside will be able to walk them to the *Orika*. It's going to be a different matter to get the bigger containers out.

"If we can link them all together with a rope or a chain, we can secure them to a sturdy wall, then cut a larger opening through the main cargo hatch and the airlock to haul everything out," Karl suggests.

"If we destroy the airlock," Hoogs says, "this bird's never leaving orbit again."

No one says anything. While it may be true, the likelihood anyone will ever be around to try and fix it is, among other things, not our problem.

The comment goes unanswered, and Hoogs seems inclined to drop it. I'm standing next to him, the magnetic grippers of our boots making us and the rest of the boarding crew the only things touching the floor in the hangar. "Then just have the *Teibo* move into range, open the hull, and we can each grab a box and use our suit jump-thrusters to push us out through the airlock and into the *'Bo.*"

The group agrees on it being the best idea and we relay the plan to Zeta. Vitruzzi and I start moving the smaller cargo to the *Orika* while the rest tether everything together in preparation. In another forty-five minutes, we're all ready for the *Teibo*.

"What the . . .?" Venus's incredulous query comes through our radio, followed by several seconds of silence. I'm about to decide she forgot she was broadcasting, when: "That's just not right!"

"Venus, what's your status?" Vitruzzi asks, her eyes fixed on the expanse of space outside the breach we created.

"Cap'n, I'd say we have at least one visitor. I'm reading another ship moving toward us."

"Zeta, are you picking anything up?" V asks.

"Yeah, oh yeah," she replies. "Sure am."

"No, dammit," Karl cries. "Not a chance! This boat's been out here for weeks. No way another ship randomly shows up now."

"How long until they arrive, can you tell?" Vitruzzi asks.

"Soon," both pilots respond simultaneously.

Karl and I exchange a glance. "V," he says, "maybe Venus should unlink. She's a sitting duck if they're hostile."

Vitruzzi nods and passes on the order.

"Guys, what about you?" Venus asks. "What happens if they board?"

"I think we'll be able to handle them," Vitruzzi answers. "You two need to put some distance between this boat and yourselves—right now. Keep eyes on and transceiver links up. If you don't hear anything, come back in two hours and do a sweep. Most importantly, keep yourselves clear of engagement. The colony can't afford to lose you or those scouts."

She turns to the rest of us. "The only people with rights to this salvage are the people who own the ship. If it's them, and they can prove it, we'll leave in peace. Otherwise . . ." The statement hangs, but we all know what it means.

I quickly unharness the T-Max laser I carry for outer-atmosphere jobs, everyone else copying the action with their own choice of firearm. We could open a black-market dealership with the range of weapons among this crew. "We don't want to give away our numbers," I remark. "Looks like good vantages from along that wall, up there on the catwalk, and . . ." I gesture at several potential cover positions.

"I'll stay put. Talk to them," Vitruzzi says.

"V, do you want—?" David starts.

"Yes," she answers before he can finish.

"Okay"—he nods—"we'll cover you."

The crew moves out to wait. Karl and I take the uppermost story, while Hoogs, a stringy marvel with chameleonlike powers, finds an out-of-sight niche to occupy on the main deck, and David digs in near the hull's primary hatch. Desto and Mason stand beside Vitruzzi. It's most likely whoever is out there will see our hatch demolition on their own scout pass. They won't see our ships, so they won't expect anyone else to be on board, which gives them every reason to take advantage of the invitation of an already open door. It's possible that they could even decide to go on by once they've seen another salvage crew has already come through. But if they don't, and they enter through some other means, we'll have plenty of time to regroup and confront them from new positions.

Twenty minutes later we hear them make contact. Judging by the lack of possible landing zones we'd observed on our own pass, they've chosen the same spot to cling on that Venus had. Time seems to pass at the rate of ice freezing in hell before the first three come through the opening. My weapon's sight locks on the instant the leading helmeted head becomes visible.

They immediately see Vitruzzi and company holding weapons at the ready. The visiting trio pause, taking in the rest of the bay, then wisely show their empty hands. Vitruzzi gestures for them to approach. There's no mistaking their disgust at getting to the ship too late to claim the salvage—not to mention having guns pointed at them.

When they're closer to Vitruzzi, she signals to them to turn on their coms, then says, "Sorry to say it isn't your lucky day, folks. This ship is ours."

The one in the middle tries to negotiate. "We've come a long way, lady. Any chance we could split some of the take?"

And there we have it. Admission that this isn't their ship to begin with. All that's left is a peaceful resolution to the situation—or whatever kind of resolution they'll take—and Vitruzzi can send them on their way.

A subtle flicker in my peripheral vision distracts me from their conversation, and I look around in time to catch another stranger coming through the upper bay hatchway. He doesn't see me nestled between hull reinforcement struts and moves to a flanking position near the rail, drawing a weapon of his own.

Dumbass.

He's just a kid, about twentyish. Old enough to be brave but not old enough to be smart. I don't want to kill someone who really doesn't have to be, so I give him a chance. Sneaking up and placing my gun barrel on the back of his helmet—where I apply just the right amount of pressure to grab his undivided attention—I lean near enough for him to hear me through the helmet and say, "That's a very clever idea. Exactly what I would do, in fact—find the high ground and get the drop on us."

I can see Karl across the bay with his hand in the air, asking for a status update. I raise a gloved thumb, then take a step around the kid so that he can see my face. But I don't lighten the pressure of the barrel against his head. "Now ask yourself this question. Are you ready to be remembered as a clever *dead* guy that *used* to be on their crew?"

I see the shock in his face, but he doesn't stall when putting his weapon out in front of him and releasing it. It floats there, unconcerned with the reasons why it's become suddenly weightless. I take a swipe and gently nudge it behind us and out of reach. "We're just going to stand by until they figure it out, roger?"

He nods. Not so dumb after all.

"So you just want the cargo? We get anything else on the ship?" one of the guys below is saying.

"That's right," Vitruzzi answers.

The three of them appear to confer while taking not-quite-surreptitious glances at the upper walkway. I pull my new friend to his feet and we wave down at them. "Deal," says the first, finally convinced to see things our way.

They regroup and start scouring the rest of the derelict while we linger in the hold, waiting for the *Orika* and *Teibo*. My O2 meter has dropped uncomfortably close to red by the time they arrive and we've filled them in on what had gone down. The other salvaging crew doesn't bother us, and we make quick work out of getting the cargo lines set up and the equipment moved aboard the *'Bo*.

Vitruzzi and I are still in the hold, just getting ready to jump out with the last large cargo bin. She's untying the line from the deck as I prepare to hail Karl to get ready for us when my feet suddenly begin to feel funny. Not funny exactly, more as if they're vibrating. As if, in fact, the derelict's engines are being cycled for flight. The other salvagers can't be trying to initiate flight operations. Can they?

SEVEN

I turn to Vitruzzi in alarm, about to warn her that we need to get out of here posthaste, but the next second I'm lifted to the top of the bay, shot from the floor like a cannonball. Vitruzzi gets pushed up against the ceiling next to me, and the cargo tether, bin still attached, zings out of the hold like a harpoon. There's a rumbling explosion from the direction of the engines, and I realize, somehow, *impossibly*, the ship is moving.

Frantically, I yell, "What the hell, V? Are we diving? Don't they realize this boat has no flight controls? Or airlock?"

Realize it or not, the fact of the matter is that we've been blown out of stasis. What had I said about them not being dumb? Scratch that. I don't know which direction we're going, but I do know we have to get off this beast before it disintegrates. The foredeck beyond the cargo bay had evac pods, and I grab Vitruzzi's suit, pointing in that direction.

"Come on! We'll be able to set up a transponder when we're outside so the crew can find us." If we're lucky.

At least one engine is online, but the ship's not moving too fast for us to pull ourselves through to the foredeck. The evac pods are two-seaters, and Vitruzzi and I shove ourselves into one. It's like putting sausage into a sausage casing, our bulky suits making the fit, already claustrophobic, worse than my worst nightmare shoved inside a coffin. But there's no other choice.

We're fumbling with the safety harnesses like idiot orangutans when the ship is suddenly hit by what feels like a planet. The hull absorbs most of the impact, and the e-pod's close confines protect us, but the jolt isn't what I'd call pleasant.

"Shit," V says. "We just broke through atmosphere."

We're on a one-way trip to Eruo Pium—not my first choice for an impromptu vacation—with maybe four minutes until impact. Her harness is latched and she reaches over to slam mine closed, then pulls the manual lever that releases us from the ship's belly, gambling that there's still enough time to escape before gravity smears us over the moon's face.

The velocity of our launch is instant and brutal. I feel as if I've swallowed my teeth, and the pressure on my chest makes breathing impossible until the pod's auxiliary pressure stabilizes. Slowly, the speed reduces to within the range of what human bodies can tolerate, and the light outside our pod window port grows brighter.

I'm just about to relax and start pondering what our next step is going to be when something slams into us, jarring both Vitruzzi and me hard enough to make my jaw clack, and knocking us into a new trajectory. A few red lights blink on the small control console, letting us know that things are going—or have already gone—awry. The only thing left to do is hang on and hope the speed dampeners still work.

A minute later another jolt pulls our descent up short, then we're drifting. The e-pod's base thunks to earth, and we slowly tilt over. My stomach lurches as my last meal threatens to evacuate. Then it relaxes, letting me off with a warning.

The impact is far less jarring than I'd expected. For just a second, we both remain motionless, taking in the newfound stillness and silence, the contrast almost unbelievable after the chaos of the last . . . Jesus, has it only been ten minutes?

Yanking my helmet off, I take a greedy gulp of air. At the moment, I don't feel much pain, but I know that's going to change later. The torque on the emergency pod and our helplessly suspended bodies, caused by whatever had hit us just after crashing into Eruo Pium's atmosphere, hammered my muscles and joints hard, but it hadn't killed us. That's something at least. Still, the minute I have a chance to do a full assessment, I have no doubt I'm going to be sorer than I care to imagine. I might even cry.

"Aly, we're down. Can you move?"

"That sucked," I groan.

"Are you hurt?"

"No, don't think so. You?"

"I'm all right."

She tries getting the coms up and running to see if either of our shuttles is near while I crank at the harness to get it off. They'll know we went down, but the likelihood they'll be within com range is narrower than my firing group. As for the other salvagers, they may be down here somewhere too, but there's no telling. If I remember my Corps training well enough, the type of bug-out we'd just had could sometimes result in as much as a 50 percent casualty rate. V and I made it, so the math isn't in their favor.

She curses and gives up on the com when the control console's last light goes dark. "Dammit. Come on, let's get out of here."

My gloved fingers fumble clumsily at the harness lock, but depressing the release button results in stubborn resistance. It feels jammed, probably from playing bumper ships. As I struggle with the straps, the feeling of being buried alive starts to settle over me like so much stale grave dirt. My throat begins to close up and my hands tug frantically, not doing any good, but there's no stopping them. I can't handle small spaces, and the present small space is getting more stifling by the second thanks to this goddamn harness.

"Hey, hey, Aly, calm down. Let me help." Vitruzzi reaches for the buckle over my chest and deftly cuts me free with the blade she keeps in the space suit. The straps holding me in loosen, but it barely helps. We're inside what amounts to a bullet casing for humans. The only way I'll ever be okay in a capsule this small is when they put me in my burn box for cremation. Even that thought makes cold sweat ooze from my armpits.

"Open the hatch, V," I whisper through a throat that feels stuffed with sand. "I gotta get out of here *now*."

She unbuckles and searches for the hatch handle. We were lucky; the pod fell over with the hatch faceup to the sky. Vitruzzi pulls on the release and nothing happens. She yanks harder, then resorts to kicking at the base of it, trying to jar it free. Whatever had struck us must have jammed the release mechanism; the thought makes the muscles in my jaw clench painfully. Did we survive the destruction of the cruiser just to die trapped inside this metal coffin?

Need to get out, need to escape before it's too late. Need some air. Need—

My focus starts to collapse into tiny pinpoints of light as the volume of panic inside my head goes up another few decibels. Without thinking, I reach for the T-Max I'd tucked between my knees and point it at the release mechanism, ready to shoot my way free if that's what it's going to take.

Before I pull the trigger, Vitruzzi shouts, "No!" and yanks it from my grip. "The frame's buckled. If you do that, you're just going to waste your charge. Take a deep breath and let me think, Aly."

Easy for her to say. *I need some—Calm down, Aly—I need some air—Just cool it, okay. You're going to be okay—NO! I need some fucking air!* This mantra continues, my brains heating to a boil, about to spill over.

Putting one knee into the seat, Vitruzzi turns around and gets into a half-standing, half-squatting position in order to reach into the containment bin overhead. *Need some air—Chill out.* While I tightly grip the material of my pants just above my kneepads and think about breathing in, breathing out, she searches inside. *Hurry up, V. Hurry up. HurryuphurryuphurryUP!*

"Got it," she says, then gets back into her seat. "Put your oxygen back on. I'm going to burn through the hatch."

"What?" I'm barely holding myself together and she wants me to put something even more constricting over my face?

"You have to. The fumes will make you sick. Here . . ." She reaches over to help me with the helmet, and I grip her wrist.

"No. I'll . . . I'll do it. Just be quick."

There must have been a toolkit or emergency prep box in the bin because she has about two fistfuls of E-10 wax that she quickly rolls into long strips and sticks to the shell in a circle big enough for us to crawl through. While I stare at the circle of wax hard enough to ignite it with pure freak-out urgency, she pulls her own helmet on and shocks the wax with the igniter. As it eats through the layers of metal, insulation, and thermal tiling, acrid blue smoke fills the cabin, and my heartbeat finally starts to slow. Surviving spacecraft explosions, firefights, atmospheric reentry in a tin can, and near-fatal midair collisions are all child's play compared to being turned into a human sardine. I keep telling myself it's all in my head. It doesn't help, but when daylight starts to shine through the circumference of Vitruzzi's homemade hatch, my throat begins to loosen up and let more oxygen actually reach my brain. *Sweet Jesus, air!*

Before the burn-through stops, she pushes herself almost into my lap—the hatch is on her side—and kicks the disconnected metal outwards. It gives after three good punts, and I have to stop myself from wrestling her to get outside first.

Where apparently the fun is just beginning.

We've barely put our feet on the ground when dirt kicks up in an abrupt flurry just a couple of meters away. At first, I think I must be suffering from aftereffects of the claustrophobia, but then more dirt swirls into the air and I don't need a lessons-from-the-war manual to know what it is. We're being shot at.

We both dive down beside the pod, but I catch a quick glimpse of who's firing. An open-topped hover-runner is about fifty meters away, closing the gap between us at its top speed. My brain does an automatic calculation, and I take a knee and bring my T-Max up for a shot in one fluid motion. I'd seen two people in the cab, a man driving and a woman standing up and firing at us from above the front dust shield. My first shot hits home, and she flies backward into the HR's cargo area.

My second shot goes into the vehicle's body. It apparently takes out the steering electronics board because the thing keeps moving at top speed—right over the top of us. Just before I duck, I see the driver working frantically to get the vehicle turned, but it doesn't happen. The base of it clips the pod's shell and the whole thing first gains a couple more meters of lift, then tilts over sideways. Its magnetic power mechanism blows and the HR crashes down just past us.

Vitruzzi closes on the driver and puts a bullet between his eyes before he has a chance to apologize.

And I thought the Admin was hostile.

I walk up to the HR and look inside. Both occupants are dead, their blood splattered about the cab. The woman looks to be in her early to mid-forties and the driver just a touch more. Neither wears any kind of uniform, and they're both emaciated, so it's probable they're just settlers or scavengers; the system is full of them now. Without a second thought, I strip them of their weapons. The woman had a carbine AK-80 like mine, which I lament is still on the *'Bo*. The activator that limits its users to only soldiers is disabled, shedding a ray of light on an otherwise gloomy situation. The man had only a laser-firing sidearm, which is out of charge and useless.

Stepping away from the disabled vehicle, I comment, "What a mess. Let's get the transponder up. I'll stand watch if you want to work on it."

She doesn't say anything, and I turn to see if she'd heard me. She's kneeling by the dead man, staring into his face intensely.

"V?" I try again. "We need to let them know where we are. There's no telling how long it will take them to find us, and there could be more scavs around."

I catch a sound and jerk my head up to scan the area. We're in a relatively flat plain, most of the ground around us dry but covered in a stunted, crackly grass. The landscape rises into a line of foothills about a kilometer to the north, and with the dampness in the air, I'm betting Eruo Pium's ocean lies on the other side. Sparse signs of people are evident, mostly just crisscrossing vehicle tracks that extend east–west. These, and the way the hover-runner had arrived so quickly, tell me that we must be close to some sort of outpost or settlement. Another glance at the dead couple is all it takes to hammer a nail of dread deep in my gut.

Then I see the source of the sound; a track vehicle lumbers toward us from the northeast. They can't go faster than a few kilometers per hour, but they're coming from the same direction as the HR. They'll be here within a couple of minutes. There's nowhere within a reachable distance for us to run, and our only cover is the pod and the overturned HR. Track vehicles usually have thick steel bodies and are very, very hard to penetrate with regular arms. Dammit, I did not plan to spend my day in multiple firefights. I should never have left Keum Libre.

"More company. Get ready," I tell Vitruzzi as I crouch with her behind the HR and dig in to wait. The newly acquired carbine has an almost full energy clip, so I should have enough rounds between it and my T-Max to keep the tracker crew occupied. For a while.

The tracker grows noisier, then suddenly quieter as the engine cuts to an idle. I look around the rear of the HR and see the passenger door of the cab swing open.

"You all okay?" a man shouts from the opened door. "We saw you coming down. Anyone hurt?"

So their angle is to check us out and see if we need help. I'm touched. I nudge Vitruzzi's shoulder—she still hasn't said anything—to indicate she should follow my lead, and keep my eye on the tracker. If we stay quiet, we should be able to draw at least one of them out and reduce their numbers.

"We have a medkit if you need it. Don't be afraid. Our settlement's just a little way from here. Food, water, aid, whatever you need. Hello?"

No one climbs out of the tracker, so I try to entice them. "My friend's injured. Looks like a broken ankle. Do you have a splint?"

"Yeah. Yeah! We have that. Come on over and I'll get it for you."

"No. I can't leave her here; please bring it."

No one moves or says anything. Then, to my utter surprise, a man jumps down from the cab and starts walking toward us with a splint in one hand. I don't see any weapons on him. Despite the tracker and the med supplies, the man looks like he could recently have been napping in a pile of dirt. He's filthy and ragged and as thin as the other two we'd shot.

He stops about five meters away and says, "Here," while holding the splint out.

Before I realize what's happening, Vitruzzi stands and moves past me toward him. She holds her pistol limply in one hand, and she's walking as if she's about to shake hands with the man. Has she lost her mind?

I jump forward and grab her by the shoulder, intending to pull her back behind cover. As soon as we're both in the open, someone else in the tracker opens up with a rifle, the shots low and aimed at our legs. Fortunately, the man approaching us ruins their field of fire and they miss, but I shove Vitruzzi as hard as I can back behind the HR and dive for the cover of the e-pod with the rest of my momentum. Hitting the rocky soil with my knees—and sending a silent thanks to the god of combat for my kneepads—I get into a good firing position in anticipation of V hammering them with cover fire from her own T-Max. I wait. And nothing.

Risking a quick look over the pod, I see her still crouched behind the overturned hover-runner. She's dropped the pistol beside her in the dirt and is hugging her knees like a child that's seen something scary in the dark. I don't see any blood or wounds anywhere.

Mystified, I shout, "V, you okay?"

I take the opportunity to get a couple more rounds at the tracker, which do no good, but she still doesn't respond. Dammit! She's freezing on me. I've seen it before, but she's the last human on the planet I would have expected it from. From here, I can't try and shock her to her senses. All I can do is yell at her and hope for the best.

"Vitruzzi! Pick up that pistol and cover me. I'm coming to you. Do you hear me?"

No. Goddamn. Response.

Pushing my back into the pod, I take a second to analyze the situation. Options, options. There are always at least two, but a lot of the time one of them is dying. The tracker crew isn't doing any firing. Just waiting us out. They know we have nowhere to run, and they'll have a clear shot if and when we break cover again. So *that's* not an option.

There was a time when I never left my rack without explosives. What happened to the good old days? As I look around, all I have at my disposal are rocks, sand, dead-looking grass, and broken shards of atmo-shield from the pod. Nothing that goes boom.

Another quick peek shows V hasn't moved. A round flies uncomfortably close to me, but I have enough time to see she's adopted the look that every person in the system knows at this point after the war: the thousand-yard stare. The only thing she's seeing right now are the horrors inside her own mind, both the real ones she's witnessed and the ones she's imagining on her own. Fuck. It's worse than I expected. And from Vitruzzi, one of the most level-headed and stalwart women I know. My day just went from bad to absolutely drowning in used toilet water.

Except . . . maybe there's some fuel left in the pod's tank. It uses combustible fluid in its reverse thrusters for slowing down when it gets near earth. Vitruzzi and I hadn't used up all the supplemental oxygen either. I might, just might, have what I need for an old-fashioned package of fuck-you. If the hull is as damaged as it looks, there's a chance I can get the O2 tank off and roll it under the tracker.

The one piece of luck I have is the fact that the pod's hatch is on my side. Pulling out my bolo, I lean inside and start attacking the upholstery of the seats. Soon nothing's left but the frame. It's fused to the steel cabinet that houses the O2 tank, but that's okay. The small toolkit from the overhead bin gives up its screwdriver, and I'm able to disassemble the interior of the seat enough to get to the steel cabinet's door.

It's been quiet for too long, and I pop out of the pod to see what might be sneaking up on me. Vitruzzi—same. Tracker—still quiet. Diving back in, I'm inside the cabinet in seconds, but discover that the pressurized O2 tank is bigger than the cabinet's opening. It's made to be refilled but not removed. Goddammit!

"Aly."

I jump back out and the sweat pours off my forehead, momentarily blinding me. "Aly," Vitruzzi says again, and to my relief, when I blink the sweat away, I see her looking at me. But the expression on her face is about as close to panic as I've ever seen. "It's over."

"No, we'll make it, V." Trying to make the most of her lucidity—who can guess how long it'll last?—I prompt, "Look inside the hover-runner. Is there anything in there like a grenade? Something we can toss at those cocksuckers?"

She stares at me like I'm from another planet for a minute, then turns her head to look inside the damaged vehicle.

"Give it up, ladies! You come out, we promise you won't get hurt."

Fantastic. We've arrived at the deal-brokering stage. I take a short second of pleasure knowing that their *not* knowing what we're up to is making them more edgy than we are. That second ends quickly, though, because I also know they'll get sick of waiting soon. That tracker could start up any minute and roll right over us.

"V! You have to hurry. Is there anything in there?"

She doesn't answer and appears to be going catatonic again, so I give up thinking and just start doing whatever my instincts suggest. After I crank the refuel cap and interior valve off the side of the pod with my screwdriver, my nostrils are hit by the tank's heavy, oily fumes in a nauseating wave. Next, I yank my utility vest off, followed by my jacket, and finally my shirt, tying the latter around the end of one of the internal support bars from the seat and shoving it down into the fuel tank. It comes back out dripping thick amber gel, which I light up with my portable torch. Black smoke immediately fills the air, the lack of a breeze making it hang around me in a gag-inducing cloud. Not that it matters. Hucking a nearby rock over the top of the pod and squeezing off a pair of rounds as a diversion, I take a quick—possibly final—breath and stand up with my flaming torch.

One solid swing of the carbine launches the blazing shirt onto the tracker's window screen. It hits with a satisfying splat that shoots burning fingers of flame across the screen and down the front. The fuel gel isn't going to burn itself out soon. With my momentary advantage, I streak to the hover-runner. Vitruzzi gives me a look so dark and full of despair that I can hardly believe she's the same woman. What happened? What sent her over the edge?

Not that I have time for worrying about it now. Yanking my jacket back on, I can see from my original vantage point that the guy who'd come out has retreated back into the cab. Time is short; they're not going to wait much longer. Scrambling through the meager entrails of the hover-runner and the former occupants' clothes gets me nowhere. Turns out that's okay, though. Before I have time to get more than averagely frustrated, another voice comes from the tracker.

"Friend of yours?"

People always describe it as a sinking feeling in your guts when you realize you're totally screwed, but right now, what I'm experiencing feels much more like a gas ball of rage exploding in my guts.

"Say something, scav!" This is followed by the sound of someone grunting in pain.

Then a new voice says, "Are you survivors from the *Galatea*?"

Goddammit. It's that kid I'd let go. The one who didn't want to be a clever dead guy.

"We have more of your buddies in the back of the tracker," says the tracker guy. "If you don't come out, you'll get to listen to them die."

Buddies? That isn't exactly the word I'd use to describe the other salvage crew. But . . . still, they could have survived. Or the scavenger could be lying. It could just be the one kid. I'd let him go once; is it my fault he wasn't capable of making it on his own?

But that's not me, not anymore. I can't let them die for us.

Leaving the carbine and T-Max in the dirt, I grip Vitruzzi's shoulder once again and pull her up beside me, our hands holding up the sky.

EIGHT

THE WAR

Of the approximately fifteen thousand soldiers originally occupying the PCA *Celestial*, more than half are foot soldiers—the ones with boots on the ground. And that's all it takes, combined with the might of a fleet cruiser and all of the ordnance and weaponry at its disposal, to take control of a moon or a planet with a population of more than a hundred times this. Corps training, Corps strategies, but most of all, Corps resources, are that good.

But we're down to about ten thousand now, after Medina's command early in the war to "restructure" the Admin-loyal troop faction. I'll say this about Medina, she's thorough. Her effectiveness scores as a fleet commander must have been among the highest in the prewar Corps. I still have a hard time believing she was central to the anti-Admin pockets of resistance ever getting off the ground and organizing. Someone this good at being a soldier is rarely anything but.

Still, she's clearly as shrewd and politically competent as any Admin Director. It took more than polished lockstepping and persuasive order-barking to become the commander of one of the Corps's twenty-five fleet cruisers. In her position, she'd have been a regular attendee of Capital Strategic Planning Summits, and would have had the ear of most of the leading Ministry advisors. Which is how she had everything she needed to raze their entire bastion to the ground.

I'm on the bridge rotation of my navigation team when Medina enters, ready for her new shift SITREP. I should be on the R&R we'd been offered, but the one constant truth about being ship-side for R&R is that boredom is a hundred times more insidious and soul crushing than nearly any human enemy. For that reason, I'd reentered my name on the duty logs. It's better to be on flight-deck duty than sitting around waiting to get called into battle or hanging back when a company returns from combat and watching them pick the grit out of their skin.

We've remained in orbit around Broon, one of Spectra 6's satellite moons, for the last forty or so hours, hiding on the moon's dark side with all the *Celestial*'s cloaking systems running to keep the settlement and incoming and outgoing ships we're surveilling from knowing we're here. Another reason I've kept myself busy is because we're just a few hours' flight time from our old home, Agate Beach. The knowledge that we're so close to what was the only place I had ever truly felt was home tugs at me, making me restless and more than a little dismal. I know I'm not the only one. Karl and Vitruzzi have had hair-trigger tempers since we got here. It must be so much worse for them. Agate Beach was their settlement, their life, for several years, before it was all ripped away. Ultimately, the Admin's decision to arrest the Beachers and make us all outlaws had resulted in this war—though, knowing what I now know about the organized resistance Medina, Quantum, and many others had been planning since the Soldier's Rebellion, it's clear the war was coming no matter what. Destroying Agate Beach was the ignition, but the fires had already been set to burn.

But I try not to think about it—Rob Cross's betrayal, Rajcik's mad mission to destroy the Admin, Bodie's death. None of it can be changed now. If there's a future, we have to target it, because there's nothing left in the past worth holding on to now.

Lieutenant Steward salutes Medina out of habit, then prepares to brief her on the last six hours that have passed since her off-duty rotation.

"Commander, they don't appear to be any stronger than we initially assessed from our drone passes. Heat signatures and visuals suggest no more than three thousand bodies, and our mission analysts report an estimate of about eighty percent active combatants."

"What do we know about their fighting force resources and equipment pool?"

"We cross-checked the data from both our drones and scouts and calculate their air forces to consist of only three active armed craft, forty unarmed craft, and fifty to sixty land craft. They have no detectable surface-to-air or surface-to-orbit weapons. The analysts predict the usual number of personal weapons."

"No, they wouldn't have surface-to-air ordnances. This is a makeshift settlement. Probably an outpost they erected hastily to refit damaged ships," Medina says.

"That could be the case, Commander," Steward agrees. "We've noted a number of troop transports, mostly former Corps but a few civilian, coming into and out of the settlement. Their behavior indicates supply transfer, but we haven't been able to get close enough to get a solid fix on what they're doing."

"How much time is elapsing between takeoffs and landings?"

"Minimal. Between twenty minutes and an hour. A few remain overnight, but none have stayed for more than a day or two."

"That kind of quick turnaround isn't the behavior of damaged ships coming in for fixes," Vitruzzi cuts in. "It's possible they've set up a casualty collection point. They may be bringing wounded in for treatment."

Vitruzzi showing up on the bridge out of nowhere is nothing new. Since the war started, she's made it a point to be involved in most of the major operations' planning, in one way or another. I haven't missed that her visits usually coincide closely with Medina's debriefings—particularly if any heavy actions have been predicted. Vitruzzi's lack of trust in the war commander may not be explicit, but it's definitely implied. So much so that tension between the two has become a topic of discussion among all of us who've crewed with Vitruzzi since Agate Beach.

Medina cuts her eyes in Vitruzzi's direction, then turns to face her. "You have a good point, Doctor. Steward"—she turns back to her LT—"is that population count steady, or does it fluctuate?"

Steward spends a few seconds manipulating information from his console, then pulls up a series of graphs on the holoreader. The three of them look it over for a few seconds before Steward speaks. "This output plots the ship traffic patterns," he says, pointing, "and this one, the population approximations based on different calculation variables. The pop counts lag behind by about thirty hours. We don't have enough intel readers in the area to keep a steady flow of data, so we recalculate new baselines every six hours, then build a new population count data set from that, which accounts for the three-hour lapse. Numbers show a slight rise when new ships arrive, and intermittent larger drops, but without being able to do an actual person-by-person head count, we can't tell who's coming or going."

"So the information here is three hours old?" Vitruzzi asks.

Steward hesitates before responding, and his eyes remain on Medina until the CO nods slightly. "That is correct."

Vitruzzi says nothing, studying the graphs. From where I'm sitting in the navigator's bench, I have to turn away from my controls halfway to watch them. Medina's gray eyes land on mine, holding them, knowing that I'm eavesdropping. "Anything else, Lieutenant?" she asks, still staring at me.

Steward continues, "No, Comm—"

"Have you sent any scouts to follow the outbound ships?" Vitruzzi interrupts.

"Our primary objective has been to surveil this post. We don't have the resources to send long-distance scouts," Steward responds.

"So you're saying you don't know who's down there, what they're doing, where they're coming from, or where they're going."

Steward's carefully controlled neutral expression cracks for a moment, but his silence is the answer Vitruzzi expected. She addresses Medina, "Commander, it doesn't appear to me that we're doing any good by sitting up here making wild guesses. They could be doing anything down there. I think we need to put someone on the ground to take a closer look before we decide on any action."

Ever calm, Medina's eyes remain steady and clear as she nods her head. If she resents Vitruzzi's unsolicited advising, she doesn't let on. "I agree. Lieutenant, muster a force of thirty bodies, armed, and six battle-ready troop transports."

"Medina, I think you misunderstood me," Vitruzzi says. "Going in there hot isn't what I had in mind. If we want intel, we can certainly get that without inviting—or instigating—a firefight."

"As always, I appreciate your feedback, Doctor. I'm sure we can avoid bloodshed if this colony is nonthreatening. As you said, we need to get closer first to assess that."

"Of course, but we can get close enough with one ship and a crew disguised as refugees or freelancers. We can see they're mostly nonmilitary from the intel Steward has. There's no point in—"

"Vitruzzi, this is my call. And it's been made." Medina's voice is like a steel trap that's been sprung. There's no arguing. "Since you're here, would you like to update me on our overall medical and casualty status for the day? If you need to get back to the med-deck, I understand. I can make my rounds down there per usual later. So . . .?" Medina lets the question hang, very much done discussing anything to do with Broon with Vitruzzi present.

NINE

The crash of the *Galatea* is like the old-Earth fairy tale of manna from heaven for these scavengers, but cleaning up after it seems to be just another day on the job for them. Two other survivors from the salvage crew and a handful of other people—settlers maybe—had been brought back to their camp on the track vehicle and locked inside this crudely built shack V and I now inhabit, the pieces comprising it scavenged from a hundred different derelicts and other debris. Despite its haphazard-looking construction, the walls are strong and unyielding to our efforts at breaking out.

When I say *manna from heaven*, it isn't irony. This group looks like they've been here awhile, probably from the early days of the war, and in a camp this far from any food sources it's obvious from the start that they're willing to eat whatever falls into their laps. I've heard about gangs of people going this far over the edge. I would have been more than happy to never witness it firsthand.

After a short trip in the tracker, I'd spotted at least two more shacks like ours when we arrived just under an hour ago, and that unmistakable stench of burned bodies clings to the camp like mustard gas in a trench. Most of the shack's occupants, like Vitruzzi and me, are basically uninjured, but everyone isn't so lucky. A woman with one side of her head badly swollen has been in and out of consciousness since we were rounded up.

All the captives have been tossed together and I scan the filthy room, trying to assess who may be the best assets in case an opportunity for escape appears.

"Hey, kid," I whisper to the survivor from the other salvaging crew who'd boarded the *Galatea*, "mind telling me what the hell your crew was thinking when they cycled up that derelict's engines? Because, I don't know about you, but I would have preferred dying of old age to being made mincemeat by a bunch of half-lunatic cannibals."

He looks up at me from where he sits with his chin on his knees across the shack. The dirt covering his face and the wide-eyed, almost guileless, expression on his face make him really look like a kid barely old enough to join the Academy. For someone like me, adapting to a war wasn't that hard—I've always been a soldier of one kind or another. But his life now must be one-eighty from what it had been two years ago. I'm too busy figuring out how we're going to survive this to spare much sympathy at the moment.

"Hurley, my boss, wanted to know if it had enough power to bother trying to salvage it," he finally says after giving the question time to sink through his undeniable shock. "We couldn't get the feedback gauges to work, so he thought he could force output from the engines, which should have back-fed their specs to the flight deck." He pauses. "I guess he got his wires crossed . . . or maybe the ship's systems weren't working right."

"You think? Maybe you should have assessed the damage before . . ." I stop myself. This kid isn't the reason I'm pissed. He's just a convenient scapegoat for my frustrations. "Anyway, did either of the other crew with you make it?"

"I don't know," he says simply.

"You two want to cut the chitchat?" another one of the captives says. "We don't want to draw attention."

I turn my head to glare at the speaker, the shed's dim interior light vaguely illuminating a medium-sized man with blond hair and thick limbs resting against the wall farthest from the door. He doesn't hold my eyes.

"Kid." I get his attention again after a second. "Want to help me with something?"

Luckily, he's still aware enough that I'm able to recruit him to help me find structural weaknesses in the shack, at least somewhere we can punch out an opening to try getting some fresh air and hopefully a visual of what awaits us on the outside. Keeping busy helps me do two things: take my mind off the small, crowded space, and hold off the muscle soreness the crash caused that lies in ambush just at the edge of my nerves.

The *Teibo* and *Orika* crews know we went down; there's no doubt of that. But the low chance of them being able to locate us easily doesn't leave me with much hope. Even if we weren't in hot water at the moment, Eruo Pium is a reasonably big moon, and our e-pod's trajectory lost some of its predictability thanks to whatever we'd hit that knocked us out of our dive. V and I are going to have to get out of this mess on our own.

The sound of metal sliding against metal freezes me from trying to work free the edge of one of the thinner steel sheets welded to the wall, then a shaft of light comes through the doorway at head height.

"Everyone back up." The short barrel of a carbine appears in the peephole to help us make the right decision. Almost everyone moves toward the rear wall, but the two men with Blondie linger near the door, planning to attack anyone who opens it.

"I see nine bodies and I know there's eleven in there." The small space erupts with the carom of a shot being fired, and one of the prisoners at the back falls to his knees, grasping his shoulder. The rest of us hit the deck in a panicked knot of limbs.

"Get over here!" someone cries, and the two hiding out of the peephole's sight back into the throng carefully.

"Good." The door is pulled open. A group of three, all armed, stand outside with their weapons pointed. One of them enters and trains his rifle barrel at me where I half squat against the wall. "Come."

Why me? Do I just have a face that begs to be interrogated? I certainly can't look that appetizing, having barely more meat on my bones than the locals. Vitruzzi and I exchange a glance, her eyes looking dead, and I step outside.

They walk me to a gazebolike structure, the journey enough to let me take a good, long look around the camp. In truth, it's more of a semisquare compound, about two hundred meters end to end. With the exception of the prisoner confines—only three total—most of the structures are barely standing, and the ones constructed out of primarily steel components are badly rusted, making the place a tetanus incubation hot spot. However, they've used this to their advantage and built a shambling, shoulder-high barricade around the area that's clogged with spikes and sharp corners. Getting out could be just as hard as getting in.

We pass by a lander discarded against the barrier, displaying the same eight-digit ship ID as the *Galatea* derelict. The hull is battered with small-arms fire, and it looks like one of the engines flared out, incapacitating it. I guess now I know why the transporter's crew didn't make it back.

One of the scavs notices me looking around and backhands me across the mouth. The skin of my top lip splits and bleeds, then I'm pushed onto a stool and surrounded by gun-toting savages on three sides.

The biggest of the three stands in front of me, looking me over. His face and the backs of his hands poking out of his ragged sleeves are badly scarred, an obvious indication of having once been, but most likely no longer, a sun-head. Given the lack of civilization on this planet, I doubt there's much of the drug to be found anymore. The real surprise is he'd survived the detox.

He asks, "Who are you?"

"Your fairy godmother."

This is followed by a protracted silence that allows me enough time to think up a brief will and testament, then he begins to laugh in short, choppy grunts that quickly prove whatever mind he has left is missing a few important bits. Just as quickly, he stops, and says seriously, "You must be Corps."

I give him a short, disgusted chuckle. "Don't you get it? There is no Corps anymore."

Since the end of the major fighting, the Spectras have been left to themselves, and what's happening right now is the reason why. Anyone who lands in a Corps ship or wearing Corps uniforms is attacked. The Spectres don't trust anyone who used to be part of the Admin, and who can blame them? Problem is, the only long-range ships that are still operational and have energy are either overtaken or abandoned Corps ships. Consequently, since no one likes their search-and-rescue or salvaging op to turn into a suicide mission, the Spectres have been left to fend for themselves. Enclaves of scavs that have turned to cannibalism, like this one, are the result.

"No one is Corps, or Admin, or a soldier. We're all just survivors, like you," I go on, not expecting any sympathy.

"We saw the ship—" Another pause, this time punctuated by a massive twitch in his right cheek, as if the skin is trying to jump off his face in a gruesome rebellion. I can't help but be a little horrified. After a second, he slaps that side of his face, then grips the flesh with his hand, apparently trying to get it under control. Oh, yeah, he's a poster child for the delights of being a solar stoner. "—go down. Straight into the ocean," he finally finishes, pointing with his free hand out toward the west. "A big one, like a fleet transport."

Interesting. The ship had gone down at sea, and Eruo Pium only has one. Whatever previous crew owned the *Galatea* are lucky they weren't still on it. If not treated, the water on this moon is toxic to humans. Even too much water vapor from waves or wind can be harmful. This fact also explains a little about why the scavs here have turned to cannibalism; they can't eat the sea life, and I didn't notice any Mr. and Mrs. Pioneer–type vegetable gardens.

"Yeah, so? Like I said, the Corps is history. If you're worried about anyone coming in and threatening your, uh, settlement, don't. There's no one else up there, and Eruo Pium isn't exactly anyone's idea of a fun getaway."

His un-twitchy eye glares at me ferociously for a few seconds. One of the other abductors—a hunched, squat man with enough loose skin, dirt caked into its jiggling folds, that it is clear he'd once been on the fat side of corpulent—encircles one of my wrists with his own hand. The skin around his fingertips looks gnawed and infected, like maybe they've become his new favorite after-dinner snack. Yanking my wrist free earns me a snarl, and he raises his fist, ready to strike.

"Bulgaç, hands off," Twitch says. "This one knows something. She just needs some incentive to tell us."

Relaxing more and getting comfortable—I could be here awhile—I say, "What could I know? You saw what happened. My crew was in the ship that went down. You picked us up. I've never been to Eruo Pium"—*and hope to Christ I never have to come back*—"and don't know a goddamn thing about the planet except the sea's poisonous to humans. Besides wanting to get the hell off this rock, I don't know a single. Other. Thing."

"Wrong!" His breath assaults my face like a rancid acid bath as he leans over me. "We picked up chatter. There are other ships, and they're coming. We want to know where you're meeting them."

Picked up chatter? "You mean a transmission? Is there a satellite in your orbit?"

That broken laugh again, like he's gagging with every breathy expulsion. I know *I'm* gagging on his every breath. "Ha-ha. I like this one. She thinks like a scav."

Without a hint of what's coming, his broad hand is at my throat, lifting me off the seat, and hurling me to the ground like a sack of shredded meat. My knees and elbows groan in protest. "Take her back to the shed and bring me the other one. The one we picked her up with. The juicy one."

As I roll over, a boot connects with my diaphragm, sending every molecule of air spewing from my lungs in one giant spasm. Clenching my guts with my hands, I writhe in the dirt for a second, black spots doing the cha-cha-cha in front of my eyes. " . . . f'n bas . . . tard."

Someone wrenches my arms up behind me and drags me to my feet. "Walk."

Forcing my legs into a shamble, I do as he says, encouraged by an occasional shove. As soon as my abdomen unlocks and air starts to flow back into my system, my vision clears. Vitruzzi is in no shape to be interrogated. She hasn't said a word since she came apart at the crash site. If they get their hands on her, she's as good as lunch for them.

Twitch follows behind. Too busy calculating the odds of getting to either his or Fingernails's sidearms before getting myself turned into the appetizer, I almost miss the sound of a tracker engine approaching. It isn't until a voice coming from the cab yells, "Ferenzi," and a hand on my shoulder stops my progress that I notice it.

The tracker—the same one they'd picked all of us up in—stops at an idle about ten meters away, and a woman jumps out.

"Hold her," Twitch tells the two men with us and skulks over to the truck.

An animated conversation takes place between him and the driver, her hands waving frantically at the rusted barrier between us and the sea beyond. I'd smelled its somewhat fetid odor as soon as Vitruzzi and I landed, and the occasional flurry of a breeze confirms we're just southeast of it.

"Close the barrier!" Twitch suddenly cries, turning to us. Neither of my other two captors does anything for a moment, so Twitch pulls out his sidearm—a modified Bowker O9, it looks like—and points it at them. "MOVE IT, YOU FUCKWITS!"

Dumping me like last night's stale beer, they start running to an opening in the barrier, waving their arms to advise what few other scavs are in the area. The tracker's driver follows them, leaving the vehicle where it sits. Twitch spears me in the back with the Bowker's barrel, directly on top of the scar left by Rajcik, and propels me toward the shed. Whatever's going on has him spooked, which, despite the situation, gives me a tiny spark of hope. Enjoyment even. Survivor of the war or not, this is one vile scav who's just wasting oxygen.

We reach the shed. Trying to save myself another cheap shot in the kidneys, I fall to my knees and cower, giving him a comfort zone to fish for the keys to the heavy chain and lock holding the door closed. That and the noise of the barrier gate clanking shut and being fortified with a backfill of whatever junk they can find distract Twitch enough for me to suddenly shift around, sweep my fist up to nail him in the crotch, and follow through by gripping the butt of the Bowker he's reholstered.

TEN

Smashing in his surprised grill with the stock turns out all his lights, and he crumples next to me. None of the scavs notices, and I crouch to retrieve the key Twitch has dropped to the dirt. Quickly unlocking the chain, I swing the door wide and whisper-shout inside, "Everyone, get out and find cover. We're taking over the camp."

Shock peeks through the grime streaking most of their faces, and I hold up the Bowker, pointed skyward, to help them grasp the situation. "This is it, people. Time to run!"

Vitruzzi is the first up, slipping through the opened door with all the stealth and reflexes I've come to expect from her. She spots the downed scav and quickly rifles through his filthy jacket and pants cargo pockets, coming up with a folding knife. Opened, it's about the length of a butter-knife blade, but looks sharp enough to carve up much tougher material. It'll have to do.

I steal another look at the group of scavs working on the barrier—

And my heart goes into a tailspin.

"Aly, what in the name of bloody Christ are those things?" Vitruzzi gasps, but my brain is barely able to interpret what my bulging eyes are seeing.

A torrent of some kind of multilegged crustaceans, like crabs but with long, scorpionlike bodies complete with hooked tails, pours over the wall en masse. It looks like a waterfall of ocean vermin, except their bodies are the size of German shepherds. They have four eyestalks that seem to retract until the eyes wave only centimeters above a hard-shelled, thick forebody, and two sets of hand-sized gripper claws extending from their flanks about half a meter to either side. As gross as they are, and as many as there are, they still don't look all that capable of doing much damage.

Then why are all the scavs screaming?

The first wave, at least a dozen of them, has hit the dirt inside the compound before I unfreeze. And I finally see it. One of them seems to rear up, almost like a Sufi doing a backbend, and long, wickedly jagged plated pincers unfold from its thorax, grabbing ahold of a scav with each and sawing through the unlucky bastard's leg and neck with the ease of a surgical knife.

Ah, *that's* why the screams.

The things move faster than I could have dreamed possible, almost floating over the ground on who knows how many centipede legs. The twenty or so scavs begin to scatter like terrified rabbits, the monsters in pursuit.

"Get to the tracker!" I manage to yell, and bolt.

A meter and a half from the tracker's still-open door, a creepy-crawly darts at me. My first shot blows off at least two eyestalks but doesn't penetrate the shell. At least it slows down—just enough for it to do its bizarre rearing thing. Those pincers start to reach out, and I shoot straight below the plates they're connected to. As I do, a hole, maybe a mouth, opens near the top of its underbelly and spits at me.

A cloud of tiny white darts emits, and I spin sideways to try and avoid them, feeling, nonetheless, a few of them sink into my side. The pain is like white-hot needles being rammed into my ribs and the back of my firing arm. But my shot hit a soft spot and the thing tumbles forward, greenish-red ichor beginning to saturate the ground beneath it.

The shot draws the attention of the scavs, and when they realize I'm not one of them, three begin running toward the tracker. Vitruzzi jumps into the cab and I pull myself in behind her, closing the door and leaning from the side window to aim at the scavs. I don't need to fire, however, as their sprint is easily overtaken by the local fauna.

Vitruzzi is hammering on the control console, and I risk a glance behind me.

"There," she says as the whine of the opening rear cargo doors drifts into the cab. "Get us closer to the shed."

The engine is still running and I follow her directions, hearing the satisfying crunch of a crushed crab shell as I drive over the one that came at me. The rest of the creatures have spread out, following anything that's running, but haven't keyed in on the tracker yet. I get the vehicle as close to the open shed as I can, and V shouts, "Get in the back! Hurry!"

Once the other abductees start to come out, telling them to hurry is wasting breath. One look at the crab-things and they rush into the back, three of them carrying the unconscious woman.

"Go to the other sheds," V says. "We have to help."

"We have to get the hell out of here!"

"Just do it!"

The tiny crab darts stuck in my side make my skin feel as if it's being slowly peeled from my body, and I'm grateful the tracker has a steering ball instead of a wheel as I spin toward the next shack. V jumps out and gets lucky with the key from our cell's shed on the lock while I cover her with the Bowker. But there are nothing but bodies inside. Inside the third shed, we find . . .

Four kids. Jesus. Vitruzzi and another of the prisoners haul the kids inside the back of the tracker, then V jumps into the cab and closes the rear door. Her face has gone intensely pale and slightly greenish, like sea foam.

"Go."

My tour of camp had given me the impression that the barrier's thinnest spot is its northeast wall, so I maneuver the steering ball toward it and press it down for acceleration. It isn't a fast vehicle, but the heavy steel body keeps out the monstrosities teeming through camp—both kinds. The scav with an appetite for his own fingers breaks from his cover as we pass, grabs the rear bumper, and uses the cargo door's hinges to pull himself up. As I'm watching through the rearview screen, a crab grips one of his legs and climbs him before he can get all the way aboard. Severed bits of him leave a trail behind, and what's left finally comes free and drops to the ground as I push the tracker into the barrier. Drooping skin folds or not, the guy had had a hell of a grip.

The barrier's rusting plates of metal and discarded junk give way easily under the tracker's relentless pressure, and we hit the grassy plain outside, slowly gaining speed until we max out at the vehicle's limit, forty kilometers per hour. The earth is bumpy and uneven, and a long, slow whine clanks from the tracker's undercarriage after we've gone a few klicks.

"Looks like this is as far as we go for now," I tell Vitruzzi.

She barely dips her head in acknowledgment and continues staring through the window at the scrubby hills beyond.

Pulling to a standstill, I leave the engine running. "Look." I have to speak with more force than I normally would just to get her attention. "V. We're out of the woods. Those crab-things aren't going to get this far, and I highly doubt there're any more scavs in the area. And the best news . . ." I pause, hoping for a reaction, but get none. Sighing, I finish, "Is that they have a receiver, maybe even a transmitter. They said they heard chatter after we went down. Which means there's a working satellite up there somewhere. I propose running a recon back to the camp later on and see if we can find their unit. We have a better chance of getting rescued if we can send a message. Are you reading me?"

She nods.

For a second, I just stare at her, trying to assess what had put her in this wicked state of mind and what I can do to change that. She's just sitting there like a zombie, and finally, I snap. "I don't know what the fuck your deal is, Vitruzzi, but you need to get your head back in the game. We're in some serious shit—"

She slaps me so hard my opposite temple whacks into the back of the cab with a dull thunk. Fury and boggled disbelief paralyze me, and I stare at her with my hand pressed against my burning cheek and reopened split upper lip. Almost immediately, her face relaxes from the mask of rage that had slipped over it to genuine regret.

"I'm so sorry, Aly. I don't know . . ."

I finally find my voice. "What the hell was that for?"

"I don't know," she repeats, sounding completely believable. She really doesn't know what she's doing, or why. Vitruzzi, for all her stalwart and controlled composure, has cracked.

A knock at the window behind me draws my attention. It's the kid.

"You think we're in the clear?" he says, his voice muffled through the window's composite material.

Shooting him a thumbs-up, I return my attention to Vitruzzi, a hundred different thoughts about what to say to her tumbling against each other in my head like sand on a stormy beach. She's leaning forward with her elbows on her knees and her head in her hands, her hair coming loose from the braid it's normally held back in and sticking to her damp and salty cheeks. My stomach does an uncomfortable flip-flop at the sight.

Unable to conceal my anger, I say, "Let's check on our passengers."

ELEVEN

"God, what a fucking mess," one of the refugees, a youngish, dark-haired woman named Cari, says as she looks over the cannibal camp. "I don't think we have to worry about the scavs anymore." She tosses a disgusted look in my direction.

The tracker's night beams wash over the inner courtyard, glistening off puddles of viscous fluid that look like oil, but which we all know are blood. A few mangled bits and pieces of the scavs dot the area. And that's it. The crabs must have dragged off the bulk of their victims. I shudder, not at the gore, but at the memory of the creatures. If the critters back on KL give me the creeps, those crustaceans were enough to make my blood freeze. I'm just hoping they stay gone until we get gone.

When we'd made our escape I'd hardly been worried anyone from the camp would chase us. It seemed the whole entourage had been out trying to fight back the crabs. If any had survived, they had more to worry about than trying to hunt down us escapees. Regardless, with the extra two weapons I'd found in the tracker's cab, a pistol and another carbine, and help from the passengers, we'd stayed put and set up a watch until dark, keeping our six covered.

The kid from the other *Galatea* salvagers—I finally got his name, Ryan—turned out to be a big help with the tracker. The engine was fine, but its fuel cell was low on water. He told me we could use seawater if we needed to. Lucky for us, we'd only been a klick from the high-tide line. After a discussion with the rest of the refugees, some who'd seen the Admin ship drop into the ocean, our best guess is that the disturbance caused by the crash may have been what sent the crab-things onto land. Apparently the cannibals weren't the only predators in the area with a taste for human flesh. The most important thing is that it looks as if they'd returned to their normal hunting grounds before we came back.

We'd lost the unconscious woman just before dark. With no medical supplies, there was nothing Vitruzzi could do for her, and the swelling on her brain went critical. The two men with her explained that they'd been abducted by the cannibals while out on a long-range search for resources, downed ships, scraps from orbit, things like that. Vitruzzi bandaged the arm of the man who'd been shot by the guard—a superficial wound, fortunately for him—while they described their own settlement that lies over six hundred klicks to the northeast. Others from their group had run into the cannibal enclave months earlier but escaped without being detected. These three had been desperate and foolish enough to travel on their own without sufficient firepower and been hijacked. The price could have been all three of their lives instead of just the one woman, but I hadn't needed to offer my opinion on it. They already knew.

"Ryan—you stay on my ass and hold that Max at the ready. Cari, keep that 'bine tracking along the edge of our light. Anything that moves gets a bullet. Copy?"

Ryan nods, and Cari waves the affirmative from the tracker's roof. I glance back inside the cab, where one of the dead woman's friends is driving, and give him a nod. We push forward, walking slowly while the vehicle follows in our rear. Our destination is the main building—or rusted shack—where I'm hoping the former inhabitants' communications equipment is kept.

The camp is eerily quiet, the air heavy with mist. Despite that, the disquieting stench of dead bodies lingers lightly, as if the back of my nasal passages have been permanently stained by the smell. The tracker makes the only noise. I have to admit that I admire how quietly the kid walks over the packed sand and rock. Nothing moves in my periphery, and I keep us moving forward. Only twenty meters to the shack.

A carbine being fired explodes through my focus. A blossom of dirt spikes up about eight meters to my left and lingers in the thick air and light of the tracker's beams.

"Cari?!" I yell, needing to know what she's firing at.

"I thought I saw movement," she replies as the tracker halts.

"Thought or did? Now is not the time for guesswork." Keeping the irritation out of my voice takes more energy than I can spare. I'm tired, hurt, hungry, and at my limit. The fact that everyone else is too doesn't reduce my frustration. At all.

"Uh . . . thought."

"And now?"

"It's, uh, clear."

Swallowing my suggestions for what she can do with the next round of guesses she may have, I wave my free hand at the kid and start moving to the shed again.

Before we reach it, I note that the door hangs ajar on slightly bent hinges. It looks deserted, the inside blacker than the barrel of the pistol I carry. There's no way I'm walking in there without light. No way.

"Kid, go to the back of the tracker and ask Vitruzzi for her VDU."

He hurries around the vehicle, and I keep pressing forward until the tracker's front end is only a couple of meters outside the doorway. Movement is limited to a few shadows bouncing around the interior, which only increases my nervousness. Shadows? Or men with guns? Or worse—critters with pincers the size of my forearm?

Ryan comes back and hands V's wrist communication unit to me. Turning the display on and setting the screen to full bright, I press up against the shed's exterior wall, crouch, and flick the VDU inside. It comes to rest near the shack's center, throwing a strong white glow up to the ceiling. Nothing moves. This could go well, after all.

The kid tries to move past me, apparently judging the lack of movement to mean all clear, but I grab his arm and pull him up beside me. Pressing my fingers against my lips, I stare hard at him, making sure he stays put. I cup my hand behind my ear to indicate he needs to wait and listen, and we hang tight for three full minutes before moving again.

Finally, I pick up a nearby pebble and toss it in, waiting for any response. Still nothing. After turning the display on my own VDU up and cautiously moving inside, I strain my eyes to catch any surprises.

The place is trashed. Consoles lie scrapped on the floor, toppled from makeshift workbenches, their wires jutting in every direction.

"Sonofabitch," I whisper, dropping my arm, still holding the pistol, to my side. Our chances for contacting the scouts just dropped to zero, and I don't have the most positive outlook about spending what could amount to weeks on this rock waiting for them to find us.

The kid steps over to a cracked screen and picks it up, eyeing it critically. He puts it back down and looks over the heap, then moves toward the back wall behind the workbench. "Huh," he grunts.

"Jubels," I shout at the driver of the idling tracker. "Back up. There's nothing in here."

Could the day get any worse?

"There never was."

Turning back to the kid, my expression makes him flinch. "What?"

"There never was anything in here. This"—he sweeps an arm over the broken equipment—"is all just junk. There's no power coming in."

"You're saying there may be another com setup somewhere?"

"Well, yeah. If they were telling the truth about picking up a transmission, there has to be. Right?"

Right. But where? Everything in this camp looks as stripped and bare boned as their recent meal du jour. Before I open my mouth, he says, "What about that wrecked lander? It has to have a comsys. Could be what the scavs were using."

Where did I find this kid? Once more, he could be right. This camp looks like no more than a junkyard where even the junk is too run-down to be considered refuse. Besides the tracker, the only other thing that isn't totally derelict is that landing craft.

Waving him forward, I reply, "Let's check it out."

I KNOW I'M NOT THE only one who feels a monumental sense of relief as the landing lights of not only the *Orika* but also the *Teibo* descend out of the sky like twin dei ex machina.

The kid was clever, just as I'd originally thought. The lander's receiver worked just fine, but the transmitter had required some TLC and very ingenious jury-rigging of the tracker's fuel cell to feed power to the lander before we'd been able to send a signal. My electronics skills are enough to help me arm an explosive device or short out a lockpad, but Ryan turns out to be a jack-of-all-trades. He figured out what the transmitter needed and how to get it done within minutes, and now that his shock has worn off he hasn't shown any signs of fading in the twenty or so hours since we'd met aboard the *Galatea*. I grow happier with every passing hour that I hadn't shot him. His kind of handiness is the mark of a true survivor, someone who'd made it through the war by being adaptable, smart, and quick on his feet. Just the kind of asset—and person—we could use on KL. Depending on what kind of provisions are left on the scouts, and whether or not this kid has anywhere else to call home, I may make a case for bringing in another stray.

Our ships locked on to our signal within a couple hours of Ryan's magical fix-it skills. The junction box kept overloading, so we couldn't maintain a conversation with Zeta on the *Teibo,* but we had managed to give them our coordinates. We've rotated standing watch, two per shift, since then. This isn't the first all-nighter I've pulled, and I'm still on watch while the suns' glow begins tracing the scouts' hulls as they drift onto a flat landing area just outside the compound.

David and Karl are the first ones to come through the main gate, where we'd cleared away the hastily piled-up obstructions.

"I can't even tell you how glad I . . . *oooph.*" This is all I get out before Karl has me in a hug so tight I think he might dislocate my ribs.

"Dammit, Aly," he says. "Don't do that to me again."

My right arm is pinned against the spikes still embedded there, and I suck in a breath as he squeezes me tighter.

"Shit, are you hurt? Let me see your lip." He pulls back and stares squinting into my face. His hand comes up and gently cradles my cheek as he glares at my upper lip. "Where else?"

"Nowhere. Just these . . . I don't know . . . crabby, spikey things in my side. I'm okay. Really."

David's face rearranges into that frustrated-at-having-been-freaked-out older-brother smirk, and he steps up. "I'm glad you're safe, Twig. You said V isn't doing well? Where is she?"

Indicating the tracker with my chin, I answer, "She's back there. Been sleeping all night. She's not hurt, didn't take a hit or anything, but she's just . . . off. You know, the twenty-meter stare in a ten-meter room type of off."

"What the hell happened down here?" Karl asks, finally looking around and taking in the scenery.

TWELVE

"Whoa! Hey, get a room." As I walk inside the *Orika*'s main cargo bay, Zeta and Desto have themselves entwined in an amorous embrace so flamboyant it could make a *kagema* blush. "There's a kid present for God's sake!"

Desto lets his hands fall from Zeta's ass, and she turns to smirk at me. "Kid here? C'mon, Aly, I know you're not that puritanical. This kid"—she pats the small bloom of her three-months-pregnant belly—"isn't going to grow up with any illusions about where she came from, anyway."

"And what's wrong with the room we're in?" Desto adds. "Plenty of space for everyone in here. What do you say, sweets?" He winks at me.

Zeta laughs and gives him a playful slap on the cheek. "You're going to embarrass her, Bomani."

"I swear, *Bomani*, I can't believe you're breeding, especially since every other ex-Corpsmember in the galaxy still shoots blanks."

"Ha!" He snorts, gently taking one of Zeta's hands in a gesture I find surprisingly sweet and protective. Desto may be a letch, but there's no doubt of their love for each other, or that he would do anything for her. "The Corps should have known better than to think they could drown the power of my epic swimmers."

I pass by, shaking my head. "A soldier can't even walk through her own scout without feeling like she was just violated when you're around."

"Aly, you quit being a soldier the first time you saved someone's life," Desto says, and his deep laughter follows me through the inner hallway as I make for the locker room.

I've just finished filling the two crews in on everything that had gone down during these last few hours for V and me. No one was surprised; we've all seen or heard the stories about camps like this one. After I introduced them to Ryan, Karl woke Vitruzzi, and Desto and Zeta came back aboard to start the preflight routine, freeing up the rest of the crew to begin attending to the mostly low-priority wounds, mild dehydration, and extreme hunger of the remaining fugees. We are all exhausted, even the crew that had been searching for us. The word *relaxation* doesn't exist when your friends are in trouble and you're not sure where they are or how to help them. It had all turned out for the best—this time. The scariest part, and the one we all work hard to ignore, is that if anything were to happen to us out here, no one on KL would ever know.

Once in the locker room, I drench a towel in hot water from the reserve tank and grab the hem of my shirt, already gritting my teeth against the pain I know is coming when it brushes over the embedded crab spikes.

"When we're ready to launch, it may not be easy to keep them off the ships."

I spin around and find Quantum standing in the doorway, his unreadable gaze assaulting me. His comment catches me totally off guard. "What?"

He moves to the window port that gives a view of the exterior and flicks his hand at the group of eight adults and four kids still milling around the tracker outside. "The fugees. We don't have provisions, or room, to bring them all with us. We'll run out of food and water at least a week before we arrive at KL."

I take a seat on one of the benches. Fatigue is beginning to make my limbs heavy. "Have you said anything to V or Karl?" I look back through the port, where my view settles on Ryan helping one of the children with the lid of a water bottle.

Quantum's right, and he knows I know it. However grudging and hostile our understanding of each other is, Quantum and I are similar in our pragmatism. In a world that has come to rely on fact over feeling to survive, this shared quality has made us ideological, if not actual, allies.

"Erikson, Vitruzzi is not capable of being trusted with the kind of decision that has to be made about them. She's—"

"Hold it, Quantum. You watch what you say about her."

His eyes flash with anger, but intelligent anger. The man is genius, and not just intellectually. He's clever and cunning. "Look," he continues, "you know I'm right. She needs a . . . vacation. Some time away from the pressure she's under from running her personal little fiefdom."

"She doesn't need a vacation. She needs a shrink. But that doesn't matter. She's the leader on KL, her and Brady. They call the shots, that's how it is, and this conversation isn't happening without her. Come on."

Fucking stingers aren't going anywhere for a while, it looks like.

Once outside, I lean against one of the *Orika*'s ramp struts and catch David's and Karl's attention, waving them over. When they get close to us, I say quietly, "Quantum just brought something up. I want to get your opinions on it."

"What's up?" Desto asks, emerging from inside and wiping sweat from his forehead.

Quantum stands beside me and sighs as if it pains him to have to repeat himself, then says, "You've thought about the next steps? We used up a lot of resources looking for Erikson and Vitruzzi. We'll have just enough to get back to KL, *maybe*. And then, there's them." Without even attempting to conceal the gesture, he waves a hand toward the group.

David gets it immediately and bites his lower lip, clearly unhappy with the implications.

"Hmmm . . . we can't leave them here," Desto says matter-of-factly.

"We can't take them with us," Quantum replies.

"Shh!" I warn. "David, will you get Vitruzzi and Venus? There's no need to freak any of the fugees out. Not with a bunch of kids."

"I think Mason and Hoogs are doing a perimeter sweep," he says. "I'll get them too."

"No," Desto says. "Aly is right. We don't want to freak everyone out by having a huddle behind their backs. Lets talk this over nice and quiet."

After Venus and Vitruzzi join the rest of us and Zeta in the *Orika*'s galley, the debate starts heating up.

"The majority aren't even from Eruo Pium. They're settlers who crash-landed on their way to Obal 6," Vitruzzi says tonelessly. "And they need our help getting off this rock, where they have a chance."

"Vitruzzi, *you* may be in the search-and-rescue business, but the rest of us are concerned with our *own* survival," Quantum says.

"Yeah, we know what you're concerned with," Vitruzzi responds angrily, the first spark I've seen in her in what seems like weeks.

"Does it matter?" Quantum continues, looking around at the rest of us from where he stands by the freezer. "The reality we're facing is simple: limited food, limited time, and limited risk avoidance. If anyone else sees where aiding a group of refugees fits into that equation, now's a good time to explain it."

It's hard to meet the rest of the crew's eyes, but I know where I stand on this one. *Sorry, Ryan.*

Finally, David says, "A few of them are from the settlement they mentioned, somewhere east of here, at least. We can take them back and drop off the rest with them. Give them something from the salvage to barter with."

"David's right," Karl says. "We can't just abandon them out here. You agree, Quantum?" His face is a mask of neutrality as he turns to the wire-rat, but I know what's going on behind his eyes. *You started the war that caused this, you bastard.*

Karl and I have had many late-night conversations about the events that had brought us into this situation and started the war between the Admin-Corps and the vast numbers of non-cits that were taking the brunt of the Admin's "policies." Policies that included a lot of people dying. Ultimately, the only one to blame is the Admin. They brought the fight to themselves when they started treating people like petri dishes. Despite that, however, Quantum was the one who unleashed the first salvo, so to speak. He helped organize the anti-Admin-Corps forces and pushed the button that set everything that's happened in the last eighteen months in motion. I'm not saying what he did was right or wrong, but if he hadn't, David and I would be either dead or still running black-market smuggling deals on the fringes of the system. Which may as well be dead. And Vitruzzi and Karl and the rest of the Agate Beachers would be fugitives or dead, too. Wasting time hand-wringing and judging all the scenarios as good or bad doesn't do any good; they just *are*.

At least, that's where I stand on the issues. But something happened in that war that hit others deeper, more in the heart than in the guts, and Karl is one of them. He's not as used to the darkness people have within them. Seeing the cold and methodical ferocity the Corps adopted in dealing with the uprising took even world-wise people like him by surprise. The way the humanity of Admin-controlled Corps soldiers bled away in the face of battle, turning them into conscienceless automatons instead of people—it took a toll, on almost everyone. The result is that now survivors are looking for answers and searching for reasons to explain what had happened and why. Finding someone to blame is part of, if not the healing process, at least the reconciliation process. Being able to blame one person makes it easier to ignore the ugly possibility that it's really *every* person that is to blame.

So Karl harbors an unspoken resentment for Quantum. The only thing that keeps him from acting on it is the fact that he knows, deep down, that Quantum is too small for that much blame, and Karl would waste the rest of his life trying to dole out the remainder of it.

Quantum's fixed gaze doesn't waver from his. "If that's the group's vote."

After another minute, it's settled. Desto and David volunteer to apprise the fugees of what we can offer them, and I, hopefully, can take care of my own thorny issue.

"Aly, can you help me prep the *'Bo* for takeoff?" Zeta asks. "Venus is helping Karl sort some of the salvage."

Sure, why not? These spines aren't going anywhere.

ONCE WE GET AIRBORNE, I finally get the moment I've been waiting for.

Standing next to the full-length wall mirror, I slowly begin pulling the synthetic fabric of my less-than-optimal-smelling shirt first away from my torso, then over my head. When the rag grazes my skin, I grit my teeth. It feels as if tiny needles are stabbing into my lats and rib cage, and the material tries to snag on them as it comes up. Dammit, what had those crabs been made of? If I didn't already hate multilegged, crawling and clacking minimonsters, this experience would be the defining moment.

Dropping the shirt to the floor with a sigh of relief, I crane my head around to try and see what the hell I'm up against. Three of the fugees stand around the benches, doing their best to clean the grit of their own captivity off. I'm not sure if what they're doing would be called ogling or gawking, but they aren't even pretending they're not watching me.

"You want to take a picture, boys? Or would you prefer an ass-kicking to remember me by?"

The blond one reminds me of a schoolyard bully whose body has outgrown his brains. He'd been the most vocal and angry when we'd told them they couldn't come with us, but none of the fugees could argue that we had any responsibility to take them. They know the deal out here. Everyone looks out for themselves first.

He snickers and says, "Sweetheart, with an attitude like that, you're just asking for someone like me to set you straight on some things."

Can this be happening right now? I'm half-naked, bleeding from at least three places, my torso is a chaotic tableau of unattractive yellows, greens, and blues, and this guy wants to first drool over me like a poodle with a puppy treat, then threaten me for not appreciating it? After I'd saved his ass? I momentarily entertain the wish that the Admin had started a weapons research program to develop bombs that only killed stupid people.

Muttering, "And if you had the capacity for complex thought, I'm sure you'd be the man for the job," I dismiss him and return my attention back to examining my side.

"What did you say?" he asks, but I ignore him.

With my arm in the air and my head twisted almost into my own armpit, I catch a glimpse of the small, spiny projectiles, about a quarter- to half-centimeter long, running in a line just at the base of my rib cage and up. I reach around with my right hand and gently feel for them. It stings like crazy when my fingers brush over their tops, but the searing pain that happened when I was first struck has at least dulled. The things feel brittle and a little flexible, not quite as stiff as fine wire.

"I said, what the hell did you say, girlie?" Blondie has come over beside me and leans over me, his breath hitting my face and making me flinch a little. "You got something to say, you go right ahead."

I ponder it for a minute and flip a glance toward his friends still by the benches. They're all part of the five-person crew that had crashed on the way to Obal 6, these three, the woman named Cari, and another older woman. Neither of the other two men will look at me. Blondie catches my glance and grins obnoxiously, assuming he's scared me.

Finally, my voice giving away my utter disinterest in him or anything he has to say, I advise, "If you value anything down here for any reason, you'd best find someplace else to stand. Someplace where I don't have to look at your ugly fucking mug."

The surprise on his face when he realizes I have a modest but laser-torch-sharp bolo knife pressed against his nuts should be entertaining, but I realize with resignation that I've seen this kind of idiot wake-up call too often to be moved one way or another by it anymore. The goal is simply to send his stupid ass on its way so I can start pulling these damn spikes out of me. They're making me cranky.

"Erikson, is there anything I can help you with?"

Blondie turns his attention to the locker-room entrance. Quantum has come through and is holding the pocket of his jacket as if to reach for something inside. A quick glance lets him know I'm all set.

Blondie's hands go up in a warding-off motion, and he takes a slow step back. Before he thinks of trying anything else, I reach down into my boot without looking away from him and withdraw a Sub-Oss, just for some added incentive. Without another word, he spins around and joins his mates, the three of them hurrying out past Quantum like they're late for lunch. Good fucking riddance.

But at least it was a distraction from these damn stingers. I should be grateful, actually. Now I'll feel much less bad about stranding them in some far-flung, sketchy colony that probably hasn't seen running water or electricity in a year.

As if reading my mind, Quantum walks toward the sink, then says, "Now you understand my reasons."

"Quantum, if you keep showing up while I'm in the locker room, I may have to interpret your behavior as a threat."

Ignoring the comment, he continues, "You're just holding on to a broken idea. The old system no longer applies. Now it's every person—"

"For themselves," I finish for him. "Thanks for the sociology lesson. Now, do you mind? As you can see . . ." I wave the knife at my blemished flank before resheathing it and the Oss.

"I want to talk to you about something." He pulls off his jacket and rolls up his sleeves before turning on the wash powder dispenser.

"Can it wait?"

"No." Facing me, he says, "I know what that machine is."

"You mean the thing we have in the hull? What is it?"

"A seed sequencer."

My expression must show my confusion, so he continues, "A generator, of sorts. It takes raw materials and creates new seeds for crops, for food crops. Do you see what that means?"

"Yeah, it means we're going to be better off than ever at the colony. We can produce whatever we need. But how do you know?"

"Hoogs accessed the *Galatea* commander's drive and found his directives. That Admin ship was in the Spectras to drop off the seed sequencer. What we have in the hull was the only thing on the transport that fits the description. I looked it over, and I believe I can operate it."

I'm still hung up on the first thing he said. "Why would they drop something that produces crop seeds in the Spectras? There's hardly enough viable soil in most places to grow anything worthwhile."

"Not on the other side of this moon."

"Huh? It's barely . . ." He's looking at me expectantly, waiting for me to understand. And then, I do. "They used the soil compound, didn't they?"

His lips thin out as he presses them together in a look that reminds me of a dead snake. "The recorded directives clearly outlined the fecundity and success of their soil enhancement project. The Admin intended to begin planting synthetically generated seeds within the year. The year before the war, that is."

How many people had lived on Eruo Pium? How many had the Admin snuffed to test their poisonous compound?

Feeling my guts go hollow with disgust, I ask, "So what does any of that have to do with me?"

"KL is too small, too disorganized—and most of its settlers are war casualties with too many injuries—to be able to fully deploy the capacity of the seed sequencer. In other words, the colony isn't capable of sustaining itself. I want your help to convince Vitruzzi to let me take the soil compound and the sequencer to Obal 6."

I laugh, assuming he's joking.

His stare grows cold. "We can't expect to live on salvaged food stores and canned vegetables forever. We have to begin working toward a long-term solution."

Cutting the laugh off like a gangrenous limb, I ask, "How does the soil compound count as a long-term solution, Quantum? It's poison. You know that. It kills everything—for years—before it becomes inert. Where would you even use it?"

"Obal 6 is a big planet. They may be willing to deploy it to help provide for their remaining population, and to plan for more growth."

"No. That's crazy. We don't fully understand it. You can't just let this stuff loose out there. People could get killed."

"Why do you care about a few hundred people? How many did we just see killed in the war?"

"Exactly, there's been enough death." I know he's an opportunist, but I never thought he had it in him to be so incredibly callous. "We don't need to increase the body count. It's time to put the system back together, not add to its decay."

"You have to under—"

"No! You have to understand—this conversation is over." I turn back to the mirror, keeping an eye on him in the reflection.

After a pause, he says, "Don't make the mistake of believing the war is over, Aly." Rubbing his hands against his pants to dry them, he finally leaves.

What the hell does that mean? The war *is* over. That's why everything has taken on these wonderful new dimensions of fucked up. What war is he still fighting?

Clicking on my VDU, I scroll to Karl's channel.

"What's up, lover?" he says.

"I'm in the troop locker room. Do you think you could swing by and help me with something?"

"Yeah, be there in a minute."

Trying to shake off the conversation, I pick up a pair of splinter forceps I'd snagged from the med-bay and clamp onto the first spine. Something tells me I'll be finding myself in the midst of Quantum's war sooner or later. No reason to start with my flesh looking like a porcupine's hide.

THIRTEEN

After sleeping the sleep of a war veteran on farm animal tranqs for a couple of hours, during which time the two scouts take flight to Eruo Pium's remaining settled colony, I wake up to the sound of running feet outside the berth Karl and I share. My guts go on a roller-coaster panic drop, but my mind quickly registers the giggling shrieks that trail behind the footsteps. Those kids we'd picked up must have slept less than I just did. But I thought children were supposed to need to recharge?

Karl's leg is draped over mine, and he snorts, still asleep, as the last of the laughter fades down the corridor outside. Like me, this is the first chance to rest he's had since before we boarded the *Galatea*, and I take a second to just enjoy being next to him. From being a soldier, to deserting and becoming a criminal, then to fighting a war, and now scratching out existence as a scavenger (which is an ugly word for it, but I promised myself no more lies, not even to myself, when Rob Cross had come back into my life and nearly wrecked it) in a system full of equally desperate scavs, I have a habit of living every breath like it will be my last. And no one can blame me for stealing a few minutes of peace to appreciate this man who had saved more than my life; he'd saved my soul.

My stomach rumbles and reality penetrates through my tranquility. Trying not to wake Karl, I reach inside the gear loft over our bunk and retrieve my VDU to tap out a message asking Venus how much time till we arrive at the colony. She responds with less than an hour to go.

Deciding that it will be better to be awake and alert than still be horizontal when we get there, I gently nudge Karl until his sepia eyes open, and he smiles up at me.

"We there?" he asks.

"Not for an hour or so. Thought we'd grab a snack and get ready."

His arms wrap around me and he pulls me on top of him, then starts nuzzling my neck. "Delicious," he whispers through his exploring lips.

Giggling, I play-fight him off. "Not that kind of snack."

"But it's the only thing that sounds appetizing."

We're interrupted by the children's laughter and echoing feet running down the corridor again, this time in the opposite direction. "I thought I'd dreamed that sound," Karl says.

"Nope, they've been playing around out there for a while. They barely slept. It's like they're not even human."

He rolls onto an elbow and looks at me with a bemused expression. "Have you ever thought about it?"

"About what?" Then I realize what he's asking. "Having kids? Didn't joining the Corps pretty much ensure that wasn't something either of us ever *had* to think about?"

"Come on, Aly. The Corps doesn't even matter anymore. Nothing is the same as it used to be. There're tons of kids like them in the system, ones who need homes, safety, people to look out for them." He pauses. "So, have you?"

The concept is so foreign to me that my next words come directly from instinct, not contemplation. "What's there to think about? They eat, sleep, cry, and want things. Basically the same as every adult in the worlds. That's not really much enticement, if you know what I mean." His face closes off in frustration, but he doesn't say anything. "Besides, can you imagine me as a muh"—I can't quite get the word out—"guardian, some kind of role model? I could teach a kid to shoot from prone and reload faster than average, but—"

"I know, lover. I get it. It was just a thought. Come on, let's get some grub."

After dressing, we walk to the mess and find Mason and Hoogs already there and occupied with teaching the children how to unload and reload a weapon in combat time. I give Karl a meaningful look, *See?*, which he emphatically ignores. The oldest girl looks only about eight, and the youngest boy maybe six, but it's hard to tell beneath their rags and malnourishment what their real ages are. I'd joined the Capital Military Corps Academy when I was fourteen, the youngest age you could enter, but the grim awareness in these kids' faces shows an intensity of understanding and wisdom that is years beyond where I'd been at their ages. Eight-year-olds with guns. The oldest girl points the pistol Hoogs hands her directly at me before he pulls the barrel aside and warns her not to, and I quickly decide to keep my distance from the children. Looking into her eyes—even for an instant—had been like looking into a ghost's.

"Are you cold?" Karl says.

Before I can ask him why he'd think that, I glimpse the goose-flesh that has sprung up on both of my arms, wrists to shoulders. "Nah." I shake my head. "Just . . ."

He stares at me, waiting for me to finish my sentence, but I don't know what to tell him. That I had a sense that, even though we'd rescued these kids from a gruesome end, I still feel like they're doomed? That I felt a sudden certainty that the last war was the final war humanity would ever fight, because we're *all* doomed?

Stepping over to the rations cabinets, I enter the code only the KL crew has and grab him and me ready-to-eats. Handing one over, I let him know I'm heading to the bridge. I don't want to eat in front of those hungry kids, with their shining eyes crawling over me like grave beetles.

When we'd divided up for the flight to the colony, I'd been relieved that the only ones coming with us were the kids and Mason. The rest of the refugees stayed with the *Teibo* after we'd transferred all the essential salvage aboard the *Orika*. None of them had seen the kids before, and the children who weren't too traumatized to tell us their story said they hadn't seen their parents since their transport ship had been attacked, less than a week prior. Before those cannibals had been eaten alive by the swarm of crab-things, they must have bragged to each other about their good week of "salvage."

Trying to shake the creeping feeling thinking about those children and their parents' fate has given me, I join Venus in the cockpit.

She's at the pilot's console, spinning a small object around like a top on one of the flat displays.

"Hungry?" I ask, dropping a nutrition bar on the console between displays.

"Thanks! All clear in the rear?" She chuckles at her pet joke and picks up the object, which I can now see is a ring made of some kind of matte-textured metal.

Nodding, I bite into my own bar and perch on the edge of the navigator's seat. Trying not to be obtrusive, but curious nonetheless, I comment, "Pretty baubley, what is it?"

"Molybdenum and titanium alloy. It's a piece off the *Sphynx* that Jer welded into a ring for me."

"A . . . ring? Like, are you engaged or something?"

"Yeah." She says it with the gushing joy of a kid getting her first magbike, her happiness nearly too big to be contained in the small cockpit.

And it suddenly hits me—in spite of all the losses, deaths, uncertainties, and just the way almost everything in life has become so *hard*, there will never be a total loss of hope, never be a total loss of what it means to be human. When the scale of everything is out of proportion, happiness and enduring optimism adjust accordingly, but they do not disappear. The realization is a weird contrast to the gloomy feeling I'd just had about the kids, and the competing extremes give me a moment of cerebral vertigo.

I take another bite and chew it, clearing my head. "I'm really happy for you, Venus. He's a good guy. Actually, he's a great guy."

"I know," she states as a matter of fact, then chomps into her nutrition bar.

I lean forward and start cycling through feeds and data to get a sense of our landscape. "Older satellite images show that it was a fairly good-sized mining colony," I mention. "Wonder how many people are left?"

"We'll know in about three minutes. It's just on the other side of this range. Snap in, Aly." After confirming by radio the distance and a good landing area with Zeta on the *'Bo*, she makes a general announcement to our crew over the com that we'll be landing shortly.

As we crest the peak of a barren, snow-dusted, twenty-five-hundred-meter mountain, light from two of the suns breaks into weird shadows through our viewscreens, draining the cockpit of any real color, turning everything a simmering sepia brown, like rust. For a few seconds, Venus's hair appears to be aflame in the glow, and I realize mine must look just as fiery to her. It will be night again soon, or at least nightlike for a few hours. This side of the mountains looks like it will be colder than the cannibals' side.

She pushes the engines harder, expertly taking advantage of the thermal currents coming down the back side of the mountain range, and the mining colony comes into sight within moments. The *Orika*, like all ships based on its model, is sleek, solid, and built to take a beating. Mostly interplanetary, they have a range of a few hundred thousand kilometers on a full nuclear-core load and the capacity to carry 750 cubic tons. Mostly, they were commissioned by traders and shippers for local jobs. Nearly one of every five non-Corps vessels in the air were ASHTs—Admin Starclass Hypermaneuver Transport Craft—prior to the war, and being one of the most resilient hull designs ever made, more of them survived it than any other model.

Despite the *Orika*'s notable carrying capacity, room for personnel is spartan at best. A central shower, a galley that carries up to fifty days' supply of meals and beverages, a rudimentary medbay, a private captain's bunk, which Karl and I are sharing on this run, and a separate general sleeping bunkroom for up to six crewmembers make up the living quarters. Only three people are needed to fly it at once, but backup mechanics and cargo handlers are usually included on the manifest. If something happens in space and you need to keep flying, someone has to staff the engine ports to keep it going. Fortunately, most of the shipping lanes were well trafficked enough before the war that a broken-down vessel was rarely left in the lurch for long.

After the war, these shipping lanes provided the easiest pickings for scavengers and salvagers (though, in reality, I'm not sure there is any difference). We picked up both the *Teibo* and the *Orika* herself from one of these orbital highways. The Beachers may have been backwater-planet dwellers, but their combined mechanical ingenuity and engineering moxie are among the best I've seen outside of the Obals. Something about living tangential to the "civilized" world brings out qualities in people that seem to be dormant within those whose lives were a clear path of steady and consistent submission from the cradle to the grave.

Sometimes those qualities are extraordinary. Other times— horrifying.

We start a circle around the mining settlement, giving me time to take it in, though we plan to land a few klicks away—just to be safe. It must have still been functioning before the war. Scattered mining equipment and drill pieces dot the area and line the southern edge of a pit in the earth that could easily swallow both the *Orika* and the *'Bo* and still have room for every building within the community. It's as if the moon were hit by an asteroid, the crater almost too deep to see down to the bottom, particularly in the spreading twilight.

Both scouts come to rest north of the colony. We don't want to invite trouble or give them an easy target if they're primed to fight. The fugees will have to walk the rest of the distance, but they shouldn't complain. They're getting a couple of bins of water and some food, a couple more bins of medical supplies—even precious antibiotics, at Vitruzzi's insistence—and everyone gets a weapon and a couple of clips of ammunition. It's a lot to carry, but they'll find a way. After we're prepped to leave, that is. Vitruzzi's one other requirement is that the orphaned kids come back to Keum Libre. It'll make rations tight for the trip home, but without someone to look out for them, their fates out here are easy to guess. After Karl's and my earlier conversation, I'm wondering if he's thinking we should be part of those someones.

None of the refugees had been happy about our plans to leave them behind, even the ones from the mining colony. I can't blame them. Regardless, postwar fact number one: altruism is as dead as the Admin. What had Quantum said? We're not in the search-and-rescue business? That's the absolute truth. They should be able to make the best of things here, maybe acquire enough salvage of their own to barter for a ride off and a better chance next time a ship comes through. And if Quantum had been right, only a couple thousand klicks from here, there's a planet ripe for growing all the food they can eat.

I don't let myself think too much about the extremely high likelihood that not one of them knows a hoe from a combine.

With no reason to leave the *Orika*—Desto, David, and Zeta can handle any trouble—I dig into a food bar and watch through the viewscreens as we wait for the *'Bo*'s cargo hatch to retract.

And wait.

Venus stands up and stretches, then turns as if she's planning to leave the cockpit.

"Hold it," I say.

The strain in my voice stops her. "Something bugging you?"

That cold feeling I'd had earlier when looking at the ragamuffin kids comes back, but this time it moves into my spine, making my body feel rigid and brittle, ready to crack. It's the same instinct that's kept me alive for this long. Without answering Venus, I click on the com. "Anyone back there? Is the ramp on the *'Bo* open?"

After a second Hoogs gets back to me. "I'm in the cargo bay, Aly. The ramp is still closed. Can you ask them what the holdup is?"

I activate our transmitter. "Zeta, it's Aly. Need any help over there?" Venus stands behind me. We wait for almost a minute—no response.

I switch back to the com: "Everyone, the 'Bo's crew is in trouble. We need to get—" Before I finish the sentence, an engineering hatch on the other scout's underside bangs open, and five limp bodies fall to the earth. None of them moves, and they hit one by one, first stacking on top of each other and then tumbling into a disorganized heap, devoured by the ship's shadow. My heartbeat suddenly fills my ears, the blood roaring through my body and brain like a supernova. I'm outside the cockpit and sprinting for the cargo bay door before the last body has settled. Dimly, I hear Venus's voice over the intercom, telling the others what we've seen.

Skidding to a stop in front of the cargo bin where we keep the larger weapons inside the bay—the carbines, Dragunovs, and Brownings—I enter the code and scoop up my AK-80 as Hoogs lowers the cargo ramp. With everyone closing in behind him and me as fast as they can, we burst outside. But before we can reach the bodies, the *Teibo*'s jets accelerate to launch torque and force Hoogs and me to our knees, shielding our faces with our arms.

And like that, the ship is screaming forward, gaining momentum before exiting the atmosphere. Leaving a pile of corpses in its wake.

FOURTEEN

"David!" My voice rips out of my throat hard enough to hurt. I'm pulling him over onto his back while Mason and Karl untangle Desto and the others. "No, no, fuck, David, no."

"There are no injuries, no wounds. No . . ." Vitruzzi says, kneeling down and patting their bodies intently, checking their eyes, their pulses. "No, wait!"

Frantically, she yanks open her medkit and withdraws a breath scanner, which she holds over Desto's mouth for a few seconds, staring intently at the readout screen. Her body visibly sags when the device finishes its job. "Just drugged. They've just been drugged. Jesus Christ." She does the same with everyone else—Ryan and the two survivors from the mining colony—then sits hard on her ass, looking shell-shocked.

The nausea that I hadn't realized I was feeling suddenly wins, and I stagger a few feet away, retching out everything I'd just eaten in a ropy puddle of orangish goo. But it makes me feel better. Walking back to David's prone form—though now my brain recognizes the movement of his chest rising and falling with breath—I take off my jacket and cradle it beneath his head.

"What the fuck . . .?" Karl begins, but none of us has the answers.

"Let's get them inside, get some fluid in them," Vitruzzi says. "It was a GABA. They should be conscious within a couple of hours."

The six of us carry them inside. After a short wait, just as Vitruzzi predicted, they begin to regain consciousness, and David is the first to awaken. The twilight outside has darkened to an inky blanket, though the air is thin and cold. We've buttoned up the *Orika* to keep out both the chill and any settlers that could wander out this far to see who we are.

The scout ship's infirmary isn't big enough for all five of the patients, so we laid the two fugees and Ryan out on the extra crew bunks we'd screwed into place in the storage room for salvage runs, and keep watch over David and Desto in the crew's berth. Eleven adults and four children is nearly triple the ship's normal crew size, making things much, much tighter than they ever should be.

"What do you remember?" I ask David. "What happened after we left the scav camp?"

Vitruzzi monitors his vitals and vision as he blinks confusedly. I glance toward her nervously, my query written on my face: *All clear?*

"It's wearing off fine. Nothing permanent to worry about," she says, then moves over to Desto's bunk to check on him.

At first David is groggy and seems unclear about what had happened. "Are we home?" He scratches the back of his neck, then finally focuses on me. "We still on Eruo Pium, Twig?" Then: "Jesus, I'm thirsty."

Vitruzzi had thought of that too and hands him a container of water as I answer, "Yeah. You and the rest of the crew were drugged, knocked out. Do you remember anything?"

After a long drink that seems to bring him back to the here and now, he says, "Desto and I were sitting in the mess having some food. Quantum and one of the fugees came in, and Quantum . . . he asked me if I wanted anything from the ration locker. I remember hearing it open behind me, seeing the fugee walk by Desto, something sharp in my . . ." He reaches behind his head and scratches again.

"David, look toward the wall," I say, then study the skin on the back of his neck when he turns. A tiny scab, the size of a needle prick, shows faintly just to the left of his spine. "Bastards. You said Quantum was be—"

"HAAARRUAH!" Desto shouts and grabs Vitruzzi's wrist so hard I'm afraid he's going to snap it off.

"Desto! Relax, it's me!" she yells, putting her other hand to his chest to try and calm him. Just like David, he starts to blink, trying to focus, then lets go of her.

"What the fuck!" he hollers. "What the . . .?"

Vitruzzi quickly explains what David described as I pass him the water container. Venus comes and leans through the doorway, her face tight with concern. As Vitruzzi wraps up the story, she says, "The two colonists are awake too. And him." She points and Ryan steps into the doorway beside her, looking dazed and close to falling over. Beyond him, I catch a glimpse of two of the fugee kids standing in the corridor, their somber eyes wide and questioning.

"Have they said anything?" Karl asks. Then, looking suspiciously toward Ryan, he follows up: "Is Hoogs on the flight deck?"

Venus nods. "Yeah, he's still trying to hail the *'Bo*, but . . ." She shrugs, the corners of her mouth drooping in frustration. "They told me variations of someone grabbed them from behind, then they woke up here."

"You think Quantum had something to do with this?" Mason asks from where he leans against the wall next to Desto's bunk.

David swings his legs onto the floor, ignoring my comment to take it easy, then sits up slowly, gripping the bunk support bar with one hand. "Maybe, unless there was someone else in the room. I only saw the one fugee, the big, blond one who looks a little like—"

"Where's Zeta?" Desto cuts in.

Vitruzzi looks hard into his face, silent, but I drop my own eyes to the floor.

"Where is she, V? Where the fuck is she?"

"We don't know. We think she's still aboard the *Teibo*."

His face flushes an alarming shade of purple as he jumps out of the bunk, nearly busting his melon on the sleeper above him.

"Wait, just slow down. You're not ready to—" I start, but he's not listening, already pushing past Karl and heading toward the doorway.

"Why isn't this thing in the air, Venus? What the hell is everyone standing around for?"

The fury in his voice is frightening, and I see the kid Ryan stumble back to get away from what he must think will be an onslaught. It might take the whole crew working together to bring Desto under control—I don't want it to come to that. Before he can start barreling toward the cockpit, Karl jumps forward and grips one of his wrists, pulling him to a standstill. Karl puts his other hand on the back of Desto's neck and brings their faces close enough to stare eye to eye. "Calm down, brother." His voice is rock solid but compassionate, almost serene. "You gotta smooth out, get still, think this through. You're not going to help her by losing your shit. We will figure this out. But first you need to get it together."

Desto licks his lips, his eyes fused to Karl's, then slowly backs away, relaxed enough for Karl to release his grip.

"Uh." The voice comes from Ryan. Everyone turns to him, surprised, like they'd forgotten he was there. He swallows and reaches out to the wall as if needing support. "I walked in on them while they were planning it."

"Planning what?" Desto growls.

The kid's face is pale, but he soldiers on. "The big one, the blond guy, and your crewmember . . . Quantum? They were talking about hijacking the ship. Said they could use the cargo to barter for something. I didn't, uh, I didn't get what they were talking about. But when they saw me, the blond one grabbed me and then, um"— he looks helplessly at Venus—"then I was here."

"That sonofabitch," David sneers.

The conversation between Quantum and me in the locker room bubbles to the surface of my thoughts. "I think I know where they're going."

FIFTEEN

I just came off my last rotation at the nav bench in the latest six-hour on-duty–off-duty cycle and head for the squad's utility closet. First order of business: get even with Desto for the nauseating stench he doused my body armor in. I've sprayed at least a bathtub full of degreaser and caustic cleaners on the plates, yet the odor of cheap cologne still hits my olfactory bulb like a haymaker when I take a deep breath, but now with the added infusion of cancer-in-a-bottle chemicals. My turn. He'll know exactly what I mean the next time he puts on his combat suit liner and has to suck in lungful after lungful of the cleanser they use in the galley ovens. Nothing like spending a few days trapped inside a bubble of odor that smells exactly like singed hair and burned grease. Unoriginal as the plan may be, the beauty of it is that Desto's size will make it hard for him to find a replacement at the last minute before going out on an operation. I shake the bottle of liquid with glee just thinking about it.

On the way back to my unit's berthing area, I decide to pass through the med-deck to check on Dan Hoogs, who I've become quick friends with since being on the *Celestial*. He took one in the shoulder on our last excursion, but it's healing fine. In a few years the ghost of that impact will sink into his bones deeper and deeper until, in his old age, he'll feel like the bullet took up permanent residence. My own shoulders ache in sympathy. I've hit the deck enough times in my life—in firefights, escapes, life-and-death two-steps—using my hands and knees to break my fall, that pain and my joints are on a first-name basis. The likelihood of either of us living to be old enough for it to matter, small as it is, serves as a tiny—scratch that, *nano*—comfort.

While I pass by the chief medical officer's station, the sound of familiar voices raised in an exchange best described as *heated* stops me short.

"It was a goddamn massacre, Medina." No doubt that's Vitruzzi, and she is clearly pissed. "And you intended it to be from the start. They were nothing but civilian and military casualties, not an organized fighting force."

I hadn't heard the outcome of the operation on Broon, but I'm sure it's what they're discussing. Last I knew from the discussion

I'd overheard on the bridge it was supposed to be a surveillance mission to establish the outpost's status.

Medina: "They were potential combatants. This *is* a war. Do I have to remind you?"

Vitruzzi: "That's bullshit! They were *noncombatants*. What you did was murder wounded people and take their supplies."

Medina: "They were Admin Loyalists and sympathizers, which makes them enemies. We give no quarter to enemies."

There's a long pause, then Vitruzzi continues: "No. I am a doctor. I won't allow you to do this. Not again."

Medina: "Dr. Vitruzzi, what you are is an asset. When you stop being an asset, you become expendable. Have I made myself clear?" There's an extremely loaded pause, then Medina continues, "One more thing. Before you and your previous crew decided to blackmail the director of the Ministry of S&E, we had a plan for hollowing out the Admin from the inside. An organized rebellion under my command might have been able to accomplish the goal of a newly formed system peacefully. But you chose an arrogant and absurd vigilante approach, and this war is the result. Maybe you don't like it, but you can't deny that we are in this situation because of you, and someone has to finish it."

I don't have time to get the hell out of there before Medina walks through the doorway, nearly coming nose to nose with me.

"Erikson," she says, her face unreadable.

What is there to say? She pushes by me, and I swing aside to let her pass without a word. As I turn back, Vitruzzi is already on her way out.

"Aly." She stops, the heavy vein that descends from her hairline to between her brows prominent, and seems to consider something deeply before continuing. "Do me a favor, get Karl, Desto, Venus, everyone from the old crew and meet me in Brady's and my bunk in twenty minutes. We're leaving."

THE DISCUSSION WAS BRIEF. Not one of us had the stomach to continue fighting Medina's style of warfare. Brady recommended we bail and join the group of original Agate Beach colonists who'd stayed put at Keum Libre when the war broke out. Others from the Beach had joined the scattered anti-Admin fighting forces or tried to make it back to Spectra 6, their home. We didn't hold out much hope of seeing many of them again, but we'd all had to make our own choice.

By that week's end (six months ago), the plan was in full swing. Medina hadn't so much been consulted as informed of our imminent departure. Vitruzzi, Desto, Brady, Doug Mason, Karl, David, Venus, Jeremy La Mer, and I were splitting off with a few months' worth of supplies and materials and going our own way. No one who knew the plan—though we'd tried to keep it as quiet as possible—had dared to stop us. Not even Medina had tried, but then, how does the unelected commander of a no-longer-military vessel declare a mutiny? Allegiances in any war only run as deep as the fighting force's beliefs; and this war, this large-scale slaughter of the very foundations of our system and civilization, hadn't left much to believe in beyond survival. Medina knew it. And she'd known the second she tried to curtail the rights of anyone on that ship who had fought alongside the rest, the slaughter wouldn't be in the air or on the ground. It would be at her feet.

A handful of our closest friends had joined us at the last minute, including Dan Hoogs. To everyone's surprise, Quantum had elected to join us too. My own reservations about bringing him— the guy, after all, had once kidnapped me and threatened to kill me—didn't amount to much. Someone with his wire-rat skills, as well as the ability to pilot many types of crafts, was an asset we couldn't pass up. And so he came with us. And so . . .

SIXTEEN

My disclosure of what Quantum and I had talked about on the 'Bo is met with all the warmth of people being told they've been selected to test a new enema probe. Not surprising, given the already nonexistent feelings of affection for the wire-rat, despite the fact that he'd helped us get the upper hand on the former director of the Ministry of Science and Engineering, before the war.

"So we're going to Obal 6 to get the ground-down piece of shit," Desto states, rubbing the back of his neck and preparing to leave the bunkroom. "And then I'm going to tear him fifteen new assholes."

"It's not that easy," I say, trying to take him by the wrist and slow him down. Though direct action is my usual course as well, the issue isn't as simple as flying in with guns blazing.

"Aly's right," David says. "Our food and water *might* be enough to get us to Obal 6, but then what?"

"Then what? Then we stomp that conniving bastard into bone powder." Desto glares at each of us in turn. "Since when does this crew decide going after one of its own is too difficult?"

I continue, "I'm not saying we don't go after Zeta. I'm just saying we need to think this through. All we know about that colony is that they're buttoned up tighter than the Fortress, they're armed, and they're not friendly to anyone who can't offer them something better than a hungry mouth to feed or another body to protect."

"The big question is what Quantum plans to tell them. Yeah, he has the—what did you call it, Aly? Seed sequencer? They'll see the utility of having it," Karl says. "But what will he tell Obal 6's colony leadership about Zeta?"

I give him a sharp look to warn him that following that train of discussion isn't going to help right now, but it's too late. He's scowling like he's just swallowed a squirming insect and avoids looking in Desto's direction. What would any unscrupulous person who's kidnapped someone and forced her to fly a stolen ship to a potentially neutral, but definitely not co-conspiratorial, colony do to cover up his crime? Easy: kill her and make it look like an accident before she ever gets a chance to out you.

To Desto's credit, he takes it in stride and responds calmly, "That's exactly what I'm saying. We have to get there before he does, or we're writing her off. And my kid."

"I'll get us up," Venus says, turning to head to the cockpit.

She stops when Vitruzzi says, "We have other kids to worry about now."

"What?" Everyone's face shows the same shock as mine. "What are you talking about?"

Vitruzzi slumps against the wall—when had her posture turned into an S with a broken back?—and won't look at anyone. "These four kids only have us. We have an obligation—"

"To help our crew!" Desto nearly yells.

"Yes, Desto"—she straightens and looks him in the eye—"we can go to Obal 6. We can try and convince them we're the good guys and Quantum is the bad guy. Maybe they'll believe us. Then what? We have no more food, no more water, so we give them everything we have in the cargo bay to buy enough to get us back to Keum Libre. And we're back to where we started. Barely holding on, resources dwindling. For all we fucking know, Keum Libre isn't even there anymore. Some other scavs could have gone in there and wiped it out." Her voice starts to shake, and she takes a deep breath. "Don't you get it? We're fucked. The whole goddamn system is crumbling. We might be too stupid to lie down and die with it, but maybe that's exactly what we should do."

Karl scrambles over to her and puts a hand on her shoulder, soothingly, an old friend trying to offer support. She shrugs it off. No one speaks as she looks around at our faces. I've seen people crack before. The dark shadows from being too strung out to even sleep anymore that crowd into the hollows under her eyes, the way her 1.8-meter frame can barely hold the meat that hangs from it, the edge to her voice when she speaks, like the fading scream of a jumper before they hit the sidewalk—Vitruzzi is a walking case of nearing the terminal breaking point.

As if someone's drawing a curtain away, I'm suddenly thinking back to PCA *Thor's Hammer*, a long-range patroller tasked with joining a convoy of gunships sent out to suppress mutiny on the PCA *Frontline* a week after the Soldier's Rebellion broke out in earnest. I remember his eyes the most—my squad's heavy gunner, Enlistee First Class Tollhut—the way they had darted around the bunkroom like a mismanaged marionette. "We can't board her, not a fleet ship! he'd said. We can't fire on our own people!"

I'd been called out of the navigator's seat down to the armory bay to help calm him down. We'd gone through the Academy and boot together and had served in the same company for the prior two years on the *Hammer*. He trusted me, and more importantly to our command, I was the only one who could fit through the narrow opening between the bunks and cargo bins he'd piled around himself like some kind of last-man-standing barricade.

"What's going on, Tollhut? What's with the drama?" I may be good at fitting into small spaces, but I'm no psychologist when it comes to talking someone off the ledge. Which was rammed home that day.

"That's one of our ships, Erikson. They want us to shoot our own brothers." He stood near the back of the bay behind several hanging racks of bugsuits. I caught glimpses of him moving around and heard clicks and bangs while he spoke, but I couldn't tell what he was doing. "You're always talking about it; can't you see? This is where the line is drawn. *This* is what separates the humans from the monsters in Corps uniforms."

Yeah, I'd known exactly what he was talking about. The story they were feeding us was the Rebellion was a bunch of disgruntled soldiers taking over a few scattered ships. But then it became more than a few ships and more than a few soldiers. Fighting was breaking out on several stations, even on the Obals, and despite how hard our COs tried to keep us from knowing all the details, the stories poured in with every transmission we received and every port we docked at. Something big was going down, and the Corps was beginning to fracture like an overstressed viewscreen in deep space. Tollhut wasn't the only one who thought being asked to fire on our own Corps brothers and sisters was insane.

But what could I tell him? I hadn't known then what to say any more than I know now. I'd rattled on about his duty to his comrades and his duty to justice, and he didn't want to hurt anyone, did he? And blah blah blah. All the while, he'd been putting on a bugsuit—or Goldblum Squad Leveller suit—the heavy-fire body weapons we used for urban terrain seek-and-destroy missions.

When I heard Tollhut say "Switch to full-auto," I jumped behind a crate. When he fired a cement-mixer explosive through his barricade, I'd been knocked unconscious. I'd woken up with David screaming into my ear that we had to get off the ship, we were going down. The *Hammer* never fired a shot on the *Frontline*, and besides us, I never knew how many others made it clear of the ship before it blew. And David and I had spent the rest of the Rebellion trying to stay ahead of the Corps.

Vitruzzi's eyes look just like Tollhut's had.

She's as close to the edge as you can get before falling into the abyss, but I don't know what to tell her. The doomsday shiver from just a little while earlier works its way through me again. I know exactly what Vitruzzi is going through, and I have nothing to offer her. What if she's right? Shaking off that thought, I offer in a voice that's barely above a whisper, "Don't say that kind of thing, V. Yeah, shit's hard, life's not all bubble baths and daffodils, but we just have to keep going. Sometimes survival is as good as it gets."

"Right," she answers, almost accusingly.

"Eleanor, come with me. You need some time to get your head straight," Karl says, turning aside and waving a hand toward the doorway to try and convince her to go. The room suddenly feels like it's shrinking around us.

Finally, without looking at anyone, she pushes past Karl and walks down the corridor toward the cargo bay. No one follows her.

Desto glares after her and the rest of us exchange a knowing look. Mason breaks the cold silence with his always practical observations. "We're going to have to dump the two fugees and keep the salvage we were going to give them."

Nodding thoughtfully, Karl says, "This is their colony anyway, so . . ." I know we're all sharing the same relief that we don't have to ditch them somewhere dangerous or unwelcoming. Then again, we have no idea what life is like in this colony. And there's still Ryan from the *Galatea*. Karl is looking at him, no doubt pondering his fate.

Before someone else does, I make a decision and turn to him. "Guess what, kid, this is your lucky day. You get a choice. We can either drop you here, or you can join the crew. What'll it be?"

To his credit, the look on his face is more excitement than abject terror, and he only hesitates for a second before responding, "With you," then adds hurriedly, "and don't worry, I'll pull my weight."

I try on a grin that doesn't get far, but it's better than nothing because he relaxes a little. "You already have."

Nodding his agreement with the addition of a new crewman, Karl says, "Venus, let's move out."

SEVENTEEN

We can easily outmaneuver that flying brick, Venus. Why not just shake him off?" David comments from the rear of the flight deck.

"Yeah, I could. But the two *escorts* at our six are military-class scouts. They could yo-yo around us like we're standing still."

David pushes up closer and looks at our radar, finally seeing the tiny specks of the ships that have been dogging us since shortly after we broke into Obal 6's atmosphere. The red glowing specks they make on our nav interface are marginally less worrisome than the equally red but much brighter power-diverter malfunction indicator on the main console telling us we can choose to land within the next couple of hours, or the choice will be made for us.

"Fuh . . ." He trails off, realizing what Venus and I already know. These two scouts are equipped to take out a squad of ships our size if they want to.

"Unidentified transport craft, you are in controlled airspace belonging to Bogotan. What are your intentions? Over."

Venus and I look at each other. Finally, contact.

I respond normally, as if anything is normal anymore. "Bogotan, we are a salvage operation from the Alpha Quadrant with an imminent system malfunction. Request your permission for an emergency landing. Over."

There's a delay, presumably while the scout communicates with someone else. Then: "Negative, scavs. You need to keep on moving."

"This got hostile way faster than I expected," I comment, already running my hand along the nav console and pulling up landscape schematics. In case we have to break for it.

"How far from the city are we?" David asks.

"Just under ninety klicks. We could be there in ten if we didn't have to worry about getting turned into missile kabobs."

"So we could potentially force them to fire on us over their settlement if Venus works some of her magic?"

"Yeah, I mean, we could, but . . . the way she'd have to fly, those kids in back might get tossed around too much—"

"You have one minute to divert, scavs, or we will take aggressive action," the scout warns.

"We are in a situation up here, people. Get buckled in as tight as you can. Things are about to get fun," Venus announces to the crew, then clicks on an audio autocounter that plays over the onboard intercom to give the deadline. David hustles from the cabin, slamming and engaging the cockpit hatch.

"Thirty seconds . . . twenty-nine . . . twenty-eight . . . twenty-seven."

"Aly, you just let me take over," Venus says excitedly, like a kid that just heard their shiny new bike doubles as a rocket racer. "I can handle them."

"Sixteen . . . fifteen . . . fourteen."

I give my harness an extra tug to make sure nothing gets pinched by a loose strap when our g-forces suddenly turn me into a five-hundred-kilo rag doll. A pinched-off boob would give an entirely new meaning to the phrase "on my tits."

"Nine . . . eight . . . seven."

"What's your plan?" I ask.

Venus's head tilts slightly sideways in thought, like an attentive pup. "I haven't quite decided yet."

"Venus . . ."

"I could pull an Ivan, but we'd just end up dead in the air with no place to go but down." She taps the control stick pensively. "Nah."

"Venus . . ." A bit more of an edge in my voice this time.

"Maybe cut the engines, pop the air brakes, and let them fly on by?" She glances at me the way somebody asking for an opinion might—but really not. "No, that's way overdone."

"Four . . . three."

"Dammit, Venus! Can we do anything like that with the power diverter on the fritz?"

"Probably not. We're probably going to die in a meteor of fire." With that, she flashes me a quick grin and cocks an eyebrow. "Just playing, Aly-oop. We're golden."

"One."

"Oh, sh—" I begin, but before I know what's happening, g-forces slam me into my seat, cutting off my breath and slapping my head down with force enough I'd have bitten through my tongue if I weren't lucky. *Hope those kids are squared away.* Apprehension—and a spine-crushing amount of g's—make my throat tight.

Venus yanks the stick hard back, firing us into an insanely steep climb straight up. The ship groans and shudders violently in protest but holds together. Venus's hand darts to the throttles and flicks the port engine to idle. The *Orika* slews sideways. Impossibly, the g-forces get worse, and my grip on consciousness starts to slip.

With barely a strain to her voice, she announces, "High-g pitch-back turn." She glances out the port window. "Should put the sun at our backs too. The old ways still work, y'know?"

She flings the ship hard uphill and turns the belly into the wind. Our airspeed drops to nothing, and the other ships shoot by, far underneath us.

The world through the viewscreen spins wildly: ground, sky, cloud, a blinding flash of sunlight, now ground again. Through my diminishing vision, I see a double pulse of light and two streaking vapor trails.

Venus grunts. "That's two missiles we won't have to worry about. Now, the fun part."

She straightens the controls and slams the port throttle forward again. Instantly the g's relax, and I desperately suck in a breath. My vision comes back to normal, and our speed climbs rapidly as we dive back down like a bird of prey.

Venus rolls the ship a few degrees, then pulls hard back on the stick again. The g's hit once more but not quite as strong. Her eyes dart to the radar, then back to the viewscreen. Eyes narrowed in concentration, she calmly says, "Give me the ventral thrusters when I ask for them, please."

I'm already too sick and oxygen deprived to ask why. Then the enemy ships appear in our viewscreen, dead ahead. The thought *suicide run* flashes in my mind, but then she pops the nose of the ship up.

"Ventral thrusters . . . *now*."

She flicks the throttles back with the dexterity of a concert pianist, and we level out barely meters above their ship, with the blast from our thrusters reflecting off their hull and against ours, giving just enough extra cushion to keep us from slamming into them. Even so, I think I felt the slightest impact, like we actually touched.

Almost as if she's in my head and hearing my thoughts, Venus says, "We did. I misjudged it by a couple meters." She shrugs and continues straight on. "One of those scouts is a newer pilot. He wasted his missiles on a wild shot when we did our climb, then he couldn't stick with us. His leader is smarter." She grins her silly, slightly wild grin again. "So he wouldn't fly into the blast of what he thought was a kamikaze run."

She snaps the controls hard over and jams the throttles to their stops. With a rending screech, we slide sideways off the top of the other ship, roll upside down, and pull hard up, down—shit, *whatever*—toward the ground. The world outside does another sickening psychedelic kaleidoscope routine, and I feel my last meal, maybe *literally* my last meal, looking for a way out.

"Yep, here he comes again," she calmly announces. "His angle on us isn't too good, but it's close enough that he'll probably try a—yeah, thought so. Missiles inbound." An earsplitting buzzer nearly drowns out her last few words. "They'll be on us in a few seconds."

We're pointing straight down at the ground with the engines screaming at full thrust. A thin layer of wispy clouds is in the distance, far below us, then all of the sudden it isn't, and the ground is perfectly clear, colorful, and getting more so by the instant.

"The nice thing about the really fast missiles," Venus murmurs, "is that they don't turn well."

I close my eyes, suck in a breath, and grit my teeth, just in time for another assault on my senses as she makes yet another maneuver that smashes all my internal organs into what feels like chunky tomato soup against my pelvis.

Dammit, I wish he'd just shoot us down already.

Through the pain and what I hope is a silent scream on my part, I feel a couple small jolts, like driving over bumps in the road.

Venus says cheerfully, "Missed. I'll bet that lead scout must be getting pretty frustrated by now. We're over the city, by the way."

I open my eyes as the last hills and trees flash by our sides, and we break out over Bogotan, slowing and dropping in altitude enough to make shooting us down here guaranteed to damage the city. "That's the craziest set of flying you've put me through yet," I comment, my voice a reluctant rattle. "I hope everyone's okay back there."

Venus replies, "They'll be fine. I left the gravity compensators on full back in the hold."

"So you just needed to turn it off here in the cockpit?"

"Yep." She climbs to get a little bit more altitude and take the engines back from redline. Then she relaxes a bit more in her seat. "Well, no. I just thought it would be funny. You probably didn't know it, but you can make some really nutty faces." Without missing a beat, she keys the radio. "This is the *Orika* to Bogotan, requesting landing clearance. Or we can just slam into midtown. Thanks for your attention. Over."

Venus looks as relaxed as a cat in a sunbeam. If I could take the cue from her, I would, but my skeleton currently feels like it may have recently been used to support a skyscraper.

"We're on approach," she notifies the crew. "Should be landing in about a minute. The kind people of Bogotan are more likely than not going to be welcoming us in full splendor, so I suggest we do the same. Out."

Our high-speed approach only allows for a limited glimpse of the infrastructure, but our nav scopes record everything and create an instant three-dimensional map. On the two-week trip here, the crew used every hour studying the archival images and prints of Bogotan. As a smaller city with limited manufacturing, it had missed most of the systematic destruction of first the uprising masses, then the Admin when they went through the system and razed all communication satellites.

With a radius of just under five thousand kilometers and a surface of 75 percent water, Obal 6 is the smallest Obal in the system and had the lowest population density of the Admin-ruled planets—now, given its low priority during the war, it may have the highest. To citizens, it had always been thought of as the backwoods Obal, the kind of place an eccentric old aunt or moonshining pappy would have settled down.

On my last trip, just before the war, we'd been brought here by Quantum to take advantage of the vast web of citizen-owned communication satellites, our intent being to blackmail T'Kai, former director of the Ministry of Science and Engineering—though now I think of him simply as the reason the human race just got blasted about a thousand years back toward the Stone Age. This time we'd dropped out of orbit into its atmosphere on the planet's dark side and flown over two of its five major continents. The destruction, even from ten thousand meters, is unreal. Blackened craters mar the landscape where most of the major cities used to stand, and those that weren't annihilated seem to have fallen to ruin through inside fighting, loss of civil structure and leadership, or just abandonment.

Depending on what side people took after the mass-broadcast revelation of the Admin's policy of using citizens and soldiers as biological test subjects, the cities had become too dangerous, especially for citizens who were known to have been former Corps or higher-ups in the Admin echelon. Some say half the system's population died, some say more. What I know is—there's no one left to take a head count.

"Easy. Easy, now. Just cool your jets a little, people. We aren't that scary."

Venus is talking to herself, but her audience could be the scouts now hovering on our wings as we glide to a landing zone on the settlement's edge. Two smaller ships, retrofitted citizen-class compacts, were apparently also scrambled to "welcome" us, and the *Orika* is now covered from four angles, making escape impossible.

The skids hit the earth and the hydraulics settle smoothly. Venus has already unstrapped her harness and heads toward the cockpit exit without a glance back. I unlock too and rise to my feet but have to blindly reach out and grab the back of the navigator's seat to keep myself from pitching headfirst into the console. My legs take a couple of seconds to decide if they're still part of the team, then I'm finally able to follow Venus out.

Karl meets me in the cockpit's antechamber, his face nearly as blanched as my own must be. "You okay?"

"Yeah." I give him a grin. "You?"

"Someday I'll get used to Venus's flying." I raise my eyebrow at him, and we both force a short giggle. "Or maybe not." His face turns serious. "Look, Aly. I'm . . . I don't know how to say this, but I want you to follow my lead on this. Eleanor's not . . . herself, and Desto, well, you know. I don't trust either of them to make sound choices right now, so I'm taking point."

I nod, feeling more relieved about his plan than I'd expected.

"I'll back you up too, bro," David says, joining us from the crew deck below. "And I know Hoogs and Mason are on board. We all heard V . . ."

He doesn't have to elaborate. I'd told Karl about the way Vitruzzi had reacted when we crashed back on Eruo Pium, the way she froze up when the hovercraft attacked us. It's clear the word got around. After her meltdown before leaving the mining colony, the rest of the crew isn't taking chances.

"They'll be knocking on our door soon. Let's get it together," Karl says.

The hold is secure for now, but anyone with the proper motivation and a high-output plasma torch can get inside in no time. The crew gathers, ready to implement part two of the plan.

Which is to say—improvise.

"Desto, I clearly remember you being present when we said we were going to try this with no guns. Did you forget how to count?" Karl says.

The father-to-be stands in the hold next to the manual hatch release, waiting for us, and his body bristles with barrels and blades pointing in every direction.

"You know they outnumber us by a few hundred. We're not going to handle this thing like kamikazes," Karl finishes.

The hard set of Desto's face makes me think this isn't going to end well. The eight of us, nine if we count Ryan—but he strikes me as too smart to jump into this kind of fray—could restrain a man of Desto's size, if we're willing to take a few hits. After all, none of us wants to get shot before we even have a chance to get off the ship, but we're guaranteed to be bruised and bloodied, and—

Desto swings the Thresher over his shoulder and drops it on the deck, his eyes peering at the rest of us like a judge passing sentence on condemned heretics. The rifle clatters loudly in the tight space, and he sends a carbine and TorcherMax to follow it. His hand goes to the Sinbad on his right hip and stops there. No glare ever promised more pain if anyone steps up to challenge him.

Drawing a breath that doesn't quite hide his relief, Karl turns questioningly toward Vitruzzi. She has the four children drawn up around her like a squad of miniature soldiers. Despite their malnutrition, the most hollow set of eyes in the group is Vitruzzi's. She stands near the rear of the hold, letting Karl run the show.

"Why isn't anyone demanding we open up?" I wonder aloud.

"Maybe they're waiting for an invitation," David replies, surreptitiously pulling his jacket tighter around the pistol in his shoulder harness. In this crew, a decision against carrying guns is really a decision against carrying *visible* guns. Some people have lucky rabbits' feet, others have lucky firepower.

As if on cue, Desto depresses the hatch control and the ramp begins to lower.

"Remember, they're not our enemies," Karl says quietly.

Right, I think, *because if they were, they would have fired missiles at us.* But pointing out the obvious would be counterproductive at the moment.

"Wait, where's Venus?" I spin around, searching for her, but don't see her anywhere.

The ramp hits the tarmac outside, and no one says a word. Is she hiding? We hadn't talked about leaving anyone on the ship—too late now.

I shiver, suddenly hit by a blast of dry, cold air. It feels like the planet has been locked inside an icebox for the last year, but anywhere feels that way after Keum Libre's humid sweatbox climate. My muscles clench in protest. Cold muscles slow down reaction time—I'll need to keep moving to stay limber.

From where we stand, the tarmac appears empty. If anyone waits for us, they're holding back until we're clear of the *Orika*'s relative cover.

"Hello?" Karl calls into silence. Nothing. "We're stepping outside. We are nine adults and four kids total. Our intentions are peaceful."

Another blast from the icebox whistles up the *Orika*'s crew deck corridor, but nothing else.

Karl nods to me where I stand on his left, then to Desto and Mason, on his right, and we amble as a group down the ramp, our hands remaining visible. It feels like we're walking off the edge of a cliff.

I sense a movement far to my right and glance over. The older little girl, a blonde-haired one of about seven, has left the bunch circling Vitruzzi and moves up to Doug Mason. She grabs his big, rough hand in one of hers and squeezes it, as if she's trying to reassure him. Doug smiles down at her. When he does, his face opens up in a way I've never seen—never even imagined—and for the first time, I realize that Mason could be someone's kindly uncle, or their dad. He'd had a wife, another soldier, but she died in a friendly-fire accident prior to the Soldier's Rebellion. This is the face of Mason who might have been—if so many things had turned out differently. The girl—was her name Cassandra?—tugs at his hand, then reaches up toward his neck. He squats and scoops her off the ground like she's made of feathers and sets her in the crook of his arm. She leans in to hug him, and he rubs her back.

Shaking off the odd feeling seeing this new, or, not new but *other*, Mason causes, I pull my attention back to the moment. Out on the landing tarmac, nothing stirs. The four ships standing guard on us maintain their hover but don't land.

The curly headed younger girl, with features close enough to Vitruzzi's that she could be the doc's daughter, looks around the empty tarmac. "What happens now?" she asks in a voice teetering between curiosity and fear.

"What the fuck?" Desto says. "Is this some kind of ghost town?"

"If it is, those scouts are some of the liveliest ghosts I've ever seen," David replies. His head swivels as if on bearings, evaluating the locations of the sentry ships.

Mason juts an elbow into Desto's bicep. When Desto glances at him to see what's up, Mason scowls, then glances meaningfully at the top of the girl's head.

"Shih—I mean, damn, sorry, man."

Everyone's attention turns back toward our surroundings. Besides the scouts at our periphery, the place could be abandoned. But the breeze carries the sound of some kind of machinery, possibly the steel plant on the north end that we'd all seen on the town's schematics.

"I'm cold. Can we go back inside?" one of the little boys asks. His dark hair and the gleaming blue of his eyes remind me of Cross.

"We can soon," Vitruzzi promises him. "We just have to find whoever lives here first. They may have . . . a friend of ours may be here, and we need to find out."

The boy's lip wrinkles back in resignation and he looks at the ground. Something about his childlike disappointment tickles my funny bone, and I grin. David gives me a curious glance. Shrugging, I say, "Well, if they're not going to bring us a 'welcome to the neighborhood' fruit basket, we may as well go to them. Desto, you ready?"

He starts to walk forward but stops when David rests a hand on his shoulder. Desto glances back at David, who slowly shakes his head. "It has to be a trap."

"Doesn't matter. We're here, they have all the advantage. We can't just stand here with our thumbs up our asses and wait for them to bring us some nappies." Desto's severe expression communicates a resolve that nothing short of a missile through the middle of him will dampen. He's right. There's no changing our minds now.

My voice sounds tinny in the cold air. "Let's do this."

We've landed on the original docking tarmac. Forty meters ahead is a brick and steel berm, fifteen meters high, designed to protect the dock control buildings from the blasts of exploding engines or skidding out-of-control ships. A heavy steel gate, wide and tall enough to accommodate large track vehicles or trucks, leads through the berm to the town beyond. Both the gate and sections of the berm are marred by dents and gouges, showing the age and heavy use this airfield had seen, at least in the past, if not currently. Bogotan had once been a reasonably busy city, but Desto is right—it feels like a ghost town now.

"Through there, let's go," Karl says, leading the way to the gate.

Standing up close, it towers above us about six meters. There doesn't seem to be a man-door anywhere, the gate the only way through. It remains as closed and sealed as an airlock at our approach, and David steps forward. He knocks. The ridiculousness of his maneuver is enough to burst the tension running through me, and I can't help but chuckle. Shrugging and grinning too, he puts an ear to the door.

"No porch light," he says. "Maybe we're early? They could still be out grocery shopping for the dinner par—"

Before he finishes the quip, the sound of a rattling and ill-kept engine begins somewhere deep in the berm. Involuntarily, I jump a little and reach to my belt—where no weapon hangs. Muttering a curse, I back away a few paces, mirroring what the rest of the crew is also doing.

The seam in the middle of the two gate doors begins to gape as the opening mechanism pulls them apart. I feel utterly naked and exposed. How did we think this was a good idea? How? What they failed to do with the scout is going to be laughably easy with us just standing here like idiots. My breathing starts to feel shallow, as if panic is setting in. *Think of Zeta,* I tell myself. This is about her and about doing what we can to help her. If we didn't try—and Desto didn't mow us all down for being cowards—we wouldn't be human. We're doing what's right, what we have to for the sake of our existence. Survival isn't the only thing.

Convincing myself of this is going to take a lot more than a self–pep talk, however.

The grating sound of the poorly maintained gate reaches into my throat and drags claws across my insides, and my vision begins to narrow. This isn't right; something is about to go terribly, irretrievably wrong. I'm having a hard time breathing, and it's getting worse. Like someone is squeezing my lungs.

"What's wrong with her?" I hear one of the children ask, but his voice sounds far off.

I begin to turn around, ready to sprint back to the *Orika* and pick up the weapons Desto had left lying on the cargo deck, the feeling of dread sinking into my core and making my whole body feel heavy. And then—*Why am I lying on David's feet?*—a shroud covers me.

EIGHTEEN

"Aly. Aly." Karl's voice parts through layers of cobwebs encasing my brain.

My eyes slide open and he's there, leaning over me, concern filling his sepia eyes and his hand cradling my neck.

I'm fine, I try to tell him, but it comes out: "Mfffmmf."

"Can you sit up?"

Wherever we are, there's enough light to see clearly that I'm lying on a military-issue cot, like the one Venus keeps in her maintenance bay on KL's ocean platform. The rest of the crew are scattered around me, sitting on or standing near more cots. I reach out and Karl grabs my hand to steady me as I pull myself into a sitting position.

"Where are we?" I ask.

He shakes his head. "Dunno, exactly. Some kind of school building."

"A school?" It's as if he'd said we're in a cotton candy factory; my mind is too fuzzy to process or make any sense of what he's saying. I remember standing at the landing-field gates, panicking. Had I passed out? The two things don't add up. "Why a school?" is all I can manage.

"Whatever the reason, they want us alive," Mason says from a couple of cots away.

"What happened?"

From the bunk next to mine, David explains. "You forgot to take out your filter. The air is good here and you didn't need it, so you were breathing almost pure oxygen, plus your blood pressure hadn't fully regulated after all the fancy flying Venus did. You blacked out right before our escort arrived." He drops the offending apparatus on the cot next to me, and I stare at it as if it's an alien that had until recently lived in my skull.

I blink a few times and take a couple deep breaths, and the last of the fog starts to clear. "You're saying I fainted?"

"And scared the shit out of all of us," Karl adds.

David nods. "Then colony guards rounded us up and brought us here." He smirks, but not in amusement. "You really missed out on the fun. We've been waiting for about ten minutes for"—he shrugs—"something." He peers at me closely for a couple more seconds, then stands. "You're all right. Now, let's see what we have here."

Everyone has been disarmed, down to our last blades, but the locals left us alone otherwise. So the situation is simply that we're being held inside a school gymnasium, at their mercy until they decide otherwise. So far, our improvising leaves a lot to be desired. We spread out and begin to sweep the room, leaving Vitruzzi seated with the kids while Karl moves up to the main doorway, keeping an eye out for company. Walking along the vista-screen that covers the back wall, I search for the control booth that runs the giant image player schools use to help students train for different sports. The material of the screen is hard but thin, but that doesn't matter because it's probably backed up by either cinder block or something equally solid. I come across the control panel at the far end, but instead of being in another room—where we might get lucky and find an exit—it's just an interface box on the wall for loading and operating new training programs. Frustrated, I turn toward the others, hoping for different results.

"Anything?" I call.

Desto doesn't respond, and I realize I've lost sight of Mason. As I scan the massive rectangular room for him, my eyes catch on a doorway set into the wall on my left—which Mason is coming out of.

Immediately breaking into a jog, I stop short of him when he shakes his head. "Just a bathroom," he says.

"Hey! Company," Karl shouts and starts backing toward the cots, which are all clustered a few meters from the main entryway.

We quickly group around Vitruzzi and the kids, ready for whatever. As ready as you can be, that is, when you're trapped in a high school gymnasium, shipless, weaponless, and until recently, unconscious.

The doors retract smoothly, sliding into the grooves in the walls on either side, revealing three silhouettes. The light outside is much brighter, punctuating the overall dimness surrounding us and nullifying any sense of safety or protection—no matter how false— the dark might have given me.

The three enter, one man slightly in the lead. He's lean and tall, all angles, with sharp elbows and long, thick-jointed fingers, a pointed nose that looks like you could use the ridge of it to cut the heads off small animals, and straight, broad, but almost dainty shoulders. His whole body resembles a delicate but deadly medieval torture instrument. Even the blue of his eyes is piercing, though they are heavily bloodshot.

Despite his thinness, nearly gauntness, his approach is deliberate and stern. He walks like a man who is used to being listened to and who never makes a move without a purpose. He walks like someone no one fucks with, and I'm utterly certain that our foray into Bogotan is not going to be dull. Hasn't been so far, in any case.

This man—obviously the honcho—and his two flanking musclemen plant themselves a meter in front of us. The crew stands in unison, mentally and physically alert and ready for whatever's coming next. Before saying a word, he looks at each of us individually, and as his bloodshot blue eyes look into mine, the intelligence in them bleeds through like a strobe light on a dark night.

Breaking the silence, he asks, "I'm glad to see everyone on their feet. Is anyone suffering from any immediate needs? Injuries, thirst, hunger? Any chronic medical issues that require tending?"

A query about our well-being is about the last thing I had expected, especially with the amount of authentic concern in his voice. I glance at David questioningly. *Did I hear that right?* His raised eyebrow shows the same level of surprise.

"Anyone? No? Okay, that's good news." He turns his head to the man on his left, a brawny, scowling meat sack that oozes militancy and rage like a bad skin infection. "Van Heusen, their meal, please."

The muscleman returns to the door and steps out, and our captor continues, "Please, everyone, let's all sit and discuss the circumstances we find ourselves in."

None of us move, not about to let our guards down, and he and the other bodyguard continue to stare at us—him with calm but detached concern, the meathead with a blank gaze that could belong to a robot.

"I see," is all he says.

A second later, the first guard comes back through the doorway pushing a plastic, four-wheeled cart in front of him. The smell of warm bread nearly knocks me off my feet, the reality of how hungry I am immediate and severe. None of us has eaten a decent meal in a few days, having been worried and diligent about rationing to hopefully make it back to KL. A tsunami of saliva rushes into my mouth.

Without waiting for the go-ahead, the four fugee children swarm the cart, ignoring Vitruzzi's urgent "Hold it!"

The blue-eyed one who reminds me of Cross uncovers a platter, and exclaims, "Cinnamon rolls!" Then looks inside a box: "And comic holos!" He seems more delighted about the live-action comic holographs than the cinnamon rolls. The guard whispers something to their leader.

"We intend to provide for everyone, I assure you," Skinny says. "We wouldn't have fired on your ship if we'd known you had children aboard."

"Why did you fire on us in the first place? Who the hell are you?" Desto asks, the longevity of his patience shorter than my eyelash.

"Desto," Karl says and moves his hand in front of him in a *calm down* gesture, then he regards Skinny. "Look, we don't know who you are, but you have some explaining to do. Firing on an unarmed transport ship without cause? What kind of people do that?"

Vitruzzi and Mason hover over the kids protectively while Skinny takes his time responding. All four of the children have helped themselves to the rolls and dig in with fervor while watching the action holo, which they've set up on one of the cots.

Skinny steps over to the cart the man he'd called Van Heusen brought in and opens up the sliding door on one side. The smell of warm bread gets stronger, and I see plates and carafes inside. He gestures to it. "Help yourselves. We've brought coffee, eggs, toasted bread, and, I believe, some fruit." When none of us move toward the cart—despite what I'm certain is naked longing on our faces—he sighs and continues, "I understand your anger and confusion. That's natural. We fired on your ship with engine phase bots that would disable you and bring you down, but not harm you. Surely you understand our need to keep our population safe?" He gestures at the food again. "Please. You don't need to be concerned. We are all too short on allies in this new world."

A gurgle of hunger twists through my stomach, the noise audible to everyone in the room. Shit, if I'm going to die on this planet, I may as well do it on a full stomach. Stepping up and grabbing the cart by the handle, I pull it closer to the crew and pass them plates and forks. No one hesitates to take one.

After we all dish ourselves up, completely emptying the food platters, Karl says around his first mouthful, "We're here for one reason and have no intent to stay. Two weeks ago, a friend of ours was kidnapped, along with the long-range transport ship she was piloting. We think the kidnappers brought her here, so we came to find out. That's it. Is there anything you can tell us?"

Hanging on Karl's words, I study our captors, hoping to read some good news in their faces. The thugs stay cool, but recognition flits over Skinny's face.

"You know something," Vitruzzi says, seeing the same thing. "Tell us."

"Ms. Zeta Abrams, flying the *Teibo*," he states, and my guts knot up. "She's already on her way to your home. Keum Libre. She's fine. Almost four months pregnant, too."

What? How would he know that?

"What the hell are you talking about?" Desto asks, his tone betraying a confounded and barely harnessed rage.

The guards react. Van Heusen reaches behind his back and withdraws a set of stun sticks. Thug Two does the same. Each stick is good for two loads, but the more important thing their choice of weapons tells me is that they don't want us dead. But why should we believe Zeta had been sent back to KL if they're holding us captive?

The questions keep piling up. "Answers, Skinny," I prompt. "It's time for some goddamn answers."

"Yes, of course." He smirks self-consciously and his eyes blink rapidly in a tic of some kind. Yet their focus on us never wavers. "First off, I am—or was—Port Control Authority Deputy Jim Whitmore. Now I'm just Jim, and I help keep safe and secure the last colony of consequence here on Obal 6. These men are Daimler Van Heusen, who heads Bogotan's security crew, and Jono Zabriskie, another of the colony's important members. I want to assure you that you are not captives here, and that we fired on your transport merely in an attempt to keep you from endangering the city." He clasps his hands together in front of his waist, almost wringing them. "Obviously, we have much to learn."

"Zeta, how did you know she was pregnant?" Desto demands.

Looking surprised, Whitmore responds, "Well, she told me. Over dinner the night before she flew home, which was three days ago. She was quite exhausted after the trip here, being one of only two pilots among the crew she arrived with, and—"

"Quantum and the fugees. Where are they?" I break in.

Whitmore smiles patiently. "I'll come back to that. I think you're all first concerned with the well-being of your friend, as anyone would be." I have to grit my teeth at his not-quite-condescending tone. "As I said, she was quite tired but understandably in a hurry to get back to your home moon. She and the others explained the situation regarding your salvaging operation, which is quite harrowing. We gave her the resources she needed, and she went on her way. After hearing Ms. Abrams's story, we anticipated the possibility of your arrival, but unfortunately, our airspace security team is jumpy—for good and obvious reasons. I can't apologize enough for the way things have developed."

"You sent Zeta back to KL," Desto reiterates, "on the *Teibo*."

"Yes, that's right."

"She's on her way home—alone. On the *Teibo*. A ship that requires a minimum of two to crew. That what you're saying?"

Desto rises from his bunk and looms like a multikilo colonnade about to crumble into them. Van Heusen says, "Easy, scav. Don't give me a reason."

"Desto," Karl says quietly to get him to calm down, then turns back to Whitmore. "Answer him." Then, as an afterthought: "*Please*."

Whitmore steps up to the cart and casually pours himself a cup of coffee while continuing. "Ms. Abrams's crew—"

"Kidnappers," I cut in.

He glances at me and sips his coffee. "Yes, if you insist. Quantum and the other men did not harm Ms. Abrams, which she was explicit about. The dynamic between them was unfortunate, of course, and this colony doesn't tolerate that kind of aggression"— *unless someone's flying a transport ship you don't recognize*, I think—"but we did listen to their reasoning."

"But didn't you try shooting them down the way you did us?" Desto inquires, reading my mind.

For the first time, Whitmore shows signs of impatience, placing his cup down hard enough to make the coffee splash lightly over the rim and onto the cart. "No, they did not appear to be as threatening. They hailed Bogotan from several kilometers distant and landed, then waited for our security team to reach them."

"You can't expect us to believe a goddamn word you have to say unless—"

"Desto, let the man speak," Vitruzzi cuts him off, an edge in her voice that I haven't heard since the war.

"This is bullshit, Vitruzzi, and you know it! Where is that son-ofabitch now? This talking head is just stalling until . . ."

From the corner of my eye, I catch Van Heusen aiming his stun stick at Desto. Things are about to start going much worse for us if he doesn't cool it. For just a second, I consider letting Van Heusen take him out. Then think better of it.

"Hold it, Bomani. Just chill." I turn to Whitmore. "Look, we've been through some rough shit lately. This hemming and hawing isn't going to get us anywhere fast, so let's just cut to the chase, Whitmore. We need to know our friend is safe. What can you do to assure us, and when are we getting out of here?"

Karl gives me a grateful look and his shoulders relax just slightly. Mason has stepped in front of the group of kids, who've stopped watching the holo and stare wide-eyed at the exchange. The thought flits through my mind that their adult selves are going to contribute brand-new colors to the spectrum of psychologically damaged. "So?" I prompt.

Whitmore links his hands behind his back and steps out from behind the cart toward Desto. "You're the father, I presume. Please believe me, I understand what you're going through. I have two of my own. Sons." He steps closer to the group of kids, and Mason tenses for a moment, staring hard at Whitmore. But he drops a shoulder and lets Whitmore by, where he puts a hand on the blue-eyed boy's shoulder in a fatherly gesture. The kid doesn't flinch, but he doesn't smile either. He just looks at the adult emotionlessly. "I wish I knew where they were."

No one speaks for a moment as Whitmore continues to look at the boy, and his eyelids do another series of fast-paced blinks. Finally, he turns to face the rest of us. "I understand your worries, so I'll just give you the details you want. Ms. Abrams went back to your colony with one of our pilots and a third crewmember to assist. We plan to send a team to pick them up within the week. And they're also going to retrieve this soil amendment compound your former colonist Quantum told us about, along with the cache of raw materials other members of your colony previously retrieved on a salvaging run. Quantum is going to assist us in recreating this world."

"I'LL KILL THE BASTARD."

No one responds to Desto's pronouncement. I glance at Vitruzzi to see her reaction to the news that Quantum has bought his place in this colony with the soil amendment compound, and for the first time in what seems like weeks, her expression shifts into the Vitruzzi from before the war.

"You can't do that," she says.

Whitmore looks surprised. "We can't do what?"

"You can't use that compound. You don't know how to, or what it's capable of."

"Miss . . .?"

"I'm Dr. Eleanor Vitruzzi, previously the head of R&D in the Ministry of Science and Engineering. My expertise is in the field of cyber- and bio-physiology with considerable overlap with virology, immunology, and disease research. So when I tell you that you *can't* use that soil compound, I know exactly what I'm talking about."

"Dr. Vitruzzi, I-I am, I would say, I am *grateful* to meet you." For the first time Whitmore's in-control attitude gives way, revealing a postwar survivor with the same hanging-by-a-thread worries everyone has. "We in Bogotan are doing our best to stay out front of any catastrophes of the nature of which you are so skilled in coping with—"

"I don't want to hear it. You have no idea what you're dealing with in terms of that compound. I don't know what Quantum told you, but it can't be the truth. The man is a calculating opportunist, nothing more. He didn't like the way we run our colony on Keum Libre, so he looked for the easiest out and he took it—without regard to the health of a pregnant woman, I'll add. The fact that you've listened to a single goddamn word he's said to you, knowing what he's done to get here, says all I need to know about your judgment. And I'm telling you, that compound *cannot* be used."

Shit. Vitruzzi's tactician skills must have been another casualty of the war. But none of us disagrees with her approach.

"Doctor, I understand your opinion, but based on Quantum's explanation, it has the potential to become a vital link in replenishing the planet's food supply. It could save thousands, even millions, of lives. We cannot let a useful resource like—"

"No, you're not listening," Vitruzzi cuts in. "This soil compound isn't a resource. It's a poison that we don't fully understand."

David adds, "If it were deployed and you lost control, no one knows exactly what could happen."

"Actually, we *do* know exactly what will happen. The survivors of the KL prison settlement saw the results of the Admin's testing firsthand. An extinction-level event on a scale we haven't seen since the terra-forming disasters of last century." Vitruzzi pauses, then adds, "Or the war. "

Van Heusen speaks up: "Then we don't lose control. It's that simple."

"Simple?" V says. "Have you been paying attention to anything but your own ass for the last twenty-four months? *Simple* doesn't exist, not anymore."

Karl tries to cut in. "Eleanor—"

"No, goddammit! You're talking about—"

"That's quite enough, Doctor. Please." Whitmore's posture is tense, but his voice hasn't lost any of its calm. "This is a necessary and important discussion. My biggest hope is that we can carry it out in an amicable and thoughtful way. But first, let us get our team back with the compound. We can evaluate next steps then. Together." He turns to the man he'd called Zabriskie and says, "Jono, can you ask Korine to bring them coats and hats? It's autumn on Obal 6," he explains, turning back to us, "and I'm assuming you don't have many warmer clothes."

"Does that mean you're not holding us?" Karl asks.

"No, of course not, Mister . . .?" When Karl doesn't respond, Whitmore blinks rapidly, gets it under control, then continues, "No. This isn't a prison, as I've already explained. We'll afford you the same hospitality I would hope you'd extend us if we came to your settlement. As far as we're concerned, Bogotan and the people of your settlement are not enemies. This is about cooperation, not antagonism. You're free to stay here, in this building, while you're on Obal 6. Come and go as you please. As long as you don't endanger any of our colonists, we will make sure you have what you need until our colonies reach a mutual agreement."

He pauses and reaches for his coffee cup but doesn't pick it up. "My ultimate hope, however, is to integrate. Pool not just our resources, but our people." He returns his blink-free stare to all of us. "We are not factions, we are survivors. We all need each other to ensure a future."

BEFORE WHITMORE AND HIS men leave us in the gymnasium, he informs us that his people had attempted to "secure" the *Orika*, but she was locked up tight. Everything they tried to open it had ended up with the hatches either remaining locked or reversing as soon as they started to release. We all know it's Venus, still inside and keeping herself barricaded in as long as she can, but we don't tell him that. Karl lets on that it's the security system and nothing more, and given that it's our vessel, no one's getting aboard but us. Looking dubious, Whitmore makes the decision to drop it—for the time being—and exits.

"I don't care how much Whitmore acts like sweet old Uncle Fred, we have to get the hell out of here and back to KL before— who knows what," David says.

"Yeah, of course, we all agree that's the case. And if we play nice and Desto doesn't step on his dick, we can probably do it without anyone getting hurt." Karl stares hard at Desto as he says this, but his message is loud and clear to all of us. Between Desto's rage and Vitruzzi's bouts of . . . *ineffectiveness*—to put it nicely— we have double the number of loose canons to cope with, which is twice more than we want. "I don't think Whitmore wants any trouble either," he finishes.

Desto cuts in, "What he wants and what he asked for are two different things, Karl. You heard him. He's letting that bag of recycled meat vapor walk around free. And—"

"He's letting us walk around free too—"

"—after what he did to Zeta, he can't be trusted. Hell, V, you said it yourself. The guy has no judgment; he's off the hook and we don't know what's really going on here."

"I'm not saying we have to trust him, but we're in his kitchen. We can't start cooking his food behind his back and hope he doesn't notice." Karl looks at all of us in turn while he speaks, and I roll my eyes at his analogy. He shrugs, knowing how ridiculous it sounded.

"I'm not suggesting we do anything behind his back," Desto continues. "We take our goddamn ship and leave. If anyone tries to stop us, we blow their fucking balls off. *After* I rip Quantum's off with my bare hands."

"What did I just say about not stepping on your dick?" Karl's reasonable tone begins to show strain, but he takes a deep breath before continuing, ignoring Desto's grimace of fury. "If we do that, we'll get shot down, or worse, get stranded midtrip when we run out of fuel. And what about food? And them?" He waves a hand at the kids, then turns and looks off toward the far side of the room, thinking. Turning back, he scrubs his palm over the heavy stubble lining his cheeks and chin, then says, "Look, maybe we need to take a mental time-out. We've been at war for almost two years; our first reaction is to fight. But . . . maybe we're past that. Maybe we have to *let* ourselves be past that. Maybe this is the first chance we have—the first chance *people* have—to start picking up the pieces. If we handle this carefully, calmly, *rationally*, everyone might get what they want."

The crew is quiet for a minute, all of us listening thoughtfully. Impulsively, I grab one of Karl's hands. It's cold inside mine but begins warming up quickly. He turns to look at me, having to tilt his head down because I'm so close. The warmth and gratitude in his eyes make it impossible for me to drop mine.

And I realize—this is it. This is the reason we have to stop fighting, have to stop running, and have to start finding a way to, as Whitmore put it, "recreate this world" together. People helping people. We have to give up the divisions and the factions and the war and the hate because of what I see in Karl's face when he looks at me. There *is* more to our lives than surviving, ticking off the minutes until we're all dead. And he's standing right in front of me.

Turning back to face the group, I say quietly, but firmly, "I'm with Karl. This isn't about shooting our way out of here. It's our opportunity to try something new." My eyes find Desto's. "Think about your kid, Bomani. If you ever want to meet her, you have to be willing to give yourself, and the rest of us, a chance."

The muscles in his face are as tense as a rebar armature. If his stance were any more rigid, he'd be a statue; only his nostrils move, flaring in the anything-goes moment between giving up or blowing up. Finally, he spins around and grips one of the cots, hurling it into the emptiness of the gymnasium with a rage-filled yell. One of the little girls begins to whimper, and Mason pulls her closer to him, letting her squeeze against his leg as he gently strokes her hair. No one says anything. No one dares.

Desto's back stays to us as he glares into the darkness, his shoulders heaving and shuddering and—and . . . is he crying?

I glance toward Karl. His stare rests on Desto's back as he begins to take a step toward him. I reach out and put a hand on his forearm. Turning to me, Karl cocks an eyebrow questioningly. "Let me," I whisper, giving his arm a light squeeze.

"Hey, man." I speak as gently as I can after walking up to Desto. "Zeta's going to be fine, all right? She's tough and she's been through worse. We're going to get home and you'll see that you're worried for no reason. These people seem on the level, you know? They have no reason to hurt anyone."

There are no tears on his face, though his shoulders still quake and his breathing comes in quick gasps. The lack of actual tears doesn't surprise me. I have a hard time imagining he could be capable, but I've been wrong about others—grown men, tougher than titanium plating, breaking down in ways that are usually devastating and never pretty. War does strange things to people. It gets to a point where you have to start expecting it.

"Bomani, you okay?"

He takes a deep breath and finally looks at me, managing a stunted half smile. "Yeah, Aly, I'll be okay."

Reaching up, I put a hand on his shoulder, hoping the contact will be reassuring, followed by a smile of my own, hoping it looks more encouraging than it feels. "All right, then."

Unexpectedly, he wraps a rough and callused palm around my neck and pulls me into a hug. My arms barely reach around his wide, muscular torso as I hug him back. It's a moment of pure, genuine affection, bringing home more than ever how much my crew has come to mean to me. We're all in this together, no matter what. No war, no fighting against gangs of crazy, desperate, or greedy scavengers, and no hardships or scarcities are going to get between us again and break this group up. We stick up for each other, through whatever this chaotic system can throw at us.

Releasing me, he turns fully back to the group. "We need a plan."

NINETEEN

We sketch out something rough and digestible that won't draw anyone's suspicion. The first thing we have to do is ensure Venus knows we're okay and find out if she is, too. Which means a trip to the *Orika*. From there, we hope to have more options and information that will illuminate a long-term solution.

Volunteering, I go to the gymnasium door through which Whitmore and his meatheads had entered. It opens freely, but the one called Zabriskie is outside on guard. He looks at me expressionlessly when I step into the hall.

"So," I begin, very aware of my innately poor negotiation skills, "we're wondering if we can check out our ship. Make sure everything is, uh, being taken care of, and get some of our stuff."

"No."

Okay, this is going to be fun. "Whitmore said we're free to do as we please." God, it's like I'm a child arguing with another child.

"Yeah, you can run around Bogotan. But not together and not without a guide."

"Which is you."

"You got it."

"And our weapons are . . .?"

"Secured."

"Uh-huh. So why can't we get on our ship?"

"Whitmore told you. We're trying to work out a deal with your colony. We don't need more talking heads in the mix making things difficult."

"We're not goddamn talking heads, we're people—wait." I stop myself. Pissing off this guy will get me nowhere. "How does access to our ship make things difficult? We can't communicate with KL anyway. Unless you're telling me you have working satellites." His silence is answer enough. "You do, don't you? So why not just contact KL from here, why send some of your people with Zeta?"

To the cynic—a.k.a. *realist*—in me, it seems obvious. They're going to hit Keum Libre with an attack if Brady doesn't give up the soil compound willingly. They must be using Zeta as a negotiating chip, and Whitmore had probably been lying about sending a ship in a couple of days to pick up the crew he's sent to accompany her. They must already have backup in the air, ready to hammer KL as needed. It's vital that I inform the crew of my suspicions ASAP. This could be the info we need to decide on a game plan. Knowing they have a working satellite is a very, very good piece of information.

But dammit, Whitmore had seemed so reasonable.

"Look," I continue, "we'll stay off the flight deck and out of the com room. Just let us get to our belongings, changes of clothes, et cetera. If we're stuck here, it just makes sense. And it's *polite*."

It will be a risk to let these people near our stores and weapons—not to mention the risk of exposing Venus—but if we can reach out to her, we can covertly establish a communication protocol, as well as give her a sense of what's going on out here. She may not know if we're alive or dead, and Venus could do something to compromise herself if she stays in the dark too long. An ace in the hole is only good for us if she's playable, after all.

"Wait one," Zabriskie says and gets on his com. After talking with whoever's on the other end, he clicks off and says, "You'll have an escort in an hour or so. Until then—" He juts his chin toward the gym door.

"You're a prince," I comment before heading back inside, but inwardly I'm relieved. Besides, being held hostage here beats the shit out of being held hostage by cannibals. I'm a lot more comfortable with the menu, at least.

BEFORE OUR ESCORT—who end up being Van Heusen, Zabriskie, and to everyone's surprise, Whitmore himself—arrive, I quickly sketch out my suspicions to the crew about a potential attack on KL by Bogotan if Brady doesn't do what they want. We don't have any time to fully grasp all the implications of this before the gym door swings open and Van Heusen steps inside. The ambidextrous draw holster sporting two pistols draped over his shoulders captures my attention immediately. What made them switch from stun sticks?

"Which one of you is the pilot?" he asks.

We hadn't discussed what would happen if this question came up, but Karl immediately steps forward.

"Okay. Then, you, you, and you," he says, pointing to me, David, and Ryan. "The rest stay put."

"Only three of us can go aboard?" Hoogs asks.

Van Heusen doesn't bother to answer, just steps to the side so the three of us can get past him.

Sighing with exasperation, I give Karl's hand a quick squeeze as I walk by. "Back soon," I promise.

As I approach the entryway, Desto's weighty shadow follows. *Oh man, don't fuck this up, Desto.* Van Heusen cuts him off before he steps through the door behind me, and I turn on my heels to be ready for whatever happens.

The two men face each other, and Van Heusen, no shrimp, is nearly eye level with him. One of his hands already clutches a pistol grip. "Are you deaf, scav?"

Desto stares at the security chief coolly, but I see murder in his eyes.

Seconds float past in a dream—or nightmare—then Desto smiles at the other man, all of his white teeth bared in mirthful savagery. "Don't forget my shaving cream, Aly," he says, then abruptly turns around and rejoins the others.

I rein in the sigh of relief wanting to slip from my lips, and head into the corridor. The three of us had wrapped up in the hats and coats the woman named Korine brought us, and I'm grateful for them as soon as we step outside. KL and Spectra 6 are warm year-round, sometimes oppressively so; the only way I'm going to get used to this type of cold is if we're here awhile. I just hope that doesn't happen.

Expecting to walk to the landing zone, I snug my synth-wool hat down tight and recheck the zipper on the coat to make sure none of the penetrating breeze can slice through. Instead we're loaded into a ten-seater land trans. Whitmore drives while Van Heusen takes the backseat and Zabriskie the front. For a moment I wonder if the gym is now guard-free. Not likely. This group hasn't shown a hint of bad strategy yet.

Algol A and B are in full view, the sky perfectly crisp, cloudless, and blue. The city streets and buildings extending in every direction look just as well-maintained and clean as they must have been before the war—possibly even cleaner. With fewer people living here, less garbage and fewer signs of consumption mar the cityscape. The moment takes me back to life before the Corps and before this war, and I remember what it was to be a citizen of the Obals in a society that was orderly and peaceful. Out of nowhere, my emotions suddenly feel ripped in half. On the one hand, I'm hit with a wall of sadness and a sense of loss that makes my chest tight and my eyes hot in their sockets—so much devastation, so much waste. But on the other hand, I'm surprised by a sudden clear-headed sense of hope, almost excitement. This is another chance, a new system with new opportunities to get it right.

But can we this time?

The drive lasts only a few minutes. With ordinary prewar traffic, it would have taken at least triple that in a city this size, and David and I use the time to examine the area's layout and organization. No matter how good your sat-maps and schematics are, things always look different from ground level. Occasional lights pepper the buildings, few of which show signs of battle. The mag-rails and streets all seem to be untouched as well. It's as if the war bypassed Bogotan, and I see why they've made it their home. Yet few people walk the streets. Much like Agate Beach and even KL, I'm sure the city's inhabitants have little free time, occupied with getting and keeping the basics of survival up and running.

Reaching the southern edge, we get our first exposure to the scars of the war. This side of the berm safeguarding the city from the airfield, which I hadn't seen after landing thanks to my fun with the nasal filter, looks like the gateway to the apocalypse. A ten-meter-high wall of earth and steel had been—there's no other way to describe it—*melted* and turned into a standing wave of fused metallic obsidian before it could collapse into a puddle. The damage extends down the length of the berm from one side of the gate about fifty meters before I recognize an impact crater. Odd. Based on the shape and angle of the crater, the missile that had caused it came from inside the city, as if someone was trying to make the berm impenetrable to those coming from the airfield. Was it the city's attempt at self-defense, the occupants trying to turn this wall into a stronghold that would keep attackers out? A large contingent of ground forces would most likely have come from a strike from ships using the airfield to get their teams close. The other option would be to send forces inside using the city's major streets and thoroughfares. I'd bet my favorite carbine those locations are well guarded, maybe even blockaded, too.

In any case, their aim had been off. The giant gate still works, as we'd already seen. Yet it leaves me wondering why a city filled with people who were so worried about outside attackers that they tried to destroy their own points of ingress was never, in fact, attacked.

We approach the cargo hold hatch, Whitmore, Van Heusen, and Zabriskie trailing the three of us. The wind kicks up, rasping against my exposed cheeks with a gritty feel of dust, but it smells clean. The Obals always make you appreciate good air, and the war hadn't damaged O 6's atmosphere significantly if it's still this fresh. I have to admit, KL is starting to look a little Paleolithic by comparison. It's possible to walk around without a breathing filter there, but after a while the thickness and particulates in the air clog your throat and lungs enough to make you feel like you're trying to breathe underwater. Uncomfortable, to say the least, and who knows what the long-term effects would be.

"Just have to enter the opening sequence," David says, approaching the *Orika*'s outer panel, which gives access to the manual entry keypad. If Venus is still inside and saw our approach, she'll be able to override the safeguards that keep anyone else from getting aboard after David keys in his code.

"Nice and easy, scav," Van Heusen warns.

I'm really starting to not like this meat sack, and the dirty look I throw over my shoulder at him must make that obvious. "We're not scavs."

"Course not, dollface," he says, and puckers his lips at me in a disgusting leer.

"Eat me, d—"

"That will be enough," Whitmore interrupts and glances meaningfully at Van Heusen, whose face returns to a scowl.

"Just open it," he says to David.

The inset latch to open the panel sticks for a few seconds before David is able to prise it loose and slide the panel open. He enters his key code and steps a bit to the side, staring hopefully at the hatch. The hydraulics inside instantly begin humming, and the ramp lowers smoothly.

"How did you do that?" Zabriskie asks, suspicion triggered. If they hadn't been able to open it with simple bypass algorithms, there's no way a key code should have worked.

Without missing a beat, David responds, "Facial recognition." I have to stifle a chuckle at the unintended truth of that.

The ruse apparently works. Zabriskie's expression remains doubtful, but he doesn't ask any more questions.

"Before we step aboard," Whitmore says, "I'd like to assure you that we are not pirates and your belongings will not be taken. If there is anything you'd like to share with the city, we'd be happy to have it. And if you have any weapons aboard"—I look at him sharply, already bracing for the conflict that's coming if he asks that we hand them over—"please leave them be. You may take them when you leave Bogotan, but you understand that we aren't willing to invite the kind of problems they may cause. Aside from that, for efficiency's sake, please separate into three groups, and one of us will accompany each of you."

"That's not really going to do any good, Whitmore," David explains. "Ryan isn't a regular member of our crew. He doesn't have anything aboard and isn't familiar with everyone's property."

Whitmore looks thoughtful for a short, blink-frenzied moment. "I'm sure there's something he can gather for your group." His eyebrows rise questioningly.

David thinks about it, then capitulates. "Sure, yeah. Ryan, can you hit the galley and grab as much of our rations as you can? If you need a backpack, you can pick one up from the crew quarters. Which means"—he looks at Whitmore—"he'll need to go with whomever picks up our personal gear."

Rations? That's a laugh. What's left in the galley could probably be carried in just Ryan's pockets. We'd stored some backup provisions in the cargo hold, just in case, and would have broken them out today if we'd still been on the ship. Before Whitmore had come to escort us from the gym, we'd all agreed that it's best to leave them unmentioned and aboard, mostly for Venus's sake, and in case we have to make a break for it. It's a 140-or-so-hour flight from here to KL, and there isn't enough food to keep all the adults and children well fed (we'd agreed to give the children full rations, but the rest of us would go hungry), but if just a couple of us are able to break free, it will be enough to sustain whoever does.

"Aly and I should both get the crew's items," David says. "I'll take the main bunkroom while you go through the spare and your cabin."

I nod agreement and he starts aboard. Whitmore beckons at Van Heusen to go with him. Ryan follows, Zabriskie on his tail.

"You and me, then?" I ask Whitmore.

"Is that all right with you?" he asks nicely enough.

Without responding, I step inside the hold where the cargo bins are all still tied down exactly as we'd left them.

Van Heusen asks, "What's in all these?"

"Our stuff," David replies bluntly and with finality.

Van Heusen starts to say something, but Whitmore cuts him off with a steely look. The six of us move through the main corridor toward the berthing room. Whitmore and I continue past it as David and Ryan veer inside with their escorts. I enter the cabin Karl and I share, absorbing every detail visible, hoping Venus had left a message or indication of her status.

The room and the rest of the ship are chilly, barely warmer than the outside air. She's not running any power, knowing it would give away her presence. As soon as I think this, I realize that the top blanket from my and Karl's rack is missing and conclude her bunk must already be stripped. Whitmore wouldn't know anything about my blanket, but I hope a bare bunk in the main berth doesn't give her away.

After stuffing a few hygiene items and some clothing in a bag I'd pulled from the under-bunk storage drawer, I suddenly see what I've been hoping for. The digits on our universal clock, which runs on its own battery, flash the hour. The seconds are ticking past in regular time, but as soon as they reach *00* and the minute should increment by one, it flickers, then returns to the same time it was just on. I move slowly, trying to make it look like I'm searching for something, doing my best to veil the attention I'm giving the clock. Then it happens again. Same time. It has to be Venus, but what's the number sequence for?

"You're a soldier, Ms. Erikson. Aly—if I may. Is that correct?" Whitmore's question surprises me, and I glance to where he remains in the doorway. "Your life experience has forced, perhaps *offered*, you a unique and practical perspective on this kind of situation."

"Yeah, sure. What kind of situation is that?"

"Making choices. Choices that mean the future for humankind."

What the hell is he talking about? I stand up straight and give him my attention.

"The good of one cannot supersede the good of all. If we allow that to happen, even the one will lose. I know you understand that."

"Whitmore, I swear you couldn't have been a dock supervisor before all this. You sure you weren't a teacher, or maybe a priest? If you have a point, would you just get to it?"

He grins with genuine amusement. "A soldier, like I thought, a woman who appreciates directness. So I'll be direct.

"It is vital that we here at Bogotan acquire this soil amendment compound that your, uh, former . . . cohort described. And why? What I propose is doing the greatest amount of good for the greatest number of people—with one caveat. The greatest number of people with *the greatest chance for success.* This is a variable that no amount of numbers, no allowance for attrition, can subvert. And we no longer have the numbers to consider attrition an acceptable factor. We cannot live with an expectation that our gains, our human successes, will accumulate enough in the long term to allow us to thrive. If we don't start thriving en masse right now, *today*, too many will die for us to possibly regain the worlds we came from. We will fall back into chaos, disease, starvation—in short, the return of a Neolithic human existence."

His reference to the Neolithic, reminiscent of my earlier thought about KL seeming Stone Age compared to Bogotan, jars me. His tone of voice is more convincing than his words could ever be, and strangely, I realize I'm paying attention. Acutely. No sharp remarks form behind my lips; no arguments; no naysaying. Am I really listening to this?

"I am no savior, Aly, no beacon of modern mankind, sent to save the world, delusions of grandeur. I am none of that. I am a father aching for the loss of his children, a husband who is tormented by his feelings of gratitude that his wife died before she had to witness all of this, and a believer in the better side of humanity. What we've experienced, this war, it was more than enough to drive anyone to their limits. Those of us who haven't gone a little mad with what we've witnessed must already have been crazy to begin with. And that, that right there, is the new normal."

I move a little to the side and lean against the wall in order to cover the clock. Whitmore doesn't seem to notice. His hands are clasped tightly around his midsection, twisting together in a severe wrestling match, as if he's trying to keep them from flying away. His clear blue eyes almost bug, the intensity and sincerity of his gaze unmistakable. His uncontrolled blink is completely absent. He believes every word he's saying—and . . . so do I? Do I?

"I don't want to hurt anyone. I want everyone who has emerged from this civilization-ending tidal wave to have the same freedom to rebuild everything we've lost. Why else would we have given up so much of our old way of life, the little comforts we had under the Admin's system, to salvage Bogotan? We have running water, we have order, we have the beginnings of commerce, we have satellites to communicate with anyone else who may be able to listen. We are putting the pieces back together. And everyone here knows we're doing what is most important, most vital, for humanity, for our present, and for our future. Our short-term inconveniences mean *nothing* in the face of long-term survival. Long-term thriving. We want to keep going, Aly, but we need every bit of help we can get. We need you and your crew's help. We need your settlement's help. And most of all we need the help of what tools of civilization remain."

He takes a long stride and reaches out to put a warm, gentle hand on my shoulder. We look at each other, me speechless, him searching, and that same sincerity remains in his face. "Will you help us?"

TWO THOUGHTS RUN THROUGH my brain in quick succession, the latter snapping at the tail of the former. *This is exactly what Karl was talking about: put aside the fight so we can all start relearning how to live normal lives.* Followed by: *When Bodie first analyzed the data to the soil compound, he found communications about making it commercial. Could we have missed something on KL? Could it actually be used safely? Does Bogotan have people who can figure out how?*

I move my eyes to stare pointedly at his hand, staying silent until he removes it. "Help you how, Whitmore? We already told you the compound is dangerous. No one who created it is still alive, and everyone who's seen it in action says it's deadly—even the data says that. Like Vitruzzi told you."

"And I understand that. But it has incredible effectiveness, according to Quantum."

"The only side effect being the massive kill-everything-else-first issue."

"Science didn't die with the war, Aly, we will of course study it before using it. You can help us by—"

"Convincing my crew to go along with you, right?" I've had this conversation before. He almost flinches at my interruption, unsure how to respond to such aggressive bluntness, so I use the dead air to continue. "And what's in it for me?"

"What do you mean?" He actually seems surprised. He's not an idiot, but the priority list of the criminal-enterprise educated doesn't come naturally to him. So I help.

"Give my team back our VDUs, and let us contact our colony on Keum Libre. You have working satellites; I can't think of a better use to put them to." *And this is your chance to prove you're not bullshitting us.* If we don't let the rest of the colony know where we're at, when Zeta gets there, they'll have to assume we're still stuck on Eruo Pium and send out a pointless rescue mission. *Or is that what you want, Whitmore? To get more of our people and ships away from KL to thin the herd, make a takeover that much easier.*

His response comes quickly, too quickly for my suspicions to increase. "Can I have you and your crew's word that you won't put our city and people in danger?"

"You have mine," I promise. "And I'll talk with the others."

"I appreciate your candor, Ms. Erikson, and your sophistication." He reaches out to shake hands on the deal.

"Just don't fuck with us," I warn, ignoring his hand.

TWENTY

Hot coffee steams beside me on a table. After a second, I wrap both hands around the ceramic mug and cradle it like a precious gem, trying to get heat back into my body. Once we'd returned to our "accommodations" in the high school and dropped off the collected goods, Vitruzzi, Karl, and I were immediately taken by Whitmore to their satellite link up, this time being led on a walk through the biting cold for about a kilometer along the street. The communications hub resides in an office building like you'd find in any business district on any of the Obals. *Used* to find, that is. I'd lost feeling in my fingers about halfway, despite rounds of blowing on them and then jamming them into my armpits to keep them out of the wind.

Other than letting everyone know we were going to get in touch with KL, I hadn't had a spare second to tell them about Whitmore's and my arrangement before we left to send the transmission. I filled in Karl and V on the way, my teeth chattering to add a dramatic flair to the story. They got the picture regardless, and the relief on their faces about getting back in touch with the colony is as visible as mine. For Whitmore's sake, he better not have been misleading me.

Zabriskie sits beside Korine, a slim, middle-aged woman, at the communication console. The two of them have been sending out hails to KL's satellite frequency every three minutes for the last fifteen, and we're just waiting for Patrick or whoever's on watch to respond. Karl's arm hangs over my chair's armrest, his warm hand on my thigh. Vitruzzi sits to my left, still and straight-backed, as if preparing to give a speech. She hasn't said much since we'd arrived planet-side, and I keep meaning to find a few minutes to check in with her. Something on Eruo Pium had spooked her and sent her even further inside whatever dark mental cave she's been withdrawing into lately. I'm afraid if someone doesn't start to pull her back out, she might stay there for good.

There's no time like the present.

"V, look, I know you're not happy with the plan"—giving up the soil amendment compound—"but I don't really see that we have any other choice. You know? We need to get home. Let them worry about it." I wave vaguely toward the window overlooking

Bogotan's city central. "Besides, remember what you and Bodie read in the data logs from the Fortress?"

Pain stabs me deep inside, despite the time that's passed since Bodie was killed. Some people you never get over losing, I guess. The thought makes me glance at Karl, who catches the look and lifts a querying eyebrow at me. Giving him a half smile to tell him I'm okay, I continue, "The data said the compound had commercial potential. Maybe Whitmore's people can figure out how to make it safe."

"Maybe, Aly," she responds. The look she gives me could make a psychopath feel guilty. "Or maybe not."

Had I made a mistake? Taken too much liberty by making a deal that will ripple throughout KL and affect everyone there? No. Vitruzzi has shown that her ability to take meaningful initiative is flawed. If she were operating normally, I could have referred Whitmore to her. If she were operating normally, *she* would have been the one he'd spoken with. But she's *not* operating normally. She's barely operating at all, and someone has to pick up the slack. If my decision turns out to be less than optimal, at least I made one. Someone has to.

"Fair enough," I reply after a second. "But it's not our problem anymore. Let it go; let someone else handle it."

I'm talking about the compound, but I'm also talking about everything Vitruzzi takes on. It's too much, running a colony, a hospital, and everything else. She has to realize she can't hold herself responsible for the way things are or the way things in our system go from here on out, or she's going to burn out. Already is burning out.

"Let it go? You're giving *me* advice, Aly? You know, that's about as meaningful as—"

"Jim, we're getting another incoming ping from"—Zabriskie cuts himself off and glances toward the three of us—"uh . . ." He looks at Whitmore significantly, eyebrows arched.

But whoever's contacting them is not what I'm thinking about right now. "What do you mean, Vitruzzi? My advice is as meaningful as what?"

"Forget it," she says, her eyes as cold and distant as the dark side of a moon.

"No, I want to hear this."

"Excuse me," Whitmore breaks in. "I need a few moments. If you all wouldn't mind waiting outside, just through the door there. The foyer has comfortable seating, and it's warm. This shouldn't take long. We'll get you immediately if your settlement responds."

"Sure," Karl says and rises from his seat, pulling me up by the hand. His grip is tighter than it needs to be. When I glance at him, the message in his expression is as clear as if he were speaking aloud: *Give it a rest, Aly.*

Once we're in the foyer, I pull my hand from Karl's grip and confront Vitruzzi. But I have to give myself some credit; I try to keep my tone benign. "What's on your mind, V? I'm just trying to help."

She seems to deflate right in front of me, like I'd stuck her with a pin.

"Why?" she asks, her expression morphing to neutral, as if we're discussing the merits of eighth-inch screws over quarter-inch screws. "Why are you trying to help? And why should I go along with it? Haven't I done enough?"

"Done enough? What do you mean?" I look toward Karl, the question *Do you know what she's talking about?* in my eyes.

She sighs. "Maybe you're right. Give it to them. Give them anything they ask. I'm out of this. Done. It's not up to me, and I . . . I can't be responsible for things anymore."

I can feel my mouth hanging open, but nothing comes out. Am I really hearing this? Her . . . confession? Is that what it is? Because that's what it sounds like—and it's exactly what I'd been thinking moments ago. But her words do nothing to relieve me. Instead, her newfound flexibility, or rather, disengagement, sounds like defeat at a visceral level. Like she's giving up. Vitruzzi, giving up? It just doesn't compute. Can't be true.

"I . . . what do you mean you need out? Vitruzzi, there *is* no *out*, not of this. People need our help. The compound might be it."

"*Our* help? What happened to 'survival is as good as it gets'?" She looks at the palm of her hand, as if examining it for profound truths that she no longer believes exist, apparently. Then she chuckles. "Survival isn't even that good anymore, Aly. If you don't believe me, ask those corpse-eaters on Eruo Pium what they think."

This conversation has moved beyond surprising to outright weird. "The cannibals? What—?"

"Dr. Wyss. That's who I'm talking about."

Karl and I exchange glances, both of us equally clueless.

She goes on: "We worked together in the Medical Sciences Research facility on Obal 10. His work on developing neurological recombinations was one of the breakthroughs that helped us build cyber-prosthetic limbs. The big joke in the lab was that he put the mind in our matter. Ha-ha, funny, right?"

I have to take a step back. She's not going to be talked down from this ledge until she's gotten whatever it is that's jacking up her frequencies back to a manageable level. If that means letting her brain download a bunch of crazy, well, it's not like Karl and I have anywhere to be at the moment.

A tornado of apprehension brews in the back of my mind, but I nod quietly. Vitruzzi is a boulder—has *always* been stable and strong—that's finally showing signs of cracking.

"He was brilliant. And his family was beautiful." Vitruzzi circles the ring of chairs ringing a center table as she talks, her movement keeping me off balance and fidgety. "Marie, his wife, and their twins, Sammy and Margriet—they'd have been about sixteen or seventeen now. They would come to our neighborhood cookouts, and the twins showed Evie how to ride a magbike. Evie would never listen to John or me when we tried to show her things like that. She was too stubborn."

Evie and John? That's right, her husband and daughter who'd died in the Crowers Croup outbreak before the Soldier's Rebellion. Giving it one last shot, I try: "V, now isn't really the time for a trip down memory lane." Her black eyes hit mine and hold them, and I give up. There's no reasoning with that empty space.

She stops pacing and grips the back of a chair, facing me. "He had a brilliant and capable mind, Aly. A solid career and family. There was nothing monstrous or depraved in him." She sits, collapses really, into the overstuffed seat. "But that's what he became and now he's dead and it's *my* FAULT."

Karl's turn. "Calm down, Eleanor. I don't know what you're talking about, but I'm sure we can, uh, we can fix this, okay?"

Dammit, I wish Brady was here. This is a level of loony that I'm not used to. Her eyes are more focused and severe than I've ever seen them, not like the eyes of someone about to lose their shit, but her voice, what she's saying—this isn't the Vitruzzi I know. I'm damn certain this isn't the Vitruzzi *anyone* knows.

"I had to shoot him, you know. You were there." She stabs me with another black look. "He was going to gun us down in the middle of nowhere and serve us up to those cannibals as if we were wild game. But when I saw his face and realized who he was, it all suddenly became clear to me. There was no way I could ignore the truth anymore. No matter how fucking ugly it is."

"You mean that guy in the hovercraft?" I ask, who it is she's talking about finally dawning on me. "The one who tried to run us down as soon as we got out of the emergency pod? You knew that guy?" The odds are almost impossible. "V, that had to be someone else, someone who just looked like the doc you used to know."

"Do you think I could make a mistake like that, Aly? We worked together for ten years. His kids used to play with Evie. I know his face as well as I know my own, and I shot him because if I hadn't, he'd have killed us."

"I've killed a lot of people, and believe me, when it's either you or them, it gets easier. Trust me on that."

Her short laugh is brittle. "You know what never gets easier? Losing your kid. But when I think about what I let happen, what I *caused*, I'm—" Her body contorts; her arms cross her chest, and she crunches forward like some huge weight has been dropped onto her shoulders. The anguish in her voice in the next sentence scares me more than any words I've ever heard. "I'm glad she isn't here. I'm glad she's dead."

This is the part where I'm supposed to walk over and hug her and tell her everything is going to be okay. Except—I don't even know where to start. Looking at the suffering and pure battle fatigue hacked into every groove of her face, I realize: if everything is going to be okay, it takes a more creative imagination than mine to figure out how.

"V, I'm not sure I understand what you're talking about. But whatever it is you think you let happen, there's time later to figure out what to do about it. But right now—"

She cuts me off. "What I let happen is the war. Medina was right when she said it was my fault. *You* were right when you told me not to trust Rajcik. If I hadn't believed any help fighting the Admin, even from a psychotic criminal, was better than none, the war wouldn't have happened. *I'm responsible for the war, Aly.* I'm the reason so many people are dead."

When she stops speaking, the silence draws out the same way it does after a dying person's last gasp of breath. She thinks she's responsible for the war, for the millions dead. She holds herself accountable for something that's so far outside of her ability to control that it's absurd. Crazy.

Unfixable.

"Eleanor, you are so completely wrong about that," Karl says, disbelief straining his voice. "The war was coming whether we worked with Rajcik or not. He was the catalyst, but you were not the cause. You have to be cra—"

I grab his arm to stop him, but Vitruzzi breaks in first. "Crazy?"

The sound of an incoming ship, something bigger than an intra-atmosphere shuttle, cuts off whatever disaster heads our way. We all instinctively look toward the ceiling, tensing against the possibility of an air assault. But it isn't needed. The ship passes, flying west toward the landing field.

Just as it glides over, Whitmore exits the com room. He catches the looks on our faces, drawing the conclusion that the ship must be the reason for our troubled expressions. "That was another of Bogotan's associates, and I need to go and meet with her. But first, your call to Keum Libre. A man named Patrick Brady is waiting to speak with you."

Finally, a break.

BRADY'S FACE LOOKS LIKE the man went twenty rounds with the devil and lost every single one as Vitruzzi fills him in on everything that's happened to us since getting separated on Eruo Pium. Inexplicably, now that we've reestablished contact, a sudden feeling of calm, even optimism, settles over me. Knowing Zeta and the settlement are safe, and just a few days' flight time away, I start to think we could actually get out of this okay.

"I thought . . . Christ, I thought we might have lost you, Eleanor. When Zeta got here with just the 'Bo, and the story she told us . . ."

"I know. I know, Patrick. But we made it. We're fine. All of us. No injuries. And the Orika is still sound."

"Good. When are you coming home?"

Vitruzzi doesn't look at Whitmore, and I have no idea what she's thinking. We haven't had any time to regroup or discuss our plans or options. Everything is happening with the speed, but not the predictability, of dominoes falling.

"Listen, we'll come home as soon as we can. But I want you to do one thing first. Copy everything in the data storage from the lab at the landing platform that has to do with the soil compound. Take that and the compound and the cargo from Karl and David's last run and bring it all here, to Obal 6."

"Are they holding you hostage? Is that what this is?" The transmission's static and fluctuating volume as it bounces through fields of space debris give the rage in his voice a raw, primal edge. "Because if it is—"

"No. We're free to go. It's just a matter of trade. We give them the compound"—she turns her dark eyes on Whitmore—"and they give us what we want in return."

Brady is smart and he knows Vitruzzi well. There's more going on here than she's letting on—even I hadn't anticipated her turning this into a barter—and he's picking that up. "We've discussed at length the issues with that stuff, with what it might do. Why are you considering turning it over to this other colony?"

The obvious answer: we don't have a choice. If I know Brady, he's already assuming that, but Vitruzzi offers a different angle. "They have more of a chance of making it viable than we do, Patrick. I think it's time to get rid of it—and I'm . . . tired of being responsible for . . ." Her voice loses its momentum and she lets the sentence hang.

Her sudden silence isn't like her, and Brady's expression shows his confusion at first. "We're getting a bit of breakup, Eleanor. Repeat that last."

"That's it," she says. "It makes more sense to give it to them than to keep it."

Brady's eyes stray past her to Karl, who leans close to the video feed camera with a hand on the back of Vitruzzi's seat. "What do you think, Karl? Is this a good idea?"

"If it's not, the KLers aren't the ones who need to worry about it," he says matter-of-factly. "We're just ready to get home. If you can send the *Teibo* back, we'll load both ships up with supplies and come back. Soon as we can." He pauses to let Brady process this, but the time is taken up by a sudden disturbance out in the foyer.

"Motherfucker, you better be ready to shoot me, because you're not going to like what I do to you if you don't."

Oh shit. Desto.

Whitmore rises quickly from the chair he'd taken near the back of the room and rushes out to the foyer.

"Wait one," Karl tells Brady, then follows Whitmore, with me right behind him.

Zabriskie stands outside the double door, partially blocking it, his pistol aimed center mass at Desto.

"What are you doing here?" Karl asks.

Desto's expression is grim, and he stares at Whitmore as he responds. "Let me talk to Zeta. And I'm not asking."

"Jono, lower your weapon," Whitmore demands. Zabriskie's face is as blank as a dead monitor, but he drops his arm, his thumb resting on his pistol's safety, but not engaging it. "Of course. Of course. I understand completely. Korine"—he turns to face inside the com room—"please keep Mr. Brady's connection active. Mr. Desto, come inside. And I apologize for not considering your situation."

Desto looks surprised. He'd been ready for a fight, not an agreement. But that doesn't slow him down. Seconds later, he's seated in Vitruzzi's vacated spot.

"Pat, how's Zeta? Can I talk to her?"

"She's completely fine, Bomani. Don't worry. She's over at the platform right now, just taking care of postflight details. I know she'll be upset she couldn't be here to talk with you herself."

"Well, tell her . . . tell her I'll see her as soon as I can. And thanks, Pat."

"No problem. You okay?"

"I will be." There's a sinister undertone to this statement that I catch, even still standing in the foyer.

He stands, leaving the chair pulled out for Vitruzzi to reclaim, and walks out to where the rest of us wait. For the first time since Desto had woken up on Eruo Pium after Zeta had been kidnapped, the ferocious grooves carved across his forehead have relaxed.

"So, uh, everyone okay back at the gym?" I ask him, knowing that his presence here means one of two things: he'd been lucky enough to sneak out while whoever was left to guard the rest of our crew at the high school had their pants down, or that guard is meeting his or her maker as we speak. I hope like hell it isn't the second possibility.

Desto swings an arm loosely around my shoulders. "No one got hurt that didn't need to be."

"What—?"

"It's all good, Aly. Our sentry just had a demonstration of some hand-to-hand he didn't previously know, but he's not hurt. Much."

Whitmore and Zabriskie look alarmed at these words, but Desto merely stares at them. "Korine, send Stybar over to the school to check on Rodriguez," Whitmore says, and no one else speaks until Vitruzzi comes back into the foyer a few minutes later.

"Whitmore, Patrick is sending our ship back with the compound and the people you had accompany Zeta. They'll be here within four days. Now, let's talk about what you're giving us."

"No, Dr. Vitruzzi." The words come from someone new. "Let's talk about what else you can do for us." Five people have entered the foyer. The first is Commander Medina.

TWENTY-ONE

"You've got to be fucking kidding me," I spit.

The group of us who flew with her during the war grow instantly mute, our surprise at this unexpected reunion cutting off any other reaction like a guillotine. She seems to realize the effect of her presence but keeps her military bearing as stiff and unreadable as ever. Van Heusen and one other soldier enter with her. I recognize his face as her apparently still next in command, Lieutenant Steward. Then comes the next backhand.

Quantum.

Oh how we've waited to see this betrayer again, a walking bag of viscera that needs to be spilled. Karl's hands clench into fists beside me as I involuntarily twitch forward, but I stop myself before doing anything that will lead to nothing except a bottomless pain cave. Desto, however, doesn't have the same hesitation.

"Strahan, stop him!" Vitruzzi's voice echoes clearly through the bowl-shaped foyer.

Karl tackles Desto from behind as the enraged father-to-be stalks toward Quantum with single-minded purpose, his stride amplifying his dead-set intent on revenge. But for Karl it's like gripping an elephant, and his assault results only in Desto's sharp elbow connecting with his collarbone as the larger man tries to shake Karl off.

Hardly seeming to notice what he's doing, Desto promises, "I'm going to kill you, Quantum. Say your fucking prayers."

"Jesus, big guy, you gotta get ahold of yourself," Karl says, his teeth clenching against pain as he maneuvers between Desto and the newcomers. "Little help here, people!"

That's all it takes to galvanize Vitruzzi and me. She rushes up and grips Desto's shoulders from behind, while I use my body to help Karl block him. Karl links his right arm with my left to create a barrier. Vacantly, I realize every weapon in the room is pointed at Desto, and there's no telling how much military discipline this security force has. A single nervous finger is all it will take to send a flurry of projectiles that will turn us into a collection of holes surrounded by blood and bone.

"Out of my way, so help you," Desto grunts, his eyes wide and unwaveringly focused on Quantum.

"Think about this," I say as calmly as I can. "The only way this ends is with you dead."

"I don't care."

"Yes, you do. Because you're going to get us killed, too. Is that what you want?" His eyes leave Quantum for a split second and bounce to my face. "You just heard Brady—Zeta is okay. So lock this revenge shit down before she has to bury an empty goddamn box."

An evil-sounding chuckle oozes from my right, and Van Heusen stands a couple meters away, grinning. He catches me looking and says, "We're this close to having us a roast."

My stomach twists into a sickened knot. *A roast?* This man, whatever kind of soldier he may have been before the war, is now pure monster. I don't even want to consider what he may have done to survive, yet my brain shoots up a high-contrast memory of foul-breathed Twitch the Cannibal from Eruo Pium—sometimes my imagination is a curse.

Desto takes a deep breath and lets it out, then puts a hand on Vitruzzi's, still on his shoulder. "It's all right, V. I'm good." But his face shows the moment is merely an intermission, not an end. He steps back toward the com room door and crosses his arms over his wall-like chest, and the rest of us relax. Slightly.

Quantum hasn't moved at all, choosing to stay at a safe distance outside the potential crossfire of the security team. Medina watched the entire seconds-long encounter with patient reserve, just waiting for the right moment to continue talking.

And that hopeful feeling I'd had when I heard Brady's voice transmitting from KL?

That's gone.

"I DIDN'T ANTICIPATE OUR paths crossing again so soon, Vitruzzi, Strahan . . ." Medina's eyes take in the room, lingering for a moment on those of us who'd served under her. "Everyone. And under these circumstances. It's only been what? Six months?"

Our initial shock drains out of the moment, and the four of us find a suitable place to sit, stand, or seethe. She displays a calm and appropriate smile that seems to imply, *We are all friends here. There's nothing but water under the bridge between us*, and continues. "I suppose the good news is that the war is truly and unequivocally over. And we are at a new frontier in human history."

Dramatic, but also the truth.

"What are you doing here, Medina? What's this all about?" Karl says from his seat near the foyer's deserted central desk. Desto is parked behind him, leaning against the counter, and I stay close to him just in case. He has returned to normal—or as close to it as he's likely to get with Quantum in the room and still drawing breath.

"That's a question I'm about to answer, Tech Sergeant," Medina says, "if you'll let me."

"I'm not a soldier. You can stop calling me sergeant," Karl cuts in.

Her eyes hold his steadily for a breath before she continues, but none of us need to have it spelled out: something bigger than a straightforward exchange of resources is about to go down. Medina is obviously the person pulling strings in the colony. Whitmore had faded into the background the minute she'd entered the foyer, and Van Heusen is looking to her, not the former dock supervisor, for orders. What we'd all originally assumed was a citizen settlement is nothing but a land base for Medina and anyone still serving with her. Which changes things. How, though, remains to be seen.

"Let me just give you the highlights. Shortly after your group de . . . camped"—I'm sure she was about to say *deserted*—"the volume of fighting engagements, as you probably know, began to diminish, fewer and fewer Admin and Corps Loyalists stayed that way, and those of us controlling the larger forces began disarmament talks. In these last six months, we've achieved a peace of sorts. We don't have the system-wide organization to celebrate this victory with the proper gravitas, but we can all finally draw a breath unburdened by continued destruction. And now we have to look to rebuilding."

Her posture isn't exactly guarded, but still as stiff as ever. Thinking back, I realize I'd never even seen the woman sit down anywhere but at the command bench or let her shoulders drop or wear anything but her uniform. Along with this awareness, the memory of something Vitruzzi had said to Medina back on the *Celestial* just three months into the war surfaces. *"We can continue to fight our brothers and sisters who fell on the wrong side of the rift, or we can begin the process of laying down our arms, laying down our differences, and picking up the pieces together. Rebuild. If we don't, no matter who survives, we've all lost this war."*

So Medina is finally seeing the wisdom in peace over force—at least that's what she seems to be saying, but right now, I feel like I'm choking on the message instead of swallowing it.

Vitruzzi speaks up, voicing what I'm sure we're all thinking: "Understood, Commander, but I don't remember ever voting to put you in charge."

Medina's response is quick and final. "Democracy died when János Rajcik dropped a terra-shattering bomb on Obal 10."

Vitruzzi flinches.

Karl responds sharply, "Then let's restore it."

Medina shifts her gaze toward the wall, as if searching for an argument that will put an end to this off-topic, at least to her, debate. "Serg—Strahan," she starts, looking up again, "if it were as simple as a quick show of hands, we'd all be happier. But since it isn't that simple, and won't *ever be that simple*, we need to start talking about what is, not what was. Hmm?"

The condescension packed into her last statement could only be missed by a deaf person, but it has her desired effect. Our attention cements to her.

"Good," Medina continues. "The crew of the *Celestial* and I have been hard at work throughout the system helping to find and secure everything we need to create and sustain a viable new home. A safe and ideal place to begin a new centralized government, or at least, centralized within limits. With the remaining human population widely scattered and badly organized, Whitmore and I have agreed to make Bogotan that location. We've been working together for these last few months, and we have one hundred percent agreement about what steps to take to get this quadrant of the system back on its feet. I'm sure you've worked out for yourselves that we see the seed sequencer and the soil amendment compound as necessary assets for the fastest and most efficient means to feed a new and growing population."

"What kind of population do you mean, Medina? We have refugees on KL that were turned away from Bogotan because of minor handicaps," Vitruzzi says, her voice finding that old edge. "Doesn't your 'efficient' system have room for people like that? Or is it just for those who are willing and able to march to your fife?"

Whew! I've been known to be abrupt and stubborn, but I think she just won the award for being the most deliberately antagonizing non-cit this side of the war. It's clear now that Vitruzzi hasn't forgotten Medina's actions that led us to leaving the *Celestial* in the first place, or forgiven her for them. The medical station on Broon; the way Medina had ordered its annihilation instead of trying to help the injured. The doctor in Vitruzzi couldn't let that slide if her life depended on it.

And given Medina's presence here, it probably does.

Medina's hard shell doesn't crack, but she's no longer giving Vitruzzi even a fragment of her attention. "We need people like you to help us achieve what we're hoping to achieve. More importantly, we need your cooperation." She lets that sink in, then goes on, dropping the commander's voice and sounding like a regular, needs-driven, hope-filled person. It's a tone as bizarre coming from her as an opera singer's voice coming from Desto would be.

"Erikson, Desto, Strahan . . . Vitruzzi, it's not about fighting to win. We're all fighting to survive at this point, and none of us can do it alone. Your colony on Keum Libre, while noteworthy for lasting even this long, isn't going to last forever. You don't have the human resources, nor even the means to enforce any kind of security, to support the colony indefinitely. You must see that. Bogotan has factories, textiles, metals. Munitions. But what we need now is *people*.

"We need to get together on this. If we couldn't do it during wartime, I pray to any potential powers that may be that we can do it while we have some peace."

She's sounding eerily like Whitmore had when trying to convince me to help sway my crew to his point of view earlier. The two of them are as thick as thieves. Another brief memory surfaces, something Medina had said as soon as the main Corps posts on Obal 8 and Obal 3 had fallen. Some of the *Celestial*'s crewmembers had started advocating for an armistice, but Medina, the unyielding military tactician, had commanded the fight to continue until all regions of resistance were broken—or as she'd put it, "*burned in the refuse pile of dogma and antihuman apostasy.*" She might have been in the uniform of a Corps officer, but her true core seems to be made of an almost Straussian idealism. I can see from my crew's expressions that they know it, too.

She goes on: "What I propose is that we all join in one colony and bring the rest of your settlers on Keum Libre to Bogotan. And yes, before you ask the question, I do mean everyone, even the disabled and sick."

She finally winds down, giving us a second to absorb her proposal.

"Maybe we're happy where we are," Karl says after a few ticks of the clock.

Medina reacts, but not in words. Her body instantly transforms from friendly and collaborative to her default rigid military decorum—stance aloof, back rigid, and eyes as unreadable and glassy as an artificially generated human avatar.

"Why should we agree to relocate to Bogotan?" Karl continues, not in the least deterred by her visible frustration. "What's in it for us?"

"Let me make it easy for all of you to understand." She deliberately unzips her Corps-issued officer's jacket and pushes the material back, revealing the tactical vest, holster, and pistol beneath. "I let your crew leave the *Celestial* because I didn't think you had a chance in hell of surviving on your own. I considered it to be cutting dead weight. Now I can see I was wrong, but that doesn't matter. And believe me, I'm not going to make the same mistake again.

"The Admin was an experiment that failed. If the war is going to mean anything more than the destruction of hundreds of years of civilization and progress, we cannot fail like that again. Bogotan is where we're restarting; it has to succeed. And to succeed, we—and that means all people—have to be unified."

"With you in charge," Desto states and flashes the kind of smile at Medina that a large predator shows its prey just before sinking its incisors into its throat.

"Order can only be achieved through the rule of law, with someone to facilitate. Do you think it's possible to keep peace between hundreds of divergent groups of scavengers when they're all competing for the same last resources without unification, without shared goals? Do you have any idea what people have become, what's going on in this system?"

My eyes flick back to Van Heusen, catching his stare of unconcealed contempt for the four of us. I *do* know what's going on in this system, and looking at the sadistic guard, I can guess what would be going on in Bogotan if people like Whitmore, who at least seems reasonable, ever lose the initiative.

Medina's next words hit like an ambush. "I am not going to let everything fall apart, regardless of the resistance—whether from your colony or any other. I'll kill anyone who tries to stop or gets in the way of what we're trying to build." She unsheathes the pistol, and Van Heusen and Steward copy the action. "Make your choice now. We have a lot of work to do."

FOR A SECOND, I THINK I must have misunderstood her. But the Bhishma 10.3 mike-mike in her hand acts as a bullhorn until her words finally, irrevocably, sink in, and the skin hardens like ice over my entire body.

"Medina, could I have a word with you?"

It's Whitmore speaking, and the sound of his voice gives the rage whipping into a frenzy inside me somewhere to focus. My head swivels jerkily toward him, as if on a broken servo. He'd lied to me, bald-faced and so convincingly. I'd bought every word, and performed like a perfect puppet for him. I'd trusted him enough to convince Vitruzzi and Karl to do the same, and we'd called Brady, asked him to bring the compound and deliver it like an early Christmas present directly to Medina, putting the whole colony in jeopardy. Now we can't even get back in touch with them to warn them. How stupid could I be?

Medina ignores Whitmore's quiet request, her cool gaze riveted to us, waiting for someone to make a hero move so she can sic her dogs Steward and Van Heusen on us. He tries again, "Commander Medina. I need to speak with you *now*."

"It can wait, Whitmore." She never looks at him. Addressing us again, she continues, "I know it's a lot to take in, but I need you to understand your options, and what specifically is at stake. Do you?"

"Fuck this," Desto says, stepping toward our former commanding officer.

"Wait, Desto," Karl warns. "Nothing can go wrong right now that won't be made worse by you doing something stupid."

Clenching his fists, Desto assumes a pose of quiet, simmering deadliness.

I'm about to open my mouth and say something, though I'm not sure what it will be besides categorically offensive and probably suicidal, when Vitruzzi says, "Let me guess, Medina. Anyone who isn't an asset is expendable. That's what you told me, right?"

"Not anymore, Doctor. Anyone who isn't an asset is a liability. And we no longer have the luxury of allowing liabilities."

Vitruzzi doesn't hesitate. "We'll cooperate."

Medina is too smart to believe our subservience will come that cheaply, but she relaxes the finger cradling her pistol's trigger. "Of course," she goes on, "it would never come to that. I don't want to turn our new social order into a dictatorship or even an oligarchy any more than anyone else. I had no doubt you'd see the reason and inevitability of our two separate colonies joining together. We have to remember, I know you'll also agree, that the next few decades aren't about us, they are about creating and protecting our future. I'll let Jim fill you in on our plans." She dips her chin at the former dock controller, then motions to Steward, and the two of them exit. Quantum, who's said nothing this whole time, disappears with them.

My mouth is as dry as the engine housing of an overheated skiff as I say, "Vitruzzi, you can't seriously be willing to go along with this."

"Do you have an alternative proposal, Aly? One that doesn't get everybody on KL killed?"

My eyes jerk away from her, knowing she's right, but my rage isn't going anywhere. I turn it back on Whitmore.

"You double-dealing bastard. You knew about this, didn't you?"

His face is unreadable, but that blinking tic of his eye is going full throttle. "I-I . . ." he starts, but quickly stops himself. One hand goes to the side of his face and rubs near his twitching eye, trying to force it to calm down, but the effect is just the opposite. Abruptly, he turns to Zabriskie. "Jono, escort them back to their quarters. I need to talk to Medina."

Zabriskie nods and opens his mouth, but Van Heusen cuts in and gives the order. "You heard the man. Everyone back outside. And don't do anything I'd love to make you regret."

TWENTY-TWO

Night has spread its blanket over the city by the time we leave. The walk back is a little over ten minutes long, and I mentally prepare myself for the biting cold before heading outdoors. It's easy enough. My inner supernova of fury at Whitmore and Medina keeps me warm. As the others pace ahead, I find myself in step beside Zabriskie, whose stare is no warmer than the weather.

"Help me understand this, Zabriskie. How can a whole postwar settlement think massacring others is the solution to a new system of the worlds?" The cold breeze pulls most of the fire from my words, and I hear the underlying confusion and fear that are hiding in them. I hadn't even known they were there.

For a few seconds, it seems like he's going to ignore me. But then: "You fought in the war, right?"

I nod. Almost everyone fought in some capacity or another.

"Then you must get it. People are scared. There's no such thing as situation normal anymore. You find your tribe and you watch each other's backs. Sometimes that means others . . . well. More than a few of us here have learned the hard way that nothing can be counted on now." His jaw goes taut for a second, as if he's clamping it closed on something he doesn't want to say, but then he continues. "Not even people you thought were allies."

"What do you mean?" I ask, but his face has reverted back to brick-wall blankness. After another few steps, I blurt, "You realize that there's four of us and two of you, right? We can escape any-time we want."

"And you realize we're not the only ones watching you while we enjoy this leisurely stroll, right?"

We're passing an alley, and the wind screams down it with a freight train's whistle as he speaks. But I hear him. Loud and clear. Plenty of rooftops and high windows make our trip down the street a sniper's wet dream. Changing the subject, I ask, "So what's your story? Are you from Bogotan? Were you in the Corps before?"

"No, I was a citizen. Worked here with Whitmore in the shipping yard."

"You have a family?"

He doesn't answer that question. Which leads me to wonder, what exactly had happened to Bogotan during the war? The image of the damaged landing-field berm comes to mind. What had they been fighting against? "Was Bogotan Admin-friendly during . . .?" He knows during what.

"We were just trying to keep from getting wiped off the map."

"Is that why you tried to disable access to the city from the landing field?"

He looks at me sharply, not expecting my insight into their tactics. After hesitating for a second, he answers, "We thought we were under attack, so we took action to try and protect ourselves." He goes silent, again with the tight jaw, before saying, "Turns out things aren't as discrete as good-guys–bad-guys anymore."

I'm still pondering what he means by that when we reach the high school. As we step up to the front doors, they push open and two guards exit. The second one sports a swollen-shut eye and the start of what will be a bruise on his temple that would make a prizefighter wince.

"Asshole," he mumbles as he passes Desto and makes for a land trans parked on the street.

"Zabriskie, make sure they're locked in tight. Don't want them doing more of this, do you?" Van Heusen asks with a nod of his head toward the battered guard.

"Who's on watch tonight?" Zabriskie asks.

"I am. Back in a couple of hours to relieve you." Van Heusen's steel-blue eyes fall on me and he gives me a wink. "And you too, dollface."

Before he gets to the first riser on the stairs, Karl tackles him gut level like a rhino. Van Heusen had no idea it was coming, and his breath exits his body in one heavy expulsion. They fall sideways on the building's stoop almost at Vitruzzi's feet, Karl on top of Van Heusen, slamming his right fist into the man's nose and breaking it. The crunch is amplified by the crispness of the air, the wind having ceased to blow for a minute.

"Hey!" Zabriskie yells.

Karl jumps off the downed security guard just as Desto is about to intervene. He spits on the concrete as he glowers over Van Heusen, every muscle in his body daring the man to retaliate.

Van Heusen sits up and grasps his nose between his palms. Two streams of blood cascade down around his mouth, giving him a clown-faced sneer, and his squinting eyes seek out Karl's face, landing there and digging in like a pit bull's teeth. Zabriskie has his hand on the butt of his pistol but hasn't drawn it. For the first time, his face shows something besides neutral detachment as his lips tighten, and he glances around the group quickly, taking it all in.

With a casualness that completely belies the intensity of the moment, Van Heusen puts a hand to the ground and pushes himself to his feet, leaving a bloody handprint behind. I step forward a pace, ready to jump into the fray if needed. Four of us and four of them, but we can get to their weapons almost as fast as they can in such close proximity.

Van Heusen is enough of a soldier to realize this. Wiping the back of his hand across his top lip and smearing the cold-thickened blood across his cheek, he promises, "See you soon, scavs."

Karl opens his mouth and I grip his arm to try and stop him from speaking, but he says anyway, "Looking forward to it."

"GODDAMMIT, DOES SHE LOOK like she needs a knight in shining armor?" Vitruzzi hurls the words at Karl as soon as we're inside. "What the hell were you thinking?"

I don't need anyone to speak for me, but keep quiet on this. No need to add fuel to the fire. And speaking of fire, Vitruzzi's anger is a good sign. Like she lanced a boil back at the satlink room and has new freedom from her self-induced burden of guilt. Let's hope it lasts. We're going to need everyone operating at full capacity in the coming storm.

"What am I thinking? Where were *you*, V? They're blackmailing us and holding us hostage. This is bullshit! Patrick is getting ready to walk into a trap, and Medina has turned into a primitive warlord that's about to put her enemy's heads on pikes. We have to make plans, to figure out . . ."

"That's what I'm talking about, brother," Desto says. "We need to bust the hell out of this rat hole and get back to KL before something happens."

"Jesus, people!" Mason snaps. "Did you forget about them?" His hand waves toward our four fugee kids, who sit as a group on his bunk, their eyes eating up the scene with the same avidity with which the kids had eaten every morsel of food they'd been given since we'd found them.

Vitruzzi's anger evaporates instantly, and she goes over to them and crouches. "It's going to be okay. We're just trying to discuss what to do next while we're staying in Bogotan. Everyone all right?"

"Dr. V, we don't want any more bad things to happen," Cassandra says, taking the hand of the youngest boy, sitting next to her on a bunk.

"I know, kids. Neither do we," Vitruzzi says simply.

"You want to tell us what the hell's going on?" David says. "Medina's here?"

The four of us spend the next fifteen minutes filling David, Hoogs, and Ryan in: we'd (well, *I'd*) made a deal with Whitmore to give up the soil compound, we'd contacted Brady to deliver it, Medina turned up and threatened our colony with death or worse, and we're all pretty much fucked if we don't dance to her tune. I'd be the world's best con artist if I could convince anyone that they take it well.

"Can we get Venus to launch an attack from the *Orika*?" David's proposal is the first on the table.

"Maybe, if we could get in touch with her," Karl says. "At least we know she's still tucked safely away."

"Yeah, but for how long?" I ask. "She doesn't know what's going on. She might get some ideas of her own. The longer she's in the dark, the twitchier she'll get. I know I would be."

Karl responds, "But she had to have heard your and Whitmore's conversation on the *Orika*. She'd have turned on the com as soon as she opened the door for David. As far as she knows, right now we're all working together. That should keep her from doing anything too, I don't know, too *Venus*."

Somber nods from the group, more hopeful than certain.

Before the conversation continues, the door opens and we all spin to see what's coming. Korine enters, pushing the same cart from earlier, piled with food, plates, and a couple of carafes, presumably our dinner, followed by four more armed guards: two men, two women. They already have their weapons hot.

Korine pushes the cart to within a couple of meters of us, then says in a voice that barely rises above a whisper, "I'm going to need to ask that those children come with me." She doesn't look anyone in the eye.

"What? Why?" Mason says.

One of the guards, a thick-framed meat bag with a face like a hyena, takes a pace forward and says, "You can ask Commander Medina about that." Casually, he taps the side of his pistol's trigger guard.

Korine looks like someone just told her her mother died. "I promise you, they'll be well cared for. It's just until we . . . you . . . the situation gets settled. I'm not going to let anything happen to them, okay. They'll be safer if they're not with . . . not here. Please, you understand?"

Glancing at Vitruzzi, I can't read anything in her expression. Her face is as blank and shrouded as the surface of the ocean. After a second, she crouches again near the cluster of kids and says, "It's okay. These folks are going to get you out of here and into some-place a little warmer and cozier. We're going to pick you up in a couple of days, after more of our friends arrive."

Cassandra speaks again. "No, we don't want to go with strangers. We want to stay with you and Mr. Mason!" She jumps off the bunk, nimbly avoiding Vitruzzi's hand as she reaches for her, and wraps her arms around Mason's waist as tightly as if he were a raft and she were about to go over a waterfall.

Mason's nutmeg-brown eyes squint in an expression that might be pain or might be hate, it's hard to tell which. But when he pulls the girl's arms away from him, he does it with a gentleness that's nearly reverence. Squatting, he looks into her face. "Don't worry," he says, "a lot of good folks are going to be looking out for you while we sort things out. Okay? Come on."

He stands up and holds out a hand to either side, waiting for the kids to grab them. The oldest boy does, and after a second, Cassandra does too. Vitruzzi walks over and takes the hands of the remaining two. The littlest girl starts to cry when she tries to let go of her hand and pass her over to Korine. Eventually, the four are led out, and the door is closed with finality.

"We're going to make that bitch pay," Mason says, talking about Medina.

The eight of us pick at our food silently, like it's our last supper.

TWENTY-THREE

"Don't make the mistake of believing the war is over, Aly," Quantum had said to me, back on Eruo Pium. And apparently he'd been right.

I lie in my bunk thinking over the past few hours, mostly pondering one simple thought: this is what it feels like to be between a rock, a hard place, and a shit sandwich. Around me, everyone else does the same. I doubt any of them are asleep. We'd discussed as quietly as possible the idea of trying to fight our way out of this holding cell together when the Bogotanites switched guard, but the question had been: Then what? Even if we get the *Orika* off the ground, without La Mer to hack Bogotan's satellite, we can't send a message to Brady in time to stop him from launching from KL and delivering the soil compound as planned. Plus, this settlement has their own armed ships, and none of us are naive enough to think the only things they're capable of firing are engine disablers. And finally, we have to assume whatever remains of Medina's attack forces is stationed aboard the *Celestial*, which can't be too far out. It hadn't taken long for us to decide, reluctantly and with extreme prejudice, to lock down our instincts and sit tight until Brady gets here.

But there's still Venus. After I'd mentioned the numbers she'd left on the universal clock in my bunk to the crew, we'd realized they are a secure transmission frequency. David confirmed this, having noticed she'd done the same in the main berth. If we can get a radio or our VDUs, we'll be able to communicate with her again. Knowing Venus, she feels safest and most in her comfort zone staying aboard the *Orika*, and we know she's keeping it buttoned up tightly. But without the ability to contact her, whatever intel she may be able to glean from the landing field and whatever news we could share with her are useless.

Just like the Admin's tactic in the war, Whitmore and Medina recognize that strictly controlling communication effectively controls just about everything else. I wonder, though, if they get it: the Admin still lost.

IT TAKES FOUR DAYS for anything to happen. And when it does, the sucker punch to the gut is like nothing any of us has ever felt.

Zabriskie, flanked by several guards—the usual situation lately—opens up the gymnasium door sometime in the midmorning, as far as I can tell. "Your crew has arrived."

The flood of relief we all feel, though immense, is so intermixed with anger and fear, it's hard to know if the news is good or bad. It's good they weren't taken captive and then executed, something no one would put past Medina at this point, but bad because now they're as stuck in this web as we are.

I catch a glimpse of one of the other guards; Blondie, the mind-like-an-amoeba ringleader of my locker-room-buddy fugees—the ones who'd stared at me like I'd been giving them their own personal striptease after the cannibal camp escape—stands among the security detail. Medina must be actively recruiting more bodies to help discharge and enforce her rule. Her selection leaves a lot to be desired. The scav carries an unholstered Sinbad pistol and wears a basic Corps uniform kit: tactical equipment vest with ammo pouches, lightweight upper body armor, kneepads. It's as if he's expecting to assault an enclave of dissidents, not a group of salvagers who'd saved his ass from being someone else's lunch, literally. The remaining detail, six total, are similarly attired, making it clear that they are fully prepared for us to be, well, a little miffed.

Karl seethes. "I see you've brought along your kennel mates, Zabriskie."

Zabriskie remains detached, but I forget about him a second later as Patrick Brady, Zeta Abrams, and Jeremy La Mer rush through the door. The gym instantly fills with cries of joy as we swarm each other, hugging with the lack of restraint only the desperate can feel.

Our security detail keeps its distance as we all mingle together, letting us reunite on our terms. It doesn't appear our arriving crew have been mistreated, yet they don't seem at ease. After the initial flurry of welcome, I look at La Mer and my stomach immediately drops into my feet. I rush toward him and embrace him as if our entire lives have led to this moment.

"Keep cool," I whisper into his ear. "I don't know what they've told you, but Venus is safe. She's hiding on the *Orika*, and they don't know about her. We have to keep it that way."

I pull away from him and stare hard into his eyes, making sure he'd heard me and understands what I'm saying. We hadn't discussed what to tell Brady and the crew about Venus, never expecting that they'd be allowed to reach Bogotan so quietly and easily. But La Mer's reaction surprises me. "I know," he says.

"Did—?" I stop myself before blurting out anything that would jeopardize Venus's anonymity. He's nodding at me, confirming what I want to know—she must have been able to get a transmission to them, probably as they'd landed at the airfield.

His cold hand is still wrapped around my wrist. I feel his fingers slip inside the hem of my sleeve, and something even colder is pushed against my arm. It feels small, no bigger or heavier than a bolt nut. La Mer's green eyes stay fixed on mine, waiting for a show of understanding. I nod just enough for him to see. It's either a diminutive explosive or a com device; either way, it's a method of creating organization, or organized chaos.

"Baby, you shouldn't have come," Desto croons to Zeta nearby. "I don't want you putting yourself into danger. Not for me."

He holds her so close their two bodies are nearly fused, making me wonder if she can breathe. But from my vantage it looks like her arms are clamped around him just as tightly. Brady and Vitruzzi stand together, arms laced around each other's waists and their foreheads touching as they share an overwhelmed moment of relief.

This is as all right as it's ever going to get. The thought seeps through my mind, leaving me feeling like a sack that's been filled with lead. Heavy, dull, immobile. I reach over to Karl and grasp one of his hands. Behind us, the gym door closes and we're left alone.

"WE WERE DETAINED THE instant we landed. Medina and her jackboots took over the *Nebula* and started moving everything out and onto a Corps ISPS." Brady and the crew stand and sit in a cluster around the bunks as he fills us in on what they know. "They told us you were safe and, in short, that you'd all agreed to relocate the entire settlement here."

I snort loudly, unable to contain my disgust.

Brady's expression tells me he couldn't agree more. "Yeah. I could tell things were fucked here, more or less, the minute Zeta got to KL and explained what had happened on Eruo Pium, and Whitmore's *envoy* explained his proposal for bringing the compound and data here. When we finally got your transmission"—he squeezes Vitruzzi's hand, which he hasn't let go of since arriving, tightly—"we started planning."

"Planning?" Desto asks. "Planning how and for what?"

"For any contingency. We rigged the soil compound with about twenty kilos of explosives camouflaged inside three extra drums that they don't know are dummies. There's one remote detonator on the *Nebula* and . . ." He turns his head to see if anyone is watching through the window in the door, but it's all clear. Waving to everyone, he draws us closer, then pulls a small device, like the one La Mer had given me, from its hiding place in his armpit. "Most of you should have one of these transmitter pods now. Their effective range is up to about two klicks, though we haven't been able to test them completely."

"It's a detonator?" Ryan asks.

Brady and La Mer look at him curiously, and I realize they have no idea who he is. Zeta breaks in, "We picked the kid up on Eruo Pium; he was one of the fugees." She looks at him. "Glad to see you on the crew."

Ryan nods shyly.

Brady continues, "That's exactly what they are. Of course, we didn't know Medina was a factor in this—"

"None of us did," David adds.

"Yeah, that's what I figured. But as soon as she met us in the landing field and sent troops on board the *Nebula* without so much as a 'would you mind?,' my gut told me whatever's going on here, you've been under coercion since the beginning and she's behind this whole game. I thought about blowing her to hell as soon as we landed, but . . . I don't know what the game *is* yet, exactly."

"It's pretty easy to explain," Karl says. "She wants to turn back civilization's clock to the Roman Empire."

"And we get to be the Christians she throws to the lions," Hoogs adds.

After a second to take this in, Brady says smoothly, "About what we thought. This is the reason we left the *Celestial* in the first place. Too bad we didn't just kill her then . . ."

But no one had ever really believed things would go this far. I suppose this is what metaphysicists refer to as the wheel. What goes around, comes around.

Karl responds, "As I see it, the question is, how are we going to link up with Venus and get the hell out of here? We can blow Medina's ship with the compound you rigged on our way off this rock if we can just get to the airfield."

"What if she's not in it, though? She'll just mobilize the *Celestial* and come after us. And Keum Libre," David says. "Not to mention, if that compound is as deadly as it seems, it could kill everyone in Bogotan if it's spread. An explosion might not render all of it inert."

No one has a response to that. It's a fact.

He looks around. "I don't know about all of you, but I'm not prepared to kill a bunch of bystanders. Enough of that happened in the war. I'm done with it."

Something from Rob Cross's final message, a recording he'd left for me to watch after he was dead, whispers in my head. *It's just the way of the worlds. It's a fucking mess and the best we can do is try to survive.* It had made sense to me at the time, but not anymore. Survival at the expense of so many lives, maybe innocent lives, isn't survival. It's lunacy.

As if reading my thoughts, David continues, "Besides, we don't even know if these people are all on board with Medina's plans, or just as caught up in it as we are. Like those kids from Eruo Pium. Whatever we do, we have to get that compound away from here. For good."

The silence that follows his declaration this time is reluctant, almost grudging. But the faces of my crew show agreement, unanimously.

Finally Brady says, "If we have a chance, we have to try." His statement goes without question. "We have to stop both her and Whitmore, and I propose—"

Karl jumps in. "I really don't think Whitmore is the issue. I don't think he knew about her intentions."

I look at him, surprised. "Whitmore was standing right there when she told us she was going to wipe us out if we didn't serve ourselves to her on a platter."

"Did you see the surprise on his face, though? The way she shut him down when he tried to get her attention?" He's speaking to me, but he looks around at Desto and Vitruzzi, too. "He looked to me like a prisoner under a spotlight, dazed. He didn't know she was going to take it this far. I'm sure of it."

Brady rubs a hand along the gray sandpaper of his chin and meets my blue eyes with his hazel ones, waiting for Karl and me to suss this out.

I take a second for a breath. "Maybe, Karl. But here's where I agree with Medina—in this situation, whoever isn't an asset is a liability. If he's running this colony, he's going to have to fight for it. Our only goal is to protect our own. If he and his people get in the way, that's not going to slow us down. I'm not ready to wipe out the entire city of Bogotan"—I nod to David, showing him I agree with his determination—"but I'm also not going to stand aside if any one of us is threatened."

Our eyes hold for a moment, and I hope he can read my thoughts in my expression. When he says, "I'm with you. We just don't want to put anyone in harm's way who doesn't need to be. All of us are going to have to make an effort to leave the noncombatants out of this," I know he has.

The rest of the crew nod, but I know at least a few of us are sharing a thought: there are no innocents in this. We—and by *we* I mean *everyone*—have lost the luxury of staying neutral and not picking sides. It's gone too far, too much is at stake, to think in any other terms but black and white.

David picks up the thread. "The biggest problem we have is the fact that the *Orika*, even if we get to it, is low on supplies. We won't make it home."

"The *Nebula* is fully powered and stocked. Enough for us all," Zeta comments.

"Good." Karl nods excitedly. "Then if we can just get control of it, we can get out of here. Venus is just one person, so it may be easy enough for her to slip clear of the *Orika* without being seen and meet us there."

"And then what? Run back to KL and wait for Medina to show up with shackles and bullets?"

At the sound of Quantum's voice, all eleven of us turn our heads toward the door so fast we must appear to be a single remote-operated unit. We've been so involved in our discussion, no one saw or heard him enter. He stands at the door, now closed behind him, arms held out, palms up, showing us he's empty-handed. Yet if I've learned anything from Quantum, it's that everything about him is a threat, from his mind to his intent to his schemes.

"What are you doing here?" Hoogs says, the first to break through the stunned silence.

"I ask again: And then what?" Quantum says, ignoring Hoogs. He takes a couple of steps forward, gauging the group to be too frozen in surprise to impede him. "If I've learned one thing from this war, it's that those who want to win never stop fighting, and those who just want to live end up doing little more than dying. So your crew has to ask yourselves, who do you want to be? The winners?" His thick eyebrows arch in a way that makes his always-smug expression that much more antagonizing. "Or not."

"Are you trying to make us think you want to help us, Quantum?" I watch Desto, wondering what he's going to do. For the moment, he remains standing behind Zeta, his hands resting on her shoulders, the muscles of his jaw straining against his skin.

"Think what you want. If Medina isn't stopped, the system just fought a war for nothing. The Cabinets of Directorates may as well still be in charge of deciding who is free and who isn't, and Kurosawa T'Kai may as well still be treating soldiers and non-cits like lab rats. *I* started this war because I wanted to change things, improve humanity. Maybe I'm too ambitious, but at least I have the balls to try."

"And now Medina is just trying to reinstate the status quo," Brady says flatly. "That it?"

For the first time, Quantum shows something like an emotion. But it's not anger or resentment, which wouldn't have made me think twice; it's the look of a puppy that has been smacked unexpectedly by its owner. He glances around at the crew, uncertainty and hesitancy making him drop his eyes to the floor more than once, and he has to clear his throat. But when he speaks, he's back to normal: cold, calculating, deadly sincere.

He puts his hands down slowly, and lets his stare rest on Jeremy. "And you, La Mer, when you were still Axone and part of the network that almost brought the Admin down in the first Rebellion, I remember you from that time. And I remember all the high ideals you had. Are you still that person? Or did you stop standing for anything when you fell for that loopy pilot?"

Is this his idea of a rallying cry? A glance at La Mer tells me he's on the verge of doing something brash, but he's not a fighter, so it's a guess as to what. I step in to cut it off. "How did you get in here?"

Quantum responds, "Not everyone in this city is behind Medina. In fact, most aren't, but they're too afraid of her to stand up against her. They originally resisted any Admin—former or not—months ago and tried to keep her out. But they failed." Thoughts of the partially destroyed landing-field wall and Zabriskie's earlier statement—"Turns out things aren't as simple as good-guys–bad-guys anymore"—run through my head, finally making sense. "Even former citizens are smart enough to know when they are outgunned and outsmarted. I have allies, others who think Medina is taking things to places they don't want to go. Who think she is just the seed of a new Admin. Few want that. They will help us put a stop to this."

Brady, ever the pragmatist, says, "Get to the point."

With a dip of his chin, Quantum steps amid the group and continues, "Medina is only part of the problem. She still commands the *Celestial*, and while a ship that war-ready still flies, it will always be a threat. We need to take Medina down—cut the head off this particular snake—and make the cruiser obsolete so no one can step in to take her place."

"And you have a proposal on how to do that," Karl says.

"I always have a plan," Quantum responds, implying that we are too incompetent to think beyond anything more complex than our next meal, and not caring in the least that every word that comes out of his mouth makes everyone in this room detest him more. "Medina will be coming soon to collect those she wants to take back to Keum Libre to recruit the rest of the settlers for her rebuilt Admin. You'll tell Venus to create a diversion at the landing field, during which time you'll board the *Nebula* and escape."

I start at his mention of Venus—*how could he know she's there?*—then realize he must have known she was still aboard the *Orika* all along. If she's not with us, where else would she be? His shrewdness, as misdirected as it always seems to be, still never fails to catch me off guard. But the fact that he hasn't already given up Venus to Medina or her echelons, more than anything else, tells me he's not playing us. At least, not any more than he's playing Medina. But that doesn't mean we can trust him or count on him as an ally, as loyal. Not for a second.

"We've already gotten that far, Quantum," Karl says. "Have anything better to suggest?" His sneer doesn't hide his loathing, but then, Quantum is used to that.

"Then Aly and I will get aboard Medina's landing ship and take it back to the *Celestial*—which she will obviously marshal to destroy you and make dispatching the rest of the colonists easier—where I will disable the ship and stop her."

"Wait, what?" I blurt. "Why me?" It's not fear that makes every cell in my body resist his plan; it's the idea of being alone with Quantum on a fleet cruiser, forced to follow whatever scheming lead he takes. Not fear at all. Just pure survival instinct.

"Because you're the only one small enough to be hidden inside a cargo box and taken aboard undetected who also has the training to use a bugsuit." He looks around slowly at the rest of the crew, then brings his eyes back to mine. "And you're the only one I trust."

It's at this point that my brain stops engaging and goes into a tailspin while pondering the full implications of the words "small enough to be hidden inside a cargo box." He might as well have said "small enough to count worms in a corpse condo." As I consider the reasons to protest, each less convincing sounding than the last—*I'm not a coward, I just feel like I'm choking to death on my own heart when stuck in small places*—the conversation swirls around me . . . Medina still considers Quantum an asset and confederate . . . he'll have free rein of her ship . . . when it's time to put the plan in operation, he'll vent a nerve agent throughout that will knock most of Medina's troops inert . . . I'll take control of the bridge, using the Goldblum to go on the offense and deal with any remaining alert troops, then he'll put the ship in stasis long enough to give the rest of us time to rally more help from KL and get back to take control of the cruiser, its arsenal, and its multitude of adjunct attack ships . . . if the plan fails, we can blow the rigged compound from inside and destroy the cruiser completely, while Quantum and I escape in evac pods—overhearing this part sends me into a shuddering spasm—and the crew can track our emergency transmissions and pick us up before emergency life support gives out.

As the conversation advances, arguments and counterarguments from the group dwindle until none remain. There is no other way to stop Medina, or to ensure the fatal compound is never deployed. And whether the crew believes Quantum is being honest or not, his plan is our best chance for at least getting back to KL and warning the rest of the settlers about what's coming.

My attention comes back to the moment when I feel Karl tug gently on my arm. "You don't have to do this, Aly." His voice, crackling with emotion, carries throughout the room.

I turn to look into his eyes first, then around at the others. Finally, turning back to Quantum, I ask, "Isn't there another way of getting me on her landing ship?"

He stares blankly at me, not answering. Answer enough.

I take a deep inhale, then let it out, hoping no one notices the slight hitch and tremble as the breath leaves my lungs. "Then I'm in . . . I guess."

Quantum reaches into his jacket, pulls out a radio, and places it on the nearest bunk. "Call your pilot and tell her to be prepared to distract Medina's crew and get herself to the *Nebula*. I'll get prepped to leave."

"Hey Quantum," Desto says and steps from behind the bunk Zeta still sits on.

The wire-rat stands his ground as Desto approaches, and to his credit he barely flinches when he intuits the bone-crushing swing Desto aims at his jaw. No one tries to stop the father-to-be this time. After a moment, Quantum picks himself up off the floor, spits a puddle of blood at his feet, and makes for the door, wobbling slightly. He turns before leaving and says simply, "Be ready. This will happen fast."

Vitruzzi shakes free of Brady's hand and hurries up to the wire-rat. This time, she narrows her eyes and his face tenses, preparing for anything. Instead of striking him, Vitruzzi leans close to his ear and says something, but I can't make it out. Quantum nods his head, then exits.

Of all the questions yet to be answered, the one my mind keeps going back to is: Why would Quantum say he trusts *me*?

BRADY AND LA MER TRANSMIT to Venus, knowing she'll be monitoring all frequencies. When they reach her, they fill her in on everything that's already happened and is about to happen. While they discuss possible methods of distraction, the rest of the crew settles in, the tension and stress of waiting for something to go down already growing unbearable within an hour of Quantum's departure. The hardest thing about a plan, any plan, is the time that elapses before it can be put into motion, the questions that arise, the fears that worm into your guts and take root, feeding and growing fatter on every uncertainty and doubt that fractures your equilibrium. With no outlet to bleed off the infection of nervous energy but sitting and waiting, the situation is even worse.

Karl and I sit side by side on one bunk, enjoying the closeness of being together. We've been talking about every detail we can remember of the *Celestial*'s layout from the fourteen months we were aboard, calling out potential advantages or potential weaknesses of Quantum's plan. Neither of us brings up what might come next, all of the what-ifs: What if I or Quantum is caught before I can take the bridge? What if the plan fails and we have to implement the soil compound backup plan? What if that fails? What if it doesn't but I can't get to an evac pod and escape in time? What if I do, but the crew can't find me in all that vastness of empty space? And worst of all, what if this whole plan is a lie cooked up by Quantum for some ulterior motive?

What if these are the last moments Karl and I will ever spend together?

As the night progresses, our ideas and voices slowly fade, most of the crew grasping at the potential for a brief, though guaranteed to be restless, sleep. I'm stretched out on my side on the bunk, one of my hands lightly rubbing Karl's lower back as he sits and stares absently at the door. Seeming to realize how quiet it's become, he glances around him, then reaches into the inside pocket of his jacket and turns his body to the side, facing me.

"Aly, there's something I want to . . . um . . . I want you to have." He reaches behind him and pulls my hand from his back, then drops something into it.

I open my fingers and see a ring like the one Venus had been wearing, the one La Mer had given her.

Before I say anything, Karl continues, "I had Jeremy make one for us. I want you to know how much you mean to me, how much I love you."

As the full meaning of what he's saying hits me, a shiv of fear pierces the center of my chest. My voice barely squeezes past it. "Karl, what—? We . . . we don't have time for this kind of thing." I know it's not the right thing to say, but the fear—fear of losing him, fear of losing everything that matters to me—short-circuits my ability to think clearly or to say what I mean.

But he knows me, and he can hear the truth of my feelings in my heartbeat. Calmly, he says, "Aly, this may be the only time we have." And he lies down beside me on the tiny military cot and wraps his body around mine while I place the ring on a loop of utility cord and hang it around my neck.

TWENTY-FOUR

Medina doesn't make us wait for long. Only for a few hours after Brady, Zeta, and La Mer arrive, in fact. The inside of the gymnasium is like a vacuum where no noise or outside light penetrates, and when she opens the door and steps inside, we're like newborns that must reacclimate to a world outside our insulated one. Now after so many long hours cooped up—some of us in this holding cell, the rest aboard the *Nebula*—we embrace the knowledge that we'll be leaving Bogotan soon. Alive or dead.

Whitmore and a retinue of eight armed guards, including my favorites, Van Heusen and Blondie, come inside with her. Quantum lingers at the back of the group, scowling. No one seems to be paying him any attention.

Without ceremony, she says, "By now you've all had the time you need to discuss your options."

She flicks a quick nod to the gunmen assembled in a single line along the far wall, and each draws their sidearm of choice. I feel cold sweat break inside my armpits, though I know at this point we're not going to put up any resistance. Karl stands on one side of me, his shoulder touching mine, and David stands on my other. Between the two of them, I feel almost invincible, but I've heard the ticking of enough battle countdowns to know it's only an illusion. The dead aren't winners, just losers who don't have to care anymore.

No one has spoken, but Medina continues as if she already knows the answer. "Dr. Vitruzzi, Brady, and Desto will travel with us to Keum Libre. Takeoff is in one hour. Come with me, please."

She spins around, preparing to leave, but my eyes go to Quantum, anxious for a signal to put this grand plan of his under way. What I see doesn't reassure me. He raises a hand to his chest, pressing it there with one finger lifted in a *stay put* gesture. Easy for him to fucking say.

What happens next is more of a surprise than anything I've seen so far. Whitmore reaches out and puts a firm hand on Medina's shoulder as she takes a step toward the door. He looms over her by at least a head, but his gangly form is still somehow *less* than her stocky, erect military persona.

"Wait, Medina. I won't let you do this."

Medina comes to a standstill, but she doesn't turn around. Van Heusen's feral blue eyes stare at Whitmore, and the muzzle of his raised pistol targets Whitmore center mass.

"We talked about this, Jim," Medina says.

"No. No, *goddammit*. I will not allow you to . . . to make yourself the leader of a new Admin, not after what—"

Medina turns around quickly, knocking Whitmore's hand off of her shoulder and following through with a short chop to his midsection. Whitmore's eyes bulge comically as he doubles over, gasping. For the first time since I'd met her, Medina's face shows something new, a side of her I'd hardly have believed existed if I weren't witnessing it. The animal rage of a pit viper about to strike transforms her usually benign but hard features into something too shocking to be feared, too horrible to be ignored.

As Whitmore clutches his stomach and tries to catch his breath, Medina looks Van Heusen in the eyes and says laconically, "Shoot this bastard. In the face."

"No—!" I yell, beginning to step forward before David and Karl both stop me.

Van Heusen doesn't hesitate. Whitmore is dead before he hits the floor.

Medina faces us once more, but my gaze goes back to Quantum, desperate. He remains as he was, his gesture to wait firm, his eyes meeting mine with a ferocious command to follow his lead. I almost don't listen, almost rush into them, throwing my life away over disbelief that the woman who had started this never-ending war had merely done it out of insanity, not idealism, not something more pure, more rational.

But with Karl and my brother next to me, I'm not ready to die. Not today.

Medina's features are smooth and stern once again, no sign of the monster coiled beneath her skin. "If you had any questions about how far I'm willing to go to ensure humankind's continuity, I hope they have been answered. Follow." The command, meant for Vitruzzi, Brady, and Desto, is incontestable.

The three of them look around at the rest of us, then begin walking to the door. Vitruzzi kneels down and puts her fingertips to Whitmore's wrist before passing by. She knows he's dead, but I read something in the action that gives me a tiny jolt of hope. Vitruzzi isn't too far gone. She still cares, she's still *her* underneath the trauma that's been scrambling her circuits. She is still strong beneath the damaged exterior. I hope it lasts long enough for us to see the end of this.

Two of the security detail grab Whitmore's legs and drag his body out behind the rest of them, leaving a repulsive smear along the floor. As soon as the door closes, Karl grabs the radio.

"Venus, it's Karl, come in."

"Karlie," she answers immediately, "time?"

"Yes. Medina is heading to the landing field with Brady, V, and Desto. When they get there, light up the Venus show."

"Roger. Jeremy?"

He grabs the radio from Karl. "Yeah, babe."

"Love you. Don't forget that I like the vanilla frosting better than the chocolate when we get back, okay?"

"I won't."

THE DOOR ONLY REMAINS closed for a few minutes, the remaining eight of us pacing and holding ourselves back from trying to bum-rush through it and race to the landing field. If V, Brady, and Desto get on Medina's ship, we may never see them again. The one predictable thing we all know about Quantum is that he doesn't waste time on sentimentality. The three of them are as good as dead if they're not part of the plan. And he'd made the plan crystal clear. It's him and me. No stragglers, no flexibility, no loose ends.

As our nerves strain, nearing the breaking point, Mason says, "Venus will be able to slow them down. It's at least one element in our favor."

But is it the only one?

As this thought passes through my head, the door opens, and Zabriskie, flanked by at least two visible guards just outside, steps in. "You all need to come with us. Now."

"Why?" David asks.

"Just come." Zabriskie's eyes are lit by an urgency I haven't seen in him before, and my nerves warn me that our old friend Chaos is about to strike.

"Whose side are you on?" David says, his stance rigid and ready.

Zabriskie crosses the distance between the two of them in four long strides. All of us prepare for a confrontation; even the air seems to be alive with coiled energy. I see David's nostrils flare, but Zabriskie stops short of him, and then—does something totally unexpected.

"Take this," Zabriskie whispers and holds out a VDU, then reaches in his jacket and pulls out two more. "Here," he says, looking at Karl and me, both standing closest to him. "We're getting you out of here."

At the mention of "we" my eyes jerk toward the doorway where the other two guards have entered. Neither of them holds weapons in their hands, but both look nervous as hell.

"Who are you working with?" David repeats, not yet willing to take Zabriskie's com device.

We all feel David's paranoia. Could this be a setup? Is Medina looking for an excuse to ghost us so it will appear to have been self-defense to the rest of the KLers if they're brought back here? Why hadn't Quantum told us to expect Zabriskie if he's in on the plan? Without confirmation, it's impossible to guess what Zabriskie has up his sleeve, which leaves us with one last decision-making tool: our instincts.

Stepping up to the colonist, I take one of the VDUs, then turn to the rest. "What are we waiting for?"

"Aly—" Karl says, alarmed.

"We don't have time to debate this. We have to act."

Zeta takes my cue and grabs another VDU from Zabriskie, and the rest's resistance dissolves like salt in water. Everyone begins grabbing what gear they've brought, and we follow Zabriskie out, moving not quite at a double time. The other two men are already down the hallway and at the front door, peering outside. For what or who, we're stuck guessing.

Zabriskie fills us in on the way. "Whitmore wanted to set you free days ago while we figured out a plan. Now that he's dead"— he makes eye contact with the men outside, who nod an all clear, then pushes through the school's front door without slowing— "we're just improvising. Medina is making unilateral decisions. Trying to run Bogotan without consensus or even discussion. Quantum says you can help us stop her."

"Why should we trust you?" I ask as we rush into the street.

He opens the rear cargo hatch of a transport truck. Inside, I catch a glimpse of a cargo container about the size of a squad arms locker with the words Communications Backups stenciled on the side. "You don't have a choice but to trust us. We're taking you to the landing field so you can get the hell out of here, and—" He breaks off when his VDU lights up.

Quantum's voice: "Zabriskie, do you copy?"

"Zabriskie here."

"Is she in the box yet?"

"Negative, the crew is loading up. ETA to the landing field is ten."

"Affirmative." My own VDU pings to life and I answer. "Aly," he says, "your crew needs to get your pilot in action. There's not much time left."

"Roger. What did you mean by 'is she in the box yet'?"

My screen goes black without him responding. Not that he needs to.

Zabriskie and one of the men with him open the cargo container and begin pulling out weapons. Carbines, Dergs, a couple of Sinbads. He motions to the crew. "Get what you want and get in the back. You"—he passes me an AK-80, my always trusted weapon of choice, and a few clips of caseless—"jump inside there once we get everything out and lie down. I'll get you on Medina's ship."

I swallow hard, checking the action on the '80 and loading the first clip. My eyes hold his steadily while I shake my head. "I'm not missing this fight."

Wisely, he doesn't argue. The crew grab the guns and get in, Zabriskie pulling himself into the covered bed with us. The vehicle is already moving before he gets the cargo gate closed. "This truck is heading straight for the *Kongjù*, Medina's ship. I'm supposed to leave you on the city side of the landing-field gate before we go through, and your pilot is supposed to do whatever she's going to do. The truck is completely armored, so you can use us as a shield until we get to the *Kongjù*. But no one stays inside except Erikson, or we'll never get her aboard. Everyone clear?"

No one says a word; the only sound now is the dull whump of the fuel cell engine and the tires humming on the road. I look around at their faces, seeing the same severe dilation of their pupils, the same controlled breathing, the same fierce warrior mask as mine. The kid, Ryan, has been through some shit, maybe even had to kill others to survive, but he looks more scared than the rest of us. This is a real battle, with real soldiers. The kind of bloody razing mess that he's used to as a scav fighting other scavs, while it was probably always gruesome, would never have had the same methodical, purposeful intent to destroy as what he's about to encounter. Almost all of us in the bed of this truck, and even more of Medina's crew, were trained by the best to be efficient killing machines. The Corps never stinted on doling out ruthlessness, and no one kills better than its graduates. I just hope the kid is prepared for it.

My eyes fall on Zeta, then quickly bounce away. She was a civilian before the war and had left that behind for her own reasons and joined the colony on Spectra 6, but now she's just a survivor like the rest of us. A fugitive in a system where no one is anything but. Fugitives from reason, stability, maybe even hope. What chance her and Desto's kid has was already limited, but now . . . now I don't want to think about what could, and probably will, happen.

Zabriskie's carbine lies across his knees. He leans forward, leaving his hands on the stock and the barrel to keep it from falling, and says, "You know you're putting the whole mission in danger until you get in that crate."

"I told you, I'm not missing this fight." I don't bother mentioning that I'm more afraid of being stuck in that black box than I am of being shot point-blank. "Another gun could be the thing that keeps the people I care about alive."

His seawater-green eyes stare into mine for several seconds, his face only a puff of breath away. Then he leans back, reaches into his jacket, and pulls free a small plastic bag, which he tosses at me. "Quantum told me to give you those. Vitruzzi asked him for them. Sedatives. If you don't get killed before you get aboard the *Kongjù*, take three. Quantum will come get you when it's clear. Save the rest in case it's longer than . . ." He shrugs.

The bag lies in my lap. I look inside at the handful of white pills, then put three in my breast pocket for quick retrieval. If Vitruzzi were here, I'd kiss her.

Someone from the cab hammers on the divider and the truck slows to a stop—our cue. I promise Zabriskie, "Get to the *Kongjù*'s ramp, I'll meet you there."

"Fifteen of Medina's on the tarmac, looks like the three going to Keum Libre haven't boarded yet. They're standing over by the supply dump with four guards on them," says a voice through Zabriskie's VDU. He glances around to make sure we've all heard it, then slides open the rear door and drops the cargo gate. "Good luck. We'll keep it slow so you can use our cover."

"What about Venus?" Hoogs says. "Shouldn't she be doing her magic trick right now?"

We look at each other impotently. Finally Karl says, "We can't wait. Mason, La Mer, and I will go after the crew. Zeta, just stay low and get your ass to the *Nebula*." Karl's obviously been having similar thoughts to mine. "Aly, you do what you can to help Zeta, and make sure you get back to this truck without being seen. Ryan, you stick with David and Hoogs. Cover us from the rear." He stands and the rest of us do the same. Giving it one last shot, he gets on the VDU Zabriskie had given him. "Venus, I don't know where you are, and don't respond to this message if it will compromise you, but we're about to come in hot. The *Nebula* needs to be ready to launch ASAP." He gives it a second, but there's no return transmission. Nodding once, he says, "Let's do it."

TWENTY-FIVE

Not being able to see anything on the other side of the truck is unnerving. But what's worse is the lack of surprise, the lack of distraction. The lack of the Venus show. What could have happened? If she's been compromised or killed, this fight is already over. I may still be able to get aboard Medina's ship and rendezvous with the *Celestial*, but it may not help Vitruzzi, Brady, and Desto. If they die, and if Venus is already dead, the fallout will be much, much worse than just shattered morale. They—along with Karl and David—compose the core of my world, the people I most care about, the people I will never hesitate to put my life on the line for. If I can't keep them safe, the whole hellish fight will be for nothing.

Locking these fears deep inside, I press forward, following Zeta so closely our hips touch as we shuffle along. The line is Karl, Hoogs, Mason, Zeta, me, David, Ryan, and La Mer at the rear. The truck is long, made for carrying large loads, and conceals us easily. Zabriskie's collaborators informed us that all of Medina's squad is busy with loading a resupply cache to take to the *Celestial* and guarding Vitruzzi and the other two. The cargo brought by this truck is the last expected on their manifest. From our enemy's perspective, the arrival of Zabriskie is situation normal.

I'd had a brief look across that landing field after the gargantuan gates rumbled open. The *Orika* is still where Venus had planted it, its state of disuse and general beat-up condition making it look almost like a monolith from ancient times despite its short tenure in Bogotan. Immediately beside it, only thirty meters distant, sits the *Nebula*, a slightly bigger craft. Towering behind the two of them looms the much larger battle-ready fleet attack ship, the former PCA *Kongjù*. I'd been a navigator on it myself during the war and know full well its capacity for rendering the *Nebula* and *Orika* into scrap without even needing to engage its heavy artillery. Seeing it for that split second had made my guts turn to ice. The only chance Venus has is to outmaneuver it. Karl can fly it if Venus is somehow out of the picture, a thought that sends another freezing stab of anxiety through the middle of me, but he doesn't have her preternatural, sometimes miraculous, talents for making a craft do the seemingly impossible. Yet if the *Nebula* makes it into the air, maybe Medina will just let her go. After all, Keum Libre has no defense against a fleet cruiser and its arsenal, all at Medina's disposal, and she must know that. Whitmore's men, the ones who had delivered Zeta, then returned with the crew, could easily have reconned KL during their stay and figured this out, and Medina surely debriefed them. Even if part of our crew splinters off in the *Nebula* and gets to KL in time to warn the settlers of Medina's coming, there's nothing, not a goddamn thing, the settlement can do to stop her.

That part is up to me.

We can't be more than fifty meters distant of the cluster, and David, Ryan, and Hoogs disengage and silently run behind a vehicle parked toward the edge of the ship takeoff zone to take up long-range backup firing positions. No shouts or words of warning come from ahead to indicate they've been spotted. A relief. The *Kongjù*'s engines start to cycle, sending a low-pitched throbbing rhythm through the ground and up into my feet. The rest of us continue to plod forward, then the truck stops and Zabriskie jumps clear of the back.

A voice from in front of us: "Zabriskie, is that the last of the supplies?"

"Yeah, Quantum's parts."

"Okay, one sec and I'll send the loader over."

Where the fuck is Venus?

Karl turns around to face us, meets my eyes with his for a heartbeat, and I read the go signal coming before he says anything. The slight breeze blowing up from the south feels warm against the coolness of my skin. My nostrils flare as I draw in a deep breath, calming myself and preparing to let the battle-drunk veteran that I usually keep suppressed deep within me once again inhabit my body.

He turns back toward the front of the cab, peers around, and lifts his hand, ready to wave us into action. Just before he does, the sound of voices raised in some kind of confrontation carries to us.

"What do you mean 'shut her down'? The commander wants her up in the air to be added to the *Celestial*'s armada. I mean, who wouldn't want this ship, this *absolutely gorgeous hunk of machine*, among their squadron?"

Venus? Really?

Unable to stop myself, I slide up beside Karl and cautiously peer around the cab. He turns to look at me, his eyes shining full moons of surprise.

It *is* Venus. Dressed in a mishmash outfit that is part Corps uniform, part civvies, obviously trying to blend in with the bustle of security personnel finishing up the final supply run, she stands less than fifteen meters in front of us, just at the base of the *Nebula*'s open ramp.

"Nobody said nothing to me."

If it isn't my old friend Blondie.

"Hmmm, must have slipped her mind," Venus replies, her voice as dismissive as if she were a queen speaking to an idiot serf. And then I finally hear what I'd been too keyed up to recognize over the dull thump of the *Kongjù*'s engines—the *Nebula*, too, is online, her internals whirring into flight mode.

"Don't I know you?" Blondie says, leaning forward.

Those of us who realize the risk Venus had taken to show her face flinch in unison. She must be crazy, but sometimes crazy is the only option. I catch something out of the corner of my eye and turn just in time to reach out and grip La Mer by the sleeve as he tries to pass us and help Venus. *Don't*, I mouth, warning him. She may not have played all her cards yet, whatever the hell those are.

Within sight ahead of us, the pile of supplies Zabriskie's man had spoken of, where Vitruzzi, Brady, and Desto are waiting to board in the company of three guards, sits forward of the *Kongjù* and just between the *Nebula* and *Orika*. A track loader rolls down the *Kongjù*'s cargo ramp. The remaining supplies are small, not requiring a loader, and I realize it must be coming to us. If Venus has a move to make, it *has* to be now.

The onetime fugee reaches out and grabs Venus by the arm. "You're that pilot that came from Eruo Pium, I know it. Come with me."

It all happens as fast as the speed of light, and as slow as drowning.

As I watch, Brady and Desto tackle two of the unprepared guards watching over them, while Vitruzzi opens one of the boxes sitting near her and pulls out several weapons. The cue given, Karl takes aim and fires at Blondie but misses. The guard's reflexes are sharp, and he runs behind the *Nebula* at race speed, leaving Venus behind him. She immediately sprints inside the safety of the ship's hull, out of the line of fire. From behind us, I hear David open up with the rifle he'd taken from Zabriskie's cache. Hoogs and Mason take up firing positions behind and under our truck, and the squadron of soldiers under Medina's command scatter or sprint to the only place that offers them any protection on the mostly flat, open landing field—inside the *Kongjù*.

By the time the last bullet's echo fades Desto, Vitruzzi, and Brady have annihilated their guards and taken shelter in the safety behind one of the *Kongjù*'s external missile chutes. We can't know for sure how many others are inside the attack ship, but no one is leaving its interior without being in direct line of fire from those three. The squaddy driving the loader, the four guards with Vitruzzi's group, and three others are down on the tarmac, and we haven't taken a single casualty. The box of guns Vitruzzi had accessed could only have come from Venus, or maybe Quantum, and while it wasn't nearly the bang-up surprise I'd been expecting, I'm not complaining about the results.

But nothing is stopping Medina from calling for backup, which could be seconds away.

And I still have to get onto first the *Kongjù* and then the *Celestial.*

David, Ryan, and Hoogs read the situation and risk closing the gap by running across the space and rejoining us behind the truck. Zabriskie had jumped inside the rear, and his two compatriots are keeping a low profile in the cab, sitting this one out.

"What do we do?" Ryan asks, out of breath. I can see panic and excitement starting to squeeze in on him, turning his decision-making skills and reflexes into granulated powder. Can't have that.

"Calm down, kid," I say. "We need everyone focused and relaxed. Don't let yourself get distracted, read me?" His jittering eyes cut to me, and I force myself to grin at him, passively, showing no teeth. *Just another day, nothing unusual, no need to worry about it being your last*, my expression tells him. "If anyone comes at us, just pick your targets, take a deep breath, and squeeze the trigger. Remember those three steps. That's all you gotta think about. Okay?"

He nods. If the kid gets killed, I won't be happy, but getting shot with a stray bullet because he can't keep his nerves in check will piss me off even more.

My focus returns to the team as Karl moves to the truck's rear and slams a fist against the gate. "Zabriskie, listen up. You have to get this truck to the *Kongjù*. There's no way that loader is coming our direction. Put yourself in between the ramp and the *Nebula* so our people can make a run for it."

Zabriskie responds, "On it," and we hear him speaking into his VDU: "Medina and Steward, this is Jono Zabriskie. I'm stuck on the landing field with Quantum's supplies. The loader can't get to us, so we're bringing the truck to you. Do you read? Over."

"That's a negative, Zabriskie. It's too hot out there. Stand fast until we give you the all clear."

"Dammit," we hear him growl under his breath, then: "No can do, Steward. We're not going to sit here and wait to get shot. Out."

Fuck me, he's quite the gambler.

Karl says, "We'll give them cover fire from the *Nebula*. Stay low and get up beneath the ramp. That fugee may have a good position from the rear of the ship, so make sure the ramp is between you and him. Zeta, you follow me. Head straight for the cockpit. Venus will need your help. Let's move."

As I get into position to run, he steps in front of me, forcing me to stop. "Except you, Aly."

"Karl—"

"We have this covered. Stay here and watch our backs. Once we're all in the *Nebula*, you get on Medina's ship." He leans forward and kisses me on the lips quickly, before I can argue, then straightens. "I'll see you, lover—*soon*."

David wraps me in a brief side hug. "Good luck, Twig. Give that bitch my regards when you see her."

Then Mason squeezes my shoulder: "You got this," and Hoogs says, "We'll be there when you need us." La Mer: "Luck, Aly." Zeta says nothing, just gives me a long, hard hug, and even Ryan says: "Thanks for what you did for me. Good luck."

I don't know what to say, suddenly realizing I couldn't say it even if I did, the way my throat suddenly feels gummy and stuck fast. Finally I squeak out, "Go get back our crew."

I take a knee and get a bead on the direction Blondie had run. The crew rushes past me, and I watch enrapt as they make a few feints up the ramp. No shots are fired, and soon they've all disappeared into the shadows inside the hull.

I hear Zabriskie behind me: "Time to move, Erikson."

Standing, I'm about to make my way to the truck's cargo bed, but suddenly my legs feel weak, wobbly. I lean against the side of it for a second, fighting back dread, struggling not to believe that I've just said goodbye forever to the people I love, forcing my god-damn game face back on. Remembering the pills Vitruzzi had asked Quantum to get me, I reach into my pocket and dig them out, quickly popping all three in my mouth and dry-swallowing them. It's the only way I'm going to find the will to get inside that box.

A second later, I shamble to the rear. Zabriskie sees me and leans out with a hand extended, ready to help me up. I reach out to take it—

—and he points a pistol straight into my face and fires.

The thunder, so close to my head, nearly blows my eardrum out and I fall backward onto the ground, landing on my ass, reflex-ively trying to scoot away, wondering why I'm not dead. My hand hits meat and I jerk my eyes down, realizing that I can't push any farther away from the truck because there's a body behind me.

Blondie?

"Erikson, come on!" Zabriskie yelling at me just adds to the confusion, and I turn my stare back to him dazedly. "He must have snuck by them. Your friends are in the clear, but we've got to go!"

I push myself up and stand and shake my head to clear the ringing in my left ear, then turn around to glance back at the very dead fugee. Zabriskie hit him neatly in the temple, leaving a slightly gray, perfectly round, upraised ring around the hole in his head. His eyes are open, the moisture already being sucked away by the dry wind.

Zabriskie has the lid to the cargo box open and waits for me impatiently. Looking into it, I feel like I'm looking into an abyss. But even an eternal plunge into emptiness would be better than a second stuck inside this casket. I can't look Zabriskie in the face, too hard to yank my stare away from that box waiting to swallow me whole. The *Nebula*'s engines begin to whine louder, their de-parture now only seconds away.

"What are you waiting for?"

His words float to my ears from far away. I try to swallow, but my throat sticks. I pass him the carbine, put my hands on the cold metal side of the bin, stand still for a few breaths, then swing a leg over. Once I'm lying flat inside, a sudden and incredibly welcome rush of calm tingles out from my midsection, like a wisp of pure oxygen flowing through me. Either the sedatives or wishful thinking kicking in.

"Quantum says he'll come get you as soon as it's clear. It'll take about ten hours to get to the *Celestial*, so you're looking at about twelve hours in there. There's a bottle of water and another empty one if you need to piss. Just stay calm, take it easy." Can he see the fear in my face? He passes me the carbine, which I lay beside me. He stares at me for several seconds, his face moving through a range of expressions I previously wouldn't have believed he was capable of. Finally he lands on what I take to be confidence, his brow knit sternly and a twist at the side of his mouth that's part smile, part scowl. "Make your people proud, Erikson. Bogotan's too. We're counting on you."

The nod I give him is abrupt and short, all I can manage in my state of approaching paralysis.

The lid closes and I have the scope light of the carbine switched on before I even realize I'm doing it. Sound from outside is severely muted, but the truck is already moving forward past the subdued roar of the *Nebula*'s engines, then it hits the base of the *Kongjù*'s ramp and starts to tilt.

My heart is trying to explode through my chest. "Count," I whisper to myself, "one hundred, ninety-nine, ninety-eight, ninety-seven . . ."—*breathe, breathe, breathe*—"fucking ninety. Eighty-nine, eighty-eight, eighty-seven . . ."—*just fucking breathe*—"eighty . . ."

We've stopped, but at this point, counting aloud to myself is my only conscious awareness. I block it out, everything, crushing the worries—that the Nebula will never get off the ground, that Vitruzzi, Brady, and Desto won't be able to get to the scout, that the mission will fail and Keum Libre will become the killing field of a tyrant, that I'll die in this box—into a dark corner where I can't think about them, can't think about anything except: "Sixty, fifty-nine, fifty-eight, fifty-seven . . ."

When my brain finally fuzzes out completely, I don't know if it's from panic overload or sedation, but I don't care. The relief is all that matters.

TWENTY-SIX

Is it perverse to have grown bored after being trapped for hours in the dark, just waiting for Medina's crew to either find me and put an end to this slow descent into panic-slash-death or run down the *Nebula* and unleash all hell on them? The crushing terror that gripped me at first once the lid closed dulled to unconsciousness soon, then became a sort of malaise when I awoke that I thought only people who'd consumed horse tranquilizers could feel. Now, after the past ten hours and forty-six minutes in this sarcophagus-sized crate, I can't seem to get worked up by the very real possibility they are going to be my last.

I have Vitruzzi's magic anticlaustrophobia pills to thank for that, which have left me adrift inside my drug-induced subterranean mental maze, and surfacing only brings awareness of one simple thing: my muscles are beginning to feel a little cramped. My hidey-hole is only about 2 x .5 x .5 meters in area, so moving around isn't exactly easy. Other than the capped bottle I'd managed to use as a latrine, the only things in here with me are a bottle of water, the energy bars I still had in my equipment vest, and my AK-80. Plus the last four remaining sanity-saving pills.

I've popped two every three hours, and they've magically transformed the anxiety and panic that would ordinarily have sent me clawing through the steel lid with my fingernails into a blunt-tipped afterthought. The aftereffect has been, besides cramps, flat indifference. And I'll take it. Knowing I only have a few pills left, though, turns the dial on my anxiety meter up enough that I've re-initiated the countdown from a hundred in round after round just to keep my mind off it and . . . other things. Like memories.

Some might call this brief calm before chaos an optimal time for introspection, but I try to keep my stampeding-rabbit thoughts in a white-noise cloud, or on things like the bruise on my left big toe that will probably make running a lot harder—if I get a chance—and the way my lips are starting to feel a little like sand-paper. But when the panic starts to creep in and I pop the pills, their power sends acid tendrils through my brain that eat away the barriers between my life now and my life as a child, letting memories I wish I didn't have spill into the present. It's a side effect I find much more unpleasant than stiff muscles.

My father's face—his thick, manicured, rust-colored beard, which always smelled of the acrid tonic he used and always made my eyes water; his murky blue stare, which would land on me with an almost physical thud when he was angry; and his ladder of wrinkles, which grew as deep as caverns at times, cascading from his hairline to his brows—loomed out from the well I'd sunk it in as I'd emerged from the first pill-induced fog. I hadn't thought of him in years, since before I'd even graduated from the Academy and been sent to my first duty station on Obal 8. He'd come to David's ceremony but skipped mine two years later. I hadn't been disappointed. We hadn't spoken since I'd joined.

As I cross my legs and press the back of my head and shoulders against the cargo box to try and sit up some, that phantom smell of beard tonic hits my nostrils out of nowhere, jolting me. The memory trailing along behind it is so vivid, it seems like it is happening again. I'd been eight years old and had just been picked up by my father from a neighbor's house. I don't remember her name, but she'd been the single woman living a few blocks away, just leaving for work, and had found me crying on the street after wrecking my magbike. Harald—the only name I ever used for my father—had been forced to turn around from his own work commute and come get me.

In our kitchen, he'd bent down and put his big, heavy hands on my shoulders and shaken me once, twice, three times, hard enough to make my head snap on my neck—despite the fact that I'd been cradling my broken arm since I'd fallen, gamely holding in the tears that I hadn't been afraid to shed until he came home.

"I told you to take the city trans to your summer classes, and what did you do?" Shake one. "You go chasing after David, trying to follow him to Preflight Club. Again!" Shake two. His muddy eyes stared into mine. "When are you going to learn how to at least act like a good daughter?" Shake three. And finally I'd begun to wail, each shake making the greenstick-fractured bones crunch in exquisite, sparking pain.

"What?!" he'd yelled. "Now you're crying because you know what a useless little girl you are?" He'd shoved me into a chair. "Jesus Christ. You'll never know how badly I wish your mother had taken you with her when she split." He leaned down again, and I could smell the beard tonic even through my sniffling nose, almost strong enough to gag me. "If you're ever going to be any good to anyone, you're just going to have to get tougher. You stay home by yourself today until I get back from work. Then I'll have time to take you to get that arm looked at. Unless you're just faking it." He'd risen, put his jacket back on, and warned me as he walked out the door, "Stay out of trouble, or that arm is going to feel like a love tap if I have to knock off work early."

It had been David, home within a few hours after his Academy-sponsored Preflight Club, that had called a friend's mother to take me to the neighborhood medical clinic. Of course, I hadn't said my father had left me home with a broken arm; I'd made up a story about skipping summer school and breaking it while riding my magbike. In reality, I'd just been grateful David got me sorted out so I didn't have to spend any more time in Harald's presence than necessary.

Memories like this one push me fighting and clawing back to consciousness. I don't want to think of my childhood. That's long over and long forgotten. Or I thought it had been. I'd risked a lot, taken more chances than a reasonable person should, to get as far away from it as I could. Now, sitting in the dark and still smelling the smoke in my clothes and hair from the brief firefight in the landing field, I'm beginning to wonder if my recklessness hadn't just been about escaping, but had also been a lack of a reason to live. Survival instinct, yeah, I definitely have that. How many times have I shot someone faster than they could shoot me just so they'd fall and I'd still be standing? But what was that for? What had I had to live for that made my trigger finger faster and my aim straighter than all those others?

The answer to that question was never more clear to me than after I'd met Karl and the rest of the Beachers, my new crew. I've always had David to look out for and to look out for me, but back in the Corps and when we worked for Rajcik, he was it, the only thing that mattered. Now I have family—something I've never had before—people and a life and home of my own on KL, even if it is a spider-infested jungle with a downed fleet cruiser for its hub.

And there's more. That instinct to survive hasn't gone any-where, but it has changed. The addendum "at all costs" that used to apply is gone, just like my fears of being betrayed or hurt—the only "gifts" my father ever gave me. I still *want* to survive, of course, but when I look inside myself—and where else have I had to look in these last few hours?—I realize that I'll do whatever I have to now to protect those who matter to me. My crew. My family. Even if it means I'm stuck on this ship and going down with it. I'll do it. I'll do it for them.

Fully awake for the first time in hours, I notice the way the stale air inside my storage box suddenly assaults my nose much more strongly than before. The pills are wearing off, and my heart does an uncomfortable somersault-y *bap-bap* in my chest. Involuntarily, I rattle my hand, which is closed in a protective cocoon around the last four tranqs. The tiny *tick* sound they make is only minimally reassuring. Almost before I think about it, I pop two in my mouth—then I spit them back out into my open fist, still dry, thanks to sedative- and fear-induced cotton mouth. It's almost time. I have to get my head straight, can't be wandering around out there with only half my faculties activated. I have no alternative than to try and deal with the claustrophobic panic currently trying to rip open my chest wall like a glass-clawed parasite.

A quick glance at the counter on my VDU tells me the length of my captivity: eleven hours, two minutes now. I'd felt us dock with the *Celestial* about forty-five minutes ago. Even in my haze, I think I would have known if the *Kongjù* had pursued the *Nebula*, but the flight had been smooth. A ship this size can't make the type of aggressive, split-angle course changes that Venus and the nimbler Nebula could have, so maybe they'd seen no reason to give chase. If they had, and Venus was forced to switch to an evasive flight pattern, she'd have used up so much power at once that she'd have had to scale back on output for several hours after the initial evasive burst. Then Medina would merely have had to stay on course and once again close the gap while they were vulnerable. But there's been no change in the regular hum of the ship's engines until the *Kongjù* docked and shut down, so I believe—pray, more like—that the plan is progressing as hoped. Maybe miracles are real.

I guess I'll find out when it's time to take the bridge.

CLAMMY SWEAT OOZES FROM my forehead and the palms of my hands, and I can almost feel the air pressure increase as the walls and floor of my box collapse in on me too slowly for the eyes to see. Whether it's time or not, I'm putting the next mission phase into action—before I go batshit psycho.

I've spent the last hour stretching and tightening all my muscles, limbering and waking them up in preparation for moving through the ship. I'm done waiting for Quantum. Rolling to my side, I turn on the VDU glowscreen for some light, put my hand on the latch, suck in a slow, deep breath, adjust my '80 for fast deployment, and press the inner release.

It doesn't move.

Okay, a little stuck, so I push a fraction harder, imagining the relief I'm going to feel when it depresses. But there's no give. Was it . . . is it possible . . . it's been locked? Why would Zabriskie lock it?

I freeze, trying to get a grip on the situation before torrents of adrenaline block my ability to think clearly. A drop of sweat slides down my temple and along my ear and plops onto the floor of the crate, looking through my hyperfocused vision like a bottomless pool; then another falls, and a jolt of electricitylike pinpricks dance up my spine and flush across my back, forcing an involuntary shiver to rip through me. When my hand slides through the cold pool of sweat in front of me, the dike gives out.

I slam my palm against the latch as hard as I can, not feeling the shock run up my arm, then flip my carbine around and hit the latch with the stock—again and again, not hearing the clang, not feeling the vibration, not caring that my breath is coming in loud, raging gasps that surely must be audible, even over the polymer-on-metal noise of the weapon and lid. Suddenly, I'm six again and my father has locked me in the trunk at the foot of my bed as punishment for running off to look for my mother. Terror so extreme and so clear it could almost be mistaken for rhapsody explodes from the center of my body, turning every sense and every perception into a singular desire for escape.

Heaving over onto my back, I bend my knees into my ribs and wedge my feet and hands against the cover, preparing to press as hard as humanly possible against it until either it breaks away or my hips and arms splinter into a million shards. Just as my shoulders begin to scream in protest—it opens! My father's face appears in the space over the rectangle of light above me, and my first instinct is to let a kick fly, then I realize—

"Quah-Quantum?" He barely has time to get out of my way before I propel through the opening and thud to the floor, wheezing in great, rasping breaths.

"Erikson. Would you mind doing us both the favor of calming the fuck down? Someone is going to hear you."

Though his words pierce through my straitjacket of panic easily, my brain takes a minute to catch up to the fact that it's really him, Quantum is standing in front of me—not my father.

Even as I realize it, the only thing I can think to say is: "What the hell took you so long? I nearly started this show without you."

He looks up and down the storage bay as he responds in a hushed voice, "You aren't smart enough to do this on your own. Now come on."

Still too shaken up to be pissed off at his statement, I lean heavily against the wall beside the storage box for a second, trying to regain some calm. Avoiding a last look inside its hateful interior, I reach in and feel around until I clasp the butt of my '80 and withdraw it. With a glance around, I take in row upon row of the soil amendment compound drums, all lined up inside the storage bay like sleeping soldiers of the plague, awaiting orders to inflict mass destruction on innocents. Reaching into my jacket, I run a finger along the tiny detonating unit La Mer had passed me. A click of its button would unleash hell.

Not waiting, Quantum steps outside the exit hatch, then turns and motions for me to follow him. *I'm okay,* I tell myself and tighten my grip on my carbine with slightly trembling hands. But after I take a single step forward, the hatch suddenly slides closed—me on my side and Quantum on the other.

Van Heusen steps into view from behind a row of drums, nonchalantly pocketing the remote hatch controller he carries. "I knew that bastard was up to something, but I'll deal with him later."

The nasal growl of his voice, compliments of the broken nose from Karl, makes my teeth want to grind. My carbine is already aimed center mass, but, insanely, he's stepping toward me.

"Go ahead, Erikson. Take a shot." He sees my indecision and laughs. "That's right. You know this ship, don't you?"

I can't shoot. He knows it. The discharge of a weapon aboard will trigger the ship's alarms, and this mission will be over before it starts.

"Stay the fuck away from me, Van Heusen."

"But that's not what I have in mind at all. I've been waiting to get some time with you for a while. Scav or not, you still look tasty to me."

His words barely register as I assess my options. Between his greater size and his body armor, a hand-to-hand encounter has a low chance of ending well for me. I can't blow what he has for brains out, and there's nowhere to run but deeper into the storage bay, but then where? Fleetingly, I think about the detonator in my pocket. No, not that. Not yet.

He takes another step forward, and I add a little more bend to my knees, the carbine not wavering. Surprise ripples across his face. He pulls a knife from his equipment vest. The overhead lights flash dazzlingly along its tang. I flick my eyes over his shoulder toward the hatch, hoping to see it opening.

"He can't get in," Van Heusen says, reading my glance. "It's just the two of us."

"Do you know what this stuff is, Van Heusen? What it will do?"

He takes a half step forward, but I remain firm. Backing down isn't going to gain me anything.

"Do I look like someone who cares if a bunch of weak citizens get turned into fertilizer? That's all any of us are anyway. Worm food—"

He takes another step as he speaks, and I drop to a knee and roll into his legs, forcing him to career to the side. He reaches out and belays his fall with a hand against one of the compound drums, then spins around. I've already scrabbled to the hatch control panel and jam the "Open" command.

Not happening.

He comes at me fast but light, a boxer's approach. But we've had the same training, all Academy soldiers did. I dance away from a jab from his left to my ribs, and block the knife coming toward my chest with the carbine. The thud of his wrist against the stock tells me the nerves there will be sizzling, and I let his next left make contact against my cheekbone as I drive the carbine barrel into his right armpit and knock the knife in his weakened grip free. It flies toward the cargo crate and hits the side with a dull echo, but my senses are busy trying to come to terms with the buzzing pain in my cheek and temple.

With his right arm temporarily numb, he uses his body to smash into me, forcing me up against the hatch. I can't move enough to strike or leverage my carbine, but there's nothing between my teeth and his face.

He screams as I bite into the skin below his eye and tries to pull away. As he does, I grab him around the shoulders, letting my carbine fall to the side and hang by its strap, and wrap my legs around his waist. He wanted a close-up-and-personal, that's what he's going to get. Stumbling backward with me attached to him like a rabid dog, he loses his balance and goes down on his ass. My weight coming down on top of him pushes him flat and compresses the breath out of his lungs in a high-speed purge, and I release my bite, rear back, and smash my forehead into his injured nose. This time, blood pours from it like a fountain instead of a trickle, and he grips his face with both hands, unable now to even scream, rocking his body from side to side in blunt, brutalizing anguish.

I walk to the knife and pick it up almost leisurely, then move back to him. His eyes, which had been squeezed shut, now open a sliver—in time for him to see the kick I launch into his midsection below the base of his torso armor.

He grunts, and I rear back for another one. "What's that?" Kick to the gut. "Did you say you're enjoying the time we're spending together?" Kick to the wedding tackle. "Well, good. So am I." Kick to the head. This one lays him out cold.

"You done, Aly?" Quantum's voice pulls me out of the moment, and I spin around to face him. The hatch is open again; no doubt he'd found some way to bypass it. After assessing me for a brief moment, he says, "Let's put him in the cargo box."

Van Heusen won't be awake for a while, if ever, and he definitely won't get out of there on his own. The metallic-electric taste of adrenaline coating my throat and tongue is unpleasant, but the surge of it in my bloodstream wiped out the last of my jitters from being stuck in the container. Task complete, Quantum and I speed out of the storage bay and down a corridor toward a bulkhead about ten meters distant. Quantum keeps his eyes forward, and I watch our rear, thankful the remaining area is empty. When we reach the hatch, instead of opening it, he climbs (surprisingly nimbly) up the adjacent wall using the housing of an electrical console and pushes a 1 x 1 ceiling panel aside, then pulls himself up. His hand drops through and waves at me to follow.

"No. No way," I mumble, my throat already tightening the way I imagine the walls will if I get in there.

His head drops through the hole, a sneer plastered across his mouth. "Get your ass up here. Or would you prefer to see all your friends smeared from one end of KL to the other?" His voice is gravelly and uncompromising. "You know I've never liked you, Erikson, but we have a job to do."

The comment almost makes me laugh. Since he and his companions had kidnapped me on the streets of Tunis City almost two years ago, I've never exactly teemed with affection for him either. The scar on my left hand from his oh-so-unsubtle way of driving his intentions home while interrogating me looks almost like an arrow pointing to my middle finger. Thinking of it, I stifle the urge to put that finger on display in a similarly unsubtle message. Instead, I say, "The feeling is mutual. But I'd say we're in a situation where what we think of each other"—or how strong our urge may be to strangle the shit out of each other—"is irrelevant."

He nods, as if I'd simply capitulated, says, "Then shut up and quit stalling," and retreats back into the vent.

"Wait!"

"I don't have time for th—"

"No, hold on. Do you know anything about my crew? Did they make it away from Obal 6?"

It seems like an hour ticks by before he answers in a voice that betrays absolutely nothing, like the voice of an android, "Yeah. They made it."

I could press him for an answer, make him say something that will assure me of the truth, one way or the other, but a different part of me—the part that might simply give up if they hadn't—isn't really ready to know. Convincing myself that Quantum's strangely toneless response was merely because he doesn't actually care if my crew is dead or alive is easy enough; he has no stakes in their survival. But the other problem isn't so easy to resolve—how am I going to do this? Crawl from one tiny space into another? It's like being liberated from hell just to be flung into an incinerator. *Figure this out, Aly. Too many people are counting on you for you to indulge in phobias. Put yourself in someone else's shoes. How would Karl make this happen?*

Thinking of Karl helps. I imagine his eyes, the way his smile reaches them when I run my fingers through the hair on his chest, and the trick starts to work—helped along by whatever tranq residue still swims in my bloodstream. *It just has to last a little longer,* I tell myself. Keeping a mental picture of Karl's face in front of me, I push the carbine around to hang on my back and grasp the electrical console. *Like getting on an elevator. No big deal.* My knees and the joints in my shoulders protest as I try to copy Quantum's monkey impression, even with my hefty dose of adrenaline. I knew I'd be a little stiff, but if this doesn't fade quickly, I'll be an easy target once the real ship takeover begins. As I reach over the opening's lip to pull myself up, my grip starts to slip on the slightly oily surface. Just before I fall, Quantum grabs the straps on my vest and hauls me over the edge with a grunt. I lie still on my stomach for a moment, listening—almost hoping—for the tromp of boots below us.

"How you like me now?" I rasp.

"Less and less."

"Fuck you, Quantum." The anger helps, and I take a second to wonder if he's provoking me on purpose. The man has never shown much skill in the social interaction department, but right now I don't care. I need to get through this. I *could* get through this.

It could happen.

He rummages through his jacket, then passes me a new VDU. "I've reconfigured it to block tracking signals and piggyback onboard frequencies so we can communicate without being 'seen.' Wear it so I can reach you."

He turns and begins crawling down the vent shaft.

"Wait. Where are we going?"

He doesn't stop. "You'll see."

We push through the ventilation system for twenty minutes, enough time for me to vacillate between panic and control half a dozen times. Every time it starts to get bad, I randomly berate Quantum for leading us on a wild goose chase, for getting us lost, for being too slow—anything I can think of to get him to respond with equal rancor in that grating hiss he has and yank my mind out of its spiraling descent.

He stops crawling all of a sudden. My focus elsewhere, my hand comes down on one of his ankles and twists it roughly.

"Pay attention!" he barks as I shift backward.

"Sorry."

Looking at his VDU, he ignores the insincere apology, then grabs the edge of another panel and pulls it aside. Without a word, he lowers himself. The sound of his boots hitting a metal floor doesn't echo. Wherever we are, the space is small. Fantastic. But it has to be better than this vent shaft.

Once I drop inside, he informs me it's an anteroom to the bridge's main electronics pipeline. The space is tall enough to stand in, with enough room for two people to sit side by side if their arms are touching—except Quantum has filled half the floor space with electronic panels and two portable control terminals. He's brought in an ammo crate from somewhere and uses it as a bench, leaving only enough room for me to stand behind him.

It's clear he's been busy. In the year-plus I'd been a crew-member on the *Celestial* I hadn't even known this was here. "Let me see if I have this right." Though the space is dark, the consoles' screens illuminate enough of the area to give me my bearings. It feels a little like being in the cockpit of a one-person scout between stops on a planet-to-planet hop. "You started setting up . . . whatever it is you've set up, long before shit went down with Bogotan."

"Right." The impatience and sarcasm sizzle on his tongue like nuclear bacon. "I already told you, I always have a plan. Now do you want to play some more catch-up, or are you ready to hear what comes next?"

"There's something I want to know first." A sound in my tone catches his full attention, and he turns, laying reptilian eyes on me. "So why do you?"

"Why do I what?"

"Trust me."

He snorts. "I *don't* trust you, Aly. I don't need to. Because you're predictable. That's why I wanted you on board with me."

A rare moment of thoughtfulness settles over me, and I comment quietly, no challenge or anger in my voice, "Quantum, you gotta know, when this is all over, we can't just let you go. You're going to have to answer for some of the things you've done or let happen."

His pale brown eyes glitter, but no words pass through his thin lips. He's going to play this till the end. Hell, he probably already has a plan for how to escape not just the *Celestial* but the rest of us, too.

So: "What do you have in mind?" I finally ask.

He returns his focus to the consoles, commenting dryly, "Those who cannot use oxygen responsibly will have it taken away."

TWENTY-SEVEN

The plan is impossibly simple. Full frontal assault, take no prisoners. After studying the armory through onboard surveillance cameras, linked into by Quantum, and identifying the security personnel guarding it, I loaded directions on my VDU (this time I insist on making the trek by using stealth and going through regular corridors, not the ventilation system), and now stand before the vault to the one weapon that can actually give us a chance at stopping Medina and saving KL.

The trick will be getting to the bridge, where the most rigorous onboard security is concentrated. But that's where Quantum's wire-rat genius will save the day. With partial to full control over most of the ship's systems, he's managed to route their nerve-agent tank lines—a Corps favorite for maintaining crowd control during a riot—to their main life support air lines. Exchanging the agent for their air, he'll knock out everyone in the main hull of the ship and buy me a surprise-free trip to the bridge, which, with its own separate and unlinked ventilation system, will still contain awake crew. The good news: I'm only going to have to kill the eight to ten people on the bridge. The bad news: I have to make sure I don't damage too many of the ship's controls if we're going to salvage it. KL will never have to worry about defense again if the *Celestial* belongs to us. And once I suppress any resistance from the flight operations crew, between my nav skills and Quantum's piloting and programming skills, the two of us will be able to control the *Celestial* for as long as it takes for the *Nebula* and more settlers from KL to get here and back us up. With their help, we can revive the *Celestial*'s remaining personnel but keep them firmly controlled until we decide the best course of action for dealing with them. No one wants unnecessary bloodshed. If we've learned anything, it's that we have to live by justice, not revenge, not power, not rule. Another war like the last will be the end of us.

Jesus, I'm starting to sound like Whitmore.

As the access door to the weapons vault tries to slide closed, it catches and hangs on the left boot of the crewman I'd assaulted to get inside, now lying unconscious on the ground. He'll have a hell of a headache, but he'll live.

"Dammit, Quantum, this sonofabitch is heavy. Give me a second to get him inside before you close the door," I whisper through my throat mic.

The hatch slides open again, and I give the guard a solid heave. His body clears the door, leaving only a small smear of blood from his split scalp outside. I need a few minutes to suit up. Hopefully no one wanders by and notices it.

And there they are. Fourteen bugsuits hanging in their ready harnesses. But one is all I need to wipe out the crew on the bridge. I haven't worn one in months, but these machines are basically self-operated. It's just a matter of ensuring their plasma catalyzer tanks are topped off. Usually a remote operator runs the bugsuit installation program for outfitting soldiers, but they can be donned solo if one is limber and determined enough.

The interior of the bay is laid out in a minigrid along the fleet ship's bottom level. A cruiser sports twenty to twenty-six bays, ranging in size from a typical shopping-center warehouse to the gargantuan hangar where surface fighting crafts are stored. Each separate bugsuit vault has on hand the quota intended to outfit one attack ship for a quick-assault op, and the contents of a single bay of this size are usually all that are needed to get the job done.

There's no better single-combat weapon for a lone fighter with plans to take on a small army. As long as those plans include potential suicide and a high probability of personal injury.

The suit is made of a lightweight composite breastplate, backplate, and reticulating arm covers with flexible-fiber full sleeves. The fine mechanism and wire system that controls the user's motions nests between a solid outer plate cover made of the same composite construction material, and an inner graphene mesh that covers the user's skin. Individually, the arm units weigh about as much as a carbine—no big deal.

The weapon's weight factor comes from the energy pack in the backplate. The generator, battery, and materials for creating plasma projectiles add about fifteen kilos, and the helmet another eight. It's not that much to carry, but it's a shit-ton when speed and agility are necessary. The designers, of course, knew this, and given the rarity of foot soldiering on the modern battlefield, there's no longer much need to manufacture small arms that prolong firefights. The bugsuit isn't made for drawn-out contact and leapfrog advances. The bugsuit is made to wipe out every living being within a ten-klick radius in the shortest amount of time possible. A suit operator can potentially stand still in a moderately protected location and plant plasma projectiles into walls of opposing forces in no more time than it takes to drink a canteen of water. And the accuracy of each shot is flawless. The suit's full-auto feature takes the guesswork of a human's brain out of targeting and leaves it all up to the helmet's optical processor—which is where it gets the name "bugsuit." Using a system of bug-eye lenses and autonomous computing, the suit identifies objectives and sends signals to the user's central nervous system through sensors and stimulators in the graphene-mesh sleeves and helmet connection points. The lenses have the ability to focus on things panoramically and at different depths simultaneously, much like a fly's compound eye. This allows it to calculate risk and choose optimal targets and evasive maneuvers for the user and then stimulate the body to bring the arm-mounted weapons into position or get out of the way of potential incomings, effectively turning the user into an autonomously controlled extension of the suit.

The firing armatures are wrist mounted, and most of the heat dissipation happens before the projectiles leave the barrels. Yeah, your back gets a bit sweaty, but most of that is from the compact battery and generator inside the backplate housing nestled between your shoulder blades. As plasma projectiles are basically soundless, users' ears aren't damaged from the firing tubes' explosive power, though the helmet includes nerve-sensing soundbuds to gauge the user's inner ear function as a backup balance sensor. All the user's physiological data, from their lifemarkers to the suit's nerve sensors, are fed into the helmet's processors to help feed the weapon's analytics and maximize shots-to-kills ratio.

Bugsuits' manual operations come from either voice-code-recognized verbal commands or the fire control button screens inside protective covers that are mounted along the radial surface of each wrist. By selecting "manual," "semi-auto," or "full-auto" verbally or manually using the control buttons, users can decide the firing directives for either barrel separately. Of course, given the nature of having a suit that can control your arms and targeting, the only way to have it work at full effect is to set it to and leave it on full-auto.

The suits hang from their cradles along a ten-meter stretch of one wall with the helmets mounted above them. Fourteen suits at full charge are estimated to be all that's necessary to fully neutralize a complement of up to a couple hundred conventionally armed units, i.e., soldiers. Plasma projectiles don't have much trouble knocking over fully armored troops and burning them up from the outside in.

Checking the first suit in the row is a bingo. Fully loaded and ready for wear. I step onto the half-meter-high platform beneath it and operate the controls to lower it over my head. Flexing and bending in uncomfortable ways, I finally get the body sections on. The helmet is attached via hinges to the back piece, and I adjust it to get the fit just right—wincing as it bumps against my bruised cheekbone—latch all connections, and engage the calibrating system.

When it gives me the cue, I say, "Manual. Semi-auto. Full-auto. Engage."

A mild *ping* sounds in my helmet to alert me the voice system is online. For forty seconds, more *ping*s of different tones cycle through my ears, then a hollow, robotic voice says, "All systems online and ready for deployment."

Go time.

My VDU reads one minute till Quantum puts the nerve-agent part of the plan into effect. I retrieve a facemask from my cargo pocket and fit it beneath the helmet, then wait for his signal. Pushing the bugsuit mounting controls aside, I begin taking calm, deep breath after calm, deep breath. Karl's and David's faces appear in my thoughts. If they and the crew made it out of Obal 6's airspace and the potential gauntlet of attack ships Medina may have deployed, they would be within range to transmit to KL's satellite from the *Nebula* by now and warn the settlers to prepare—either for self-defense or possibly for evacuation. If I see any of them again, it could be on another world. But it doesn't matter. As long as we put a stop to Medina's madness. For good.

A slow-building, low-pitched warning alert begins chiming through the ship. Someone must have triggered it when their mates began taking unexpected midday naps. I'm anticipating one or two lucky soldiers to have reached a mask before their lights went out. But when they see me, it's their luck that's going to run out. Despite the sparseness of the bugsuit hardware, these beauties do have a way of making a woman feel invincible.

TWENTY-EIGHT

On Quantum's mark, I triple-time like a whirling dervish on speed through the hull, not taking a breather until I reach the main hatchway to the bridge. I pass only a handful of lights-out senseless personnel in the corridors, not a single person lucid enough to engage me. It gives me a second to reflect on how flawlessly every plan Quantum has been part of has gone down. In a perfect world, he should've been an ally. But here, even with a temporarily shared goal, I suspect it's every man and woman for him- and herself. Shaking off this unsettling thought, I contact him.

"At the bridge. Ready to go. Out."

The flight control cadre must know that things in the main part of the ship are not right, but I cross my fingers that no one had time to inform them exactly what was happening. The next phase is up to Quantum. He'll launch a ghost brigade to make the bridge scramble to ready the *Celestial*'s exterior defenses. Of course, it'll just be interference on the ship's radars and intercept systems, but the crew won't know that right away. The surprise will distract them enough for me to make my dramatic entrance. I should be able to achieve 90 percent casualties before they even know I'm inside.

"You have between five and ten minutes, Aly," Quantum says through my helmet's receiver.

"Hold it. You told me you were keeping the crew gassed until we get backup from KL."

"And if the nerve-suppressant tanks had been full, I would've."

I have a second to wonder if this is Quantum's way of fucking with me, but immediately dismiss the idea. No human I've ever met has less of a sense of humor than him.

"Better hurry," he continues. "Remember, I'm opening the hatch thirty seconds after my mark. Ghost brigade in three . . . two . . . one . . . mark."

So Quantum's plans *aren't* always flawless. This is not the moment I needed to have that reality check. "Full-auto," I tell the suit.

The hatch opens soundlessly, as well maintained as everything under Medina's command has always been. The first crewman to see me looks shocked, not understanding how the bridge could be isolated and operating normally one second and overrun by a bug-suited soldier the next. His shock lasts less than a heartbeat.

The sound of plasma guns isn't loud, but it is unmistakable. Almost immediately after the first man goes down, three more fall, then the rest begin diving under anything that might give them cover. A couple have the instincts to reach for their weapons, but the bugsuit's targeting-and-triage system takes them out first.

To their advantage, the bridge is two levels high, and those on the lower deck, generally the flight navigator and two to three operations personnel, are protected—with the exception of the two who rush my attack to try and stop me. And fail. I dart inside and take a position behind a waist-high observatory counter that flanks the commander's bench on the left. Medina. Where is Medina? She should have been right here. Behind me, the hatch closes, locking in the bridge's air supply and locking out the quickly normalizing gassed air from outside. This tells me that Quantum hadn't been exaggerating; time is short.

Unless he's still working with Medina. But no, if that were the case, he's had a hundred chances to kill me since releasing me from the cargo locker, and there's no way Medina would sacrifice the bridge to an assault. *Then maybe he's trying to let the bridge crew finish the job after you do most of the wet work.*

This thought takes my mind immediately off the task at hand. What exactly is Quantum's motive in all this? He wants Medina dead, of course. Her intent to essentially enslave the rest of the settlers to help her build her private world had definitely sent him to the other side, which happens to be our side; but in the end, Quantum has consistently shown who he ultimately sides with: himself. A team player, he is not. And the idea of the greater good doesn't get past his survival filter. Not like Whitmore and Zabriskie. Or even Vitruzzi.

Cool it, Aly. He can't fly this beast without you. He needs you.

We'll see about that. But first, I have to get control of this situation. The dead pilot who'd been at the bench isn't Medina, and neither are the other crewmembers who'd gone down. If she's not on the bridge, she must be in the hull, and she'll be awake soon. I have to get the bridge wrapped up immediately and then regroup with Quantum so we can come up with another plan for dealing with the rest of the *Celestial*'s crew.

Raising my head just enough for the optics on the bugsuit helmet to clear the top of the observatory counter, I let the suit assess the bridge. The eyepiece gives me enough information to tell that no one still breathing is dumb enough to show themselves. They all know what their odds are. A console next to the pilot's bench suddenly sputters, shooting sparks from an electrical fire. The sharp smell hits my nose, and blue-tinged smoke begins to lift toward the ceiling's vents. Less than a second later, an internal foam deploys, ending the fire. Using the sound to cover me, I dash forward toward the upper-deck railing, a solid enough barrier to protect me, and prepare to blitz the stairs to the lower level.

ZING! A bullet strikes the back of my helmet—just a glancing hit—and nearly knocks me off my feet. Using forward momentum, I careen toward the railing and spin around—thanks to the suit's prerogative—putting it to my back so I'm facing the direction the shot came from. The suit's already controlling my arms and has the target in sight, a crewmember near the blown console. She goes down, and, unable to recover my balance, so do I, right on my ass. Breathing hard, I scoot backward until I'm pressed against the railing's half wall and out of anyone on the lower deck's line of fire. That was too fucking close for comfort. The bugsuit is better in wide-open spaces. I'd forgotten about that.

That's seven down, which leaves from one to three to go, unless they had some bigger meeting going on. My monocular system display informs me the helmet's rear optics have taken damage; too much, they're out. Now the suit can only give me about a 240-degree field of visibility. In other words, no one has my back.

I switch over to semi-auto, leaving the bugsuit in control of only my left arm, roll over to my stomach, and get my knees under me in a crouch. With the ample cover afforded to the remaining crew below, and my now limited visual advantage, I'm less keen to drop down the stairs and start a death disco. The nav bench is down there, too, and if that becomes collateral damage, the ship won't be as easy for Quantum and me to manage. There's a backup nav bench, but it's in the ship's belly, which is off-limits until we take the rest of the crew out of commission.

Quantum again: "Aly, what's your status?"

"Typical," I respond in a half whisper. Then, more loudly: "Sixty percent down. The rest are hiding."

"You have maybe three or four minutes before the crew starts to wake up."

"Thanks, that's so helpful. Why don't you come lend me a hand?"

No response. Also typical.

I glance to my side down the stairwell and immediately take fire. They miss. They aren't dumb; they know I can't get to them unless I come down, and I can't come down by any other means than the stairs.

Fucking standoff; god I hate these. My eyes wander to the doused and steaming nearby console. Unless . . .

"Quantum, come in."

"Here."

"Can you reverse the ventilation in here? Send the used air back?"

"Wait one."

"If you can, shunt it all into the lower deck. Smoke them out."

"Wait one," he says again irritably.

No problem. Take all the time you need.

"Done. But you need to create more smoke if you're going to affect them."

That I can handle. "Roger. Just shut off the self-activating fire retardants."

Reaching back inside my cargo pants pocket, I remove the gas mask I'd stuffed in them before entering the bridge and put it back on. From the cover of the railing, I open up on the overhead lights, the nonessential electronics hardware, and anything else that looks like it might pop, sizzle, or melt. At first, all the gray-blue smoke starts leaving through the outflow vents, but then it stops. A few seconds later, a wall of it flumes up from the stairwell next to me, quickly leaving the deck in darkness. I shove away from the railing back toward the observation counter, hoping to get a better view of the stairs and anyone who comes up them. The only way out is through the main hatch, and if they don't want to choke to death, that's where they're going to have to go.

I hear running footsteps beside me. *What the—? How did—?* Before the thought is complete, the observatory counter starts taking direct fire. Pushing off the floor, I roll-stumble to the relative cover of the commander's bench. The floor is a hockey rink of warm blood, and I end up on my stomach when the hand I place down to brace me slides out from under me. Not important. My ears strain for the sound of whoever is still running around in here with me.

A metallic clink off to my left, maybe ten meters. I pop up from the bench—taking a moment of satisfaction from the fact that I know he can't see me any better than I can see him—and let the bugsuit find my target. Its burst of fire is displeasingly short. My stalker didn't stay visible for long. He's good at this game.

"You know no one can access the bridge to help you, right?" I yell. "They're all getting their beauty sleep. If you're smart, you'll drop your weapon and join them. You can still live through this." I count ten seconds while waiting for a response, but none comes. "I don't want to have to kill you. It's your choice." I give it one last shot. Some people have a well-developed sense of reason, after all.

But not this guy. I sense something dropping down over me before I feel the impact against my left arm, which reflexively goes up to block whatever's coming. It strikes my arm—*What is that? A fucking console? It weighs at least twenty kilos!*—and a sickening crunch vibrates up my wrist, to my elbow, and lodges in my shoulder like a cleaver of fire. I fall back with the console on top of me, pinning my, at minimum broken, arm against my body. I have to get the bugsuit off semi-auto. If it spots a target and tries to fire with my left arm, the pain sprinting its insidious journey through my nervous system right now is going to feel like a candy-wrapped peck on the cheek.

"Manual!" My voice cracks, and what would have been a scream comes out a windless shriek. But the tech is flawless, and my visual display unit tells me I've been switched to manual.

New problem. Commander Medina stands above me, the black bore of her sidearm demanding my attention.

"Don't move," she says through her own gas mask and steps with her entire weight on my still-functioning arm. A girdle of pain cinches down, simultaneously shooting from the arm pinned across my chest and the arm she stands on, meeting somewhere in the middle of my sternum and constricting my already burdened rib cage.

Her face and scalp are bleeding heavily from at least three places, turning the navy blue of her uniform a sticky black. She must have caught a spray of broken glass or poly-composite. In a way, it's a relief to see Medina, even if she's the one who kills me.

Not everyone who had remained under her command when we'd broken off to settle KL had been bad people. I'd hate to be killed by someone I'd once liked and considered a compatriot.

"I know you're not here alone, Erikson. Where is the rest of your team hiding?"

"If I told you that, you'd kill me." I have to force the words through the heavy weight compressing my chest.

She grinds down with the sole of her boot, making me cry out. "Where?"

Tears of pain and anger spring to my eyes. "Probably enjoying a nice, hot bubble bath."

"*Where?*" This time she puts her free hand flat on the console and presses down. I try to lock my chest against the pressure, not wanting to lose precious air, but the agony of my arm forces me to make a noise that sounds to my ears like the grunt of a dog being hit by a speeding land trans.

She lets up the pressure, and tears start flowing down the sides of my head. I squeeze my eyes shut as battering rams of nausea choke me, and my skin flushes first blisteringly hot, then icily frigid.

"Last chance," she says. My eyes open to the darkness of her pistol's barrel.

"They're . . ."

She leans forward at the waist just a hair.

"Right behind you," I finish.

She whirls and fires, facing Quantum, who fires back at the same time. The woman crumples backward, landing beside me, gasping and gurgling through a mouthful of blood. Her head falls to the side and her eyes come to rest on my face, then go blank.

There's a noise like a laundry bag being tossed into a pile. The room is beginning to clear; Quantum must have reengaged the outflow vents before dropping in. Craning my head up, I first see a ceiling panel halfway across the deck that's been removed— Quantum's ingress point—then see him lying on his side at my feet, grasping his midsection.

"No, no, no," I mutter. Bracing my free hand against the side of the heavy console, I give myself just a moment to pre-regret what I'm about to do, then shove the unit off. A nova of pain freight trains through me, and I go black.

But I'm back in seconds, according to my helmet-mounted VDU. Remaining still for a moment, panting and taking bets against myself whether I or the pain-soaked nausea is going to win, I try to get enough of a grip on myself to stand. Winning the fight for now, very, very slowly I sit up.

It takes more time than I'd like to recover from that maneuver. *Harden the fuck up, Aly. This isn't going to get any easier.* Every nerve fiber in my body tuned in, I try to detect other signs of life on the bridge but hear nothing. If there are any more crewmembers, either they're too scared to come out, or they've inhaled enough of the toxic air that they've blacked out. If I'm going to be able to defend myself, I need to get this bugsuit, now rendered useless thanks to my injuries, off. The weight isn't much, but it's enough to hold me back. Gingerly, I disconnect all of the helmet links and remove it, letting it drop beside me. My hand brushes against a bump on the back of my head, which makes me wince, and I feel blood matting my hair. Whatever had tagged the optics must have nicked me too, but the wound is mild. Nothing compared to my arm.

And it hits me—I'm not getting anything off, not with only one functioning hand. The left arm, definitely broken, is also dislocated, though only at the shoulder, not the elbow. That at least is something to be grateful for, but the satisfaction is short-lived. How am I going to fly this thing? The controls can't be handled without authorization, and Quantum—

Shit!

"Quantum, man, you okay?"

No, he's not. He's still on his side, leaking vital fluids at a rate that I wouldn't be able to stop, even with the help of a full medical team. Gutshot.

"Quantum?"

His eyes, sharp and clear and tortured, find mine. "This wasn't supposed . . . to . . . to . . ."

"Wasn't part of your plan, huh?" I whisper, surprised to discover a hint of sorrow, or maybe just regret, in my reaction.

It occurs to me that if I hadn't told Medina Quantum was behind her, she might not have got off the shot that killed him. More likely, though, she'd have shot me point-blank when he had fired into her back instead of her chest. The thought quickly follows: I'm sure Quantum wouldn't have cared. Which in turn puts definitive limitations on my own survivor's guilt.

The problem is, in my condition I can't climb back into the ducting to look over his hacked systems controls and figure out a way to undermine the remaining crew or keep them from carrying out their original mission. Not on my own. When the crew wakes up, whoever's in charge will immediately start searching for the saboteur, and I doubt, after this havoc, they'll be in a negotiating mood. And Van Heusen is still out there. He's proven his appetite for carnage. Which leaves KL still vulnerable. Even if Quantum weren't down, there's no telling how much time I have left to turn the tide of our completely FUBARed plan, but I'm sure it's not enough. It's never enough.

There's only one thing I can do: I have to destroy the ship from here.

The thought provokes a wave of such intense exhaustion that I can't move for a few seconds. Because destroying the ship means I'm not going anywhere. I'm trapped.

My body feels denser, heavier than a neutron star, and I don't have the will to even think about other options. There just . . . aren't any. Is this what Vitruzzi feels? It suddenly seems so clear, so obvious—why keep fighting when there's nothing left to fight for? All I can do now is try to ensure Keum Libre at least has a chance. Leaning against the pilot's bench, feeling the warmth of the blood trickling from the back of my scalp against my neck, I close my eyes and take a minute to let my mind go blank, just let everything go.

A single thought comes to me, a memory of the way Karl's hair had smelled during those three months living at Agate Beach before Cross showed up and betrayed us all, before the Corps killed Bodie, before Rajcik dropped the bomb that pushed Quantum and Medina to start the war, before everything fell apart. We'd worked hard that summer, and his hair had always smelled of warm sand, sweat, and the soap he used, something both musky and sweet. That smell had lingered with me all day, like perfume, like the scent of pure happiness. I couldn't get enough of him. I'd let myself believe it would last forever.

I've never luxuriated in the illusion that anything, any part of ourselves, continues on after we die. If humans had an everlasting spirit or soul, why wouldn't we have come to some kind of enlightenment by now? Why do we continue making the same mistakes century after century? Because it's just one life. One brief, rushed life, and I know, now, that these will be my life's last minutes. The one thing I want to keep with me until my final moment is that memory. The smell of warm sand in Karl's hair. And what he means to me.

A chime pings on the array behind me, jolting my senses back to the present. Am I going into shock? No, got to get on top of this. There is still work to do. Intentionally and abruptly, I grab the pilot's chair and yank myself to my knees. The scream from my arm and shoulder seems to echo throughout the bridge, though it's only in my head. Sweat pops to the surface of my skin, from my scalp to the soles of my feet. Gritting my teeth, fully alert again, I pull myself onto the bench and scan the flat screens arranged in front of me. Vertical holocontrols will make this easier, and the first thing I do is activate them. The glowing blue, red, and green lines of the ship's control system menu rise before me. Without thinking, I select "Communication," wait for it to activate, then input the sat-link codes to transmit to the *Nebula*. I want to know what happened to them. And . . . I want to say goodbye.

"*Nebula* crew, this is Erikson." Transmit. Wait. Repeat. "*Nebula* crew, this is Erikson. Do you read?"

Remembering to engage the video-link, I click it just as Karl's face comes into view in front of me.

"Aly!"

He can't see me yet, and for a moment I'm glad about that. I can't speak, the knowledge that this is the last time I'll ever look into his shining sepia eyes rendering me paralyzed and devastated. But I swallow, activate the feed, and reply, "Karl."

"You okay? You must be okay, right?"

"Yes. Right now it only hurts when I bleed." I don't mean to be funny, but how do you tell the man you love that you're going to be dead within the hour?

"Aly, what—?"

"Listen, Karl, it didn't work out here like we planned."

"Okay, but it doesn't matter. You're alive, that's what counts. Aly, I've been going crazy—"

I cut him off again, not liking myself for doing it, but time's getting short. Do you have to hurt the ones you love to save them? I don't like the answer, but I don't have a choice. "Listen, there isn't time. I have the bridge, but I'm trapped and Quantum's dead. It's just me now—the *Celestial*'s crew are still in the picture—and I have to blow the ship. It's the only way."

"Okay, get to an escape shuttle and set your coordinates. We'll come back for you."

This time I don't cut in. I want to hear him out because his voice gives me a second of hope. I wish I could live the rest of my life in that second. My good hand goes to my neck, pulling the cord with Karl's ring free from my shirt. My fist clamps around the circle of metal, warm from my skin. "Babe, I-I don't think that's going to happen."

"It'll only take us about a day to get to you, maybe two. You can hold on that long, right? How badly are you injured?"

He isn't listening to me. For once I don't mind. If I don't do this now, I'm going to lose my nerve. Leaving Karl's feed open, I go to work on the pilot's console. It won't be enough to just blow the compound drums with La Mer's detonator. The *Celestial* is a lot bigger than the *Nebula*, where he'd built and tested it, so there's no guarantee it will even work. Even though I can't control flight systems without crew authorization, I can still access maintenance systems. I'm going to sabotage the ship, burn out the engines and force an overload that will start an irreversible series of internal malfunctions and melt this intergalactic death trap from the inside out. I have maybe five minutes until the crew starts to wake up, if that. No matter. This ship is doomed.

"Aly, do you hear me?" Karl's been talking to me while I concentrate on the ship's destruction, but I haven't responded. "We're already turning back. Just send me the coordinates you're at now."

His eyes are so sincere, so calm, but the dark fear—or is it fury?—lying behind them is another face of the Karl I know. The Karl that has seen battles and blood, wars and violence, and has fought through them all with the same stoic and indomitable resolve each time. The steel in him that will outlast any foe or enemy he confronts. It's that hard-burning, powerful rage that I'm counting on to get him through this next battle. I may not have told him enough, but he became my reason to go on, my reason to live and face every new tragedy and fight. He was my strength. Now he has to be that for himself.

"Karl, I can't make it to the escape shuttles. There isn't time. Tell David goodbye for me, okay? And keep the crew safe."

"I don't know what you're talking about. Are you saying you're too hurt? Can you get an IV in?"

He's going to keep denying what he's hearing until the ship turns into frozen space-borne carbon. I don't want his suffering to be the last thing I see, or mine his. "Karl." This time something in my voice catches him, makes him take a breath of silence. "Be strong. And remember that I love you."

I turn off the feed before he can respond.

Leaning back into the pilot's bench seat, I let my eyes fall closed, the thump of pain from my wounded arm settling into rhythm with my heartbeat and dulling enough for me to just sit here for a few last seconds and count them. With no other living people on the bridge, it is completely silent, even the constant ambient hum of the ship's engines and life support systems seeming to have faded away. Most of the bridge's lights were blown out, and behind my lowered eyelids I can almost imagine that I'm suspended in space, already free from the entrapments of my body and its suffering. In another moment I recognize what this feeling is, though I'm not sure I've ever really felt it before. Peace.

TWENTY-NINE

Noise like screws rattling in a plastic box jerks me out of my semi-consciousness as abruptly as if I'd been shot. Before my eyes focus, something hits me in the leg and bounces off. As I bolt upright the shrieking in my arm pitches to a new fervor, and then I see what happened. Quantum is awake, not dead like I thought, and staring at me with eyes lit feverishly bright. A medkit lies at my feet.

"Take it," he says, his voice no thicker than a spider's strand. "Morphone Z. It'll kill the"—he squints and sucks air through his teeth as if in sudden pain—"kill the pain. Get to the . . . to the . . ." Unable to finish the sentence, he waves toward the front of the bridge.

"What, Quantum? I'm not quite prepared to hurl myself through the viewscreens."

"There's a fucking e-pod under the nav bench." Somehow, even dying, his voice still manages to carry the *Why am I surrounded by such towering stupidity?* tone. "I already set the ship to blow from my link up."

It's as if a Glower missile just hit me in the forehead. "You mean you programmed it to self-destruct?" Then another thought smacks me. "How many escape pods are there?"

"One."

So he *was* going to let me do the dirty work, destroy the ship on his own, then take off using the escape pod and leave me here to die. Or maybe he never thought I'd make it in the first place. Which leads back to the fact that he'd set me up to take the fall while he got out in one piece. I've been right about him all along. But . . . but he didn't have to tell me about the pod. Should I be grateful, or just put him out of his misery for good? One look at him tells me that's going to happen within a few minutes anyway, no matter what I do.

"How long do I have?"

He mumbles something, but I can't hear it. The puddle he's lying in hasn't stopped growing, and the strong smell of blood swims in the air like aerosol. He knows he's already dead, that's clear.

My heart speeds up, and it takes me a minute to recognize why. I could still make it through this. There's a chance—a tiny, almost imperceptible one, but a chance—I could still make it out of this.

Decision made, I ease off the seat and try to crouch low enough to get to the medkit. If I bend over, the weight of my busted arm pulling against my dislocated shoulder could make me pass out. Grinding my molars together, I dangle my good hand and scoop up the kit, then straighten. I don't know if I have time to call the *Nebula* back and tell them what I'm doing, but Karl said they'd already started to double back. If I get out in the pod, they'll pick up my emergency beacon. They'll come back no matter what. I know they will.

I hope.

The world wavers in my vision for a second, the edges of it bleeding dry of color, then it comes back into focus. I take the ramp down from the pilot's bench to the main deck and reach the navigator's array, sparing one last glance at Quantum. His eyes remain open, but they don't follow me. After reaching the bench, a few seconds of exploration reward me with access controls to the emergency sardine can—which is basically what it is.

I don't have the time or energy to care if the deck is clear of danger. If there's anyone else breathing down here, they can take their best shot. Right now, I just want to get out. Regardless, a lifetime of surviving prompts me to do a quick scan. Nothing moves.

I gaze through the hatch that's slid open beside the nav bench into the coffin-sized pod and let the idea of staying aboard the *Celestial* until it blows tease through my mind. If this is truly the only escape pod on the bridge, it must have been built to evacuate the last person left in the case of attack or total ship failure. There aren't many weapons powerful enough, with the exception of the Mini-Nova of course, to instantly obliterate a ship this size. Any attack or malfunction would generally give the bridge crew enough time to get to their nearby evacuation-pod bays.

A heavy thump at the bridge's main entry echoes across the deck. They're awake. I only have a minute or two until they find their way through—that's *if* Quantum jammed up the hatch. Acute claustrophobia aside, I'm not fitting into the pod's cradle while still in this bugsuit. It has to come off. Which means I'm about to suffer. A lot.

I drop the medkit on the console display and thumb the release catch to open it, but it won't budge. The kit looks abused and probably hasn't been opened in years. As Desto would say, what kind of fuck salad is this? With my one usable hand, it's hard to get a grip on the box to work the release tab. Squinting in frustration, I end up picking it up and slamming it hard against the console, breaking both the console and, thankfully, the kit's latch. Everything flies out across the console table, but I manage to slam my palm across the morphone syringe before it gets away.

Pulling the cap off with my teeth, I press the flat delivery end against my neck just below my earlobe and hit the button. A tiny spike of pressure against my skin, followed by a moment of what feels like ice running down my neck, then heat. It'll take a few seconds for the narcotic to kick in, but there's no time to wait. I can hear a dull whine coming from the entry. They're cutting through.

I take a deep breath and don't hesitate, yanking first against the chest buckles that hold the bugsuit on, then the sleeves. Before I start to pull my arms through, I use my right hand to grip my left arm just above the elbow, and simultaneously drop to my knees and press the bad shoulder into the nav table's solid edge.

Okay, Aly, just a quick yank and a push and your humerus will be reseated. You're not getting into that tin can with your arm hanging by the socket like dead meat. On three, two, one . . . OW JESUS FUCKING CHRIST THAT FUCKING HURTS . . . SHITI'MGOINGTOPUKE . . . OHHOLY . . . OH, that's a little . . . oh, okay, I'm okay. It's all okay.

The head of my humerus slips back into place with a wet sound just as the morphone hits like a tidal wave of pure bliss, sending the spiking pain to a dark, lonely corner at the very edge of my brain. I'm even feeling a little happy. Until I look into the waiting bucket of terror that will take me into airless oblivion.

A shudder runs through the floor of the bridge, subtle at first, but quickly building in intensity. Quantum's destruction sequence beginning? It has to be. No more time to wait.

I quickly pull my broken arm through the bugsuit sleeve, feeling it but not feeling it at the same time. That hand is completely numb and won't grip the wrist of my right-arm sleeve. So I hold onto the edge of the nav console table and pull myself to my feet, step on the hanging suit arm to hold it down, and perform a wriggling dance maneuver that eventually gets the unit off. It takes less than a minute, but a high-pitched, whining buzz has begun emitting from all the electronics on the bridge, threatening to turn my inner ear into jelly, and the remaining lights waver between off and blazing. I sit on the edge of the open emergency pod hatch, dangling my feet inside, then slowly slide into the tight passenger cradle. The pain and fear of small spaces sing in a deep, fading baritone in my head, but the tune is drowned out under the morphone ocean. If the e-pod thrusters get me far enough away to clear the debris and flak from the vessel's self-destruction, I'll be lucky. But the morphone drowns that anxiety, too.

Once I'm nestled and buckled, I press the syringe against my neck once more. If I don't live through this, I'm not going out screaming. I'm doing it in quiet, unbroken serenity.

Just as my lights start to fade, I activate the release sequence and emergency beacon, and let fate decide what to do next.

THIRTY

Flutter, flutter, flutter.

I shake my foot, trying to get the cat at the end of the bed to go away and stop tickling me with its whiskers.

". . . awake . . ."

Flutter . . . flutterflutterflutter.

"Would you stop!" My eyes slowly peel open, the lids nearly gummed together by what feels like years of being asleep. It's not a cat, it's Karl. He stands at the foot of a bed—a med-bay gurney?—lightly rubbing the tips of his fingers along the sole of my bare left foot. "Whuh . . .?" The words *what are you doing here?* stick in my similarly gummy throat.

"Welcome back, lover." He smiles, and, whether it's just a trick of memory or an actual sense, I smell the warm sand and sweet soap of his hair drift to me.

Besides the tickle in my foot, my body is gloriously absent of any other tactile sensation. Blinking with the cinder blocks that compose my eyelids, a glance tells me I'm wearing a sling on my broken arm.

"How do . . . does . . . look?"

"How do you look? To be honest, terrible. But you'll live." That same mischievous grin.

Apparently morphone doesn't block feelings of annoyance. I scowl, or think I do, it's hard to tell when my face feels like a drenched, dripping sock, and try again: "My arm. How's my arm look?"

"V says your wrist is sprained and you have an impacted fracture of the ulna, but you'll be doing push-ups again in less than a month. We found a hydro cast in the *Celestial*'s medical supplies, and she's going to fit it for you when you're a little more awake."

A subdued but no less disturbing jolt of apprehension slams through me. He sees my expression and says, "Don't worry. We're safe. There's a lot to catch you up on. But let's wait till the morphone wears off. You have enough in your system to knock out even Desto." He steps up and brushes his hand along my unbruised cheek. "I'm sorry I woke you up. I just couldn't wait to see you again, hear your voice. Go back to sleep now, okay?"

It isn't hard to convince me.

DESPITE THE BRILLIANCE THAT had been behind Quantum's plan, I've never been happier to see one fail so abysmally.

Desto sits cross-legged on the *Nebula*'s galley floor, detailing everything that had happened between the fight at Bogotan's landing field to when they'd picked me up in the e-pod, unconscious but apparently raving about being buried alive. His leans back, relaxing against Zeta's chair and lightly rubbing her calves, which are draped over his shoulders. "It took us thirty-six hours from your transmission to reach you, but you were still out. Once we got you inside, Vitruzzi sedated you with something to counteract the morphone but keep you from totally losing your shit. You kept shouting 'not the trunk, not the trunk, not in the trunk, Harald.' I have no idea who Harald is, but you clearly didn't like the guy much."

He stops there, letting the pregnant pause pressure me into an explanation, but I'm not going along with it. As far as I'm concerned, I'd left my recollections about my father aboard the fleet cruiser. Some things should stay buried.

After a minute, he continues, "I've never seen anyone who's spent so much of their life flying in dinky scout or attack ships so afraid of small spaces."

"It's different on a ship," I start to explain, then stop. Those without phobias just can't understand. That's what makes them phobias; they have no rational explanation. I change the subject. "So you and V and Brady got to the *Nebula* okay. Did any ships follow you from Bogotan?"

"We had one attacker on our tail, but Zabriskie sent one of their own ships after it."

"Zabriskie?" It had become clear to me that most of Bogotan's people weren't keen on being under Medina's thumb, but I'm still surprised they'd get into any active engagement with her and those under her command. What if Quantum and I had failed and Medina discovered their complicity? She'd have done to them what she'd threatened to do to Keum Libre. Maybe the Bogotanites were tired of living with fear and compromised ethics. Sometimes taking a stand, even if it means dying, is better.

"Yeah. The Bogotan scout took care of Medina's attack ship, and we were halfway to KL when you called."

David, who's been working behind the galley counter to try and make something more appetizing than nutrition bars and endurance gels, jumps in, "We thought our nav-system had failed when we got into range of your emergency alert. The sky wasn't filled with debris from the *Celestial* like we expected. The cruiser was just sitting there, fully inop."

"Powerless and dark and as cold as the grave," Desto says.

"We thought you'd been tricked into sending that transmission to Karl, and we basically just floated there, waiting for Medina to send out a squadron to dust us." David sticks a finger in the bowl he's mixing things in, licks the yellowish substance from it, and wrinkles his nose. He comes around the counter and holds the bowl out. "Desto, could you taste this? What's missing?"

Zeta grimaces. "Get that . . . whatever . . . away from the pregnant lady! You do not want me to get sick. It makes me crabby."

"Get it away, quick!" Desto says, making melodramatic warding-off gestures, and Zeta play-punches his shoulder.

"Sorry." He brings the bowl to me. "Help me out, Twig."

"You know I love you, brother, but . . ."

"Gah! Bunch of cowards." He retreats back behind the counter and slams the bowl down.

Desto picks up the thread. "We waited, ran some hull scans, but it seemed like no one was home, then found you floating nearby. After hanging back for a few hours, just waiting to get blown out of the sky, Brady made the call. We picked you up and got you on board. When it was clear you weren't going to be able to tell us what happened for a bit, we decided to go exploring.

"Everything on the *Celestial* was offline. Power, engines, life support. We broke in through the secondary small-ship airlock and tried to minimize pressure loss to make it easier to figure out what had happened. Didn't matter though; one of the aft engine rooms had a small leak from a minor explosion. The whole place was a ghost town.

"Most of us went in, and it took about three hours to reach the bridge. We found Quantum and Medina's bodies, and every other crewmember we ran across was dead, too. Jeremy dialed in to the ship log and figured out what Quantum had tried to do—and he mucked the beast up pretty bad—but it never fully destructed. I guess fleet cruisers have enough stopgaps that it was able to shut down the sequence Quantum programmed to sabotage it. Unfortunately for the crew, not before the life support systems were totally blown."

"So it's salvageable?"

"Jeremy and Mason have been working their asses off to try and answer that question, but we think so. That kid Ryan has been pretty helpful, too."

I repeat, I've never been happier in my life to see a plan fail so abysmally.

THE MOST UNEXPECTED THING imaginable happens over the next six months: life goes on. Though the idea of "normal" is never going to mean anything again, unless you consider disorder and random surprises normal, the settlers of both Keum Libre's colony and Bogotan's pick up the pieces and resume.

I heal, as I so frequently spend time doing, and Karl and I return to being partners in short- and long-range salvage ops. Jono Zabriskie takes over leadership of Bogotan, setting up a representative council to oversee daily life and operations there, giving everyone a voice in their own future as well as a sense of stability. Keum Libre and Bogotan set up a system of trade and aid—just like Quantum had originally proposed, but not in the backward, old-school, subversive process he had attempted. Some Bogotanites move to KL; some Klers move there.

David meets and falls in love (finally, the guy had been like a monk during the last few years) with one of the transplants, a former major in the Stellar Corps, thus proving to David that not all officers are self-serving bottom-feeders—while simultaneously proving to me, though David will never admit it, that she can command him just like she'd formerly commanded the lower enlisted serving under her. I *like her*. And though nothing will ever diminish the bond of family between David and me, Olamina, or just Mina, soon becomes like a sister to me, and the two of them join most of the salvage trips Karl and I take.

As for the two of us, we continue to call KL home, completely content with our off-the-grid, seminomadic lifestyle. I've found that the vastness of the ocean just down the cliff from KL and even the trees and neotropical jungle surrounding the settlement still feel more unconfining and open than a city. And after everything, I can't seem to get enough of open spaces.

More importantly, Vitruzzi has started to heal. Less than a month after we returned to KL, Zabriskie's people made contact with another fleet cruiser. Unlike Medina, the man in charge had been both a civilian and pro-Admin—until the war. Whatever the cruiser's crew and inhabitants had gone through, they'd reached the same conclusions as Bogotan and KL—either we all work together or we all die alone.

One of the crewmembers is a psychologist who specialized in combat-related disorders. She meets via satlink with Vitruzzi several times a week. I'm no brain debugger, but I think that whatever had triggered the reverse of Vitruzzi's downward spiral has been helped by seeing the way things are improving between Bogotan and KL, and the weekly discovery and influx of survivors from all over the system who want nothing more than to find ways to put the worlds back together, peacefully and with minimum competition or struggle. It's probably also helped that she and Brady have adopted two of the kids we'd picked up on Eruo Pium. Those kids may be scarred by all they'd been through, but if anyone can raise them, it's someone with scars of their own, someone who can empathize. And Vitruzzi and Brady have plenty. Even Mason took in the little girl, Cassandra, and her brother, their quick attachment to each other a surprise to everyone.

Speaking of Mason, not everything has been roses and rainbows. Both he and Hoogs have moved on, deciding Bogotan suits them better. I miss them, but it hit me even harder when Venus and La Mer decided to relocate as well. It makes sense; La Mer's technical savvy is put to much better use in their colony, which has more intricate engineering needs than ours. And of course Venus wouldn't hear of being apart from him. Fortunately, we've seen them a few times since they departed, the constant traffic between the two colonies making it easy. As a bonus, Ryan has stayed, and no one can claim the kid isn't damn near as adept in the mechanical and electronics arenas as La Mer. We're lucky to have him.

I'M KICKING BACK IN the lounge area on the *Andromeda* after a two-week salvage op when David runs in.

"What are you doing?" he asks.

I give him the look I reserve for people who ask stupid questions. "Reading."

"Yeah, but what's that?"

"Uh, it's a book, Bright Light." It isn't as easy as it sounds to make sense of a question that has such an obvious answer.

His expression shifts from curiosity to exasperation, as if I'm the one asking stupid questions. "I can see that, Aly. What I mean is, why are you reading a book made of paper? And where did you get it?"

Ah, now I see. "Venus brought a few boxes of them from Bogotan. She says they have a nostalgia library with at least a few thousand." I hadn't seen a book printed on paper since I was a kid and we'd visited the Tiptree Memorial and Archive Center. David, obviously, hasn't seen once since then either. "I guess they have a thing for vintage. I'm kind of starting to see why."

"Yeah? Why?"

I have to think about how to put it into words for a second before responding. "I don't know. There's something about the way it feels in my hands. The way I can flip the pages and create a little breeze. The smell of glue and wood pulp. It makes me think of . . . simpler times." A little embarrassed at waxing poetic, I drop my eyes to the book, then glance back at him. The smirk I see on his face confirms my instinct to feel a little silly.

"Well, you better keep them locked up," he says through the smirk. "Some of these heathens may be inclined to use them as fuel."

"Noted. So, mind if I . . .?" I wave the book at him, annoyed.

"Yeah, but you may want to come to the med center. Zeta's about to pop."

Three hours later, David, Karl, Brady, and I stand outside Zeta's room. Vitruzzi comes out, tells us she's sleeping, everyone's happy and healthy, and to come back later. She looks more like the old Vitruzzi than ever. I don't know if it's because of that, or because of my gladness that Desto and Zeta and their new kid are all doing well, or because of some other unexpected, even unimagined, relief that we've somehow made it through the worst of everything, still whole, still human, but I suddenly wrap my arms around her and hug her like I've never hugged anyone but my brother. Almost surprisingly, she returns it, and we stand that way for a while.

The door opens and Desto comes out. V and I let go of each other, and I look at the bundled-up little girl in his arms.

"She's as beautiful as her mama," I tell him.

"Aly," he says.

I look into his face and see the tears streaming from his eyes. Tears of such rejoicing happiness, so unexpected from such a lifelong warrior, it's almost hard to look at him. "What?" I manage, feeling my own eyes start to swim.

"That's her name. We're going to call her Aly."

ABOUT THE AUTHOR

Tammy is an inveterate verbarian, who spends her day surrounded by the written word, both hers and others'. As an ex-paratrooper with the 82nd Airborne Division, her stories are often as gritty as a grunt's pile of three-week-old field gear. Her military science fiction novel *Contract of Defiance* is the first book in the Spectras Arise Trilogy and debuted to acclaim in Spring 2012. *Contract of Betrayal* is the second in the trilogy, and the final book, *Contract of War*, completes it. When not hunched like a Morlock over her writing desk, Tammy runs and bikes silly miles in the playground of Southern California and spends an inappropriate amount of time watching Henry Rollins videos on YouTube. Feel free to visit her blog and sign up for her newsletter to be the first to know of contests, new releases, and special events you might enjoy at {www.tammysalyer.com}, or stop by and say hi on Twitter {@TammySalyer}.

ALSO BY TAMMY

NOVELS

Contract of Defiance, Spectras Arise Trilogy, Book 1

Contract of Betrayal, Spectras Arise Trilogy, Book 2

Contract of War, Spectras Arise Trilogy, Book 3

Conviction: A Spectras Arise Novella

SHORT STORY COLLECTION

On Hearts and Scorpions: Four Twisted Tales of Love and Lust

SHORT STORIES

Artificial Fate

Creepers

No Suede Soles in Hell

Indulgence